THE LAST ARK

Harvey Price

Publisher: Harvey L. Price, Jr
Hoquiam, Washington

Quotations: From BHAGAVAD GITA,
translated by Stephen Mitchell, copyright © 2000 by
Stephen Mitchell. Used by permission of Harmony
Books, a division of Random House, Inc.
Excerpt from p. 56 from THE ESSENTIAL
KORAN by THOMAS CLEARY. Copyright © 1994 by
Thomas Cleary. Reprinted by permission of
HarperCollins Publishers.
Permission granted by Bukkyō Dendō Kyōkai,
Tokyo for quotation from THE TEACHINGS OF
BUDDA.

ISBN: 978-0-9819220-0-3

Library of Congress Control Number: 2008906883

Manufactured, printed and bound in the United States of
America by Minuteman Press, Olympia, Washington;
and by Phil's Bindery, Seattle, Washington.

FOR JEANNIE

CONTENTS

APPENDIX 1

APPENDIX 2

APPENDIX 3

ACKNOWLEDGEMENT

It would not be right for this book to venture into the public arena without expressing the most profound gratitude to my family members and friends, both of whom have dealt with me for years as I whined about wanting to write a book someday. Their infinite patience and forbearance was crucial for this book to be published. Specifically, I wish to thank my wife, Jeannie, for listening and making needed corrections to every word herein. Her support and encouragement was, and always will be, at the core of each day. To my sons and sister, Steve, Ben and Kathy, I am forever indebted for their unrealistic and unfathomable faith in me. To my dear friends, Nancy, Ken and Katy, I am ever-amazed at their unflagging encouragement and tireless efforts to help me finish this book and to gain some familiarity in using a computer. And, likewise, to Tom and Liz, I am ever-grateful for their untold numbers of hours rewording, correcting text, making countless suggestions and pushing me to finish this project. Without all these dear people, I'd still be whining.

FOREWORD

This book contains three distinct volumes: The Last Ark, The Confinement and The Emergence. Each of these separate texts has an accompanying Appendix, which provides the primary source material for that particular volume.

The timeframe encompassed by this book extends from November 19, 2010, until June 30, 2015, the date this project was commissioned by the Global Union Governing Body. It is a chronicle, or more precisely, The Official Record of Events. It was compiled, written and edited by Fred Wailand.

The intention and hope for commissioning this book was to provide a detailed record of what occurred during those years and, thereby, possibly help future generation's better care for themselves and for their world. There is some attention to detail; it is not meant to be tedious. The intent is to give a factual accounting of what occurred. Only you, a future reader, can work to prevent our species' existence from vanishing forever. This is their gift to you.

THE LAST ARK

PART I

ONE: THE VISITOR

It was nearing midnight, on November 19th. His eyes opened fully, shifting side to side, trying to throw off the net of deep sleep. The night's stillness gave his bounding heart an echo. Shadows were frozen in place. The deep hush stayed the young coyote's cries, as they roamed through the blackness. All living things became paralyzed by a Presence. It was as if the endless desert expanse had become an immense cathedral. Rather than incense and myrrh, this sanctuary had the fragrance of sage, creosote bush and the ever-present reminder of the desert heat. There was an unnerving quiet about. And starlight gave this sanctuary its light. "It's started again," he said aloud. "It always seems to begin this way: first the silence. Then the stillness and chilling sense that I am not alone."

For the last seven years, since a few months before his wife's death, he had lived in the remote desert region, east of Cadiz, in one of the last remaining strips of undeveloped land in America. It was just off old Highway 66. Its isolation was soothing, giving him comfort and peace.

They had found an old abandoned homestead

1

cabin in the area, probably built in the 1930s. It had been partially completed. It was someone's dream. Maybe for someone, it was their dream fully realized; who knows. He thought we tend to judge others too harshly when it comes to acting out their dreams. For him, it was enough just to dream. For it to be a finished product was unimportant.

Eighty years ago, this highway at night was a necklace of lights, stretching from horizon to horizon. People then were traveling to and from California, each hoping to start fulfilling their dreams or leaving behind ones that were much beyond their grasp. Up until recently, there might be one or two vehicles pass by his cabin each day. But some time ago the bridge washed out three miles up the road towards Needles, and even though the bridge was repaired, very little traffic now came or went along this stretch of roadway.

The cabin, as they were called in these parts, was not like one would imagine, set back in the woods of the Northwest. Instead of being made of notched and caulked logs, it was covered with tar paper, mismatched plywood and weatherboard strips of various shapes and shade. In places, even cardboard was used to cover odd gaps. Each occupant over the years had added his or her own touch to the exterior, seemingly to always leave whatever the last person had patched.

It had three rooms, if the bathroom was counted. The shed-like roof was low. Even at its highest point, it required all but the smallest adult to stoop when entering the front door. A large wood burning stove filled the kitchen area and provided whatever heat was needed in the colder months. The summer, which in other places would be three months, here lasted at least six to seven months. And it came with such intensity that the old water cooler just gasped through those endless days. The cooler had long needed repair, with the mineral deposits giving it the appearance of a large chunk of whitish-gray ice. But he didn't seem to bother much with repairs and upkeep those days, so its effectiveness lessened with each passing heat season.

Of recent months, in fact, even extending into this last year, a certain resignation had crept into his life. He used to think it was due to the punishing heat. But now there was a disquieting uneasiness and fearfulness that was becoming stronger each day.

He sat upright in bed, swinging his feet quickly over the side. He sat there, rubbing his forehead, with his elbows resting on his knees. He had been in a deep sleep, as often would happen at this time of night. And the two beers that he had before going to bed added to his dulled unsteadiness. He hesitated to attempt standing.

"What's happening to me?" He wondered out loud. "Am I finally losing my mind?" Over and over again, as he had after the three previous episodes like this, he recalled the strange events of the last four or five months.

It all seemed to start with those floaters. For years the technicians who tested his eye sight would ask him about the large and numerous floating objects in both of his eyes. He always told them he couldn't remember not having them. Only rarely did they seem to become larger or more noticeable. He just told them it seemed associated with increased eye strain at work or doing close work such as drawing. They were no bother to him.

Then, without any apparent cause, he began to experience an extra large, darkened blotch in both eyes. It would linger, usually off to the side of his visual field. Blinking did not seem to move it. Rolling his eyes didn't shift its position. Often it would hold its shape; unlike the usual spots he had which altered shape and position constantly. After he turned his head away, whatever it was would be gone when he looked back.

It was at this point he returned to the local optometrist in a nearby town for a recheck of his eyes.

"There are no changes in your eyes from the last visit," the optometrist told him. "You don't even need to get a new pair of glasses, which is a change for you. You seemed to have needed a new set each time I saw you. But not this time. Everything is fine."

Hearing that, he went on his way and tried to pay no further attention to his eyesight and the various apparitions he'd been having.

That was until two months later, when he was driving along the usually deserted stretch of roadway about six miles from his homestead. Suddenly, he had a reoccurrence of a 'floater' to his right side. But more disturbing, it actually appeared to be outside the truck window. And the form did not move when he shifted his visual field. It seemed it was only gone after he had passed it by. Looking out his rearview mirror, there was no sign of the blackened form. But since that first episode, he had two more similar experiences.

The eerie silence would begin about the same time each night for those last couple of weeks. It lasted over an hour each time. Once it even occurred during the midst of a screaming sand storm, which commonly occurred this time of year. Midway through the storm, everything just stopped and the stone silence began. Then just as suddenly, the storm resumed, in full fury exactly one hour later.

Before this episode, he was unaware of the silence. If anything, it seemed pleasant. It just seemed a little quieter than he had usually known in this deepest part of the desert. It was later that he noticed that the length of time was different for each uninterrupted silence. It was like a forced hush. Over time, as anyone who has ever been in total silence knows, it became like a storm inside his head. After four or five nights of this, there was also a strange sense of peacefulness associated with it. But his gnawing fear and growing sense of losing control wouldn't permit that kind of delusion to become fixed.

The silence seemed to come only at night, or maybe he was just too busy during the day to notice any such change then. And oddly, it seemed that each subsequent episode was possibly longer and the silence even deeper. Now after two weeks of this, he knew that this was not just a case of cabin fever. All his senses told him this was no coincidence of nature. It was too regular and too predictable in its onset and pattern.

It was like Someone or Something wanted him to realize there was an impending visitor or visitation and did not want him to panic beyond what any mortal, isolated in the vastness of the Mojave Desert, might. Already, he was becoming hesitant and anxious about going to sleep at night. He found himself staying awake longer and longer each night, trying to prolong the time he was awake and alert. It was the awakening into the silence that so mystified and haunted him. He felt vulnerable. And he was beginning to have the steely taste of fear each night.

He had examined everything around him closely. There never appeared to be anything disturbed inside his cabin or about his property. Nothing ever was out of place. And yet nothing was beginning to appear quite the same. He could only sense this. He couldn't see it.

As he sat on his bed, trying to clear his thoughts, he scanned his living room and kitchen area. The stove had now burned down to glowing embers, barely seen through the cracks in its firebox door. Airtight it wasn't, nor could it ever be again. Odd piles of dishes were on

5

the kitchen counter, stacked and waiting for their weekly scrubbing. On top of the small round oak kitchen table were stacks of papers, open and unopened letters, and bills in scattered heaps. Two mismatched chairs rested at different angles around the table. The small refrigerator was his only other appliance, other than the water cooler and wood stove. Using an electric generator made it impractical to have much else in the way of electrical equipment; anyway, most of the time he only had refrigerated items in the summer. The winter cold kept his perishable food edible enough until he finally ate it. But most food that he bought was canned, packaged or dried anyway. By a process of trial and error, he had simplified his life to this level.

The kitchen cupboard doors stood ajar, at different angles, as if he had left them in a hurry to go somewhere. The walls were covered, alternately, with white plaster and yellowish-brown wallpaper. Haphazardly nailed or tacked over them were some paintings, photographs, letters or notices to remind him of long-ago appointments or deadlines. It all had a soiled appearance, like the inside of an old roadside filling station. "Dingy" would probably best describe the area for any visitors who might have come, but, now, even they were few and infrequent.

This was all he and his wife had toward the end of their lives together. Theirs was never a busy household. Having a house guest or family member in their home was a very special occasion. Usually, it was just them. During their years together, there was a descriptive phrase circulating frequently in discussion groups regarding couples who were as close as he and his wife were. They would have labeled it a co-dependent relationship. He would have found that term somewhat puzzling, even patronizing. For both of them, their relationship was filled with love and respect for one another. Their home, however simple or sparsely furnished, was a sanctuary, both for themselves and for anyone who came to stay or visit. Theirs was a bond that withstood many changes and hardships, both in where they lived and worked and in the tragedies resulting from poor health. Her long-term illness, ending in her dying from cancer, and the death of their only child years before, had a profound impact on him. He knew he would always love and miss them both. And it felt right that he should. His was not a lonely and insolated life now. It was, to him, simply a solitary one.

He had sometimes wondered why, given his enjoyment of being with people, and his ability to laugh and joke, did such a quiet conclusion come towards the end of his life. It just wasn't to be that he would be surrounded by others. He had no regrets or feelings of resignation. To him, life was like a journey in the mountains, along a narrow dirt road, traveled often at night, with only a dim light as a guide. The joys, companionship and love or the tragedies, loss and isolation were either the wondrous vistas during the day or the dangerous curves navigated at night. All were mostly beyond his will or ability to understand. All he could do was to try steering as true a course as he could along the way. He believed in a God, and he loved life, but both remained mysteries.

Moving from the small bedroom in the cabin to the living room to sleep was a decision he made soon after his wife's death. Sitting there on the small brass framed bed, the one possession he treasured, he turned his gaze slowly from the kitchen area to the doorway, leading out to the porch. And at that moment his breathing stopped. His heart began to pound even harder, almost out of control. He moaned in fear. There, framed in the doorway, was a dark form, moving effortlessly into the living room. There had been no sound of the door opening beforehand, and even then, it was still shut, like he left it before going to bed.

"Who are you? What are you doing in my home?" was all he could manage hoarsely to cry out, before fear paralyzed him, and he began to tremble uncontrollably. Not being around people that much these last few years, to have someone appear like this was terrifying to him. He was not an especially brave person, in his own estimation, and it seemed at this moment that he might lose control of his bowels as well.

The blackened form replied in a voice that resonated throughout the room and seemed to rattle anything loosened, stacked or unhinged. "I have been observing you for a long time. And now I need to speak with you. Time has become an issue in what I have to tell you. There is not much left of it left. And you will have much to do."

The dark figure continued, "I know you will have many questions and concerns, but first let me speak. Maybe by my talking, you will find yourself calming down somewhat. First off, I mean you no harm. And none will come to you from my hand. But others have a different plan in mind. And that brings me to the reason for my being here. Your life, possibly all life as it now exists, could cease in the months ahead unless something dramatic is not done to try and reverse what now seems almost inevitable.

"Briefly, let me share with you why this is happening. Too many people of this world are losing their collective sense of humor. And believe me that is essential for everyone to have. It gives you the best hope of living responsibly and peacefully with each other. And too many are losing the sense of being connected to one another, to the other species you share this world with, and to Something that exists beyond your daily, earthly pursuits. How this catastrophe may occur is still unclear to me, but daily I become more aware of so many having this awful intent.

'But more specifically, I need to explain to you why I have appeared before you tonight. We have a mission that you must undertake immediately. We must try to halt what is driving this spiral of planned death and destruction. My hope and plan is to begin a process that might reverse the feelings of worldwide alienation and distrust, before they result in uncontrollable evil intentions. And I have chosen you to start the plan in motion."

Still sitting, half slumped on his bed, with his mouth gaping open, shaped neatly like a petrified scream, Clem gasped and stuttered, "Am I still asleep?"

"No", replied the shadowy form.

"Who are you? What are you? Where did you come from? Are there more of you coming here tonight?"

"The answers to your questions will be come in due course," the stranger replied. "Right now, you just need to understand that no harm is going to come to you personally by my hand. And for the present moment, we have to begin preparations for you to undertake a journey. I am going to have you, and maybe one other person, start trying to revitalize the population around you. You will be the messenger to the people, not by what you say, but by what you do. And if that approach does not work, I will have to resort to implementing another, much less desired one. For now, we need to alter somewhat your general appearance before we get too much further along."

"Wait a minute!" Clem was finally able to blurt out. "I don't remember volunteering for anything, and I didn't invite you here. This can't be happening to me. I've had it with this dream I'm having! Enough of this!"

With that, Clem stood, somewhat unsteadily to

be sure, and made his way ungracefully to the doorway where the shadowy figure stood. Ignoring that the form may be still there, Clem opened it and marched through, without touching the dark figure. He did notice, however, a strange sensation as he passed what he had thought was the dream shadow. Once outside, he felt reassured and more relaxed. "Now then," he thought, "that dream is over". Looking up at the night sky, ablaze with starlight, from horizon to horizon, it was a great comfort for him. He felt relieved.

"Feeling better now?" came a more serious voice from the doorway.

Hearing what he thought was the dream voice, Clem's bladder, or more exactly, all his sphincters, reacted spontaneously.

"Maybe I need to start over again with you," the voice resumed. "Maybe if I give you a small demonstration of the importance and urgency of my visit here, you will better understand my intentions. I see there is real doubt about whether I am serious or even exist. So, let us start by your saying something to me, whatever comes to mind." And at this point the darkened form, while Clem's back was still turned away, reached forward and held Clem briefly by the shoulder. The touch was so light, and the shock of what was taking place was so profound, Clem never noticed.

"Oh! My God, please help me...please forgive me, and help me!" Clem intoned in a whisper. But it was spoken in fluent Russian, a language he had never heard nor ever spoken. Spinning around to face the shadow, he stuttered, "My Lord, what is happening to me?" And, again, this too was spoken in a language he had never heard before. Yet, it was understandable to him, when he spoke it.

"That's right," the figure said, moving away from him and back onto the porch. "You have spoken and understood perfect Russian. And if you name any other language, you will be able to do the same with it. You now have the ability to speak and understand all the languages of this world. And there will be other surprises in store for you as you go along, so don't be too shocked when they occur.

TWO: PLAN B

Janice and Sid Blackwell lived in a small house close to the Hoquiam River, about two miles out of town. Their home was surrounded by young forest of Spruce, Douglas and Noble Fir and Cedar, with Alder scattered throughout their property. The presence of Alder most likely indicated that the old growth forest had long since been harvested by long-forgotten, but hardy, men and women. True, the native people of this area had, blessedly, left the landscape relatively untouched for thousands of years. And that should be acknowledged as the soundest judgment and strength of all who have peopled this region. But, sadly, these brave and industrious native people seem to be caught up in the lure of building more and bigger gambling halls and resorts. This easy money and lifestyle, which is derived from gambling, when it's compared to the remarkable and innovative life of their ancestors, is a complete antithesis. Equally distressing, certain members of the majority population in the area now appear intent on denuding the region for housing projects, golf courses and commercial ventures. If the land and the trees could talk, the conversation would be woeful.

It was December 1st, and the rainforest was soggy. Even when it was not raining, there was often the dripping sound of water falling from the branches.

Little streamlets were everywhere. And the mat of downed autumn leaves and old conifer needles was a spongy carpet. The ever-present fragrance this time of year was of the wet. It was not a monsoon wet of the tropics, with its heavy scent of mildew and decomposition. Rather, it was a softer smell of cedar and fir, mixed over the eons of their accumulated growth. In this part of the forest there was no time for jungle rot to develop, with its rankness. Here the dramatic change of seasons kept the landscape scoured and the air filtered. And the first snow of the season was fast approaching the Blackwell's farm.

As usual when Sid was not working in the woods, he had to spend time managing the effects of November's rain storms. He was about to head out to the back of their property to fill sandbags and place them along their fence line that divided their property from the land bordering the river. They lived along the lower stretch of the river that was influenced by tidal changes from the Pacific Ocean. And in recent years, more so in the last couple, they had noticed flooding was more frequent along the river. It occurred both here and in town during a heavy rain combined with a high tide. The dikes were no longer high enough in town. And now their land was starting to flood as well.

"How long will you be out back?" Janice called out, as Sid lifted his shovel and gathered up a bundle of reinforced plastic bags to be used as sandbags.

"Probably a couple of hours are all. There aren't more than 15-20 bags here to fill and stack. We'll probably have to go into town to the fire department and get some more later today," he replied.

"Take care, then," she answered. "It's getting pretty boggy out there now."

Janice watched him slog along the wet pasture, appearing to heave each leg out of the soggy ground as he inched his way toward the river. He was a strong and robust man, and she was very proud of him. He didn't finish high school, but chose to follow the work path of his father and grandfather, that of farmer and tree faller. For the last twenty-one years, he had worked in the woods of the Puget Sound, cutting timber for all the major lumber companies. All the while, he still worked their small farm. She knew that these skills would not be passed on to their son and daughter. His work world was disappearing, like it was for so many others. Corporations owned much of the land and harvestable timber now. And they outsourced any work they could to the cheapest labor pool. Then, once the land was exhausted and denuded, they would often sell it to the highest bidder for residential or resort development. Time to work the land and the woods was not on his side. He was a dear and gentle man, and she loved him as much now as when they first met.

As he passed from view, she decided to walk out to the highway and see if their Seattle newspaper had been delivered. It was their morning paper. In the afternoon, they also had the local newspaper delivered for keeping up on nearby news and events. Today she wanted to check the paper's classifieds for any ads regarding puppies. Their black Labrador had died last week, and their children wanted a brown Lab for their next pet.

Once she got the newspaper and got back to the house, she settled down on the living room sofa and started sorting through the paper for the classified section. Once she found it, she scanned for pets and animals, but nothing interesting was being advertised. With nothing particular in mind, she shifted her attention to the general announcements and job wanted ads. Just then, something strange and seemingly out of place got her attention. It was an oddly worded offer:

"Enter a chance to be chosen to attend a free, international, investigative Symposium of urgent importance on 1st -8th. Spend seven days and nights in the warmth and sunshine of Southern California's Mojave Desert. All expenses will be paid for you and your family, if you are chosen. Simply fill in the requested information and answer the following questions. E-mail and air mail your reply no later than this December 5th. Families selected will be notified on December 26th. Please use only one type written page, providing your names, address, telephone number, email address, occupations of answers to the following questions. How do you cope with stress? What gives you your deepest happiness? How well do you interact with strangers and new situations? What makes you laugh? Send to: www.amrebkeepers.com and to Amboy Rebuilders and Keepers, Ltd., P.O. Box 439, Amboy, CA. 95100. U.S.A."

She laid the paper down in her lap and stared out the picture window that overlooked the back of their property. It was a peaceful sight, no matter the season or the weather. She wondered out loud, "Is this a hoax? Could there be anything to it?"

It was so curiously worded that she reread it a number of times, wondering why someone would ask such questions, and then why would there be this free symposium for a family? And all of this to take place in the desert…none of it fit together. Her puzzlement grew. She was bright, but circumstances at the time she graduated from high school, prevented her from attending college, even though she would have easily been accepted to any she would have applied to. Once she completed high school, she began work at a cookie and candy factory in her home town of Bismarck. She had always loved to read and to draw any humor possible out of day-to-day life. Her northern plains upbringing had instilled a determination, honesty and generous nature in her that brought a unique perspective to this offer. It intrigued her. She decided she would try for it and surprise her husband and family with a free trip, if they were accepted.

She knew that Sid would be a couple of hours, at least, working down by the lower fence line, so that would give her time to get started on her reply.

She found a used insurance notice which was blank on the back side and began scribbling all the names of her family, their ages, occupations and the other requested information. Then, taking the next hour, she composed her answers to the questions. Once that was done, she went over to their computer and typed up her response. It took some rewording and changing the letter size, but she finally got it all on one page. Looking out the window, again, she checked to see if Sid was on his way up yet. There being no sign of him, she read aloud what she had written and then e-mailed it. It read:

"Rural Route #1
Hoquiam, WA 98760
(942) 367-9876
E-mail: jbsb@pugsnd.com
Janice Blackwell, age 39, homemaker,
          mother.
Sidney Blackwell, age 49, logger, farmer,
          father.
Tim Blackwell, age 16, student.
Kathy Blackwell, age 14, student.
1. For me there are two kinds of stress. Long

term, e.g. a difficult and dangerous job or caring for someone you love who is very ill. And short term stress, e.g. witnessing a house fire, a tornado, someone collapsing in front of you. For the long term stress, I must take one day at a time, not focusing or worrying about the next. Do the best I can and be as organized as possible. And praying daily for guidance and patience, trying to find some pleasure and satisfaction in what I am doing each day. For the short term stress, it involves the same skills as those used in managing the long term, but condensing them into split second decisions and actions. Perform the "ABC's" of the situation, whether it is CPR or evacuation. Stay focused on the moment. Do not be preoccupied whether you are doing the right thing. And always, in either situation, be aware of the safety of yourself and others. But if risking your life is part of the ABC's, then do it.

2. Happiness, for me, can be associated with my surroundings, e.g. a choir singing in a church or a cathedral, music playing in my living room. It can be due to being with my husband or my children, not doing anything in particular. Or it can be interacting with others or being somewhere, e.g. a conversation with strangers of similar interests, being in the woods and sensing all around you. It can be when I am alone or with others.

3. My interaction with strangers and new situations depends on the circumstances of our meeting. It can be cautious and reserved in a stressful situation, or it can be welcoming and inviting in a social one. I am curious by nature and like to listen to others. I like to tell stories,

so I also like to talk. I am much better one to one. It is difficult for me to enter a function with a large group of strangers and start interacting. Generally, new situations do not overwhelm me, but I have noticed as I get older, that I am more hesitant and less carefree when confronted by them.

4. I laugh when I feel comfortable with those around me, giving me the freedom to say, without thinking ahead, things that are oddly connected with the subject being discussed. It can be an exaggeration, a comparison, make believe, enlisting a pet or wildlife in a conversation (imagining what they might say in such a situation). I laugh at humor initiated by others, especially when it is an unexpected surprise, a unique perspective, or a turn of phrase. And I always like a good pratfall. Exaggeration and make believe can be funny either in cartoons, writings, on stage or in social circumstances. I enjoy laughing and trying to get others to do so as well."

Next, she addressed an envelope, put a stamp on it, walked out to their roadside mailbox and raised the red flag, signaling there was a letter to post. Just as she got back into the living room, she heard Sid close the back door. Another busy day was about to get started, and this strange message and reply was soon forgotten. In fact, in the days following, she tried to find the same notice in the paper.

Unnoticed by Janice, if not most of the other inhabitants of the planet, this same announcement appeared only this one time in scattered newspapers in every state, province, region and canton on in all of them, it was on that same December day.

THREE: GETTING ACQUAINTED

Associated with his uninvited house guest's linguistic, slight-of-hand, Clem also noticed he felt a certain calming effect as well. The raw fear and panic was subsiding.   Maybe it was resignation to his impending fate, or to something else, but it was definitely noticeable. However, he now needed to get out of his night clothes and take a shower. At this moment, he was mostly embarrassed. And he was hungry.

Slipping back into his cabin, trying hard to avoid looking at the dark form standing inside the front doorway, he went straight into his bathroom, removed his dirty clothes and took an almost endless shower. Finishing that, he shaved, changed into his last set of clean clothes and headed to the kitchen stove.

"Would you like to have some fried eggs and bacon?" Clem called out, as if the shadowy figure was somewhere a mile down the highway, rather than still standing inside his front door.

"It's been eons since I have," was the reply.

"Well, if you can make me talk and even understand all those foreign languages, seems like you could apply that same nose-twitching, ear-wiggling magic to yourself and have an appetite. It sure couldn't hurt you. And if this business you mentioned is so urgent and important, a little food might spark you up. What do you say?"

About now, the visitor began to wonder if this hands-on approach, with someone like Clem, was the smartest move. Maybe the quaking, mumbling Clem was a better choice to work with. "Get someone relaxed, and free will takes over. I'll never learn..." The visitor's expression appeared to say, if Clem could have seen it. "Ok, I'll try, but make my eggs scrambled," came the reply.

"Kind of picky for a shadow," Clem mumbled, thinking that he was talking to himself. But, of course, even the flutter of a butterfly wing could be heard by the visitor. But no reply was made, and the remark was ignored.

After he finished cooking the meal, both sat down at the small kitchen table and ate silently. Clem had cooked nearly a dozen eggs and half a package of bacon, along with toasting seven slices of bread. He covered everything on his plate with ketchup, a habit that became more pronounced as he aged. Food seemed to have lost a lot of its flavor, and using ketchup spruced it up enough so that he at least would eat something.

When they finished eating and Clem had poured his third cup of coffee, he leaned back in his chair and asked, "What do folks call you? You must have a name. With this big agenda you have hinted at, it must be an important sounding name, certainly nothing like mine."

"For now," came the reply, "you can just call me 'B', for that 'big agenda', as you describe it. That ought to do for now."

Clem shrugged and nodded, "Well, 'B' it is."

He had noticed whenever he forced himself to glance briefly toward his visitor, which was not frequent, due to his persistent nagging fear and reservation about who B was, the form of B appeared shapeless and not well defined. There were no distinct facial features or hand movements. The figure before him was like a shroud, but not entirely filled in; it was like a cloud or a shadow that spoke and moved with some purpose. Clem didn't feel comfortable staring, so this impression was the one that lasted for much of the time they spent together in the days, weeks and months ahead.

(Throughout many years, your chronicler of these pages has wondered why Clem was chosen by B for this most fantastic undertaking. By this writing, and probably for evermore, the reasons can only be a source of conjecture. No one will probably ever know what B's motivation was to choose him. What follows are my own thoughts on the matter. One of the reasons Clem was chosen for the tasks he was soon to undertake, was his natural ability to accept whatever was revolving around him. His questioning nature was more to seek how things worked, not to probe the reality around him. This, along with his other traits, after he was observed for some time, led to his being selected. He had an intelligence that was untapped, along with a unique way of adapting and improvising. He approached problems from a fresh perspective. For the missions ahead of him, he seemed well suited for the tasks. His years of isolation had only improved those traits. And now it was time to describe to him what lay ahead.)

Then, as Clem recounted to me, B began explaining to him the following. "As you are finishing your coffee, let me describe for you in more detail what is going to be your essential role in the process ahead. You will be my messenger, my scout, my bringer of tidings to all you meet. And in the course of all this, you will be meeting many people, literally touching them, as it were. Additionally, you will have to use organizational skills that you never knew you possessed. You will know more about each phase of this process as it develops. For now, let me say there are to be two plans of action that will be set in motion simultaneously. You will be involved in both, but each in a different capacity.

"Speed is most urgent now. Even I am unsure exactly how much time is left before events career completely out of control. We will begin by going somewhere and finding you a suitable wardrobe to wear, spend some time improving your appearance, and then you will begin.

"I will be passing on to you certain abilities that will not be immediately obvious to you. You, in turn, will need to physically touch each person to pass some of these same abilities on to them. The effects will be more dramatic the stronger the touch or hand shake, or the more frequently they are contacted by you. I am hoping that whoever is touched by you will be prompted, by what they then experience, to reach out and touch others around them as well. That is absolutely necessary for this phase to be effective. Just like the passing of the flu virus in a pandemic, I hope this method of transmission will be as rapid, but certainly not as dangerous. On the contrary, it must have the totally opposite effect. It has to bring people together. Motivating people to reach out to one another is the issue here. Right now you are the sole person with this ability. In studying you, I found you are the only person that I can fully trust not to abuse it, as tempting as it may become.

"Once you have performed this mission, you will then return here to help with the backup plan. But I have to hope it will not be necessary to fully implement the alternate plan. I am going to have you lay the groundwork for this backup plan today, before you depart on your first venture.

"Now, to expand a little further on why all of

this is necessary, as I mentioned to you earlier, when I was introducing myself...."

"Excuse me," Clem interrupted, "I believe that I missed that part. All I remember is just seeing you and having everything I ate or drank try to get as much distance from me as soon as possible. It wasn't like you spent much time with formal introductions or niceties. If you are going to have me take that same approach with the folks that I meet, I believe I'll pass. Try the next hermit down the road."

"There was no way that you could be forewarned about my actual speaking to you," B replied. "You did have those visitations from me, as the blackened form, over these past months. Those were to prepare you, somewhat, for my actually speaking to you."

"Pretty subtle," Clem responded.

"Be that as it may, we are now linked together, and you need to have at least some general idea as to why. Terrorism, warfare, political stalemates, destructive capabilities in the hands of insane despots, a general gridlock of government institutions and its leadership, and a loss of the peoples' willingness and ability to calmly, and with good humor, interact with one another have brought your world to a tipping point. And soon it will snap. Very soon, I am afraid. And unless a surge of renewal and composure is infused into this world of yours, minimal to no life may be all that is left.

"I need you to pack your everyday personal articles, such as a toothbrush, comb, and any medications that you take. Put them in a bag of some kind, and we need to leave right now. You've eaten, slept some, and now it is time to start. I will see that you get everything else you need, once we get into a nearby city."

Feeling his choices were well defined and any

attempt to argue or protest was hopelessly futile, Clem nodded his head, got up from the table and packed the few items he thought he might need for the journey ahead. The sun was rising as he closed the cabin door.

FOUR: GETTING STARTED

The worn condition of Clem's pickup truck was much beyond its years of service. It was a motorized wreck. Whatever color it used to be could only be found in the Department of Motor Vehicles files. It had to be on record somewhere, but not on its surface. Sand blasted for years, blistered and charred from the intense heat, it was now a yellowish brown, superimposed on some malignant rusting process. The truck bed was already rusted through in many places. The dashboard and seats had long since lost their over-stuffed padding. He had to use old blankets to cover much of the seats' exposed inner springs. And the odor upon opening the door was a combination of smoldering shoe leather, a dusty basement and a dog kennel long overdue for some cleaning.

In fact, Clem had had two dogs up until a few months ago. They were his constant companions. But the coyotes would eventually tease each of them out into their trap and take them. He had tried everything to insure their safety, even using the truck cab as a temporary shelter. With the loss of his last dog, he decided it was too cruel to have one. It was a sad decision for him.

As he sealed the plastic grocery bag with his toiletry articles, a couple changes of underwear and loaded it into the bed of his truck, he called out to B,

"Well, I guess I'm ready to head off. Do you want me to start the engine?"

"Yes," came Bs reply. "We need to be on our way."

Surprisingly, the truck engine snapped to and started with the first turn of the ignition key. With a grinding of gears, Clem backed up, shifted into first gear and headed out onto the old highway. It was about a hundred yards from his cabin. Once on the highway, they had about 20 miles to travel before getting to Amboy, the next closest settlement.

Amboy had had its days in the sun, both literally and figuratively. When Route 66 was in full flower, Amboy was a sought after watering hole. Built by a huge, dry lake basin, some of which was still mined for salt, it was also a railroad water stop when steam locomotives were in use. Unfortunately, time marched on rather cruelly for Amboy. The Interstate Highway was built north of town about fifteen miles, and salt began to leach into their water supply. And the passers by all but vanished.

Salt was their only major natural resource. Scattered small hard rock mines were also found in the area, with their hillside tailings seen here and there. But their commercial value was minimal to Amboy's ultimate survival. Other dry lake basin communities in that region of the Mojave Desert were fortunate enough to have many other valuable mineral resources in their dry lake beds to mine. They provided additional mining jobs and a reprieve from becoming another western ghost town. Amboy, sadly, was fast heading in the opposite direction.

Traveling about 50 miles per hour, now the truck's top cruising speed, they bounced along the roadbed heading west. B broke the quiet since they had left the cabin announcing, "You will need to conduct some business in Amboy. There are two chores that I need you to do there in preparation for what has to be done later.

"First, I need you to stop at the post office, and tell the clerk there that she can expect a large amount of mail to come into her station in the days and weeks ahead. And that she will probably need to order ahead some more post office bags to store the incoming mail. As the mail arrives, she should just have the bags delivered to your residence. Tell her to leave them on your front porch. They will be safe there.

"Then, and this is a little more complicated, I need you to go to the restaurant/motel office across the street from the post office and ask for the owner. Even though the facility is in a rundown condition, instruct that individual that we will need to reserve all their rooms for the month of February. To pay for this and other expenses, I am going to give you a debit/credit card, but you will use it as a debit card only. Using this card will be the way you will pay for what I request you to do in the months ahead."

Handing him the plastic card, Clem looked at it with general interest. He had had a credit card before, but the term "credit/debit" together was confusing to him. He had no idea how 'debit' applied to his using the card. For him in recent years, it had been cash and carry. His financial horizon was limited to whatever cash he had immediately in hand. To him, it seemed like B was being too trusting and assuming too much about what he knew and didn't know. Already, he was beginning to feel overwhelmed at the developing scope of this venture. His voice had some quiver to it when he said, "Thanks for trusting me with this. But you'll need to tell me when and how to use it, to make sure I don't make any mistakes."

"Don't worry, I will," B responded. "And you

will do fine. But as you are about to pull into the post office parking area, I need to let you know about another aspect to this journey we are starting. To you, I am visible, although I realize it is fuzzy. Others around you will not see me, unless I chose to make it possible. And at times I will be in your presence, but you may not know it. Because of that, you will need to be a little more careful how and when you speak to me, especially when someone is present, or we are in a crowd. For the time being, I will be beside you, but as we proceed, I will need you to perform certain duties on your own."

Hearing all this just added to the anxiety that had been building since Clem was instructed to see the postmistress in Amboy. He was getting a little too much information all at once. But he tried to put on his bravest front and nodded. By then, he pulled up in front of the post office.

Amboy's post office resembled a concrete block house restroom in a bygone era city park. It long ago had its last coat of paint, and it appeared that it was white wash at that. There were large flakes of paint coming off, revealing an aged, concrete gray underneath. The only thing that was new and crisp was the American flag, atop a high pole to the side of the building. The flag alone, blurred the building's presence, and made the setting official. Inside, on one half, were banks of unused post office boxes, and the other half was framed by an eight foot long counter top. Behind the counter stood Rose, the postmistress in Amboy for over twenty-five years. Her longevity was due in part to her husband's job, as one of the few remaining workers at the nearby salt mine. These days she opened at dawn, sorted what little mail there was, greeted any customers that wandered in, and closed down by 10 a.m. She kept summer hours the year around. The heat dictated her hours of operation.

As Clem walked in, she greeted him with, "Clem Newberry, where have you been? You haven't been around here in months! Harry and I thought that you might have taken ill or something. Have you been away?"

"Nope," he answered, "I've just been staying closer to home lately. Weather turned colder sooner than usual, and I found myself keeping my own company more. But now I am going to be taking off for a while. I've got some business to attend to out of the area, and I probably won't be back for a few weeks anyway."

"You going to see family?" she then asked.

"Well, not really," he said hesitantly. Because it was at this point he realized he was going to have to begin speaking about the mission or venture or whatever you call it, that he was embarking on. He didn't want to be telling lies to cover himself. That would get too confusing for him, and it just wouldn't be right.

"Believe it or not, I have been asked by someone to assist in a rather important and complicated project. And it's going to require that I be gone for a while. I can't really reveal the details of it yet, because I am still not too clear myself what is going to happen. But it is because of all this that I am coming in to see you today. I need to ask big favor of you, and if there is payment due in advance, I certainly will pay you.

"Sometime pretty soon, there will be mail coming in to my post office box, under a different heading, and there will be a lot of it. And, if you will, I need you to bag it up, and whenever a bag is full, get someone to take it out to my place and just leave it on the porch. You'll probably need to send in a request for some extra bags to handle the volume that might be coming."

"Is there anything illegal about any of this,

Clem?" she snapped back.

"No, no, nothing like that Rose. It's all very important business. In fact, after I leave here, I have to go across the street and make arrangements with Hazel and Ray to reserve their motel for the month of February."

"All their rooms for a whole month!" she exclaimed, with less challenge in her voice.

"That's right. And the mail that will be coming here is directly related to the motel reservations. But don't ask me how or why yet, because I don't know. But I do know that it's important. You can trust me, Rose. I'm really too stupid to be involved in something dangerous, criminal or underhanded. And, as soon as I know more, and when I am back in town, I will fill you in. In the meantime, do you need a deposit for the mail that will be coming?"

"No, that won't be necessary. But you should know that the postal inspectors will be suspicious if anything other than regular mail comes. If it is as you say, there will be no problems getting it all to your place. And I would like you to stop by, and let me know what's happening as you find out more."

"Thanks Rose. I will stop by, as soon as I get back from my trip. See you later, then." And he pushed open the door and headed out to his truck.

As he exited through the doorway, he overheard Rose say under her breath, "If that doesn't beat all. Clem involved in some kind of venture. What's next?"

Getting back to his truck, he soon backed it up to head across the old highway to the motel. As he turned the truck around, B asked, "Did you have any problem?"

"Not really," Clem answered. "I have to get used to the idea of saying something truthful, while not really knowing what I am talking about. But Rose is going to cooperate with your request anyway. She'd like to know more about what's going on when I know. This makes sense to me."

"Good," B interjected rather enthusiastically, Clem thought. Then B added, "At least we are now underway. Pray, dear fellow, that this all works."

"B, if I knew a good prayer, I would have started saying it constantly, starting about 1 a.m. this morning. But I never had too much to do with that business during my life. Then again, if I had, it probably would have come in handy now and then."

"I know," was all B said in response.

Pulling up in front of the Roadway 66 Motel, the only motel in Amboy or anywhere else for at least 150 miles of desolate old highway, it was clear that a night's lodging here was something most people avoided. It looked like no one had stayed there for years. It was a typical 1940's or 50's two story structure. Built in an 'L' shape. It, too, had the brownish tan color of the desert. In places where the prevailing wind did not hit the surface full force, there was a faded sky blue color. The asphalt roadway up to and around it was pitted by pot holes, some quite deep and deserving respect. They also were an indication that roadway maintenance was not a priority here either. There was a tattered balcony surrounding the second floor, and a swimming pool in the front that had not been used in years. Behind the main structure there were six duplex, two bedroom cabins. The main building had 63 two bedroom units.

Gas pumps located under a large overhang, framed the front of the restaurant, which also served as the motel's office. The restaurant was partitioned by a large set of folding doors. The rear portion, behind these doors, would seat approximately 100 people. In the main restaurant area, where the office was located, there were twenty tables, fifteen booths, and a large counter that would seat eighteen more customers. Altogether,

Clem figured later, there was seating for about 275-300 people, if you included both the front and rear sections.

Parking off to the side of the building, Clem walked around and entered through the restaurant door. Walking up to the combination cashier and registration counter, he rang a bell that had a roughly written note attached, announcing, "Hit me if you want help." He banged it sharply, figuring whoever was on duty might be some distance away or even asleep, there being little business most week days. On weekends there was a little more traffic through the area, with travelers taking short cuts through here going to and from Las Vegas. Today was Monday, and it was quiet.

After waiting some time, he hit the bell again, twice. And almost immediately a man, in his mid 60's stepped through the doorway. His face was somewhat bloated, and he had darkened areas under his eyes. It appeared that he had not shaved for two or three days, which was not all that uncommon for folks who lived in these parts. He was somewhat overweight. But the biggest indicator that his health was in decline had to be his slow and labored movements, like he was walking through deep snow. His speech was often halting, with him having to pause to find his breath, even after speaking a few words. Clem was not a student of health matters, other than those associated with his own family's history, but he knew enough to recognize that Ray's was not at its peak. Everyone in Amboy wished he would stop smoking.

"Morning, Clem," Ray, the motel and restaurant co-owner, gasped. "What brings you in this time of day, and all fired up to keep banging that bell? I have to say we've missed not having you in here lately for your usual lunch. It hasn't been the same without you. What's up?"

"Well, Ray," Clem began, "I've got a big

opportunity for you and a big favor to ask of you. Maybe I'll start with the opportunity first. I need to reserve all your rooms here in the motel for the entire month of February.

With that, Ray acted like he'd attempted to swallow his entire breakfast with one bite. He spontaneously coughed and blurted out, "What is heaven's name are you talking about? Clem, you hardly have enough money from day to day to buy yourself a cheese sandwich and a cup of coffee for lunch, much less talk about reserving this entire motel for a month. This must be a joke."

"No, it isn't, Ray. I'm serious. And I will insure the reservation with this card."

Now, up to this time Clem had not thought about the ramifications of what he was embarking on. With Rose he simply made the offer to pay her something. But with Ray, he was going to have to pay him with cash or show good faith somehow. Neither of which he, personally, had. To try and bluff Ray was a waste of time or worse. He had to convince him that B was not a hoax. And for himself, that this was not some sort of cruel, cosmic joke. Handing Ray the credit/debit card that B had given him, he tried to look commanding and business like, but there was a slight tremor in his hand.

"Clem, I will have to run a check on this card. And I'll tell you now, for you to reserve the motel for that period of time and with that many people, you'll have to pony up some advance money. I'm sorry, but as you can see, we are in no shape to receive that many people without some major refurbishing and repainting. But you can't be serious, are you?"

"Sure am," came the quick reply. "It's an important meeting with people and families coming from far away. (This was nothing he had been told, but it seemed ok to say it, given the comments B had made to him earlier.) I am not sure how long anyone is actually staying, but the individual making these arrangements has instructed me to have you block out everything here for that entire month."

"Well, before this conversation goes any further, I am going to run a check on this card you gave me." With a quick swipe through the countertop, card entry box, he waited to see what message came up. The digital screen indicated, 'Processing' had been initiated. Then the message appeared, 'Enter Amount'. Seeing that, Ray knew the card was at least not bogus. But he wondered how Clem had come by getting it.

"Alright, Clem, it does appear your card is active. But where exactly did you get it and from whom? I need to know that it is not stolen or lost."

"It was given to me to use by my contact individual, who goes by the name, B. I don't know anything else about him. I am just following his instructions. I do know that it does not involve anything illegal or immoral, so you don't have to think that. And I know, as I said before, that it involves something very important. But what it is exactly, I can't say."

"Can't or won't?" Ray interrupted.

"Ray, it's like I said to Rose just a few minutes ago. I am just too dumb to be involved in some scheme. I really don't know any other details, other than what I've told you. And if you would like a deposit or something for good faith, just tell me what it is.'

Ray thought a minute, looking away from Clem. This offer did have the hint of opportunity about it. And if he were to get a down payment, enough to upgrade the motel somewhat, it wouldn't hurt to at least play along for now. But he'd need a considerable amount to begin the sprucing up.

"Clem, I will need $25,000.00 right away to start getting the motel in shape enough to house that many people. And I'll probably need another $25,000.00 in another month to get supplies, food and linen in stock. But I must add that if for some reason your plan falls through, this money is non-refundable. Is that clear?"

"I understand," Clem answered. "Now, go ahead and do whatever you need to with that machine to get you started."

Shaking his head, Ray then entered the $25,000.00 amount into the card entry box and pressed 'debit', as Clem had instructed him to beforehand. Then they both waited nervously to see what followed and within about ten seconds, up popped the screen, asking for an authorizing signature. Ray seemed to turn pale and uttered a low gasp. "Clem, you need to sign this."

In rather neat script, Clem signed his full name, Clement L. Newberry. And in another ten seconds, the cash register buzzed and up came a script, indicating that the "Roadway 66 Motel and Restaurant" had just been credited $25,000.00.

Ray leaned back in total surprise. This little man came in here, like he had done a thousand times before. But in two short minutes he had changed everything in Ray's universe. It was then that his manner and mood changed completely.

"Right! I'll get started on getting the motel and the area around here straightened out and cleaned up, with some new paint and carpet. This must be important for this to be happening like it is. I bet it's some kind of government thing."

Clem was relieved this first assignment was about to be completed, and now he was in a hurry to get outside before he did something wrong. So in reply, he said, "Thanks for your help, Ray. I should be back here in another 3-4 weeks to see how things are going. You and Hazel take care of yourselves."

"And the same back at you, Clem."

Clem turned and headed toward the doorway, while Ray immediately exited into the living area to share the bountiful news with his wife. Lying by the doorway, as usual, was Amboy's resident dog, Jake. Everyone who came in soon met and petted Jake. He was an old fellow, probably 15-16 years old. General opinion had it that he was a mix of Labrador, Great Dane and German shepherd. True enough, he was very large, but he was also extremely gentle. He had eyes that followed your every move, and he held your gaze, not shifting them nervously, like most animals do. His look had an understanding and compassion that comforted all who spent time with him.

Clem, as usual, reached down to scratch and pet him. At some point, he apparently also even took one of Jake's paws and gently shook, probably emphasizing a heartfelt greeting. That gesture, and all the touching of Jake, had a wondrous aftereffect. Looking into Jake's eyes after this, Clem quietly said, "Hey, there, dear Jakie, it is so good to see you. I hope you are doing ok. I'm going to be gone for a while, so take care of yourself my friend."

And to Clem's astonishment, and as B had forewarned him, he heard in reply, "Thank you, Clem, I will try."

Being mildly confused from all the recent excitement, Clem reared backwards, momentarily losing his balance. In a kind of stumbling motion, he pushed open the restaurant door and made his way back to the truck. Surprisingly, in his relief to be done with this phase of B's plan, he soon forgot all about his experience with Jake. There was just too much to do and to think about.

FIVE: ROUTE 66

The desert around Amboy is both fascinating and stark. Nearby, there is an ancient, dormant volcano cone, with its river of black lava extending out to the highway. Barren hills, even a small range of mountains, ring the basin that Amboy struggles to survive in. In the early morning sun, shades of red, orange, yellow and off-white can be seen, each color representing rocks whose minerals were exposed through the area's long history of uplifts, earthquakes and volcanic activity. When there is enough soil to permit vegetation, creosote bushes dominate the landscape. And scatted amongst them can be seen yucca plants, ocotillo and choya cactus. Of course, if there is enough rainfall during the preceding winter months, spring brings a glorious display of wildflowers carpeting this entire region.

For Clem and B, however, it was now approaching mid morning and the bright sunshine distorted and faded the colors that would have been seen earlier. And a haze began to form that partially hid even the surrounding hills and mountains.

"Clem, I need to ask if you have a driver's license or some form of identification, and also if you possibly have a passport? I should have asked sooner, but the urgency to get underway did not leave us time to discuss some details."

"Whatever I have," he replied, "is in that glove

box in front of you. That's where I keep all my valuables and personal papers. It's my safety deposit box. I don't really have much need for official papers, so whatever I have, doesn't take up much room. You might look to see what's there. From what I recall, it seems like my driver's license should still be good. I think I had it renewed about three years ago. If my memory serves me at all, my wife, Elizabeth, and I did a little traveling to Mexico before she became bed bound. And we got passports to make that border crossing easier. She's been gone now over seven years, but I think there may be about a year left before it expires. But you can check."

Opening the compartment, B was able to confirm that Clem did have a valid driver's license and passport. There was still a year before the license expired and eight months before the passport did.

"Everything is fine," B reported. "And my next request is that once we get into a reasonably large enough community, we need to find you a store to buy some clothes, a carry bag for your extra clothes and belongings, and probably get a couple of other items I'll mention later. Also, be on the lookout for a travel agency. You will have to book some flights. You will be gone for a while."

"I figured that," Clem responded. "I told Rose at the post office that I could be gone up to a month. Was that about right?"

"Almost to the day. I will be with you until your first flight takes off, but then you will be on your own. By then, you will know exactly where and when you will be traveling, what to do, and how to do it. So you will not need me. There are other things that I need to do while you are away. And there is one other errand that I just thought of. When we pass through the next city, of any size, I need you to find the local newspaper office. We have some business to conduct there as well.

"If possible," B continued, "we need to get all these errands done and be in Los Angeles, somewhere near the airport by this evening. You will stay there overnight. Then you will start to work tomorrow, when you arrive at the Los Angeles airport terminal. From there you will go to New York City, by way of Chicago. After being in New York and New Jersey for two nights, you will fly on to London on Thanksgiving Day. For the remainder of the trip, I will fill you in later when you make the reservations."

As B was outlining all these travel plans, Clem was struggling to remember it all. However, he did think his anxiety was less noticeable. A definite calm seemed to take control when he sensed he was becoming overwhelmed. It was puzzling. All of this happening to him, and he was almost beginning to enjoy it. He turned his head slightly to glance toward B, but, as before, there was nothing distinct to see, no expression, no hand gestures, just a form and a voice. At that moment, his daydreaming was interrupted by his noticing a roadside marker, indicating Barstow was nineteen miles further.

"Barstow is probably a big enough city to accomplish all that you have mentioned," Clem announced. "We'll be there in about 25-30 minutes. But make sure to remind me after we finish all the chores, to get gas for the truck before we head off to Los Angeles. We'll just make it to Barstow with what's left in the tank."

Once inside the city limits, Clem began to look for any sign of a newspaper office, travel agency or department store. The first thing he found was a department store. Pulling into a large parking area, he nervously asked B if this store would do, and how would he like to handle the next phase of his plan.

"Are you going in with me?" Clem asked. "Or

do you just want me to get whatever I think I need?"

"Yes, I am going in. But remember no one will see or hear me. Again, I caution you not to speak to me if someone is near or watching. The last thing we need is for you to appear addled. Just be natural and try to relax. You will select two sets of sport coats and trousers, with dress shirts and ties to match. Then you will need one pair of dress and one pair of comfortable shoes. From here on, you will only wear these clothes outside your cabin. Once we finish here, we will find a barber shop. And when they are done with you, you will put on a set of your new clothes. Then we will proceed with the other contacts you have to make today."

"Got you," Clem answered. "I'm relieved that I took the time to take a shower earlier this morning, before I put on these new clothes."

Entering the store, these two entities, one looking a little thread bare and unkempt and the other quite invisible, proceeded to the Men's Fashions section. That was a phrase that seemed somewhat stuffy to Clem. If he had to characterize the world he had parted ways with a few years ago, he would have said it was an odd combination of being more dangerous and yet being less able to cope with the danger due to a softening of character and will. For him men don't wear fashions. They simply wear clothes. But, not wanting to disappoint B, he just muttered under his breath, "Oh, well, here I go.", and headed towards a clerk standing behind a nearby counter.

"I need to purchase some clothes today. Would you mind helping me pick them out?" Clem asked somewhat nervously.

The clerk, a young man in his mid twenties, looked at Clem as if he might be addressing someone else. He was not planning on this job being his vocational pathway. It was simply a part-time job over the holidays. He thought being indifferent to the individual before him was the natural thing to do, given his circumstances. He just appeared not to hear him and looked through him without a reply.

Clem, aware of this snub, would not be put off nor become angry. It certainly wasn't the first time he'd been treated like this in stores or businesses. Instead, he noticed that the young clerk had one hand on the counter, with the other hand resting on top of it, leaning away from the public he was supposed to be helping. Clem, with an easy, graceful move, reached out and gently touched the young man's hands. And, instantly, he became aware of the clerk's name. Quietly, he asked again, "Alan, would you mind helping me?"

Upon being touched, Alan would later describe the feeling as if he were taking a warm, soothing shower, after coming inside from some bitterly cold journey. Now he looked at Clem, with a sense of being with someone who was an old and trusted friend. "Sure, of course, it would be my pleasure to help you. What do you need today?"

Clem realized B had told him strange things would occur when he made contact with others, and, without a doubt, this clerk now had a different attitude. But he didn't have time to analyze what occurred; he needed to get some clothes. Immediately, he outlined for Alan what he needed and the three of them worked through the process of selecting and purchasing his wardrobe. Again, Clem used the debit card. But this time he was more confident in using it, but he still fumbled sliding the card and pushing the necessary buttons. Alan graciously helped him. And at this point, even the other clerks were noticing a change in Alan's customer attentiveness. It sure wasn't the usual Alan.

Once their purchases were complete, Clem asked Alan if there was a barber shop nearby.

"There is a new hair dresser salon downstairs in this building," he offered. "I hear they do a nice job. Just take the escalator down to the lower level and turn right. It's down the corridor on the left. And I don't think you'll need an appointment, if you try going there now."

Clem gathered up the bundles of clothes and shook Alan's hand, thanking him for his patience and kindness. Together Clem and B ambled off in the direction of the hair dresser shop. If Alan had watched them a little longer, he might have noticed how Clem seemed to leave an unusual amount of space between himself and the counters on his right side. He was carrying the bags of clothes in his left hand, and leaving a wide space between him and whatever was on his right side. And sometimes, it appeared his head would turn slightly to the right, as if in conversation. But, again, no one noticed.

Haircuts were low on Clem's list of 'must do's'. Fortunately for him and for others around him, his wife had cut his hair all the years they were married. After her death, he purchased an electric trimmer, which he used to shave off all his hair, whenever he thought it needed cutting. He would do this every two or three months. But more recently, he had let that lapse. His motivation for self-care was minimal. It was easier to tie it in a pony tail, tuck it under his hat or just let it hang over his shoulders. It was a tangle when he walked into The Perfect Look Hair Salon. B had tried, before they entered the salon, to prepare him for the looks he would get. He also instructed him to ask for a professional cut, wash and manicure. Lucky for their tight schedule today, there was no one waiting ahead of him, and within two hours he was done.

As Clem got out of the chair to pay for all this work, he asked the hair stylist, as he had learned they were called, "Is there somewhere I could change my clothes?"

"You could use our large changing room, if you like. It is in between shift change and break time, so no one would bother you," she answered.

Thanking her, he gathered up his recent purchases and entered the large area at the rear of the salon. It was scattered with lockers, a couple of old arm chairs, a few collapsible metal ones, a large table with coffee mugs, lunch sacks and an old empty chocolate candy box. Throughout this room and the work area, Clem noticed, there was a pervasive odor of hair products, almost like ammonia, he thought. Looking around, he saw that the restroom was off to one side. Placing his bags on the floor, he got out a brownish gray tweed sport coat, gray slacks, a light blue shirt and tie. Once he had changed into these and deposited the old clothes he was wearing into a large waste bin, he put on his new socks and dress shoes. And he looked at himself in the mirror for the first time. He thought he was looking at a total stranger.

Maybe it should also be noted that the hair stylist, who worked on Clem for those two hours, was now experiencing some strange symptoms. She now had a deepening calmness. Her workmates were more approachable. It was easier to laugh, to find humor in what someone said or did. She, by all measures, was simply more relaxed. As the funny little man left that she had just worked on for two hours, she shook her head. It was like he was about to suddenly leap from the ground and click his heels together.

As Clem closed the salon's door, B commented, "You look much better now. For the business ahead, you will not attract as much negative attention, and, more importantly, you will be better accepted and more likely to get the results we need. Now, you need to purchase a suitcase before the leave the store, and then we have to find that travel agency and a newspaper office. We must go to both before their business hours are over today. The travel agency will take the longest, so we should try to find the newspaper office next."

As they left the store, Clem asked one of the sale's clerks if she knew where they could find these two places. Fortunately, he was told they were both close by. In fact, a travel agency was in the same shopping complex as this store. They were also given simple directions to the local newspaper office. Placing his newly purchased suitcase, or grip, as he called it, into the bed of the truck, they got in and drove immediately to the newspaper office. Along the way B outlined for him what needed to be discussed with the newspaper reporter.

Once they entered the front door of the Barstow Herald, they were immediately standing before the Reception Desk. It appeared to serve as a barrier, preventing unwanted entrance into the offices' interior. Clem, looking rather important to the Receptionist, asked if he could please see one of the staff's investigative reporters.

The Receptionist, realizing this visitor may have some important news or business to conduct with the newspaper, inquired, "Do you have an appointment, Mr.?..."

"No," Clem answered. "But it is urgent that I speak with someone immediately about a serious matter that is about to get underway. Please see if anyone on your staff is free to see me now. I am unable to wait due to the urgency of what I have to say."

Sensing the immediacy and sincerity of his manner, she replied, "Well, then, let me see if I can find someone at their desk who might be able to help you." Turning sideways to the reception counter, she pressed some buttons for an extension and began talking to someone. After a brief exchange, she turned back to Clem and said, "Fred Wailand, who is actually our Senior Investigative Reporter, said he is free to see you right now. Just go through this doorway on my right, and he is in the first office on the right."

Thanking her, Clem steeled himself, and made his way into the newspaperman's cluttered office. If was like something Clem remembered reading about in a dime mystery novel. There were stacks of papers, books, and magazines on shelves, on the one desk, on a table across the room and on the floor. Behind the desk sat a middle aged man wearing a New York Yankee baseball cap and a polo shirt with the words written on it, "We have a dream". Under the words were detailed renderings of a whale, baby seal, some dolphins, and other fish, all lounging around a den-like room, each drinking a beer, with two men dressed like fishermen, serving them. His desk also had a computer on it, scattered folders and a couple of ash trays. He looked up at Clem as he entered the office. The look gave Clem the impression that this was a no nonsense kind of person. He looked at Clem without smiling; there was no "how are you doing?" nor any greeting whatsoever. He simply cocked his head slightly, narrowed his eyes somewhat, and asked, "Yes?..."

Clem introduced himself. Then, unrehearsed and spontaneously, he said, "I believe I have a story for you that will be one for the ages. I have an offer to make you the sole chronicler for a series of events that will probably reshape all our lives forever. You and you alone will have access to this information as it unfolds. But the only catch is that you cannot print anything until you are given the ok to do so. It does not involve anything illegal, immoral, or foolish. I am about to draw you into a confidence that requires strict secrecy. And you will be paid for all your time and effort, starting with today's request. But first I have to have your word that none of what I tell you or ask you to do will be printed until you are given permission to do so. Will you agree to that?"

Clem knew that this was a major step for him to take, not clearing with 'B' what he had just offered. But there was no prompting or gasps from his guide and mentor. Unless he turned around, he would not even know that B was still in the room. That being the case, he felt comfortable proceeding with this conversation as he thought best. What he obviously didn't know was that B, indeed, knew what was taking place with Clem. And that it was deeply satisfying. The gradual transformation of this desert hermit into the spokesperson, who had to now adapt and communicate in an untold number of upcoming new and challenging circumstances, was just what B had hoped for. No prompting was necessary.

Over his many years as a reporter, both in New York City for the "Tribune", and then later, as he had to keep moving westward to try and find the right climate to lessen his wife's worsening breathing problems, in St. Louis at the "Times" and now in Barstow at the "Herald", Fred had never been approached in such a manner, with such an outlandish offer. He was skeptical at best. The fellow standing in front of him was well dressed and well groomed, which at least said he wasn't there for a handout. And he did offer to pay him. In this way, the "Herald" was not out for expenses for his time spent. And things had been a little slow around here lately. So, he thought, what harm will it do to at least listen to this guy?

"Sit down, Mr.?..."

"Newberry, Clement Newberry is my name," Clem answered rather stiffly.

"Then sit down, Mr. Newberry, and fill me in on your offer. I can give you no guarantee that I will help you, but at least I will respect your confidence. And I may take some notes, if that is ok."

Relieved at his being given the opportunity to at least describe what was needed; Clem agreed to the note taking and sat down. He then proceeded to tell him what had been done thus far in Amboy, and what now needed to be done. Afterward, removing from his coast pocket what he had written down earlier from B instructions, he handed him a short list of a few cities and countries from around the world. Even though abbreviated, it was impressive. Next, he gave him a rough outline of the message that needed to be printed in a newspaper of his choice in each state, province and canton across the globe. And finally, following his giving him this material, he got out the debit card B had given him and laid it on his desk.

Looking across the desk at Mr. Wailand, Clem could sense a mixture of shock, skepticism and maybe even some fear. "This is a massive undertaking for me," Fred responded. "It could take me days to determine who to contact and how to complete the transmission of your message. And the language barrier is just staggering!"

Hearing this, Clem knew what he had to do to win over this reporter's support and help. He asked, "Would you please humor me by answering one question? Do you speak Russian?"

"No!" came the puzzled reply. "Besides being able to recognize some Russian dance and symphonic music, I have no grasp of that language nor do know much about its culture. Why do you ask?"

"Then, I have one other favor to ask of you. Would you please shake my hand?"

Shrugging, as if this whole episode was about to

surge out of control and become a farce, with a sigh of resignation, Fred reached out and shook Clem's hand.

Lowering his hand once that was done, Clem repeated, in fluent Russian this time, "Let me reintroduce myself. I am Clement Newberry. And I am pleased to make your acquaintance."

To his shock and almost horror, the reporter understood perfectly what he had just heard, and in response replied, in perfect Russian, "I understand you perfectly, for God's sake! What have you done to me?"

"I just shook your hand, is all," Clem replied. "But the act of my shaking it apparently has some kind of effect on a person. I'm beginning to see that the effect is not always the same. Touching someone has one effect, shaking their hand another, or by using both hands to touch them, it has even another. Right now, I am unable to predict what the result may be. It's like, if I need it to have one particular effect, that's what will happen. But I am sure it could never be used for evil or devious purposes. Apparently, it can only be used in the pursuit of goodness. And I might add that it wouldn't surprise me if now you were able to communicate in any other language you needed to."

Still shocked, and with a veteran reporter's innate drive to establish confirmation, Fred reached out for his telephone and pressed the extension for one of his associates who had migrated to the United States from Bosnia three years ago. He had started working for the "Herald" last year. When the connection was made, he asked, in a language totally foreign to him seconds ago, "Omar, this is Fred Wailand. I just wanted to call you, and see if you were having any luck with that story about the accident out at Camp Irwin?"

"Fred! Is that really you?" Omar exclaimed. "When did you learn our language? I didn't think you knew anything but get-the-facts, keep-it-concise, meet-the-deadline in English."

Flustered, but not wanting to tip his hand on what was unfolding around him, Fred fabricated, "It's an old habit of mine. I try to pick up a bit of language from a country that is getting extensive news coverage. It's really just a hobby of mine."

"Well, you had me going there for a minute. You've got the inflection and dialect down perfect. But, anyway, I am going out to Camp Irwin this afternoon to finish up on that story. Thanks for asking. I'll talk to you when I get back." And the conversation ended, much to Fred's relief.

Looking up at Clem, this seasoned reporter was transfixed. "I don't know what to say. You have done something so unbelievable. If I wasn't sitting down, I believe I would have probably fainted from the shock of all this. Who, again, are you? Where did you really come from? And what in heaven's name is all this preparation and planning leading to? Do you work for someone else?"

Only adding to his amazement and confusion, B had decided, at this point, that it was time for his presence to be known. Standing behind Clem, who by this time was perched on the edge of his chair, B's form suddenly took shape, and he addressed the newest member of Clem's team, "Yes, for me."

Even Clem was taken by surprise by B's decision to reveal himself, but it was nothing compared to the shock and gasp that came from Fred. "Ohh…what is happening? Who are you? What are you?"

Shaking his head, he closed and rubbed his eyes, and looked up again. He still saw two figures, one sitting and the other, almost like a shadow, standing behind him. Trying to gather his senses and fall back on his skills as a reporter, he managed in a loud whisper to say, "Something important is about to happen, isn't it?"

"Yes," B replied. "Clem has chosen to bring you into his confidence in order to move forward with the plans that I have outlined for him. And I approve of his decision and choice. You, like him, will only know what I need you to know at any given time. For now, it is urgently important that you begin the process of identifying, then notifying the various newspapers over the world to print this message. And as Clem stated, in a month or so, he will be contacting you about further details. You will keep all this confidential. To do otherwise would put you at great risk. Make no mistake, there is great danger associated with mishandling what you are about to embark on. Do only what is requested at the time. Now we have to go. Clem will give you funds to get started, and he will purchase a portable telephone immediately and give you his number. Call him if you need to follow up with anything."

Clem then touched the debit card he had previously laid on Fred's desk, asking "would $10,000.00 be enough to start you off and pay for your time and the various expenses? I will authorize more as you need it, once you get underway."

"Certainly," Fred said. "But you realize there is no way that I can predict what the actual costs will be. I will keep a record and call you when more is needed."

"Fair enough," Clem answered. "Just call me if you need more or if there are questions. The telephone will really be the only way I have to communicate with you in the days ahead. If nothing else, you can speak to me to reassure yourself that this is not a dream. Like you, I was, and still am, in shock. But B's appeal is so urgent, it leaves us no option but to try to do what is requested. For now, God's speed to you."

After saying that, Clem and B left the reporter's office. As they closed his door, Fred briefly shook his head and then immediately shifted his position in front of his computer. Striking some keys, shifting the cursor, and clicking on various internet sites, he was now positioned to make a list of newspapers over North America. He had begun his portion of this mission.

As they drove back to the large shopping center where the travel agency was located, Clem turned towards B and asked, "Do I just get tickets for this first portion of the trip, and then have the travel agency forward the other tickets to me once I am in London?"

B was silent for a moment, and then answered, "I am sure that is probably what will have to be done. The time it will take to make all the necessary reservations and secure the tickets will make it impossible to do all of that now, particularly, given our tight schedule for the remainder of today. Just give the travel agent your schedule and these directions."

Clem was then instructed further on his itinerary, with places and dates after he left London. It was now getting hard for him to keep it all organized, but at least he did have the assurance that B would be there in the agency office to prompt him, if he made a mistake or forgot something.

Arriving back at the shopping center, Clem scanned the stores, looking for the travel agency. Before he made the complete circuit around the parking area, he spotted a small office. The Far Horizons Travel Store was squeezed in between a laundry mat and a pharmacy. He parked the truck as close as possible in front of the agency. Then once again he glanced towards B, hoping to get some signal or indication of his approval. But there was nothing more than the hazy form, without expression or definition. Each of these encounters Clem had with the public gave him a little more confidence, but a nagging fear and apprehension persisted. He had little idea what this was all about. All he really knew was that what he was doing apparently was going to be dangerous in some way. Or at least that was what B implied when he spoke to the reporter.

Once Clem entered the travel agency, he noted there was only one desk. There was little else in the way of furniture present. Travel posters lined the walls, beckoning would be travelers to far off destinations on the Mediterranean Coast, the Caribbean Islands, or to the fiords of Norway. Besides a few chairs in the waiting area, there were two small tables piled with brochures and information packets. Travel magazines were available in slotted wall shelves. The one desk had the usual commanding computer and some tablets for note taking. The office had a fresh fragrance, owing to there being potted plants and flowers placed everywhere. That was the most striking feature about the office. It was very welcoming.

Behind the desk, standing up as Clem entered the office, was a neatly dressed woman. Clem figured she was in her late forties or early fifties. She, as it turned out, was the sole employee and owner of the business. Her hair had a golden sheen, and was pulled back, as he remembered his wife calling it, in a French bun. Her facial features were remarkable for her high cheek bones, easy forthcoming smile, and an olive complexion that was present, no doubt, the year around. She was wearing a white sweater, which set off her features. She appeared relaxed and at ease, which helped give him the confidence to proceed with his business.

"Good afternoon," she announced in a rather melodic voice. "My name is Cynthia. How can I help you? Do you want to plan a flight, a cruise or some train travel today?"

Stuttering somewhat, he replied, "Uh, well, ..I ...actually need to make reservations for multiple flights, if I can."

"Certainly! Won't you take a seat?" Then sitting down, she arranged her desk for note taking and pulled closer to the computer keyboard. "Will you be traveling within the States or overseas?"

"Both. And I shall be doing so for about a month. In fact, it will involve transferring in and out of many countries and laying over in only a few." Saying this, Clem, right away recognized that he would also have to bring this individual into his confidence. There was no way she could comprehend and accept such a task, without some explanation. And, again, because B was positioned behind him, he had no way to confirm any agreement with this plan.

"But first, I feel it necessary to introduce myself and give you some insight as to why this travel plan is necessary. My name is Clement Newberry. I have been asked by a significantly important party to undertake a mission of grave importance. But, honestly, I do not know all the reasons why nor fully, what all is involved. But it has been made clear to me, as it soon will be to you that I must try and complete this journey. For confirmation of what I am saying, I have also enlisted the help of Fred Wailand, over at the "Herald". You could speak with him, but only do so in the strictest confidence. That, as he was told, is paramount. And as I told him, this does not involve anything illegal or immoral.

"For now, I need you to schedule me a flight out of Los Angeles tomorrow at around noon. That flight will be to New York City, by way of Chicago. There needs to be a stopover in Chicago, and then later that same evening, I need to complete the flight to New York. I will need lodging reservations for a hotel near that airport for tomorrow night, and then at a hotel near the Newark airport for the next night. From Newark, I need to fly to London, then to destinations throughout

Europe, the Middle East and Asia for the next two weeks. After that, I will need you to schedule one week of flights to cities in Africa and one week of the same in South and Central America. I have a list of places here that I will give you. And finally, I need to return to Los Angeles before Christmas. Later on, during this upcoming January, you will most likely need to schedule flights from many countries to Los Angeles. From there, the reservations would include a shuttle flight to Palm Springs and eventual bus transport to Amboy. But I will give you more information on that later."

Then Clem followed up with a full description of what had happened to him since B's appearance late last night and the various arrangements he had made up until now. He finished up by saying that all of her time and the reservations would be paid for in advance using the debit card he then showed her. But he pointedly left out any mention of B, figuring that would only convince her that he was a crackpot.

"My goodness, Mr. Newberry, you sure have a way of getting someone's attention. Are you really serious about this, or is this some sort of prank one of my square dance friends put you up to? Besides, if you were serious, I don't speak all the languages necessary to make detailed arrangements like what you have in mind. You will need to go through the United Nations or find somebody much more knowledgeable than me."

"It will seem awkward and forward for me to ask," Clem answered, "but, if you will, let me demonstrate to you how you will be able to do as I have requested. But I will need for you to shake my hand. Again, there is no harm or trick intended. I would even step outside onto your front sidewalk, if being more in the public view would give you a better sense of your safety.

Looking at him for a few seconds, Cynthia saw,

like Fred did, that he was well groomed and neatly dressed. He appeared to speak well, although maybe a little stilted, like he was saying the lines of a play for the first time. He seemed earnest enough, and his body language so far didn't indicate a threat or menace. And she always had a streak of adventure and daring that kept her on the edge of danger, but safe enough to not ever be harmed or injured. All this considered, she held out her hand toward Clem.

"Thank you," he sighed. Taking her hand, he gently and briefly shook it, and then hurriedly let it go.

Then, as with Fred before, he asked in flawless Russian, "See, did that hurt? Now you will possess unusual abilities that you did not have before."

To her shock and amazement, she replied in equally correct Russian, "My Lord, I understand you perfectly. How can this be happening?"

And once again, B reappeared at that instant. "Do not be too alarmed at my sudden appearance, but I think it best to reveal myself to you now before we take too much more time with Clem, here, trying to convince you of the importance of this matter. He calls me B. Who or what I am is not the issue at this moment. You will have an opportunity in the near future to know more about me, but for now my presence here and the special abilities you now possess should be enough to reassure you that a crisis is at hand. Please follow Clem's instructions and know that no harm will come to you, if you keep what you now know and what you will be doing in strictest confidence. That is of utmost importance. Now, I'll let Clem continue."

After that, Cynthia shook her head side to side, and rubbed her forehead, pulling her hand back over the top of her hair. "I will try," she stammered, "to listen and do what you request, but I cannot guarantee that I will be able to do it all as you want. I will have to take more notes, and get the times and dates down in more detail."

After the details of Clem's itinerary were completed, to her amazement, even in this most hectic and overbooked time of the year, she was able to book him on the flights and times and to destinations he wanted, getting him all the way to London. That, in itself, amazed her. Clem then handed her the debit card, and they completed this transaction. He asked her if depositing another $25,000.00 into her business account would cover at least the first couple weeks of reservations. She agreed it would. Finally, arrangements were made for him to call her back with his telephone number, once he got his cell phone. At that point she directed him three doors down from her office to a Radio Shack, where he could purchase a phone.

Their business concluded, Clem again shook her hand, but this time she appeared more hesitant taking it, fearing what else may happen from touching him. Clem smiled at this, but reassured her that nothing further was to happen by touching him. But to Clem's surprise, B actually went over to her and appeared to speak with her privately. At least it was the closest to someone he had witnessed B getting. Not wanting to stare, he exited the agency, and headed on down to the store to purchase his telephone.

He and B eventually climbed back into the truck and drove off. Within a few blocks, they stopped briefly to fill up with gas at a service station on old Route 66. And soon thereafter, they merged onto the west lanes of Interstate-40. Their next destination was Los Angeles.

PART II

SIX: LAX

The remainder of the drive into Los Angeles was uneventful, aside from one stop at a medical supply office in Pasadena. There was almost no conversation between Clem and B. Clem was trying to imagine what and how he could perform the job that B was asking of him. He knew he had to try and touch as many people as possible for the plan to work. But, with the strict security that now was commonplace, and how any odd behavior by passengers or the general public was subject to immediate investigation, Clem knew he had a problem. B had offered him no advice or suggestions. That seemed to be a pattern, now that Clem thought about it. The task was outlined by B, but Clem had to try and come up with a way to accomplish it. Touching hundreds, even thousands, of travelers in airports around the world seemed like a blue print for being arrested in every stop he made. But as he drove in the silence, he focused on the options available to him. And then it struck him.

"I've got it," Clem exclaimed, with a chuckle. "I think I know how to make my way through the crowds at the airports you want me to go to. But first I have to make a stop before we get to a motel near the Los Angeles airport."

To Clem's surprise, there was no reply. Clem just shrugged and thought maybe
B was dozing and hadn't heard him. He decided not to pursue it any further and simply watch out for a store that sold medical supplies.

As it was getting late in the afternoon by the time they were nearing Pasadena, Clem pulled off the freeway and began looking for a store that was still open. Within a few blocks of turning onto Colorado Boulevard, he saw a medical supply office with an "OPEN" sign still in the window. Turning into a parking lot beside the store, he parked and as he got out of the truck, called out to B, "this should only take a few minutes, I hope."

He went inside and scanned the store for what he needed. By the front window in a floor rack, filled with crutches and canes, there was one white cane with a red tip. It was collapsible. That was even better. He could carry it unnoticed when he was not masquerading. Next, he found a turntable that had various sizes and shades of sunglasses. He tried on a few and selected the pair with the darkest tint. Having found what he needed, he made his way to the cashier.

"Find everything you needed?" the clerk asked.

"Sure did," Clem answered. "And I am so relieved you were still open for business. Saying that, Clem knew he could not discuss why he had selected the items he had. Remembering what B had said to the reporter, he realized the less people knew about what he was doing, the better for everyone. Paying with his debit card, he quickly returned to the truck.

Just then he remembered that he had not yet contacted Fred and Cynthia to give them his cellular telephone number. He reached into the truck bed where he had secured his new suitcase with all his travel clothes and personal effects. Reaching inside, where he stuffed the phone, he also found the new telephone number that was to be his own. Closing up the suitcase, he climbed back into the truck cab.

"I need to quickly call Fred and Cynthia to give them my number. I nearly forgot to do this."

Again, his comments were met with silence from B. By now, Clem was convinced B was in a deep sleep, probably worn out from all the traveling and excitement. He pulled out a business card from his shirt pocket and dialed Fred first. There only an answering service available, so he left his name and number. It was awkward doing this, and he stammered a few times. Still he hoped the message got through. Then he dialed Cynthia's number, and to his surprise she answered right away. "Cynthia, this is Clem Newberry. I am just calling to give you my telephone number."

To his surprise, and then dismay, she replied, "Oh, Clem, I am so relieved you called when you have. I have a lot of information for you. And I have a major change in store for you. First off, the reservations have all been made. It was simply amazing how quickly, and without any confusion, all of it was completed. My guess is that it being so straight forward had something to do with B. It was stunning to me after all these years of doing this work. So that's done.

"Now for the shocker. I am coming with you! I need to know where you are staying tonight, and I'd like you to make a reservation for me as well when you check in. I will soon be leaving my office to go home and pack. Afterward, I'll head off immediately for Los Angeles."

Taken totally off guard, and being a person used to routine and structure in his life, this news was far from what he had expected or anticipated. How could she have done this without asking him? Or why hadn't she asked B? All he could do was to shout back into the phone, "You did what?!!…"

"Like I said," she responded, in a calm but determined voice, "I made duplicate reservations for this upcoming month's travels. As I rethought what you and B talked about doing, I knew there was no way you could do it alone. It was too obvious. The airport security would immediately pick you out of the crowd. You needed a companion to make it look casual. And, besides, I felt that B, if not you, would understand."

Turning to B, Clem exclaimed, "B, Cynthia has made reservations for her to accompany me on this trip! She says it will make me look less obvious and help accomplish what you want. She never even asked us! What do we do now?!" His exasperation was only too evident.

At this, B did stir, and the shadowy form shifted position. "That is a great idea! Tell her I am very pleased that she took the initiative to do this. And tell her that we will make arrangements for her tonight at the motel, and that you will meet her in the lobby tomorrow morning at 9 a.m. Tell her I am proud of her."

Clem shifted the telephone back to his ear and repeated what B had told him. He was stunned. "I will need to call you once we get reservations at a motel." He said in an almost apologetic tone. "How will I get in touch with you?"

"Here is my cell phone number." She quickly replied and with great relief in her voice. "I'm sorry to have shocked you, Clem. But there was no other way to tell you. I hope you will eventually understand why I did what I did."

Clem realized his feelings were hurt by this seeming snub of his role in this venture. But as he recalled how today began, he knew that his role then and now was to help and not to try and become some central figure.   Self-importance, he knew, was a deadly emotion. This, he had learned years ago. Now it was time to recognize its subtle signs and regain his perspective. B was directing this matter. He subsequently replied, "Sorry for my reaction to your news. The more I think about it, the more I realize it will improve our chances of doing what B has requested. I'll call you later. So long for now."

"Good bye, Clem," came her final reply.

Clem tucked the telephone beside him and started the engine. He turned out of the parking lot and eventually reentered the freeway, anxious to complete this final leg of the trip to LAX.

After another hour of driving, and without Clem noticing, B did glance at Clem's recent medical supply office purchases. Not commenting on that, B suggested to Clem, "You must be getting hungry. Do you want to find a place to eat? You have had a full day, with nothing to eat since you made yourself breakfast."

"Come to think of it, I am hungry," Clem answered. "And what's more, it's getting on to 7 p.m. But because we're close enough to the airport right now, maybe we can find a restaurant close by our motel." After saying that, he glanced up and saw a large billboard sign, advertising reasonable rates at a nearby motel on Century Boulevard. Since they had just gotten off the freeway, and were now on that street, he was relieved to have this day come to an end. Eating something, anything, sounded great.

"Let's head there B. It's probably only a few blocks down this street."

The motel was just off the main street. It was older, but it had an atmosphere of comfort. The inner courtyard was overflowing with shrubs, flowering plants and palm trees, along with the usual swimming pool. Once inside the lobby, Clem was able to make arrangements for two rooms for the night. He let the office clerk know the second party might be coming in much later. After taking his suitcase to the room, he asked B if he wanted to accompany him to the restaurant. B declined, letting Clem know that eating breakfast with him this morning was a very rare event.

After dinner at an adjacent restaurant, Clem returned to the motel. He remembered he had to call Cynthia with the name and directions to the motel. Once he had done that, he showered again, hung up his clothes for tomorrow's trip, and with mounting exhaustion, climbed into bed. It wasn't his nature to brood over past events, and even with all that had happened today, tonight was no exception. He was fast asleep within one to two minutes.

Meanwhile, the drive into Los Angeles for Cynthia was simply long and tiring. She knew the route well, having been raised in Culver City. She was able to gather together all the tickets, itineraries, her passport, some changes of clothing and get them all either in her carry-on bag or in a mid-sized check-in suitcase. She decided she would just wear the same clothes she had on today for tomorrow's trip, and then change once they got to New York City. What she hadn't told Clem was that she had registered them both as husband and wife on the tickets. She thought that would make their traveling together less conspicuous. She would have to tell Clem about this as soon as they met. And as preparation for this, she got out her old wedding band and put it on. Once everything was in order, she left Barstow about 7 p.m., just as Clem was pulling into the motel. She had not been driving too long when her cell phone rang, and it was Clem. He sounded less agitated this time. The call was brief, but reassuring.

Her registration at the motel was routine, except for the issue of getting permission to park her car for the next month. Clem had not yet addressed that, so it became her job to arrange for both his truck and her car to be impounded, as it were, for this period. The motel was not thrilled about it, but they changed enough to sooth even the most edgy manager. Cynthia knew a bargain when it came along. She also knew when someone was taking advantage of a situation. This was one of those times, but there was little she could do. Finally, she made reservations for her and Clem to stay there upon their return in four weeks.

Her room was on the main floor, next to the swimming pool. It was too cold outside to swim. So she took a shower, ate a power bar and drank some herbal tea, then briefly read a magazine she had brought along. She fell off to sleep with the magazine in her hands and all the lights still on. It was a deep and dreamless sleep.

The next morning Clem and Cynthia met in the motel office at 9 a.m., as planned. It was somewhat awkward at first, with Clem suggesting they go to his room for any last minute instructions they might need for the trip. Prior to their leaving the motel office, he asked if they could reserve a seat on the 9:30 shuttle to LAX. That done, they went back to Clem's room to meet with B about any final details.

"Are both of you packed?" B asked. Each nodded 'yes'. "Did each of you get something to eat for breakfast?" And, again, both acknowledged they did. "Then Cynthia, you need to understand what Clem plans to do," B continued. "He is planning on disguising himself as a blind or nearly blind individual. His plan is to be less conspicuous, as he touches anyone. Your being together also helps prevent that possibility. And I presume that you made reservations for the two of you to travel as husband and wife?"

Cynthia nodded 'yes' to that as well. Clem, in turn, reacted with a quick head turn towards Cynthia, but sensing the acceptance of this arrangement with B, he made no comment.

"You both have the same abilities to affect the individuals that you touch. As with you, each person touched will experience a new sense of being connected to those around them. But you will not passing along the language skills that I entrusted you with. Those are only for a select few, and they are only for a given period of time. But that could change as circumstances warrant. My admonition to each of you is to touch as many people across the world as possible in the month ahead. I will be here when you return. You will not see me until then. Now you must take your things, and be on your way." Saying this, B was gone. There was no time for questions, good-byes, or see-you-soon. It was simply time for each to begin their mission.

Collecting their suitcases and carry-on luggage, they got on the shuttle and rode to the airport terminal. During the short ride, Clem got out the sunglasses and white cane. He unfolded the cane and instructed Cynthia to always walk on his left side. Being right handed, it would make it easier for him to manage the cane that way. Once they stopped at the American Airlines terminal, each got out and proceeded to remove their luggage. A red-cap at the front of the terminal spotted Clem getting off the bus, demonstrating some awkwardness with his cane and luggage. Right away, he saw a nice tip.

"Good morning, folks. Can I help you with those bags and get you checked through?" he asked.

Clem, feeling very nervous and far out of his element, nudged Cynthia in hopes she'd know how to respond to the question. Sensing this, and realizing it was to be her role anyway, given his pretense of blindness, she immediately responded, "and good morning to you, sir. You surely may help us. We are on our way to Chicago, on the noon flight. Let me get out our tickets and identifications for you to check us through."

Working quickly and efficiently, the red-cap processed their tickets and checked in their luggage. Turning back to them, he said, "here are your tickets, I.D.'s, and claim tags for the luggage. You and your luggage are checked through to New York City, by way of Chicago. That's a pretty long layover in Chicago. I'm surprised you couldn't get a quicker connection."

Cynthia, knowing that it would be awkward for Clem to pretend to get his wallet, went ahead and tipped the red-cap, replying "thank you so much for your helping me and my husband. We won't need further help. We are early enough that we can walk through the terminal and then through the inspection/security areas, rather than have you take my husband through in a wheelchair."

The red-cap thanked her for the tip. They had him check both their stored and carry-on luggage through to New York City, which seemed kind of strange as well. But with the on again-off again security regulations, maybe it was the smartest thing to do, he thought As they strolled off, he called out, "Take care and have a good trip."

For Cynthia and Clem, having their hands free from carrying any luggage, gave each of them more opportunities to reach out and make contact with others. And that had already begun with Clem patting the shuttle bus driver and with Cynthia shaking the red-cap's hand when giving him the tip. It should be noted, however, that there was to be no immediate surge of good will with their touching others. It did not have the same potency as with the earlier contacts. B had wanted sudden changes to occur at those times. Now, to allow his ambassadors safe and anonymous travel, he had insured that the effects would take a few hours to reach their maximum effect. And this same delayed effect would be present when those individuals initially touched by Clem and Cynthia began touching others. So far, all the shuttle bus driver and the red-cap noticed was a calming effect, which in itself was unusual, given the hectic early morning rush around LAX.

If someone had a security camera focused solely on this couple, it might have become fairly obvious that something strange was happening. Cynthia would swerve side to side, touching someone to ask for directions to one place or another, while Clem, with his white cane and sunglasses, would falter, stumble and touch those nearby, pretending to regain his balance. It was an awkward ballet, to be sure. But this was their first attempts, and before long they had perfected their movements, hiding any obvious looking, staged appearance. But there were mishaps, to be sure.

One in particular happened soon after they entered the LAX terminal. It was a lesson that both of them never forgot. As they approached a waiting area of gates for various flights, sitting in a chair, which faced the pedestrian traffic walking along the concourse, was a truly blind individual with his seeing-eye dog, lying quietly beside him. Cynthia was walking, as she previously had been instructed, on Clem's left side, with Clem sweeping his cane along in front of the seats the blind man was occupying. Both were focused away from the seats when Clem accidentally scuffed the dog's tail with his foot. It was only the lightest touch. But that's all it took. It turned out that animals were much more sensitive to Cynthia or Clem's touch. Jake could testify to that. The effects were immediate and dramatic.

Immediately, the dog sat up, not being held by his handler, and proceeded to rush away with Clem. He was actually behind Clem, as the foot traffic was heavy, and the dog could not get beside him. As a result, Clem had no idea what was unfolding. Passing by a restroom, Clem nodded to Cynthia and indicated he needed to go in there. With cane in hand, sunglasses on, he pretended to wave the cane appropriately and shuffled his way into the toilet area. And behind him was the seeing-eye dog, dragging all his leash paraphernalia. And rather than have the rather determined, military bearing and erectness so ingrained in these amazing animals, he was like a puppy. So here was Clem preparing himself to do his business at the wall urinal, with this dog jumping up and down behind him, barking, and being just your usual, happy-go-lucky dog. At first Clem tried to ignore him, but obviously it was a scene beginning to attract some attention. Adding to the confusion was the entrance of the dog's rightful owner and several good Samaritans coming to retrieve the dog. Meanwhile, Clem was seriously into his business by now, and the urgency of it wouldn't allow him to stop and referee this evolving calamity, which he had been totally unaware was unfolding.

All he could do was face about and try to ignore the fiasco going on behind him, like he was an innocent victim of very-happy-dog-stalking. Once the owner was led over to the dog, whose name by the way was Regal, which Clem feared from now on would not fit his new personality, he was able to take his leash and lead him away. As the owner turned to leave, he did apologize for the embarrassment, stating that he'd never had the dog act that way before. Clem could only nod, keeping his face turned away. He was just relieved he hadn't pet him like he did Jake. Then Regal may have been shouting for joy! Clem shuttered at the thought. At least, he concluded, I just brushed him.

What Clem never knew was that Regal, or Happy, as his new owners renamed him, was soon retired from seeing-eye duties and was adopted by a family with three children. It was even said that their long-term family cat, whose personality had always been aloof and distant, after having one encounter with Happy, in which Tuffy, the cat, swiped the nose of Happy, was ever-after also transformed into a mindless, happy-go-lucky ball of energy. It was true, ultimately, in that household, the dog and cat ruled from then on.

But Cynthia and Clem did finally board Skyways Flight #239 to Chicago about 11:40 a.m., leaving behind 137 souls that had been touched by them at LAX.

SEVEN: BALLARAT

December in Ballarat, Victoria, was often sweltering. It was called the Garden City. And it was centrally located in the Garden State of Victoria, Australia. So what made Ballarat special? Unlike the zeal which gripped city planners and developers in the United States to demolish and erase so much of our country's heritage, Ballarat had steadfastly kept and maintained its past. It began its recorded history with one of the world's greatest gold rushes in the mid-nineteenth century. It was a jewel of a city. Located on a worn mountain plateau, the city was scrubbed regularly by the winds and rains from the Great Southern Ocean. It left this place so rich and pure in color that one had to say whoever chose to define the different colors of this world had to start in Ballarat. And yet, there were spring-like days when, if you found yourself at a family reunion in one of Lake Wendoree's many park areas, the dazzling haze-like quality of the colors made you think you were part of a painting by one of the old masters. There was a haunting quality of light, buildings, people and weather that was unlike anything else, anywhere.

Geoffrey Graham was taking his early morning walk to the nearby news stand on Sturt Street, across from the Ballarat Base Hospital. He only lived two blocks away in one of the older sections of the city. His usual routine on a day like today was to let the family sleep in, while he got a paper and walked down to Lake Wendoree to read it. On the way back, he would stop by the local bakery shop and get some fresh rolls for the family. Today was Friday, when they had their rostered day off or RDO, as it was called. It gave them a three day weekend at least once a month. He and his wife were both mining engineers. They often had to be away throughout the week, scattered over this vast country, performing surveys and trouble-shooting for various mining companies. Each of them grew up in Ballarat, and both went to the Ballarat School of Mines. It was the premier university for geology and mining engineering in the country. And they had never desired nor wanted to leave the area, once their work life began.

Today, like any other RDO, he opened up the Melbourne newspaper, scanning the headlines. His main interest was to be found in the classified section. They desperately needed a new truck. Their present Ute, or pickup truck, was falling apart from all the unpaved roads they had had to drive over the last four years. The Australian Outback was the Great Leveler of all human inventions and aspirations. But Geoffrey and his wife, Patricia, both loved it for its untamable vastness. But now they needed another truck.

As he scanned the advertisements, he found no ads for trucks that interested him, but his eye caught an oddly worded and misplaced offer (see Appendix 1, fig. 1, "The Newspaper Offer").

He reread it numerous times thinking there had to be something else on the page that described in more detail what this was about. But this was all there was. And, most of all, he thought it was just another scam-like offer that the United States was so famous for. Soon enough, he resumed his search for their truck replacement, and the offer's impression was lost.

As usual, he stopped by the bakery shop to get the bread rolls, but today he added some sausage rolls to have with their picnic lunch. He thought the day was too clear and beautiful not to take a picnic out into the bush somewhere.

Once home, he found that Patty, as he called his wife, was already up and moving about. "Great day for a picnic," she called out as he walked into the kitchen.

"I was thinking the same thing. I even stopped by the bakery and got some supplies. If we have an extra bottle of wine, we can take it as well. We'll pick up some drinks for the kids as we head out."

"Good thinking, chappy," as she affectionately called him. "For now, let me get my bearings, have a hot cuppa, and read the newspaper for a while before the kids get up."

"Ok, I'm going to clean up, shave, and try to sort out the truck before we head off. We've got so much stuff in it now; there's no room for the kids. Call me if you find anything in the paper about a new or older, well maintained Ute. I couldn't find anything earlier." And with that, he handed her the newspaper and headed down the hallway.

Preparing her first cup of tea for the day was one of Patty's deepest pleasures. It seemed strange that with all the competing influences there were, sporting events, social gatherings, theater performances, family outings, work life challenges, it was still that first cup of tea of the day that brought the most consistent pleasure and comfort. We try too hard to be entertained, she thought. Give me a cup of tea any day.

Like Geoffrey, she sat back and lazily opened the newspaper and began to read. It was some time before she got to the classified advertisements. And when she did, immediately her mind, trained as a

71

geologist to notice anything different in her surroundings, focused on the offer to go to Amboy. She, likewise, read and reread it. For her the Mojave Desert had always been a magnet of great interest, located in that desert, for the family to explore, were the wonders of Death Valley, the great dry lake beds with their vast mineral deposits, and Joshua Tree National Park. "What's this all about?" she wondered out loud. "Could it be legitimate?" she added. They weren't asking for any information that was compromising or endangered your identity, like taxation identification numbers. She wondered if Geoff had seen it.

Impulsiveness was not her manner, but for some reason which she later could not describe logically, she decided while Geoff was getting ready, she had some time to try and prepare a quick answer to this offer. What harm could it do? And besides, they had always wanted to go to Disneyland and see the Grand Canyon. They had weeks of holiday time stored up. Reaching down beside her lounge chair, she pulled up her lap top computer and began to write. 'This shouldn't take long,' she thought:

> "325 Kline St.
> Ballarat, VIC 3342
> Australia
> (05) 3881-4632
> E-mail: pbgraham@geomail.au
> Patrician Boyd-Graham, age 32,
>   geologist/mining engineer.
> Geoffrey Lynn Graham, age 31,
>   geologist/mining engineer.
> Colin Graham, age 5, student.
> Karen Graham, age 6, student.

1. It is my nature to analyze the reason why a particular situation may be stressful. Then I

most often will develop a strategy to work through it. Generally, I just take a stressful situation as a challenge rather than as an obstacle. I deal with stress by not letting it get to the point that I have to cope with it. I treat it as a short term issue only.

2. Being with my family gives me my deepest happiness. But a close second is discovering something new while exploring for minerals in the substrate found in the Outback, and then in devising a way to extract and refine it. And next to that is developing a new method to accomplish a given task or solve a problem.

3. Oddly enough, being an engineer and scientist, I obviously work best with uniformity and structure in a controlled environment. But personally, I welcome new situations and the challenges each presents. Both my husband and I seek out and enjoy being involved in a variety of social events, and in meeting new people. Growing up in the same area together, we have lots of friends and have always liked making new ones.

4. I laugh when anything clever and unexpected occurs or is said, especially if it involves political or social commentary. My husband and I have a continuous banter that we think is humorous. We sincerely enjoy each other's company and think the other partner is truly funny."

After completing the entry letter, she e-mailed it. And then she went over to their desk and shuffled through it until she found an envelope. Addressing it and putting what she thought was enough postage on it to satisfy the Australian Post authorities, she put the envelope in their porch mailbox for the postman to pick up later that day.

By now, the kids were up and making a dash for the kitchen to get something to eat, and Geoff was done in the bathroom. It was her turn now to get ready for the day. Passing her husband in the hallway, she gave him a peck on the check, saying, "it's going to be a beautiful day, luv."

Smiling broadly, he pinched her on the bum, replying, "They always are, with you in it."

EIGHT: EUROPE AND BEYOND

Once Cynthia and Clem had settled into their seats for the flight to Chicago, she reached into her purse and brought out a single piece of paper. She had dreaded giving it to Clem, knowing it would probably overwhelm him, as it had her, when she had first compiled it. But he had to see what lay ahead for them. Without a word, she passed this next month's itinerary to him. And then she put on the earphones that had been provided to them by the flight crew, turned on some soothing music and shut her eyes. She knew Clem would need some private time to digest the enormity of what lay ahead. (see Appendix 1, fig. 2, "FAR HORIZONS TRAVEL STORE, Confirmed Itinerary for Cynthia Garr and Clem Newberry.")

Clem reread the list over and over. To see what lay ahead was beyond his ability to grasp. He had never even heard of so many of these places. The distance they were traveling was staggering. And trying to make all the connections, all the while trying to accomplish what B wanted, touching as many people as they could, safely and discretely. He let out a sigh, leaned back, closed his eyes and tried to get some preparatory sleep. He felt desperate at that moment. It was all just too overwhelming.

Their arrival at Chicago's O'Hare Airport was

rough, due to a snow storm that was to hit the area within the next twelve hours. The winds caused the plane to shudder and shake, so much so, it scared both Cynthia and Clem. They were relieved when it touched down safely. The total count of passengers and crew touch: three. It was not a very promising start to their journey, both commented to each other later.

Donning his dark glasses and cane, they both exited the plane into the gate area of the airport at 5:40 p.m. The departure flight to Kennedy International in New York City was at 8:30 p.m. That gave them some time to stretch, relax a little, and touch some travelers going to destinations mostly in the mid-western United States.

Cynthia proclaimed, as they entered the main concourse, "Let the dancing begin."

Clem, smiled broadly hearing this, and relaxed immediately. He realized, more and more, how grateful he was Cynthia had taken the initiative to come along. "You bet, let's reach out and touch someone today!"

For the next two hours they weaved their way back and forth along the maze of corridors, Clem sometimes faking a stumble or just lightly bumping into someone, and Cynthia reaching out to get someone's attention for directions. At the end of this period they decided to freshen up, get something to snack on and go to their designated departure gate. They felt better about their efforts. And they knew all the folks they had touched today were going to feel immensely better in a few more hours.

From Chicago, their flight was smoother to New York City. The storm front was behind them all the way. They were staying in a hotel near Kennedy Airport. By staying there, they could go back to the airport tomorrow and catch a shuttle to La Guardia Airport and then onto Newark, without wasting so much time. And as usual, Clem was discovering, Cynthia had made the most practical arrangements. In each hotel where they stayed along the way, which were not many, she had arranged for them to have the same suite but separate bedrooms. That was a great relief for Clem. It was not that he was such a lofty or principled individual, but his years of living alone in the cabin, had imprinted in him the need for some privacy. For Cynthia, the arrangements allowed her to be more relaxed and lessen the chances for any confusion to develop in their relationship. And yet, it still gave the impression that they were married, and she could continue to walk beside Clem wherever they went without attracting attention.

The next day and a half in New York and Newark, New Jersey's airports were very hectic for them. The crowds were almost overpowering. It wasn't necessary to pretend much. Just walking, with an occasional weave, would put you in contact with an onrushing mob of scurrying commuters and travelers. By the time they had gotten on the plane bound for London, they knew they had touched hundreds of people. They were now well on their way and were feeling more comfortable with what lay ahead.

When they finally landed in Rome at 4:10 p.m. a week later, they were completely exhausted. Each wished they had more time to spend in Rome, just to rest up, eat some decent food, and establish a more regular daily routine. Their bodies and brains were so jet-lagged they had little idea what day or time of day it was when they arrived. They had slept in waiting areas and ate in airport kiosks and bars, when not trying to reach out to all around them. They hardly knew each other any better now than they did at the start of the trip. Luckily, there were no mishaps or obvious mistakes made to call attention to them.

Once shown to their suite in Rome, they agreed each would go shower and sleep in their respective beds until dinner time. Then maybe after that they might try to meet and go downstairs to eat in the hotel's restaurant. But neither one gave the other any assurance that might happen. Sleep was all they could think of at that moment. Before they parted, however, Clem mentioned it might be a good idea for them to call the front desk and arrange for their travel clothes to be picked up to be laundered and pressed. Cynthia heartily agreed, so a call was made. Each changed into their bathrobes and set their well traveled suits outside the suite's door. They requested they be returned by 8:00 p.m.; that done, it was time to shower and get some sleep on a mattress.

Probably driven by the instinct to eat properly to survive, both Cynthia and Clem awoke, got dressed and met at their hallway door simultaneously. They laughed at their eagerness to get something not prepackaged to eat, in a non-airport setting.

As they entered the low lit, overly upholstered, oak paneled restaurant, it was clear that they were either too early or too late for dinner. There were three customers sitting at the bar and maybe two other couples sitting in booths. As the hostess came to greet them, Clem asked in flawless Italian, "Are we still able to order dinner at this time?"

"Of course you can. Is there anywhere in particular you'd like to sit?" she asked in reply.

"In a booth, if we could," Cynthia answered, also in Italian.

"Right this way, then."

The rest of the meal proceeded at a normal pace, with the weary travelers exchanging impressions of their trip so far. It was like neither had the will nor motivation to ask anything of a personal nature. It was almost a business-like atmosphere. Finally, it was

Cynthia who broke the ice, after the main meal was finished and cleared. They were each having a cup of coffee, when she asked, "Could you tell me a little about yourself, Clem? I really know nothing about you, and here we are traveling completely around the world together. Certainly, that must vouch for the persuasive powers of B, to have a single lady traveling all this way, with a single gent, and know nothing about him."

Clem kind of sighed, and turned his head slightly away from the table, as if thinking where to start. Then turning back, he looked at Cynthia and noted the sincerity of her expression. Her look put him at ease, and he began with, "I was born in west Texas. My family had a small farm or ranch, as they used to call them in those days. We did have a few beef cattle and usually a milk cow or two. Mostly, it was just dry, parched land. I had a brother and a sister, both of them younger than me. I had to set about working when I was pretty young due to my family's meager income. I started working when I was about 12 or 13, mostly on the neighbors' farms or ranches. Then I got on with the oil riggers, working as a roustabout. Eventually, I met my wife, and we married when we were both under age. But both of us saw it as a chance to leave our present circumstances and make a better life for ourselves away from Texas.

"So, within a few months, I joined the Army. It was probably one of the best things I ever did. My wife, Elizabeth, and I were able to be stationed overseas in Germany and Japan. I was in the infantry and saw some combat in the Middle East. That left me having some sleepless nights, but I didn't regret having been in combat, for the reasons we were there. My feeling was we were just trying to help people have a better life than the one they'd had for centuries. But, I guess, in the scheme of things, who's really to say what's right for another country or people. It seemed right at the time. I served in the Army for nine years and would have stayed in until my retirement, if I could have.

"But the first of two terribly sad events began my last year in the service. Our son, Dallas, was diagnosed with cancer. He was eight years old when diagnosed. I had to be discharged from the service to be close to a hospital that knew how to treat his illness. I was discharged out of Fort Polk, Louisiana. Luckily, I was able to get into a welding program at the shipyard in Gulfport, Mississippi, after my discharge. We had already started taking Dallas to the Tulane Medical Center in New Orleans, so I could drive to work from our home in Mississippi and easily commute to New Orleans for our son's care.

"He was a treasure of a boy. And I realize that all children are. His humor, his giving and loving manner were a source of daily joy for me and my wife. He loved to talk, and as you already know, I'm a big listener. He could chatter for hours on end, it seemed. Elizabeth and he would have the greatest fun together. He had many friends, but he always seemed to be happiest when he was with us. Then the treatments started, the radiation, the chemotherapy, followed by the bone marrow transplant. In a terrifying sequence, over a period of just weeks after his transplant, he had a heart attack; his heart stopped; he was in a coma for a month; he had a stroke with paralysis on his left side upon waking from the coma; and he developed what they called, 'graft versus host' syndrome. All his skin and mucous membrane lining around his mouth, eyes, nose blistered, scabbed and began to fall off. The pain was unbearable for him. And that condition never let up. He lived for another two years like that. Most amazing of all, though, was that after he came out of that coma, he was different."

"How so?" Cynthia asked, obviously moved by his account so far.

"I can't really describe it too well. He was just different. It was like he had been somewhere else all that time he was in the coma, and he was just coming back for a visit. It was as if he had been touched by something that purifies you. His eyes were so restful and reassuring. His voice was low but commanding. You paid attention to everything he did or said. It was like you didn't want to miss anything. I guess he was like an angel. When he died, my wife and I grieved for years. We had lost our only child, and he was such a precious one at that.

"Life, for us, did go on as best as we could manage after that. Eventually, I got a transfer out to the shipyard in San Diego, California. We liked living there. And we did find some happiness. I treasured her; and heaven knows I didn't deserve her. She had all the qualities I didn't. But she loved me. And then, she, too, became ill. She passed away over seven years ago. It wasn't too long before her passing that we up and moved into the Mojave Desert to my cabin. She passed on a few months later.

"I'd pick up an odd job here and there to make ends meet, mostly helping Ray and Hazel at the restaurant and motel. And then along came B. I truly am nobody. I am invisible in any situation, in any place or in any crowd. But, you know, that's ok by me. I guess I'm really one of the luckiest people alive, when it's all said and done. I've been loved, and I have learned how to love. What more is there to life than that?"

"And I guess that's about it for me. So what about yourself? Can you tell me anything about where you're from or anything else?"

Cynthia did not say anything for a while, but

that was not a problem for Clem.   This kind of conversation was not something he knew much about, nor had he even participated in that often, so her silence did not cause him concern. He just thought maybe she would rather not talk about herself. But what he did not know was how touched she was by what he'd said and how he'd told it. Here was this little man, sitting before her, unknown to the rest of mankind, short of herself and maybe a handful of others, who was charged with trying to resurrect the common good of humanity through his touch. And there was not a hint of self-importance. She, too, sighed and began.

"Thank you, Clem, for sharing that with me. I am deeply touched by what you told me. My story is neither as interesting nor as engaging. I was born in Culver City, California. I had two brothers, both older, who protected me like I was a china doll. We did a lot together. I played sports with them. We hiked, biked, swam and surfed together. After high school, I was able to qualify for a scholarship and went to UCLA. I majored in marine biology. It allowed me to continue my love affair with the ocean. I ended up working for the State of California Department of Fisheries and Wildlife. It was while working there that I met my husband. We were married for six years, but with each passing year, we grew steadily more apart. We shared the common bond of our work, but little else. Our separation and divorce was cordial and with very little trauma.   Probably the most traumatic event of our marriage was when it was discovered that I had a uterine malformation which prevented me from conceiving. Despite some experimental surgery, I was left unable to have children.

"Over the next fourteen years I stayed with the same Department, and I began traveling overseas as part of my job. By then, more of my duties involved speaking with various governmental agencies about what we were doing to prevent ecological damage to our own coastline, wetlands and rivers. Because I was single, I traveled a lot. And I enjoyed it. There was never anyone that I really had a serious relationship with after my divorce. Work pretty much consumed me. And then, toward the end of that time, I had to start taking care of my mother. After an early retirement, I had enough money to set myself up in the travel agency in Barstow, where you and I met. Ultimately, I had to place my mother in a retirement home. She still lives in Culver City, and I go see her as often as I can. The travel business suits me fine. I'm my own boss. And I still love to travel. So that's about it for me."

Clem nodded his head and gave her a rather bashful smile, and just said, "Thanks for sharing that with me." Cynthia could sense he was groping to say more, but just didn't have the words. Coming to his rescue, she reached out and gently patted his hand which was resting by his coffee mug. At this, he looked at her and said, "Well, I know you must be as bushed as I am. Why don't we finish our coffee, and head on up to our room and see if we can sleep non-stop until we have to leave day after tomorrow."

Cynthia smiled at his response, and replied, "Great idea. I'll race you to the room."

Their stay in Rome was far too short, but they were eager to get started on their next leg of the journey. Their plane to Istanbul left Rome at 6:30 a.m. on November 29, and from there they went immediately into Beirut. It had been years since Clem was in the Middle East, and he had some anxiety associated with coming back into the area. But soon they were on their way to Mumbai, India, having had no particular problem, except that under no circumstance did Clem ever touch a woman in these Muslim countries, even when he was disguised as a blind tourist. It was too much a risk to do so. Cynthia was able to manage that aspect of their job without incident. And, as they had hoped, almost before they knew it, another week had passed, and they were arriving in the Sydney International Airport on December 6, for a two night stay.

However, the customs officials in Sydney were some of the strictest they encountered along the way. One agent became alarmed at the number of stops they had before reaching Australia. It was only Cynthia's quick thinking that prevented them from having to reveal their real purpose for travel. Touching the custom agent was impossible. It would have been considered a hostile action. So, in her most pleasant and worldly manner, she responded to the agent.

"Well, haven't you seen others here before us with this same pattern of multiple stops in various countries in a short period of time?"

"No, Ms. Garr, I most certainly have not," he replied in a crisp, officious manner.

"Well, there you go, Clem," she countered. "We're ahead of everyone after all. You see, sir, we are in an international race to see who can stop over in the most countries in the shortest amount of time. And by you questioning us, this must mean that we are in front of everyone else. Isn't that great, Clem!"

Clem, trying his best to play along with Cynthia's ruse, said in the most enthusiastic voice he could muster, "Can you beat that! And we were definitely behind when we were in Beijing two days ago."

The custom agent then made two mistakes, if he was planning on pursuing this issue further or even making an arrest. First, he quickly glanced back over their passports to see if and when they were in Beijing, and seeing that they were, he lowered his suspicion level enough to dip Cynthia's passport down toward the counter for her verification of other stopovers. And secondly, in doing so, she was able to touch his hand, in such a way as to appear she was assisting him in any further verification he might need. But, rather than use one hand, she made it a point to touch him with both her hands simultaneously. This immediately had the full effect on the agent. It was like he had lost 25 years of worry, stress and resentment. In fact, after this contact with Cynthia, he wasn't too sure he wanted to be a custom agent any longer. A day filled with suspicion was not suited to his new outlook. Instead, sensing the mission they were on, he heartily welcomed them both to Australia, and encouraged them to make contact with as many people as possible. They, too, encouraged him to do the same.

And so it went, through the next week of their travel as well. It all passed very routinely until their flight left Monrovia, Liberia, on December 14. For some reason, maybe due to the flight being so long before it arrived in Rio de Janeiro, both Clem and Cynthia let down their guard and didn't keep tabs on everyone they were touching. And it was a flight, unlike most they had been on, that was filled with an already fun-loving group of people. The atmosphere was festive to begin with. The problem started when both Clem and Cynthia began overlapping their touching on the same person. The feeling of good will, connectedness and general well-being became infectious and overwhelming to all the passengers and flight crew. The joy was boundless. It was like a scene out of a summer camp song fest. The plane seemed to move up and down, as if to the beat of whatever was being sung. And it lasted for eight straight hours. Upon their arrival at the debarkation gate, this same behavior was still ongoing when everyone exited into the airport terminal. Clem and Cynthia, aghast at what they had done, quickly melted into the crowd. But it did seem like the shortest flight they had the whole month.

The final week was uneventful, except for some symptoms of high altitude hypoxia when they stopped over at the La Paz airport, en route to Lima, Peru. Mainly, it was headaches and some nausea, which they figured would have gotten much worse if they had had to spend the night there. The airport in La Paz was sparsely populated anyway, and they were only able to accomplish a few contacts while there. But, overall, their week in South and Central America seemed to go well.

When their flight landed back at LAX on December 21st, however, they were totally exhausted. It was all they could do to catch the shuttle back to their same motel, register and request two additional nights lodging as well. They knew neither one could make the drive back to Barstow or Amboy right away. As much as they both wanted to be back home, they had to rest from their trip. Besides, Clem had said nothing to Cynthia en route, but he noticed something was wrong. He just didn't feel well. At first he thought it was the airport food and the grueling schedule that was causing him the stomach pain and occasional diarrhea. But then he noticed some blood in his bowel movements as well over the last day or so. And his energy level had been dropping steadily. But he thought that would sort itself out once he got settled again and got some needed rest. Basically, his approach to caring for his own health was to shrug it off, and this episode was to be no different. After his experiences with his son and wife's illnesses, he was not interested in any contact with organized medicine.

He noted later that getting to that motel and

being able to sleep undisturbed for the next two days was the tonic he needed. By December 24th, he was feeling much better, eating well and ready to drive home. Cynthia decided to stay in the area to be with her mother over the Christmas holiday. So for the first time, before driving off from the motel, they gave each other a warm and meaningful hug.

Cynthia spoke first, knowing his shyness would probably inhibit his saying anything at this moment. "Thank you, Clem. Thank you for being the gentleman you are, for letting me share this momentous trip with you, and for showing me a side of you few will ever know. It's been an honor to have this time with you."

In response, Clem could only say, "I am so glad you came. I couldn't have done this if you hadn't been with me. You are a lovely lady. No matter what happens in the months to come, I'll never forget this time we had together and your kindness. Thank you as well." Then they each drove away.

NINE: MONROVIA, LIBERIA

Albert and Dada Nugama were both attending a regional educational seminar in Monrovia. It was the closest place they could go for the quality continuing education courses they needed and wanted, outside Ibadan, Nigeria, their home. They probably could get nearly the same material in Lagos, but it was such an over-crowded city now, and the flight to Monrovia was easy and a break for them. Ibadan was about 80 miles from Lagos and had a population of nearly four million. Luckily for both of them, the University of Ibadan was an excellent university. And it provided them ready access to the newest discoveries and developments in the areas they taught. The seminar in Monrovia was more about teaching methodology.

They were secondary teachers; each of them had been teaching 8th and 9th year students for nearly twenty years. They loved the challenge and the reward of seeing their students become progressively enthused about their studies and preparing them for the upper grades. Many of their past students had gone on to the university and become influential citizens in Ibadan. But they were quick to tell anyone that there was no secret to their success. It simply resulted from their desire to continuously upgrade their teaching skills and the body of knowledge of their respective subjects.

They were never completely satisfied with their past year's lesson plans and were always trying to gain insights and information on new ways to teach their material. Albert taught mathematics and biology. And Dada taught language arts and composition. Both earned the reputation of being very demanding, but fair and helpful.

They left their children at home this trip. It was a first. But Ariesa was seventeen and Edree was sixteen. Each had a birthday coming up in a couple of months. Each promised not to get into mischief, and they seemed ready to handle the responsibility of caring for each other. Besides, it had been years since Albert and Dada had been anywhere by themselves. The seminar was to last three days, with eight hours of classes each day. They would spend four nights away from home. Their first class started Friday, December 1st at 8:45 a.m., and it ended at 5:45 p.m., with an hour for lunch.

Getting back to their hotel at 6:30 p.m., they had a quick dinner at a nearby café. Neither was particularly hungry, given the pace of the day's classes. They both ate too much for lunch. When they came back to the hotel, Albert stopped by the kiosk and bought an evening newspaper, the Monrovia Post. He would probably read the newspaper until he got sleepy, and then call it a day.

Once back to their bedroom, Dada prepared to take a shower, leaving Al to his newspaper. He invariably read the classified section first. Being a biology teacher, he was always interested in seeing what plants, animals and fish might be for sale. Maintaining and making additions to his garden and aquarium in their suburb home in Falade were his hobbies. He started scanning the newspaper as Dada showered. But, in the middle of the classified section, set off in an eye-catching space, as if reserved just for this announcement, was something that intrigued him. It read: (see

Appendix 1, fig.1, "The Newspaper Offer").

Setting down the newspaper, he looked out their hotel window. "Why not try?" He asked himself. "It will only cost me for the airmail stamp to send this to America. If I write something now, I can use the computer in the hotel lobby and e-mail it tonight to that Amboy place."

That decided, Albert opened his ever-present briefcase, and took out a writing pad and pencil. Adjusting the pad on the desk, he began to compose:

"3618 Palm Drive W.
Falade Township
Ibadan, Nigeria 6340
(7) 663-4211
E-mail: anugama@falade.ni
Albert Nugama, age 41, secondary
   teacher math & biology.
Dada Nugama, age 40, secondary
   teacher language arts &
   composition.
Ariesa Nugama, age 17, student.
Edree Nugama, age 16, student.

1. Probably because our life in Nigeria has always been filled with unexpected and difficult situations, whether from overpopulation, scarcity of goods and services, unpredictable transportation, or governmental delays and confusion, we have become accustomed to facing new situations with a minimum of stress. To us, stress is like when you have the flu or a head cold. You just deal with it until it plays itself out. It rarely causes us to expend any extra energy, effort or thought to deal with it. I guess we may approach daily life with a more relaxed attitude than some others do.

2. Our happiness is being together as a family. We trust, believe in and love each other. Out of that love, flows the deepest happiness one can know. And I cannot respond to this question without saying that our teaching also has provided us great satisfaction and happiness.

3. Interaction with strangers and new situations is easy for my wife and me. After 20 years of teaching and being exposed to hundreds, if not thousands, of new students and their families, we have learned to analyze and adjust quickly to new situations and to newcomers.

4. I laugh at the stories and jokes that my wife and children tell me. And I laugh at my students, once they have started to adapt to my classroom and do or say something that I think is funny. It puts them at ease, and they realize that I sincerely respect them, even though I expect a great deal of them. Humor and laughter are essential components of rewarding and productive communication."

By the time he had jotted down this information, Dada was out of the bathroom and getting into bed. She asked, "What is that you are doing?"

"I have just entered us in a contest to fly to America for a week, all expenses paid. It is somewhere in the state of California. You have to write a page of information and answer some questions, then, I guess, they decide from what you provide them, if you are selected or not. I figured it wouldn't hurt to try. I can go down to the hotel lobby, after I read to you what I have written, and e-mail it per their instructions. Everything has to be submitted by December 5th. Here's what they asked, and how I replied."

Once he had read it to her, she smiled and said,

"Sounds ok to me. It all seems rather odd, but what harm will it do to try for it. Now, go on down stairs and submit it to them, and then let's get some sleep. We've still got two more days of classes ahead of us."

Once they got back home, Albert did airmail the same information to Amboy, California, and then essentially forgot all about it.

TEN: THE SEARCH BEGINS

Before he began the seemingly impossible task, as outlined by B, Fred needed to get back in touch with his wife and daughters. It had been two or three days since he had contacted them, and he liked to communicate with them daily. Truth be known, he hadn't really wanted them to go on their month-long trip back to Norway. It was Freda, his wife's, birthplace. But it was the first opportunity that they could afford to have their two daughters visit her homeland, and they each wanted to see it. Besides, after their last eight years of home schooling, they deserved some kind of reward. They never got much of a summer break, like the public educated kids. And it appeared they were both doing well, according to the regularly scheduled, state-sponsored testing that was required. So, despite his mood changes the week prior to their leaving, they all reassured him they would be fine and merrily flew off two weeks ago for their month long holiday. Without fail, he had been e-mailing or calling them every day up until now. But his work load had recently piled up, and he had become slack keeping in touch.

He began with typing out his usual greeting "How are you? What are you world travelers up to? How much I miss you." He closed with, "love and kisses to all." He then e-mailed the message to Freda's laptop computer. She, despite being on holiday for the month, still had obligations at New York University's School of English Literature. The laptop kept her both in touch with Fred, and it allowed her to update her lesson plans. She tried to teach, for one quarter each year, at least three different classes. It was to keep her mind challenged, she maintained. The students she had in her graduate school classes were bright and demanding. And she had always loved teaching. But more than that, she was passionate about her writing. A published author of some fame, keeping her connection with New York City was one of her conditions for relocating further west. Barstow had seemed like the nearest place to the moon she could imagine when they first got there. But she adapted quicker than Fred. Her experience as a migrant allowed her to adapt more readily to new and unpredictable circumstances, and how he loved her for her ability to be so resourceful, adaptive, and understanding. He had to be one of the most difficult men anywhere to live with. He treasured her.

Getting their message off, he then decided to begin the search for newspapers around the world. It seemed like a task too broad in scope. First off, he decided he had to get an atlas for each country world-wide, probably using an internet search engine. Then he would cut and paste next to each country, the states, provinces, cantons or whatever classification that country gave to their next level of authority, below the national one. Once he completed that, he looked up the capital of each state and did another search for the newspaper with the largest circulation in these cities.

He worked through the night, ever aware of B's admonition that the notice had to be in these newspapers on December 1st. By morning, as the "Herald's" receptionist was opening the front door, he had just completed the list of over 500 newspapers. His ability to understand all the languages, after his contact with Clem, was what enabled him to complete this task so quickly. Whatever this was all about, he was now convinced it was too important not to follow through to its completion. But he would work on the actual newspaper announcement when he got back to the office, after he went home and got some sleep.

When he did get home that morning, he quickly checked his home computer for any e-mails from Freda, and happily for him, there was a message from her. Nothing in it was out of the ordinary, just that they were having a grand time and wished he was there. By now, so was he. Quickly, he heated up some oatmeal, covered it with butter, raisins and brown sugar and consumed it in a few gulps. He headed into the bathroom, showered and eagerly slipped into bed. He was ready for sleep.

But, it didn't come. Instead, it was like his mind had shifted into an even higher gear. It was like sleep was something his mind was shunning, like trying to make himself jump into an ice-covered river. Soon, he realized it was hopeless.

"Wouldn't you know it," he muttered. "Ever since that handshake with Clem and talking with those two, I've felt like a race car engine. I guess I might as well try to finish this business, and get it all sent on its way."

Deciding that, he went back to the refrigerator, got our some apple juice, poured himself a large glass, and sat down at his computer in the den. Off and on, he had been trying to expand the newspaper offer outline Clem had given him in the office. Now, in earnest, he edited it until he felt satisfied with the final product. Finally, he sat back and read what he had written. (see Appendix 1, fig. 1, "The Newspaper Offer")

After rereading it several times, he knew it was useless to attempt going back to sleep. Determined to get this phase of B's plan completed, he decided to shave, dress, and head back to the office. It being Thanksgiving Week, there were fewer staff members around, and it would allow him the uninterrupted time to finish what he had started.

For the next fifty-one hours, Fred worked continuously on this project. With each submission to a newspaper, he had to provide the text, give the one single date that it was to be printed, provide the debit card number for them to bill, and give his home e-mail address for a confirmation. He started with the English speaking countries first. It eliminated the easiest and fastest to contact. From there, he went continent by continent, ending up with South and Central America, unaware that he was following Clem and Cynthia's itinerary of overseas' flights, to a large degree. The final count of newspapers the offer was submitted to was 515.

By the time he had finished, it was Thanksgiving Day morning. The newspaper's offices were completely dark, aside for the light in his office. But he had done it. It was such a crazy idea to begin with. And he had little faith that any meaningful responses would come from it. But, at least, he had completed his part of the plan. Now he could rest. The only other detail left for him was to travel out to Amboy and to arrange adding the offer's e-mail address to their computer out there. He hoped that the staff at the motel or restaurant already had a computer. He would take an extra one he had kept, after he replaced the older one Bernice had used. He thought he'd go out on Saturday to get that all set up. That would leave some time before the replies to this offer, if any, would start coming in. Also, he thought he would go by the post office in Amboy and introduce himself to the staff there. It would be some time before Clem got back to Amboy, and he hoped he could at least have the e-mail and most of the air mail letters in some order when he returned.

The drive over to Amboy on Saturday was relaxing. Heading toward Needles, then taking the cutoff to Amboy was straightforward. Once there, he parked outside the restaurant. There were a couple of other cars parked there, with some people casually walking around the building. It did not look like anyone was inside. Fred opened the restaurant door and walked up to the counter and tapped on the bell.

"Be there in a minute," called out a quick and chipper female voice. And sure enough, within less than 15 seconds, a neatly dressed woman in her mid-to-late fifties came out, announcing, "Boy, has it been a busy day today, even for a Saturday. Now, how can I help you?"

Fred was taken off guard, somewhat, by her ease of movement and clarity of voice. The surroundings here in Amboy not just hinted at, but shouted: "slow, lazy, defeated, escaping, stay away." But his first contact was with someone who was eager and excited to be alive. Reaching out his hand to introduce himself, he replied, "Good morning. My name is Fred Wailand."

Hazel, Ray's wife of thirty-three years, took Fred's hand with a firm grasp and shook it slowly, looking at him with penetrating blue eyes. Immediately, both she and Fred understood. "You've been touched by Clem," she exclaimed.

A feeling of recognition and understanding radiated through Fred, and he responded, "You're right. How else could two people feel and sense what we did with that handshake? When did you shake his hand?"

"Oh, he didn't. He spoke to my husband, Ray. Clem shook his hand. It wasn't until Ray came to me and gave me a hug that I, too, experienced the reassuring calm and connectedness to others."

Fred was immediately relieved he could just

proceed with the reason he had come to Amboy and not try to maneuver around what Clem and B were about. He proceeded to say, "I have been working on a project for Clem." But, then, he became hesitant what exactly she might know of B, so he thought it best to avoid mentioning that aspect of his assignment. From what B had said, he should use caution in discussing any details. "There is a possibility of a large number of e-mail responses coming into Amboy, from around the world, starting in a few days. I came out to see if you might have a computer, and if you are connected to the internet and can receive e-mail."

"Yes, we are, and we do. If fact, I was just sitting down to correspond with one of our children when you rang. Do you need our e-mail address?"

"No, but I will need to change yours for a brief time. I am sorry for the inconvenience. Can you let your friends and family know right away? I will then amend your current e-mail address. It shouldn't be in place for long, but I know it's an imposition."

"Is this about the mob of people supposedly coming here for a month on February 1st?" she asked.

"Yes, it is. And from these responses, a decision will be made which families are selected to come. I have no idea how many replies will be e-mailed. The offer instructs them to reply by e-mail and then by air mail as well. I brought a computer from home in case you didn't have one; it was my daughter's. And I also brought twenty packages of bond paper to print out any replies. The instructions were to send only one, typewritten page. If there are more pages than that, they are disqualified, and the e-mail reply will not be printed. I will get extra printer cartridges, as well, to handle the possible volume.

"How many responses would you estimate there might be?" She asked, rather nervously this time.

"I couldn't say. I mailed the notice to over five hundred newspapers around the world. It is supposed to be published on one day only, on December 1st. The replies have to be sent back no later than December 5th. So you could start getting e-mails any time on December 1st. I actually plan to take time off from work to be here, if you don't mind. If the response is slow or the announcement does not attract much attention, then I will probably leave. But if it is heavy, it might help if I am around. Would that be ok?"

Now it was Hazel's turn to be overwhelmed. "Sure, I guess. It's hard to grasp, right away, what you are telling me. Do you think our computer and printer can handle the possible traffic, if it is heavy?"

"What I'll do is set up my daughter's computer and printer so it is there for back up. And I will go ahead and purchase another of each just in case. That's actually a good question. I hadn't thought of that. If the response is heavy, I can imagine someone will need to be sitting here twenty-four hours a day for those five days. We'd have to work in shifts. Is there someone else who could help us?"

Somewhat recovered from the shock of it all and reassured that Fred would be around, she answered, "Well, Ray is not real savvy with the computer, but he could easily be shown how to print out the messages as they come in. And I know Rose, over at the post office, has her own computer and could help when she is not busy with her work over there."

"Good," Fred exclaimed. "That means we each could work a six hour shift, if it came to that. I would be around all the time to trouble-shoot and fill in when needed. Is there a place I could stay for those days?"

"Let me get Ray for that. I think it's about time to get his input and advice on all this. Ray! Oh, Ray!" she shouted. There was no reply. "He might be outside, doing work on the motel somewhere. He has just been swamped with repairs and upgrades since Clem was here a few days ago. Let me go out the back door and call him. He won't mind being interrupted."

Once the three of them got together, it was decided that Fred would take a room in the motel for those days. And because he needed to talk to Rose about post office matters, and the office was closed that day, Hazel called and invited her and her husband over for lunch. They could then meet Fred and discuss whatever issues he needed to with her.

The lunch became a special memory for Fred. He became part of a community which was bound together by something none of them neither understood nor felt compelled to question. Instead, there was an easy banter, like people who had been close friends for years. As problems arose, each person presented a perspective in solving it that invariably led to an easy consensus. It was finally agreed that Fred was to come over on November 30th, five days from then. He was to bring all the extra supplies that might be needed for the computer and stay through December 6th, to make sure all the replies had been received. Likewise, he was to check with Rose at the post office daily, after the 3 p.m. mail truck delivery, to sort out the replies and help bag them. For now, they thought it best to separate them by country only.

Following lunch, Fred was taken back into Hazel and Ray's living room, behind the restaurant, and he was able to switch their e-mail address. Prior to that changeover, Hazel sent out a blanket notice to their family, friends and business connections of this interruption. In addition, she requested that no one send any e-mails during the December 1st -6th timeframe.

As Fred concluded his very successful first day in Amboy, he noticed Jake lying by the front door, as he was about to leave. He reached down and petted him. Jake then awoke from his afternoon nap, looked up and appeared to nod. But Clem was to be the only one who knew of Jake's unusual ability. And that's the way it stayed.   But Fred did notice that there was something very different about Jake. However, the whole day had been wonderfully different. And besides, it was time for him to drive back to Barstow.

ELEVEN: MASSANDRA, CRIMEA

December along the coast of Crimea had about the best climate that the subcontinent of Russia could offer its most powerful and ruthless or its most lowly and deserving. In particular, Massandra had been the destination of choice for the former. December's rainfall was somewhat more than most months of the year, but at a little over 3 inches, that was balmy compared to what was happening in Moscow about the same time. And that was not to mention the temperature difference between the two regions. The Black Sea was a climate buffer, and the coastline from Yalta to Massandra was what most Russians day dream about throughout the year. And that was no different for Philip and Theresa Lieska.

They and their two children, Natalia and Peter, plan all year to be in Massandra throughout the month of December, living in their time-shared dacha. For the children it was like having Christmas throughout the entire month. And for their parents, it was a welcome and needed escape from the ever-present, high pressure of their careers. Philip was a guest concert pianist with the Moscow Symphony Orchestra. During this last year his assignment was to perform Shostakovich's First and Second Piano Concerto's. He had to give multiple performances of each of these taxing works throughout the Symphony's season. And in between teaching his students at the conservatory, he had been trying to focus on his composing. That was now his first love in music. Playing the piano had always been his emotional outlet, but recently the composition of music had taken command of his musical talents and expression. He actually hoped, during their month long stay in Massandra, to be able to complete his first musical score. But first and foremost, he wanted to enjoy his family, being together without the pressure of work and living in Moscow.

Theresa was equally involved in her work. She divided her work time between her painting, teaching art classes at Moscow State University, and working as the Scenic Adaptation Director at the Moscow Arts Theater. Like Philip, she enjoyed the time she could just compose her own paintings and drawings. But to help with the family budget and to keep their children in private schools, she had to work outside her studio. Coming to Crimea each year was a joy to her. The brilliant sunshine, the many colors along the hillsides rising from the shoreline, the sea's changing moods with the passing storms, and most of all, seeing her family relaxed and happy, all this gave her memories that lasted for the rest of the year.

They arrived about 1 p.m. on December 1st, and spent the rest of the afternoon unpacking and getting beds made up, dishes stored, cookware cleaned and ready to use and just walking outside in the blessed warmth. Philip was the first to come inside after making his customary walk down to the water's edge. He had purchased the Yalta newspaper on the way back home and settled down to read for a while before he started preparing dinner. He wasn't that interested in world events now that they were starting their holiday, but he did glance through that section. Politics and government activities offered him little comfort. Soon he was studying the housing section of the classifieds to see how much inflation had affected the rentals and purchases in the area. And then he noticed, set apart from the other advertisements, a paragraph announcing an offer. He stopped and began to read it. (see Appendix 1, fig. 1, "The Newspaper Offer.")

Philip reread the offer repeatedly, shaking his head more vigorously after each time. 'What an offer!' he finally thought. Aloud, he exclaimed, "Theresa and I have always wanted to visit America. And we could maybe extend the trip after the meeting and visit New York City, go to the Lincoln Center, hear the New York Philharmonic Orchestra perform, and see the Metropolitan Museum of Art...what's the harm in trying. Besides, I'm sure we can get time off from work to attend."

Thinking it was at least an hour before he needed to start preparing the evening meal, he walked over to his desk, already covered with finished and unfinished musical scores. He gathered them up, placed them on a side chair, found a piece of notebook paper and began to write:

"21 Drazhinshk Ct.
Massandra
Yalta, Crimea 21311
0012-031-494-01-33
E-mail: phillies@crimea.ru
Philip Lieska, age 32, pianist and
    composer.
Theresa Lieska, age 30, artist.
Natalia Lieska, age 8, student.
Peter Lieska, age 6, student.
1. After growing up in a society experiencing severe restrictions on our personal liberties, and

later when our country began to change, still being imprinted with the need to be cautious and aware of what I said and did, stress management was an integral part of my survival. Even now, there are long lines waiting for a particular food or household item or when you have to conduct some official government business. Ever since I can remember, I have coped with it all through my love of music. It has always calmed me and kept me focused on what was important in life.

2.   My deepest happiness is when I have uninterrupted time with my family. Second to that is when I feel I have mastered a musical composition well enough to perform it with the orchestra and play it before an appreciative audience. And lately, that same satisfaction is possible when composing my own music. In short, I have many ways I experience happiness. Most consistently and often, it is with my family.

3.   My life and work has not required that I become very involved with a variety of strangers or new circumstances. I enjoy interacting with people I've never previously met or traveling to new places and having new experiences. But I cannot comment, with any consistency, on my approach to these events.

4. Probably because of my experiences growing up in a rather closed society, I laugh most readily at the unexpected, the exaggerated, the absurd, at caricatures of people and events, and at the funny things that my wife and children do and say."

After writing this, he read it over and thought to himself that it was probably too brief and wouldn't even be glanced at. But it was all he felt needed to be said in answer to these questions.

Just then, Theresa and the kids barged into the house, giggling and shouting. "The holiday has officially begun," he thought happily. Theresa came over to the desk and gave him a long hug. Peering over his shoulder, she asked, "Who are you writing to now? We've just arrived, and you are already at work!"

"Not at all," Philip replied. "I am entering us in a contest or a promotion, or something that I'm not sure how to describe. But they will pay for our family to travel and spend a week in America! I just couldn't pass up the chance to try. I know how much you'd like to see America and visit New York City and the museums there. So I just finished writing up my response to their questions and instructions. Here, read what the newspaper says and what I wrote."

She sat down on the nearby sofa, with the children plopping down around her. It was quiet for the next five minutes, while she read both the newspaper offer and then what Philip had written in response. At last she said, "Oh, Philip, how wonderful it would be if it happened. I am so glad you saw this and took the time to write a reply. It looks good to me. Let's e-mail what you've written right away. I brought my laptop, and I don't think it needs to be recharged to use. Let's get this sent off, and air mail the letter tomorrow." And without any hesitation, their reply was sent off to Amboy.

TWELVE: THE RESPONSES

As promised, Fred drove back to Amboy on November 30th. Once he entered the motel office and saw Rose and Ray with their spouses, he sensed that the tension of that small band of drafted participants in B's plan was almost too much for each to bear. "This was Amboy, for crying out loud," he thought. "Each of us came to this part of the world to escape the world or to find some healing, not to become the welcoming committee for a United Nation's assembly." Lucky for him, Ray, Hazel, Rose and Harry were trying their best to be helpful and involved. He just wished Freda could have been here, but she wasn't to return from Norway until December 14th.

Ray gave him the key to his motel room, and he drove over to the motel and unloaded his personal belongings. Realizing that it was going to take him some time to hook up his daughter's computer and to get the printers, copier, CD disks and extra paper sorted and in place, he decided to head back over to the restaurant immediately thereafter. Once he got all that paraphernalia sorted and hooked up, and then took Ray and Hazel's computer out of their office and installed it with the other equipment in the rear dining area, he decided to call everyone together. They were still very nervous, and he wanted to try calming them by beginning the instruction on how to download and copy the responses as they came in. He was relieved nothing would start coming, if any ever did, until tomorrow.

It took a few minutes to get everyone, with their coffee in hand, seated around the large table with the two computers and all the necessary supplies. Feeling relieved about how, so far, everything was proceeding according to plan, Fred rather nonchalantly turned on Hazel's computer, to demonstrate how easy you could click on the internet icon, and presto, be on line and ready to receive incoming email.

"See, that was all quite straight forward, wouldn't you agree," he prompted all of them sitting there. With his back to the computer screen, he obviously couldn't see what Rose did. And with some earnestness in her voice, she asked, "That isn't right is it? Your e-mail 'inbox' says you have over 11,000 responses!"

Spinning around, like his feet were not even in contact with the floor, Fred scanned the screen's sidebar, which listed any e-mail activity. And sure enough, it reported there were now 11,234 responses waiting to be read.

"Oh, no! I forgot that November 30th here, is December 1st as you travel west across the International Date Line. Those are responses from the South Pacific and Asia! We've got to start right away, this minute, downloading these replies! Folks, Amboy is now on the world map! Get something to drink or to snack on, and get comfortable. We've got some work ahead of us. I'll take the first shift, in hopes we can get the bulk of these replies copied and deleted. If any of you are available right now, one of you can start making separate piles for different countries, as I finish with copying their response and copying it on the disk. And maybe a couple of you can bring in tables and get them set up for us to sort and stack on."

And so it went day and night for the next week. Not infrequently, a reply would have two or three pages. Those were automatically discarded. And some failed to include their e-mail address. Due to the timeframe necessary for notification, they, too, were eliminated. This editing process lessened, to some degree, the amount of printing and copying that was necessary. All total about 15% of the responses were disqualified for one reason or another. But by midnight on December 6, when the process shut down, they had tabulated over 67,000 responses from over 150 countries. This small band achieved a staggering feat. And it was soberly acknowledged that Rose would have about that same number of letters routed through her post office. She had forewarned the San Bernardino Regional Office of a potentially large influx of mail. But no one imagined it would be this much. They were going to have to help Clem sort, as well. No one person could do that much in the little time he'd have, once he returned from his trip. And by December 4th, those letters were starting to pour in from Canada and the U.S. With each passing day, mail arrived from more countries that were further away from Amboy. Again, the restaurant became the center of sorting and storage of responses.

Fred had to leave on December 7th, to return to Barstow for a few days' appearance at work. Even with him telling his editor that he was covering the story of a lifetime, it was clear that the newspaper's management was becoming less understanding of his commitments. He sensed that there was a limit to the amount of time he could devote to this story. But he also knew that it was more than just a story. Coming to that conclusion helped him make the next decision. He would definitely come back to Amboy and stay for another week. He would return there tomorrow and be back home in time for Freda and the girls' return from Norway on the 14th. He straightened up the house, washed his clothes, and stocked some groceries for their return. But, given the overwhelming, world-wide responses to the newspaper offer, he had no choice but to return immediately to Amboy.

It was another whirlwind week for him and the small band in Amboy. Letters poured in from all over the world, some that could not be matched to any preceding e-mail reply. They, too, were discarded. Each respondent had to follow the directions in the offer exactly as requested, otherwise the constraints of time and distance and the process of how and why particular families were to be selected, would become totally ineffectual. In the course of this last week, between all of the Amboy crew, they were able to match e-mail to airmail letters for 75% of the replies. The tables in the rear dining room were covered with the thousands of replies, each now separated by country of origin and then, as much as possible, by occupations. Whatever letters were received between now and December 26, their arbitrary cutoff date, could easily be matched to the e-mail responses with the system they had set up. With a great sense of pride and accomplishment, they had a little party the night of December 11th.

At 5:45 p.m. on the 14th, Freda and the girls drove up the drive way in the rental car they hired at LAX. They were so relieved to finally be back in their own home. Fred let them get comfortable and get some rest before he shared any news about what had been happening to him. And they were so eager and excited to tell him all the details of their stay and trip, it seemed rude for him to do otherwise. It was a thrill for him to have them back. Even though he had been extremely busy, he hadn't realized how deeply he had missed not having them around. It was a warm and hearty homecoming. His surprises could wait until later.

THIRTEEN: THE LIST

Clem got his truck out of impound and drove off from the motel on December 24th. The extra two night's stay had helped both Cynthia and him regain some energy and strength. They were about at the end of their endurance from this long trip when they arrived there. He was amazed how well Cynthia managed to perform the task B had outlined for them. She had volunteered for it, after all. He was drafted. But it was over now, or at least it would soon be once he got back home to his cabin outside Amboy. It was 9:10 a.m. when he drove off.

Once he got out of the worst of the freeway congestion, somewhere outside Fontana, B again made his presence known. Probably because of his lingering fatigue, Clem was not as shocked as he normally might have been.

"I want to thank you, Clem, for what you and Cynthia have just accomplished. I realize how very difficult it all was, but each of you did it with style and with such grace. I am proud of you both. And I wish there was time to show my appreciation in some way other than by just saying 'thank you', but we must go on. I still need your help. If you will, I need you to please find a store somewhere along the way. I'll need you to purchase a tape recorder and some tapes. Once you have done that, I need to discuss the next project with you."

"Ok," Clem replied. "I just hope I am up to the task."

Pulling off the freeway, he found a nationally recognized, pharmacy store on a corner and purchased what B wanted. Before he pulled away from the store, he set up the tape recorder and inserted a 60 minute blank tape. It was ready for any recording that was needed. Soon they were back on the highway, heading east toward home.

"What we need to do now," B began as they entered the flow of traffic, "is for you to turn on the recorder, and then you can listen to what I have to say, as it is recording. At any time, please interject suggestions that you might have. We are going to start compiling a list, by occupation, of who will be selected for the symposium, or of who might be needed in case of an emergency, if the symposium cannot proceed as planned. Also, I will need you to contact Fred and have him meet you tomorrow morning at the Amboy restaurant. You will have more sorting to do then."

Clem had been dreading this part of B's project. This sorting seemed too much for one or two persons to do. He sighed heavily at the thought. But, returning to the task at hand, he was puzzled, as always seemed to be the case when he and B began these work sessions. Finally, he said, somewhat jokingly, "Ok, boss. You talk, and I'll listen. That's something I do especially well."

The taped conversation went on for the rest of the trip back to Clem's cabin. By the time they had arrived, the 60 minute tape was full and B had departed, but not before telling Clem to expect a return visit later this evening to discuss the list after he had finished compiling it. Up until this time, it was all a blur to Clem. He had concentrated more on the driving than on what B had talked about. Any suggestions he offered, seemed disconnected. He tried hard not to be discouraged by all of this.

Parking his truck, he retrieved his cell phone and called Fred's number and left a message for him to meet him at 8 a.m. tomorrow at Ray and Hazel's. Realizing that tomorrow was Christmas Day, he suggested that Fred bring his family along as well. And while he was at it, he called Cynthia's number and left the same message. He knew she would not be back home yet from visiting her mom, but it felt right to at least invite her.

Now it was time to see what shape his cabin was in after his hasty exit over a month ago. It took him a while to get the inside in some order. He then made a late lunch, sat down at his small desk and began listening to the tape. It took him three hours to finally organize the list to include all that he thought B had wanted. It incorporated 75 couples, accompanied by their 150 children.

Now that the list was completed, he and Fred would have to meet tomorrow and go over it. It was not entirely clear to him why they were doing so at Ray's, because at this point he and Cynthia had no idea what the Amboy crew had been doing since they had been traveling. But, at least he had done his part. Now he was going to sleep. Enough was enough, he thought. Just before lying down, he would read over the list in its entirety. It read: (see Appendix 1, fig. 3, "The Occupations List").

Once he had this chance to see the list all together, he became upset. His years of being an outsider, of being a marginal reader and student, of having too many jobs due to poor learning skills and abilities, gave him the feeling that B had ignored the working man and woman, those who were the bedrock of any land. To Clem, the list was elitist, composed of the best and the brightest. To him, they always seem to have the special privileges, even though it's the working class people that make it all possible. He felt humiliated and angry reading it.

And unsure if B was in the area or not, Clem exclaimed. "This just isn't right. Even when things are seemingly falling apart, the privileged few still get all the breaks. It just ain't fair. All my life I've been seeing this happen, and now I am a part of it. It makes me mad. I don't want to be involved in this anymore. Why did you do this?"

B had expected that there might be some reaction from Clem after he finished this final draft of the acceptance list. And he was beside him when he completed it. It was now time to provide some needed comfort.

"Clem," B said in the most reassuring voice, "I am aware of your distress and disappointment. And you, of all people, deserve to know my reasons for what you have written down. I have chosen those groups, not based on accomplishment, status, or privilege, even though it has to appear so. I had eight guiding principles in deciding who should be selected. Those principles were: to be of good character; to have the ability to laugh at one's self and find and express humor in one's daily life; to be able to interact with others easily and comfortably; to have skills or knowledge that is needed for basic survival or ones that need to be saved or recorded; to have the ability to teach and share with others these skills and knowledge; to have the ability to plant, nurture, and harvest foodstuffs for sustaining life; and to have the love, patience, and skills to mother and to husband children, so that they might become mature, caring and thoughtful of others. And my reason for choosing so many teachers was that they can both teach and reinforce all these qualities and skills, insuring that they pass on to the next generation. And most of all, that life, an abundant and good life, could possibly happen in the future. And, believe me; I plan on being a much more visible presence in the hope of achieving that outcome…

"I realize the list is weighted in favor of science and technology. But that is where the vast store of knowledge has come from over the last two hundred and fifty years. The humanities, art, music and writings have not been as expansive. They are of equal value and importance to me. Actually, I must admit, they are more important. I tried to include individuals who could carry on these skills, as well, but just fewer of them. But they, too, must be prepared to teach, inspire and coach the children. Imagine if you will; this list represents what would have been written and painted on the walls of caves or canyons, on papyrus scrolls or Rosetta stones to record a passing presence. I am not trying to reward a class or group of people. I am trying to save some but, if that fails, then to record the presence and the possible passing of a people. I, at this moment, can only hope that it will be more than just a passing.

"And if it becomes necessary to enlist their support, I will be including military personnel and their families. I must confess a bias here. Of all the institutions in this country, or even elsewhere, I have been most impressed with their character, their devotion to duty and to the citizens of this country. They stand apart from the general population, which has become nearly obsessed with matters involving business, finance, consumption of goods and services, and on becoming or being a success and achieving self-importance. There are certainly exceptions. Many individuals and groups have worked tirelessly to improve and prevent the catastrophe that now seems inevitable. For their dedication and deep love of life, for their concern for those around them, for this planet, and for their trusting faith and hope that they could make a difference, I reserve for them my greatest adoration. They are the blessed ones, and they shall inherit everlasting life. Make no mistake about that.

"These military people, on the other hand, blend moral purpose with economy of organization. It's their genius. They realize their role is to be of service and provide protection for the greater good of the citizenry. They risk and give their lives in the service of that role. And certainly, there are others who perform these same functions. But, as a group, they are, for the most part, selfless and brave. I wanted them included, not for their battlefield experience, but for the influence they will have on the selected families as a whole. They can provide protection, if needed. But most importantly, they provide organizational resources and skills for survival. If it comes to that, they will be incorporated into the governing process as the group evolves and survives beyond the calamity that could happen. I make no apologies for including them. They are fine, almost noble, individuals. I only wish the general population, of good and decent souls, could have been included as well. There was no space left.

"And I have definitely not forgotten those you mourn at this moment, the poor, and the huddled ones, those struggling to make life work; the ones who have despaired and given up hope. The ones who have worked so hard and diligently all their lives, only to find themselves in hopeless circumstances due to ill health, death, calamity or fewer natural abilities. These are the ones for whom I grieve the most, and I always have. By its very nature, life has a disturbingly high chance of failure. That is why, and I shall one day speak more about this to you, the Kingdom of Heaven has its place.

Sometimes, only hope can sustain and be offered to people. It is for these people that I have my greatest love."

Once B had spoken, Clem was quiet for a while. B recognized his need to let what had been said be sorted out. Finally, Clem said, "I think I understand, B. But I am afraid all of this is becoming too overwhelming for me. You have taken me into your confidence. But I am a very simple man. I'll try hard to do what you have asked of me, but I don't think I'm going to try and understand what you've said. I feel pretty tired lately. That's why I came back to my cabin to rest. You know, I don't think I'll be asking you any more questions."

FOURTEEN: NOTIFICATION OF THE CHOSEN

Unaware that Fred had followed up on Clem's cell phone call, when Clem arrived at Ray and Hazel's restaurant on Christmas morning, both Fred and his family, Rose, Harry, Hazel, Ray and Cynthia were already there. They had arrived around 6:30 a.m. Clem arrived at 7 a.m., thinking that he might get a jump on everyone and have some coffee and maybe a donut before the meeting started.

"Merry Christmas, Clem!" the cry went out, as he entered the restaurant.

"Come in world traveler and have some breakfast with us. We were beginning to wonder if you would ever get here," Ray chimed in.

As he passed through the doorway, Cynthia came up and hugged him, quietly adding her greeting, "Merry Christmas, friend. It seems strange not running from airport to airport with my blind companion."

"And Merry Christmas to you, Cynthia! How did you find your mom?" he asked.

"About the same, I guess. But she did seem pleased to see me. We had a good visit, but short. I wanted to get back home as soon as possible. But then I got your message to come here this morning. It's funny, more and more my home seems to be where you and I are."

Clem smiled at her, and then found himself blushing. He knew she meant nothing suggestive. Probably his blushing was more in response to his feeling the same way. By now, he thought, there was a definite bond joining them.

The atmosphere was festive. Adding to the merriment of the occasion were Fred and Freda's two girls, Bernice and Megan. They were energetic, enthusiastic, and at ease with all the assembled folks. To Clem, it was the nicest Christmas morning he could remember since the death of his wife.

From 7 to 8 a.m. they ate a huge breakfast prepared by Hazel and Ray. As they each settled down to drink their last cup of coffee, tea or cocoa, Clem slipped back into the motel office and photocopied ten copies of the list he had finished last night. He made a copy for each person.

Coming out of the office, Fred bellowed out, "Ok, Clem, what do you have for us now? I had a feeling you might have other plans for us this morning."

Tipping his head down in embarrassment, Clem knew he was going to interrupt the wonderful Christmas spirit that everyone was so enjoying. He knew he had to. B would be here this afternoon to select the families that would be coming for the symposium. But he also knew that Ray and Rose and their spouses had never witnessed seeing B. Because of that, he had to try and steer this final selection process carefully.

"Well, I'm sure sorry to be interrupting such a grand meal and celebration. I hope we can resume all of this, as soon as we've completed one last chore. I'll just pass these copies around to each of you. Take a few minutes to look them over." (see Appendix 1, fig. 3, "The Occupations List".)

Each person there, even the girls, studied what was handed to them. It was soon clear to each, just by the listings if nothing else, that this represented something more important than they had expected. Realizing the awkwardness of the situation, Clem explained that his contact had supplied him with this list and would be here later this afternoon to make the final selections. Because of his contact's wish to remain anonymous, the folding doors into the rear dining room would be closed once they had completed their task. In short, the list they were looking at was to be an additional factor, if not one of the most important ones, for choosing who attends the symposium in February. But he knew it left many unanswered questions. He didn't encourage any either.

"Since I don't know what you've been doing here while Cynthia and I were away, I can only assume that by Rose's mail bags not being stacked on my front porch, as was earlier planned, that the replies to the newspaper offer are either here or are still in her office. And that they still need to be sorted. Fortunately, I also assume that there probably weren't many replies."

At this, giggles and some laughter broke out. "Listen, Clem, before you go much further, there is something you and Cynthia will want to see. Come on, let's open the doors to the rear dining room and take a look inside," Fred eagerly called out.

Standing up, all the Amboy crew then followed Fred and Clem over to the folding doors. With some exaggeration and fanfare, Fred swooped wide open one of the doors, revealing to all standing there twenty tables, each eight foot in length, and fully stacked with replies to the newspaper advertisement.

"As you can see," Fred announced proudly, "while you were gone, we've also been pretty busy here in Amboy. Now with these lists that you've provided us, we can refine the division and sorting into more specific stacks. At least we can have them separated by country and the occupational categories you have listed here, e.g. science, teaching, engineering, humanities, medicine. We won't have the time or space to separate them further into exact job titles."

Both Clem and Cynthia were visibly overwhelmed at the sight before them. Obviously, Clem had misjudged what the response would be. While he was trying to gather his senses, Fred suggested, "To make this process go as quickly as possible, why don't we divide the workload into ten workstations. Each of us will sort and restack two tables. I think our daughters can do this sorting as well. It shouldn't take us too long to wrap this up. I bet we can be done by noon."

All present nodded in agreement. And for the next three hours there was very little conversation or chitchat. Everyone knew this was a task that needed to be done quickly and well.

As predicted by Fred, by noon all of the crew, except Clem, had reassembled out in the main dining area and were getting warm-ups for their drinks. Christmas time in the Mojave Desert can bring a deep chill, and today, even with the brilliant sunshine, it was cold outside. The rear dining room was not heated. The hot drinks were a welcome treat for all.

Soon, Clem finished restacking his last table and came out, closing the doors behind him. Before he exited, he did arrange with Hazel to get a small table, and he placed it just inside the folding doors. Relieved, he poured himself some needed coffee and sat down beside Cynthia.

"There," Clem announced, "that should do it. What a remarkable job you fine folks did, getting all this organized and sorted. And what a great bunch you are to work with and to be around." All present nodded in agreement, patting each other on the back, and quickly resumed their chatter and laughter.

Just then Cynthia called out to Ray and Hazel, "Are you taking volunteers for Christmas dinner preparations?" Her offer was accepted, and everyone pitched in to set tables, place decorations, spread out a few gifts, and prepare the meal. The afternoon passed joyfully. Their holiday had begun.

No one knew when B came and did the selecting of families. The closed doors to the rear dining room remained unchanged. They did notice it had been quiet in there all afternoon. But come about 3:30 p.m. someone saw that the folding doors were ajar. Knowing that he had closed them tightly, Clem walked over to see if something had happened that they hadn't noticed.

Opening the doors slowly, he saw there were now two stacks of replies on the small table, with written notes on top of each stack. And there was a separate note addressed to Fred's family. Clem called Fred over to read all the notes.

As Fred took the notes off the stacks, he read the one from the smaller stack first. "Fred, please notify these families this afternoon. It is already December 26, where they are." And on the taller stack, it just said, "Notify these families tomorrow." The separate note was sealed, addressed to his family. He gave that one to Freda to open. She opened it and read aloud, "Fred, you will note there are only 74 families in these two stacks; your family is be the 75th."

Freda was surprised when everyone in the room began to clap and congratulate them. No one felt anything but genuine pleasure and pride that Fred, Freda, and their daughters had been selected to attend the symposium. Everyone knew that Fred had recently lost his job, and they knew how hard he had worked preparing for the meeting in February.

For Fred and his family, shock was their first response. No one was too sure what it really meant. But

Freda commented that at least they could now write about the symposium as attendees. But certainly, they laughed, it was no prize for them to spend a week in the Mojave Desert. They had already lived in Barstow for six years. For his part, Fred was overjoyed. Now he could write an accurate firsthand account of what took place.

But the celebration was short lived for now. Fred realized he had to respond to the 28 families for whom today was already December 26th. Immediately, he excused himself, and went over to the computers in the back of the rear dining room. He closed the folding doors behind him, knowing he would need privacy to complete the acceptance letter. He hoped B would assist him in the details of the letter, and said aloud, "B, can you advise me on how you want me to write this letter and help me with a few issues that it raises?"

Appearing immediately, B answered, "Of course, Fred. Let me outline for you what I would like to have written."

As B spoke, Fred took copious notes. When B had finished outlining the letter, Fred asked, "Is there some way you can make a lasting impression with the selected families, so you can insure their full cooperation with all you are asking them to do? You mentioned that we need to pack our belongings for a possible long term emergency. Do you still want that included as well? There is an element of threat about that portion of the letter that will startle and dismay everyone."

"I understand what you are saying. And, yes, I expect they, and you, will be disturbed by that request. But, like you and the others here in Amboy that I have appeared before, I will reinforce the contents of this acceptance letter, leaving no doubt in their minds that they need to do as it requests."

And after saying that, B was gone.

The feeling Fred had after this discussion with B was not one of ineptness or of being overwhelmed. It was a feeling of grief. The letter was intended to salute those selected and then to give them detailed instructions as to what they needed to do. Yet, by its very nature, it was more soberly announcing, although silently, to the rest of humanity, that they weren't selected. As he composed the last draft of the letter, frequently tears would form and fall into his lap as he typed.

After finishing the editing, he finally leaned back and reread what would be sent to those selected families. (see Appendix 1, fig. 4, "The Acceptance Letter") It was now time to type in the e-mail addresses of those families that were accepted and then type the final version of the letter on Rose and Ray's computer. Their computer was the one with the proper e-mail address on it. He planned on copying each address and letter to them on a disk and download that onto his own computer; he wanted to begin a file for each family. It was clear, even now, that tracking all this correspondence and the responses was going to become impossibly confusing unless it was organized and filed. Once the e-mail acceptance letters were sent off, he then would have Cynthia and Clem help him address and airmail the 74 letters to the selected families. It was important that dual notification was given and acknowledged. Already, Fred was beginning to realize how sobering and awesome this whole endeavor was becoming. He knew something ominous was probably awaiting everyone.

Fred did not wait around for any responses. He figured that the main objective of today's efforts were to get the acceptance notifications off to the families that were on the other side of the International Date Line. That being completed, he wanted to shut it all down and return to the Christmas celebrations.

The rest of the day and night were spent opening the few gifts for the girls, singing, dancing, laughing and endless conversations. Clearly, this group was now an extended family circle. Even Jake had double helpings of food and treats. As the evening shadows from the surrounding mountains lengthened across Amboy's dry lake bed, Clem quietly asked Jake if he wanted to take a walk outside. Clem's revelation involving the seeing eye dog at LAX reminded him that Jake did have unusual abilities, and that he should now ask him if he'd like to do something. Jake happily agreed, and they spent the next hour strolling and chatting. This walk and their talking, as impossible as it all seems, strengthened a bond that future events would only deepen.

By midnight, everyone had left the restaurant and gone to their rooms in the motel. Fred's family decided that they would stay in Amboy overnight, as well, to make it easier on Fred to notify the accepted families in the morning. He was relieved that they were staying over. And the next morning he sent the rest of the acceptance announcements to the remaining 46 families.

Of the 74 families who got their acceptance notices, only two will be chronicled as to what happened and their reactions. Their reactions were fairly typical of what most families experienced. It could be said that between all of them, the full range of human emotions was felt upon receiving this notification letter.

In Ballarat, Australia, December 26th, is Boxing Day, a national holiday. Geoffrey and Patty Graham had both taken another RDO for Friday, December 22nd. That day, plus the next four days, gave them a nice five day holiday. Like they had for the previous three years, they chose to spend that time in the little village of Apollo Bay, Victoria. It is located on the Great Ocean Road, with magnificent views of the ocean and the surrounding cliffs. Being December, at the height of Australian summer, escape to the cooler coastal area became an established tradition for them.

Both realized that the notification for acceptance as a participant in the Amboy symposium was scheduled to come on the 26th. For that reason, Patty took her lap top computer with them, just in case they were selected. It seemed a highly unlikely eventuality, but they treated it like buying a Tattslotto ticket: 'you can't win it, if you're not in it.'

Because the time difference between California and Victoria, Australia is seventeen hours, when Fred finally sent the email notices to the selected families, it was 5 p.m. in Amboy and 10 a.m. in Apollo Bay. Because this was the Graham family's last day by the ocean, they all slept in. Gradually, the kids awoke and started watching cartoons on television. This was followed by Patty, who had the usual mother's sixth sense that her charges might need extra mothering today. They were not spoiled kids, but they were kids. And they knew the ins and outs of getting attention and being naughty. Today, Patty thought, might be just one of those days. They had to drive back to Ballarat today, and they might be a handful.

Because she was still groggy from getting up, she automatically turned on her lap top to get the news form the Melbourne newspaper website. And there flashing, as she completed the internet sign in, was a message that she 'had mail'. Her dulled state prevented her from anticipating that it might be from Amboy. But once she saw the senders address, she knew exactly who it was from. Nervously, she clicked on the inbox and up came Fred's acceptance letter. She only read the first paragraph, and then jumped up to wake Geoffrey.

"Geoff! Geoff! Wake up! Hurry! Wake up! We've got a reply from Amboy, California, saying we were accepted! Quick, come read the entire letter with me."

It was like someone had poured cold water on him. He sat up and was standing almost before Patty could get out of his way. "Great!" he said. "What a wonderful surprise for all of us! Let's go see what they have to say," was his immediate response.

Together they quickly printed off the letter and then sat on the sofa to read it. The kids sensed their anticipation and excitement. They cuddled themselves, one on each side of their parents. And then the full reading of the letter began. By the time they had finished it, they were in shock. This was not like anything they had thought it was. It asked too much of them. The symposium sounded fascinating, as did the free trip to America. But placing in storage all the requested items was impossible and inappropriate, to say the least. It was an outrage.

"Who do these people think they are, demanding this?" Geoffrey exclaimed angrily. "They must be crazy to think we'll do what they are asking!" But as he was expressing his frustration, an invisible presence was felt simultaneously by all the family. Nothing visible was evident, but each knew that they were not alone. And at that moment, Patty turned to Geoff and asked, in fluent Russian, "What is happening? Do you feel the same thing I am? I sense we are not alone!" And Geoff replied, in equally flawless Russian, "I have no idea. But I agree, something or someone is here, but just not visible." Then each of the children spoke, but they spoke and were easily understood and responded to, in another language, fluent Japanese. What followed for the next 30 minutes was a cascade of languages, spoken and understood by all four of the family members. Some languages they had never even heard before, but still understood and spoke them effortlessly.

Then the presence was gone, but not the ability to speak whatever language they chose to. Their previous anger now turned to confusion and anxiety. What was going on? They knew whatever it was, it was far beyond anything they could understand or explain. And it punctuated the message in their acceptance letter. They knew what it said was important and should be followed as written. They weren't sure at this point how to go about gathering together the items listed. But at least they understood nothing further may come from organizing and storing it. They had to begin.

And it was after another 30 minutes, a feeling of calm and well being settled over them. Without expressing it to the other, each knew this was no ordinary trip to a place called Amboy. Quickly, they packed up their Ute and returned to Ballarat. All the way back they discussed what to store and what to take with them. As they pulled into their driveway at home, Patty turned to the children and reminded them "You are not to tell anybody about this. I think you have an idea how important all this is." The children nodded their heads. And they never spoke of it to anyone.

It was late afternoon on the 26th when Philip got the acceptance e-mail from Amboy. He and his wife had tried to stay busy all day to avoid getting too anxious about the passing deadline to hear about whether they were selected to attend the symposium. Between walking into town to shop for groceries, walking along the beach, and bicycling up into the surrounding hills of Crimea, the family stayed occupied. When the e-mail came from Amboy, Philip was just sitting down to try and compose the final movement of his new piano concerto. He had worked diligently on it through the month they had been here, and it was nearing completion. Theresa had also been working this last month on her painting, trying to get ready for her first individual showing of her art work. It was scheduled to be exhibited this upcoming May in Moscow.

When the e-mail came through, Philip was overjoyed. He read it non-stop, not waiting to get Theresa. This was a mistake. The latter part of the letter astonished him. He could not believe what he was reading. He felt disappointed. It seemed like a sham, some kind of promotional gimmick, like a time-share offer or a pyramid scheme.

Discouraged, even somewhat despondent, he went out on their veranda to call Theresa to come in and read it for herself. By chance their children were with her, and they followed her in as well. They sat on the floor by the love seat Philip and Theresa were on. She read the letter aloud for the children to hear as well.

When completed, she turned to Philip and said, "I don't understand. What is going on here? I thought the newspaper notice said it was a symposium?"

"That it did!" Philip replied emphatically. "This business of packing our belongings and other equipment is confounding."

And, like happened with the other 74 families around the world in this 24 hour timeframe, an unmistakable, yet unseen, presence came into their midst. And for the next 30 minutes, the four of them spoke and understood ten to twenty different languages, none of which were ones they already knew.

This astonishing new ability was followed by a sense of calm, well being and connectedness to those around them. It was like some magical conversion, they said later. Or even like the deepest religious experience. And they all knew what they had to do. The letter was to be followed exactly as written. The airmail letter would be forwarded to their Moscow apartment, because within hours of receiving their acceptance notification, they were preparing to return to Moscow.

Philip gathered all his notes, musical scores, compositions, various small musical instruments to take with them back north. And Theresa assembled all her paints, brushes, easels, frames, instruction booklets, and texts kept at their dacha to take back as well. They planned to be packed and ready to leave for Amboy come January 30. They would arrange for travel visas as soon as they returned to Moscow.

PART III

FIFTEEN: AMBOY

Amboy, in February, was beginning to feel out of control, particularly if you have not lived in the deep desert before. Whether you arrived by bus, train, car or motorcycle, you had a sort of dread when you arrived. True, the surrounding barren mountainsides and heat waves simmering off the dry lake bed were ominous enough. But it was the heat, whether present or yet to come, that herded your fear. The area was imprinted with the ravages of it.   In the deepest recesses of everyone's psyche, the desert reigns supreme, beyond the prospect of your living in the area that had frigid temperatures, tornadoes, hurricanes, or even tsunamis. Some people who lived in it would brag about doing so, and some even appeared to enjoy it. But each one, somewhere within their clutch of fears, harbored an uneasy pact with the desert gods. The desert looked deadly. And it was.

For the residents and upcoming visitors, soon to become residents themselves, it was obvious that the temperatures were too hot for this time of year. Each year, it seemed, it just got a little warmer. But in Amboy, they had passed 'warmer' long ago. It was either cool-to-cold two to three months a year, and then it was hot. Experiencing warm sunshine was something you did at the beach. Not in Amboy.

Today the business and governmental representatives of Amboy, Ray, Hazel, Rose and Harry, came together with Clem, Cynthia, and Fred's family to review the roster of families that would start showing up in the next five days. It was 10 a.m. on January 27th, and already Ray had to turn on the air conditioner to make it more comfortable inside the restaurant.

Because Fred had been the primary correspondent with the families and had organized most of the activities prior to their selection, he was the logical one to present the list of those selected for everyone's review. It was hoped that by everyone assembled studying the families' names, their occupations and where they came from, the newcomers would be made to feel welcomed sooner.

"I will be circulating a list of occupations and where the individuals are coming from. There are 75 families, including mine, encompassing 150 occupations. Students are not counted in the occupational totals. There are also 150 children coming with their parents. We'll discuss the list after you have had a chance to look it over. Clem, will you be so kind as to pass these around?"

"Sure, be glad to, Fred. I'm anxious to see what you've been up to these past few weeks." Clem replied.

Then each person took time to read over the following: (see Appendix 1, fig. 5, "Accepted Applicants' Occupations and Countries of Origin")

After giving everyone time to thoroughly look over and digest who had been selected, Fred decided to lead the follow-up conversation, starting with some observations of his own.

"You'll note if you add them up, there are 37 countries represented here. However, even though 43 of the 150 adults and their children are now living in the United States, we estimate at least half this number are either naturalized citizens from another country or are first or second generation immigrants. It became obvious in the selection that America is the true melting pot that others have claimed it was. The selection process involved trying to match the most qualified family members, that is, the wife and husband, in the same profession or job description. When that was not possible, the attempt was made to assure that we selected the most qualified individuals. And those selected had to respond to the questions asked in a way that met the standards that had been set. The guidelines and standards were high, which hopefully will insure a highly motivated assembly that is gifted in their respective fields, compatible with others in what could become an indescribable set of circumstances, and open to the mysteries and events that might unfold in the weeks, months, and years ahead.

"I am sure you will have questions and comments, just let me say one more thing. The agenda or program for the symposium is ready for your review. I will give you that handout, along with the listing of family members and their room numbers after we've had a lunch break. But, for now, do you have any questions or comments about this handout?"

"What about being able to understand all these different languages?" Ray asked. "Coming from all these places, it will be impossible for me to understand them."

"Good question, Ray," Fred replied. "And at this point, I'm in the dark on that point as well."

Saying that seemed to cue B's presence at that moment. And as would be expected, it came as a total shock to everyone assembled there, even Clem, Cynthia and Fred.

By now, there was no way for Clem to measure the shock that came over people who had never seen B. It was, certainly, life transforming in itself; and that B just appeared, where nothing but space was there before, didn't lessen the impact any. His form, as always, was shapeless. It remained a shadowy blur. Invariably, at the onset for any of B's appearances, people would rub their eyes, thinking initially they were having floaters, just like Clem did. But then B speaks and puts that possibility to rest. Clem had noticed that B's voice had ranges of volume and tone, depending on the subject and the audience to be addressed. Today, as it turned out, it was reassuring, calming, and appreciative.

"Good morning to each of you," B began. "A few of you, Clem, Cynthia and Fred, I have met before. But for the rest of Fred's family, Hazel, Ray, Rose and Harry, I need to introduce myself. I took the name B one night last November, after my first conversation with Clem. And you may call me that as well. Most importantly for this moment, let me assure you, as I have others, I mean you absolutely no harm. On the contrary, my sole purpose for being with any of you is to prevent further harm to anyone, as much as that now will be possible. Soon enough we will know which direction that hope and purpose has taken. I would expect within the next week, something definite will be known about how well the world wide travels of Cynthia and Clem succeeded.

"For now, let me say how proud I am of each of you here today. You have been extremely patient and preserving during what had to be an oddly mysterious time. Now I shall begin to unravel some of that mystery for you."

About this time, Fred's daughters, Bernice and Megan, became somewhat overcome with the presence of B. Even though their father's touching them had the same effect as Clem's had on him, they were still entitled to be quite emotional at this moment. It was more a matter of a swoon, rather than a reaction from fear and anxiety. True to the wonder of adolescent development, with its heightened sense of awareness, psychic energy and spiritual openness, they realized who and what B was, more so than anyone else in the room. And B was keenly aware of this. Both girls also knew that B knew. In response, both bowed their heads, which was unnoticed by the rest of the transfixed group. Without their being able to see, B smiled at their recognition.

"When Fred sent the acceptance letters out to the selected families," B continued, "he stated that there would be something that accompanied the letter which would convince each family that what they were reading and what they needed to do was real and important. I quietly visited each family, although not visible to them as such, and through my touching each of them, they now can speak and understand any language you might hear once they arrive. Each one of them has tested this out within their own family. That ability cannot be passed on, except in my presence, as was the case with Clem and each of you.

"So, Ray, in answer to your question about how will you be able to understand what these family members are saying, that will not be a problem for you or anyone else in this room. You possess that ability as of today.

"The choice of who is coming, from where, and why certain skills or talents were important was all my decision. My hope at this stage of this mission is that there will be no need to have anything other than this symposium, as outlined. Then the attendees will publish these discussions and recommendations, and let the impact of those publications take hold everywhere. All this is dependent on whether Cynthia and Clem's efforts were broad enough in their outreach and had the effect needed on certain key individuals. For now, we are proceeding on the assumption that their trip was a total success.

"Know how grateful I am for your work. I realize you are tired, probably even exhausted. You must take heart, though. The importance of what you are doing is beyond measure."

And saying that, B was gone, leaving the room of people quiet and reflective. It was clear to all that their lives were changed completely by these past moments together.

SIXTEEN: THE SYMPOSIUM'S AGENDA

The lunch was a mix of excitement and awe. Clem, Cynthia and Fred had enough prior exposure to B to be somewhat less overwhelmed with his spontaneous appearances. But they were still stunning in content and timing. Today, at least, there were no bombshells or changes in plans or long trips to take somewhere. So they were relieved. And it was comforting to know that all of their past efforts were not part of some choreographed dream state.

The meal lasted over an hour, with each person sharing their reactions to the news and B's appearance. But with the common goal well fixed in everyone's mind, there was no fear or anxiety. Soon jokes started to be told, and laughter replaced serious discussions. Ray and Hazel had fixed cold cut sandwiches and iced tea for lunch. They had essentially closed down the restaurant and motel after Clem's initial visit to reserve the motel for February. They limited their services to simple counter lunches thereafter. There was too much to do between then and February 1st, to be providing full service. This meal was their first social event since Christmas. With just a few days remaining before the symposium started, they were ready for the influx of families.

Fred noticed that everyone was done eating and

was relaxed. That prompted him to excuse himself, while he got the Symposium Agenda outline and the list of individual families with their room numbers. First, he distributed the "Agenda" outline, while they sat around the dining table, announcing as he did, "Ok, folks, here is the last bit of information you'll be getting from me today. This Agenda is the only one that might need any discussion." (see Appendix 1, fig. 6, "The Symposium's Agenda")

Asking that they reserve comments and questions for a minute, he then handed out the list of names for the 74 families, which included their home of record, and their motel room number. His family was not listed due their commuting from Barstow, part of the time anyway. After passing out both sheets of information, he asked if there were any questions or issues that needed to be discussed. He emphasized that today being January 27th they only had a few days left to complete last minute arrangements.

Clem then reminded everyone who had particular responsibilities to check the bulletin board next to the main dining room entrance for any changes or updates. He then volunteered what he had done or had left to do. Because he was placed in charge of coordinating transportation, he outlined that he had contacted local airlines to alert them that there would be 300 travelers arriving at LAX on February 1st, and that they would need their shuttle service to Palm Springs. Then he had called a private, bus transport service in Palm Springs and arranged for seven buses to be on standby at that airport to transport passengers to Amboy. Likewise, he had made the reverse arrangements for the families when they left on February 8th. He emphasized that Cynthia, when making the reservations for all the families, had been able to coordinate their arrival at LAX to approximately the same time of day. And she would also be available to make connecting reservations during the week they were here for their return or to other destinations for an extended holiday.

He also added that one of his other responsibilities was contacting someone in the area, who had a stable of horses that could be positioned in Amboy for the families to ride. He had been able to get someone who had fifty horses in the Lucerne Valley area, and they were going to transport them over here. They would be arriving on January 31st, and stay for the week. And that he had likewise arranged the transport of 100 bicycles of different sizes and configurations to be on loan for that week. They were coming from San Bernardino, and would also be arriving on January 31st.

Cynthia then interrupted to say she had been able to make arrangements through an arcade company to have about 40 play station games set up in a large room in the old school building. And that cleaning and repainting the school was almost done. She added that the school building could also be used for any group meetings that required long term discussions. Also, she was able to contact a playground equipment company, who were coming tomorrow to set up outdoor equipment and lay out areas for different sports, e.g. baseball, volleyball, tennis, miniature golf, horseshoes, soccer, football and basketball. She had arranged to have a kiosk/book store, of sorts, set up in the school building, which would be stocked with writing materials, notebooks, magazines, newspapers, some books of general interest and sundry items for health and self care. She planned to work in the store for a couple of hours in the morning and for a couple more in the afternoon.

But the main topic of discussion revolved around the restaurant. Who would help? How were meals to be served? What were the hours of operation? What would be expected of the family members as far as clean up and maintenance of the area? It was generally agreed that everyone present there that day, including Freda and their daughters, would have to be on duty for every meal. Rose agreed to limit the hours the post office was open, so she could help with two meals each day.

Ray then pointed out that there was to be no extra help for any housekeeping chores at the motel. He said an announcement would have to be made sometime during their orientation that each family was responsible for cleaning and maintaining their own room. And to reassure everyone, he said the swimming pool had been thoroughly cleaned, repainted and would be filled and ready to be used by February 1st.

It was agreed that Cynthia and Clem would be responsible for the registration and orientation when the families arrived. Any announcements about dining room restrictions or housekeeping obligations would be made by them upon their arrival. These two would also circulate in and around the games and recreation areas to maintain some order and safety. Fred would be the trouble shooter for whatever problems arose. Ray and Hazel would have absolute authority over the restaurant and motel. And everyone was to return to the restaurant at meal times to help.

SEVENTEEN: THE FAMILIES ARRIVE

No one could have predicted that the originating flights, the connecting flights, the shuttle service, the bus pick up, and the actual arrival in Amboy would go as smoothly as it did on that February 1st. It was nothing short of miraculous, Clem thought. From all over the world these families came here to tiny Amboy. He couldn't help himself, he was just so proud of what his friends had accomplished to help make this happen.

The moment that the bus loads of families began to pass beyond the small community of 29 Palms, California, en route to Amboy, they almost, to an individual, began to realize the starkness and utter remoteness of the area they were going to. With each passing mile, they saw fewer and fewer clusters of living quarters. As soon as they began the climb over the pass into the Amboy basin, it was evident there was no sign of life anywhere. The vista of the dry lake bed for miles, coupled with the sparse vegetation on the mountain sides surrounding this valley, was a powerful introduction to a stage that soon would be the ground zero for a never to be forgotten performance. Most conversations stopped when their buses passed through this pass. And then gradually the chattering would begin again, as feelings of anticipation and excitement grew.

As each bus pulled into the marked off area and

discharged the families and their luggage, there were signs indicating which direction to head for registration. Luckily, the buses seemed to arrive in about 30 minute intervals, giving Clem and Cynthia most of the time they needed to process and to direct the most recently off-loaded families to their hotel rooms. They gave each family member their own schedule for the week and a list of all the families. And soon enough the entire area of Amboy was alive with people, shuttling their belongings and children, asking for directions, getting something to drink or eat until the next scheduled buffet meal. The children discovered the school area with its game room, the playground, ball fields, bicycle rentals, horseback riding and kiosk. The adults found their way to their assigned rooms and promptly started trying to catch up on some sleep, lost over the last 24-48 hours. None of these families were spared the difficulties of preparing for both this trip and for the packing and storage of their valuables and job-related equipment. To finally be in Amboy was like slipping into the massaging, warm waters of a spa. They dissolved into recovery sleep.

Because there were no language barriers, given 'B' influence over everyone, there was an immediate and spontaneous camaraderie between all the families and the Amboy personnel. If something was not quite right, whoever was involved would enlist others to sort it out. Complaints were nil. A sense of cooperation and goodwill was evident from the onset of their arrival.

The pace of the first two days, February 1st and 2nd, appeared about right. People were able to settle in, overcome most of their jet lag, play, hike or bike, ride horses or just rest more. By the time of the banquet on the 2nd, it was clear the symposium had the energy and direction to accomplish what the agenda had outlined for them. More and more the families realized that the organizing and hosting party was very small but dedicated. And that they could use some help. Without asking, family members began to help with meal set up and clearing tables. Likewise, helping with clean up and maintenance of their sleeping quarters was divided up voluntarily and on an informal basis.

Clem and Cynthia's day on February 2nd, was spent mostly organizing and directing the kids into whatever activity they wanted to do. Cynthia kept the kiosk open longer that day, both in the morning and in the afternoon. She wanted to make sure everyone could, if possible, get whatever items they had forgotten or needed. It was all free of charge, so she kept busy most of the day. Clem, for the most part, was in his element playing with the kids and bouncing from venue to venue coaxing and encouraging them to do different activities. Both he and Cynthia had worried the most about how the children would manage throughout this symposium. Now they could rest easy, seeing that there was plenty for them to do. Tomorrow, he thought, he might take a bunch of them on a hike up behind Amboy into the mining areas to see what riches used to be taken from this area. It was a good hike and would use up some of their ballooning energy.

The welcoming buffet that night and the festivities afterward were magical, Clem thought. Fun making and good humor was evident everywhere, with everyone. Rather than end at midnight, as scheduled, the crowd poured out onto the parking area and the surrounding space by the motel and school, and they continued to party and dance. Things didn't quiet down until nearly 3 a.m. This day and night were a complete success. To an individual, everyone was looking forward to tomorrow's agenda. They were ready to organize the study groups at 10 a.m. and to get started on their assigned projects. As Clem drove back to his cabin that night, he felt such relief that it had all been worth it. It was a moment of great pride and sense of accomplishment for him. He looked forward to what tomorrow would bring.

EIGHTEEN: THE COLLAPSE

It was the morning of February 3rd, B had been pleased with the originality and dedication Clem and Cynthia exhibited during their contacts with people, now scattered across the world. In every major land mass, contact was made. And that spark of decency and good will was then passed on with every succeeding individual that was touched by the person previously contacted. Possibly the initial contact should have been a cough or a sneeze, like with a flu virus. But somehow that just did not seem appropriate or possible. It was both too manipulative and probably too impractical, to say nothing about it being unhealthy and most likely it would transmit diseases.   Through touching, it emphasized the need for humans to make contact with one another. It forced people, some for once in their lifetime, to reach out beyond themselves with the best of intentions. This Grand Plan, or Plan A, had been set in motion with the best of intentions and through the most exhaustive efforts by Cynthia and Clem.

But, tragically, it was becoming too clear that it was not working. The spreading pattern of contacts was indeed extending globally, covering all inhabited areas. But those in power, the major decision-makers, were just too isolated to become 'infected' or affected.   Their isolation protected them from all outside influences, including being touched. It was not just the rogue leaders, the ones traditionally considered despots, or the terrorists or, quite obviously, those who were criminally insane who controlled countless people of the world, who were unaffected. This same protective cordon all but insured that nothing like this could enter their circle, no matter who were the major decision makers, be they democratically elected or self-appointed. The really disturbing aspect of this failure was that it extended to both the individual leaders and also to the bodies that co-led and governed with them. They were also 'immune' or shielded from being touched. Power had become so centralized, delegated, legislated or passively acquiesced to these individuals or legislative and legal bodies that even with people by the millions being touched and changed, no significant change at this level had occurred, in the way B had hoped. The crisis was unresolved.

What B had not told Clem was that the urgency of his mission, started during that Thanksgiving Week, was driven by multiple forces, both natural and man-made. Even with the terrible disasters like killer tsunamis, typhoons, earthquakes, volcanoes, and even objects striking the earth from outer space, too many people of this world had failed to recognize how suddenly life, all life, can end. They began to treat life like it was an inherent right, to live as one pleased. Many became unwilling to accept the consequences of their decisions or actions. Personal responsibility for one's behavior was minimized. Life, to most, became framed as a given life span of so many years. It was their right. Any disease, disaster, even premature death, was to be marginalized. That sort of thing happened to someone else, not to me, was the predominate attitude. And it led to a laziness and dullness of spirit.

For now, as B had surveyed the world as a

whole, there was a confluence of events about to happen, and very soon. Clem had to be charged with another mission to prepare for implementing another course of action. B no longer had the time to survey the effects of their first attempt to alter the course of events. Now the focus had to be on preparing a precious few for what lay ahead.

As these foreboding visions were becoming all too clear to B, Clem was busy helping serve breakfast to an overflow of people. The selected families had been in Amboy two days, and some routines had been established. The first day was given up to sleeping, hiking around the mountains, bicycling to the dry lake bed or to the nearby extinct volcano. It was a time for the attendees to recuperate from their trips, and to start getting acquainted with their new companions and the surroundings. The second day was the official get-acquainted day. Gatherings were scheduled all day with welcoming speeches, entertainment for the kids, dinner and dancing for everyone. It was, as it turned out, the last carefree day anyone would later recall. And one thing was most certain to occur. Ray and Hazel's restaurant became the central gathering place. And Clem became the village clown. He appeared relieved that his official duties had come to an end. He was now the person that B somehow knew he was: an individual full of good humor.

So it was a surprise of some magnitude when, as he left the restaurant to get in his truck and make a quick trip back to his cabin, B was sitting in the front seat when he climbed in.

"Whoa, there," Clem said, reacting with surprise. He had been daydreaming as he walked up to the truck door and was startled to see B.

"Well, top of the morning to you, B. It's been about a week since I've seen you. I was thinking that you might be gone for some time. Is everything here alright?"

"Yes," B answered. "All of you have done an excellent job to this point. But, unfortunately, I must tell you that your job is not done. In fact, much more lies ahead now, I fear. The results of your travels have not had the outcome that I had wanted. And we must proceed immediately with the alternative. I have telephone calls for you to make. And you will need to start organizing the assembly of families into different groups. We have to divide them into work groups, if you will. Soon the test will come as to how well they have been chosen. Regrettably, I cannot tell them, or even you, why they will need to do what has to be done. Not now, anyway. Certainly, they will be told later. As always, each of you has to work on trust, faith and hope."

Clem could only look at him. The shock and challenge of the initial contact with B that night in his cabin gave Clem the numbed fortitude to venture into an unknown world. He had gained self-assurance as he attempted to complete the tasks that B had asked him to do. He had no previous experiences or unrealistic expectations to stifle him. Everything had a newness of sheer adventure. The eventual scope and selective nature of his assignments were not clear then. Now, in this brief exchange, he became aware that something dangerous and final was at hand. He felt his confidence fading. The look that B saw was of raw fear.

"What is it that you want me to do?" Clem asked, as he sat down, trying to appear as casual as he could. "Do I need to travel again?"

"No, that is over. Travel for anyone now in Amboy will be severely limited. What I will need you to do is to contact railroad and roadway shippers. We will have to get a large reserve of supplies stored for what lies ahead. And there is not much time.

"You will need to get together with a group of newcomers and determine what is needed. This will include food, personal, household and rebuilding supplies. All supplies will be delivered here to Amboy. That list and those contacts need to be made by no later than tomorrow. So you will need to act quickly."

"B," Clem interrupted, "what you are asking these folks to do, without telling them why, isn't right. And I don't think they will do it. Many of them have traveled around the world to be here, on the vague promise of something.   They've even packed up valuables, belongings, and their work materials. If there is something wrong, it's time to tell them. I know I'm slow and plodding, which puts me in a separate category. You can tell me to do whatever, whenever. I just seem to go along. But these newcomers are not local; they are not stupid, and they've got return tickets. If you don't level with them, they're going to leave here. I promise you that."

B paused briefly after this outburst from Clem, thinking it was certainly out of character for him to be so frank and forthright. But, he had a good point. In the midst of this storm of upcoming events and the catastrophe to come, some perspective had been lost. Clem was right.

"Ok, Clem. You are right. Make arrangements for me to address all the adults this morning at 10 a.m. Post notices wherever you think it necessary to get everyone's attention. Get the word out right away. We should leave it up to the parents how they want to tell their children. It is time they know what is happening and why. I cannot tell them everything. It is too much at one time. But, do not worry, I will tell them all that is appropriate."

"What about Ray and Rose's families?

Shouldn't they be invited too? They've put in a lot of time and effort, and I did tell them I would keep them up to date on what happens."

"Yes," B replied, "they need to know as well. What eventually they choose to do about it, I will leave up to them. Invite them as well. And thank you for correcting me on this oversight.

"Also, I need you to contact the U.S. Marine Base just over the local mountains and make an appointment with the commandant of the Base. That needs to be made for day after tomorrow. And I will attend that meeting with you as well. What I am saying is that I will be visible throughout both meetings."

NINETEEN: GIVING NOTICE

Clem didn't make it back to his cabin that morning. Instead, he went back inside the restaurant, got some blank paper and a felt-tip pen from Ray and began making handouts and posters for the change of this morning's meeting.   The original purpose of their coming all the way to Amboy was to start this morning. That was all changed now.   He removed from the bulletin board the symposium's list of the ten groups and the people assigned to each group. Instead, he tacked on a sheet, roughly lettered, with the following message:

"URGENT!   IMPORTANT CHANGE IN THIS MORNING'S   MEETING   OF   THE   TEN GROUPS. THERE IS TO BE NO MEETING OF THESE GROUPS TODAY! REPEAT, NO MEETING OF THE   TEN   GROUPS   AS PREVIOUSLY   SCHEDULED.   INSTEAD, ALL ADULTS MUST ATTEND A MEETING AT   10   A.M.   THIS   MORNININ   THE RESTAURANT.   EVERY   ADULT!   NO EXCEPTIONS! NO CHILDREN ARE TO BE PRESENT AT THIS MEETING.   IT IS THE UTMOST IMPORTANCE THAT EVERYONE IS AT THIS MEETING.
SIGNED,

Clem then went to each section of the motel, to all the outdoor recreation areas, playgrounds, ball fields, game rooms, post office, Ray's office and each window of the restaurant and posted this notice. He then notified Ray and Rose that their attendance was necessary, that they were to lock up their respective offices and come as well. He was finally able to locate Fred, who was just starting to take a bicycle ride. Clem asked him to locate and bring his wife and Cynthia to the restaurant right away. All he would say to Fred was that, as the notice indicated, it was important that they all be there as well. He did not feel comfortable telling anyone what the meeting was about or who was going to speak. Luckily, no one else checked out a bicycle, so everyone was accounted for in the Amboy compound.

By 9:30 a.m. Ray closed down the buffet line for breakfast, and he and Clem bused the dishes out to the kitchen for cleaning. Ray yelled out, in a voice that Clem had not heard since the days he used to stop by Ray's for a drink or two, and somebody was starting to get too rowdy. In those days he would raise his voice, like a mother grizzly bear protecting her young, and roar for the person losing control, to stop what he or she was doing. And if that didn't get their attention he, secondly, would bring out a baseball bat, and tell the person what would now happen. It was always very clear, very precise, very loud and effective. Very few ever tried to proceed to the second part of his outlined plan. Today, Ray was announcing that breakfast was over and so was their eating of it. He wanted them to bring their dishes over to the receiving counter and please leave while the rest of us prepared for the 10 a.m. meeting. There was no mistaking his tone, this time either. And certainly everyone did as he requested.

On their way out, the late breakfast eaters saw Clem's new notice. There were some comments in low voices, but no one ventured to turn and ask about it, after hearing Ray's no nonsense request. They each filed out talking amongst themselves, looking back into the restaurant. But all they saw by this time were six people busily cleaning up, moving tables and chairs into position for the 10 a.m. meeting.

By 10 a.m. the restaurant was jammed. It seemed to Clem there were more people than when they were all together yesterday. He then realized that for privacy, it was decided to only use the rear dining area. By the time everyone was seated, the room was packed.

Not being a public speaker, Clem was quite nervous about standing up before this group and calling the meeting to order. But he knew he had to. Rising from his front row chair, nearest to the doorway, he walked to the center of the room. He was alone, and he didn't see B. "What if he didn't come", he thought worriedly. Looking out over the audience, he finally spoke.

"Good morning, friends. I apologize for having to bring you together like this, under strange, and most likely, stressful circumstances. Some things that you have heard or seen leading up to this point have also had their share of mystery and have no doubt given you cause for alarm. Today, I fear, you will begin to know the reasons for this lack of clarity and mystery."

The audience sat there during this monologue expressionless, with some building resentment and boredom. Enough was enough, was the feeling. Clem sensed this mounting tension. But just at that moment, the moods and reactions changed 180 degrees. B was suddenly standing beside him.

Often when you witness a sudden life-threatening change in your surroundings, like a bad automobile accident, a violent crime, someone injured or killed, an explosion or fire, you can only gasp and look around to see if others are witnessing the same event. You need to check first to see if this is really happening. Then you have to take stock if you, yourself, are in danger and need to flee or what is the best way to respond. With B's sudden appearance, the meeting room was filled with gasps of surprise and the turning of heads to verify the reality of the moment. When their heads returned to see B still standing beside Clem, there was a wave of panic like the room might erupt into a fleeing mob.

Sensing this, B said in the most calming voice, "Please, please, if you will, sit back down. You are in no danger from me. As you can see, Clem still stands here quietly. Please let me speak as you begin to recover from the shock of my appearance.

"I am the one who initiated the ability you have to speak and understand any language spoken. At that time I chose, for my own reasons, not to become visible to you. I was present to each of you, as a family, the day you got your acceptance letter to come here. The multiple language abilities you gained then were my way of letting you know there was something, you were becoming a part of, that was much bigger than anything you could ever imagine. Today, that will become clearer to you.

"And first, I want you to know how deeply saddened I am, revealing to you what I am about say. You will need to cling to your family members, and telling your children will be heartbreaking I am sure. For those of you who pray, do so with sincere conviction. It will be heard. For those of you who don't, it won't be long until you do.

"For a little background on what is ahead, let me

155

quickly tell you what has transpired since the last week in November. I sent Clem and Cynthia, both of whom you have now either met or seen, on a month long trip around the world, visiting 53 cities. Their job was for each of them to touch as many people as they could. Those people would then feel compelled; by the peaceful calm and interconnected force they would have for others around them, to touch others. The hope was to reach as many people on the planet as possible, thereby easing the tensions and grim realities that face the world today. Sadly, as of yesterday evening, I realized that this strategy did not have the effect I had wanted. The leaders and most powerful or dangerous people of this world were untouched. The ambitions, delusions, revenges, conquests all remained fixed and, more importantly, they were being set in motion to bring life on this planet to the very edge of massive, if not complete, destruction.

"But at the same time I had Clem arrange with Fred Wailand to begin the process of placing that offer, in over 500 newspapers worldwide, looking for people like you to apply to attend this symposium. In my mind, I thought if the first plan worked, your gathering here would serve to begin an annual meeting of people, from around the world, to discuss, decide and publish their conclusions. And I was going to be an added facilitator, with the powers that be, to start working to institute the changes you recommended. I so hoped it might work out that way. But it has not.

"Now, I must tell you the reason you were asked to pack your belongings, reproduce and collect your work materials and place them in containers for possible shipment. It was because the world is going to experience a life-shattering series of events on April 1st, of this year. You are part of a very small group that will, I hope, survive that cataclysm.

But to do so it will require you, from this meeting until the end of March, to work night and day to prepare. There is so little time, and there is, quite frankly, an almost impossible amount to organize and complete by that date. Clem and I are going to the U.S. Marine Corps Base, located within 50 miles of here, day after tomorrow. I will arrange for them to help you. Likewise, a select group of them and their families will accompany you in your efforts to be sheltered and to preserve your lives. Additionally, there will be some Air Force personnel and U.S. Navy Seabees involved. They and their families will not be in the same shelter as you, come April 1st. But I am hoping to find someplace where they will be secure and safe enough to survive as well.

"You will need to immediately contact your shipper, who you contracted to hold your containers of personal goods. Give them your password and permission to release those containers to the Air Force personnel that are soon to arrive. And you must e-mail that approval no later than today. The shippers have to transport those containers to the nearest airport that can handle the large cargo planes that will pick them up. Those containers will then be flown to the Marine Base near here, where they will later be trucked to your shelter.

"The roads into and out of Amboy and to your shelter will be blocked off as of day after tomorrow. No one, except for shippers, will be allowed in or out. You are now confined to this area. No one will police you, either as to what you communicate or what you do. But, you must believe me when I say this. You are now in the greatest danger. If you talk to anyone, other than amongst yourselves and the military personnel assigned to this duty, and tell them what is happening to you and why, I guarantee you, I promise you, none of you will even survive to see April 1st.

"You have a most noble mission ahead. You have been selected not only to preserve the remnants of humanity but also to document its presence on this world at one time, should disaster befall every one of you as well. Each of you was chosen for a reason. You represent a cross-section of this world. Not all countries could be represented, nor could all occupational categories. There was just so much room. At that, it will be one of history's greatest challenges to somehow achieve your ultimate survival, even with your small numbers assembled here.

"You have been given the ability to speak and understand each other's languages. And you have been touched in such a way that you recognize the sisterhood and brotherhood of all people. You are intertwined. The job skills and professions that you represent are those that I hope will enable you to survive. But again, maybe your greatest contribution, and that is why I wanted you to assemble and pack the items you did for the containers, will be that you document and inscribe, for all time to come, that your race did what it did and that you achieved what you have. I do not want the final epitaph of your wonderful accomplishments and aspirations to end up being only rubble.

"You will be sheltered in a cavern about 100 miles northeast of here. It is at about 4000 feet elevation, facing east. The cavern contains a cluster of large caves, but not all of them are interconnected with each other. No doubt excavation and tunneling will be necessary to make the cavern, as a whole, habitable. All the construction work will be designed and completed by your assembled engineers and the military personnel who will be coming here in a couple of days. The caves are imbedded in a granite mountain range, but inside them the composition of the rock is primarily limestone.

That has allowed there to be tremendous expansion of the voids inside the individual caves. There are several natural, cathedral-like ceilings, making for huge individual rooms. I believe they will offer all your families, and those from the Marine Base, adequate shelter. And for those of you who are skeptical about using caves for long term survival, you might recall how early Turkish, persecuted worshippers lived in caves near Capadocia. There, as many as 2000 lived in those caves for up to two years at a time. It can be done.

"And I know all of you will be asking many questions, once all this shattering news is absorbed. What about food and water? What if I have a medical emergency? What's to eventually become of us? What about various animals? Our pets? All these questions, and any others, are absolutely appropriate to ask. Your division into work groups will begin to address each of these questions. At the end of my speaking to you, Clem will ask that you divide into four distinct groups. Each group will have particular duties to perform that are vital to your survival. And the coordinators of these groups will be meeting here with the military personnel on February 6th.

"Finally, I must say that I cannot answer all your questions or relieve your fears. It is not possible, under these circumstances. Cling to each other, pray, hope and work. Work as you never have before. I, too, grieve for those loved ones you leave behind. The immensity of the loss ahead for all of us is too large to grasp or to contemplate. We all shall go mad if we do. Please, try to focus now on what needs to be done. Grief, shock, becoming overwhelmed will have to wait. Tell your children in the best way you know how, but tell them. They are all going to be needed to work as well, and they need to know why.

"I am now going to turn this meeting back over

to Clem. I apologize for not taking questions at this time. We will be spending time together later. For now, we must all go to work."

TWENTY: PREPARATION BEGINS

Saying that, B was gone, leaving Clem, again, standing alone in front of this body of stunned families. He began, stammering, as he spoke, "I need you to understand that I, too, have just received this devastating news. I am speechless and bewildered, but I know one thing for sure. If B said it will be so, you can believe it. And I know we all feel paralyzed, but so much has to be done today... And immediately! So, if I can have your attention for just a few moments, then I'll let you go back to your children, and we will meet again in designated groups, starting at 2 p.m. We must begin to organize ourselves. I have to contact various suppliers and shippers tomorrow morning to tell them what we will need.

"To begin this organizational process, and certainly you can change how things are done, once we get underway and see that there is a better way to proceed, I need each family represented here to count out loud, '1 through 4', repeating the sequence until each family is in one of four groups.   You can begin counting on my far left, please."

Once the counting was done, Clem struggled on, "For starters, let's have those in Group number 1 meet in here at 2 p.m. Group 2 will meet in the main dining area. Groups 3 and 4 will meet in the larger classrooms or the cafeteria area in the school building.

"Between now and the time you meet this afternoon, I will try to find B and see if there are any particular problems or issues that you have to address first. I think it is safe to assume that Group 1 will be responsible for deciding what supplies will be needed. I will be working with them. Arbitrarily, just to begin with, I would just suggest you consider maybe letting Group 2 be responsible for making the physical environment of the cavern livable. Group 3 could address our health and well being while living there, considering such issues as our medical care, counseling, various activities, diversions, schooling, and whatever else might help us cope and survive. And Group 4 could possibly be responsible for trying to forecast what will need to be done and stockpiled for rebuilding, once our confinement is over. If the composition of the groups, by my four-count method, does not give the groups the right mix, then rearrange and shift it amongst yourselves. My main concern is that there is equal representation within each group.

"And there is one last thing. During this afternoon's meetings, please choose someone in each group to be that group's coordinator. As B mentioned, those people will be meeting with the Marine officers on February 6th. I wish I, or anyone else could provide you with more information or direction, but there is no one else to turn to but ourselves. B has insisted, for our protection and for the welfare of those who may follow us, that we maintain the strictest secrecy. My suggestion it that any notification you give family, friends or employers back home would only mention that the meeting here is so important that you are being asked to extend your time for another two months. I wish it were possible to say honestly what is happening to you, but you can't. That leaves us on our own. My heart goes out to each of you and to your children at this time. I hope B's occasional presence among us will provide us with the strength and courage to face the unimaginable.

"Please meet with your respective groups at 2 p.m. And don't forget to contact your shippers to give them approval to release your shipping containers to the Air Force. Bring your shipper's e-mail and actual address, along with the nearest airport that can handle the cargo planes, with you to this afternoon's meetings. Just give that information to your designated coordinator, and I will pick up those slips from them later today. We need to hand those slips to the Marine personnel day after tomorrow. We must now begin to prepare."

One member of the "Amboy Survivors", as they were later named when historians outlined the days, months, and years that followed that February 3rd announcement by B, was reported to have said, that getting the news that day was like being told every one of his extended family and dearest friends had just contracted a terminal illness and were only expected to live another 2 months.

Trying to tell their children what was happening was, according to the families, the hardest news they ever had to give them. It was not like everyone was not aware that something potentially ominous was not possible, given the dramatic moments when each family could speak and understand those languages, and then to be told to gather together their work site materials and to pack for such a long stay. But each family had tried to theorize what it all meant. None of them could have possibly guessed the finality of what they were just told. The sense of shock lasted for days, weeks, months, and even the rest of their lives for many. But everyone tried to prepare, as best as their psyche would let them. Significantly and, foretelling the strength and courage of these families, each one took their children to the afternoon meetings that day. Each decided that only by doing everything together could they have any chance of surviving what lay ahead. Most families began that night taking the mattresses off their beds and putting them together on the floor. They began sleeping together with their children. It was instinctive. Each sensed the ultimate threat was at hand. Few people ate lunch that day. Most were unable to eat and were too nervous about the meetings scheduled that afternoon.

Clem was able to see B again before the meetings began. Together they reviewed what obstacles and issues needed to be covered by Clem's group. It was the most pressing one to achieve consensus and to start implementing its decisions. Clem knew he would have to moderate this one meeting, but thereafter he was anxious that the group's coordinator perform that function. He was eager, if that feeling was at all applicable given the present circumstances, to start the meeting. Being in the position of facilitator, and the other assignments B had given him, was too awkward for him. His deep rooted shyness was about to boil over into a full blown panic.

After the meeting with B, he went on a short walk down to the dry lake bed. He needed the solitude at this time. He hoped he could keep all the details straight after B's instructions. His memory anymore was becoming like Swiss cheese, full of increasingly larger holes and getting stiffer with age. It was another hour before the meeting started, so he picked up his pace. It was good to feel the heat of the sun, particularly after all that he had heard today.

By 2 p.m. the various group venues were overflowing with the assigned families. Each family was huddled together, arms around each other, many still wiping away tears or just letting them fall. At Group 1's meeting site, Clem rose from his seat and went again to the center of the room. He had arranged ahead of time, with Ray, to tape some large sheets of paper table cloths on the front wall, facing the group. With his black felt-tip marker, he wrote the following headings at the top of the sheets, each spaced about two feet apart:

"FOOD   PERSONAL   HOUSEHOLD   REBUILDING

SOLIDS   LIQUIDS"

He then turned and began addressing the assembly. "I was able to meet again with B, and I got some additional information and guidance to help us with making this list. The guidelines provided were that there will be least three caves for us to use. For these three, there will be 75 families in each one, divided into three rows of 25 families each. Every family will have a 42 foot by 8 foot modified, metal shipping container to live in. Dividing the container, or home, as I would prefer to call it from here on, into sections or rooms will be done after they arrive here in Amboy. Furnishings will be limited, but once we know what the Marine Base can help with, we will know better how much is available to choose from. But don't be surprised if each home is furnished pretty much the same.

"There will be a common area where meals will be prepared. No cooking will be done inside your home. As you can appreciate, ventilation will be an issue. Likewise, there will have to be a common shower and toilet area. All of these facilities will be located at the front of each cave. There will also be a communal area where you could eat together or have meetings or other functions. But it's safe to assume, there will be times when you will simply want to eat in your own home.

"There will be every effort made to tunnel

165

between what appears to be three to five major caves. That would give complete access to all caves throughout the cavern complex. Also, it would provide a way to transfer goods and items between each cave. It is B's hope that supplies can be bundled into a one month's supply per cave. Most storage will be inside the cavern. Probably there will be some warehousing done outside, but that is something the engineers and military personnel will work on. Most importantly, your personal effects that are coming from your homes will be kept inside. That is important, both for your comfort and well being, but also to help you begin to organize and plan for the future.

"We need to plan for two meals a day. No doubt, there could be some snacks that are eaten in your home, during a given day, but that should not require any formal planning or preparation. There will be electrical lighting at the entrance to each cave, but there will be only scattered lights for illumination of the interior beyond that. Cooking, computer work, light equipment and some machinery use, would most likely be located only at the entrance area, but not in the interior. Your homes will not be electrified; you'll be using mostly candles for lighting. Certainly, battery powered light can be used, as long as the batteries are usable. Power outlets will be scattered, to the best of my knowledge, over the cavern, but you'll have to find out more about this later. Refrigeration, whatever little there may be, will only be available in the kitchen areas.

"Overall, as you will appreciate, ventilation and circulation of the air in the cavern will always be a concern for everyone. That and a reliable way to generate power, limits where and how many areas can use equipment that produces fumes or consumes electricity. And finally, if there can be found a smaller cave, which is adjacent to the others, maybe a connecting link can be made to it and a place can be developed for housing some pets and animals."

It was at this point in Clem's monologue that the first audible cry went up. It was from the kids. Spontaneously, many of them shouted out with joy and approval about possibly having animals. Clem smiled broadly at their reaction.

"I'm sure everyone will try to make that possible," he added.

"For now, we must focus on the supplies and equipment we will need for the 75 families here in Amboy. And I presume we will double whatever we decide to order, to cover the Marine families' needs. I would like, if we could, to take one heading at a time, as I have written them on these paper sheets. I will write up here what you suggest that we will need for six months to a year's confinement."

What follows is the summation of over four hours of discussion and brainstorming. When it was completed, Clem wrote it down so he could organize it, for calling the various suppliers and shippers the next morning. This was the final list: (see Appendix 1, fig. 7, "Equipment and Supplies for Amboy and Marine Contingents")

For the most part, Clem thought the meeting went pretty well, given the grim circumstances... It started slow, but eventually everyone was involved in suggesting, debating, arguing, and eliminating choices. And they were also able to choose the coordinators for this group. It was Janice and Sid Blackwell. They were chosen because they were both from the States, giving them familiarity with what is available locally and how best to secure it. And both had experience in the science of day-to-day living, which the group felt made them ideal for the positions.

The discussion was the most animated when it

came to how many items, e.g. gas and electrically powered tools, it would be practical to have. It was finally impressed on everyone that conveniences, that had been taken for granted before, were to be very scarce or non-existent hereafter. The availability of electricity and gas were two of the major ones. Likewise, in determining the amount of building materials to order, assuming that one day in the distant future an above ground structure would be possible, it was finally decided that a standard house design would be used. It would have 1200 feet, and be 30 feet wide by 40 feet long, and it would have rafters for the roof framing. Using rafters would allow extra room in the attic for another room or for extra storage. The roof would be covered with slate and the exterior of the house would be brick, both of which would help extend the house's lifespan. Including the 160 Marine families, it would require ordering materials for 235 families. But, again, it was emphasized amongst the group, that this type of conventional style home may not be practical to build any time soon. But at least it was in everyone's future interest to at least have the material available to use. It gave them hope.

The group understood that their work had just begun. Ahead of them were the overwhelming jobs of preparing an area near by the motel for sorting and packing the supplies and equipment as they arrived. It was also in this area that the shipping containers would be placed. The group would eventually be packing this material in each container for delivery to the cavern. Once the Marines were involved, they hoped they would have earth moving equipment to help clear the cactus, which was so difficult to remove by hand, and level an even larger area. No one really had any idea how big in scope this whole operation would be. But the Marine involvement gave them some needed confidence.

Throughout the meeting, it gave Clem great comfort to see that the children were present. They participated in the discussions, and their suggestions were seriously considered and many adopted. Their presence and energy would be critical.

Once the meeting was adjourned, Clem made the rounds to the other meeting sites, gathering the names of those chosen to be the coordinators. He shared the list of rebuilding supplies with the coordinators of the rebuilding group to get their input and to make any additions to the list. The group assigned to the health and well being of everyone in the caves decided to see if they could arrange to get the needed medical supplies from the Marine Base hospital. Otherwise, it would take too long to order and receive what they needed. The group assigned to make the physical living conditions manageable had many suggestions and ideas, but they were limited in what they could do until they had access to the cavern. All the groups agreed that they would pitch in to help whichever group had the most pressing job to complete at the moment. For now, it was Group #1.

Fatigue was building by this time, and Clem nearly forgot about the family's shippers' addresses, etc. He found Fred back at the restaurant and asked him to collect the needed information about the shippers from the families. He reminded him that he had to give that information to the Marine Base personnel when they met. They agreed that once Fred had that material, he would give it to him sometime tomorrow.

Clem then decided to drive home and eat something there. He needed time alone to sort out the lists and to decide who was best to order from. And he wanted to limit the number of suppliers. The more that were involved, the harder it would be to keep track, and the easier it would be to have a security lapse of some sort. So, he decided to use three major shippers: a grocery chain headquartered in Phoenix for food, drinks, household and personal items; a large building supplier in Barstow for delivery of tools, generators, windows, doors; and the railroad company who owned the nearby rail line for the larger, bulkier building materials such as cement, mortar, roofing, bricks, lumber, plywood, plumbing and electrical supplies.

The rail delivery would be directly to Amboy. The railroad company's main trunk line passed through there, and rail sidings were already in place to park any railcars for unloading. Additionally, he figured, they would have to drop off 343 empty 42 foot shipping containers! It would require one container of food and personal supplies per month for each 26 families. There will be 235 families, times 12 months. That comes to 108 containers. Then they need 235 more containers for each family's living quarters. That brought the total number to 343. Clem was staggered by the scope of all this.

The groceries, personal items and building material deliveries, which he hoped might be packed in shipping containers whenever possible, would have to be by truck. Any of those extra containers would come in handy later for outside storage of non perishable materials. Not having a telephone, he would have to return to the motel office in the morning to start ordering the supplies.

It was midnight before he was done with processing all this information. He fixed a sandwich, drank some juice and fell into bed. He was asleep within minutes. Unaware, as he began a gentle snoring, B appeared again in his doorway. Watching Clem for a while, B nodded and whispered, "You are doing well, Clem. Sleep now, my friend."

The next morning, February 4th, Clem was in

Ray and Hazel's motel office by 9 a.m. They knew that he had a major job ahead of him, so they cleaned off their desk. As Clem sat down to begin the calling, they closed the office door and wished him good luck. And for the next five hours he talked continuously to the various shippers, arranging shipment to Amboy by truck and by train. His easy going manner was a great asset during all this. He did not get overly excited or frustrated by being put 'on hold', with different delays while confirmations were made or with transferring calls. He just plodded through it all. And when he was finished, he had arranged for the shipments to start coming day after tomorrow. By now, he had no idea how B's debit card could handle all this, and it always came as quite a surprise to each of the shippers. But each was pleased the money was readily available, and each contract was quickly agreed upon, once they were assured of getting their money. For anyone who asked why all this was coming to Amboy, the answer he gave was that it was a major government project. And right now only civilians were involved, but it needed to have the highest priority for immediate delivery.

It was 2:15 p.m. when Clem opened the office door into the restaurant. Ray met him there, and asked, "Would you like something to eat, Clem?"

"Thanks, Ray, I really would enjoy some of your soup about now," he replied.

"My pleasure, Clem. Just sit down at the counter and rest your weary bones. You've lost some weight over this last month or so. We need to fatten you up."

At that, Clem smiled and nodded. He was so relieved to have this finished. All that was left now was getting the information from Fred and driving B over to the Marine Base tomorrow morning. They'd need to leave about 9 a.m. to be there for their 10:30

appointment. For now he had the rest of today to eat and rest. "Make that one really large bowl of soup, Ray. I may sit here and eat all day." And at that point, Jake ambled over and lay down at Clem's feet. Looking at each other, they both winked.

PART IV

TWENTY-ONE: MARINE CORPS BASE

As Clem was driving across the salt pan and up the rock-strewn mountain sides over from Amboy to the valley where the Marine Base was located, he reviewed in his mind what he had found out regarding their upcoming meeting.

The Marine Base's commanding officer, Brigadier General Eric Stanfield, had been recently given the command of both the Desert and the Oceanside Marine Bases.   When Clem made the appointment to meet with him, he advised the commander's receptionist that this meeting was urgent, and that the General and four of his most trusted officer staff should be present as well.   There had been some reluctance expressed by the appointment secretary, but urged on by Clem's tone and persistence, she elected to proceed with scheduling the appointment and let General Stanfield make the final decision who would meet with Clem's party.   Being new to the Base, the General decided to go along with it, thinking it was to appease local community leaders.   The appointment was confirmed for February 5th.

B was present and visible during the trip over to the Base, and would remain so during the meeting as well. But once they arrived at the security gate, Clem was the only one visible. His clearance at the gate was routine. The General's office had already notified them of Clem's appointment. But once he was inside the sprawling Base, he became immediately disoriented by all the signage, some with only initials, others with abbreviations and odd words, and many with arrows at every corner. Just by chance he noticed a small sign with an arrow pointing straight ahead, indicating "Base HQ". Relieved, he managed to eventually find a parking place, labeled "Visitors Only", amongst many military vehicles.

Once inside the Headquarters Building, he asked for directions to the General's office. He was escorted by a Marine who met him at the front door. Clem had worn one of his dress suits that he used on his world-wide trip, but at that, the crispness of the Marine's uniform made him feel underdressed. It was an understated, but impressive atmosphere. It declared an efficiency and dedication to fulfill its mission, whatever that might be. But rather than intimidate Clem, he was comfortable being there. Realizing that B was beside him, but still not visible, he shifted more toward the wall in the narrow hallway to allow room for B.

They had arrived at the Headquarters on time. Clem had barely sat down in the Waiting Area, when the door opened into the General's office and out strolled General Stanfield. He was trim, of average height, with a close-cropped hair cut. There were hints of gray breaking through his dark hair. He had an easy smile, but behind it, one could sense it was not to be interpreted as faintness or reserve. Stepping up close to Clem, he stretched out his hand and vigorously shook it. And then, as had been the case so many times before with others, he, too, was transformed by Clem's touch. The General sensed it immediately. And at that moment B became   visible   to   him.

B spoke first. "It was at my request that Mr. Newberry called your office. Presently, only you and Clem can see me. I will also become visible to your assembled officer staff, once we are inside your office and Clem shakes hands with them during your introductions."

General Stanfield, obviously shocked and confused with this unexpected course of events and with B's strange manifestation, nodded and turned, reluctantly stretching out his hand to usher each of them into his office. "Please," the General said, "come in and meet my fellow officers."

Clem followed B into the room and as the General entered the room behind them, he began introducing each of his Officer Staff. Clem, in turn, shook hands with each of them. The four present were Col. Priscilla Roberts, Logistics; Lt. Col. Jason Black, Mission Operations; Maj. Miles Stanlowski, Material Command; and Maj. Nancy Gilcrest, Personnel Affairs.

As each was experiencing the Clem-initiated transformation, B appeared at the end of the mid-sized, oval meeting table that each were to sit around. There was a collective gasp as B appeared. At this same moment, General Stanfield closed and locked the meeting room door. It was a windowless room.

"Please be seated." B requested in a softer voice than what Clem had been used to hearing. "I realize that you are, and will remain for a time, stunned by what is now happening. Certainly, Mr. Newberry, here, can relate completely to your surprise and shock. Imagine if you will, in his case, I appeared in the middle of the night at his remote desert cabin!

"I should start by saying that my appearance to you is limited to few individuals. Who or what I am is not as important right now as what I have to tell you.

One day you will know better who I am. There is not time for that now. Rest assured that I am not some alien being, nor do I intend to harm you. On the contrary, my recent efforts have been to try to save everyone, everywhere.

"Sadly, my first plan did not work. The sense of connectedness and good will that you are now experiencing since Clem shook your hand was something that I tried, through him and his associate, to spread across the planet. They visited designated cities around the world, touching all the people that they could. My hope was that those they touched would, in turn, touch others and pass on this good will and the diminished drive to control and conquer others. But even after millions of people eventually were changed, it was not enough, or more specifically, it was not focused enough on the isolated decision-makers of this world. Events remained unchecked, spiraling out of control. The time is too short now to devise another plan that would avert the inevitable. That is when I asked Clem to contact you and convene this meeting.

"What is discussed here will have to stay here, for reasons that will become clearer soon enough. There is no way now to stop what is about to happen. All we can do is try to prepare for its aftermath. Even I cannot predict the scope and extent of what will occur. You are to take your instructions from me only. You will tell others your orders come from a "higher authority," and leave it at that. There is to be no discussion or argument. They must do what you ask or order. As you say, this is on the strictest 'need to know' basis.

"The other groups, not represented here now that will be brought into this confidence, are air crews from McChord and Fairchild Air Force Bases and Seabees from Port Hueneme. We will need four plane crews, and their support personnel from each Base, for transport and for refueling. I presume you can bring these planes and crews here, given the capacity your airfield now has. It will make it much less complicated to have them based here when you start the actual missions that I will outline later. The Seabees should provide about fifty personnel, along with their construction equipment. The eventual sheltered relocation for all these individuals will have to be a different one, from the one you and your personnel will come to by April 1st. And I will not be present when you have their officers come to a joint meeting in Amboy on February 8th.

"Now, what is your role to be? You will need to alert five different operational units, which I have assumed would include no more than 31 personnel each. The units needed are Engineering, Transportation, Medical, Reconnaissance and Communication. The five of you here would make up the senior leadership component. Included in the ultimate relocation would be the spouses and children of all these Marines, as it would be for the five of you. I have figured that the total number of individuals that would finally be relocated from here would come to 640.

"You are to begin immediately by sending your Reconnaissance unit to the Providence Mountains northeast of here. There is a state recreation area with a large cavern, located at the end of a dirt road. You are to seal off that road from both the north and south direction. On the southern end, seal it off at the Interstate 40 exit northbound and southbound toward Essex and Amboy. If you find someone working there at the Cavern or visiting there, tell them you are involved in an upcoming large military training exercise that is to last an extended period of time. If you should determine someone may become a security risk, you may not be able to let them off the premises until all the relocation is completed. Handle these matters as you think best. The strictest secrecy is your mandate. Next, you will need to seal all roads, leading into and out of Amboy. Have the Marines stationed at these roadblocks allow only authorized deliveries and designated individuals to pass through.

"Once the region is sealed off, then you must begin immediately transporting supplies for that unit to be self-sustaining until April 1st. Then, you are to send in the Engineering and Communication units to design, modify and outfit the cavern for 940 men, women and children to occupy. This number includes you as well. The openings into the cavern have to have the capacity to be tightly sealed. You will need to construct storage areas within the caves. And at least two reinforced, covered storage areas will need to be constructed outside the cavern. One of these outside warehouses, the smaller one, should be adjacent to the cavern wall and have a connecting passageway into it. The larger warehouse will have metal shipping containers with non-perishable rebuilding supplies, large construction equipment, stackable materials, large bladders filled with various petroleum products and emergency vehicles. Both warehouses will have to be tightly sealed from the outside. Finally, if possible, see if your Engineers and the Seabees have the capacity to drill into the immediate area for a water source. It would be a great help if one was found.

"You will be transporting enough goods and supplies for six months to a year's confinement in the cavern. And once the major construction work is completed inside, the Medical unit needs to set up their receiving and treatment area.

"There needs to be some kind of ventilation system installed, with filters and scrubbers. There can be no direct contact with incoming air, unless it has been screened and filtered. You will need to have the ability to monitor the outside environment, without having to go outside the walls of the cavern. Toilet facilities, sinks, and showers will have to have direct access to an outside wall. A sewer and water delivery system have to be designed and constructed as well

"Next, of the 940 individuals to be housed in the cavern, 300 are here from around the world. They are made up of 75 families, each of whom has a metal shipping container stored near their home of record. These have to be moved and stored in the cavern as well. Before I leave today, Clem will give you a list of the shippers and airports, around the world, where these containers can be picked up by the Air Force. You will need to coordinate with these shippers the pickup time and exact location. The 75 families have given authorization to the shippers to release the containers to the Air Force personnel. This has to be done as soon as the planes are relocated here on Base. It has the highest priority. Once they are here, the Transportation unit can move them to the cavern straight away.

"When the air crews are finished, you should arrange for their family members to be relocated here as well. As much as possible, this Base should be the center of operations to reduce the risk of wider exposure to the public and to the media.

"Clem, along with his groups in Amboy, is putting together the list of supplies that all 235 families will need for this period of confinement. Deliveries will only be made directly to Amboy, by way of trucks and the railroad. We will let you know in one to two weeks when you need to start transporting them, as well, to the cavern. You will be getting a copy of that list of supplies from him today, as well. Look it over, and if you see items you need to add, just let him know. Then by the last week in March we need to transport your families and the ones in Amboy to the cavern. All this must be completed, and the caves sealed by April 1st.

"Finally, can you think of any place that would be a large enough underground shelter to accommodate approximately 1000 people? I would hope that if you did, you could then offer to some of the personnel, under your command here and elsewhere, the possibility of survival.   I would strongly suggest you include personnel from the Coast Guard, Navy, and Army as well.   Let me be quite honest, no one has a 100% guarantee of survival in the next months ahead. What has led to this climax of events does not lend itself to ready rescue or survival. Your guidelines for who are chosen should be those of good character, possessing skills needed to rebuild, having immediate family members with them and being able to maintain strict secrecy. No one should know more than is necessary. Do you have any suggestions on where such a shelter might be?"

"I have an idea," Major Gilcrest interjected. "Is the nuclear waste depository at the Yucca Mountain Facility in Nevada still mothballed? I don't believe it has ever stored any nuclear waste material due to environmental issues."

"Good idea," General Stanfield exclaimed. "I will contact the Nuclear Regulatory Agency and see what, if anything is happening there.   And I will certainly try to get something moving in that direction. I want to try to keep as many of my people from harm as I can." Then the General asked B if they could given any indication what to expect come April 1st. "It would help motivate and make priorities easier to establish, if we knew."

"Simply put, General," B answered, "imagine your worst nightmare."

What followed was a silence that probably scared Clem more than anything since Thanksgiving

Week. Here were some of the most courageous and capable people one could assemble, and they had become pale, with far off gazes of despair. They had the look of gallant warriors who had been told their forces had lost everything. The silence could not have been more forlorn. He was shocked and overwhelmed.

"Yes, and I am truly sorry to be bringing you this news. Even Clem, who I have trusted with so much these, last weeks, had no idea the scope of what was ahead. I have chosen to incorporate you into this plan for many reasons. Maybe someday, when this madness ends, I can share more with you. For now, we have no time. Please be about your tasks.

"You assembled here are to come to Amboy tomorrow at 11:00 a.m. for a meeting with representatives of their work groups. Together, you can begin to merge your needs and coordinate timetables. And following that on February 8th, there will be another meeting of representatives from the Air Force and Seabees and your staff in Amboy at that same time.

Call Clem at his telephone number listed on the sheet of the shippers, if you have questions or further needs. He will let me know immediately.

"One last thing. I will not appear to your staff outside this office, and you should not divulge my presence here today. Before you transport your families, we will all gather at your Base Chapel, and I will speak to everyone then. Now, we must go. There is so much you have to do. Complete this mission. So very, very much depends on its outcome. And I thank you for your time and dedication to duty. With all that said, B was no longer visible. Clem then stood, said a brief good-by to each officer and left.

TWENTY-TWO: OPERATION PROVIDENCE CAVERN

After General Stanfield had shown Clem out of his office area, he returned to his Officer Staff with the gravest demeanor. Continually wiping away tears that were unresponsive to his status and rank, he walked to the blackboard side of the conference room table. All four of the seated officers were both glum and tearful. None had spoken a word since B had left their presence.

In complete resignation to the awful news they had just received, the General whispered, "God in Heaven, grant us the strength and will to do what now seems the impossible. Please bring a measure peace to those of us who might survive what's ahead, but most of all, we pray for those who won't. We beseech you, be ever merciful and forgiving, granting them the comfort of knowing that awaiting them is your heavenly kingdom. Amen."

After picking up some chalk from the blackboard, he slowly turned toward his officers and spoke with more effort and volume. "Ladies and gentlemen, we have received our orders, and we must begin to implement them. You and I, better than anyone else at this moment, realize the improbable nature of the tasks we've been assigned. But I believe all of us, despite the enormity of what we've just learned, would like to see some shred of goodness and hope survive what's ahead. We must try. Never underestimate the depth of my sorrow for you and your families, and for all others beyond this room. And I never will yours. Let's begin.

"First off, Jason you will need to contact your Recon company commanders and have them select and assemble their best personnel for an immediate operational-ready platoon. They will need to deploy by 1600 hours today. At the same time, Miles you will need to coordinate with Jason and the Captain in charge of his platoon, to insure that have enough supplies and material to last them for a two month operation. Provide them with the transportation and equipment to be self-sufficient for this timeframe. They will need enough extra vehicles to guard three roadblocks 24 hours a day, allowing in or out only those with proper I.D., and who are on official business. Have them take two bulldozers and two forklifts with them.

"Nancy, I need you to get the names of these Marines and notify their families that they will be deploying during the last week in March. Also, notify them that there will be a joint meeting, prior to that departure, in the Base Chapel of all the families who will deploy. Have them arrange to pack their personal belongings, clothing, sundries, and valuables. They will need to prepare both for extreme cold and extreme heat. Tell them it will be for a one year deployment with their spouse. Then I need you to assemble the operational manuals, texts, all materials related to the duties, functions, and organization that are used by all the major commands on Base. We should begin storing this material, and the associated equipment, that is used by the personnel who perform these jobs. In other words, we need to be able to teach others how to perform these many jobs, and what you store will be their instruction material.

"Priscilla, you will have to locate empty shipping containers and the personnel to load them as the supplies and equipment are assembled. We will set aside any that are loaded and ready for delivery. Once the Providence Cavern is secure and able to receive them, then we will transport everything there.

"Next, I need each of you, whose area of responsibility oversees Transportation, Engineering, Medical or Communications, to do the same as Jason has to do today for Reconnaissance. The best and most reliable Marines from each of these operational commands must be selected to form the individual platoons. You are then to meet with the Captains of these respective units and outline for them the urgency and scope of what is ahead. They, in turn, will brief their platoons. Each individual must know what is going to happen. Miles, you will have the added responsibility of circulating within these units and determining what equipment and supplies they will need. That list will become more precise and more focused once all of us meet with the Amboy personnel tomorrow. Finally, all the names of the personnel in each platoon must be funneled to Nancy for family notification, just as we will be doing with the Reconnaissance platoon.

"That's probably enough for now. We will have plenty of time to rehash all the details of this operation tomorrow. Meet me at the helicopter pad at 1030 hours. We will shuttle back and forth to Amboy to reduce travel down time. And we can discuss any issues that need to be addressed in Amboy during that flight. And just for a reality check, tomorrow is February 6th. I fear the countdown of days is going to become a nagging presence for the next two months.

"While you are completing these assignments, I will get in touch with the Air Force Commanders at McChord and Fairchild Air Force Bases and at Port

Hueneme Seabee Base and begin the transfer of their personnel to here. I will also contact the California Department of Highways to inform them of the road closures. I am going to explain that it is a military priority of the most urgent and secret nature. And on that note, if any staff or visitors are at the Providence Cavern when your people arrive, just coax them out with the same explanation. It makes no sense to confine unnecessary individuals there.

"And that should do it for now. Collect your thoughts and impressions for our briefing tomorrow, when we travel to Amboy.

"My thanks to each of you. You are the best of the best. God's speed to all of us."

Each officer saluted and filed out of the General's office. As they were doing so, he picked up his intercom phone and asked his Receptionist to get him the telephone numbers for the Air Force and Seabee commanders. This part was going to be a little more delicate to manage, not having the freedom to divulge more than was necessary or appropriate. National defense and the need to know were usually enough justification to satisfy most commanders when they had to relocate their assets off base. He hoped that would be sufficient now. Luckily, this was not a period when transport planes were tied up shuttling personnel and material to some theater of operations overseas. It was a rather non eventful time for large military operations. The recent change in political and civilian leadership changed the large scale involvement overseas, at least for now. And remarkably, he was able to secure four aircraft each for transport and refueling from their respective Air Force Bases, along with the support crews for each. They were to fly out on February 7th, arriving at the Marine Base by 1700 hours. And it was further approved that their families could be temporarily relocated here as well. And the commander of the Seabee Base said he would hand pick his finest personnel for the job ahead. They would leave by convoy in the afternoon on the 7th, arriving at the Marine Base by 2300 hours, provided the traffic was not too congested between there and here. Their family members were also to be temporarily relocated to the Marine Base. It was decided that any big equipment that might be needed later, that was not being transported with them, may have to be flown to the Marine Base.

His final call was to the California Highway Department. They were not happy about the closure and wondered why it had to be for so long. General Stanfield had to do some dodgy explaining, to avoid creating more interest in the closures. Basically, he said, given the present climate of terror threats and the need to train troops under very difficult and realistic conditions, it was necessary for national defense to close off these areas for the extended period of time. He likewise notified the National Parks Office of this closure to insure that no official got too concerned about what was happening.

In the meantime, Lt. Col Jason Black had met with his Officer Staff at Recon Headquarters. The complement of officers for this command was already gathered in the Report Room for a briefing on a recently completed training exercise. Col. Black outlined that he needed a platoon of their best men, led by one of the assembled Captains, to report to him by 1530 hours for a briefing and then for deployment to their new duty stations by 1600 hours. He explained they would need supplies for a least a week, with additional supplies to come later. Realizing what was ahead, he added that they also needed sixteen concrete barriers for roadblocks. They would be transported with them, and then they were to be off-loaded where they were to

186

establish a secure roadblock. Finally, he said they needed to take extra vehicles to travel back and forth to relieve each other at the three check points. And as an afterthought, he instructed them to also have two tractor trailers accompany them, loaded with two smaller bulldozers and two oversized forklifts.

Puzzled by his orders, the officers agreed anyway to execute them right away. Their prompt response was essential for the personnel to be selected and outfitted enough to begin their operation within the given timeframe.

By 1530 hours, outside the Marine Base's Mission Operations Command Center, the convoy of vehicles, including four semi-trailers loaded with concrete barriers and hoists to unload them and two tractor trailer rigs loaded with two bulldozers and two forklifts, was parked. Captain Pete Mendoza was the commanding officer of the platoon. Included in their convoy were the extra fuel and water trailers, pulled by the six deuce and a half trucks, loaded with their every day supplies. There were twenty-two vehicles in all.

Col. Black addressed the assembled platoon, as they stood around the lead vehicle. He explained that they were embarking on a highly secret mission that no one, outside their immediate family must ever know about. Moreover, they were to communicate with them alone where and why they were being deployed. In addition, not even their command structure back in the Recon Headquarters would know what they were doing or where they were. To emphasize his point, he said both their lives and those of their families depended on their honoring this confidence.

He concluded by saying the remaining personnel, after setting up the three roadblocks, were to go immediately to the Providence Cavern and secure that area. Anyone they found there was to be told there was a military exercise taking place, and they were to exit the area right away. No one outside their immediate group was to enter that area, other than those with proper identification and conducting official business. And this applied to all the roadblocks as well. Some directional signage would be printed and posted that would detour travelers well before the actual roadblocks to lessen the number of denied entries. In conclusion, he instructed Capt. Mendoza to meet him in Amboy tomorrow at 1300 hours for further updates and instructions.

Saluting one another, the group mounted their respective vehicles, and the convoy headed out of the Base perimeter toward Amboy. Most of the personnel in this platoon would never return to the Base. Their new home for themselves and their families was to become the Providence Cavern.

By 1700 hours they had reached the outskirts of Amboy, where the roadway merges coming from the Marine Base and heads either into Amboy or west toward Barstow. Stopping the convoy, Capt. Mendoza had one of the semi-trailer trucks unload four of the barriers on the northern side of the railroad tracks. All vehicle traffic would be stopped here. There were two concrete barriers extended from the median strip across one lane and over the paved shoulder. Then fifty feet beyond that lane barrier, the opposite lane was blocked the same way. It was agreed that leaving this space between the barriers would allow enough room for passage of the commercial, delivery trucks. One bull dozer and the two forklifts were driven off their semi-trailers and left near the post office. Four Marines were stationed at the roadblock with a supply truck, extra water and fuel and two humvee vehicles.

The same procedure was repeated three times on exits coming off Interstate 40. One roadblock was northeast of Amboy, preventing traffic from coming south off that exit. The other roadblocks were further east along I-40, at the Providence Cavern and Essex exit. Both the north and south roads were blocked at that exit, essentially sealing it off completely. This roadblock was also only guarded by four Marines, just like the other two. It was easy enough to monitor traffic coming off this exit, attempting to go south or north, with the one outpost. An unmanned roadblock was erected on the dirt road heading east from Cima Station, north of Kelso. The actual barricade was on the ridge top of the Providence Mountains, just before one would be able to see the Providence Cavern compound. Lookouts would be posted to observe this area, and if there was any likelihood of trespassers, then Marines would be stationed there as well.

This dispersal of twelve Marines at these checkpoints left nineteen more to be stationed at the cavern. It was 2200 hours by the time all the roadblocks had been established and the remaining convoy pulled into the cavern area. It had been a long day for the platoon, and no effort was made to erect tents. They just bivouacked by their vehicles for the night. Tomorrow morning a proper operation center could be established.

And certainly all this activity did not go unnoticed by the newcomer families now living, rather than just visiting, in Amboy. The sight of military equipment and the establishment of a roadblock, with patrols, gave grim reinforcement to what B had told them. But the children of the families lost no time running over to where the Marines were now stationed. It became clear that both military and civilian status would merge into a familiar and supportive atmosphere. Each was there to help take care of the other. The children brought food and gaiety. The Marines brought a sense of structure and protection. No sense of threat between the two existed then or thereafter.

TWENTY-THREE: FEBRUARY 6TH MEETING

The five Marine officers met at the helipad at 1030 hours. General Stanfield had arranged a Chinook class helicopter to transport them to Amboy. It gave them the room and privacy to talk freely. And upon securing their seat belts, he asked for a progress report on what had happened yesterday after their meeting with B and Clem. Each officer outlined their progress thus far.

As the helicopter was preparing to land on the old Route 66 highway, just beyond Amboy's scattered buildings, the General reported to his staff who he had contacted yesterday. He emphasized to each of them that from here on all transport, whenever possible, should be done at night to reduce the element of exposure and the risk of a breach in security. Given the gravity of what they were doing, no one doubted that if any of this preparation and activity were to be exposed, untold chaos would result. They all nodded in agreement to this new order.

If the families selected to attend the now-cancelled symposium had any doubts up to that point that their lives, they were now exponentially changed. The sound and sight of that Marine helicopter, approaching and landing on the roadway, deafeningly removed any of them. Once the downdraft of blowing sand settled and the engine was shut down, the Marine officers exited the chopper and walked toward the restaurant. It was a sight of memorable contrasts. Marine uniforms, military aircraft, scattered drab, struggling-to-survive buildings huddled close to the road, and hundreds of adults and children standing on or along the old highway. As nothing else could up to this point, it visually confirmed to all there that their mission had immeasurable importance.

Clem met the Marine officers at the restaurant door and led them into the rear dining area. Fred, Cynthia and Clem had arranged four tables in a large eight foot square, with chairs for sixteen people. Not wanting to be disturbed once the meeting began, they had pitchers of water and coffee on the table.

"General, please, would you and your fellow officers please sit in the remaining empty chairs?" Clem requested. "The meeting has not started, but everyone was anxious to begin once you arrived. Maybe now it is best if we all introduce ourselves before we get started."

The General and his contingent sat down, nodding to those sitting around the table. Clem then asked each person to introduce themselves and indicate what responsibilities they presently had. Cynthia and Fred said they were part of the organizing committee for the symposium and were there to help facilitate arranging anything the civilian community might need.

Following the introductions, Clem performed what he hoped was his last official act. He suggested that for the most efficient use of their time, someone needed to be elected, appointed or volunteer to be the chairperson. All there agreed by nodding their heads. He then asked if there were any suggestions as to who it might be. Geoffrey Graham spoke up, suggesting that he thought it should be General Stanfield, at least until everyone was relocated inside the cavern. Then, he added, at that time the whole process of governing and decision making would need the most detailed review by everyone, including their three judges, to be followed by a community wide election. And again, there were nods and audible expressions of agreement. By voice vote, the General was unanimously voted the Director/General of the Amboy Relocation Committee.

At this point the General stood, clearing his throat of the chronic sinus drainage he was ever-plagued with, and said, "Maybe it would be best to begin this morning with myself and the other officers bringing you up to date on what we have done so far. Then we need to hear from your various coordinators what has been decided and done. For later discussion, I might suggest we keep our comments or questions limited to what needs to be done, how best to do it, who best to do it, and by when it has to be done. If we can frame our comments that way, maybe we can come up with the quickest and most efficient way to find the solutions. So, I'll start, and then we'll proceed with Lt. Col Black on my left.

General Stanfield began. "I have contacted the State and Federal folks about the roadblocks into the Amboy and Providence Cavern areas. I presume you are aware your personal effects that you left behind will be flown into our Marine Base. Preparing for that, I spoke with the Commanders at McChord and Fairchild Air Force Bases, and those crews are arriving at our airfield tomorrow. Clem gave us a copy of your shippers' addresses and contact numbers. I also contacted the Seabee Base in Port Hueneme, and they are sending a complement of 50 personnel, along with earth moving and drilling equipment. They are coming by convoy and will arrive sometime tomorrow night.

Additionally, I contacted the Nuclear Regulatory Agency in Washington, D.C. about the status of the Yucca Mountain Nuclear Waste Repository and whether it is still in mothball status. I then requested a meeting with them on February 10th. Our hope is to open up that huge underground facility for the Air Force, Seabee and other personnel as a long term shelter. It would serve as a refuge for a total of 250 families, made up of 80 Air Force families from Fairchild and McChord, and 20 from Nellis Air Force Base, 50 from the Seabees, and 25 each from the Coast Guard, Navy and Army and another 25 from Camp Pendleton Marine Base. That would bring the total to 1000 individuals housed in that underground facility. We will not be arranging supplies or equipment for them. They will be notified, as they arrive at our Base, about the April 1st deadline, and then they will be given the responsibility of organizing their own shelter's survival gear. I have planned on meeting all these individuals on February 12th. I think you will appreciate that if these people are working to save your lives, the least we can do is offer them the possibility of survival as well. And like us, they will receive the "Clem treatment", as I call it. They will experience the same transformation as all of us sitting here did. And they will be sworn to the strictest secrecy. Any breach of this security will be fatal to all of us and, more importantly, to the noble cause this mission is trying to achieve. So, that's it for me for now. Jason, I guess you're next."

"My responsibilities are to oversee the Mission Operations Command at the Base. Starting yesterday, after learning about the April 1st deadline, a Reconnaissance platoon was formed, with Capt. Mendoza as its leader. His personnel were able to briefly tell their family members about this deployment and why. He is coming here today at 1300 hours to report on their deployment of roadblocks and securing the Providence Cavern perimeter yesterday. As you can see, they already have a roadblock established just west of you. I have also arranged a meeting with the Commanders of the Engineering, Transportation, Communication and Medical Commands to have them select a platoon of their best individuals and a leader for each platoon. I will then be meeting with those units on the following day for a briefing and assignments. They should be fully operational by February 10th. And that's it for me right now. Nancy, I guess it's your turn."

"Because my responsibilities are to manage the Personal Affairs Office, I am now in the process of collecting the names of all the Marines who are now on station with the Recon platoon. By February 10th, after Lt. Col. Black's meeting with the other platoons, I will be given their names as well. I will then proceed to notify their families, all of whom will be living on Base presently, that they can expect redeployment by the end of March. I will further instruct them to begin packing their most valuable possessions, clothes, and personal effects for a one year isolated deployment. And to follow up on what their active duty spouses tell them, I will also have a meeting with all of them to go over a rough outline of what is happening and the need for secrecy. There will be a meeting of all the Marines and their families in the Base Chapel on March 23rd, at 0900 hrs. At that time B will explain to them, as it was to us, what is happening in much more detail.

Once the Air Force and Seabee personnel arrive, I will likewise get all their names, and then notify the Pentagon that a transfer of their families is necessary to our Base. I hope that the family relocation will be completed by February 20th. The other military personnel and their families from Pendleton, Navy, Coast Guard and Army facilities will also arrive on February 20th. They will all be housed in the old BOQ buildings until they leave. And then all of them can begin preparing for their stay in the Yucca Mountain shelter.

Finally, I am beginning work on getting all the manuals, books, documents and equipment related to the functioning of these commands assembled and ready to move to the cavern. Like you have already done, we are going to try to gather together all the pertinent information and material that could be used to instruct and/or tell a story about who and what we are about. So that's about all I have. Miles, you're up."

"I am responsible for the Material Command, in other words, getting the supplies and equipment together for the units to do their job. Primarily, at this point, once the Engineering, Transportation and Communication units have been formed, I will then coordinate with them what they will need and arrange to get it to them either from our Base or from our Pendleton Base or possibly from the Seabee's inventory. Generally, I'd guess we are planning to have three separate, but interconnecting, caves for all our families to live in. There will be 75 families in each of these living areas. And, we hope, at least two more caves are somewhere in the complex. One would be for general usage and storage, and the other, again we hope, would be much larger than any of the other caves. It could be used for cavern-wide meetings, group meetings, social gatherings, a medical facility and clinic, school classrooms and a small library. Initial reports are that there are three to five caves in the complex, with maybe one or two with interconnecting passageways. And it is my understanding that two or three of the caves already have openings to the outside. But we will know more specific details, once all of our engineers start their work. And that's it for me. Priscilla."

"My area of responsibility is Logistics Command. I have contacted our Storage and Maintenance Units to check on how many empty storage containers we now have. At this point I am told they can locate 27. I also learned there are about 112 empty ones at Camp Pendleton that could be transported here, if need be. I understand that Clem has ordered 343 from the railroad company to be delivered here as soon as possible. They will be used for our homes and storage of daily expendables. No doubt we probably will need more than our 27 for miscellaneous storage. But Clem reports there should be more containers that come with the various supplies he has ordered, and we could use them, and the ones from Pendleton, to supplement what we will have on hand.

"It's important for you to know that all of these will be positioned here in Amboy for packing into and for modification as our homes. It will be easier to do all that at this location, with the rail and truck deliveries coming here. I see that some of you are already clearing off areas for preparations of one kind or another. We will need a lot of cleared space, and that is why we had our people drop off the bulldozer and the forklifts yesterday. I will arrange to have other forklifts available for you to use, whenever you call for them. You're going to need them, believe me. And the engineers should be helping you to clear the brush in the next few days. That does it for me. I guess it's now your turn, is it Janice and Sid?"

"Yes," Janice replied. "Sid and I have a few things to add to your reports. But before we do, let me for the moment, presume to speak for the families who have just arrived here for a totally different purpose. And now we find ourselves in a fight for our lives. Hearing your reports and having you here, gives Sid and I, and I'm sure everyone else here, increased confidence that maybe, just maybe, all that has been outlined can be accomplished. Thank you for joining with us. I assure you we will do our part.

"As to what our group, which is focused on the supplies we will need, has done, I believe Clem has given you the list of items that we need immediately or that can either be stored inside or outside the cavern. I understand Clem has ordered from the truck and rail shippers everything you see on that list. And I believe he added what your 160 families would need as well. We did wonder if you have any extra furniture for our families. We were reluctant to order that until we had met with you. In conclusion, shipments by truck should start arriving today. So if any of those empty containers you have could be brought over, we would gladly start stocking them. And that's it for us. Albert and Dada, I guess you're next."

"Thank you," Albert acknowledged. "Dada and I are helping coordinate the group concerned with the physical livability issues associated with being in these caves for a long period of time. There are four items that need to be brought to your attention, in order that they can be addressed as we go forward. And as an aside, my wife and I, growing up in Nigeria, know too well about the hardships of living in over-crowded conditions. There are small things that can be done to make it more bearable. First, we need to work with your engineers in designing and building the interior of the shipping containers that will be each of our homes. Again, privacy is paramount in their design. Next, we need to discuss the interior lighting, at least having enough to illuminate the immediate living areas 24 hours a day. The storage areas certainly don't need that capability. Then, it is an understandable worry for all of us where the toilets and showers, if any, will be. What kind of privacy is practical? We'd recommend self-contained units, like you would find in a recreation vehicle or in a passenger train sleeper car. Along with that is the issue of running water. Could the Seabees and your engineers, or even ours for that matter, try to drill a well, either within the cavern or just outside it? Maybe there wouldn't be that much water available at any one time, but to have it on a rotating basis or with some guidelines of restricted or rationed usage, would be better that just having water meted out from a bucket or a bladder.

To conclude, we need to be especially aware of the effect of this confinement on our children. Can you find or develop an adjoining space, off to the side of all the living quarters that could possibly house animals and pets? No doubt the pets would have to be limited to just dogs and cats, but even that would cover the majority of household pets most people have. And I suppose that's all we have for now. I guess it's your turn, Theresa and Philip."

"Yes," Theresa nodded, "and Philip and I jointly coordinate the group charged with addressing the physical and mental health and emotional well-being associated with our trying to live in the upcoming conditions. Most important for now is that our medical/surgical staff and other health care professionals are asking if they can secure medical supplies from your staff and hospital. Is that possible? And then could they coordinate the delivery of care with your medical staff? In other words, they would like to join together in having one medical clinic and service for all the cavern's inhabitants.

"We will be developing a kind of calendar of social events that could be held in the larger cavern for everyone to attend. And we are planning adult education classes for developing skills necessary for rebuilding and surviving the conditions we find, following our confinement. Certainly, the children will have to resume their regular classroom studies as soon as possible. Our teachers are beginning to meet now to determine how this can best be done, and again, these classes would be held in a larger cavern, provided there is one.

"Finally, we need to have the capability of delivering music throughout the living areas, at least during what would be normal waking hours. The batteries on any portable recorded music devices will just last so long. We need speakers wired throughout the area. And we hope there will be those amongst us who play some kind of musical instrument. We have a list on the bulletin board for any that can to sign. Philip would like to request a piano be moved into the larger cave for entertainment, if one should be found. Maybe a stage could be built in that area as well. Does that cover everything we've discussed thus far in our group, Philip?" He only nodded his head, but he was very proud how well his wife handled this report. "Ok, then, that's it for us. It must be Patty and Geoffrey's time."

Geoff spoke for this final report. "We are coordinating the group responsible for rebuilding, once we are able to exit the caves permanently. And there are two major components to that process, which we've identified thus far. One is making sure we have listed and are now ordering the necessary materials and equipment to do most of what we will need. I think all of us understand that there will be huge gaps in what would be needed at that time versus what we thought we would need. That cannot be helped or that gap reduced. We have to trust our ingenuity and ability to adapt and develop new ways to address issues that arise. But, be that as it may, we must try and do our best to plan for eventualities. You have been given the list of what we have decided and ordered so far. Please come back to us with any additions as soon as possible. As has been said here today already, we here in Amboy will be responsible for ordering supplies, e.g. food, drinks, personal and household items. You at the Marine Base may be providing medical supplies and furniture and some building materials for immediate use. And we here in Amboy and you at the Base are both involved in deciding what rebuilding materials and equipment we will need.

"The other major issue before us is to breakdown into stages the priorities for our rebuilding and recovery, after our confinement ends. As a guide, I will outline for you what our group has decided, in the order of importance:

"1. Infrastructure building (water, sewer, septic, power, proper location of home sites, schools, clinic and roadways of some kind.).
"2. Dwellings of some kind.
"3. Develop some kind of food source (cultivate fields and crops, home gardens, orchards, livestock and fish husbandry). We are even considering livestock, which brings up the issue of whether it will be possible to have any farm animals in that cave area that might house pets. To have selected beef and dairy cows, chickens, pigs, goats and sheep to start off with would be wonderful.
"4. Outreach, Rescue, Exploring. These can only come once we have tried to insure the survival of our families from the caves.

"And that pretty much sums up what we have discussed in our group."

General Stanfield continued making notes for a minute after Geoffrey had finished his report. Once done, he looked up and commented, "Good work, everyone. In a brief timeframe, you have managed to outline many, if not most, of the major issues facing us. Now, let me speak to each group's concerns, as best I can. And it appears we will have enough plans in place to proceed full speed ahead for the next week or so.

"First off, Col. Roberts, we need you, as soon as we get back, to contact the Storage and Maintenance Depot and have them arrange transport for at least nine of those empty shipping containers over here today. And while you're at it, it seems to me we're definitely going to need more containers than we either have on hand or that have been ordered through the railroad. That so, I need you to also contact the Pendleton Storage Depot and arrange for our Transportation personnel, as soon as they are selected, to begin ferrying those 112 empty containers over here to Amboy. If supplies are supposed to start coming here today, we need to start right away providing them the units to pack into. By my quick calculations, the rail shipment should take only one train load. Most trains now are two miles in length, with each railcar approximately sixty feet long. With each railcar double-stacked with containers, they could easily ship all 343 at one time. When that train arrives, we've got to be ready to remove them and place them somewhere. All this is a high priority right now.

"Lt. Col Black, when you speak with the Engineers tomorrow, have them stop by here first, before their deployment to the cavern. They will need to do a survey to bulldoze large areas around this complex, on both sides of the roadway. We need to have plenty of room for the number of containers that are coming. Also, have them bring another forklift and teach some of the Amboy individuals how to use them.

"Janice, as far as your request for furniture from the Base, I anticipate that will be no problem. I am sure we have enough unused items scattered, stored and lying around to furnish all the living quarters. But it will be Spartan. What you will have most likely will be single beds, trundle beds, fold-out kitchen tables, wooden storage cases, and four chairs. And I feel certain we can provide blankets, sheets, and towels for everyone as well. I might suggest, and certainly not without compensation, that Clem speak with the owners of the motel and arrange for your families to take pillows and extra bedding, etc. with them to the cavern. I will request that the Marine families do the same thing. Everyone, it seems, has that favorite pillow. Without it, our lives will be just that much more difficult. As far as any other furniture, that will probably have to be left up to the imagination of the individual families. They will have to improvise from what they bring with them into the cavern.

"Albert, I'll instruct some of the Engineers to stop in to meet with you on February 8th. They can work with you to design a simple and effective floor plan for the living quarters' containers. And, again, I am sure we have enough lumber, drywall and insulation scattered around the two Bases to be able to frame in all the containers. We'll shoot for March 23rd, as the date to move furniture in, after all the remodeling is completed. To be realistic, that may be after the container units have already been positioned in the cavern. We'll see what works quickest, doing the furnishing here in Amboy or in the individual caves.

"Likewise, I will make sure Engineering speaks with you regarding lighting in the caves. Your reasoning is sound. They can also speak with you about your sewer, shower, toilet and water concerns. Between them, your own engineers here, and the Seabees, someone will start surveying where best to drill a well for water and where and how to construct a sewer system. The area for pets and livestock can be mentioned at that time as well. But no promises can be made on that suggestion. What you said made good sense, but we have no idea yet what space we have to work with.

"Theresa, I will speak with our Chiefs of Surgery and Medicine at the Base Hospital. I know they will be very interested in working with your medical staff. As far as supplies and equipment, we can manage all that. And I will let them know that as well. I will ask the Engineers to examine the cavern and pick the largest cave for your assembly area. Quite likely, we will probably have to tunnel into some of these caves, both to explore what additional space we may find, but also to enlarge the openings to allow passage of the shipping containers. And I really like your idea of having speakers throughout the caverns for broadcasting music and announcements. And from what I have personally heard about Philip's playing, I will see to it that a piano is installed in that area. A stage of some kind is appropriate to consider as well.

"Geoffrey, I will also have a group of our Engineers and Seabees speak with you on the 8th, about the building materials issue. And at this point I want to emphasize to everyone, we will need all your engineers, scientists, every individual and specialty assembled here, to be involved in every phase of this process. They are free to come with us, as we pass through in convoy, just flag us down to stop. We need all of you. This definitely is not just a military operation. It can only be described as an urgent, civilized society operation. My people will be instructed, if that is even necessary, to consult with, to work side-by-side with, and to depend on your people. We desperately need each other's abilities, talents, and efforts to accomplish what lies ahead. And I'll say no more on this subject.

"Further, the orders for building materials that Clem arranged with the railroad and building supply chain should include enough for our Marine families as well. We have none of those items either present or in enough quantity to rebuild with. But, without a doubt, we will have to erect at least one very large warehouse outside the cavern to store all that is coming."

It was at this point that Clem, most reluctantly, spoke up. "General Stanfield, if I may, with everyone's permission here, I need to add some items to the list I gave you yesterday. Since that list was made, people have been coming up to me with ideas and suggestions. I need to present them to this group before I call them in. What has been suggested are: indoor/outdoor carpet for the floors of the living quarters; two large and two smaller braided rugs to go over the carpet; seed, plants, and saplings; baby formula, two extra electrical generators, canning and preserving equipment and supplies; and most importantly, doubling the amount of food supplies ordered thus far. People are telling me that having just enough supplies for the time we are confined in the cavern, leaves us vulnerable to starvation during the period we are trying to rebuild, cultivate, plant and harvest foodstuffs. Many have also mentioned that everyone will have to revert to a Great Depression Era pattern of recycling everything possible. If we can do that, it will certainly avoid accumulating unnecessary waste that we somehow have to discard. All packaging, cardboard, cans, glass and plastic containers, even paper and plastic wrappers, would need to be saved. Who's to say if there will be any of this kind of material available to use, once our confinement is over. It can all be cleaned, broken down, and saved in the containers that we empty monthly. Finally, and with the gravest reservation, I must mention I have also been requested to add body bags to the reorder. And that's all I have."

Like everyone else in the room, the General was taken off guard by Clem's announcements. He, and each person sitting there, found themselves nodding their heads in agreement to what Clem asked for. It was shocking to hear the additions. They, alone, painted a picture of how extreme the time ahead was to be. Shaking his head, the General quietly said, "Yes, Clem, proceed with those requests. We have no choice but to try and prepare for every eventuality. Thank you.

"And with that said, I think we can bring this first meeting to a close, if there are no objections. I'm sure you feel as I do, it was a productive and worthwhile exchange. At no time will anything be done without everyone in this room knowing ahead of time. That's my promise.

"Now, I smell something cooking. I'd like to try some Amboy food. Heaven knows before much longer, that's all we'll know. So, there being no objections, this meeting is adjourned. We will meet again at 11:00 a.m. on February 8th."

It was a leisurely lunch for the assembled committee. Ray had set aside some tables to accommodate all of them in the main dining area. With the comings and goings of hundreds of children and adults, no one paid much attention to them. It was obvious the Marine officers were enjoying the Amboy families. It was not festive; the news of the last 24 hours precluded anything like that. But it was not demoralized or dejected either. And, as always, the children were the key to the air of perseverance and good will. It was highly infectious.

The General was so enjoying the camaraderie that he let Jason go out to meet Capt. Mendoza to get a report of how they were managing at the roadblocks and the cavern. The report was routine, in that no major obstacles or confrontations had occurred. There was no one else at the cavern when they got there. And anyone they turned away at the roadblocks were mildly irritated at the inconvenience, but quickly accepted that they would just have to detour or give up their plans to see the cavern at this time. Each roadblock and the contingent at the cavern had set up tents and were beginning to make permanent bases of operation. Their first orders of business were to scout out the area, set up observation posts, and erect their operational command equipment. However, the Captain's report on the cavern was more fascinating. Lt. Col. Black knew after getting this information, the Engineers would have some sorting out to do in the next few days.

He then informed Capt. Mendoza that the other units would be arriving sometime late tomorrow afternoon or evening to set up camp. From here on, the two of them would either communicate in person at the cavern or by telephone. Col. Black then thanked the Captain for getting the platoon in position so quickly.

By the time the helicopter left Amboy, there were three semi-trailer trucks pulling into the motel parking lot with food and drink supplies from the warehouse in Phoenix. For now, all that could be done, until the empty shipping containers arrived, was for anyone who could, to help unload the trucks and stack the contents in various school classrooms.

The nine empty shipping containers arrived at 4:45 p.m. and were placed off the road in front of the school. Still to be decided, was where and how to position and load the many containers in the weeks ahead. Clem, for one, was very relieved that shipments were starting to come in. He had just completed making calls to the various shippers about the additions to their lists when the first supplies arrived. He felt he could relax a little now that the process was under way.

By 1500 hours Lt. Col. Black was back at the Marine Base and meeting with the commanders of the Communication, Engineering, Medical, and Transportation Commands. He explained to them, in the briefest terms possible, that he needed each of them to select a leader and the best personnel from each command to make up a platoon for immediate deployment. He requested they provide him with the names of these individuals. He, in turn, would be giving these names to Major Gilcrest. His final orders were that these selected individuals were to meet with him at 1000 hours tomorrow in the Logistics Command Theater for a briefing, and then they should be able to deploy tomorrow at 1600 hours.

TWENTY-FOUR: FEBRUARY DIARY

February 7th:-1000 hours- Lt. Col. Black met with the Captains and their platoon personnel from the Transportation, Communication, Engineering, and Medical Commands. This meeting lasted one hour, in which time strict secrecy of their mission was emphasized and the projects that needed to be completed immediately were outlined. Col. Black asked that for any supplies or equipment they might need, beyond what they were taking with them today, they were to contact him only. He would expedite their getting it. They were dismissed and were to deploy later today. And like the Recon unit, they were each instructed to inform their families where and why they were going, and that their family members were probably going to have to work in Amboy in some capacity, as well.

-1030 hours- The first of 42 more truck deliveries arrived from the food warehouse and the building supply store chain.

-1600 hours.-The four commands left by convoy, heading to Amboy and then on to the cavern. They were to unload another bulldozer and fork lift in Amboy and did a quick survey of the area.

-1700 hours-The arrival of huge Air Force transport and refueling planes caused considerable excitement throughout the Marine Base.

-2000 hours-All the Marine personnel arrived at the Providence Cavern.

-2330 hours-The late arrival of the Seabee convoy only added to the second guessing by the Marine Base grapevine. But because the Seabees were gone by the next day, and the planes left on the 10th, the speculation soon died down, much to the relief of General Stanfield and his staff.

February 8th:1100 hours-Again, the helicopter landed on the stretch of highway just west of the Amboy motel. This time, instead of just the five Marine officers, there were also two Air Force Colonels and one Seabee Lieutenant. As on the 6th, they met in the rear dining room with the four couples representing the groups in Amboy. For the most part it was a meeting to introduce the newest members of the Team. General Stanfield had already briefed them on their mission and why all this was necessary. And as everyone else before them was, the three newcomers were in shock and very quiet throughout the meeting. They had arranged later today for the General to inform all their personnel of the gravity of what was ahead and that their families would be joining them at the Marine Base. No new business was brought forward, pending their discussions with the Engineers later today. Philip and Theresa did ask Clem to call a vendor and see if different outdoor scenes could be ordered that would be attached to the walls inside the shipping container homes. Further, they specified that the dimensions had to be no taller than six feet and no longer than ten feet. And after some discussion, they also asked him to see if they could get a couple more that were much larger to be mounted in the largest cavern. The most detailed discussion, however, revolved around the Air Force picking up and delivering the Amboy families household containers from their overseas locations.

-1300 hours-A group of nine Engineers arrived from the cavern; two were to speak with Geoffrey and Clem about supplies that would be needed for rebuilding after the confinement. At this time they were in agreement with what had already been ordered. Most of what they needed now was earth moving, tunneling, digging and drilling equipment. They did request that Clem meet with them later to arrange getting the materials they would need to erect two large exterior warehouses. The construction of those would begin as soon as the material arrived. The actual building and remodeling within the caves would probably not begin for another one to two weeks.

Simultaneously, two Engineers met with Philip and Theresa, and they ultimately agreed on the interior layout and front door modifications for the shipping container homes. (see Appendix 1,diagram 1, "Floor Plan for Converted Shipping Container Living Quarters").

At the same time two Engineers met with Dada and Albert to discuss the cavern's lighting, wiring, sewer, kitchen and water needs. Lt. Javitts, the Seabees' commander, was also present. They were to start exploring the possibility of a well site immediately. All agreed the issue of animals or pets was a low priority just now, but they would keep it in mind as the work progressed inside the caves.

While all these meetings were taking place two Engineers were busy clearing brush and leveling the surrounding area for the incoming containers. Once an area was sufficiently leveled in front of the school, another Engineer instructed three Amboy families how to operate the forklifts. And they began moving the empty containers that had been delivered on February 6th, and thereafter, to that area for the immediate loading of supplies to begin.

-1400 hours-Helicopter left for Marine Base. General Stanfield met with all the Air Force and Seabee personnel immediately upon his return and gave them the terrible news and the plan for them and their families to deploy to the Yucca Mountain Facility. This was followed by his briefing them on their lengthy mission ahead to pick up the Amboy families containers.

-1600 hours-The first bus load of Marine Base families arrived to begin eight hour shifts, stacking and loading containers. This began a 24 hour a day schedule for the next month.

-1800 hours-Engineers finished their work in Amboy and headed back to the cavern complex, with the bulldozers loaded on their truck. The Seabees' convoy was readied and left for the Providence Cavern. They picked up 53 adults from Amboy to also begin work at the cavern.

--2200 hours-Under the cover of darkness, the Transportation platoon began ferrying equipment to the cavern from the Base. Once there, they rested until dawn, then they began to convoy back and forth all night, each night, material and equipment for either Amboy or the cavern. It was a pattern that repeated non-stop for the next three weeks.

February 10th: 0500 hours-General Stanfield flew to Washington, D.C. in the fifteen seat Marine Corps jet to meet with the Director of the Nuclear Regulatory Agency.

-1000 hours-Meeting with Nuclear Agency was an unqualified success. The Facility had been totally shut down; even the thousands of workers at the research center there were relocated to facilities in Idaho and Tennessee. The timelines for ever storing any nuclear wastes kept being postponed. It went from 2010 to 2017, and finally, the entire project was just mothballed and essentially abandoned. Without divulging the actual reasons for using the Yucca Mountain Depository, General Stanfield was able to convince them that his units needed to train and modify it slightly for war games. He assured them that no permanent structural changes would be made to the facility. Silently he thought if events were not to unfold like B had said they would, his career would end in blazing disgrace.

-1400 hours- The General's plane took off, returning to the Marine Base. He phoned Lt. Col. Black and Major Gilcrest to let them know what had happened and to have them inform the Air Force and Seabee personnel. It would reassure them that they and their families at least had a chance to survive what lay ahead.

-1800 hours-All the Marine, Seabee and Air Force units were now fully operational.

February 10-17th:1400 hours-Air Force flights were coordinated around the world to pick up containers at the designated airports. As they would return to the Marine Base, the Transportation unit would be there to offload their cargo and transport it to Amboy for storage. These containers' final relocation to the caves would not be until March.

February 12th: 0800 hours-General Stanfield met with the Pendleton Marines, Navy, Army and Coast Guard personnel who will be working to upgrade the Yucca Mountain facility. They are informed that Major Gilcrest has already been in touch with the Pentagon to get orders cut for them to be stationed at this Base. And that their families are to be transferred here as well. Before the families arrived, however, each of the active duty personnel will be moved to Yucca Mountain to begin preparing it for long term residency. He informed them of the awful news B had told him and swore them to secrecy, both for theirs and their families' safety. It would take them five more days to get together the needed supplies, material and equipment they would need to begin the remodel.

February 17th: 2230 hours-The Army, Navy, Coast Guard and Pendleton Marine personnel left for Yucca Mountain in a large convoy of vehicles, under the cover of night and using little traveled roadways. With them, besides the supplies, materials and equipment, there were semi-trailer trucks loaded with three search and rescue boats to eventually be used for rescue and reconnaissance; two disassembled, small prop-driven airplanes; two disassembled helicopters, along with large bladders of airplane and boat fuel, lubricants and gasoline.

-2330 hours-The last transport and refueling plane landed with their cargo of stored valuables, materials and equipment for the Amboy families. They were quickly off-loaded and placed on trucks that sped off to Amboy. Exhausted and relieved this agonizing mission was completed, the crews headed to their quarters to sleep and eat for the next three days.

February 20th: all day-Families of the Air Force, Seabee, Navy, Coast Guard, Army and Pendleton Marines arrived at the Marine Base. Some were reunited, although briefly, and with little discussion or divulging the mission ahead, with their loved ones about to depart either to Yucca Mountain or back to the Providence Cavern. The families were surprised how relieved and excited their spouses were to see and hold them. Not knowing what awaits them in the near future, they welcomed the attention and were eager to be joining them the last week in March, somewhere in Nevada, for their next deployment.

-2230 hours-Air Force crews departed with their eight planes for Nellis Air Force Base in Nevada. With a modest amount of stealth and a major shroud of secrecy, they were met by twenty personnel at Nellis. The Nellis crew arranged their parking and secured the aircraft, and from there they all drove off in military vehicles to Yucca Mountain. Both the 80 Air Force personnel from the Marine Base, along with 20 from Nellis, drove off under the cover of night, tainted as it was, with the bright lights of Las Vegas. Inside the plane's cargo holds were truck loads of food and other supplies for their use and storage. This material, as well, was off loaded and trucked immediately to the same destination.

February 28th: 2100 hours-The Seabees left the Providence Cavern, having completed their assigned tasks, in the afternoon of February 27th. They spent that night with their families at the Marine Base. The next day, when they were not restocking supplies and equipment for their next assignment, they visited with their families. In the evening, they again had to convoy for the last time, leaving their families behind for about another month. Their destination was the Yucca Mountain Repository.

TWENTY-FIVE: THE CAVES

When the Recon Marine unit arrived at the Providence Cavern on February 5th, there was no way to know exactly where the cavern was. The night was only lit by starlight, which in itself was breath-taking in a deep desert environment. They would have to wait until morning to see where the cavern's entrance lay. With the sound of coyotes calling one another, each remaining Marine of the unit spread out their sleeping gear on the ground by their vehicles and tried to sleep.

Every one of them were seasoned enough to adapt quickly to whatever orders and assignments they were given, but none of them were even remotely prepared for this detail. Capt. Mendoza told them before they left the Base that something terrible, but no one knew exactly what, was going to happen on April1st. And that they had to prepare a site to offer refuge to the people in Amboy and to some Marines and their families. They were assured they and their families were in that group. While that offered a little comfort, now that they had time alone to absorb what it probably meant, it wasn't much. Little by little the effects of the total blackness and the silence, with the occasional coyote wailing, lulled each into a deep, exhausted sleep.

By dawn, Capt. Mendoza was dressed and had prepared some coffee for his unit that was still sleeping.

He knew each of them from previous missions and was comforted by the experience and maturity they brought to the tasks that lay ahead. He needed to make radio contact with his outpost overlooking the northern road into the cavern area and with his teams at the roadblocks. Then he had to get the remainder of his personnel ready to enter the cavern complex.

It took little time to confirm that all was quiet at the roadblocks. Quickly, with the smell of coffee in the air, the remainder of his platoon arose, washed enough to feel more alert, ate a breakfast MRE, and drank some of the Captain's soup-like coffee. Putting on their gear, they assembled around him for orders.

It was agreed that with the now-visible entrances into the cavern, they needed to take three sets of flood lamps into each entrance. Depending on what they found, they would take the flood lamps further into each cave and illuminate the interior. The orientation of the cave entrances were lying in a north-south direction, with their openings facing east. The entrances were approximately eight to ten feet above a sloping, sand drift. This sandy base then sloped further down into the valley below, which extended 10-12 miles into the distance. From the entrances of the caves, it was a remarkable vista to look out over. At the southernmost end of the outcrop of this particular mountain formation, where they camped last night, it sloped down to level ground, again to a sandy base. The northern end of this formation extended for some miles to the north and merged with an adjoining east-west oriented range of mountains.

The first order Capt. Mendoza gave for the morning was to have the bulldozer clear and build a firm roadbed around the front and south side of the cavern. The ramps into each cave entrance needed to be constructed first, so they could begin the survey of the interior. He also directed the bulldozer operator to spend the rest of the day clearing away scrub and cactus, laying out a large storage and assembly area adjacent to the southern end of the cavern complex. Their unit would then shift their base of operations and position earth moving equipment there. At this point, he was not sure what, if any, exterior structures might need to be built.

By 0800 hours the ramps to the entrance of each cave were completed enough to allow the six member teams to enter each cave. Capt. Mendoza went with the middle group. As hoped, the entrance areas appeared dry and uncluttered. Even though this was a State Park, it did not have many visitors. And, apparently those who came, respected the beauty of the area and kept it in pristine condition. Without much effort, each team was able to pull their floodlight trailers into each cave and then turn them on.

For them, as for anyone who has ever had the experience of emerging into a darkened cave, then suddenly having complete illumination of nature's sculpturing handiwork, it was a sight of almost incomparable beauty. Nothing in anyone's terrestrial experience prepares him or her for the subterranean world's evolutions. Time and water play the biggest roles in this process. But one has to admit upon viewing these hidden worlds for the first time, the hand of mystery itself, has to have been involved in its creation. For nothing that easy to explain could create the sight these Marines saw.

The three caves did not interconnect with the other. True to what B had earlier reported, once inside, it had a limestone composition. This meant the interior could be leached away in vast quantities, leaving large cavernous spaces, decorated with spectacular formations of crystals, stalactites and stalagmites. And then the lights were turned on, all these were present in abundance, especially in the southern most cave. The ceilings were vaulted, but more so as the caves extended northward. The available floor space of the individual caves appeared to expand, as well, going from the southern to the northernmost cave. By the teams rough measurements, cave number one, as it came to be called, was about 200,000 feet^2, the middle cave, number two, was about 262,500 ft^2, and cave number three, at the northern end, was close to 280,750 feet^2. The colors inside varied from pure white, to yellow, to green and rose. You could spend time staring at one particular spot in any room and find wonder in the colors and shapes that were to be discovered.

Maybe, most importantly of all, upon their examination of the caves, was that there was essentially no odor present. It appeared to have been moisture free for countless millennia. This finding was a major relief to all the Marines. Each one, separately, as they admitted to each other later, was dreading finding the area dank, with uncontrollable and ever-present mold and mildew. They were all relieved at what they found.

By 1100 hours, when the three teams reassembled outside the cavern to report to Capt. Mendoza, it was clear there were only three caves. But, maybe with some excavation and tunneling, other areas could be found, and then it would be possible to artificially subdivide the three very large caves they just explored. In summary, they hoped between these two modifications, the cavern would accommodate the number of people, the special areas and all the storage that was needed. Only the engineers, once they came on scene, would really be able to determine this. To their surprise, the teams exploring both number one and number three caves had noticed that their inner walls, facing south and north respectively, had a hollow echo when they struck them. They hoped this might indicate a void existed behind each wall, which would give them the necessary extra room for the soon-to-come refugees.

Supplied with this information, Capt. Mendoza ate a quick lunch and left for his meeting in Amboy with Lt. Col. Black at 1300 hours. He made a quick sketch of what they had found thus far, but he wanted to wait to show it to anyone until the Engineers came tomorrow to have it verified, and they filled in their own projections and findings. Until they arrived tomorrow sometime, he would have his personnel continue to explore the area in and around the cavern. And, of course, the bulldozer operation was to continue non-stop.

By the time he got back from his meeting in Amboy, his staff was already setting up the new camp. An immense area had been cleared and prepared at the south end of the mountainside, housing the cavern. As he drove up, the bulldozer was now busily working on the roadway into each cave entrance. The operator had found an outcropping of decomposed granite that he was grading over the roadway to give it more firmness for the heavy traffic and usage to come.

Later that evening, aside from a hand or two of cribbage or poker, the unit was in bed and asleep by the time dusk turned to darkness. The emotional and physical effort to climb in and around the caves, and the growing awareness of all that had to be done, was exhausting. The men were drained. But this night's sleep was more restful for all.

All day February 7th, was divided between examining the interior of the cavern and the southern perimeter of the outside edge of the cavern complex to see where the best place might be for a possible tunnel. In their minds, it probably would serve more as an emergency exit, rather than have some functional use. Instead, the latter would prove its more valuable use. This same probing was done along the caves' interior walls, as they sought the most likely places where tunnels might be dug. Gradually, with rotating the lookouts and guards along the incoming roads from the north and south, doing the prep work along the roadbed around the cavern, and refining their findings along the interior and exterior cavern walls, the day passed quickly and some calm was being restored within the unit.

They knew the other units were to arrive around 2200 hours, so they spent considerable time enlarging and grooming the space for the four other command centers, their tents, latrines, supplies and equipment. When the other units did start showing up, the Recon group had even set up more flood lights and helped orient and direct the traffic into the prepared areas. While the new arrivals were getting settled in, the commanders of the four other commands met with Capt. Mendoza, and he briefed them on his unit's findings and shared with them his rough diagram of what they found inside the cavern. In the interest of time and effort, it was this same diagram, expanded on and filled in with more detail, which was used and eventually distributed to the incoming families during their final orientation before being transported to live in the complex. That diagram, too, is included in this material for any future reader to study. (see Appendix 1, diagram 7, "Cavern Complex with Chambers Shown") This is a photograph of that original hand drawing, which was found decades later inside a desk in the Communications Room of Cave # 5. (see Appendix 1, diagrams 2 and 3, "South Half of Providence Cavern"; diagrams 4 and 5, "North Half of Providence Cavern"; and diagram 6 for a schematic rendering, as well, of the caves.)

The other platoon commanders were: Capt. Margaret LaRue, Transportation; Capt. Eric Chan, Engineering; Capt. Ian Murphy, Medical; and Capt. Hasna Eunis, Communications. By 2345 hours that night each of them had enough information so that first thing in the morning they could begin to explore the cavern complex for themselves and then begin to assign duties and request whatever other equipment they needed that was not brought in that night. It was decided during this meeting that whatever unit was not fully engaged in working and setting up their own particular equipment, those extra Marines and Amboy personnel would be shifted over to the Engineering platoon for them to use however they needed them. It was obvious that Engineering had the most immediate objectives to meet. These needed to be completed before the other units could fully devote their full complement of personnel to their particular assignments.

By mid morning on February 8th, it was clear to Capt. Chan what had to be done immediately inside the caves: level and compact the floor surface of caves # 1, 2, and 3, excavate tunnels and enlarge cave entrances. He and eight other Marines left at noon for Amboy to meet with their representatives and help complete leveling the ground for their containers and teach them how to use the forklifts. They took a transport truck with them to bring back the bulldozers, given the amount of work that had to be done inside the caves. He hoped to be back by 1900 hours. In the meantime, he spoke with Capt. LaRue about her unit beginning to transport more earth moving and drilling equipment for tunneling. They needed all this immediately. That non-stop shuttling of supplies was begun at 0500 hours.

While Capt. Chan was in Amboy, the majority of his unit was setting up more flood lights, surveying for widening the cave openings and for building the roadways, the storage and living areas inside the caves. However, a few in his unit also began surveying for a possible well site outside the complex. It was determined it would be too difficult to attempt to drill inside one of the caves. And this same group began to plan and survey for an external sewer system. As hoped, Capt. Chan did return by 1915 hours, with two more bulldozers at their disposal. He ordered that his personnel were to begin working in shifts, around the clock. People from the other Marine units, and soon volunteers from the Amboy families, were enlisted to help with this 24 hour a day drilling and excavation.

Before Capt. Chan retired for the night, he needed to have one more walk through of the cavern. He had to make sure where the drilling for the tunnels was to be attempted and whether the leveling and road work was progressing according to plan. He was relieved to see that whatever formations that were water generated, developed long ago. It appeared it had been many thousands of years since the last major water source had invaded this area. And luckily, most of the formations were small and not in places that the bulldozers had to level. The ceiling did have 'tites', as the stalactites were soon nick-named, but they, too, appeared dry, secure and well out of the usual visual field. Some were actually used later for supporting the lights and the sound system. All in all, he was relieved that the amount of construction needed would not alter much of the beauty of this haven. But for the purpose for which the remodeling was being done, there was not much room anyway for regret. The work had to be completed.

A Communication Center was set up to allow linkage to both the Marine Base and to Amboy. As equipment and supply needs were identified, they were communicated immediately to Col Robert's and Lt. Col. Black's offices.

And by 2230 hours on February 8th, the convoy of Seabees arrived. Immediately, they and the Amboy personnel were separated into work shifts, and with the extra flood lights they brought, began drilling for water, excavating and building sewer lines and water lines. Likewise, some of their company was able to concentrate on tunneling and wall building inside the caves. With the addition of the 53 adults from Amboy, non-stop work was now insured. Overnight, the extra drilling equipment arrived so that by the morning of February 9th, two different drilling operations, in Caves #1 and #3, were underway to excavate into the voids that everyone was sure were there. Large exhaust fans were set up at all cave entrances to remove as much exhaust and dust from the interior. When possible, water trucks had been brought in to spray down the floor surface for compaction and dust suppression. By the morning of February 11th, the construction work at the Providence Cavern was fully under way.

And by that afternoon, the tunneling had broken through into the largest chamber, Cave #5, as it was later designated. It ultimately was calculated to have 675,000 feet^2. Once the tunnel was widened enough to allow passage of larger equipment, the surveying and leveling began. It had a towering, vaulted ceiling. The acoustics were astonishing. You could practically whisper at one end and be overheard at the other. And again, fortunately, it was dry inside as well. It was estimated the ceiling rose to a height of over 45 feet. Everyone agreed this cave would contain most of the complex's offices, classrooms, and assemble areas. The entire floor area was to be leveled, and two extra smaller tunnels were to be dug for emergency exits. Once the leveling was completed, construction of walls and classrooms would begin. And when the space for the medical services was completed, their staff would start stocking and equipping the area. The Communications Center would be set up once the dirty work was completed, which they hoped would be within another couple of days.

At the other end of the complex, Cave #1's south wall was thicker and took longer to breach. Once the tunneling was completed, they found a smaller cave of about 75,000 feet. Because its southern wall was an outside wall, it was decided to tunnel through it to the outside, for another emergency exit. Adjacent to this exit, it was decided that the Seabees would erect a reinforced warehouse to store and secure the rebuilding supplies and other large equipment once the cavern was sealed. It would have to be extremely large, by any standard, to accommodate all the supplies that were being delivered. It was decided that it would be three stories high, with a 150 feet by 250 feet footprint. Across from it, another, smaller storage building would be erected that would be flush with the mountain side. It, too, would be a three story structure, but with only 50 feet by 100 feet dimensions. Unlike the much larger warehouse, this one would have a four foot wide tunnel into Cave #4. It was hoped that the Seabees could finish these structures and the water and sewer systems by the end of February. Everyone, by now, understood the Seabees desire to leave as soon as possible to complete whatever modifications were needed at the Yucca Mountain Depository. The April 1st deadline haunted everyone constantly.

The living areas, where the modified shipping container homes were to be located, required very little construction, other than leveling and compacting their surfaces. The Engineers laid out three rows for 25 container homes each, with a wide space separating each row. The two living areas for the Marine families had five extra containers offset for the senior and junior officers.

However, it must be said, that after April 1st, it was unanimously agreed that rank had significance only as it might indicate someone had some leadership and organizational skills. Otherwise, everyone was equal. It was after that day that job duties were what mattered most. Civilian and military distinctions became blurred. It was not an official pronouncement that led to this. It was more just the need by these huddled survivors to feel equal in status and purpose. If a uniform helped identify a job that was fine. But it no longer empowered anyone over another. Rule of law did matter, and there were three judges amongst the survivors who would help reconstruct the governing guidelines. And eventually they would also help with the formation of laws of governance based on these guidelines. But any standing military, after that date, was more like a civilian law enforcement agency. Rank was replaced by a job title. MOS, or military occupational specialty, was replaced by a knowledge base and work skill.

The ability to teach that skill to others became as highly prized as the skill itself. This remnant's ultimate survival was dependent on teaching others what one does or did. To perform a job was important. But to be able to teach what you did was vital and beyond measure. If there was any status after April 1st, it was reserved for those who best taught others.

By February 20th, the next phase of building was nearing, involving construction of the interior walls, classrooms, toilet facilities and kitchens. The completion of much of this work was dependent on when the Seabees finished installing the plumbing into the caves. Once the sewer and water connections were capped off inside, the final work could be done on these facilities. It was hoped that by the middle of March these areas would be completed.

And for anyone who would have wandered, undetected, into this area during the next two weeks, they would have been astonished at the volume of traffic, activity and noise. It was a major construction site and assembly area, stuck out in the middle of nowhere. The two warehouses under construction at the south end of the cavern complex were the most obvious structures. Surrounding them were tents, earth moving equipment, stacks of boxes and shipping containers, and growing volumes of rebuilding supplies to be stored in the larger building. There were now four more days left for the Seabees to wrap up their projects.

By February 25th, the water lines were now connected to the freshly drilled well. The well had to be sunk over 2000 feet and had been measured to deliver a flow of 45 gallons a minute. That was not a high flow rate for the number of people if would serve, but with planning and some rationing, it would be much better than any other alternative. The Engineers were now connecting the water to the restroom and kitchen areas, but were still awaiting the delivery of appliances for these areas. And the sewer lines were also in place inside the caves. The sewer pumps, which were connected to one of two diesel powered electrical generators, were now attached to leach lines buried underground, extending down the mountainside. The water and sewer pump both worked off the same generator. The larger generator would provide the power to the interior of the caves. These generators were housed in a building abutting the external wall of Cave #1. There was a secure, enclosed walkway from the cave to that building, through which someone would maintain and refuel the generators. It would always be required that the individual wear a hazmat suit, due to the possibility of contamination from the outside environment. No one knew what to anticipate come April 1st, but this precaution seemed prudent. Fuel for the generators was buried underground next to their shelter, with easy access once someone was inside the small building.

By 1700 hours on February 27th, the finishing touches were completed on the largest warehouse and on the security doors into the various caves. The day before, the smaller warehouse was finished. It took the next four hours to break down and load up their vehicles, and by 2100 hours the Seabees had said their farewells to their Marine and Amboy comrades. Not knowing if or when they would ever see them again, with mixed emotions, they began their trip back to the Marine Base to be briefly with their families. They were understandably excited about seeing them, even for the short time allowed. Then they had to leave almost immediately for the Yucca Mountain Depository.

Having the Amboy families, with their engineers, scientists and just plain hard working individuals at the Providence Cavern added greatly to the success thus far in the reconstruction. And it started a process of merging the two bodies into a cooperative and cohesive whole. Ultimately, they all became inseparable. And as each phase was completed, or nearly so, inside and outside the cavern, e.g. the medical facility or the classrooms, their respective professionals began to work even harder and longer hours. It was only by the supreme effort of all the Amboy personnel, the Seabees and the Marines that their progress was so stunning. By the end of February, the external work was completed, aside from filling the warehouses with their assigned materials. With some relief, the general impression of everyone was that within the month ahead, they were guardedly hopeful they could meet the April 1st deadline.

TWENTY-SIX: DELIVERIES TO AMBOY

The delivery of three truck loads of food and beverages on February 6th was not even the tip of the supply deluge yet to come. Because Clem, Cynthia, and Fred had the best immediate grasp of what supplies were ordered, they became the unofficial directors of this operation. The families and coordinators of the four groups were still in enough shock that major coordination was just too stressful. So between that trio, they decided that all food and beverage supplies were to be unloaded by the school, and also where the 108 twenty foot long, empty containers were to be positioned for stocking the monthly ration of foodstuffs and liquids. In a separate area further east of the school, the sorting of personal and household supplies would be stocked into their respective containers. And on the far eastern and northern side of the school, they would have the 108 twenty foot containers for food once their cavern confinement ended. On the western side of the motel, in a large area yet to be cleared, the containers with rebuilding materials would be stored. They would not require any sorting. Whereas, the bulkier building materials coming by train, which were not in containers, would have to be stacked across the street from the motel complex, on either side of the post office. And that was where any large equipment would also be positioned.

That left deciding how the containers at the school would be stacked. The containers being transported from overseas with the families' possessions in them would be positioned just behind the containers to be filled with food. Given the steady uptick in heat each day, the food, personal, household and overseas' containers needed protection. It was decided that once the railroad delivered the 343 empty containers, they would stack the 235 being converted into living units on top of and around the others. To some degree they would serve as heat shields. Clem realized the railroad could deliver the empty containers any day now. Two or three trains passed through there each day already loaded with empty containers to be refilled at the docks in Los Angeles and Long Beach. And it wouldn't surprise him if one came tomorrow to be unloaded. He had also noticed that the Transportation unit was already beginning their round the clock transports to the cavern complex. With their pace of deliveries, he estimated they would start bringing the 108 empty containers from Pendleton within the next week. And he guessed it would take them seven days to complete that job, once they started. They would use their eight transports, each loaded with 2, twenty foot containers.

No one would be available for at least a couple of weeks to start modifying the containers as homes. By then, they hoped that there would be storage space available in the cavern for the filled food, personal, household, and overseas' containers. And at that time they could be transferred into their final berthing area in the caves. That would leave space and time for everyone to help with the remodeling of their soon-to-be homes. It was a leap of faith to think this way, but each one looked at the other and said, "What else do we have?"

Once the decisions were made how the containers were to be positioned and which to concentrate on first, the three planners focused on how it would be done and by whom. Deciding by who was the easy part; by everyone. And that included the family members from the Marine Base. They probably would need shuttle transportation to and from there, so Clem called General Stanfield to let him know of their request. He agreed wholeheartedly and said he would arrange round the clock bus transport and get family members to organize themselves. They agreed that the shuttle process should begin on February 8th. There would be one bus load arriving and departing every twelve hours.

The food, liquid, household and personal items would arrive on pallets. The supplies to be loaded into the monthly containers had to be taken off the pallets and hand loaded into the containers. This meant they had to form lines from the school storage area to the containers, along which packages would be passed from person to person. The extra supplies, for use when their confinement was over, would remain on the pallets and be quickly loaded into those containers by fork lift. And all this work, obviously, would have to be done both day and night. Flood lights from the Marine Base were requested for this activity. It was labor intensive, but Clem thought to himself, we all might as well get used to that. The future, beyond April 1st, would most likely be crowded with those kinds of days.

Sorting was the last issue before them. Depending on what the delivery was, e.g. food, personal or household, the supplies would be stacked in four different areas. From the staggering volume Clem had ordered, it was easy to predict that many deliveries would only have one or two different items to offload. The conveyer lines of men, women and children would start at each of these groups of items. From that point, Janice and Sid and their group decided how much of a particular item was loaded into each container for a month's usage. It was determined that a family of four would need approximately 38 feet^3 of food and personal items. For 26 families that amount would snugly fit in a twenty foot shipping container. The conveyer line would sweep from container to container until all 108 of the food containers had been loaded with the specified amount of that item. This same process would take place for the personal and household items being loaded into those thirty containers. All that was left of food and personal supplies, would remain on the pallets, then restacked to economize space, and loaded intact into the 108 standby containers. The priority now was the monthly food containers.

Once the three Amboy veterans had worked out this system of sorting and loading, they then set about informing the assembled families and group leaders. All the groups and their leaders, aside from the engineers, scientists and others who went to the cavern to help there, were eager to get started as soon as possible, as were the Marine Base families. Everyone, including the children, wanted to be involved in some way. Work and fatigue were preferred by all, over their having to worry and anticipate what lay ahead. It appeared Amboy was almost ready for the flood of goods that was about to descend on them.

By the afternoon of February 9th, there had been 35 more truck deliveries from food and building supply warehouses. Along with that, at 3:45 p.m. the east bound freight pulled onto the Amboy siding, loaded with 343 empty shipping containers, 235 that were forty-two feet in length and 108 that were twenty feet in length, to be removed as soon as possible. And, as anticipated, the train extended for two miles in length. Having been instructed in how to use the forklifts, the Amboy workers swarmed over the containers, releasing them from their moorings, and directing the forklift drivers in lifting and placing the containers off to the side. With the flood lights from the Marine Base available, they had it all unloaded by dawn on the 10th.

By 8:00 a.m. on the 10th, Clem and Fred were busy directing the repositioning of the already-delivered Marine Base containers and now the ones just delivered by the railroad. They were placed side by side, leaving no gaps, with the doors open toward the school. Eventually 108 lay in a huge semicircle around the school campus, with another 30 out beside them. At the same time the forty-two foot ones were placed on top for insulation. The rest, which would eventually serve as homes, were stacked in the cleared area east of the school, waiting to be stacked on the containers to be delivered from Pendleton.

The heat was a problem during the day. So it was decided that tarps would be erected along the pathway from the supplies to the containers. They would just serve as canopies, open on all four sides for ventilation. But at least they would provide shade. The workers would also rotate covering the place where the foodstuffs were being removed from the trucks. That would give shade to those individuals as well. Sid and Janice's group also directed the off-loading of the truck deliveries. During the day, the crews would work two hour shifts from 10 a.m. until 6 p.m. After 6 p.m., it would be four hour shifts through the night. Clem had made it a point to the shippers that deliveries could be made day or night. That meant that the flow of trucks was steady. More and more the families were having to become involved in directing where the trucks were to park, off load, then sort and record items received and which ones were then reloaded into the shipping containers for the cavern. Coupled with these chores was the scheduling of work crews. It was all voluntary, but then it really wasn't. It had to be done, and it had to be organized. Resting, sleeping and eating were only done when absolutely necessary. The only thing done on schedule was the work itself.

Ray and Hazel, once this process got underway, had to have food ready 24 hours a day. To do that, Clem and Cynthia became part of their staff, as did Rose and Harry. Rose's post office duties were now over. All mail was left at the Marine roadblock and then brought to the restaurant for Rose to supervise the sorting. Most of it was, obviously, for the newly arrived Amboy families. Rose had the smaller children help her with the sorting and getting the mail ready to be taken out to the Marines for sending off the next day. It was also the smaller children who Clem and Cynthia had help them with meal preparation, dispensing and clean up. They made it fun, and the children loved doing it. Many took to just sleeping in the back dining room when they weren't working. It helped them, too, to be busy and appreciated. Now that there was enough general organization of what had to be done and who was to do it, Fred was elected by Clem and Cynthia to oversee the process of checking that the proper goods were being delivered and collecting the shippers' invoices and bills of lading, once the deliveries were made.

The next stage in this whirlpool of supplies, equipment and containers swirling around Amboy was the arrival of the freight trainload of building supplies. On February 20th, at 6:30 a.m. everyone sleeping, eating, sorting or loading were startled by a long and continuous blast of a freight train whistle. In the Amboy valley, it echoed, unbroken off the surrounding rocky mountain sides, with the intensity of a hundred avalanches. The train engineer had for years wanted to do that somewhere. In any other setting it would have been a distress signal. But here, parked on a siding in Amboy, it was an announcement of arrival. The freight cars, again, extended for two miles behind the six locomotives.

For those who could remember their parents or grandparents telling them, it was like the circus train had pulled into town. Where the first train held no surprises, only empty shipping containers, this train was heaped with surprises and with the visible hope of maybe a new life to come. Everyone, absolutely everyone in Amboy, in the next few minutes rushed down to the tracks to greet the train. The train crew never had a clue what the materials were for that they were hauling. But it was equally exciting for them to see these hundreds of people pour down from the hillside toward their train.

Earlier, Fred had called Col. Roberts in Logistics and asked her if they could have two or three more smaller forklifts for both moving the pallets of supplies in the post-confinement containers and for eventually unloading the freight train of rebuilding supplies when it came. She had wholeheartedly agreed, and they arrived a few days ago. Soon they were driven from the school area down to the rail cars to begin unloading.

For most of the morning, while the fork lift drivers worked feverishly to unload one rail car at a time of lumber, bricks, plywood, insulation, piping, wind turbines and propellers, solar panels and frames, slate for roofing, coils of wiring and power poles and structural steel, many of the family members took time away from their grind of sorting and stacking. They stood and sat individually and in small groups, marveling at the wonderment of it all. There was not time to sort any of it. It was just a race to get it all off the freight cars as quickly and safely as they could. By nightfall, the cars were all emptied and the engineers, after a hearty dinner, left with another long blast of their whistle as they moved out of the valley.

Unsure what to do, Fred decided to call Capt.

Chan at the cavern to see if it could be arranged to move this material directly there without them having to try sorting and stacking it in Amboy. It was soon agreed that would be the plan. The three forklifts would also be transported there as well, once the final post-containment containers were filled with the pallets loaded with supplies. By February 28th, just when the Seabees had completed the warehouse construction, all the material from the train was relocated from Amboy, along with the forklifts and their drivers. They did not return to Amboy. They were, like others before them, permanently stationed there.

During the time leading up to February 28th, the activity in Amboy was frantic. Truck deliveries from the various vendors' warehouses, from the Marine Base near Amboy and from Pendleton poured in. There was a kind of rhythm to it all. Rather than it be called "the rhythm of life", the Amboy and Marine families described it as the "the rhythm of hope". Increasingly, the families, rather than descend into total despair and fatalism, became more united in their efforts to preserve life or at least make a heroic effort to record that it once existed, even if in the final reckoning, this may be its last chapter. Work gang songs began to be sung, some even original. Recorded music filled the school complex. None of it made the scene or work festive, but it did instill a sense of hope and determination.

And it was at this time that individual family members began to make telephone calls and to write their extended family and loved ones back home. It was time to say the things they had always wanted to. Nothing was said about April 1st or their preparations. But their messages of love and farewell were heartfelt and touching. Up to this time most had not communicated anything to anyone outside Amboy. Initially, the shock and sorrow were too much. This activity, as well, brought these families even closer together. Their shared knowledge and shared grief gave them needed comfort.

And by March 3rd, there were no more deliveries. Fred had recorded the last delivery two days earlier. And the list, compiled by Clem when he ordered everything a month ago, showed there was no more to come. And by 2:30 p.m. that day, everything was packed, labeled and sealed in the containers. It was time for them to be trucked to the caves for storage. Fred contacted General Stanfield to inform him they were done with this phase. The General said he would contact Transportation and arrange for more vehicles from the Base motor pool to help Capt. LaRue get the containers moved to the caves. It was his understanding that the areas in the caves were now ready for them. Within an hour, Capt.'s LaRue and Chan both spoke to Fred and said they would start the transfers by 1800 hours that night.

Once they removed all those containers, all that was left were the ones for the Amboy and Marine families' new homes in the cavern. They now had to be remodeled. Within the last two weeks, General Stanfield had arranged through Col. Robert's Command that lumber, insulation, dry wall, plywood and doors were delivered from the Base for this remodeling. Also delivered were as many saws, hammers, drills and welding units as could be spared. Now the Amboy and Marine families turned their attention to the remodeling job. The basic floor plan had been approved. There were 235 containers to convert into homes.

The process of remodeling was broken down into phases. This was because there was a nagging fear that they could not complete all the work before it was time to move the containers into the caves. First, the four welding units were put to work, cutting out a pattern for the front door and cutting a hole in the roof for a manually operated vent to the outside. To line and insulate the containers required that their original double door design had to be modified to a single, 36 inch door. Then plywood flooring was laid down, to eventually be covered with indoor/outdoor carpet and some thicker braided rugs. Next, there was the room partitioning, followed by insulating the walls and ceilings, and finally covering all that with drywall. And if there was time, the dry wall would be taped, sealed and painted. The welding was done in assembly line fashion, but the other work was divided into crews of five people to a container. There were 25 work crews, each devoting all their time to one container, once the welding was completed. They had until March 23rd to get as many completed, or nearly completed, as possible.

And it was about this time, during that first week in March, when Clem was strolling with Jake around the construction site, while a taking break from his kitchen duties that it occurred to him that throughout all this sorting, packing, and building, there had not been at least one major sand storm. Usually during this time of year, with the seasonal changes, the winds would become ferocious and whip sand and dust up so thick it reduced visibility to only a few feet. And then the sand and dust seeped into every crack and crevice. But there had been no wind storms. He muttered to himself, "B, do you have anything to do with that?" There was no reply, but Clem knew some unseen hand had to be helping to keep this overwhelming project on course. He marveled at how well Fred, Cynthia, Ray, Hazel, Rose and Harry had performed during all these last months. Now it was just three more weeks, and they had to be done and moved.

As a few housing units were completed, they were immediately transferred to the caves for positioning in the living areas. It was decided to place them in the back end of these areas first, working forward toward the kitchen area in unison. Everyone anticipated that the last minute rush to get everything inside would be easier, if all that was left to move in were the last front rows in each living area. By the third week in March, 175 units were completed and moved in. In an attempt to get the last ones done, or nearly so, by March 27th, the absolute deadline when everything and everyone had to be moved, all the people working in the caves, who had their jobs pretty well under control, except for maybe a few final details, were shifted back to Amboy to help hurry up the remodeling.

And it was around March 23rd, during that third week, when Fred and Clem were notified by Capt. Chan that, yes, animals and pets could be housed in a special cave area. There was a strict limit as to how many, but at least some could be kept there. Immediately, Clem made up notices, inviting all the children to a meeting that day at 11:00 a.m. in the restaurant. It announced:

"URGENT MEETING FOR ALL CHILDREN! PETS AND ANIMALS WILL BE ALLOWED!! COME TO RESTAURANT TODAY @ 11:00 A.M. FOR IMPORTANT MEETING."

Like that sand and dust Clem was dreading, this news was everywhere fifteen minutes after the notices were posted. Come meeting time, the restaurant had every child, teenager, and soon-to-be an adult in Amboy eager to hear the news. To have animals along for this journey of possible endless waiting and wondering whether you were going to survive its outcome, gave a tangible thread of hope to each of them. To them, it was like what an old wood-burning, kitchen stove used to be to families, the center of what it meant to be in a home.

So it was with these younger residents of the cavern. Animals, and the possibility of caring for them, gave each child there that same feeling of building a homestead, if not now, at least in the future.

The meeting was chaired by Clem, with Fred and his children taking notes, counting votes, and keeping Clem on track. Once it was established that as far as pets were concerned, there could only be six pair of male and female dogs and six pair of cats. All had to be just weaned puppies or kittens, and each member of the pair had to be from different blood lines. Furthermore, there was a limit on the type and number of farm animals that could be chosen. It had been determined that the following would be allowed: two pairs of ponies, two pairs each of dairy and beef heifers and young bulls, two pairs of lambs, two of goats, two of donkeys, two of piglets and two dozen chicks. The animal pairs also had to be from separate blood lines. They had to be available from the immediate area. And their choices were limited to whatever Fred and his family could quickly and easily locate. Having lived in the area for some time, it was decided that Fred would be the best one to do the searching and purchasing of the animals, their pens, cages, feed and bedding.

Clem then first called for nominations and voting for the breeds of dogs and cats that Fred would have to try and purchase in the next two days. After much discussion, the choice for dogs was: Black and Brown Labradors, Golden Retrievers, German Shepherds, Border Collies, and Blue Healers. For cats, they chose: Tabbies, White and Yellow Persians, Blue Maltese's, Blacks and Siamese's. For the animals, the children expressed only preferences, if Fred had the opportunity to get them: Jersey and Holstein dairy cows, Angus and Hereford beef cows, Belgium and Appaloosa horses, Border Leicester sheep, Nubian goats, Mammoth donkeys, Duroc pigs and Rhode Island Red's and Barred Plymouth Rock's for chickens.

For daily cleaning and maintenance, twelve empty dumpsters were to be positioned in the pen area, with the hope that one dumpster per month would serve to hold the bedding and manure from the pets and animal pens. Once full, each would be sealed and quickly pushed out the southernmost cave's exit, through the double doors, by someone in a hazmat suit. It would then roll down the hillside of its own accord. Each month would be the same. Caring for, cleaning, grooming, and feeding all the animals would be left to the children. Veterinarian supplies and text books on care of animals would be purchased by Fred. But it would be up to the children and, if necessary, maybe a volunteer from the medical staff, to help with management of the animals' health and welfare. Without hesitation, they all yelled in agreement and appreciation. They were as energized as Clem had ever seen them.

And for the next three days Fred and his family worked the area in and around Barstow to fill their shopping list of pets, animals and supplies. In each place where something was purchased, the seller had to agree to bring the animal or supplies to Amboy on March 26th. If it was any later, for any reason, there would be no purchase. That day came, and with it came an endless parade of animals, their cages, stalls, pens, their bedding, tack, their feed in boxes, sacks, bales, their medicines and instructions on care and maintenance of them.

Having arranged beforehand, Fred had personnel from Capt. LaRue and Capt. Murphy's respective units there to inspect, ok, and transport the animals, their supplies and equipment immediately to Cave #4. Along with the animals, went a contingent of the children to begin establishing a routine of caring for them. The supplies were to be located in the smaller warehouse at the south end of the cavern, the one with the tunnel connecting Cave #4 to the warehouse. By nightfall on March 27th, all the gear and animals had been transferred from Amboy to their new home. It had been a complete success. The effect on the children's morale was immeasurable. And major credit went to Alfred and Dada for their recognizing the potential importance of such a venture.

TWENTY-SEVEN: THE FINAL PUSH

The last full week of March was filled with anxiety, both expressed and hidden. There seemed so many loose ends. So much had been accomplished. But leaving undone almost anything now jeopardized their potential for survival. Everyone, by now, knew that their long- term existence in the cavern, and the success of any sustainable rebuilding after leaving it, hinged on so many unknown and unknowable factors. They had to keep reminding each other to keep working, to stay focused only on the present day's work schedule. Drifting too far into the unknown was like yelling "fire!" in a large, crowded and enclosed space. It created panic and despair. So with renewed energy, both the Amboy and Marine Base families rededicated their efforts for this last week, in the hope of getting everything accomplished.

To start this week, on March 23rd, at 0900 hours, there was the much anticipated meeting in the Marine Base Chapel for all the Marine, Air Force, Seabee, Coast Guard, Army and Navy families. The active duty family members were either at the Providence Cavern or at the Yucca Mountain Repository. And they had tried to prepare their family members, somewhat, without knowing all that was going to be said. They did anticipate, however, that for many of them their deployment would come after this meeting.

By 0900 hours, the Base Chapel was overflowing with spouses and their children. Sitting in the front was General Stanfield and Clem. To the surprise of all present, it was not General Stanfield who rose first to address them. It was a civilian, dressed in a business suit. To those families who had been doing shift work in Amboy, they only recognized Clem as one of the restaurant helpers.

Clem began the meeting announcing, "My name is Clement Newberry. I live in the Amboy area, as some of you know. My purpose of being here this morning is to introduce you to today's speaker. Honestly, though, I have nothing specific to tell you about the speaker, other than both General Stanfield and I have absolute trust in whatever we are told. Otherwise, it is all a mystery to me. All I know is that the importance and truth of what you will hear today is beyond questioning."

To this introduction, there was a rising murmur of protest. It was a reaction Clem had witnessed repeatedly before. Their time was being wasted listening to this man. Why didn't General Stanfield address them instead? He, at least, knew what he was talking about. Increasingly, there was more shifting and sounds of discontent.

Then, as if it were all staged, which Clem and the General believed that it was; B appeared beside Clem. The growing protest suddenly stopped and was replaced with a stunned silence. Everyone, children included, were transfixed, before them now stood a shapeless, dark form, with no distinguishing features. And then the form spoke.

"Please," B began. "Please understand that at this moment you are in no danger whatsoever. My presence here and the reasons for my arranging with General Stanfield and Clem to have you come here today are life-saving and life-sustaining only. Your spouses have been engaged over these past weeks in a desperate attempt to build facilities that all of you can now go to for refuge from an impending disaster of worldwide consequences. And many of you, whose spouses are working at the Providence Cavern, have yourselves been working non-stop in Amboy in preparation for this deployment.

"Before each of you leaves today, I would ask that you allow Clem or General Stanfield to shake your hand, by doing so you will experience a calm and peace that will see you through the next few days and beyond. That transformation is my gift to you. It will help you persevere in these final days before April 1st, when something beyond comprehension will occur.

"My hope is that your loved ones and you will be spared. But I cannot give you any guarantees that will be the case. Everything possible, in the timeframe given us, has been done to try and insure your survival. Many of you here will be flown later this evening to Nevada by your loved ones. From where you land, you will be transported to the Yucca Mountain Repository for long-term habitation. The families of the Marines stationed here will be bused to a facility in the Providence Mountains east of Amboy on the 27th at noon. By that time all of you will be reunited with your spouses. You will stay in these locations for a period of six months to a year. You have already packed your valuables and belongings for such a stay. You just did not know what you were preparing for or where exactly you were being sent.

"And let me say right away, under no circumstances can you, or should you, communicate this information to anyone outside this group and your spouses. To do so will mean the assured death of all of you assembled here. Not by my hand, but by the terrible hand of panicked mobs. For the sake of all civilization, tell no one what you are doing. Others before you have known, even some of you and your spouses, but everyone has been sworn to absolute secrecy.

"I now want each of you to stand, while General Stanfield and Mr. Newberry walk to the back of the Chapel. As you walk out slowly, shake one of their hands. And for the families whose spouses are not stationed here, you are to come back here with your packed suitcases by 1800 hours to be transported to the Base airfield where your flights will be waiting to take you to your new home. Please complete your packing today. And for those being bused to the Providence Mountains near here on the 27th, there will be one last orientation meeting with General Stanfield and his officers before you leave for your new home. For each of you, I offer my hope that your journey is safe. Do not be surprised if you should see me again in the future. My concern for your survival and welfare will be more visible in the time to come. For now, pray for your loved ones, and for all the living."

Speechless and numbed to the depths of their souls, each individual quietly filed out of the Chapel, shaking either Clem's or the General's hand. And as they had been told, with touching either individual, an immediate sense of well being, connectedness and calm came over them. It was intended by B to confirm what they had been told, and it succeeded. Along with the calming effect, there was also a deeper understanding.

By 1130 hours this same day, the furniture, which had been assembled at the Marine Base Transportation Depot from empty or soon to be empty living quarters, was now ready to be transported to the caves. Truck load after truck load was filled and drove off. Upon arrival at the entrances of Caves #1, 2 and 3, each load was quickly emptied. After the drop off, everyone in the cavern complex stopped what they were doing and started shuttling furniture to each container home. Beds, chairs, tables, and shelves were quickly set inside each unit. Individual placement of the furniture was to be left up to each family when they finally all arrived. As with relocating the container homes into the caves from Amboy, the furniture was likewise placed first in the rearmost homes, then proceeding forward. It took the rest of the day to complete this transfer from the Marine Base.

Meanwhile, again on the same day, at 1:30 p.m. in Amboy, another meeting was being convened. All 75 families had to have an adult representative present for this meeting. And it was assumed that all the children presently in Amboy would be there as well. Chairing this meeting were the coordinators for the two groups assigned to address the physical and emotional welfare of the families. As the main dining room filled with family members, Dada, Albert, Theresa and Philip took their seats in front. People either sat or stood, as room allowed. It was noisy up until the time Albert called the meeting to order. His booming voice then commanded attention.

In a voice that was now easily recognized, he spoke in a perfectly cadenced rhythm, his enunciation revealed a bit of British influence sometime in the past. "Ladies, gentlemen, distinguished guests, and all our children, let me have your attention, please. We have some items of business to take care of today. And the reason we are meeting now is because soon we will be rushing to complete last minute details, and it will be impossible to gather everyone together like this. For any of your loved ones not here today, please pass along the material you receive and the instructions you hear. Regimentation is not our goal. But in order to establish modest livability, even survivability, we have to set up some guidelines for all of us to follow. Additions and modifications of these will no doubt be forthcoming when the Governing Body is formed, and it begins to meet, once we are established in the cavern. But let me begin.

"Clem and Cynthia will be circulating through you, passing out a diagram of the cavern and your living quarters. (see Appendix 1, diagram 7, "Cavern Complex with Chambers Shown") On it there are notations of where various daily functions will occur. You will note where your new sleeping quarters will be by the heading, "Living Area". (see Appendix 1, diagram 1, "Floor Plan for Converted Shipping Container Living Quarters") Your exact quarters will be assigned once we all are transferred there on the 27th. And for your information, it will be a random process, consisting of numbering the 75 home sites, and putting those numbers in a container for you to draw from. Please study this map, of sorts. It will help you to not be so disoriented once you get to our new home. At a later date we will be giving you updated and permanent drawings of your quarters (see Appendix 1, diagrams 2-6, "South Half and North Half of Providence Cavern" and the "Schematic").

"Along with the diagrams they have handed out, there is a sheet that outlines some issues that I will discuss briefly with you now. The first item on that handout is that all children will be going back to school on April 8th. There will be two different school programs. One is teaching general subjects, 'the three R's', if you will. But mind you, it will all be accelerated. The second teaching program is an apprenticeship, which starts for everyone ages eleven or older. It does not replace the first program. Call it their laboratory for on-the-job training, if you'd like. It is imperative we pass on our skills and knowledge, and to do so will require we begin actual skill development early in their curriculum. None of us know what our life expectancy will be in this new world, we will soon be facing. One of our most important, if not the most important, obligations is to teach and pass on our skills to the next generation. There are classrooms, a laboratory of sorts and a library being built to aid in this teaching. But understand that our teaching does not end in these areas. We must be instructing all the time, with whatever we may be doing, no matter how insignificant it may appear.

"Shelves are being built in the areas marked on your diagram, "communal area". In these you are to stock the food, liquid and personal items from each month's supply containers. There can be no stealing or hoarding. We hope there will be enough food, etc. for everyone to meet their basic needs. Stealing and hoarding would be like a disease. It, as sure as any communicable disease, would insure the death of us all. I don't feel we need to police each other. But I do feel we need to know the consequences of anything of this nature. It cannot happen. We have to work and live on the honor system.

"There will be diesel fuel stored in large bladders in two places. One storage place will be in the small warehouse next to Cave #4. The other place will be buried underground by the block house where the electrical generators are, outside Cave #1. It is adjacent to the pump house for our well. This fuel is primarily for our electrical generators. We have personnel who are assigned to manage and fill the generators on a regular basis. The generators will provide the power for the scattered lighting and outlets inside the cavern, and for the well and septic pumps. You will find there is adequate lighting throughout the cavern during waking hours. But it will be much less during what would be our traditional night time. Otherwise, you will not have any cues for night and day. If we don't provide this prompting, each of us will become progressively more sleep deprived and develop various illnesses. Observe the light sequencing, and make sure to get your sleep when they are dimmed.

"For circulation and filtering the air within the cavern, there have been blowers installed in the rear of each cave and exhaust fans at all the exits. They will be turned on for 15 minutes at the end of each day to evacuate the accumulated fumes and odors for that day. There are scrubbers and HEPA filters also scattered through the cavern, particularly in the Medical Facility. Monitoring will be ongoing to insure the air is not getting stagnant or dank. Let someone know if you sense a change or become uncomfortable with the air.

"As you see, the kitchen facilities are in the front of Caves #1, 2, and 3. They had to be located closest to the water source and sewer outlets, just as you see for the toilet and shower facilities. The kitchen is the only area in which there will be some hot water available. There will be none anywhere else. There will be propane tanks stored in the small warehouse for use on an "as needed" basis to heat water or whatever else may be necessary, e.g. a medical emergency. But to lessen the fire dangers and for obvious practical reasons, hot water availability became a luxury. In order to lessen the chances of dysentery and food poisoning, we decided there had to be hot water available where food was prepared and dishes washed.

"Meal preparation, eating, and clean up will all be done in that immediate "Communal Area". Each family, within their group of 25 families, will rotate, for a specified period of time, the duties of meal preparation and clean up. I might suggest a week's tour of duty for the assigned period. It would allow each family time to get into the flow of the job. Certainly, others can and should pitch in to help. That will be the order of the times, from henceforth.

"There will be a Governing Body selected that each of you will have an opportunity to vote on at least once while we are occupying the caves. Each major group represented, the Amboy and the Marine families, will have their own representatives for now. For the Marines there will be six at large representatives, one from each of the 25 family Living Area compounds, five of their senior officers and five of their junior officers. That will bring their total number of representatives to 16. The Amboy families will have three at large representatives from their 25 Living Area compounds, four of the coordinators from the already established work groups, the three judges who are part of the 75 families, and Fred Wailand, who will also act as the recorder and moderator, until one is voted on from their midst. That brings their total of representatives to 11. In addition, it has been suggested that our children have a chance to be represented within this body, in order that their own wants, needs and ideas get a full hearing. For now, they can choose three representatives, one from the Amboy and two from the Marine families. That will make a grand total of 30 individuals in the Governing Body. It will start meeting as soon after April 1st, as the members are elected.

"It should be noted that there is an Office Area set aside, from which the Governing Body will conduct its business and use in any way it sees fit. It, and the Communication Center, are located in the same area, and are open to all of us, but only certain individuals will have dedicated access to these areas. It's simply a practical matter. There isn't enough room for all of us to circulate freely in these areas.

"And, finally, I have to say that I am not going

to ask for questions at this time. The reason why? I won't have any answers. I probably have as many questions and doubts as you do right now. But only by our actual presence in these caves can we begin to sort out the details. It's all unheard of, and we have no blueprint to use for what happens next. Please, as you have been, be diligent, be of good will towards others, share your hopes and fears, comfort each other, pray and hope. We will soon be moving into the cavern complex, and at that time we will have to find answers to our unanswered questions and concerns. Be here at 10 a.m. on the 27th, with your personal belongings. And we will have buses available to transport us to our new home. May God, whoever and wherever that Being may be, watch over all of us and our extended loves ones, and all of humanity in the days ahead. Thank you for your patience today."

This ended the various meetings on March 23rd. Whatever lingering doubts existed prior to this day in the military and Amboy families were now mostly replaced by somber resignation that their lives were to begin a voyage of unbelievable change and mystery.

Come March 27th, at 6 a.m., there were transport vehicles waiting in Amboy to move the last of the remaining 25 remodeled containers to their location in the Living Areas of the caves. Some were fully completed, but about ten were only partially so. These last units were to be for the senior and junior Marine officers and their families. It was hoped that these containers would be finished by April 1st, once these families were transferred to the cavern. These containers had to be moved today.

By 9 a.m. Cynthia had loaded some treats for her mom in her car, and she told everyone in the restaurant "Goodbye" for the next two days. She wanted to drive to Culver City, this one last time, to check on her mom and say her farewells. Clem suggested he would be glad to go along, just to keep her company and maybe share in the driving. But she declined, saying it would be a good time to clear the cobwebs, and besides, she loved to drive. Clem, of all people, understood the importance of needing to be alone at times. So, he awkwardly, but with great affection, gave her a hug, closed her car door, and waved her off down the road, as she maneuvered her way through the Marine roadblock. Clem thought she seemed unusually bright and cheerful today. Seeing her mom was important to her. My, he thought, how he liked that lady.

Come 10 a.m. there were now 10 buses waiting outside the Highway 66 Motel to transport the Amboy families to their new home. It was not a joyful atmosphere. Even the children knew this moment was different. They were pensive, seeking shelter in their parents' arms.

The 1200 hours meeting in the Marine Chapel for the families coming to the cavern covered the same material, with the diagram and guideline handouts, that Alfred had presented to the Amboy families on the 23rd. This meeting was led by General Stanfield. He felt it required his presence to emphasize the gravity and his involvement in this deployment as well. His family and those of the other four senior and junior officers were also in attendance. Alfred had reviewed with him the instructions and information he had given the Amboy families. And the General elected to stay on that same script as well. What else could he tell them? He knew very little else himself. And like the Amboy families, the Marine families were left drained once his presentation was over. At the conclusion, he bid everyone there God's speed on this upcoming journey and concluded with a soul-searching prayer for the strength and hope they would need. By 1445 hours, all except the Marine officers' families had boarded the same buses that had just moved the Amboy families. A few more buses needed to be drafted for the increased number of people, and within an hour, everyone was aboard and headed to the Providence Cavern. The officers' families were to wait until the last day to leave the Marine Base.

Then, at 3:26 p.m., a California Highway Patrol Officer called the Highway 66 Restaurant in Amboy, asking to speak with Clement Newberry. The individual told Ray, who initially answered the telephone, that there had been an accident on Interstate 10, east of Santa Monica, and that one of the individuals involved in that accident had listed Mr. Newberry as the person to be notified in case of an emergency. Reacting with shock and fearfulness, Ray turned to Clem, who was busy at the time finishing the last clean up from the families having their last meal in the restaurant.

"Clem," Ray called out. "There is a telephone call here for you. It sounds important. It's the California Highway Patrol."

Puzzled, then alarmed at such a call any time, but not being aware that Cynthia had listed him as her person to be notified in case of an emergency, he hurried over to the phone and answered, "Yes, I am Clem Newberry. To whom am I speaking?"

"My name is Sgt. Richard Dawkins. I am with the Downtown Los Angeles Division of the California Highway Patrol. Do you know a Cynthia Garr, Mr. Newberry?"

"Yes, I do," Clem answered, now with his knees beginning to weaken and his voice cracking. "She is a dear friend of mine. Is something wrong? Has something happened to her?"

"I am sorry to have to inform you, Mr. Newberry, that Ms. Garr was killed this afternoon in an accident on the Santa Monica Freeway. She was struck by an individual who was driving a stolen car and was evading our Patrol cars, going the wrong way on the freeway. She died instantly in the crash."

To this, Clem had no response, other than a low, mournful, heart-wrenching moan. He slumped down to the floor by the counter, still holding the telephone. "Are you still there, Mr. Newberry?" the Officer asked quietly.

"Yes," Clem whispered. "I am."

"Ms. Garr had listed a funeral home in Barstow, California. Would you like us to contact them, and have them make arrangements with our people here to have her body transported there?"

"Please," was all Clem could say.

"I am sincerely sorry for your loss, sir, and I am so sorry that you have to be informed like this. You have my sincerest apology and condolences."

"Thank you," was again all that Clem could manage to say, and he handed the telephone back to Ray.

Clem quietly, and with great effort, told Ray and Hazel, who had recently come into the area sensing something was very wrong, that Cynthia had been killed in a wreck on a freeway in Los Angeles. He mumbled something about the other driver going the wrong way in a stolen car. But, by now, he was so distraught, that the words were almost incoherent. He rose and walked slowly to the front door of the restaurant, where Jake was lying. Without a word, both Clem and Jake walked out the door together, both grateful, but each for different reasons, that at this moment Amboy was quiet again.

Man and dog walked aimlessly up the hillside behind the restaurant. Once they got to an outcrop of rocks, Clem sat down and began to cry. Certainly, the main reason for his crying was the tragic loss of his dear friend, Cynthia.   Also, he was so moved that she appointed him her person to notify in an emergency. It was, to him, the highest honor he could imagine someone bestowing on someone else. And probably he cried from sheer exhaustion.   Cynthia had been his source of motivation and comfort over these last months. Not being an overly religious man, he needed tangible proof that goodness was present in this world. She had provided that proof. And at this point, even B, who had watched over Clem, as well, these past months, elected not to intrude on his grief. Only Jake, who increasingly only spoke rarely, even with Clem, just lay quietly beside him. Directly, Clem sighed and said, "Well, Jake, you and I have a trip to take in a couple of days. We'll need to go to Barstow. Then we'll need to make some decisions after that.   Come on," he said standing. "Cynthia would want us to see this through. Somehow, I feel she is still here guiding us."   And to this, B, still invisible to them both, simply nodded in agreement.

March 28th passed too quickly. Everyone at the cavern was now aware the days seemed to be picking up speed, closing in on the April 1st deadline. There was still so much left to do. And inside the cavern, with nearly all the families inside, it was close to chaos. The level of noise was something no one had predicted. And the public address system was not yet operational, due to the speakers still being installed throughout the caves, in the Main Auditorium and in the Classrooms. This left no way to broadcast the need for everyone to lower the volume, to talk softer, to avoid yelling, and to set items down with less force.

But somehow before the day was over, the last of the equipment, forklifts, scattered containers with rebuilding supplies stored in them, wood and sheeting left over from remodeling the living units still in Amboy were picked up and transported to the cavern. All the largest equipment was driven into the bigger warehouse. The stacks of bricks and slate were stacked outside it. They were to be used for exterior facing and roofing once the rebuilding of traditional style homes was possible. The only space left in the large warehouse, now that all the materials delivered by the railroad were in there, was for the emergency vehicles yet to come from the Marine Base.

And finally, by evening, shelving was being built in the communal areas for miscellaneous storage. Luckily, there had been enough plywood to do this that was delivered earlier in the day. It gave the area a more home-like atmosphere, not having bare cave walls wherever one looked. And in that same vein, the two very large wall 'posters', much larger than the ones Clem ordered for the inside of each container home, were lightly framed to prevent curling, and hung in the Main Auditorium. One was a magnificent ocean coastline scene at sunset; and the other was a verdant, snow capped mountain, hovering over a deep valley, with scattered waterfalls cascading onto the valley floor.

The day had been frantic.

But come March 29th, there was still more storing of supplies in the cavern to be done. The bales of straw and alfalfa hay, along with sacks of feed had to be moved into the smaller warehouse. Twelve empty dumpsters, brought from the Marine Base, were rolled into Cave #4 and stored against its north wall. One of them was then moved closer to the pens and stalls, housing the calves and ponies.

The health care personnel began to organize the supplies and equipment for their facility, while teachers and instructors were doing the same thing in their various classrooms. There now was available light in all these areas, with the final wiring completed. And in the space dedicated for the library, shelves would be built from the wood delivered yesterday from Amboy. They were essential to accommodate the hundreds, even thousands, of books, papers, abstracts, and journals that everyone had gathered together to store for future use and reference.

By late morning, Clem left for Barstow with Jake riding beside him. This was only Jake's second ride in a vehicle. The first was when he was abandoned outside Amboy four years ago. He and Clem were silent. Jake did note that Clem was prone to talk out loud to himself. It was like he gave himself directions and guidance on what he had to do next. It probably came from him being alone all those years at his cabin. Soon the two of them were settled in and just rode along quietly. Their presence comforted the other.

Clem arrived at the McKissick Funeral Home in Barstow at around noon. He was ushered into a darkened room, where a casket was open, ready for viewing. Looking inside, he saw that Cynthia's body was there. There were no visible signs of the car accident. Clem, in an act of simple love and affection, bent forward and gently kissed her forehead, then whispered "How much I will miss you, fellow traveler. I pray you are at peace and with your loved ones. How I wish you could have stayed with us. It is so lonely without you nearby. Goodbye, my sweet."

And after some time just sitting beside her casket, Clem finally rose and spoke with the Funeral Director. It was agreed they would deliver her casket to Amboy tomorrow morning. Clem offered to pay for the expenses, but apparently Cynthia had already prepaid all the necessary fees. That done, with great effort and resignation, he returned to his truck. There, he found Jake asleep, and not wanting to wake him, they drove back to Amboy, one last time before April 1st, in mournful silence.

By March 30th, all ten of the senior and junior Marine officers, the remaining, preselected Medical staff at the Base Hospital and all their respective families convoyed from the Base to the Providence Cavern. They took with them a fire engine and two ambulances, each fully equipped. Once at the cavern, these emergency vehicles were driven into the largest warehouse, covered with plastic wrap, and the doors of the warehouse were sealed and welded shut.

However, just prior to everyone in this party leaving the Marine Base, General Stanfield had the baby grand piano, that was kept in the Base Auditorium, loaded onto a tractor trailer, and it was brought with them as well. By nightfall, after the piano was painstakingly unloaded and moved into Cave #5, it was placed on the stage in the Main Auditorium. The General had kept his word.

Clem, in the meantime, had one last cup of coffee with Ray, Hazel, Rose and Harry. He pleaded with them for the twentieth time to come with him to the cavern for their safety. But neither couple would change their minds. They both explained to Clem, again, that Amboy was their home. And this is where they belonged, no matter what might happen. But they did acknowledge they were proud to have been a part of what had been accomplished over these last months. For now, they preferred to pass whatever time they had left quietly and with each other. Clem, deep down, agreed whole-heartedly with them, but selfishly, he wanted their company beside him during what was ahead. But they were unmoved. Instead, they said that he must take Jake with him. Jake and Clem, they knew, had a bond that was unique, and each would provide companionship to the other.

The Funeral Director delivered the casket Clem had requested. Now it was time to load it into the back of his pickup and make his own way to Providence Cavern. Ray and Harry helped him lift it onto his truck bed. And Jake jumped up beside the casket and made it clear he wanted to stay there. Then, with little ceremony, this brave, unheralded little band, each hugged Clem and said their goodbyes. Driving away toward his cabin, Clem looked back in his rearview mirror, and watched them, as they stood in the middle of Route 66, waving at him until he was out of sight. It was a scene he never forgot.

It was dusk by the time he left his cabin, where he picked up some blankets for himself and Jake, some extra clothes, and pictures of his wife and son. By nightfall, he finally pulled into the complex. That night he slept in the truck, parked away from all the construction area. He had brought a pick and a shovel from the cabin and needed to get up early the next morning to complete the job ahead.

March 31st was, for all purposes anywhere else on the planet, except at the Yucca Mountain Repository and here at Providence Cavern, like any other day. But for these two facilities, it was their last day to prepare and then to shut, seal and lock the Repository and largest cavern doors. The two smaller doors into Cave #4 and # 1 would still be accessible to the outside world, but only under very strict and limited circumstances.

Clem awoke just before sunrise and picked out a spot for Cynthia's burial plot some distance away from the cavern complex. It was on a bluff, and yet he could still back his truck up to the spot and easily lower her casket from the truck bed to the ground. After backing up, he got out his pick and shovel and began digging. But it wasn't long before he was noticed. Clem was a favorite in Amboy and certainly not unrecognizable to the Marine families either. Word got around quickly what he was doing. And soon Fred heard. He promptly gathered up Freda and his daughters and ran out to where Clem, unaware of the commotion going on around him, was steadily digging. Before too long, each was helping him dig and then helped him gently lower her casket into the grave site. Before the casket was covered, everyone took turns honoring her with some final words. It was an overpowering memorial, given the location and the circumstances. When done, they sat on the bed of Clem's truck and looked for the longest time out into the valley below them. They were all aware that whatever was going to happen in the next 24 hours, it would forever change that same breathtaking view.

By 1800 hours, the Marines at the roadblocks were called in. They parked their vehicles outside the larger warehouse, there being no further room inside to store them. When they and any other personnel doing the final check of the perimeter of the cavern were done, and Clem and his party came inside, the doors to all the entrances where closed and locked shut. Once everyone was inside, an announcement was made by Fred over the Public Address System for each family to do a head count, making sure all their family members were present or accounted for. Within an hour, the word came back to the Office that all 941 people were accounted for, plus one large dog. Jake and Clem were the final entrants into the complex. The preparations were over.

PART V

TWENTY-EIGHT: APRIL 1ST

Maybe it was when terrorism took on significantly new tactics outside the core Middle Eastern countries that it signaled a shift in the destiny of civilization.   Maybe it was something that happened more than 2000 years ago, or in the Eleventh Century or in 1948, but nothing before this spread of suicide attacks in every Western nation did a collective sense of revenge take hold.   Revenge has to be the most violent motivation in humanity's closet of emotions.   It can know no boundaries

Moreover, many of the so-called Western countries left themselves open to more vicious attacks. Democracy, by its very design, is an engraved invitation to deranged beings set on self-destruction and the taking of innocent lives.   Coupled with that was the pathological lack, in some of these countries, of at least trying to make foreign entry and long-term residence more secure. The public and political will to do so was side-tracked. The price of keeping safe and secure was left to a very few and their sacrifices and efforts were noble, yet insufficient, without the involvement of all the people.

Now, there were multiple murderers from every

country and belief, for any cause or agenda, using whatever method that would harm the most innocents. Explosives were often being replaced with chemical and biological agents, whenever possible. And any place where people gathered was a target, anywhere.

It was during this time that a large group of these murderous, underworld dwellers emerged from their putrid, dark world and were finally able to buy, steal, and kill enough to secure nuclear weapons, the most lethal ones. And, happily for them, they were miniaturized, perfect for packing in almost any size container that would normally handle a ton of weight. The metal overseas shipping containers were perfect. Packed in a two feet of solid lead, they were absolutely undetectable by any ordinary detection system. But that was not so much a worry for them. Now there were other ways to get this devastating material around and through border crossings without detection. That had all been worked out with years of dummy shipments across all borders.

Arrangements had been finalized and the containers were on their way to 122 major cities in Asia, Africa, Middle, South and North America, Australia and New Zealand. The objective of this attack was to devastate the targeted regions' infrastructures and so destabilize them that certain religious and political factions could take over in the chaos that resulted. The triggering device was a novel motion detector and timing device that would not trigger until April 1st, worldwide. More specifically, on that day, global detonation would be at noon, Eastern Standard Time, in New York City. Manifests had been meticulously written to insure quick and timely delivery of each container. For each target city, it would be the first port of entry for that container. To insure this coordination, shipments began leaving the staging area on March 18th. There was great excitement among the planners. It was less than three weeks until they would take control and enforce a change of rule and order. Now all they had to do was wait.

What follows from here is taken from scattered firsthand accounts of people who somehow initially survived this attack and the subsequent impact. These accounts are sometimes from the survivors, but most often they were gleaned from bits of paper, tape recordings, and journal entries, on anything imaginable that someone could write on. Many were stuffed in containers to try to preserve their messages. But, most importantly, there were the observations and photographs from outer space. It took decades to collect and piece together that terrible time. Even now, building on the earlier work of Fred Wailand, the reporter and earliest historian after the Emergence, there are still major gaps in what happened. The following is the most complete description to date.

As was planned, at noon on April 1st, EST, from a loading dock in Jersey City, New Jersey, there was a sound so terrifying and loud, that for any who might later recall, it was like the earth was splitting in half. Next, there was a sound of in-rushing air, an immense sucking noise, of supersonic speed, followed by a blinding phosphorous light and finally the explosion, wind and fireball. All of the metropolitan New York City area, the New Jersey harbor cities along the Hudson River, and Staten Island were vaporized. All the cities served by ports, waterways, and international flights: Chicago, St. Louis, New Orleans, Houston, Ontario, Montreal, Vancouver, Mexico City, Panama City, Caracas, Santiago, Rio de Janeiro, to name a few, were destroyed at the same time. And this was the case in cities across the world.

The confusion was so great, that in response, retaliatory strikes were launched from every nation that had any kind of nuclear arsenal or an intact air force. From then on, cities, industrial sites, military installations, anything thought useful or potentially lethal were targets. Nothing, it appeared later, was spared from these vengeful counterattacks. No one was ever sure who was responsible, and no one was spared. Within the next 24 hours from that first onslaught of terror, the world had changed completely, forever.

But, that was not the end of it. Leading up to this atmosphere of immanent attack had been some unusual activity from our sun. The number and intensity of coronal flares had recently increased significantly. It was, as later theorized, like a cluster of smaller earthquakes before a major volcanic eruption. But in this case it was the sun that was going to do the erupting. Scientists for years previous to this had been saying that so little was known about the physics and behavior of our sun. More and more was being learned, but it still remained mostly a mystery. It was at the height of these attack-counterattack exchanges that the final hint of what was to come occurred. But sadly, no one was able to notice or record that warning.

Two hours after the first nuclear explosion, the sun shot out its usual periodic solar flare, but this time there was a series of them, each stronger than the last one. Then, all at once there was an unparalleled coronal mass ejection of gas and flame with intense energy and force. It headed straight for earth, and struck it with a glancing, cataclysmic blow, like striking a cue ball off to its side. The main force of the impact was on Antarctica, along the 30°-150° longitudinal axes, traveling east to west. In so doing, there were two immediate effects. First, the heat turned the miles' thick ice sheet into steam, water vapor and water. The second effect was that the glancing blow had enough energy to shift the axis of the earth's rotation. The new poles would now be situated closer to the 15° latitude, shifting southward over north central Greenland and shifting northward in the Great Southern Ocean, about 750 miles closer to Tasmania, Australia. Associated with this impact were tidal waves and an increased water level worldwide. It was estimated the waves generated were somewhere between 500-1000 feet high. The atmosphere could not sustain life due to the nuclear fallout, and the landscape was becoming flooded by the surge of melting water. Everywhere, the water was filled with layers of building materials, shattered trees, bodily remains, and the debris and flotsam of the 21st Century's civilizations. Life was ebbing away on earth.

Similar in some respects to the December, 2005, Indonesian earthquake and resulting tsunami disaster, where the earthquake, which left thousands injured and helpless within the flood zone, was then followed by the destructive waves, which killed tens of thousands, the horrific nuclear blasts themselves, besides killing millions of people, left a much larger number vulnerable to the 500-1000 foot wall of water that came to every coastline in the world within the next 24 hours. Three quarters of the world's population had perished within a day and a half. And another twenty percent were exposed and vulnerable to radiation, starvation, dehydration and communicable diseases within the next three to four weeks. Only pockets of survivors struggled to find some shelter and life-sustaining food and water. Those life forms able to be underground or in the sea survived the first calamity, but the impact and its aftermath took many of them as well. By estimates only, and these took years to compile, it was determined that maybe five to ten thousand people survived that first six months after April 1st. Within a year's anniversary of that terrible day, that number had shrunk to some three thousand.

Almost anywhere you looked the landscape was unrecognizable. Inland seas reclaimed much of the interior of what used to be the United States and Australia. The axis shifting had sped up the tectonic plate movements, so that the Great Rift Valley was now widening at a much faster rate, foretelling a time measured only in single years, when eastern Africa would become unhinged from its continent. And the San Andreas and Cascadian faults had spawned massive earthquakes in northern California and along the Puget Sound in Washington State. The Ring of Fire earthquake zone was fifty percent more active now with volcanoes erupting at four times the pre April 1st rate. Coastlines were unrecognizable, with the tidelands shifting sometimes hundreds of miles inland. And the atmosphere that had been initially filled with radioactive isotopes and debris was now becoming more polluted with dust from the volcanoes, fires, earthquakes and oceanic disturbances. It appeared that a period of severe freezing temperatures was in store for much of the world. The earth's climate had become completely disrupted and unpredictable.

Inside the Amboy Cavern, as it came to be called as a way to honor the shelter and its role in the survival of the small band of families, the only way outside news was available to them was through the communication link the Marines had set up. Only a skeleton shift was in the Communication Center on April 1st. That was because it took every one of the 941 people, children included, working, sometimes 18-20 hours a day, throughout those last seven weeks to get the supplies, materials, shipments packed and stored, and the construction completed by the deadline. They were all so exhausted that most were asleep on April 1st. Very few were awake at 9:00 a.m. that morning.

Besides the two communication specialists in

the Center that morning, there was General Stanfield, Major Gilcrest, Fred Wailand, Clem and B. Why B chose to be there, others only speculated about in the years that followed. Most figured it was because the forces that were to be unleashed that day could not be altered and B did not want to be alone when that happened. On that day, there was a limit that any good could do when such evil enveloped everything. All beings were victims that April day. B was no exception.

Because B had made it so clear that something terrible was going to happen on or about April 1st, the individuals in the Communication Center were naturally nervous. Around the clock monitoring had been started at midnight that day. Those on duty, however, were no different from the rest of the Amboy Cavern's dwellers; they were also exhausted from all the preparations. So naturally, they were not at their peak performance level. Each was dozing off and on in shifts. When 9:00 a.m. came, only one Marine was awake at the desk. He was scanning a number of radio and television stations, ham operators and the NORAD Center in Colorado Springs. It was at that moment he heard from a New York City radio announcer,

"My God, what's.............." and then there was complete silence.

This was followed by static and silence cascading with each turn of his tuning dial. He could not get a signal from any of the major cities, except Salt Lake City. The only other signals were from the Yucca Mountain tunnel, sheltering the other military personnel and NORAD. Within an hour and a half communication was only possible with the last two, but it was getting more difficult to decipher NORAD's messages. At times, what was heard from there sounded more like death throes, than conversation. Soon even they were silent, a victim, it was learned years later, of a precision guided weapon that destroyed the complex. The tension, anguish and desperation became overpowering for everyone. To be listening to the last gasps of a world gone mad was more than anyone could stand.

And then the sun's flare struck the earth and 11:00 a.m. The caves shook violently. It knocked everyone not already sitting to the ground. The noise was indescribable inside the cavern, and it lasted for so long each person began to scream aloud. They knew the end had to be at hand for them all, as well.

There was no way to notice in all this, but if they had, they would have seen that B, too, was in shock. Cosmic events were not predictable or controlled by anyone or anything. At this point even B had little idea what was happening. It wasn't until later that enough was known to determine approximately what actually occurred at that moment.

And yet, despite the terrifying shaking, the cavern held, no cave-ins occurred. Most things were still packed, so there was even little breakage. Everyone eventually concluded that it was an earthquake along the San Andreas Fault, "The Big One", as people used to predict would occur one day. That assumption seemed to lessen the anxiety somewhat. But the shock in the Communication Center only quadrupled after this event.

Once they all got to their feet and shook off the dust, tears were streaming down everyone's faces. Fingers trembled as they attempted to type out messages. Voices quivered when calling out their location and requesting confirmation that it was being received. Added to this was the fact that having just recently closed the cavern doors, the ventilation was still a work in progress. The air was dank. The lighting was adequate but certainly not bright. Each person there were saying whatever prayers were most comforting to them, like the sounds of their own weak voices at least gave confirmation they were still alive. Even B had moved silently back away from the cluster of individuals huddled around the communication equipment. This majestic creation was collapsing. B, unnoticed by all, was inconsolable.

Oddly, it was Clem who somehow broke the mournful spiral into utter desolation by asking, "Should we be letting the others know about what is going on? As horrible as this is, shouldn't they know as well? I know that I would. If there is a possibility that we will be killed, shouldn't they have time to speak with their loved ones?"

"You're right," Eric Stanfield answered. "I will make an announcement over the public address system, and the four of us need to spread out and inform the various group coordinators and platoon leaders what is happening and let them also help notify the others, while we set up the Main Auditorium. We should all meet there with our own families. Maybe, by all of us being together, we will find some measure of comfort and reassurance. Any suggestions on timelines?"

Nancy Gilcrest, trying to gain some composure, replied, "Why don't we suggest we all gather together one hour from now. That would make it about noon."

Everyone there nodded in agreement and slowly began to file out of the office area. Clem, in the meantime, found two engineering specialists and went to Cave #4 to get some readings from the outside sampling port. They needed to begin recording any changes in the outside atmosphere. And he would later return with that data, once the assembled families were in the auditorium. He felt that information was important for everyone to know as well.

TWENTY-NINE: THE FIRST ASSEMBLY

Until a new leader of the Governing Body was elected, Eric Stanfield was appointed, with the coordinators' approval, to speak to the assembled families. This was primarily because he was in the Communication Center when the silence and shaking began. Nancy Gilcrest, Fred or Clem could interrupt him at any time with what they knew or wanted to add. He'd welcome it. As of 9:00 a.m. today, he believed himself to be a survivor, a civilian, but certainly not a military officer. Titles were now meaningless.

Immediately after Eric made the cavern-wide announcement of the meeting to be held in the Main Auditorium, families began to pour out of their container homes, many still in their bathrobes and night clothes. They were all exhausted, dazed and afraid. Everyone was. No one knew what would happen next. Fortunately, the cavern's structure appeared intact.

As the families were making their way into the Big Room, as the kids started calling it, Philip walked through the Auditorium and up to the front, climbing the steps onto the stage. He rolled back the protective piano cover, pulled the stool up into position, and began playing the most beautiful music. It was absolutely breathtaking. The sound of his playing filled the huge room and beyond. It eventually echoed throughout the cavern.

The procession of families continued steadily into the Auditorium. They picked up folding chairs quietly, came forward into the room wordlessly, and silently set the chairs out in rows, with isles, in awed reverence. It was, of all things that could have been imagined that most horrific of days, a pastoral event that would be recalled fondly for the lifetime of those present that day.

By 1:15 p.m. it appeared all the families had arrived. Eric walked up to the stage and mounted the steps. Turning to Philip, he thanked him, and turning to the audience he motioned for them to show their appreciation. What followed for the next uninterrupted minute was some clapping, but mostly there were expressions of gratitude from everyone in the area. Throughout this ovation, Philip remained seated at the piano with his head bowed. It was as if he was deflecting any credit, letting it all pass onto the music itself. When the applause lessened, Eric began.

"Thank you, Philip. I think you must sense the gratitude that we all feel for your having played for us at this moment." Philip just nodded, then bowed to the audience and stepped down off the stage. A 'thank you' was enough for him. Personal accolades now belonged in a different era. That era had or was in the process of ending and by now, everyone sensed it.

"My friends," Eric began again. "As you have to be aware, something dreadful has begun. We may never, in our lifetime, know exactly what is occurring or why. But our Communication Center has lost contact with everyone except those at the Yucca Mountain Facility. We have no idea what caused the shaking and noise we all experienced. Most likely, we are assuming it was an earthquake, triggered by all the destruction that must be taking place everywhere.

"We do have sensors extending out into the outside atmosphere by the exit in Cave #4. Our engineers are checking the results of those figures right now. We should be getting their report momentarily. And apparently, whatever happened, it began around 9:00 a.m. or noon EST. We've checked during this last hour, and there has been no structural damage to the cavern from that shaking episode. Our new home is secure.

"Right now I see the engineers and Clem coming into the Auditorium. Give us a minute to discuss their findings, and we will tell you what they discovered, if anything."

For the next five minutes, Eric, Nancy, Clem and the engineers huddled on one side of the stage. Once they were in agreement, they decided that Nancy would speak for the group.

"Let me have your attention, please," she began. "Unfortunately, I have some very disturbing news. And we have double checked the results three times. The atmosphere outside our cavern is toxic, with concentrations of nuclear radiation that are unprecedented. It would be deadly for anyone to venture outside, even for seconds. And the levels appear to be still rising. We can only assume that there has been a massive nuclear exchange of some kind in the region. Beyond that, we know nothing else.

"For now, we are safe in here. The doors are leak proof, and we only exhaust air from inside the cavern. The large number of indoor plants and small trees we brought in will also help cleanse and refresh our air. There is no possibility of drawing outside air into the caves. We will continue to monitor these levels, and we will post any updated numbers on the bulletin board outside the Communication Center for all of us to see. And if we get any other messages or responses, other than from the Yucca Mountain families, we will post them as well.

"Now, maybe we need to disassemble and return to our homes. At this time we all need to be with our loved ones to hold and comfort each other. Further announcements will be made over the Public Address System. We must try to find some peace. May God be with us."

Once everyone had filed out, Clem was the only one left standing by the Communication Center's bulletin board. He decided to go inside and be with the only person on duty there. From now on, there would only be one individual in the Center listening for a response to the Amboy Cavern's outgoing messages. Clem and Jake would spend most of their day in the months ahead, between this room and the kitchens. Today, he decided, it was time to begin a routine that would last until the end of their confinement in the caves. He opened a few boxes, until he found the right ones, and got out the albums, tapes, and CD's of recorded music. Next, he picked out some he thought were reverent, serene and pastoral. And for the next 48 hours he played them, hoping to comfort the troubled souls throughout the cavern. It was all he knew to do. April 1st had finally arrived in Amboy.

THIRTY: DAWN

The days, weeks and months, sometimes tragically, sometimes even joyfully, did pass for the survivors, but no attempt will be made, with this telling, to record what experiences took place inside the Amboy Cavern. That account belongs to another chronicle that is still being assembled by its few remaining survivors, in cooperation with various scribes and historians. It should also be reported that the communication link with the Yucca Mountain Facility was restored, and they, too, eventually relocated to the Amboy Cavern area, as did some scattered survivors from around the world.

Although for this account, it was thought appropriate by the chroniclers of these earliest preparations and events, to skip ahead and report what was seen when a few of the survivors did have a chance to first see what lay outside the cavern, after six months of confinement. What follows was a brief description of what they found and what resulted.

Emerging from their confinement in the caves, the few individuals seeing what lay before them were staggered by the sight. Their first shock was how cold it was. It was only October, and the desert this time of year usually had some residual heat left over from the reign of summer's scorching omnipresence. But there was frost in the air. And the air was filled with a yellowish gray haze. It was like the worst mid-August day in eastern Los Angeles County. There was not a hint of blue sky. And there was the smell. It was not just an odor. It was pervasive and intense. It was a fusion of organic and inorganic, biological and chemical, plastics, petroleum byproducts and unearthly decomposition. It forced you to cover your nose and mouth instantly, for any of those who emerged initially without wearing respirators. But, most shocking, was the view of the land from the cavern's exits. Every valley, dry streambed outlet, everything under 500 feet elevation, was covered with a brownish-black watery sheen. The nearby Colorado River basin had been inundated by incoming seawater. These observers were now close to the edge of the newly expanded Sea of Cortez shoreline. And, almost as stunning, for anyone who knew the migratory patterns of birds to and from this area, there was not a sound. This was a time for the birds, charting their way southward, to stop here to feed and to drink before heading further or to settle here for the winter months. There would normally be considerable bird chatter and singing. Instead, it was dead quiet. Not a sound was heard; hardly even the rustle of any wind, even at this altitude. It was like the planet was totally exhausted; like a patient who had fought for life so long and sensed the inevitable was at hand. It was mournful. And those first few survivors who ventured forth were terrified at it all.

The radiation levels were nearly at life sustaining levels, but it was decided, given what they had seen and experienced, it was best to wait for another three months before allowing the general population to venture out. At least, they figured, it could not be any worse if they waited a little longer. Maybe some preparation in the meantime would lessen the shock of what they had seen. And so, it was another three months before anyone else opened the large doors of the Amboy Cavern again.

THIRTY-ONE: EPILOGUE

After all the commotion prior to April 1st, Clem had quietly resumed his life of near invisibility in the following months leading up to the subsequent revelations of the survivors' new world. No one really noticed him.   He, in the midst of the evolving community or nation building, as it were, was alone again.

As was so often his custom in the days following the final exit from the cavern, Clem would hike up a mountain path, probably defined ages ago by mountain sheep, coyotes and cougars, to the top of the mountain range that cradled the cavern. He would often do so to watch both the sunrise and the sunset in the same day. Taking something to drink and a snack, it was comforting for him to sit there, often for hours at a time.

It had been almost a month since the Final Emergence, as it was now called, when all the survivors opened the cavern doors and gazed for the first time at their new world.   A routine was slowly being established, but so much remained to do before any semblance of civilization could be recognized. Shock, fear, and recurring depression, each took their turn with all the survivors.

This evening, as he sat down on a chair-shaped

outcrop of granite, the sunset was being framed by a low overcast of cirrus clouds. The effect was to make the sky brilliantly red, fading to orange, dull yellow, and gray with the emerging blackness of night far behind him.

Just then B appeared beside him. It had been many months since Clem had been alone with B. It was a surprise, but no longer was Clem startled or fearful of B's presence. Theirs was now a relationship of awareness and trust. Clem still had no idea who or what B was, even to this day. It just never seemed necessary to explore or worry about such things. No doubt whatever effect B's touching him had, it certainly had a calming effect. So spending time trying to sort out B was not a priority for Clem.

B found a spot close to Clem and sat down. For the longest time both just sat quietly. Then B spoke.

"I am very pleased with how you performed the tasks I asked of you, Clem. You, unlike others in the past who I have spoken to or made requests of, have done so with grace, determination and unquestioning faith, not that the others have not been any and all of those things as well. And I do understand the need for some doubt, questioning or wayward behavior. And you had your moments of hesitation with me and my requests. That always makes for suspense and excitement for me. But in your case time was so crucial. If you had been sidetracked by too many questions, most likely this entire series of attempts to rescue would have failed or had a far different outcome. And I thank you.

"You have never pursued asking who or what I am. Probably you had some idea, and there were times you wanted to stop everything you were doing until you did know. So, maybe now I should share with you something about myself. I say this because, as you can sense, your time of graduation is at hand. You have been aware for some time that your health is failing. So, what I share with you now will most likely stay here. Full revelation is not for public consumption. But from what has happened recently, I will no longer be the remote stranger, void or spirit that people imagine or sense that I am. I must be more visible and forthright from here on. Free will is not enough."

"Well, then," Clem interjected, "who or what are you?"

"I am who I am. I am the creator of the heavens and this earth. But, most importantly for me and for you, I am also the creator of life. Like you, I too, have evolved. You could say it is my right to do so. And certainly the conception of me by your brothers and sisters over the passage of time has evolved. That initial beginning, "The Big Bang", as it has come to be called, is but a vague recollection to me. It wasn't like I hit the 'Start' button on the dashboard of the universe and then everything just mushroomed. In those times I was meddling more in cosmic forces. I'm not sure now whether I could recreate the same effect. And as to whether this debate of multiple universes is for real, I can only say, keep tuned. There are many more surprises in store for those willing and able to look into and study the heavens.

"However, my passion since its inception has been life. And, yes, there is life scattered over the universe. But nowhere, not in any corner of all the vastness of space and time, is there another place with the variety of life or the potential for its goodness, as has existed on this world. You are truly my earthly kingdom, my pride, and my everlasting joy. That is what brought me to the point of recruiting you to help me try and salvage life on this world.

"I do not have the infinite powers that some have credited me with. My cosmic phase has passed. I do not move mountains, cause ice to form, waves to splash, tides to rise and fall, comets to shift orbits or suns to cool or explode. My one real influence now is interacting with the souls of this world. With them I can communicate and initiate change. And, oh, I have grieved how the course of events detoured over these last thousands of years. As I said earlier, giving free reign to free will, and not being a more forceful and physical presence in peoples' lives was a mistake of almost infinite magnitude. It very nearly cost you and me the existence of human life on this world. You are a grand people, when you go about your daily business, sincerely caring for and loving one another. I take the greatest pleasure in that interchange. And it is true; there are many paths and ways to communicate with me, soul to soul. I have even sent, as you know, various prophets, saints, holy outcasts, and my Son to help guide you. And then I hoped that my spiritual presence would tide everything over in my physical absence. Sadly and tragically, it has not worked.

"So, and for your ears only, I pledge that my presence henceforth will not be just spiritual, but physical as well. I will make periodic appearances, like I have been doing these last few months. I still will only be able to help alter the waywardness of a given soul. I cannot physically move or change anything, nor do I want to. This is my last effort to save your kind. You are my last ark. I hope that by reassuring others that a haven of rest and peace does exist beyond this life, that heaven can even begin its formation on this earth as well, and that by my better defining what that heaven is, that it will help lessen the confusion about who and how one finds their way there. I plan to be not only a spiritual presence but a physical guide. I care and love each of you so dearly. You are also my beloved sons and daughters, each and every one."

At this, Clem was left speechless. His audience with B was too overpowering. For this simple man, whose brush with organized religion, much less with any theology, had been scant, what he was hearing and Who he was hearing it from was too profound for one human being to absorb. All he could think of at that moment was of his beautiful wife and son, and the void that their passing had created in his life. Thinking of this, he asked, "Is there really a heaven? Do you hear someone when they pray?"

"Yes," B replied, realizing the longing that question arose from. "It's like another dimension, beyond time, space, gravity, or your material world. Try to think of it as someplace where souls return. Souls do have an energy that propels them. It was not something I originally thought of, but your earliest ancestors began to hope for something beyond life. And it was that hope, that deep, purest of longings that got my attention. There was eventually such love and yearning with that hope that heaven, too, evolved. And fear not, if there are now the cosmic investigations into multiple universes, do no scoff at the likelihood that such a realm as heaven doesn't exist as well. For it does. The powers of that hope, longing and love were a source of the greatest joy to me. Heaven was their reward.

"And, yes, you will recognize others, not by physical features but through the medium of your soul. Your communication will be like laughter. It, above all else, is the language of the soul, with music providing the joyful surroundings. All this you will discover when your time arrives. And as to who makes that final journey, that is my decision. I will add, however, that it is not a pleasure palace. And those who do not qualify for the journey are primarily those who cause or champion cruelty, death and destruction. To fight and die in defense of your loved ones or your land, when it is under attack is not cruel. But to those who kill, maim or rape for conquest, whether it be for an individual or a people, they will not see the kingdom of heaven. I expect people to respect the dignity, person and property of another human being. If someone should become motivated by lust for power, conquest, or revenge, they will be denied passage. The events of the last few months have shown me that I cannot let the course of human events spiral so out of control again. My deepest desire is that all shall enter that kingdom.

"And, once again, yes, I hear your prayers. Prayer is the medium souls use to communicate with me. It need not be spoken, audible or structured. Sometimes the deepest of pure longings is prayer enough for me. I do not issue grades on who is the most articulate. It is intent and intensity that matters, not structure. Prayer is the great leveler of all. Often the simplest child-like prayer is the most readily heard. Understand; I cannot affect drastic changes with each prayer. But I will reduce the alienation and loss, and replace despair with hope. And sometimes I can do even more. Miracles do and will happen.

As all of this was being said, B noticed that Clem appeared to slump slightly. Calling out quietly, "Clem", there was no response. Then B's shadowy form reached out, for the first time, and took hold of Clem's limp body. Shifting him to the ground, B's shroud was removed and laid over Clem. B gently stroked his forehead and said, "Go home, my friend. Be with your loved ones now and forever more. Your earthly journey is over. You'll never be alone again."

APPENDIX 1

Figure 1:

The Newspaper Offer

"Enter a chance to be chosen to attend a free, international, investigative symposium of urgent importance on February 1st -8th. Spend 7 days and nights in the warmth and sunshine of Southern California's Mojave Desert. All expenses will be paid for you and your family, if you are chosen. Simply fill in the requested information and answer the following questions. E-mail and air mail your reply no later than this December 5th. Families selected will be notified on December 26th. Please use only one type written page, providing your names, address, telephone number, e-mail address, occupations of family members, your ages and answers to the following questions. How do you cope with stress? What gives you your deepest happiness? How well do you interact with strangers and new situations? What makes you laugh? Send to: www.amrebkeepers.com and to Amboy Rebuilders and Keepers, Ltd, P.O. Box 439, Amboy, CA 95100, U.S.A."

Figure 2:

Far Horizons Travel Store Confirmed Itinerary
for Cynthia Garr and Clem Newberry

Nov. 21- Los Angeles (LAX) to Chicago to
New York City (stay overnight).

Nov. 22-(2) New York airports, then to Newark
New Jersey (stay overnight).

Nov. 23-to London then on to Paris (stay
overnight).

Nov. 24-to Frankfurt then on to Copenhagen
(stay overnight).

Nov. 25-to Helsinki then on to Warsaw (stay
overnight).

Nov. 26-to Moscow than on to Kiev (stay
overnight).

Nov. 27-to Belgrade then on to Rome (stay 2
nights).

Nov. 29-to Istanbul then on to Beirut (stay
overnight).

Nov. 30-to Jerusalem then on to Amman (stay
overnight).

Dec. 1 - to Damascus than on to Riyadh (stay
overnight).

Dec. 2 - to Tehran then on to Kabul (stay
overnight).

Dec. 3 - to Karachi then on to Mumbai (stay
overnight).

Dec. 4 - to Beijing then on to Tokyo (stay
overnight).

Dec. 5 - to Manila then on to Singapore then on
to Jakarta (stay overnight).

Dec. 6 - to Sydney (stay 2 nights).

Dec. 8 - to Johannesburg (stay overnight).

Dec. 9 - to Gaborone then on to Harare then on

to Lusaka (stay overnight).

Dec. 10-to Luanda then on to Kinshasa then on to Nairobi (stay overnight).

Dec. 11-to Addis Ababa then on to Khartoum (stay overnight).

Dec.12-to Cairo than on to Tripoli than on to Algiers (stay overnight).

Dec.13-to Rabat then on to Dakar then on to Monrovia (stay 2 nights).

Dec.15-to Rio de Janeiro (stay overnight).

Dec.16-to Buenos Aires then on to Santiago (stay overnight).

Dec.17-to La Paz then on to Lima (stay overnight).

Dec.18-to Quito then on to Bogotá then on to Caracas (stay overnight).

Dec.19-to Panama City then to San Jose (stay overnight).

Dec.20-to Mexico City (stay overnight).

Dec.21- return to LAX this morning.

Figure 3:

The Occupations List

-32 university/college teachers:
        -10 engineering department
        -10 science department
        -4 law department
        -4 agriculture department
        -4 medical school department
-12 engineers:
        -2 mining engineers/geologists.
        -2 civil engineers.
        -2 mechanical engineers
        -2 electrical engineers
        -2 computer engineers
        -2 nuclear engineers
        -19 school teachers:
            -3 preschool.
            -4 elementary.
            -6 middle.
            -6 high.
        -10 scientists:
            -2 chemists.
            -2 physicists.
            -2 biologists.
        -2 cosmologists/astronomers
        -2 mathematicians.
-18 medical specialists:
        -6 surgeons.
        -6 internal medicine specialists.
-6 RN's/nurse practitioners
        -8 fire prevention/EMT's.
-6 social service/counselors/psychologists.
-14 homemakers.
-14 farmers/ranchers.

-4 artists.
-4 musicians/composers.
-4 writers/journalists.
-3 judges.
-2 historians.

Figure 4:

The Acceptance Letter

"GLOBAL PROGNOSIS: AN ALL-INCLUSIVE INVESTIGATION"

Amboy Rebuilders and Keepers, Ltd.
P.O. Box 439
Amboy, CA 95100
U.S.A.

Dear: _____ : (individual family member names inserted here)

      This letter is being sent to inform you that your family has been accepted to attend the all-expenses paid trip of seven days and nights at the Roadway 66 Motel in Amboy, California. Surrounded by the spectacular beauty of the Mojave Desert, it is a place unique in the entire world. Four round trip tickets for everyone in your family will be mailed to you within the next week. And by way of confirming your selection, you can expect a visitation from the originator of this gathering shortly after you receive this e-mail. Any lingering doubts about the importance and urgency of this meeting will be addressed during that visit.

      You will be departing on or about January 31, with everyone selected, including yourselves, arriving in Los Angeles, California, on February 1. From there you will be flown by a shuttle service to Palm Springs, California, where you will then be transported by bus to Amboy.

      Please pack for a one month stay, even though you are only scheduled for one week in Amboy. There are so many sites to see and National Parks in the region, you will no doubt want to holiday in the area, once this first week's meeting is concluded. Your return tickets are open dated for your convenience. We can help you make those extended stay arrangements after you arrive and decide what you would like to see and where you would like to go.

Certainly, you may inform your business associates, employers, employees, friends and extended family that you are coming here, and that you may be staying longer to extend your holiday. But for this next portion of our instructions, you must not tell anyone, outside your immediate family, what we are requesting that you do. To do otherwise would have life-threatening consequences for you and countless others. The details and reasons for this will be explained later, if further action were to become necessary. Do not be alarmed or let it deter you from following up with this trip. You are among a highly qualified and gifted group of families. Your participation and cooperation with what follows is of paramount importance.

You will need to begin now to pack, and have stored for shipping, the items outlined below. Then you will need to contact an overseas shipper, who is located near you, and have them pick up your sealed container for possible delivery here to Amboy. And you will need to send us in the enclosed envelope the name, e-mail address and telephone number of that shipping company. Leave with your shipper a password that only you and he will have access to. Nothing will be moved unless you agree it is necessary to do so. The shipper's information is to facilitate its removal, if that should become necessary. There is little likelihood that anything further will be done with this container of your possessions. Consider it a safeguard for your family. Above all else, you must keep this activity closely guarded. No one outside your immediate family must know what you are doing with this container.

In this container, you will need to pack clothing for an additional six months. Pack for both extreme heat and extreme cold. Also, pack any small valuables and items of personal importance to you, e.g. photo albums, small gifts, paintings, wall hangings, mantel piece memorabilia, books, recorded music. Pack extra toilet and bathroom supplies, extra medications. Finally, and most importantly, each adult must collect from his and her place of work and from your home office, if that applies, all papers, books, diagrams, descriptions of experiments, pending patents, procedures, manuals of operation, and even small equipment necessary for you to perform your jobs. Larger equipment is, of course, not practical to pack. You may bring schematics of any larger equipment, however. Photocopy where necessary. Do not be concerned that you may be committing employee or government theft or sabotage. You will not be charged or be in any danger of such, ever, if such a transfer of this material becomes necessary. And most likely, nothing further will come of this packing and storage. But, as a guide, assemble whatever you can safely store, with the objective of it eventually allowing you to teach others what you do and how to do your job. And if these containers should need to be moved, as with the packing, initial moving of them, and storage, none of this will be at your expense. Simply give the shipper the enclosed debit card number. You may also use the card number for any other expenses you might incur while preparing for this trip to Amboy.

The address that needs to be attached to your container should be:

USMC Logistics Center
Amboy, CA. 95100,
U.S.A.

And, again, we here at AMBOY REBUILDERS

AND KEEPERS, LTD., are deeply grateful for your entering into this undertaking, and we are honored to be able to send you this notice of acceptance. Please use the enclosed, self-addressed envelope to acknowledge you have received and accepted this offer. We also need an e-mail reply from you after you receive this notification to confirm your attendance. We look forward to seeing you in Amboy on February 1st.

Sincerely,

Fred Wailand, Coordinator

Figure 5:

"Accepted Participants' Occupations and Countries of Origin for the 'Global Prognosis: An All-Inclusive Investigative Symposium'"

-32 University/College Professors:
  -10 Engineering:
    -China (3) -Netherlands (1)
        -U.S.A. (3) -Indonesia (1)
        -Germany (2)
  -10 Science:
    -Italy (2)   -Norway (1)
        -France (2)   -Australia (1)
        -U.S.A. (3)   -India (1)
  -4 Law:
    -Great Britain (2) -U.S.A. (2)
  -4 Agriculture:
        -Kenya (1) -Saudi Arabia (1)
        -Indonesia (1) -U.S.A. (1)
  -4 Medical:
        -U.S.A. (2)   -India (1)
        -Australia (1)
-12 Engineers:
  -2 Mining/Geology:
        -Australia (2)
  -2 Civil:
    -Germany (1) -China (1)
  -2 Mechanical:
    -Saudi Arabia (1) -U.S.A. (1)
  -2 Electrical:
        -India (1)   -U.S.A. (1)
  -2 Computer:
        -India (1)   -U.S.A. (1)
  -2 Nuclear:
        -France (2)

-19 K-12 School Teachers:
  -3 Preschool:
                -U.S.A. (1) -Switzerland (1)
                -Japan (1)
  -4 Elementary:
      -Denmark (2)   -U.S.A. (1)
                -Japan (1)
  -6 Middle:
                -Finland (2)   -India (2)
                -U.S.A. (2)
  -6 High:
                -Great Britain (2) -India (2)
                -U.S.A. (2)
-10 Scientists:
  -2 Chemists:
                -Japan (1)   -U.S.A. (1)
  -2 Physicists:
                -Japan (1)   -U.S.A. (1)
  -2 Biologists:
                -Russia (1)   -U.S.A. (1)
  -2 Cosmologists/Astronomers:
                -U.S.A. (1)   -Israel (1)
  -2 Mathematicians:
                -Russia (1)   -Israel (1)
-18 Medical Specialists:
  -6 Surgeons:
                -Australia (2)   -India (2)
                -U.S.A. (2)
  -6 Internal Medicine Physicians:
                -Canada (1) -Egypt (1)
                -U.S.A. (2)   -Belgium (1)
                -Brazil (1)
  -6 RN's/Nurse Practitioners:
                -U.S.A. (2)   -Canada (1)
                -Brazil (1)   -Egypt (1)
                -Great Britain (1)

-8 Fire/Rescue/EMT's:
    -U.S.A. (NYC) (4)   -Israel (2)
    -Iraq (2)
  -6 Social Service/Counselors/Psychologists:
    -Switzerland (1)   -U.S.A. (2)
    -Netherlands (1)   -Norway (1)
    -Argentina (1)

-4 Artists:
    -Argentina (1)   -China (1)
    -Russia (1) -U.S.A. (1)

-14 Farmers/Ranchers/Homemakers/
    Women:
    -Mexico (1) -New Zealand (1)
    -Greece (1)   -Spain (1)
    -Chile (1)   -Iran (1)
    -Poland (1)   -Turkey (1)
    -Ukraine (1)   -China (1)
    -Israel (1) -Germany (1)
    -U.S.A. (1)   -Saudi Arabia (1)

-4 Musicians/Composers:
    -Germany (1) -Russia (1)
    -Great Britain (1)   -U.S.A. (1)

-4 Writers/Journalists:
    -Great Britain (1)   -U.S.A. (2)
    -Germany (1)

-14 Farmers/Ranchers/Homemakers/
    Men:
    -Mexico (1)   -New Zealand (1)
    -Greece (1)   -Spain (1)
    -Chile (1)   -Iran (1)
    -Poland (1)   -Turkey (1)
    -Ukraine (1)   -Kenya (1)
    -Israel (1)   -South Africa (1)
    -U.S.A. (2)

-3 Judges:
    -Belgium (1)   -U.S.A. (1)

-Great Britain (1)
-2 Historians:
-Great Britain (2)

Figure 6:

"The Symposium's Agenda"

AMBOY REBUILDERS AND KEEPERS, LTD.
"Global Prognosis: An All-Inclusive Investigation"

Symposium Calendar of Events and Agenda

February 1st: Arrival of families in Amboy by way
        of LAX and Palm Springs. Registration and
        room assignment at Motel Office. Meals to
        be buffet style. Breakfast 7-9 a.m., Lunch
        12-1:30 p.m., Dinner 6-8 p.m. No formal
        seating today for meals.

February 2nd: All morning and afternoon to be free
        time to rest from trip and see the area.
        Bicycles, playground, baseball and
        volleyball fields available, swimming pool
        and game room open. Horses have been
        arranged for short trips into the surrounding
        area. Meals as scheduled above, except for
        dinner.
        6:15 p.m.- Get Acquainted Happy Hour for
                all families in restaurant.
        7:15 p.m.- Buffet Dinner with assigned
        seating.
        8:45p.m.- Evening Program with
                introduction of organizing personnel
        and brief review of the week's
        agenda.
        9:15 p.m.- Dancing and socializing until
                midnight.
        Midnight - Restaurant closes.

February 3rd: 7-9 a.m.- Breakfast served at your
                convenience.

10 a.m.-12 p.m.-All adults to attend
organizational and overview meeting.
Children need not attend. This will
be free time for them.

Proposed outline for Symposium to be
Discussed, Modified and Approved

I. Formation of 10 groups. Each group will be meeting three times a day: morning, afternoon, and evening until February 7th, when all day will be spent with everyone in all 10 groups coming together to discuss and finalize the results of their meetings.

II. The findings of each group will be published in a special edition of five world-wide journals or magazines. Each edition will be devoted entirely to the contents of these group meetings.

III. Each group will build their presentation around three central themes: the cause(s), the implications(s), and the management, correction or reversal of the topic being discussed. There is no limit as to how long your final draft should be. It is up to each group to decide length and content.

IV. Each group should select a coordinator and/or spokesperson during the first day's meeting. Assigned areas for each group will be posted by noon February 3rd on the dining room bulletin board. The bulletin board is located on the wall as you exit the main restaurant area.

V. Everyone is to be assigned beforehand to each of the ten groups, and this list will also be posted on that same bulletin board.

The group topics are:

1. Global warming and/or cooling: climate, cosmic, human interactions and their effects on its progression.

2. Overpopulation of the planet: Can we sustain a reliable food and potable water supply? How can this issue be addressed?

3. World poverty: the progressively worsening gap between affluent and third world countries.

4. Education: whether public, private or religious. Is it working? How can it be improved?

5. Political systems: Is there a better model than now exists?

6. Health issues: Is there a best delivery system? Training? What threats have to be met.

7. Terrorism: Where is it heading? Who's next? What to do?

8. Military forces: Its role, leadership and future.

9. Energy resources: Where to turn? What to develop?

10. Technology: What's ahead? What's needed?

12-1:30 p.m.- Buffet lunch.
2-5 p.m.- Group meetings in assigned areas.
6-8 p.m.- Buffet dinner.
8-10 p.m.- Group meetings in assigned areas.
February 4th:   7-9 a.m.- Buffet breakfast.
9:30-noon- Group meetings in assigned areas.
12-1:30 p.m.- Buffet lunch.
2-5 p.m.- Group meetings in assigned areas.

6-8 p.m.- Buffet dinner.

8:30-10:30 p.m.- Group meetings in assigned areas.

February 5th: Same schedule as February 4th.

February 6th: Same schedule as February 5th.

February 7th: Same schedule for meals, but all group meetings will be combined in the restaurant area.

7:15 p.m. Buffet dinner with assigned seating and dancing to follow.

February 8th: 10 a.m. Depart for home or begin extended holiday with your family.

Figure 7:

"Equipment and Supplies Needed for Amboy
And Marine Contingents"

FOOD

SOLIDS	LIQUIDS	PERSONAL
-powdered milk	-water	-medications
-powdered potatoes	-canned juices	-bathroom items
-powdered eggs	-wine*	-parkas
-powdered juice	-beer*	-long underwear
-powdered onions	-scotch*	-rain gear
-powdered soup	-vodka*	-boots (rubber, steeltoe, walk-ing)
-coffee	-sake*	
-tea	-whiskey*	
-cocoa	-gin*	-wool caps
-ovaltine	-vermouth*	-gloves
-flour	-brandy*	-wool socks
-sugar	-liquor*	-body soap
-rice	-rum*	-writing paper
-spaghetti	-root beer syrup	-pens, pencils
-lasagna	-maple syrup	-scissors
-peanut butter	-coke, 7-up*	-notebooks
-jam, jelly, marmalade	-postum	-dividers
-pasta, noodles		-hole punches

-dried fruit (raisins, prunes, apricots,   -staplers
   bananas, apples, pineapples, pears) -coat hangers
-dried beans (navy, pinto, red, peas) -musical instru-
-dried nuts (peanuts, pecans, walnuts,   ments
almonds, pistachios, hazelnuts, cashews, -from Marine
macadamias)   Base hospital
-canned food (peas, carrots, beans, peppers,-medications

peaches, apricots, tomatoes, pickles, corn,-supplies
cabbage, potatoes, yams, berries, applesauce, -equipment
beets, ham, beef, chicken, tuna, salmon, -body bags
sardines)   -hand sanitizer
-spices (salt, pepper, curry, chili, savory, garlic,
   baking soda, baking powder, cloves, etc.)-typewriters
-condiments (mustard, ketchup, relish) -computers
-olive oil, vegetable oils   -bond paper
-vinegar (plain, cider)   -ribbon
-vegemite   -tents
-marmite   -pumping
-citrus fruit (limes,   equipment
         lemon, oranges)   -welding
-baby formula   supplies
                                        -gas powered
                                           generators

HOUSEHOLD	REBIUILDING**
-bed frames	-lumber (2X5,10.12")
-mattresses	(8,10,12,20 ft. lengths)
-folding tables	-roofing materials
-folding tables	(tar paper, slate, coating)
-mirrors	-nails, screws, bolts, nuts,
-cushions	washers, rivets, staples
-blankets	-electrical supplies
-sheets	-plumbing supplies
-pillows	-windows
-towels, wash	-doors
cloths	-cement/mortar mixer
-laundry soap	-steel rebar
-file drawers,	-hand tools (garden,
boxes	construction)
-candles	-gas-powered tools
-candle holders	(8 generators, chain
-room deodorant	saws, jaws of life
-incense sticks	-electric-powered tools

- brooms
- mops
- buckets
- waste cans
- dust pans
- dish drainer
- dishes, eating utensils
- tubs, bowls
- batteries
- hazmat suits
- indoor/outdoor carpet
- braided rugs
- toilets
- exercise equipment
- bicycles (supports, generators)
- bleach
- disinfectants
- canning supplies
- (saws, compressors)
- survey transit
- tractor with implements, tires, grease gun, jacks
- wood cook stoves
- shovel, picks, hoes
- bricks for home exterior
- home insulation material
- lamps (floor, table, desk kerosene)
- light bulbs
- wheel borrows
- wind turbines (towers, generators, propellers)
- solar panels (frames, conversion kits)
- petroleum products (fuel, (oil, kerosene, Propane tanks)
- grand piano
- pipe organ
- seeds, plants, saplings
- manual printing press

*Some restrictions on how to be distributed, e.g. rationing and/or kept for special events.
** Supplies stored in outside warehouse for use, once families finally emerge from cavern.

Diagram 1:

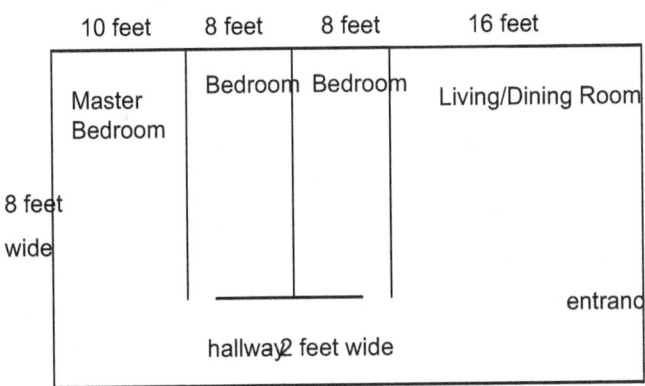

Amboy Cavern Living Unit

42 feet long

| 10 feet | 8 feet | 8 feet | 16 feet |

Master Bedroom

Bedroom Bedroom

Living/Dining Room

8 feet wide

entrance

hallway 2 feet wide

(42' by 8' metal shipping container)

Diagram 2:

Southwest Half of Providence Cavern

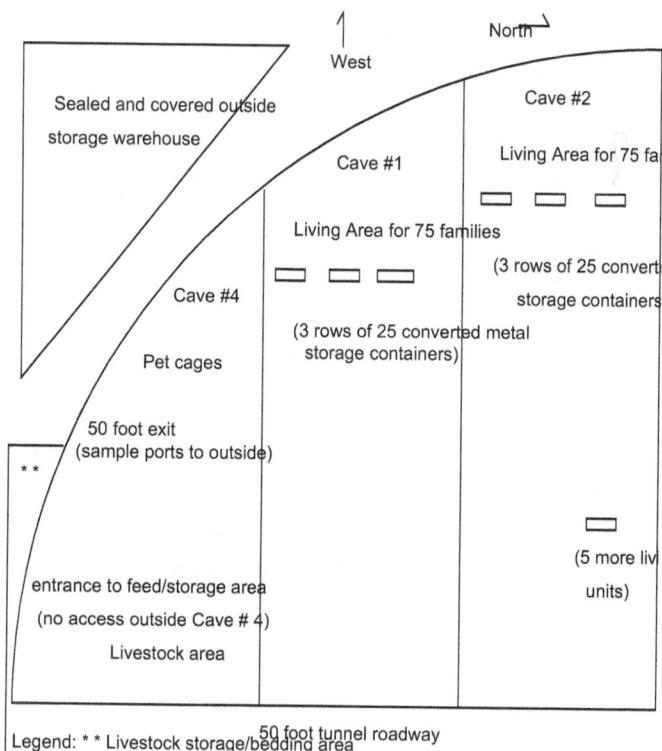

Legend: * * Livestock storage/bedding area

Diagram 3:

Southeast Half of Providence Cavern

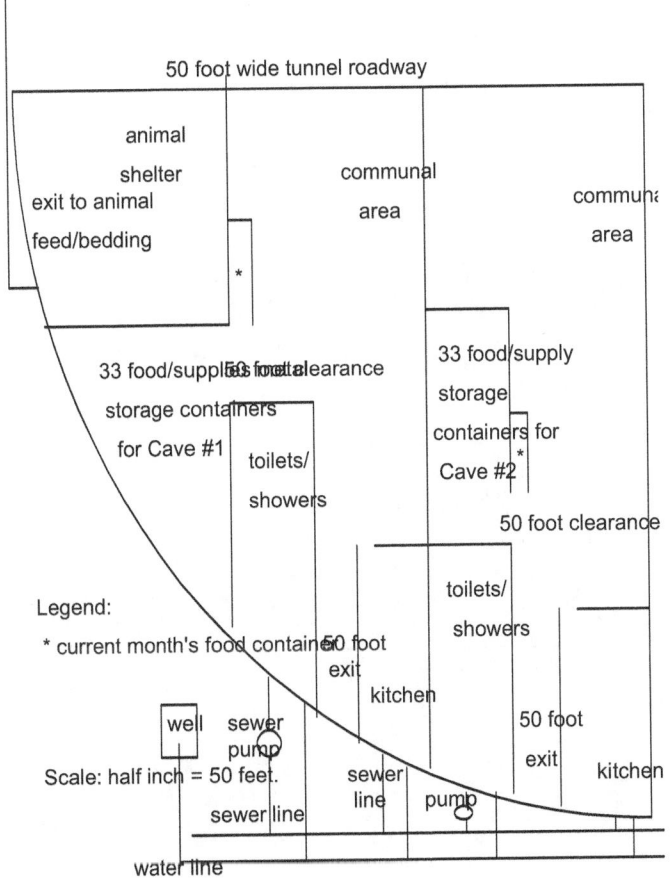

50 foot wide tunnel roadway

animal shelter

exit to animal feed/bedding

communal area

communal area

33 food/supplies storage containers for Cave #1

50 foot clearance

*

toilets/showers

33 food/supply storage containers for Cave #2

*

50 foot clearance

toilets/showers

Legend:

* current month's food container

50 foot exit

kitchen

Scale: half inch = 50 feet.

well

sewer pump

sewer line

50 foot exit

kitchen

sewer line

pump

water line

Diagram 4:

Northwest Half of Providence Cavern

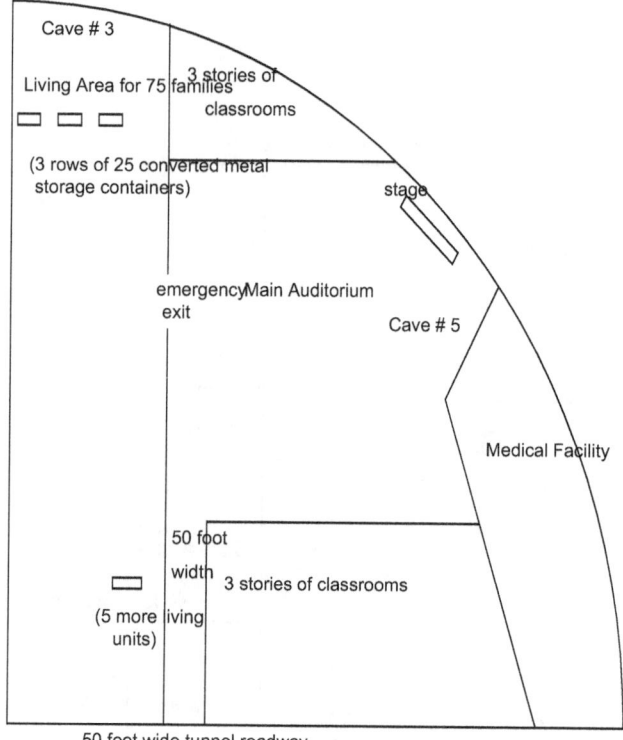

Diagram 5:

Northeast Half of Providence Cavern

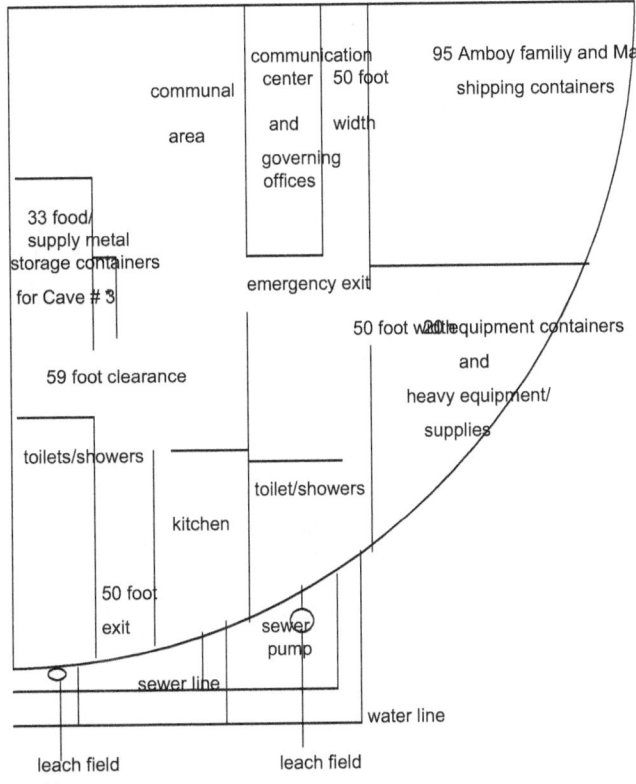

Diagram 6:

Schematic of Providence Cavern

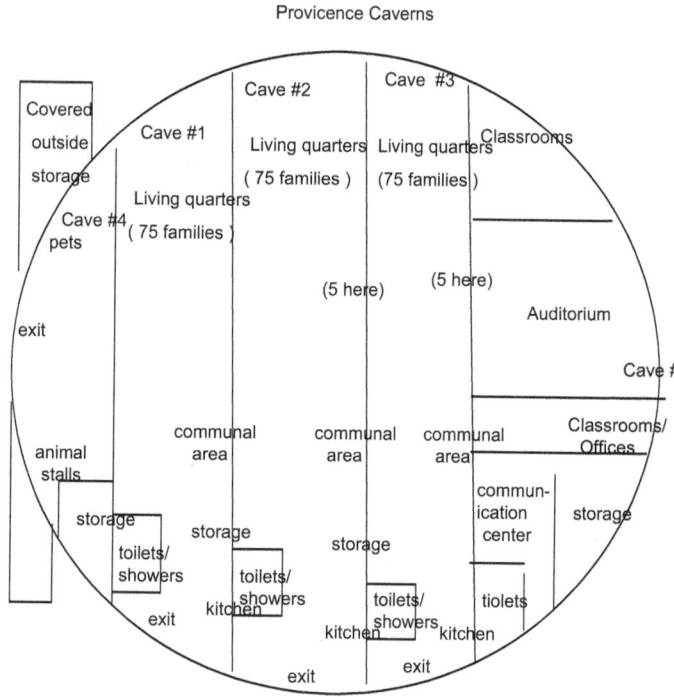

Provicence Caverns

Diagram 7:

Cavern Complex with Chambers Shown

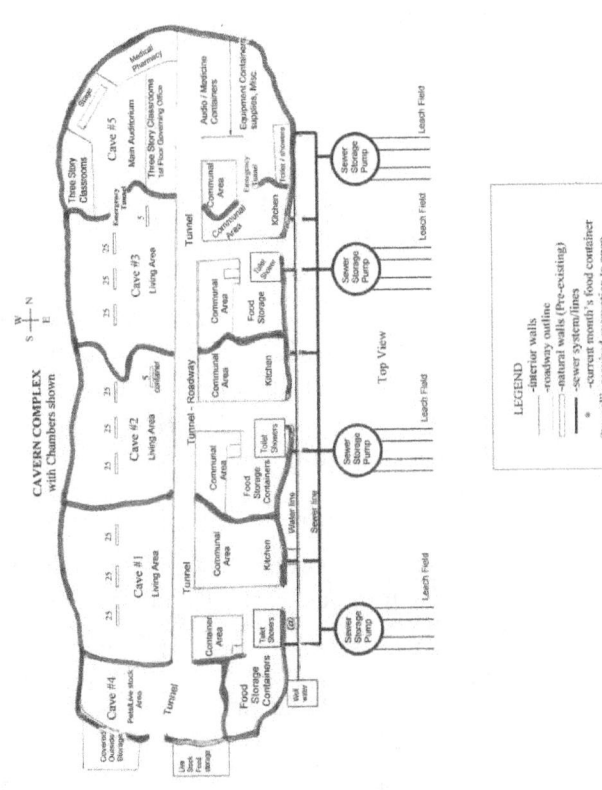

THE CONFINEMENT

PART I

ONE: PLAN C

Storms this time of year along the southern California coastline can be unpredictable. Some years there are none. Other years, the equatorial currents dictate they will come in a steady onslaught. And by today, February 6th, that pattern was well established for this winter season. This year had seen little more than tidal surges, as the storms marched inland further north.

This evening, as Lt. Ben Javitts sat with his knees squeezed against his chest, the sunset was taking its final bow. He had been sitting this way on the Port Hueneme jetty for almost thirty minutes, waiting for his wife, Michelle, to come after she got off work. He had called her earlier and asked that she meet him here at about 1830 hours. Luckily, the gentle sound of the lapping waves soothed somewhat his nervous disappointment. However, he still was not sure how to tell his wife about this morning's meeting with the Seabee Base Captain.

The Captain ordered another deployment for their Construction Battalion. This time only 50 personnel would be needed, but they would be working on a top-secret project. They were to begin immediately preparing their transport vehicles, loading them with heavy equipment and supplies for building, tunneling, excavation and drilling. Their departure was to be no later than at 1500 hours tomorrow. He was told they were to be assigned to the Marine Base at 29 Palms for at least two months. In addition, he was to be the commanding officer of the unit.

The duty assignment was the shock. It was because this deployment was coming so soon after he and his personnel had just returned three days ago from a six-month tour on Diego Garcia, the huge Navy and Air Force Base on a small, desolate atoll in the Indian Ocean. While there, they had to construct more warehouses and develop larger water and sewer capacity for the surging military population being assigned to that Base. It was his third, extended overseas deployment within the last three years.

Michelle would be devastated by this latest assignment, even though it was for a shorter timeframe. Their two children, Rhonda age 9 and Bradley age 8, had seen so little of him, and he was missing too much of their growing up. Right now, he was very discouraged. His career was putting his precious marriage and family at risk of crumbling.

Growing up in the North End of Philadelphia, on 7th St., near Temple University, he had never considered anything else but having some kind of a naval career. All through high school, he crewed for any team he could find that trained on the nearby Schuylkill River. Between his love of cycling and crewing, by the time he arrived at the U.S. Naval Academy, he was fit for most physical and mental testing that was ahead. His enthusiasm for the Navy only grew as he was introduced to his studies of mechanical engineering. Early in life, he found his nitch. And the Seabees were to be the

311

perfect match for him and his aspirations.

During his junior year at the Academy, while on Christmas break, he met Michelle, who was also a junior at Villanova University, majoring in mathematics. They were introduced to each other at a party, given by one of his old high school buddies, who attended Villanova as well. She later said it was his uniform that got her attention. He simply said it was everything about her that got his. They married after graduation. He was assigned to the Seabees, and she began her careers of teaching, as a high school math teacher, and of being a mom. Soon, she also began working on her Master's Degree. Most of that graduate work was done through internet linkage. This still allowed her to teach and, most importantly, to oversee raising their children. Her future goals, having now been a teacher at the local community college for three years, were to pursue her Ph.D. in mathematics and eventually to teach at a university. But today, her goals were to get their kids rounded up from neighbors' homes and to find her husband and then to go have dinner somewhere.

As the headlights of their well worn Chevy sedan peered down the jetty where Ben sat hunched, his mind was drifting, as anyone's does when disappointment or discouragement mounts, to visions in his past that gave comfort and allowed escape. For him, these times and harbors of safety were in the fall of the year, as he rowed or drifted down the Schuylkill River. The autumn leaves lit up his quiet passing with their brilliant colors. There was a fresh fragrance of the summer season's growth and production of leaves, berries, nuts and flowers, just before winter harvested it all. He became lost in that moment.

Abruptly, he was plunged back into the present by the voices of his kids yelling, "Dad, come on. Let's go eat." And to Michelle, echoing with, "Cast off,

Lieutenant. We're making way to a lovely dinner at Spiro's." Each of them made their way down the asphalted pathway along the top of the jetty, and as he stood, wrapped themselves around him. It was the balm he needed to coax himself out of his deepening reverie. Somehow, he thought, we'll all see this latest assignment through.

Dinner at their favorite restaurant was lively and newsy. Everyone, except Ben, chimed in with what had happened during the day and then happily recalled their hiking trip in the nearby Los Padres National Forest this last weekend. Then his turn to contribute to the discussions came.

He began with, "I got a call to see the Base Captain this morning. He asked me to come over to his office right away. It seems that the 29 Palms Marine Base has a top-secret mission that some of us here have to be involved in for a brief time. "

"For how long?" burst forth a chorus of voices, sitting around the booth.

"Just two months, this time," Ben replied, with a renewing sense of despondency. "But, I have to tell you there was something about the way the Captain informed me, and then what he asked me to do, that leads me to believe there may be more to this deployment than just a routine assignment."

"Like what?" Michelle interrupted.

"Well, he asked me to handpick out of our entire Construction Battalion just fifty of our best personnel, who would be divided into two crews, to be led by two of our best Junior Grade Lieutenants and two of our best Senior Petty Officers. It took me the rest of this afternoon to select and notify these individuals and then to discuss with them the equipment and supplies we'd need to transport. I had to wonder why we were cherry picking our personnel for this assignment. And, most importantly, he seemed to indicate there might be a transfer of dependents as well. I know it sounds crazy. But on top of this assignment coming right after my recent deployment to Diego Garcia, I have to wonder if there isn't more to this than just a simple work detail. Moreover, the level of secrecy surrounding it all is unheard of. It's not like the Captain to abuse his personnel with back-to-back deployments, unless something urgent is on the horizon.

"Are you in danger?" she asked immediately.

"No, not that I can tell by the equipment and supplies we have been asked to take, and by the fact that we are going over there in a truck convoy. We are not leaving the mainland. And the timeframe is too short to involve an overseas' deployment." What he did not say was that the Captain did order him to have his personnel check out pistols and rifles, along with ammunition. They were to travel fully armed. That, too, was another reason, but one he dared not mention, he knew this mission was highly unusual.

"When will you be leaving?" Everyone chimed in again. "And when will you know if we have to come as well?" his wife asked, in a tone suggesting some resignation.

"We have to leave tomorrow at 3 p.m., arriving at the Marine Base sometime around midnight. In addition, I would imagine there would be some kind of briefing with their Officer Staff on the 8th. I will call you by noon that day and let you know everything that I have been told. That's the best I can do under the circumstances. And you do know that whatever we are discussing now has to be kept absolutely secret. You understand, don't you kids?'

They each nodded their heads in agreement, but were confused and sad that maybe they might have to leave the place that had always been their home.

314

"I am so sorry for this newest assignment and for having to leave so soon. Heaven knows, I don't want to have to uproot you guys and move somewhere else. I know how much we all love living here. Please, let's band together for strength and encouragement. You are my life. What I do for a living is important, in so far as it helps put food on the table, just like your mom's work does. But, you all here are what makes my life worth living. Nothing else does. And I want you to know this."

With that said, spontaneously, they all stood up from the booth and gathered in a circle, hugging each other. It was not the first time Spiro's Restaurant had witnessed such a touching scene, given its proximity to the military bases in the immediate area. Everyone in the restaurant at the time that noticed this show of affection and rededication, silently and gratefully, nodded. It was a salute to this family unit and an unspoken prayer for them to have a safe journey.

The morning and early afternoon of February 7th was packed with arranging equipment and supplies, loading it up, refueling trucks, assembling personnel and personal affects. Lt. Javitts, starting at 0400 hours, spent this time assembling the names of his unit, meeting with Lt.'s JG Zelma Collins and Wally Gonzaque to double check their personnel, equipment and supply needs. He made a final call to his wife, just before they pulled out of Port Hueneme's front gate en route to the Marine Base. They did not have the most restful night, but before they did finally sleep, there was a deeper understanding and commitment to what lay ahead and to their marriage. He was ready to take command of this assignment by morning.

The convoy's arrival at the Marine Base at 2330 hours was apparently not unexpected; as General Stanfield and Lt. Col Black met him, once they arrived.

This fact, alone, told him there was a definite urgency surrounding this mission. The convoy was directed to the Motor Pool area to park there overnight. Exhausted, the personnel chose to sleep in their vehicles, rather than try to find their way to lodging on Base. Before retiring himself, General Stanfield requested that Lt. Javitts meet him at 0800 hours tomorrow in his office.

By 0800 hours both Col. Kathryn Swisher from Fairchild AFB and Col. Steven Blackmore from McChord AFB joined Lt. Javitts in General Stanfield's office. What followed was an hour in which the General discussed an utterly unimaginable nightmare. Once he had concluded his presentation, each listener was left completely drained of thought or emotion. He then added that he would be sharing this same information with their personnel at 1400 hours today in the Base Auditorium. They were to insure that all their people attended that meeting. Finally, he requested they meet him at 1030 hours today at the helipad for their trip to Amboy.

The only thread of solace any of them had was his commitment to have each of their families, including the personnel under their commands, transported here on February 20th. He emphasized the fact that they could not divulge any details to their families, other than that they, too, would be redeployed to this Base on that date. Each one, grimly understood now, why this was a top-secret mission and why silence was its only protection.

After the meeting adjourned, the General asked Lt. Javitts to stay behind a moment. He then discussed with him the meeting he had with Clem two days ago, but he avoided mentioning B for now. Knowing the 'can do' attitude of the Seabees, he decided to give him Clem's list of supplies and equipment. Ordering from that list, Lt Javitts was to arrange shipment to the Yucca Mountain Repository, provided the General could get clearance to use it. He also shared with him Clem's debit card and cell phone number. Once the General got the approval for them to use the Yucca Mountain complex, at his meeting on the 10th in Washington, D.C., he agreed to call him with the ok to begin arranging delivery to that facility. He concluded his remarks by saying, he expected the Seabees trucks would be refueled, take on any extra supplies they would need for this mission and would leave for the Providence Cavern by 1800 hours today.

Around 0930 hours Lt. Javitts had made his way back to the Motor Pool area and relayed orders from the General to get refueled and ready to leave by 1800 hours. He also informed his junior officers that they needed to tell their personnel they should all be at the Base Auditorium by 1400 hours. He then slipped into his command humvee to call Michelle. Before he did, he happened to glance over and see Clem's notes that the General had given him before he left his office. He had not had a chance to examine them before now. Pulling them out, he stared in stunned disbelief at the scope of supplies and material it encompassed. Like Clem before him, he was too overwhelmed to do more than scan it over, and then fold it up again. (see Appendix 1, fig. 7, "Equipment and Supplies Needed for Amboy and Marine Contingents"). Thankfully, at this moment, he was able to reach his wife.

"Hello, honey, it's me. I just got through with the General's briefing. It looks like we are in this for the long haul, all of us." Knowing he could not explain himself, he added, "but we can find some comfort in knowing that you and the kids, in fact all the families in our Seabee unit, are to be transferred over here on February 20th. I cannot say for how long, but I can imagine you'll have to take some leave time, anyway, from your job. I am sorry for that, but it appears that all of you coming here at this time are equally as important as our being here. The families must be together during this mission. That's about all I am allowed to say at this time, and frankly, I'm not too clear on much else anyway.

"Can't you tell me anything else?" Michelle asked, hoping to coax a little more information out of him, if not for her, at least for the kids.

"Not really. Some things I know are guarded, but most of what I know is either too confusing to me or, honestly, too unbelievable to pass on anyway. There will be someone from their Personnel Affairs Office at this Base contacting you soon, and maybe that person can shed more light on all this." He hated not being forthright with her, but he had such rigid orders of silence to maintain, and he was sincerely unclear about the overall scope of this horror, much less understanding the details of this operation.

"Ok, then, I will begin to pack some things for a short term stay, presumably at the Marine Base. The kids will, no doubt, enjoy that for a change. And I will be so glad to be with you. I can focus on my graduate studies in this hiatus, while away from my teaching. Come to think of it, I have enough time stored up; I think the college will allow me the time off, even with pay. So, then, it's settled. We'll see you sometime the week of February 20th. Thank you for letting me know ahead of time. The kids send their love and kisses. And I most assuredly adore you, my dearest."

"Thanks for being so understanding. You are the best. Kiss the kids for me. And know you are my everlasting love. Goodbye for now."

From that telephone call, events moved quickly, with the entire Seabee contingent finally arriving late that night at the cavern. With everyone now knowing what lay ahead, they arrived exhausted, with nerves stretched thin, but their work had to begin immediately.

February 10th became indelibly imprinted on both the Air Force personnel at the Marine Base and the Seabees at the Providence Mountains' Cavern. For at 0900 hours B made a stunning, surprise appearance amidst a final organizational briefing with the Air Force personnel at the Marine Base, and then at 1000 hours B did the same in a general Seabee meeting in which all personnel were attending at the cavern. The Shapeless Form, the sudden appearance and disappearance, the transformations in all the personnel, and most importantly, the message of almost plaintive urgency of their missions, all combined to change forever these two groups. Both had now been given the calm reassurance others had been transformed with, and both were given the ability to speak and understand all languages. Then B was gone.

Still staggered by what he had witnessed with B's appearance, luckily, it wasn't until 1130 hours that Lt. Javitts got the call from General Stanfield, letting him know the Yucca Mountain Repository was cleared for their use. The General instructed him to begin immediately ordering supplies, but any delivery was not to start before February 20th, well after the first group arrived late on the 17th.

The General went on to explain that there would be 100 people arriving on the 17th. The group would be a large convoy of 25 each, from Camp Pendleton and Fort Irwin and from their respective San Diego bases, 25 each of Navy and Coast Guard personnel. They were being instructed to bring with them equipment and fuel for construction, remodeling and for search and rescue missions, and daily supplies for two months. Then on the February 21st the second large group of Air Force personnel, 80 from Col. Blackmore and Swisher's flights, and 20 more from Nellis AFB, would arrive. He surmised that General Scott and his leadership staff would stay behind, however, until the last minute. In addition, they were also instructed to bring daily supplies for two months. The final large group to come, sometime around March 1st, he hoped, would be his Seabee battalion of 50 personnel. Once the three ranking officers from Nellis arrived, that would bring the final total to 250 personnel stationed at the Yucca Mountain Repository. And upon their families' arrival, this number would reach 1000. The General concluded by saying having this information, Lt Javitts would now have to arrange ordering and transporting supplies and equipment for this number of people for at least one-year's confinement. He suggested that he also duplicate Clem's order of rebuilding materials as well. It would at least give them some material to begin working with, once it was possible to exit the Repository.

And in words that Lt. Javitts never forgot for the rest of his life, the General concluded with, "I hope and pray for you all the good fortune and God's grace and mercy that can be given at this time. And I pray the same for all of us here in this epic struggle we now face. I am placing you in charge of coordinating the preparations for living in the Repository and for ordering the needed supplies. Communicate directly with me, or with Clem in Amboy, regarding questions, issues or needs. Now, go to work, son."

Lt. Javitts probably knew more than most, outside the immediate personnel who worked on building the Yucca Mountain Repository, due to his reading many articles about its development in his professional journal, written for The Society of American Military Engineers. He was well aware of the engineering challenges to build it and of the environmental issues surrounding its location. Moreover, by his familiarity with all this, he soon realized that the most practical and quickest method of transporting and storing large amounts of goods and equipment there was by rail. Further, he thought one of the three major railroad companies probably owned the roadbed in that region.

Analyzing what the General had told him, what his new orders were and that the railroad was his only option for delivery, he knew he had to dedicate time to this effort. Getting some sleep, henceforth, would be possible only when he absolutely had to. There was such a finite amount of time left before the deadline of April 1st. "God help us all", he whispered.

With some effort, he made a trek around the cavern, looking for, and finally locating his junior officers, Collins and Gonzaque. He explained to them his orders, and that they were to have total responsibility for their respective work teams. As he saw it, their primary objectives were to excavate and drill tunnels, to locate an area and drill a well for water, to construct a sewer and connect both water and sewer lines into the cavern, and finally to build the two exterior warehouses. They were to use the expertise and resource of the 53 Amboy personnel as well. For now, the two would come to him with problems as they arose, but otherwise, they were in charge. He emphasized they had to complete this work by the end of the month, no matter what.

After this discussion with his officers, the rest of that afternoon was spent talking to the Customer Service Departments of the regional railroad line serving the Las Vegas area and Amtrak. Both these contacts came after a quick telephone call to Clem Newberry to confirm that it was ok to use the debit card number for the requisition of materials and equipment he would need. It was a refreshing and reassuring conversation he had with Clem. His calmness was a welcome change. Most importantly, he instructed, even encouraged Ben, to be as innovative and far-reaching in his ideas and solutions to problems, as he needed to be. No one would question his choices or decisions. Clem had complete faith that Ben could make it all happen.

Armed with this confidence, he sat down at his makeshift desk, in his small tent beside the Providence Cavern, and calculated what was needed and how to get it delivered to the Yucca Mountain facility. He decided to divide up the ordering into two major groups: sleeping quarters, a lounge area to lessen the overwhelming stress and facilities for a kitchen and dining area in one group; and in the other group, toilet and shower facilities, food, beverages, household and personal supplies, along with materials and equipment.

He decided to tackle the last group first. The rebuilding supplies were probably the easiest to start with. General Stanfield had given him a photocopy of the equipment and material Clem had ordered from his railroad contact. And because that line and the one he was calling had merged recently, it was easy for him to ask that they pull up those invoices and duplicate that order for delivery to the Yucca Mountain facility. He requested their delivery be after the one to Amboy.

For foodstuffs, he estimated that each family of four would consume about 27 ft³ per month. That would equal 324 ft³ a year. Multiplied by 250 families, that came to 81,000 ft³. A forty-foot long boxcar had the capacity to hold approximately 2,560 ft³. He anticipated that it would then take approximately 32 boxcars to handle those supplies.

They would need twelve 32-foot long, 18,000-gallon tank cars for hazardous material: three of each for diesel fuel, unleaded gasoline, and aviation fuel; one of each for motor oil, lubricating compound and kerosene.

After some time spent sketching, drafting and

revising, he came up with a plan for the toilets and showers in this most unlikely area for humans to try and to survive in. This facility was built, after all, to house humanity's most deadly waste material, not to safely shelter people for up to a year. All facilities had to be portable. The area was too immense and unmanageable for the construction of housing, food preparation, eating or sleeping quarters or finding and acquiring a fresh water supply. It offered nothing for survival, other than the hoped for security of being deep underground in a reinforced repository, originally designed for the dangerous materials that never came.

Understanding that this is what he had to work with, his design for the toilets and showers involved the construction of external stairs up to an eight-foot wide platform over the top of each tank car, designated as a toilet or shower facility. The platform would have a narrow two-foot walkway, surrounded by a childproof railing. Beside that walkway would be six separate, five-foot square enclosed toilet and basin cubicles. In the case of showers, an entirely separate tank car would have the same superstructure, but fitted with just a shower room instead of the toilet facilities. There would be no running water piped into either the toilet or the shower tank cars. The Seabees would cut open and weld portals into the tank car for each individual toilet and sink cubicle or shower stall. For the shower, there would be a manual hand pump to preload an overhead container with a four-gallon limit of water. There would be no hot water. For after toilet use, hand washing would require occupants use a waterless hand sanitizer lotion for disinfection. In addition, to wash any clothes, a person has to bring a bucket of water up into the cubicle.

Showers would be limited to once a month per person. For 1000 individuals showering for twelve months that amounted to 48,000 gallons of water or three 16,000 gallon tank cars. For both toilet sanitation and clothes washing use, he estimated they could use only one gallon of water per day. Again for 1000 people that would amount to 365,000 gallons for the year or fifteen 24,000-gallon tank cars of water. Drinking water would likewise be limited to one gallon a day per person or 365,000 gallons in a year. Likewise, this would require fifteen 24,000-gallon tank cars of drinking quality water. That brought the total to 77 box and tank cars that the train would have to transport to the Yucca Mountain facility. As an afterthought, he would add 60 empty flat cars in this request. They would be used to transport any extra equipment or vehicles that he had not accounted for. It was some time later that Capt. Tam called him to reinforce this order of the flat cars.

Once that was organized, he called the headquarters for railroad in Omaha, Nebraska. Like Clem, he spent the next three hours ordering from his list of foodstuffs, beverages, personal and household items and rebuilding materials. He discussed with the Customer Service agent the general layout of where this material was coming to, and that there was a five mile long track in horseshoe shaped curve inside the complex. He assumed the rebuilding materials alone would encompass one trainload two miles long. In addition, he estimated the trainload containing the other supplies and equipment would be another mile and a half in length, if the flat cars and locomotives were also incorporated in that freight manifest. He specified that for the time being the five locomotives pulling the rebuilding materials would have to stay with that train, as would the five locomotives pulling the other freight train. If there were extra charges associated with that request, then they were to be added to the invoice. Also, he requested a switch engine accompany the supply train and charge for that as well.

When asked by the Corporate Headquarters what was happening that required this material to be purchased and transported to Yucca Mountain, Lt Javitts replied that it was all associated with a Top Secret National Emergency Program. In the event of a sudden and emergent quarantine of large numbers of infected individuals, this facility was to be the base of operations to protect the general population from those who were infected. Considering these circumstances, the Customer Service Department, after lengthy discussions with supervisory personnel, agreed with these requests, including leaving the engines and freight trains intact at the entrance to the tunnels. Lt. Javitts assured them that his personnel at the mothballed Repository would see to it that their train engineers would be shuttled back into their offices in Las Vegas, once the deliveries were made. Again, like with Clem, once the debit card was validated for this order, the railroad was more than willing to aid the nation in this emergency preparation. Moreover, they understood the need for strict secrecy.

That left Lt. Javitts with his final orders to be lodged with Amtrak, and then he would be done with this initial stage. In speaking with the Amtrak Customer Service Department in Washington, D.C., he began the reason for his order with the same explanation given to the freight trains' representative. Due to an anthrax emergency some years earlier in the Amtrak offices' immediate vicinity, there was no argument with his justification for what he requested.

And since Amtrak had continued its sad decline in passenger train bookings, particularly on the Superliner's cross-country routes across the mid section of the country, his request was not met with as much surprise or resistance as he had anticipated. Probably a major source of the decline was due to the apathy of the national leadership to support, financially and politically, train service nationwide. While other countries had accelerated their modernization of their rail lines and trains, Congress and the Executive Branches of government had essentially discarded any notion of promoting or upgrading this country's rail service. It was a disgrace.

Airports became log-jammed, airlines went in and out of bankruptcy or existence, and full airport and airline security was never guaranteed no matter how much money was poured into the effort. Meanwhile, passenger train travel was allowed to sink quietly into oblivion. Only Amtrak's Superliners' Coastal Starlight and Empire Builder routes remained solvent.

Taking a deep breath after his initial remarks, Lt. Javitts then added, "I need to place an order to either rent or purchase, whichever is the surest way I can get what I need in the shortest amount of time, the following. By the first week in March, I need delivered to the Yucca Mountain Repository, about 100 miles northwest of Las Vegas, 25 Superliner II Sleeper cars, 5 Kitchen/Dining cars and 5 Lounge cars. They will need to be pulled by five of your Amtrak locomotives; and they, too, will have to stay with the train after it is delivered."

The response was immediate and not unexpected. "You're joking! You want what? You can't be serious!"

Reviewing again in his mind the justification for this order, Lt. Javitts quickly refigured, to see if his requests were accurate. He planned on ten families using one sleeper car. He anticipated having 50 families, or 5 sleeper cars, in a self-contained living area. In this group there would also be included one kitchen/dining car, and one lounge car. This living area would be located on a track in a 25-foot wide tunnel, but all of these cars would be located, as well, adjacent to a spur rail line that led into a sixteen-foot wide side tunnel, which the Yucca Mountain developers had called an "emplacement drift". The spur angled off the main line on which the sleeper, kitchen and lounge cars would be parked. There also would be six freight cars in this side tunnel, each one containing the necessary supplies for two months. In addition, located in this 'drift' would be three tank cars for drinking water and three tank cars for toilet and lavatory purposes. Altogether, these twelve cars would have to sustain these 50 families for one year. The extra tank cars, to be used for showering, would have to be spaced between the first and second drift, between the fourth and fifth drift and near the entrance to the third drift on the main rail line.

After this quick review, he replied, "Yes, I am very serious, urgently so. As a nation, we must prepare ourselves, in the expectation that a major emergency could occur in the not so distant future. Your cooperation and help is essential. Can you arrange for this to be done?"

The Lieutenant was then instructed to wait for a call back from Amtrak Headquarters. At this point, no one present in their office could even begin to make such a decision. He agreed he would stand by and gave the Customer Service representative his telephone number.

He only had to wait about 45 minutes, when his phone rang and on the other end was the Vice President of Operations for Amtrak.

"Lt. Javitts, My name is George Landis. I am the Vice President of Operations for Amtrak. I understand there is an urgent need for you to commandeer a rather large number of our Superliner cars for a special train. Can you enlighten me a little on the reasons for this unprecedented request?"

"Sir," the Lieutenant began, "in wartime it has been customary for the Defense Department to requisition civilian trains, buses, airplanes and ships. This is no different. As you know, we are facing a different kind of enemy, one who has absolutely no respect for any life. With each passing day, the probability of some terrible catastrophe occurring becomes more apparent, and associated with it will most likely come a highly contagious aftermath. We have to prepare for mass isolation, or quarantining, of infected personnel. This facility at the abandoned Yucca Mountain Repository is the first in a series of these shelters that will be established nationwide. I am prepared to purchase, not commandeer as you indicated, in behalf of the nation, this train, once it is assembled.

I understand much of your passenger rolling stock is standing idle. This, in the short term, would give you some additional operational funding. Moreover, the equipment will be returned to you once the emergency period has passed. However, and I must be clear on this point, we need this train to be assembled and delivered by March 5th. That is not negotiable. And this entire matter has to remain top secret. Any leaks would be considered a federal crime; that must also be understood by you and your staff."

Once the Lieutenant had finished his reply, there was a long period of silence. "Ok, I see your point," Mr. Landis acknowledged. "The logistics are a little awkward, given the location of the Yucca Mountain facility. But I believe they completed the rail line to Yucca Mountain by circumventing the Nevada Test range, starting the transit line northeast of Las Vegas by splitting off from the main line to Salt Lake City. It begins at the town of Caliente and heads northwest from there. That line still should be serviceable. We will have your train there on or just before March 5th. My office will compute the cost of this and let you know by tomorrow. I guess, in conclusion, it is fair and appropriate to say, I just hope and pray we never have to use it for such a purpose."

"I do too, Mr. Landis. To do so will signal a terrible step backward for our civilization," Lt Javitts, replied, relieved this negotiation was ending. He was very uncomfortable fabricating this scenario, but what else could he do? Hanging up the phone, he glanced at his watch and saw that it was 1850 hours. Today had been an exhausting experience.

The Seabees worked non-stop in shifts, sometimes not sleeping for 40 hours, what with both their own work and supervising the Amboy workers and Marines. Amazingly, though, by February 27th, they were done and packed up to leave. It was, as later described, both an inspirational effort and remarkable accomplishment. But their work was only half done. Now they had to prepare their own home site at the Yucca Mountain facility. Late that night Lt. Javitts and his personnel were able to be briefly, but blessedly, rejoined with their families. Each member of the Seabee battalion that next day made sure their family members were right beside them as they replenished their supplies. It was vital to each person there, children and spouses alike, that they be together now. And each person helped unload, sort and reload. Once refueled and restocked, everyone, including their families, went to the Officer's Club, at the General's urging for dinner. It had the largest dining room on Base. By nightfall, they drove off, but this time it was to prepare what were to be their own homes. At dawn on March 1st, they pulled up to the southern gate at the Yucca Mountain Repository, soon to be renamed the Yucca Mountain Cavern.

TWO: THE FRONT GATE

At the meeting the Air Force personnel had to attend on February 10th, in which B made his shocking appearance, it was decided that the four teams of cargo and refueling planes would each be assigned a particular geographical region, or continental mass, to be more exact. Col. Blackmore's team #1 would cover Europe; Team #2 would be assigned Asia; Team # 3, Col. Swisher's team would be responsible for Africa; and Team #4 would try to manage as much of the North and South American continents as they could. It was agreed, if anyone completed their mission before February 17th, they were to contact the other teams to see who needed assistance.   And in an orchestrated effort, that would have made the finest symphony envious, by 2230 hours on February 17th, all flights had returned safely and successfully to the Marine Base.

By mid-morning on February 20th, the families of the Air Force crews had arrived from Fairchild and McChord. It was a joyous, but brief, reunion for these families. The families knew little about what was ahead, but they were aware each one was eventually to be rejoined with their loved ones sometime in the next few weeks. For now, come 2230 hours, all eight planes had to leave for Nellis AFB.

Upon their arrival at Nellis, they were met by Major General Benton Scott, the commanding officer of the Base. Along with him were his two closest associates in the operation of this Base, Col. Frances Bynum with Material and Logistics Operations and Col Alfred ('Alfie') W. Shoemaker, with Combat Support and Search and Rescue Operations. Accompanying them were Capt. Louise Matthews and Senior Master Sergeant Jesus Cabrera, along with fifteen other Air Force personnel, divided equally into three crews for Transportation, Search and Rescue and Engineering/Maintenance. They were all hand- picked either by the General or his most trusted officers. Only by enlisting the highest-ranking Officers on Base could the landing of these eight huge planes be carried out with the precision and stealth that was required. These twenty individuals were also to be sheltered in the Yucca Mountain Cavern.

With the eight planes safely landed and parked as far away from the usual runways and taxiways on the Transient East tarmac, the process of unloading the cargo planes of their trucks and equipment took about three hours. Waiting for them, parked nearby, were ten more trucks, loaded with supplies and building materials and equipment to begin refitting the cavern for their survival. The long procession of trucks and humvees, with an additional 97 workers, eased out of the Base by 0430 hours on February 21st. They arrived at the southern gate of the Yucca Mountain facility by 0800 hours.

The third major group of possible Yucca Mountain survivors was finally assembled on February 12th at the 29 Palms Marine Base. At 0800 hours, General Stanfield met with the 100 Army, Coast Guard, Navy and Pendleton-based Marines. At that meeting, held as usual, in the Marine Base Main Auditorium, with all doors secured, both General Stanfield and B spoke. The meeting lasted one hour, with the now too familiar and overpowering revelation regarding April 1st. Following this meeting, it was necessary to spend the next five days assembling supplies and equipment, and disassembling other equipment for transport. As with each group being sent to Yucca Mountain, they also had to take enough food and water to be self-sufficient for two months.

Finally, on February 17th, by 2015 hours, they had loaded the supplies, the two search and rescue boats, two disassembled Coast Guard rescue helicopters, and two disassembled prop-driven airplanes, along with half a dozen large bladders of aviation fuel, diesel fuel, engine oil and lubrication compound.

If there was one person, who could be singled out in this group, who might be the commanding officer, it most likely was the Coast Guard's Capt. Earnest ('Ernie') Tam, who had been the Chief of Operations for Search and Rescue out of the San Diego District. But two others ran a close second. They were Capt. Lilyanne O'Shay, a U.S. Navy Engineering Officer, who had just returned from sea duty on the USS Carl Vinson (CVN 70) or Col. Derek Amen with the Engineering Command at Camp Pendleton. They all recognized, however, by his well-deserved reputation as a remarkably original thinker and innovative engineer with the Army Corps of Engineers, that Major Jon Shultz could lead this expedition just as easily as they could. It probably was due to the many exploits that Capt. Tam was known for, both involving interdiction and search and rescue, that made him the unanimous choice. He was a natural leader, and personnel sought to be under his command.

So with minimal discussion, it was decided who would lead, and Capt. Tam took the lead vehicle out of the Marine Base that night. He knew it would be a slow convoy, given the type of equipment and supplies they were hauling. It was everyone's hope that by daybreak they would at least be on the northern edge of Las Vegas, missing the rush hour traffic and all the speculation that would follow. Their one mishap occurred when one of their overloaded trucks took a curve too fast, north of Cima, and ran off the pavement and buried its rear axle in loose sand. That required an extra hour and half to shift the load and rearrange vehicles to push and to tow it out of the soft shoulder. Much to their relief, they did make it out of Las Vegas just at sunrise.

From there, the topography of the landscape changed dramatically. The Providence Mountains provided an almost intimate sense of wildness and a comforting lack of civilization's littering presence. As far as you could see, the area was blanketed with scrub brush, like a bluish-green carpet, extending along the valley floor and up the mountainsides on both sides of the valley. Even though the view was expansive, it was not overpowering. It fit in your mind's eye comfortably.

That was not the case as this first group began to enter the region of the Nevada Test Site, west of the Spotted Mountain Range and into the Amargosa Valley, east of the small community of Beatty. It was stark, devoid of vegetation, almost as if all life had abandoned this area epoch's ago. The mountains, and outcrops of lesser formations, appeared to have been forged by some impatient force. This desolate expanse had to be fired quickly, and then whatever did it, had to leave. If the deep desert of the Mojave held your fears, this Great Basin area had to have been their birthplace. And then you saw the Yucca Mountain. It was a mountain shaped like the spiny ridgeback of a massive, stalking crocodile. It rose thousands of feet from the valley floor, in one long continuous and uninterrupted ridgeline. It stood alone. Apparently, its volcanic exterior was the result of violent activity from a nearby extinct super volcano, which itself was situated in a massive caldera. The entire area exuded a violent history and life-ending climate changes.

By 1030 hours on February 18th, the first of four groups pulled up to the front gate of the abandoned Yucca Mountain complex. To prevent vandalism or any harm to come to well meaning tourists, the entire area was fenced off, and posted with signage, warning: "Property of U.S. Government. Keep Out! All Violators Will Be Prosecuted!" In addition, the front gates were locked and monitored around the clock by four contracted security guards.

Capt. Tam slowly got out of his lead vehicle and stretched. Once the stragglers in the convoy had all arrived, he called out to one of the guards, as he walked up to the inside of the locked chain link gate, "Good morning, to you."

The fourth, and largest group, arrived on March 23rd. It consisted of the 230 families. Their departure time was 1800 hours from the 29 Palms Marine Base. Each of the four cargo planes, commanded by Col. Blackmore, ferried 25 families. It took three separate sorties to transport all their loved ones and their belongings to Nellis AFB. Once they arrived there, trucks and buses were awaiting them to move them directly to the Yucca Mountain shelter. By 2300 hours, the first 100 families arrived at the front gate. The others followed in five-hour intervals until late morning on the 24th.

And by 1600 hours on March 24th, Col. Blackmore's cargo planes were shuttered and secured. A final loading of possessions and official papers, documents, operation manuals and smaller Air Force equipment were loaded onto waiting trucks. Accompanying his crews were the 20 families from

Nellis. In addition, interestingly enough, this included Maj. General Scott, Col.'s Bynum, Shoemaker, and their families. It was their determination that it was best to exit the Base now, rather than try to explain all the activities of the last 24 hours.

In a sense, it was like abandoning ship, with all the crew still on board. But when B appeared before their assembled families and these officers yesterday, it was clear that no one was guaranteed survival, even with all these preparations. They were being chosen both in an attempt to maybe save some from what lay ahead and because they had been so instrumental in assisting the Amboy families. Put simply, this whole mission involved desperately trying to preserve a record of their species existence, if nothing else. And possibly, they would be the only ones to survive, if the Amboy shelter failed. The General's first duty now was not to the Base personnel, it was to those at Yucca Mountain and Amboy. These shelters were now the cradles of whatever civilization might survive. He and his staff had to leave. With the arrival of this last convoy from Nellis, the Yucca Mountain Cavern's front gates were closed and welded shut. It was 1910 hours on March 24th.

PART II

THREE: THE AFTERMATH

For the next 48 hours following the onset of radio silence and subsequent violent shaking, after the General Assembly meeting on April 1st, most Amboy cavern families stayed in their homes.   At times, probably corresponding to whenever someone awoke, one family member would wander down to the kitchen area, take some slices of bread out of their assigned food pantry area, open a can of something, sprinkle and spread something else on the bread and take whatever it was back to their living quarters for everyone to eat. The reason for there being any ready-made bread on the shelves was because someone, as an afterthought, had suggested that whatever extra food supplies Hazel and Ray could spare, they would take and use that perishable food during these first few days of confusion and adjustment.   It was not an organized or nutritious effort. For many, however, no one in the family left their homes except to use the toilet facilities.   A pall of deepest depression was seeping throughout the caves.

You could only know it was day by observing which overhead lights were on, and sometime during the day on April 2nd, the children of two families took it upon themselves to check on the animals and pets.

The families were actually neighbors in Cave

#1.   Coincidentally, one family was from Iran and the other was from Israel.   Jihan Zandi, age 13, and her brother, Ilhan, age 12, were from Malek Keyan, a medium sized town 20-25 miles from Tabriz, Iran. Like Denver, Malek Keyan was another 'mile high' city, situated at an elevation of 5,249 feet.   Both sister and brother had loved being around animals since they could remember. They spent all the time they could on their grandparents little farm outside town, where they could tend to their goats, sheep and two dairy cows.

The other half of this team was Hannah Segal, age 11, and her brother Mandel, age 14. They were from Kibbutz Ketura, 30 miles north of Eilat on the Gulf of Aqaba, or Gulf of Eilat as some preferred to call it, in the Wadi Arava North Division of the Rift Valley. It was a progressive kibbutz, with an active veterinary facility. They both took turns volunteering to work in that clinic, plus working daily after school, grooming and feeding the animals in the kibbutz's various barns and sheds.

Together with Megan and Bernice, Fred and Freda Wailand's two daughters, these six protectors became the backbone of the Pet and Animal Welfare Association,   as   it   was   later   named.   Almost simultaneously, this group had made their way into Cave #4, to find a dazed, frightened and hungry menagerie of creatures, needing to be fed and reassured. Even though the pets and animals had only been in the Cavern for less than five days, the violent shaking on April 1st had cowered them all.

For the next four hours, the six split up, each one taking a group of animals they felt most comfortable with, and each began the process of feeding, watering, and exercising. The pens and stalls were not so soiled, so not much needed to be done in that regard, but each animal responded affectionately to the cuddling and petting, along with some needed food and water. The group determined that until their school schedule and studies began to consume much of their time, they would all meet at 6 a.m. to care for, share ideas and begin some animal training. Then once school started, they would divide the week amongst themselves, each taking a particular day and all of them coming together again on Sundays. They knew others would help, so their first official act was to prepare a sign-up notice for volunteers to help. They put it on the Bulletin Board by the cavern Office later that same day. Somehow, each of them privately realized that their coming together like this signaled a vocational commitment that would bring their lives and cultural backgrounds ever closer together in the years ahead. And one day, they hoped, the pets and animals could be shown, like at a 4-H county fair exhibit, to the assembled cavern families. Finally, they hoped each animal would be adopted once everyone was able to leave this place. For these six workers the anxiety and fear of April 1st was just a little less by the end of this day.

However, so acute was the need to begin some type of crisis intervention for the vast majority of the cavern residents that Mitzi Zimmerman, the Swiss clinical psychologist from Basel, knew she and her associates had to finish organizing and implementing their plan. Her husband, Franz, was a preschool teacher, and he, too, had begun working non-stop to prepare for the start of school with Kita Satou, the preschool teacher from Japan.

Likewise, on April 2nd, within an hour or two of the children beginning to feed and water the animals, Mitzi knew she had to assemble her own staff of counselors and social workers for the crisis at hand. Certainly, she, Franz and their children were equally shocked and devastated by the news that B gave to them that day in Ray and Hazel's restaurant. Eventually, however, as they tried to struggle out of their feelings of desperation, the one small glimmer of hope this whole Amboy Cavern affair gave them was of their eventually having a home of their own. In Basel, 70% of the population rent their residences; purchasing or owning a home is not possible for the vast majority of citizens. As crude as their container home was and as emotionally spent as they were imaging what was occurring throughout the world, now that they were sheltered in the cavern, it had given them a sense of belonging somewhere. She knew it was odd, but for these days and weeks, and quite likely, for the years ahead, the reality of what they would be facing would require each person to find some small benefit, opportunity, possibility, or dream to seize and hold onto. The more concrete that source of hope, the better for now. Eventually for most families, and almost immediately for some, their religious faith would provide a major source of comfort and a measure of peace. But, with the enormity of what had and was continuing to happen, she knew from experience working at Basel's University Hospital, whose motto was "a person's psychological and social well being is of prime importance", that to begin the healing from a tragic loss required some small, visible or tangible link to the future. It had to provide a window of encouragement, something they could gaze out from and begin to visualize a future worth living. Religious faith, in those moments of greatest loss, was the bedrock that allowed you to stand at that window.

Further, she knew they had no ordained priests or pastors, no trained imams, rabbis or monks. All she was aware of was that there were some lay church, synagogue, temple, shrine and mosque leaders in their midst. Why there were no fulltime, professional church leaders puzzled her, as did the absence of any lawyers or most other health care professionals, besides the few represented here. She thought their absence must have something to do with B's overall plan for them, but the rationale for such a decision escaped her. Likewise, she did not have a clue why there were no veterinarians. Maybe there just was not enough space for them or many of the other professional specialties.

Her guess was that possibly organized religion had created more dissension and tragedy than it had given hope and comfort. The real worldly transmission of any faith is found in its believers, as they practice that faith day to day. Church polity appeared to become the beacon of so many organized religions and, too often, spiritual guidance of the needy became secondary. Rather than the light shine on the mysteries of creation and its Creator, it too often focused on personalities and decrees. Whatever the reasons for this oversight, unless B had somehow assembled other groups, like theirs here in Amboy Cavern, such traditions as apostolic succession, the continuity or passing of church doctrines from one designated leader to another in a particular organized religion, these were, most likely, effectively ended as of April 1st. The practice and transmission of a faith were now in the hands of its followers.

And for Mitzi and her staff, that faith was an integral component of any grief counseling or crisis intervention that they may have to provide. Within the next hour, she had walked around the homes in Cave #1 and assembled her staff. The team consisted of Dirk Vanbeek from Slotervaart, a suburb in Amsterdam. He had worked as a clinical psychologist in the OVLG Hospital in Amsterdam East. Next was Marianne Soto from Carboda, Argentina. She was a child psychologist who worked in an international organization that developed and operated child development centers. In addition, the final member of the team was Harriet Skinner from New Haven, Connecticut. She was the lead social worker at the Yale New Haven Hospital, a 944 bed, tertiary care facility. After Mitzi located each of them, together they walked back to Cave #5, where they found an empty room in the Medical Clinic.

"To start this meeting, does someone want to suggest how we can begin to meet this issue of deepening and widening depression head on?" Mitzi asked.

"First off, I think we have to bring the entire Health Care Team together," Dirk answered. "It appears this could have devastating possibilities for everyone, unless we address it with the involvement of all the health care professionals."

"Yes, I agree," Harriet, added. "And further, as soon as possible, we need to post on the Communication Center Bulletin Board, and then distribute to all the Living Areas, our guidelines for symptoms of deepening depression, and how we plan to address them."

"This plan has to include the children, as well," Marianne interjected. "As soon as possible the preschool program must begin. Despite all that has and is happening, we have to consider their welfare first. They are the future. And if this depression cycle deepens and extends, the hope they bring for a new and lasting beginning will be dashed."

After some reflection, Mitzi nodded and said, "Excellent insight by all of you. I would suggest we contact Drs. Minor Peterson and Zara Mahmood, our co-directors of the Medical Facility, and Capt. Ian Murphy the commander of the Marine Medical Staff and arrange a meeting in two hours with all their personnel in one of the larger classrooms. Dirk, if you and Harriet will go over to the Communication Center Bulletin Board and check the housing locations for each of the Amboy health care staff, you can then go by each home and notify their staff of this meeting. I will do the same for the Marine Medical unit. Marianne, if you will, please go by the Office, as well, and ask Clem to start playing recorded music that is less formal or reverential. I recall in paper I read somewhere, a long time ago, about Music Therapy and its potential to vector people's moods. I'm not sure I can buy into a lot of that, but I do think it would help if starting this evening, after 48 hours since the onset of the total madness outside, we can begin listening to some music that sooths and inspires. Finally, we need to have everyone, including ourselves, meet back here at 3 p.m."

By 4:30 p.m. the 36-member health care staff, including physicians, nurses, medical staff professors, and first responders from the Amboy group and the 31 members of the Marine Base hospital staff, had met with Mitzi's small committee. All 67 agreed to be present at 8 a.m. tomorrow, April 3rd, both in the Medical Facility and in the Assembly Room, to screen all the cavern occupants who came. They agreed on the contents of the notice and that it should be posted, in the kitchen and toilet facilities, as well as on the Communication Center's Bulletin Board. Additionally, there should be announcements of this screening over the public address system every half hour from 5 p.m. until 8 p.m. today and tomorrow morning from 7 a.m. until 10 a.m. Due to a critical shortage of paper goods, it was necessary to begin with this announcement immediately, thereby limiting the amount of copying that would be necessary. The notices would have to be few, but well placed. They announced: (see Appendix 2, fig.1. "HEALTH ALERT! You May Need Grief Counseling or Crisis Management".)

And by 8 a.m. the next morning, there was a line from the Medical Facility front door winding around the Main Auditorium and out past Cave #3. The health care staff had positioned themselves throughout their clinic and the Auditorium, each armed with a checklist of things to investigate and to do, if there should be a positive finding of clinical depression, as newly defined by the Amboy Cavern. In all, ten adults and four children were admitted into the hospital facility; 268 were placed into group therapy for at least a few sessions; 72 were given brief doses of antidepressants, and 116 were told what they were experiencing was within normal limits, again as defined by Amboy Cavern criteria. Everyone was encouraged to return that night at 6 p.m. for the start of religious observances, regardless of whether someone preferred strictly defined services or ones that are more casual.

Almost exactly 50% of the cavern's occupants came to the screening clinic that morning of April 3rd. There were to be stragglers over the next week, but for now, it was felt they had averted a crisis. Only time would tell if they really had. The group sessions had to be successful, and the idle time had to be reduced with classes and activities, but mostly, with they had to begin preparations for the challenges they would be faced with, once they permanently exited the cavern.

That left them trying to impede the next flood of raw emotion, which could infect everyone, boredom. The final preparations for preschool, grades 1-12, apprentice and adult education classes had to be completed. All classes were to begin on April 5th. Everyone would be teaching either a class or attending one and many would be doing both. There was so much to learn and to do, such as mastering new skills, many of which had not been used for over a hundred years, organizing the teams to scout where to resettle, preparing the area, or areas, that would ultimately be chosen for settlement, performing rescue and/or recovery work for any survivors or causalities outside the cavern, and, most importantly, developing the ability and know-how to cultivate, grow, harvest, and store foodstuffs for survival. These were not academic pursuits. A past way of life had to be relearned, and a civilization had to be retooled for a new beginning, one that was to be far different than the one they had previously known.

To work toward achieving these goals, the teachers, the third major body to meet on April 2nd, had to finalize the structure of their program and the location of individual classes. As all encompassing as their objectives were, which they had begun work on when everyone was still living in Amboy, the April 5th deadline seemed almost impossible to meet. By 1 p.m. on April 2nd, the Amboy Cavern preschool, elementary, middle, and high school teachers, college instructors and professors and 15 more credentialed teachers who had taught in communities outside the Marine Base before April 1st, all convened in the Main Auditorium, sitting in a large semicircle around the front of the stage. There were 66 teachers in all, 56 from Amboy and 15 from the Marine Base. Early on, three individuals were chosen to lead the discussions and to be the Standing Educational Committee. They were to complete the assignments as determined by the overall group. Their last assignment, before the teaching started, was to get everyone's approval for the Educational Framework Document. It would guide all of them in the months ahead. Individual course assignments and curriculums were already assigned and nearing completion.

After everyone was seated, the three rose from the audience and took their seats just below the stage, facing the semicircle of fellow teachers. Overseeing this select group was Clarice Delow, who had lived in Paris' Latin Quarter, where she could be close to her place of work. She was a Professor of Biology at the "UPMC', the Universite' Pierre et Marie Curie. And with her, was Rashid Batak from Medan, North Sumatra, in Indonesia.

He was a Professor of Agriculture at the Universitas Sumatera Utara. The last member of this committee, as noted earlier, was Kita Satou, from the Arashiyama area with its magnificent bamboo forests, in western Kyoto, Japan. She was the director of one of the largest preschools in Kyoto. Kita was chosen by the three preschool teachers to develop and coordinate their comprehension program for the 198 children aged five or under. Along with these duties, she also served with this committee for creating the overall educational design for the Amboy Cavern

Dr. Delow elected to remain seated and began the meeting with, "Good afternoon ladies and gentlemen. I only greet you this way out of habit, for as we all know, it is not a good afternoon or day or week. It is the worst that can possibly be. Probably for me, and I might presume for the vast majority, if not for all of us cavern dwellers, the only two things that keep me focused, at all at this time, are my family and the missions we have been charged with. Aside from what destruction awaits us once we are able to exit this place, the other major determinant as to whether we are able to achieve long term survival, will be who, what and how we teach and train our fellow citizens in the months we have to prepare.

"For my part in today's meeting, I have only three final suggestions to make before we begin teaching on the 5th. The first is that I would prefer we don't use titles. Formality, at this time, seems alien. The children need to be comforted first, then as time passes, challenged, disciplined, and we eventually hope, inspired. Please address me by my first name only, and I will do the same with you. Already, I have seen the military personnel in our midst shed their titles of rank. I feel we should do the same.

"Secondly, I think we must enlist the

involvement of all the remaining adults from Amboy and all the Marines and their spouses to teach in Levels 4-7. I would be glad to arrange all this, with your approval. They will be teaching what they had been doing prior to April 1st, so class preparation will not be as tedious for them as it is for us, who will also be teaching in the purely academic or theoretical Levels. Could I see a show of hands if you agree to this?... Good, it is unanimously agreed that we should involve them.

"Finally, I will have Kita pass out to each of you the Educational Framework we all have been working on for some time. If you approve, this would be the final version, and it will become our roadmap for what is ahead. Please look it over and make suggestions or corrections." (see Appendix 2, fig. 2, "Amboy Cavern's Educational Framework").

"Are there questions?" she asked, after allowing about five minutes for everyone to study the handout. There followed some discussion about where all the classes were to be held and the scheduled times for them, but the document itself was approved as written.

"Then, with that, our committee will spend the rest of today and part of tomorrow preparing the location and times for the various classes. We will also post that information on the Communication Center Bulletin Board. Classes will then begin the 5th at 8 a.m. Good luck to us all. We will meet again in two weeks to address problems and issues that have arisen since today. And thank you for your time and dedication in beginning this venture into the unknown. May all that is Holy protect and guide us. Good day."

Classes began, as scheduled, on the 5th, with Levels 1-3 meeting in the morning until noon; Levels 4-6, starting at 1 p.m. lasting until 5 p.m.; and Level 7 classes beginning at 6 p.m. until 10 p.m. The classes for the Levels 1-3 were in Classroom Building A. Levels 4-

6 were in both Building A and B, where the laboratories were located. And for Level 7 classes were conducted in the Main Auditorium, A and B Classrooms and in all the communal areas in Caves #1, 2 and 3. Later on, as the animals settled in, Cave #4 areas were used as well for some Level 7 classes.

FOUR: DANGER FROM WITHIN

It was not until April 4th that the children felt comfortable enough, and that their parents felt reassured enough about the relative safety of their surroundings, to allow them to wander at will outside their homes. Possibly the same could be said for the deer mice hidden from view in the back of Caves # 2 and #3 in their ages-old nests. Generations of mice had been born, raised and migrated out from these sites. And with each succeeding generation, their migration had taken them closer to the void of the caves. And by this April 4th, the caves' northeast walls were havens. Only by their being in the shadows of the overhead lights could they be missed. However, to curious children, some of whom had already had either hamsters or store purchased mice as pets; it was inevitable that the deer mice's lairs would be found one day.

FIVE: THE GOVERNING BODY

And by 6 a.m. on April 8th, when the temporary Governing Body had their first meeting in the Main Auditorium, they were pleased to hear from all quarters that the mental health status of all, but a few residents, was within acceptable limits.   Additionally, they were told that the school programs were meeting everyone's expectations; and that the animals were calming down, with many children signed up for doing daily chores in that area. Throughout the cavern, there was now a low hum of activity, with some occasional exceptions of yelling, screaming or just loud conversations. Serving as background accompaniment to all this activity were Clem's cavern-wide, broadcasted musical selections. For each of the representatives, however, general relief and appreciation was expressed that the initial crises had been coped with and daily routines had begun.

Once the 27 members had taken their seats, positioned around the right side of the stage, Eric Stanfield rose to address the group.

"Good early morning to each of you," he began. "I realize it is quite early for a meeting such as this, but with the class schedules, and our need for some privacy and the space to accommodate all of us, it seemed best to come here at this time. Certainly, if you can think of a better place and time, let's do it.

"You will note there are only 27 of us here

today.   The children's representatives haven't been selected yet, and this is primarily an organizational meeting.   But with your approval, we can incorporate them in all subsequent meetings, once they have elected their representatives.

"If you don't mind, I am going to forge ahead today with outlining what we need to begin organizing and accomplishing.   As you can see, I have already written on flip chart paper our agenda for today's meeting. (see Appendix 2, fig. 3, "The Temporary Governing Body's April 8th Meeting Agenda.") I would propose we go through this list now, so we can be out of here before the students begin to arrive.

"First off, the nomination and election process should be fairly straightforward.   Each of you now representing a 25 family group should immediately inform them that they need to elect two representatives. There is no limit as to how many could campaign for these offices, and you will have to run for this position as well, if you want to remain on the Governing Body. The two with the most votes will be elected.

"To prepare for this election, we will arrange to have nine boxes, one for each family group. And I'll get Clem to make individual ballots for each group, indicating who is running for the office on each ballot. Every individual 18 or older must vote, and they will be instructed to vote for only two names on each ballot. We will number the ballots to insure there are none missing or added.   In addition, I'll also have Clem prepare a list of all eligible voters, one that everyone has previously signed, and after each of us has voted, we will have to sign that list again. As has been the custom, voting will be in secret, but we need to insure that everyone did vote on April 25th. The same holds true for the children, except there will only be two representatives from the Marine families and one from the Amboy families. Here, again, Clem will see to the nomination and election process for the children, as well.

"You'll also need to explain to everyone, before the campaigning begins, that the composition of the Governing Body will be amended again, once all of us can finally abandon this shelter and be permanently relocated. Specifically, it will entail the Marine officers and Amboy coordinators being replaced with other elected representatives. These positions will no longer exist. Likewise, the Standing Committees will evolve or be eliminated, with others taking their place, as our circumstances change. But for now, we need to establish the composition and leadership of each committee so their work can begin immediately."

Following this introduction by Eric, there was a 45 minute discussion and selection process for the Standing Committees. (see Appendix 2, fig. 5, "The Global Union's Standing Committees".) It was then agreed that Eric would notify each Chairperson, giving them their list of committee members and instructing them to begin meeting immediately. They were to meet as often as necessary to have a final document or report ready for the Governing Body's final approval by April 22nd. Moreover, it was further agreed that once the children's representatives were elected, those chosen could attend any of the subsequent committee meetings.

The final order of business for the Governing Body was to address the "General Issues" on Eric's flip chart. That took the last 30 minutes of the meeting time. After that, the Level 1-3 children began to pour into the Main Auditorium. As the area filled with children, it was agreed that when the representatives met with the families to organize the nominations, they would then discuss these "General Issues" and their recommendations to resolve them.

To conclude, Eric offered a parting, "Good

work, folks. We must try to be of as much good cheer and courage as possible. Make no mistake, everyone will be watching you, taking his or her cues as to the likelihood of this venture succeeding or failing. Daily, we can't help but face the scope and complexity of what is ahead. And daily, each of us has our own moments of despair. I have been in many desperate situations in my previous life, before April 1st, but none even remotely compare to the enormity of this challenge. I am proud to be associated with each of you. Your courage, strength and perseverance help me to go forward. And I thank you for that as well. If everyone agrees, let's meet again same place, same time on April 22nd. God's speed."

April 22nd arrived in a wave of surprisingly, vigorous activity, and yet upon closer examination, it probably was more a displacement-like diversion for many. The nomination and electoral process gave most citizens an opportunity to be preoccupied with something other than coping with their surroundings. Each of the 25 family groups had at least five candidates vying for the two representative seats. Included in those five or so names were the temporary representatives meeting on this day in the Main Auditorium. They were to hear, and in some cases, to deliver the reports from the Standing Committees. Promptly at 6 a.m., Eric called the final meeting of the Temporary Governing Body to order and asked for the committees' reports.

The Education Committee was better prepared than most, because of their having to plan and implement the Level 1-7 teaching programs. The one major change for this committee was the addition of the various members who were to help with the Level 7 curriculum development and instruction. This was to be more than an oversight committee. Each of the members would be teaching or preparing contingency plans, and adapting courses to fit what was projected to be the conditions outside the cavern, once rebuilding began. Everyone agreed this committee had the potential to be the most influential in determining their ultimate survival.

The Governance and Judiciary Committee had to do the most research and long range planning. To help guide them, they recommended an all-inclusive renaming of the Amboy and Yucca Mountain facilities' citizenry. Their suggestion was: 'The Global Union' or 'GU' for short. Everyone on the Governing Body agreed that it was an appropriate name, befitting the time and composition of the populace. It was suggested that at the inaugural ceremonies on April 25th, the new name would be presented to the entire population for their approval.

And the committee submitted an outline of how the new government would be formed. (see Appendix 2, fig.6, "The Global Union's Legislative, Legal and Fiscal Principles.") Basically, it was to be a blending of constitutional and parliamentary democracies, along with the early establishment of agricultural and financial co-operatives. The inclusion of co-operatives was based on the economic reality of most pre-April 1st emerging cultures and communities in the so-called Third World. But, it was noted, that even in the economically stable countries like Japan and Great Britain, co-operatives were widely used. The values and principles, as outlined by the International Co-operative Alliance, suited the committee's goals and aspirations for the Global Union's earliest formation. (see Appendix 2, fig. 7, "Definition, Values, and Principles of Co-operatives.").

The Financial Framework Committee, without question, had spent the most time of all the committees researching, arguing over and composing a draft document. It encompassed a number of far-reaching and complicated issues. Their paper, "The Global Union's

Financial Structure Flowchart" (see Appendix 2, Fig. 4.), required major adaptation due to the realities any of the Amboy and Yucca Mountain survivors might face. In the pre April 1st world of economics, what this committee was suggesting would have been heresy. But for them, the conclusions eventually became self-evident. After Eric, the Chairman of this committee, completed their report, he nodded to Ian Murphy to make his committee's report.

The work of the Transitions Committee was not as easy to categorize or outline. Their subject matter, like the events of birth, marriage, and death, did not respond to regimentation and neat organizational boxes. With an inaudible sigh, Ian rose to address the Body. He felt the information he had to present warranted standing. There was nothing mechanical or dispassionate about their committee's recommendations.

"Probably I should begin, as our committee had to, reviewing what had taken place, cavern-wide, before this group began to meet. As you may remember, a gathering was announced on April 3rd, for everyone to come here to the Auditorium at 6 p.m. It was to complement the work being done by our health care personnel to combat serious post-April 1st depressions. Furthermore, it was hoped that by coming, everyone could find some comfort and strength from his or her respective faiths. There was no official count of how many families actually came, but it was estimated to be well over half our population. What ultimately resulted from this first meeting was that, amongst all of us assembled there, we elected to merge certain faiths. Not having any ordained or professionally trained religious leadership, we felt we had no choice but to become more ecumenical.

"Under the heading of "Catholic" were joined those families and individuals who had attended Russian or Greek Orthodox, Roman Catholic, and Episcopal services. Under "Islam" were Sunni and Shiite families and individuals. Under "Protestant" were all other Christian faiths that had evolved since the 1517 division of Christianity. And under "Judaism" were their followers, as was the case for "Buddhism" and "Hinduism". That left the largest group, those individuals and families not aligned with any particular faith or belief system, but who certainly had the same needs and desires for reassurance and hope. After lengthy discussions within their unnamed congregation, they elected to use "Universalism" to identify themselves.

"Certain guidelines have since been developed that apply to all these faiths, belief systems or gatherings. Number one, and far more significant than the rest, is that there is to be no hint of intolerance towards one another. The use of the term "religion" was even frowned up. It held such negative connotations for the divisions and destruction that occurred prior to April 1st. Ultimately, it was hoped that someday one faith, or single assembly, could be found for all to attend, celebrate or worship in. To put the finest point on this, it was recommended that any expression or act of intolerance should be considered a verbal assault or battery, just like the unwanted or unjustified physically touching or striking someone.

"The other major decision that was made by these various bodies, and it speaks more to the concerns of our committee, was that there was to be no formalized or professional leadership. Lay leadership was to be chosen from within their own ranks, based on that individual's sincerity, devotion, tolerance, and humility. In addition, for as long as this individual held that position, she or he would assist all personnel, cavern-wide, when a life transition event occurred, such as birth, marriage or death. Each faith or group will determine how long this individual stays in office. They all emphasized that it would be a rotated responsibility.

"And I would be remiss if I didn't mention the one unmitigated, and almost insurmountable, obstacle facing each faith or belief system. April 1st created an existential void in each of our lives. Given the enormity of each person's losses: Whom do you pray to? What hope can you find in all this tragedy? What is the sense of it all? What is left for us? It is totally unlike any Creation Story, of one kind or another, with which each one of us is thoroughly familiar. We were almost baptized with their content. Now, to have been witness to apparently total Destruction, what is the story that follows that? So, we have experienced Armageddon or the Apocalypse, now what? What is left? Are we just remnants, left over and forgotten, in this cosmic chess game? In addition, who was, or is, B? When do we get that piece of this tragic puzzle sorted out? Each faith or belief system and each person is grappling with the coldness of these realities, doubts and fears. And to address these questions, the final major guideline that was developed was to acknowledge, fully, our profound losses and questions, but to direct our hope and prayers to the time when we can finally exit this cavern and then see what awaits us. At that time, we hope B will reappear with some indication why this happened and what is to become of us.

"Saying all this, our committee then took each event and tried to envision who would respond and how it might best be approached. Birth was the easiest to address. It is almost purely a medical event, and we are prepared to handle that special occasion when and if it should occur while we are confined here. Moreover, before our confinement is over, we do expect there to be some births. It will be a time of celebration for sure.

"Marriage, being the second event, required more discussion. It was decided that the first step when two people become seriously committed to one another would involve a civil ceremony. One of our three judges would conduct this civil union. And at this point, it would be a legal affair.

"However, if there is either the intent to conceive or adopt a child, then that couple, it is hoped, would be married. For the child's sake, they should be. At this point, a Layperson, of whatever faith or belief system chosen by the couple, would perform a marriage ceremony and one of our judges would amend the civil union to become a marriage.

"Let's be clear here on this. One of our major missions now is to survive somehow. We hope to pass on our knowledge and skills to another generation. And most of all we hope there will be another generation. There is no place for judging what constitutes a "couple". If two people elect to have or adopt a child, and then commit to nurture that child, they warrant the designation, as of that moment, of being married. Period.

"But, for each couple to accept entrance into that relationship, it must be known that dissolution of it will not be easy. Consider "No Fault" dissolutions of marriage over, as will be tolerance of bad behavior by either of the partners. Our children will not be coddled or spoiled, but neither will they suffer physical or emotional trauma from either adult member of this union. Child or spouse abuse, like religious intolerance, will not be tolerated. Anyone entering into a marriage will have this expectation manifestly made clear beforehand.

"And that left the final transition, death, to be addressed. For this event, we envisioned involving medical staff, Lay personnel, a judge and an honor guard. Because of our dangerously confined quarters, we have to remove the remains from here in the most dignified manner we can. It was decided that we would recommend using the U.S. Navy's Burial at Sea Ceremony as our guide. The actual ceremony would be in Cave #4, using that double exit doorway to transport the remains out of the cavern. It would involve using a flag-draped coffin. And once we are free of this confinement, we can then gather any remains that had to be transported outside and conduct an actual burial ceremony in a designated cemetery site.

"Saying all this, we hope this report meets with your approval."

Albert Nugama, the Welfare Committee chair, gave the fifth report. Albert began his presentation with, "I want to thank Ian, in behalf of my committee, and probably in behalf of the rest of us assembled here, for the fine work he and his group did to arrive at the conclusions and to recommend the actions they are outlining. If there is one major objective to all this post-April 1st rebuilding, it should be to heal the infected wounds of our previous civilization. And what Ian spoke of will contribute significantly to the goal of our committee to enhance the well being of our citizens. Exposing the doubts and fears we all have, along with encouraging the hope for unity in faith and civil matters, will create a discourse throughout our people and cannot help but bring us closer together in our common cause.

"Our committee looked at three major areas: health care, safety, and social activities. For health care, we now have a committee member monitoring the services of medical care, counseling, emergency response, and routine health maintenance. For safety issues, we have someone monitoring food, water, sewage, sanitation, internal and exterior environments. Next, what we need to cover in more detail is our socialization activities. Theresa and Philip Lieska will address those with you now. Theresa, if you will..."

"Thank you, Al," Theresa responded, while staying seated. "This won't take much time to discuss, but we need to get the widest circulation of this information, in order to get the greatest response and the best results. Philip and I have prepared sign-up sheets for the following social and entertainment activities. Please encourage everyone to participate and or attend these functions. We sincerely feel, regardless of the level of talent someone may possess, just being involved in these activities, will give anyone involved a renewed sense of accomplishment and improved self-esteem. And, believe me, each of us need both, after what we have and are experiencing.

"For students, there are sign-up sheets for participation in school plays, fetes, bands, or choral groups. For adults, there are sheets for performing or participating in recitals or bands, in small or larger musical productions or in plays, dramas, or choirs. And for cavern-wide gatherings, there are dances, pot lucks, card games, backgammon, mahjong, cribbage and chess tournaments, and even painting, drawing, singing, and musical instrument competitions. We would actually like to require that everyone must participate in at least one performing activity and one social activity in the next six months. We would hope, however, that most people would be involved in something all the time we are confined here. Talent is not a prerequisite nor is success the goal. It's the involvement that matters most."

With the conclusion of Theresa's remarks, Eric then directed Geoffrey to give the report for the Final Emergence Committee.

"To be honest," Geoff began, "besides being very involved in the Level 7, Adult Education Program, there is not too much more at this point we can accomplish. We have to know more about what conditions we are facing outside, once we all can finally exit the cavern. Before that time, everyone must attend these classes and study unceasingly to get ready. But for exactly what, we don't know yet. Probably by June we will begin compiling the separate lists of our stored supplies that will be needed for certain job assignments and then start the preconstruction planning phase…

"For now, these classes are of unparalleled importance to us all. The list of rebuilding priorities that was prepared while we were living in Amboy still stands. To summarize, it stated, in the order of importance, what should be done first and what would be done thereafter. More specifically: first is infrastructure building; next comes dwelling construction; followed by developing and identifying food sources; and finally performing outreach, rescue and exploration."

By the time Geoff had completed his report and answered some questions, it was 6:45 a.m. and students were again filling the Auditorium. It was a different atmosphere from what they saw and heard after the April 8th meeting. The children were animated, talkative and laughing more. It was as a children's schoolyard was supposed to sound. The Temporary Governing Body rose to leave, eagerly looking forward to the April 25th elections and the May 1st inauguration. Maybe, just maybe…

And, as with any official meeting or discussion held daily in the Amboy Cavern, all these committees' materials and decisions were transmitted to Ben Javitts, the individual who was their communication link in the Yucca Mountain Cavern. He, in turn, would pass on this information to the various groups and individuals there who were trying to prepare, as well, for what was ahead for their families.

SIX: A TYPICAL WEEK

The following accounts were taken from the more than thirty journals that Fred Wailand compiled over the years that he and his family were involved with the Amboy, and then Global Union, survivors. His dedication and attention to detail helped create a wondrous account of what was actually experienced by those families. The records revealed personal, intimate details and broad impressions of what those times were like. Moreover, to give you, the reader, a deeper insight into that underworld they lived in, the following is taking directly from one of his journals.

"By Monday, June 4, a routine had been established cavern-wide. I usually awoke before any of the family did, but this morning, by 6:15, both Bernice and Meagan had dressed and gone to the shower area to clean up before bringing back our breakfasts. Freda usually slept in, she being the night owl of the family. And the girls had already lit the living room incense stick, and opened the ceiling vent. Both these duties are the responsibility of the first one to wake up. The cavern has kept its age-old secrets, and many accumulated odors, quite well. Even though the blowers at the back of each cave and the exhaust fans at the entrances are turned on for 15 minutes each night at 1100 p.m., the dank muskiness, and pervasive scent of the daily, overcrowded human habitation is never completely removed. And by morning, our container home always smells well occupied.

"With Freda's airway weakness, we have to try and keep odors, humidity and cold dampness to a minimum. The incense helps some with the odors. Luckily, the cavern was a consistent 65° prior to everyone moving in. But now it does fluctuate. Our engineers' have concluded the variance in our ambient temperature appears to be related to an increasingly colder atmosphere outside the cavern and the daily activity level of nearly 1000 people inside. Variability of temperature is now a given, but we try to protect Freda's airways as much as we can with extra blankets and scarves.

"This morning, once the girls had finished cleaning up, and emptying our night's accumulation of the always-covered chamber pot, they hurried back with our breakfasts. Our home is in the middle row, Row B, and its address is number 5. So our full address is: #1, B-5, derived from Caves #1-3, of rows A-C, in homes numbered 1-25. Homes numbered 25 are always located in the rear of each cave. Number 1 is closest to the cave entrances.

"Showering in the morning, using only cold water, is more a test of one's capacity to withstand torture than it is an activity to clean oneself. The danger of taking a deep chill afterwards deters many from even trying. For others, the lack of privacy limits this activity. The showers and toilet/sink areas are open bays, with only draw curtains subdividing 20 spaces for those two activities. That's twenty spaces for 75 families or 300 individuals! For some this is not an issue. However, for others, there is a cultural or religious barrier they are reluctant to cross. For now, only the hardiest take regular showers. Of all the many daydreams, the cavern's occupants have, someday to take a nice hot shower or tub bath is at the top of everyone's list. But no one wants to speculate how long a wait that might be.

"Because the two families who have the weekly kitchen detail always start preparing breakfast by 5 a.m., in order to be ready to begin serving by 6 a.m., the girls are able to walk over and get something to bring back to eat once they are dressed. We, as do all the other families, keep trays in our homes to transport the meals and empty dishes back and forth, when we don't eat in the Communal Areas next to the kitchen. We rarely eat there for breakfast, but we always do for lunch. That Area is the gossip center. And being the news reporter that I am, it wasn't long before I started our weekly newspaper, thanks to the trove of information I get at lunchtime. The newspaper isn't much, but folks seem to enjoy it and are always giving me tips to investigate. Oftentimes, it primarily serves as an avenue for the Global Union representatives to keep everyone abreast of their decisions and for me to report what I hear when I attend the meetings of the Financial and Governing Committees. And, honestly, and most importantly, it reduces the use of the Public Address System. Using the overhead speakers too much reminds everyone of the book, '1984', which was later made into a movie.

"Now that cavern routines are more settled, the two prepared meals, breakfast and lunch, are always served from 6-7:30 a.m. and from 11:30-1 p.m., respectively. Most of the month's food supplies had to be left in the shipping container for the two designated kitchen duty families to draw from for meal preparation. The shelves alongside the container in the kitchen area are subdivided for the individual families, but they mainly contain sundries, coffee, tea, and easily prepared food for the dinnertime snack. Everyone is limited to two cups of coffee or tea a day. The children alternately have either fruit juice or reconstituted dried fruit three times a week and a cup of milk daily. Because of the danger of scurvy with our restricted diet, we all take vitamin C tablets, and weekly squeeze fresh lemon juice into our tea. Adults can have a cup of milk three times a week. Even toilet paper, which is kept in our designated area on the shelves, is rationed! We can only use two squares or sheets per visit.

"By the time the girls got back with the breakfast trays, Freda was awake, and we had one of those rare occasions when all of us ate breakfast together. For all that has happened to us, Freda still looks sparkling, even in the morning after she just arises. Her humor enlivens everyone. And her curvaceous figure, even evident through her housecoat, brings out the schoolboy in me. She knows it, and she loves to tease me. How I do love and cherish that woman.

"Today, over breakfast, the conversation is about the girls school work. It seems that at first, with the home schooling we did in Barstow, they were advanced beyond their peers. But now that the accelerated pace of their teachers has gained its steady momentum, they, like their classmates, need to study and prepare for hours each day before and after classes.

"Their particular apprenticeship program is a combination of health care subjects and agriculture material. Their teachers and professors are aware of both their interests in veterinary medicine, but they wisely understand that one or both of them may change their minds. If they do, then they will be well on their way preparing for a health-related occupation apart from animal care. Their classes begin each day, Monday through Saturday, at 1 p.m. They study and tend to the animals in Cave #4 in the mornings. It apparently is quite exciting for them to work with the other kids in the cavern who also help with the animals. It has given them the opportunity to make many friends. Believe or not, they do seem happy, despite all the hardship and everlasting losses. Kids! They are such a source of joy and wonder! They aren't afraid of tomorrow. But I am.

"As they were leaving to head off to care for the animals and Freda was leaving for the Lou, I had a chance to just stand at our front door and gaze around. I had the strangest sensation that maybe, as I looked around at the stalactites behind our home and at the limestone inner walls of our cave, I am accommodating to this place. It certainly doesn't feel like our home in Barstow or New York, but maybe, like the Londoners during the Blitz, having to live for weeks at a time in "the tube" or subway, I am acclimating.

"Even the sand and grit isn't tracking into the living room as much, which means it's not in our bedding and clothing all the time now. This has to mean the ground is finally becoming compacted in front of our homes, and certainly, it already is along the main roadway, or Main Street, as it's now called. That road has a grayish-white sheen, with the overhead lights reflecting off the tiny crystals, mixed in with the sand and decomposing limestone.

"And thankfully, the noise level has diminished, since the notices went up to stop any unnecessary yelling, screaming or shouting. Now, instead, there is just a steady murmur of voices throughout the cavern, which only ceases after the personnel on duty in the Communication Office dim the lights at 11 p.m. I'm feeling like today is going to be a good day."

"And, behold, here it is Tuesday, June 5th. I overslept. By the time I was dressed enough to head over to the toilet area, as I walked out of our home and onto Main Street, I found it was teeming with preschoolers, their parents and teaching aides all heading to the Main Classroom building.

"This same surge of students and adults occurs throughout the day and night, before and after every major school program. The only change is that this parade features increasingly older students as the day progresses. By the time Freda and I head over for our Adult Education Classes, it is almost entirely adults. During these night classes, our two girls, and all the other kids in Levels 4-6, take care of and tutor the preschoolers and elementary school children.

"It's a day and evening filled with learning, reinforcement, self-testing. And it goes on six days a week. Presently, Freda's Adult classes involve planting and maintenance of orchards and vegetable gardening, subjects she knows little about, having grown up in New York City. I just started classes on developing survival skills. My work life has revolved around sitting at a computer, so I definitely need some refocusing on this area.

"This afternoon, after my meeting with the Finance Committee, I had some free time before the 5 p.m. meal, so I went to Cave #4 to check on the pets and animals. What a pleasant surprise that was. It had been some weeks since Bernice took me over there. The children had divided the area into four sections. The dumpster, for immediate use, and assorted tools for maintenance and clean up is between the door into their warehouse of animal food and supplies and the large double doorway to the outside. The larger animals are to the left of the warehouse door, with their pens sweeping around the east wall. The chicken coups are on the west side of the double doors, set apart to avoid being startled all the time by the other animals, particularly the dogs. The smaller livestock, sheep, goats and pigs are next to the chickens, extending along the south wall and occupying half of the west wall. And finally, the areas for the kittens are next to the smaller animals, separated by some extra bales of straw and feed sacks, and the puppies are along a third of the north wall, in their individual kennels. The empty dumpsters occupy the remainder of the north wall, leaving room for sawdust bedding and bales of straw piled next to the opening into Cave #1. That leaves the entire middle of the cave open for whatever large-scale activities have to be performed, such as grooming, training for showing, veterinary treatments, and just playing with the animals.

"Apparently a dumpster is completely filled in one month. Already two of them have already been sealed and rolled outside. It requires two people dressed in hazmat suits, to coordinate opening and closing the double doors to seal off the outside environment, and then quickly to push the dumpster out the outer doorway and let it roll down the incline to some nearby resting place. We hope someday to use their contents for compost, whenever we have finally set aside an area to cultivate.

"It is usually a mad dash for our family to reassemble at 5 p.m., after Bernice and Meagan's classes let out. All of us, Freda and I included, try to get back to our home for the evening meal, which is not so much a meal as a snack. Our main meals for the day are prepared in the Kitchen Area. Supper is on us, and no one is allowed to use the kitchen facilities for this last meal. Having only the two kitchen-prepared meals is part of our strategy to extend our food stores as long as we can. In addition, limiting kitchen privileges is part of everyone's attempt to maintain strict guidelines on food preparation and clean up. With our severely limited hot water availability, insuring that we are scouring dishes and cookware is a major concern. In these close quarters, an outbreak of the Norwalk virus or Salmonella could result in fatalities.

"Later, after our Adult classes had ended, Freda,

the girls and I spent some time together talking over the day's impressions and dreaming a little about the future, before we all slipped off to bed. You start to feel a chill set in once the activity in the cavern lessens. You are always glad to get into bed and get warm. Snuggling up to Freda at night is my favorite time of the day. Sleep came quickly.

"June 6th. Wednesday is the day I go over to the Communication Office to prepare my weekly newspaper, which I then attach to the Bulletin Board for everyone to read. I try to have it done by noon so everyone can read it by this afternoon.

"While I was there today, Clem showed up with Jake. It had been at least four or five weeks since I had seen them. Clem seems well enough, but continues to lose weight. His face is almost gaunt now, with his cheekbones becoming more prominent. Nevertheless, his laughter is still crisp and infectious. Apparently, he told me, he rotates working in the three Kitchen Areas, helping to prepare and then to clean up after the two daily meals. Jake stays in the Communication Office when he does this work. The two of them have a sort of bunk area, in the back of the Communication Office.

"Clem's living in the cabin those years prepared him, as probably no one else in the cavern, for an austere, but to him, a simple and comforting refuge in these quarters. My being with Clem has always been soothing. We talked and laughed for about an hour. All the while, I petted Jake, who appeared asleep. Yet I doubted it. Jake knows things and has secrets, of this I am convinced. Only Clem knows for sure.

"Because Clem and I, along with Freda and my daughters, are the only ones who have survived, of the initially recruited Amboy crew, our bond is like a brotherhood. As I left, Clem was sorting out his musical selections for the afternoon and evening musical broadcasts, based on requests submitted by the cavern occupants. And for the first time we hugged each other before parting. If these times do not teach you to reach out to one another, nothing ever will.

"I got back home in time to go to lunch with Freda. We met Janice and Sid Blackwell, a couple we have become very close to over the last month, at the Communal Area. Picking up our lunch at the kitchen counter, served like in an Army chow hall, we found a table and while eating, just enjoyed chatting about the most mundane subjects. This area has twenty long tables and benches. Each bench will seat anywhere from 15-20 people to a side. Even in this setting, it is so relaxing to be able to act normal, under these unbelievable and sometimes nearly unbearable circumstances. Both Sid and Janice are solid, down-to-earth folks from the northwest; and Freda and I are from the eastern seaboard. Our attraction to one another is like the magnetic pull of opposite polarities. Over the next years, they could easily become our closest friends.

"After lunch we all split up, and I came back home. Inside, I once again did a walk through for the 100th time, being continually amazed at where we are and how we live. Our living room area has dark green indoor/outdoor carpeting, with a large braided rug overlaying that. And this is the case in each bedroom. The one large sidewall in the living room is filled with a five foot by eight foot, self-adhesive photograph of Yosemite Valley. On the other wall, the girls painted a mock fireplace, complete with a cheerful looking fire. In the appropriate place over the fireplace, we built a wooden mantle, with some planking we confiscated, and loaded it with family knick-knacks and photos. On each side of our mantle are framed photos, drawings and paintings, from floor to ceiling. In addition, on the smaller wall opposite the front door is a medium sized mirror. It helps give the illusion of a larger room. Our furniture, like with most fellow inhabitants, is spare. However, we have supplemented our small kitchen table and four chairs with a couple of large floor cushions and a couple of beanbag-like chairs.

"The girls' bedrooms have a bed, plus two wooden boxes for bedside cabinets, and a larger cardboard box, cut and taped to make a combination wardrobe and chest of drawers. The only light inside any of the rooms is either by candle or battery powered light. We limit any candle use to the living room only, where it can be safely monitored and snuffed out when we go to bed. Out master bedroom has a trundle bed, which when pulled out and locked, makes a double bed. But it has to be locked properly into place. Throughout the night, Freda and I will have a giggle, when someone has failed to lock his or her bed securely, and at some point, it will collapse with a deafening crash. You'll hear laughter and some clapping whenever this occurs. Believe me it has happened to everyone at least once.

"Today being Thursday, it's one of my days for morning exercise in the Main Auditorium. Then I go to one of the larger classrooms, where I attend a meeting with the Governance and Judiciary Committee. Following that meeting, it's on to the Communication Office, where I work on various reports and the weekly newspaper. And finally, if there is time left, I head over to the Library to help sort and organize materials. I often forget, or don't have time, to eat lunch on Thursdays. I can get so involved in what I'm doing today. Being this involved in the matrix of this place helps me to sort and glean events and impressions for these diaries. It is a place and time that should be remembered, just as we are all trying to preserve what went on before April 1st.

"The exercise class is fascinating in its way.

Having never participated in formal exercise, it was strange for me at first. However, it is mandatory for everyone four years or older. The thinking is that everyone needs to be as healthy, and as strong as possible, whenever we leave this place. And the exercises that were chosen are designed to give us strength, endurance and flexibility. Otherwise, when we begin rebuilding, we'll be prone to various injuries and resulting limitations that will slow down our efforts, and more importantly, endanger our chances of survival. But the challenge for the medical staff in choosing our exercises was not having access to large, bulky or cumbersome equipment to accomplish these objectives. Jump ropes, adjustable height platforms, our electrical-generating cycles and regular bicycles, mounted on frames and geared down for added resistance, were what they ultimately chose. These same bikes could later be converted back to their normal configuration and be one of our main forms of transportation on the outside.

"We begin with stretching exercises to prevent injury and increase our flexibility. Our strengthening routines use isometrics in various prone, supine and side lying positions; these are accompanied by eccentric and concentric maneuvers, without and with progressive weights. Aerobic conditioning involves stepping up and down on the raised platform, which can be adjusted in higher increments, along with jumping rope and using the stationary bicycling. It takes almost an hour to do all this. The classes are being given all day, six days a week, in order that everyone has three sessions a week. And, surprisingly, within two to three weeks even I noticed a difference in my endurance. And, yes, for all you skeptics who may eventually read this, I, like everyone else who did, had their last cigarette, cigar or puff from a pipe just before the doors to the cavern were closed on March 31st... This is a non-smoking facility.

"As I walked over to begin my exercise session today, I stopped by Cave #1's entrance to talk to Arnie Davis, one of the Marine fellows who tend to generators. He was putting on his hazmat gear to head out through the smaller double doors to the generators and pumps to service them. It is a duty he and his partner perform every other day. They also check the atmospheric conditions, both inside and outside the cavern, taking readings and reporting their findings to staff in the Communication Office. Both men realize how vital these generators and these reports are for our safety and survival.

"Arnie grew up on a farm in eastern Mississippi. From what he has told me, he cannot remember a day he wasn't working. It reminds me of Clem. Folks like these two are absolutely the very foundation any society is built upon. Sometimes when I talk with him, I help him secure the last of his gear in place. It is very dangerous work, but he does it with such calm and purpose. I want to salute him every time I see him.

"And finally, after the exercising, working in the Office, and attending that committee meeting, I get to do the one thing this day that gives me the most pleasure, and the reason I often miss lunch. I get to work in the Library. By now the shelves, which were built with leftover lumber from remodeling the container homes and constructing the classrooms, are beginning to fill. The fiction section is small, compared to the nonfiction and reference sections. The Library is on the bottom floor of the Classroom Building, which houses the Laboratories. It is in a 575 square foot room. The shelves are floor-to-ceiling along three walls; the wall with the doorway has a five-foot wide entranceway. Along this same wall, there is a full-length table and assorted chairs for anyone to use. The table provides a place to do some research and study, and it holds the index card file, which lists all the material stored in the Library. Besides the shelves along the walls, there are six 16-foot long, floor-to-ceiling shelves, spaced every two feet within the room.

"By the time all the periodicals, books, notebooks, tapes, folders, microfiche, CD's, DVD's, photographs and film canisters were all unboxed and reassembled in some order, but not yet all cataloged, the shelves were 90% full. It has taken the last two months for the 75 Amboy families to unpack these invaluable resources from their containers, transported here by the Air Force. In addition, included in the Library collection is all the reference material the Marine Base transported here.

"If our children represent the future, this room contains the doorway through which they have to walk to get there. Other personnel, mostly scientists, engineers, professors and select Marine Base personnel are assembling the equipment, brought in those same containers and by truck from the Base, in the Laboratories upstairs. The logic at the time of construction was that if the Library was downstairs, and floor-to-ceiling shelves were installed there, they would serve as support beams to stabilize the upper floors. Plus the weight of all this material had to be on the ground level. Much of my writing was done in this room. It was a refuge for me.

"Friday, for me, is my 'hump day'. Before April 1st, Wednesday afternoon used to signal my workweek was almost over, but in here, I find it isn't until Friday. By today, there are only two more workdays before Sunday, our one-day of absolute rest and relaxation. I need to take Bernice over to the Medical Clinic today. She was complaining about her ankle last night, after twisting it during jump rope exercises yesterday. When I looked at it before breakfast, it was reddish, warm to the touch and swollen. My bet is that she'll have to wear some kind of air splint and use crutches for a while.

"By 9:20 a.m. she was ready to head off. But just then, one of her friends, who was new to me, showed up. He is Walt Stanfield, Eric and Ann Stanfield's younger son. I found out later he is 15. And he and Bernie appear to be just good friends. I say 'just good friends' because, presently, there is little free time for the kids to form any full-blown romantic ties. Heaven knows, though, parents traditionally have become the poorest judges of the stages of their teenage children's relationships. Whatever the case, I trust Bernie's judgment and good sense, and after meeting the boy, I was impressed with his manner. I'm sure Eric and Ann have fostered in him some decent values. So, I elected to be receptive to his friendship with Bernie, and not to worry about any future changes that may occur. This appears to be her first dedicated friendship with a boy. Let's just wait and see.

"The three of us walked over to the Medical Clinic, with Bernie leaning rather heavily on me, to protect her right ankle. Once there, we only waited for a few minutes before Dr. Minor, as everyone is now calling him, examined her. And he confirmed that it was a severe sprain and that the ankle needed to be supported and protected. After showing her some exercises and giving her directions on using cold and heat, he then showed her how to use crutches and a splint correctly. Afterwards, she and Walt decided to walk back down Main Street to the animal area. We exchanged a warm hug, and I slipped into the Communication Office for my daily check in.

"Today, I gather up all the messages from Yucca Mountain, separating them into categories, e.g. their school reports and test results, news, questions, concerns, and plans for the future. It is clear by reading all their incoming notices, over these last weeks that they are working hard to pattern their organization and preparations as closely to ours as possible. I know they must be doing this in anticipation of our being able to reunite, once this confinement is over. There is no doubt in my mind that once we are on the outside, there will definitely be added strength in numbers: the more of us, the better for all. How to accomplish and sustain that reunion is beyond me. Food production, alone, is becoming a nagging concern of mine lately. But, for now, their messages are hopeful and constructive.

"It's Saturday, and even though there are the usual class schedules throughout the day, the one blessed change this day brings is that the Adult Education classes only last from 6-8 p.m. After that, it is PARTY TIME!

"The Main Auditorium is transformed for this occasion. And the older kids delight in making this happen. The adults, after all, are still in class. Clem and the children transform the place into a grand ballroom, lined with makeshift tables and chairs. The stage is set up with a microphone, CD player, chairs, musical instruments for any existing or newly formed bands or soloists, and a list of the Amateur Hour Contestants for the evening's Master of Ceremonies. The back of the room has a long table full of light snacks and, most importantly, our ration of beer, wine, spirits or soda drinks. It's true, each of us can only have one drink, but after a week of coffee, tea, and Amboy water, it's a refreshing change and a lift. And we are marked when we choose our drink of the night. To do that, you dunk the fifth finger on your left hand in some ink-like stew that Clem brews up. The lights stay on until 2 a.m. this one night. Tonight, there are no loud-noise police to quell the festivities.

"Tonight we have a band that plays a mix of

music, but just about everyone dances to whatever is played, adapting dance moves to whatever beat is heard over the partying. We even have a square dance caller with musical accompanists. The Amateur Hour is always a huge success, especially so tonight. There was an impersonator, a juggler, three singers who were slightly off key their entire performance, a magician who was the funniest, because his tricks didn't work as he planned, so he turned that into an act in itself, and, finally, a girl, about 16, who recited some poetry from memory.

"When she began, the Auditorium was somewhat still busy with cups, saucers, and glasses clattering; with scattered sneezing and coughing; with many giggles at the perceived, but misjudged, awkwardness of what the contestant was doing; and with impolite conversations and laughter. Then her words began to stretch out over the immense room, reaching into clusters of non-listeners, quieting the clanging and snickering, muffling the shuffling and coughing. Heads began to turn toward the stage, now filled completely with this slight girl. The poet was expressing the hopes and longings, the dreams and loves that had been wrenched away from us by the events of these last months. She filled the Auditorium his words, concluding the recitation with:

> "...Only, but this is rare--
> When a beloved hand is laid in ours,
> When, jaded with the rush and glare
> Of the interminable hours,
> Our eyes can in another's eyes read
>   clear,
> When our world-deafened ear
> Is by the tones of a loved voice
> caressed--

A bolt is shot back somewhere in our
breast,
And a lost pulse of feeling stirs again.
The eye sinks inward, and the heart
          lies plain,
And what we mean, we say, and what
we would, we know.
A man becomes aware of his life's
          flow,
And hears its winding murmur; and
          he sees
The meadows where it glides, the
          sun, the Breeze.

And there arrives a lull in the hot race
Wherein he doth forever chase
That flying and elusive shadow, rest.
An air of coolness plays upon his
          face,
And an unwonted calm pervades his
          breast.
And then he thinks he knows
The hills where his life rose,
And the sea where it goes."

(see Appendix 2, fig. 9, "The Buried Life" by Matthew
Arnold)

          "There followed a stunned silence as this young
lady backed away from the microphone to walk off the
stage. Then the clapping began. It was like what
happened when Philip played the piano that terrible
April 1st day. Her recitation had spoken to each one in
the audience that night. Her name was Gloria Johnson,
the daughter of Barbara and Earl Johnson. Earl is a
Gunnery Sergeant. And the family later admitted,

proudly but somewhat embarrassed, that their daughter has recited poems, mostly from memory, to them in the evening for years. Gloria, by this unpretentious act, made the night of June 9th indelible in the hearts of everyone there. It was spellbinding.

"By 2 a.m., Sunday morning, the Auditorium was quiet and thoroughly cleaned, ready for the day's upcoming events. For 99.9% of the residents of Amboy Cavern, we all slept in this morning. Breakfast is served from 7:30-9:30 a.m. for those who can make it. And there are no weekly classes today, as I mentioned before. But there are classes, wouldn't you know, starting at 5 p.m. and lasting until 8 p.m. They are for self-expression or self-improvement, if you will, and they consist of painting, drawing, sculpturing, creative writing, woodcarving, public speaking, dancing, singing, and music lessons. It was all Theresa and Philip's idea. Everyone is encouraged to attend at least one class. And it's great fun!

"Church services are scheduled for 11 a.m., but they are purely voluntary. Followers of a particular faith can practice whenever or however they choose. It's just that this time is set aside particularly for these observances. Freda and the girls attend the Catholic services.

"Me, I'm still in the undecided camp. Like Clem, the experiences and encounters with B have left me suspended. I have questions that have prevented me from entering the sanctuary of a faith, and some day I hope to be comforted by doing so. What it will take for that to happen is one of my personal burdens. I don't really know. I well realize something cosmic, universal or life-ending or beginning has or is happening to us; and I am just unsure how to observe or worship in the face of it all.

"Lunch, on Sunday, is still at noon. Then, at 1

p.m., the performances start in the Main Auditorium. For at least one to two hours there will be recitals, chorales, dramas, dances or plays performed. I have still not figured out when these dedicated individuals have the time to practice and prepare for these productions, but they are always so beautiful. And, again, everyone attends them. Then by 3 p.m., there are the game competitions for everyone. People were playing cards, chess, monopoly, and games I've never heard of, but apparently were spawned by the Internet's evolution pre April 1st and by our adaptation to our present circumstances. It's a huge success amongst our kids, and most adults, for that matter.

"All in all, Sunday is a day of relaxation and enjoyment. The week actually builds toward it and Saturday night. It keeps our morale up. And it serves to bring us all together. More and more we are calling each other by our first names. By now there are few people we haven't met or know. The cavern is becoming a village."

SEVEN: TESTING TIME
(Smoke, Sneezing, Spoilage, Sewerage)

The drastic events inside the cavern did not start until mid June, when the main generator for the entire cavern's interior failed. This set in motion events that were dreaded by some, unexpected by most, and nearly deadly for others.

The lights went out cavern-wide around 10:30 p.m., when almost everyone had returned home from their Adult Education classes. It stopped some teachers and students who were still walking home, and it stranded a few others scattered in the Communal Areas having their last cup of coffee or tea for the day, playing some cards or just talking. And in an instant, it was pitch-black. All those who were not at home froze in place in hopes it was just a temporary problem. To move in any direction meant a sure collision with something or someone. But the darkness only intensified.

Gradually the families, who did make it home, realized that they needed to light candles, get out their battery-powered lanterns, and go outside to see if anyone needed help. In Cave #3, C-16, Arnie Davis, glad to be off duty this night, had just dropped off to sleep. His wife, Dot, soon realized what had happened, after she investigated why there was all the commotion going on outside. She ran into their bedroom, and shook him awake, exclaiming with frantic urgency in her voice, "Arnie, quick, something is wrong! All the lights are out! And they don't appear to be coming back on, like you had hoped they might, if this ever happened!"

From his years of Marine Corps service, he was almost immediately alert and on his feet. "This doesn't sound good at all. I've got to get over to the generators right away. Can you get me that large strobe light I have by the living room bookshelf?"

Within minutes, Arnie was dressed and running towards Cave #1's entrance. He had to put on his hazmat suit, before he could go outside to check on the generators. In the meantime, more and more people were coming out of their homes to check on the situation and render any assistance they could to those caught in the darkness.

While Arnie was putting on his suit, G.W. McCoy, Arnie's co-worker, and the engineer on call that night, showed up. They helped each other put on their suits, and went through the drill of opening/closing the double doors and entering the generator room. Luckily, the well generator was still working; however, they finally had to disassemble the carburetor and fuel pump on the cavern generator to locate a blocked fuel line. Fumbling for tools, and working in cramped quarters, it took over two hours for them to complete the overhaul and double check that there were no further problems. And by 1:30 a.m., the lights were back on.

However, what had begun as a simple clogged fuel line, by 2:30 a.m. had morphed into a different problem. Most families had not used their candles that much up until this night. In the case of the Michener family in #2, A-22, it was their first time to use one. As fortune would have it, the only candle they had to use was brand-new, still wrapped in cellophane. The candle was 12 inches long. Not really sure what to use to hold it, they finally decided on using a plastic drinking cup, and they attached the candle to the bottom of the cup by letting some melted wax form a base to wedge it in. To them it seemed secure enough. By 1:30 a.m., they felt comfortable that the lights were back on to stay and decided to retire for the night. However, they forgot to blow out the candle. At 2:30 a.m., their smoke alarm began to sound. Their living room was filling with acrid smoke and flames were starting to show at the point of origin, where a 5-inch candle lay on the floor, on top of some charred papers.

It was both the sounds of the smoke alarm and of the screams, coming from inside the Michener's home, which awoke and alerted those families around them that something was wrong. Like everyone else in the cavern, the Michener's kept their roof vent closed at night but, unlike most of the other occupants; they had locked their front door with a home-made dead bolt. Their container home was like a fire smoldering inside a sealed metal drum. In this closed environment, the oxygen needed to feed the fire was what the Michener family needed as well. And the fire had the odds in its favor of getting whatever there was.

Luckily for the Michener's, two months into the Adult Education classes on Fire Suppression, there were, by now, hundreds of fellow citizens who had either taken the class or had been exposed to those who had. The First Law of Fire Suppression was drilled into everyone. It was based on the premise that the Amboy Cavern was like a submarine, submerged hundreds of feet underwater. And if any smoke or a fire breaks out ANYWHERE or ANYTIME, everyone is to rush towards it, not away from it. As you are doing so, you are to gather up all the suppression equipment at your disposal or that has previously been pre-positioned and take it with you. The Second Law is someone should be immediately designated to run to the Communication Office and have this outbreak announced over the Public Address System. Doing so, alerts the Response Team to respond, and with them, they will bring other equipment to help control and suppress the fire. And in this particular case, it was the Jaws of Life.

Appropriately, the Michener's, themselves, went into survival mode once the alarm sounded and their screaming was heard. The parents herded both children into their bedroom, taking their mattresses with them. They then barricaded their bedroom door and got on the floor. But it did take time to get to them, due to the door being locked. The paramedics had to use the Jaws of Life to cut the door hinges in half. However, because the heat and fire had just about exhausted the available oxygen in the living room and two smaller bedrooms, and was beginning to migrate into the large bedroom where everyone was sheltered, once the front door was cracked open, the fire burst into raw fury.

To extinguish the fire completely, buckets of sand and precious water had to be used. It was obvious there could be no electrical service to any of the homes, but what was not known was whether there was any kerosene present. It was not recommended for household use, but the responders were not sure if it was not present. It wasn't. And within minutes, the fire was fully extinguished. The family had to be taken immediately to the medical facility for treatment of smoke inhalation, minor burns and becoming overheated. In addition, the smoldering ruins had to be thoroughly doused, then bundled up quickly and taken to Cave #4's double door exit to be discarded outside as soon as possible. The burned plastics and synthetic materials made a hazardous aerosol for any of the cavern's inhabitants to inhale, particularly those like Freda with chronic asthma.

Following an investigation into the causes of the fire, it became mandatory that anyone using a candle had to encase it in a chimney of some kind, preferably glass, and it had to surround the entire length of the candle. Next, any candle holder had to be on a wide enough fireproof surface to accommodate its total height, in case it fell over, i.e. an eight inch long candle required at least a metal or ceramic supporting surface radius of eight inches. Then, finally, no one was to lock his or her front door at night. It was senseless to do so. Anyone who enters the wrong home, if it was for illegal purposes, has no place to escape. Someone committing a crime, in these circumstances, is already incarcerated, and to escape outside the cavern meant certain, and almost immediate, death.

The Michener's were able to maintain the use of their home, due primarily to the almost Amish-like banding together of their neighbors to scrub down, sweep out, repaint, install new carpet from scraps gathered here and there, and provide replacement furniture, such as anyone had. However, none of the new furnishings included candles, and none were ever used in their household again.

The next event that was later connected to the generator failure, and ensuing darkness, centered on the kitchen area of Cave #1. It seemed that a group of families was having a final cup of coffee and a few individuals were finishing a quick, late night snack of left over potato salad. In the confusion that resulted from the generator failure, the salad was forgotten and left out of the refrigerator overnight. Because of the multiple interruptions later that night with the fire, when the breakfast crew came on duty at 5 a.m. the next morning, the youngest of the helpers, finding the salad still out, simply put it back in the refrigerator. Within the next hour, the two families on kitchen duty sat down to eat their breakfast just before the rush of everyone started. And they were pleased to see there was still some left over potato salad to eat, which they did.

By 10:15 a.m. that same morning, six of the individuals that ate the leftover potato salad were experiencing abdominal cramping and nausea, soon followed by vomiting and diarrhea. Within a few hours came the headaches, fever, with dehydration and weakness. Some made it to the medical clinic, but two were stranded in the toilet area.

Dr. Mahmood was on duty that morning, and given the brief time it took for the symptoms to take effect, after she learned about the leftover salad, she was sure they were the result of Salmonella caused food poisoning. With the Mesenger family, still either on supplemental oxygen or under observation for the aftereffects of smoke inhalation in four of their ten beds, by the time all six of the infected food poisoning cases arrived, the clinic was full. I.V.'s had to be started on both children and two adults due to their having a moderately severe case of dehydration. The youngest child was actually coming in and out of consciousness, so she decided to call Minor in on his day off. The two nurses on duty were kept busy either with filling new orders or with observation and charting. Aside from two births about three weeks ago, this day was by far their most hectic since they had been confined in the cavern. And with most of the medical staff's involvement, after three days, all the patients were discharged. But everyone in the clinic knew they wouldn't always be so lucky.

From that episode with the salad came further instructions that were posted on the wall in the kitchen area, listing the causes and symptoms of food poisoning. No one doubted that they were lucky this time. They had escaped facing irreversible conditions, which resulted from either the smoke inhalation or the food poisoning.

And within twenty-four hours after the fire and food contamination, the first sneezing, stuffy noses, sore throats and elevated temperatures started. Later, it was decided that it was due to the families responding to the fire, dressed only in their nightclothes. The result was that some of them became chilled and susceptible to viral infections. A few of the cavern's occupants had gotten flu vaccinations the preceding fall, but most had not. And before any isolation precautions could be initiated, a flu epidemic was in full bloom within 36 hours of that first flu-related sneeze.

At first, only official functions became stymied, but soon, with over 70% of the population affected, all activities ground to a complete standstill. Sadly, again, it was the very young who suffered the worst complications. Two children contracted viral pneumonia, which required a few days of assisted breathing with mechanical ventilation. In addition, many others developed either bronchitis or pleurisy. And there were some, as a result of this flu outbreak, who were still bothered with overly sensitive airways, up until the time everyone was able to exit the cavern.

By the end of June, the general impression of the cavern's inhabitants was that their introductory period of good health and avoidance of mishaps, following April 1st, was over. They became guarded, almost fearful, as to what might happen next. And sure enough, something did occur. Almost simultaneously, one afternoon, a couple of inquisitive and adventurous preschoolers, as if involved in a conspiracy but each was actually unaware of what the other was doing, took it upon themselves to see if a couple of their stuffed animals could completely disappear, if flushed down the toilets in Caves # 1 and 2. To their glee, they did disappear in one flush. But at the junction where the other toilets outlets merge into a single discharge pipe to go outside the cavern, the bears became lodged; and it was here that all passage of fluids and solid waste from upstream stopped and then backed up, until it overflowed.

Those two bears turned Cave #1 and 2's toilet, kitchen and communal areas into a hazardous waste zone and created turmoil for the residents in these caves. The only option available was to share all kitchen functions with Cave #3, and form lines outside #3's toilet facility and the toilet adjacent to the Communication Office. To identify the problem and unclog the bears ultimately required most of the Marine's engineering platoon. Both toilets had to have major excavation right up to the cavern's interior wall. Only having to do that, everyone was actually relieved. If it had involved going outside the cavern, the dangers from still elevated atmospheric contamination would have insured Chernobyl-like consequences for the personnel who ventured outside.

It was decided that there would be no posted instructions on the Communication Center's Bulletin Board, advising everyone to refrain from throwing foreign objects into the toilets, but there would be signs, with pictures of toys on them, posted in the toilet bays. Mostly, the corrective action taken involved changing the preschoolers morning litany of reciting their "thou shall not do's", by adding at the top of that list, not to put stuffed bears into the toilet.

EIGHT: A KING SOLOMON'S DECISION

Finally, after the rash of emergencies and breakdowns, everyone was relieved to have a week of calm. By July 9th, the atmosphere around the Amboy Cavern had settled back into a less expectant routine. Clem's musical selections played over the Public Address System reflected this resurgence of renewed confidence and optimism.

Being in the middle of what used to be summer, the newly born cavern deer mice, unaware of what humanity had done to their neighborhood, had now become much more active. Amongst the older generation, all the human activity in the caves had initially created alarm and reticence to venture beyond the confines of their sheltered nests. And, with the cavern's children circulating in the general vicinity, the youngest mice had not, as yet, started to venture into their immediate play areas. However, it was now summer, after all, and it was time for deer mice to wander about and to make new friends. And they did. And wherever they did, they left behind their markings, in urine and stool. Ominously, this activity had been going on for the last three weeks, as had been the exposure of both children and their parents to the aerosolized particles of their excreta or saliva.

Moreover, while it was known, at that time, that only 12-15% of these mice might harbor potentially

389

deadly disease, in the confined world of the Amboy Cavern, and with the population of these rodents in the hundreds, this left little margin for the children to avoid coming into contact with these carrier mice. In these mice, the lethal agent they carried was the Hantavirus.

Without question, if this band of cavern survivors had not battled day and night prior to April 1st to prepare this cavern shelter, and if the medical staff had had time to investigate thoroughly their surroundings for any potential hazards that they might face, warnings of all kinds could have been posted. Most certainly, they would have alerted and warned everyone to avoid contact with these rodents. But, tragically, none of that was the case.

It was on this day that the first child and adult showed up in the Medical Clinic with complaints of fever, deep muscle aching, and progressively worsening shortness of breath. Furthermore, once they got into the Clinic, it was obvious they were not stabilizing. Their subsequent abdominal pain, headaches and dizziness added to the clinical picture. Next, there followed the first episode of frank shock, with critically low blood pressure readings. Within twelve hours of admission, the first child was being mechanically ventilated to keep her alive. And the same clinical picture was repeated, sometimes with less devastating progression, throughout the next two days.

By the evening of July 10th, they had seen fifteen children and adults for the same initial symptoms and immediately had to admit eight for observation and treatment. Then the worse thing imaginable for medical personnel happened. The demand for specific life saving equipment was beyond what they had available. Within 48 hours of the first patient's admission, all eight of these patients needed ventilator support. And the Clinic only had three. Those not on a ventilator could only be manually ventilated with resuscitation bags.

A decision had to be made as to who would get the best equipment, and thereby who would stand the best chance of survival. In an attempt to accomplish this, an emergency meeting of the Global Union Governing Body was scheduled for 6 a.m. on July 11th. But, unlike any other time when their meetings were scheduled, for this one, the general population's attendance was requested. However, given the early hour of the meeting, none of Governing members expected there to be a large turnout. Prior to this morning, their meetings were always prescheduled and anyone could attend, but few did. To their surprise, by 6:05 a.m., when the elected officials took their seats on the stage in the Main Auditorium, they were sitting in front of 95% of the general cavern population.

Chairing the meeting was the newly elected, permanent Chief Executive, Eric Stanfield. There had been four other candidates seeking election for the same office. And after the votes were tallied, it was almost a tie between him and Albert Nugama. There was even some discussion about reconstituting the position as a co-executive office, but Albert said that would not work. Instead, he took one of the representative positions. He remained, however, one of Eric's most trusted and valued advisors and confidants through his years in office and each became life-long friends thereafter.

Eric opened the emergency session with, "As I understand it so far, we have an unparalleled, post April 1st, emergency facing us. Would you agree that for us to get the most accurate picture of what is happening, we should first let our medical staff give us their report?" There followed this question, a unanimous nodding of heads from those seated on stage and in the audience. "Then Minor, I presume it's between you, Zara and Ian who speaks first."

"It will be me, to begin with," Ian began, walking forward to the front edge of the stage. "Because most of those who are so critical are from our Marine families, we decided I would initiate the medical presentation.

"And to start, let me say there are eight critically ill patients in our medical facility, each of whom has, most likely, been infected by the Hantavirus. The most likely source of this outbreak is the deer mice infestation we have here in the cavern. We have had to treat fifteen individuals for symptoms that appear to confirm this diagnosis. Of the eight who are most critical, four are under the age of 17.

"All are requiring mechanical assistance for breathing. However, most importantly for this meeting, we only have three mechanical ventilators. The other patients are being manually ventilated with resuscitation bags. It is a very exhaustive and taxing use of all our personnel to try to support each patient. For now, we try to alternate using the mechanical ventilators with the others, but even that is not having the benefit we had hoped.

"These patients are having significant changes in their blood pressure, whenever we stop using the ventilators and switch to manual ventilation. They require settings that only mechanical ventilation can provide. Their cardiovascular system needs this extra support to prevent collapse. Unfortunately, we are experiencing such collapses with each changeover to manual ventilation. We are coming to you today because we will lose all eight of these patients unless we dedicate the ventilators to just three individuals. Indeed, what brought us to call for this meeting is that decisions have to be made as to who will receive the maximum, and most likely, the best chance of surviving, using the mechanical ventilators.

"You need to know something about the pathophysiology and prognosis of a Hantavirus infection; it is a virus whose onset is somewhat like the flu with fever, headaches, and muscle pain. This progresses to abdominal pain, dizziness, decreased blood pressure and progressively severe shortness of breath. The antigens produced by this viral invasion accumulate in the lungs microvasculature, and this can lead to a series of events, which results in a potentially massive pulmonary and/or cardiac collapse.

"There is no specific treatment for this condition. It is strictly supportive care, with mechanical ventilation often needed until the disease runs its course. And most sobering, the mortality rate varies anywhere from one third to one-half of those who are initially infected, with adults more likely to succumb than children. However, we appear to be seeing an equal opportunity viral organism in our midst. Maybe it's another mutation from what has been found earlier with this virus, because here, it is affecting both adults and children equally in severity.

"The virus cannot be passed from one person to another. It is only contracted by inhaling aerosolized excreta or possibly by contacting the infectious material through your having an open wound. We must begin immediately disinfecting all the interior walls of the cavern, due to our not having any idea exactly where the carrier mice are coming from. Their nests could be anywhere along our walls. A bleach solution, or even household disinfectants, will neutralize the virus, but we must begin immediately to spray and wash down these areas and any dead rodents seen lying about. Do not touch them unless you are gloved, and they have been treated with some solution. We need to trap, disinfect and seal off. It won't be easy, given the area we have to cover. Nevertheless, this operation needs to be organized and underway immediately. There is a real risk, right at this moment, of an even more serious outbreak of this disease, unless we start immediately to eradicate the source of this infection. In addition, anyone working on this clean up detail must wear facemasks.

"And that's where we stand right now. To summarize: we need guidance as to how you want any triage to be done, and we need to begin immediately disinfecting and clearing the cavern of this threat..."

Realizing the complexity and unavoidable life-shattering course they were embarking on, Eric then turned to Judge Bertha Ann Mack. Judge Mack had sat on the Federal Appeals Bench for sixteen years. And while she was not directly involved in the terribly tragic case that the President, the U.S. Congress and the Federal Court System became embroiled in, a case involving who should decide when, or even if, life-sustaining measures should be discontinued, Judge Mack was painfully aware of the choices they were facing. Furthermore, she had expressed to him her strong conviction that the Governing Body and the entire cavern's populace must be in general agreement about what is decided today.

She remained seated as she spoke, but her voice, honed by years of addressing and refereeing judicial proceedings, carried clearly throughout the Auditorium. "Thank you, Eric, and all the others who thought to assemble this Body and our citizenry before any further actions are taken.

"There are established legal precedents regarding when and who should make the decision involving the use of extraordinary medical intervention, such as initiating mechanical life support, maintaining its use, and then discontinuing it or in the initiation of cardiopulmonary resuscitation. However, maybe they are not the guidelines that we should fall back on. As with so much of our reorganizing after April 1st, we have to make choices based on a new order that has been imposed upon us.

"My suggestion would be to begin with our making a formal commitment, and with it having immediate legal authority and enforcement, that this process shall be left solely in the hands of four parties or influences. The first party, and by far the most important, would be what the patient has designated to be done. And if that patient were incapacitated, then their written instructions would be in force. Alternatively, if none were ever written or lost, then the decisions from the immediate next of kin become actionable. Thirdly, there would be whatever the patient, or again, if incapacitated, whatever his or her immediate next of kin believe that the patient's faith dictates should be done in this circumstance. Finally, there would be the patient's personal physician's medical direction and recommendations.

"No one else, no governing entity, outside authority or individual, has any business being involved in what can be a most desperate, tragic or sorrowful decision-making process. These four parties or influences, as it were, amongst themselves, by whatever instructions, prayers, advice and consensus is arrived at, must and will decide the course of care and, if necessary, its discontinuance.

"In the case of a minor, which I would suggest should be defined as anyone under the age that we require someone to perform hazardous or dangerous duties, he or she deserves to have these same rights and responsibilities, even if that age is 16, 17, or 18 years of age. And it is probably safe to say that, given our new circumstances, we will have to adjust that age threshold. There will simply not be enough personnel available age

18 or older to do all that has to be done that may be potentially dangerous. That being the case, I would suggest that we should consider establishing the threshold of adulthood at age 17 or older. Later, if the trend of hazardous responsibilities becomes shifted even further to a younger age, then this dividing line should again be lowered for defining adult status.

"And, I might further suggest that with this passage into adulthood, that there should be a ceremony, be it civil, social or both, to mark its advent. Like a birth or marriage certificate, there should be a document, marking the attainment of adulthood. It would summarize the privileges and responsibilities, attending this new status. And one of its privileges would be to decide the course of their health care and under what circumstances to cease that care.

"If the issue arose whether the individual is of sound mental status, the patient's physician would also be responsible for determining this. In all likelihood, that physician would also request a second opinion, which would be something the patient asks for as well.

"But for those under the age of 17, certainly their wishes and opinions need to be known by the family and the physician, but the latter two parties will have the ultimate decision making authority.

"And, in my opinion, from the time of conception, to birth, through the individual's lifetime and to the moment it ends, it is the beliefs, opinions and decisions of these four inviolate sources for health related issues that are sacrosanct. Any health related decisions have to be worked out within this body, even if it means tossing a coin when no clear decision can be arrived at. Amongst them are the individuals that brought this particular life into the world, and they are the ones responsible for its growth, nurturing, and God forbid, its ending, if ever that should be the case, as we are facing now.

"Maybe, for our purposes and tragically unique circumstances, there would also be a few cultural guidelines for these decision makers to consider. Along with the eventual adult onset designation and the composition of the family health care team, there would need to be certain society-related priorities. For example, we need to consider that the children's welfare and survival be considered before an adult's; women's welfare and survival before men's; and the chances of the individual's long term survivability when we are in possession of very limited human and material resources. These, as painful as they are, become factors we have to consider in our new society.

"With regard to the present set of tragic circumstances, I personally can only say you will have the fullest support of our judicial staff with your final decisions. You now know where we, as a group, stand on this issue. I might finally suggest that you get input from the clinical psychology and psychosocial disciplines on this matter."

"In conclusion, I must say that it is a source of comfort to me and my fellow judges to see this cavern-wide attendance for this meeting. For far too long governing and decision-making has been a mysterious and frustrating process. Too often, the influence of lobbyists and their money determined the direction of our government's daily decisions, a process that was foreign to our Constitution's vision of what representative government was supposed to be. Listen carefully, each of you, my fellow citizens, to what is discussed here today. And when your chance to vote comes, vote intelligently and honestly. Thank you, Eric and this Assembly for allowing our group to speak."

There followed a respectful, but warm show of appreciation for what the Governing Body and assembled families had just heard. Eric then stood and introduced Mitzi Zimmerman, and asked if she would please address any clinical psychology issues that this tragedy has created.

"Possibly none of us really heard or certainly have not had the time to digest what has just been proposed by Judge Mack," Mitzi began. "For the first time in the course of our collective memories, someone has dared to propose a common sense, yet painfully respectful, approach to some of the most private and personal decisions any of us will ever have to make.

"For our part, any contribution that our group of counselors may bring to these heart-wrenching decisions would be determined by the patient, his or her family or the personal physician as we are called upon. If requested, we would try to be a resource. Otherwise, we do not feel the need to be involved in any day-to-day decision making. In addition, as to what the final decision is as to whom, ultimately, is given the benefit of our limited equipment resources that should be up to all of us gathered here today to vote on. And thank you, Eric for allowing us to share in this discussion."

Eric then asked if any family members would like to speak. Staff Sgt. Pete and Sylvia Marzoff, were one of the families whose child did have a mild to moderate reaction to the virus. However, Sylvia was critically ill now. Pete rose from the audience and came forward to speak.

"While I know there have to be decisions made here today, based on our present circumstances and limited resources of all kinds," Peter began, "I still must plead for my wife's life. To lose her will probably be beyond my ability to cope. As each of us here knows, it is only by our clinging to our precious family members that we have managed to struggle on up to this point. Without Sylvia, her children and I will be lost. She, in her quiet way, is our strength. And, as many of you have found out in the time we've spent in here together, knowing her is to know what love and compassion is all about. Certainly, any child deserves every chance to live. Nevertheless, every adult here, likewise, is of such irreplaceable value. With the loss of any of us, we have lost their collective knowledge, and most importantly, we've lost those most precious, learned skills of loving, giving and understanding. My dearest, Sylvia, embodies all of these. I beg you to spare her life. Please, for God's sake…"

Silence and grief enveloped the Assembly area as Pete walked back to his seat to sit with his children. His moving appeal left everyone there shaken at the terrible task that lay ahead of them. No one person was going to decide who lives and who does not. Yet, with his or her upcoming vote, each adult there will now be on record as being responsible for making that choice. Each was to become a King Solomon.

While Pete left the stage, Eric again came forward, shaking his head, and as if talking to himself. In almost a whisper he uttered, "Some moments, in these days we've shared over the last seven months, are just too unbearable. This is one of them. We had no choice in the losses we suffered before and just after entering this cavern. Now we, most tragically, do. Moreover, the choices are not to save lives, but to determine which ones most likely will not survive. Please hear me when I say, at this moment, I feel at the depth of despair. I know we must go on, but I need to share with you my grief and sense of desperation."

Composing himself somewhat, he then asked, "Is there anyone else who would like to speak?"

From the front row of chairs, closest to the stage, a young woman stood, coaxing her two children with her to rise as well. She did not choose to climb the steps onto the stage, but just turned and faced the audience. The acoustics of the cavern provided the amplification she needed to be heard.

"My name is Helen Plant. My husband is Roger Plant. He is one of the adults in the clinic who is very seriously ill from this vicious virus. He became ill when he responded to calls from family members, desperate to find out what was causing their loved ones to become so ill. He apparently handled some of the infected mice, before it was known that picking them up unprotected could transmit the virus. . He didn't know that it wasn't just the fluids and solid wastes from their bodies that were infectious. Nevertheless, being the dedicated EMT that he is, he went immediately into the danger zone, while the rest of us tried to flee the developing epidemic. Now his life is ebbing away.

"Certainly, if he could speak now, and if it was one of our children who were infected, he'd say, give whatever life support resources needed to them, spare nothing. And I am sure he would say the same for any of your own children. But I can't say that. I must speak for him.

"Many of you gathered here obviously have greater minds, more technical skills and knowledge, the ability to speak, write, inspire and create great and wonderful works of art than he, but no one here can surpass my Roger's gift of selfless love for humanity. His sole purpose of living was to give of himself. And he did it in countless emergencies and routine responses to fires, explosions and accidents in New York City as a Fire Fighter and EMT. I ask each of you now to acknowledge that dedication and devotion to duty by trying to preserve his life. And I ask this not just for our children and myself but also for all of our sakes. We all need Roger Plant. Please...."

After Helen and her children sat down, no one

moved, either on the stage or in the audience. What followed were many minutes of silence, except for occasional coughing or shifting position. A quiet reflection consumed the cavern.

With an audible sigh, Eric finally rose and came forward to the edge of the stage. Shaking his head, he cleared his throat and began outlining the following instructions.

"We need to proceed with two urgent tasks, as hard as it is to gather ourselves together at this moment. The first is to begin organizing a complete clean up of the cavern. My suggestion would be that the elected representatives from each living area develop a plan within your families and begin today disinfecting and sealing off nest areas. Then we need to disinfect and bag any animal carcasses and transport them to Cave #4's dumpster. I would further suggest that you work in shifts until all this is done as soon as possible. Stop all other activities until this is accomplished. Bleach, other disinfectants, gloves and masks should be found in the individual kitchen areas and storage containers close by. While you are planning this, please don't forget to include Caves #4 and #5 as well. The representatives can meet to coordinate all the details as soon as this Assembly has completed what we have to do next.

"And the second, grim task facing us is to vote on what course of action we want taken whenever our limited medical resources are stretched too thin. Based on the testimony we have heard today, I'd suggest we cast either a "yes" or "no" vote on the following statement that I have written on the chalk board:

'We do hereby declare that in the event that our medical resources are insufficient to provide the needed care for everyone, the following sequence of distribution of these resources will be: children before adults and women before men. A child is to be defined as anyone age 16 or younger.'

"Anticipating the need to vote, Clem has prepared and numbered 451 ballots for us to use today. You will need to print and sign your name, then fold it back the way it is handed to you and mark either "yes" or "no". The ballots will remain secret and be stored in the Communication Office. No one will ever know how you voted, at least in our lifetimes. Clem will now begin handing these out to the first person in each row. Just pass the extra ones to the person next to you. A container will then be passed down each row to deposit your ballot in. Please share pencils or pens. No one will tamper with your ballot. The ballots will be counted immediately, here on the stage, to avoid any questions or accusations later. Please wait while we count, and I will let you know as soon as we have a majority either way."

From the time of the vote counting until three days later, events in the cavern cascaded one after the other. The voting results were a surprise to everyone: "Yes" 269. "No" 181. Forty percent of the population had reservations regarding the finality of this process. However, nearly everyone came to realize that it was more a matter of imposed reality, rather than any philosophical or social agenda, that dictated the outcome. The sanctity of life was uppermost in these survivors' hearts and minds. How could it not be, given what had happened on April 1st, even though they were literally in the dark as to the extent of the devastation and loss on that day. Like any self-aware beings, they just knew when great tragedy surrounded them. It is a remnant of our deepest evolutionary memory. And by the afternoon on July 11th, no matter how you voted, everyone realized this act of participation brought their new morality into sharp focus, and it gave them a taste of what lay ahead.

Because there were both Marine and Amboy

families involved in the rationing of mechanical ventilators, both Ian Murphy and Minor Peterson each took the responsibility of counseling their respective families and performing the necessary allocation of equipment. And there was no time to delay. Ian sat down with Peter Marzoff and Minor with Helen Plant. Then both physicians met with Eric, who was designated as the living will authority for the Mark and Virginia Luberaski family. There had been no time for either Luberaski parent to make any other arrangements, prior to both of them and their son, Thomas, becoming terminally ill with the virus. Eric, by default and being Mark's commanding officer, had no alternative but to assume this duty. Having this authority meant he had to speak for Sally, their six year old daughter. Helen Plant volunteered to take Sally into her home, both as an act of compassion but also to help her cope with the loss of Roger. It was an arrangement that soon became permanent.

After discussing with family members and Eric the ramifications of delaying any further, and the results of the General Assembly's voting, each agreed, with the most anguishing and soulful cries, to transfer all mechanical ventilation to the three children who had the best chance of survival. And, in the utmost confidentiality, which was not known to anyone beyond themselves, it was also decided that there was to be no further suffering, no gasping for breath, no panic or fear present, just provide them with a peaceful and serene passing with only their loved ones present. And so it was. By midnight on July 11th, five members of the Amboy cavern slipped quietly away, in the arms of their loved ones or being held by Eric and Ann Stanfield.

Moreover, under the present circumstances, sadly there could be no delay in deposition of their loved ones' remains. By 9:30 a.m. on July 12th, Eric met with

Peter Marzoff and Helen Plant to see if they wanted to arrange any funeral service and possibly a memorial ceremony for later.

To Eric's amazement, they both had collected themselves enough overnight to have suggestions and preferences for how to conduct both a burial and a memorial service. On an odd-shaped piece of paper, they had scribbled down some of their wishes, based mostly on Peter and the Luberaski's being Catholics, and the Plant's being Protestants. In addition, they requested the burial service be a private affair, for immediate family and funeral participants only. The urgency of the circumstances required that the burial services be that afternoon in Cave #4, and they agreed to this. Subsequently, it was decided to have a Memorial Service in the Main Auditorium on July 14th, in which all the cavern families could participate.

Eric directed that caskets be fashioned from any surplus building materials in the storage room off Cave #5. Along with these, he requested that a platform be built to support the caskets during the burial service. Finally, he asked that these items, along with the bodily remains, be moved as soon as possible to Cave #4 and that each casket is draped with an American flag.

The actual Burial Service, it was decided later by Peter and Helen, was to be patterned after the Burial at Sea protocol (see Appendix 2, fig. 8, "Ceremonial Procedures for a Burial at Sea" service). It was agreed that all military personnel were to wear their dress uniforms, if they had them. Arms would be shouldered, but no ammunition was to be issued. Albert Nugama would serve as Chaplin, to read scripture and recite prayers. Philip Lieska would arrange the cavern choir to be present to sing. Recorded music would be played over the Public Address System. Both Peter and Helen wanted to take part in the actual committal. It involved placing the caskets next to the double door area, then moving them to the outside of the cave. Four hazmat suits were arranged to be available so they could help with that disposition, assistance being provided by both Arnie Davis and G.W. McCoy, the two Marine engineers.

The burial service took place at 5:00 p.m. and was broadcast cavern-wide from Cave #4. It, by all later accounts, was a stately and dignified service. It was one that all present said had the solemnity of an actual Shipboard or Head of State Funeral Service.

Following this Service, on July 14th, at 11:00 a.m., the Memorial Service was conducted in the Main Auditorium. (see Appendix 2, fig. 10, "The Global Union's Memorial Service on July 14th") This service marked the end of the rash of misfortunes and tragedies.

A calmer routine returned to the cavern, which was a relief to all. And by October 1st, everyone was eager to hear what those who had ventured outside the cavern for the first time had found.

NINE: DAWN REVISITED

The excitement within the cavern by October 1st was about out of control. The youngest children had no monopoly on nervous energy. Everyone was chattering, giggling, aimlessly bustling about, or poorly concentrating and hopelessly inattentive the week before this day. The Sunday before that Monday, there had been non-stop conversations and day-dreaming by all. Nobody could or would curb their enthusiasm and hopes for what would be discovered when four of their numbers donned the hazmat suits and emerged from Cave #1 the next day.

It was decided the exploratory trip outside would occur at 10:30 a.m. This would allow time for the sun's early morning glare to pass and the evening's lingering ground fog to lift, allowing them to see the surrounding mountainsides and valley ahead of them. The radiation levels were now low enough to tolerate someone venturing outside without protective gear for a few hours at a time. Nevertheless, if they ran into trouble and had to stay outside longer, it was agreed the suits were a necessary precaution.

Once the team had completed their outdoor inspection and survey, it was further agreed that they would immediately come to a General Assembly in the Main Auditorium and report on their findings. Some families began arriving in the Auditorium by 10:00 a.m., too nervous to just sit at home and wait for the scheduled noon meeting.

There was no ceremony when Eric, Minor, Mitzi and Geoffrey put on their suits and opened Cave #1's outermost door into the previously toxic and forbidding outside atmosphere. What they saw, felt, tasted, smelled and heard has already been chronicled in a previous chronicle. It was completely unlike before April 1st, when they had access to all manner of communication and transmission equipment that allowed them to know, at the flip of a switch or keystroke, whatever was occurring the world over. Now, it was as if they had been sentenced to serve time in a high-walled prison and could only see, feel, hear and taste the smallest segment of the world around them. Their perspective was reduced to near zero. Their world had shrunk, along with their knowledge of what had happened to it. It now was solely comprised of whatever lay out in front of them upon their exiting the cavern.

The only other contact they had ever been able to have since soon after April 1st was the continuous exchange of information with their sister shelter at Yucca Mountain. Despite this limitation, they had continued daily to transmit their location and situation, hoping someone might hear them and respond. But no one did.

They had not been able to venture out before this day, due to the higher levels of radiation in their area. Maybe beyond the confines of these mountains there were blooming oases and thriving cities. However, given the findings of their five senses in this place, at this time, that seemed only remotely possible.

Geoffrey was the most puzzled and intrigued of the four explorers. He could only speculate about the formation of what appeared to be a shoreline of water off in the distance. He would need to study the topographical maps in their library to get a better idea of elevations and terrain contours in the area. Even initially, however, as he later discussed their findings with his colleagues, it appeared to him that something catastrophic had occurred during their confinement. The atmospheric conditions, coupled with this water table rise, indicated a global event had occurred. Water, in this amount, in this location, was not just the result of a nuclear holocaust. But, even then, he sensed they would probably never know what exactly had occurred to cause this stunning change.

After they spent about 30 minutes walking around the cavern, inspecting the integrity of the two external warehouses and the various vehicles left parked outside, and shifted the caskets beyond Cave #4's entrance, they realized nothing further would be accomplished by remaining outdoors. Besides, they needed to prepare their report to the families,

By noon, they had reached their conclusions. It was decided that reporting what they saw in too much detail would not be appropriate. They had little objective information to support anything they saw or experienced. Instead, they elected to report that they were encouraged, to some degree, that there did appear to be the likelihood of sustained livability in their surroundings. Nevertheless, given the still fluctuating radiation levels and the instability of the atmosphere, it would be the wisest choice for everyone to wait three more months before the Final Emergence of all families. Besides, they had arranged for supplies to last twelve months, and by January 1st, they would have only been confined for nine. Beyond this, it was agreed amongst the four explorers that no mention would be made of the water level in the distance or the cold and deadly silence. For all they knew, atmospheric conditions had possibly been improving exponentially since April 1st, and by

January 1st, there would be little of these observed effects present.

Geoffrey gave the actual report to the General Assembly at noon. It was received with polite reserve. Obviously, everyone there, including the four explorers, wanted to end their confinement today. However, he put the brightest outlook he could on what they saw, leaving out the disturbing details. To interject doubt and plant seeds of despair was not appropriate, he felt. His report concluded with an optimistic summary and encouraged them now to refocus on being ready to exit, fully prepared to explore, locate, layout and build their future community. There was still much to prepare and to learn. He reminded them, they only had three months left to get ready.

It was at least some comfort to know they were well over half way through their confinement. They hoped that the next three months would pass relatively quick and without too many unexpected events. Classes resumed at 1:00 p.m. on October 1st, and life, as difficult and confined as it was, continued in the Amboy Cavern. Everyone now dreamed what they would find come January 1st, after their Final Emergence. A few, though, were dreading the day's arrival.

PART III

TEN: MOTHBALLED YET ABANDONED

The two security guards on duty February 18th, at the Yucca Mountain Repository, which had been mothballed, so to speak, two years earlier were speechless to see what was now parked outside their front gate. And to see someone, a captain of the United States Coast Guard in uniform, no less, greet them cheerfully with a "Good morning to you," only added to their confusion and near panic. No one had advised them of this happening. While there were some rumors going around on February 10th about the possibility of the military using their facility for some exercises, those ended as soon as they began, and nothing further was ever officially or definitely said or sent to them for confirmation.   As the two men came out of their guardhouse, they just stood dumbfounded, making no move to either assist or resist.

"My name is Capt. Ernie Tam," the uniformed Coast Guard officer continued. "And we are the first contingent, of several to come, that will be arriving over the next few weeks to prepare this facility for upcoming military maneuvers. It's part of the Homeland Security Department's ongoing InterService Training Program, in case of a nation-wide emergency."

Although all this was an outright lie, Capt. Tam

had been briefed by General Stanfield regarding the content of what he had told the U.S. Nuclear Regulatory Agency Department Heads to get their approval for use of this shelter. He was not particularly comfortable at fabricating stories, particularly of this magnitude, but it was clear to him and to all the personnel in his convoy that, initially, personal ethics were to become some of the first casualties of this upcoming holocaust. In order for them to prepare an attempt to survive what was ahead, the truth had to lessen its hold on honorable men and women. Like in the pitch battles of previous wars, decent men and women were forced even to kill to protect their homeland, family and freedom. So, then, in preparation for the mindless madness and destruction of April 1st, decent men and women reshaped the truth to try to preserve a small portion their homeland, family and freedom.

"Could you gentlemen please open the gates for us? It's been a long few days, and we need to get this equipment off-loaded as soon as possible. I have the documents here from the Headquarters of the Nuclear Regulatory Agency, giving us permission to enter and take temporary possession of this facility. You may take them and feel free to call the number listed there for any verification of these orders.

"Also, I've been instructed to compensate each of you. And I believe there are four of you stationed here at this time, is that correct?"

In answer to this question, the Captain observed the first signs that these fellows were able to do more than just stare. They both nodded in reply, and the oldest one reached out and took the official papers.

"Well, then, I've been instructed to give the four of you two months' severance pay. Moreover, given that your company usually ferries the four of you back and forth from here, I'll have one of our personnel transport all of you back to Las Vegas. Your company, as I understand it, is also aware of this change and has arranged other assignments for you. Our paying you the severance money is to reduce any inconvenience and hard feelings."

None of the Yucca Mountain Repository's four guards particularly liked this assignment, and the thought of getting two months pay for leaving there was a welcome bonus, along with hearing that they also were to be reassigned away from here. The one guard, who took the transfer orders from Capt. Tam, looked them over, then stepped inside the guardhouse and made a telephone call. In a few minutes, he reemerged and finally spoke.

"Certainly, sir. We'll get these gates opened for you folks right now. And I will have the other two of our crew, along with us here, packed and ready to leave within an hour."

"Great!" Capt. Tam replied. Not wanting these individuals to poke around too much and check out their transported equipment, he immediately instructed his driver, Chief Petty Officer Dawkins, to follow these men once they were inside the gate and take them immediately back to Las Vegas once they had their gear together. He also gave Chief Dawkins four envelopes, each one containing their two months' pay in $50.00 bills. "Make sure they get these, and try to be back here by nightfall." And within the next hour, the Yucca Mountain Repository had changed hands forever.

After getting all the convoy inside the fenced perimeter, Capt. Tam requested that the various unit leaders set up camp. While there were obviously many large outbuildings surrounding the southern tunnel entrance of the Repository Complex that could have been used, given the abandoned state they were in, everyone agreed setting up their own shelters adjacent to the tunnel entrance was the better choice. Maybe this facility was mothballed, according to the official records, but in the bright Nevada sunshine, it appeared nothing more than abandoned. Nothing stays in a ready reserve condition for long when it is exposed to the intensity of the desert for any period. Two years had taken its toll on this place.

February 19th, would begin the actual exploration and preliminary planning on what needed to be done to secure this place for their survival. Capt. Tam had also been given a copy of Clem's supplies and equipment list, the same as the one that General Stanfield gave Ben Javitts. Ben had briefed him on the upcoming train shipments, on their contents, and on how they possibly could be deployed within the cavern. Ernie was not sure, when any rail deliveries might be coming, but they had to try to get some idea immediately how the cavern was laid out and start a preliminary positioning of the rail cars, should any start arriving in the next few days. He knew it would be about two weeks before Ben and his Seabees would get there. Anything could arrive before then.

By 0930 hours, the general staff meeting of all one hundred personnel was concluded. The five teams were divided into twenty individuals each, and each was instructed to report their findings at 0800 hours tomorrow in another staff meeting. The critical areas to be investigated were: the cavern's overall condition and livability; the rail bed's integrity and layout, both inside and outside the complex; whether interior lighting, ventilation and generators were present and, if so, were they operational; whether communication equipment was available or needed to be installed; and what material in the many abandoned outbuildings surrounding the southern tunnel entrance might be useful.

As the team leaders began their explorations and investigations, Capt. Tam directed his nineteen personnel to divide into pairs and each pair was to inventory one of the ten outbuildings. They were instructed to go from room to room checking and writing down whatever equipment or supplies they found. Anything of eventual use would be cataloged and referenced for later retrieval.

The reports the next day were nothing short of astounding. No one knew the breadth of this mothballed project before yesterday. Col. Derek Amen described to everyone their inspection of the cavern as follows:

"We had some difficulty getting the south entrance, multi-ton, blast doors to open. The windblown sand and grit gave added resistance to any door movement. We had to bathe the hinge mechanisms and door seams with machine oil to get them to open. It was obvious the doors were built to keep anything inside from getting out. Fortunately, upon inspection, we found the interior seals are still in good shape.

"Once inside the doorway, it appears that a boring machine must have carved out of the volcanic rock a tunnel, approximately twenty-five feet in diameter. The walls are natural rock for the most part, with some steel ribbing and reinforced concrete noted further on in the tunnel, particularly in what must have been planned to be their storage areas. Those tunnel walls are all steel-rib reinforced. The tunnel extends for five miles, in a south-north direction, but in a sweeping horseshoe shape. It angles downward until reaching the middle of that horseshoe-bend, where it levels out for a couple of miles or so, and then it angles upward to the northern tunnel entrance.

"It is in the central, level area that we found another eight tunnels, sixteen feet in diameter, extending off from the main tunnel. They were labeled

414

'emplacement drifts' at each entrance. These tunnels, as I mentioned earlier, were all steel and concrete reinforced. Everything, anywhere we looked, seemed structurally sound, but we did notice what appeared to be some water stain in a deeper level in just one of these drifts. Essentially, however, all these drifts appeared to be moisture free, as did the main tunnel.

"Interestingly, we also found three large excavated voids, which appeared to have been areas for technical work or for ongoing studies and monitoring, because there were still some benches, tables and miscellaneous small laboratory equipment in each of them. Their ceilings were well over thirty feet high. In addition, these rooms extended a good 300 feet off the main tunnel. There were no railroad tracks into these areas, but tracks did extend into each of the eight drifts I mentioned earlier.

"The northern tunnel door was, likewise, securely locked. We didn't try to open it at this time. It was clear to all of us that the rail tracks did extend through that doorway to the outside.

"Finally, we should note that there is some dankness present at that lower level. We thought with some ventilation it would be corrected enough to be unnoticeable. We did see piping and vents in that area, but left any conclusions regarding them to Capt. O'Shay's team. And that's our report for now."

Major Jon Schultz then reported what was found with their examination of the railroad tracks and roadbed. As the leadership of this newly arrived group was aware, through their discussions earlier with Ben Javitts, there would be significant tonnage resting on these tracks. Fully loaded freight trains, along with their engines, would require that the rail bed and tracks are operational. A derailment would be disastrous. Even the Amtrak train, once it was filled with the families and their belongings, would be a weight challenge to all but the best-maintained tracks. And to their surprise, the "sleepers" or "ties" were the newer concrete type and showed essentially no wear. The rails were seamless and likewise level and sound. They had no way to test the effect of rolling weight, but just by observation, the rail system looked usable for their purposes. Only by bringing a loaded train into the tunnel, possibly with a switch engine pulling a few cars at a time, would they have a true picture as to whether there was any load limit. To them, it was clear; the Repository was not mothballed due to the rail system. It was fully operational.

Maj. Shultz added that the walkway on the drift side of the tracks was paved and would allow easy passage of pedestrian traffic once the trains were in place. Because of the tunnel's extremely long distance end-to-end, he suggested it might be wise to see if Nellis AFB had a couple of golf carts and battery chargers that they could use. They would be perfect for quicker movement throughout the complex and for doing periodic, full-length tunnel inspections. However, he noted, there would be less clearance on the opposite side of the tracks, once the various trains were parked. This might pose some problems for the special tank cars to be used for showering, if access is needed on both sides of the car. The rails were a standard five foot width throughout the cavern. Moreover, the switches into the drifts were all functional.

He concluded with a brief summation about the design of the track roadbed outside the cavern. It was in the shape of a huge teardrop, with its formation beginning at a switch, about three miles before the Yucca Mountain itself. It appeared that the tracks were coming from the northwest, from Beatty, a small town about 18 miles away. At the switch, the track then formed a large, lopsided oval, winding its way into the south tunnel entrance, through the Repository, and out the north exit, completing the oval back at the switch. Presumably, all materials coming by train would have to travel from that direction. There was no rail bed coming from any other direction.

It was his conclusion that the tunnel would be livable, but there would be significant psychological issues with long-term residency, claustrophobia being the most obvious one. Others would be boredom and panic due to being confined in such a manner. Physically, there were the issues of sanitation, water and food safety, and adequate ventilation. Adequate preparation and vigilance was all he could suggest to combat these issues of livability. They had no other option.

The next report was from Capt. O'Shay. She reported that there was extensive internal wiring present, but none of it was live or operational at this time. Her recommendation was to section off the wiring, with the greatest load located at the five drift tunnels, where the Amtrak living quarters would be parked. At that point, there would be full ceiling lighting in the main tunnel and into the drift tunnels, at least as far as was necessary to illuminate the storage and tank cars. Additionally, the Amtrak kitchen cars should be fully wired for their cooking and clean up functions. The other priority for wiring would be the three vaulted areas or voids. One area would be used for General Assemblies and the Communication Office, as was the case for the Amboy Cavern; one for classrooms and one for storage. And finally, there would need to be wiring for a Public Address System and ventilation. In addition, there would need to be a separate service just for the occasional illumination of the full tunnel. This would only require sporadic light fixtures for the safety of pedestrian passage when making periodic inspection tours.

The ventilation system was extensive but, of course, it was deactivated when the project was mothballed. She recommended that this be an immediate and urgent priority to get something fixed and operational. The entire living area needed to be ventilated. There had to be some intake filtering installed and some exhaust fans at either or both ends of the tunnel. Scrubbing the air would require some engineering to insure there was adequate oxygenation and to avoid any buildup of carbon dioxide in the living area.

Finally, there were two large emergency generators located just inside the tunnel's south entrance. They only needed minor maintenance to be operational. And with both of these working, the electricity needs of the cavern could be met, understanding there would be minimal lighting after 2300 hours until 0600 hours, and no grid electricity available to the interior of the Amtrak sleeper cars.

As an afterthought, she added that it was her understanding that approximately 125 bicycle-like electrical generators had been ordered for use by the families. (see Appendix 2, ref. 1, "The Pedal-a-Watt Stationary Bike Power Generator") Each sleeper would have five of these bicycles stationed outside of it. Daily someone in each family will have to recharge the interior batteries with these bikes. This will be their sole source of interior lighting or for using any other electrical device. She expressed hope that these bicycles could be placed on the opposite side of the train from the pedestrian walkway, but they would not know if that would work until the Amtrak train arrived.

Lt. Col. La Cross echoed the concern previously expressed about the likelihood of boredom becoming a problem. Her team's inspection yielded little evidence of any communication equipment being inside the cavern. It was clear that whatever they would have, they would have to install. Her suggestion was to use the first vault area, as Capt. O'Shay had suggested, for the Communication Office and immediately begin installing a dish satellite, and possibly a microwave tower hook up, particularly with a link to the Amboy Cavern Communication Center. Through this linkage, they could download much more information and material, particularly schoolwork for the children. Not having the teachers, medical or professional staff that Amboy would have, they would be entirely dependent on them to provide material and information to use and then, in some cases, to return it to them for their review and input. Likewise, this same Communication Office would serve to link them to the outside world beyond Amboy.

The morning session's reports ended with Capt. Tam reporting that his team was able to catalog the contents in all the external buildings and found a couple that could be cannibalized for wood and materials they would need for building classrooms, tables, partitions, offices in the vault areas and platforms over the tank cars for toilet and shower facilities. There was no technical equipment remaining, but there were countless chairs of various descriptions, desks, lamps, file cabinets and shelves. In addition, he advised the group that he felt it necessary to contact Ben Javitts after this meeting and have him call the railroad and have them add 60 empty flat cars to the supply train delivery. They would be needed to load their trucks and equipment that each group was bringing to Yucca Mountain.

Everyone there sensed the urgency of getting to work immediately to prepare for what was coming. The pending mountain of equipment and supplies, and many more people, was overwhelming to contemplate. Amongst themselves they prepared a check-off work list (see Appendix 2, fig. 11, "Yucca Mountain Check Off Work List") Once the list was completed, the work was divided into crews, and work sites were set up with flood lights for round the clock work. There was a mixture of resolve and purposefulness in their manner, but the air was also filled with an indescribable dread.

ELEVEN: DELIVERIES AND ARRIVALS

No one was at the gate when the Air Force personnel arrived in their large caravan of vehicles. It was 0800 hours and Capt. Tam's work details were already in place, scattered throughout the tunnel and the outside building complex.   The front gate was not locked, however.   Probably this was someone's oversight Col. Steven Blackmore thought, as his lead truck drove through it.   In a way, it sent a small shiver down his military-oriented spine, indicating they might be heading into a slack, poorly disciplined situation. Nevertheless, his reservations could not have been further from reality.

By the time of Col. Blackmore's arrival, on February 21st, the work crews, including all senior officers, had been toiling for hours. In fact, they worked non-stop. Pulling up in front of the campsite area, just west of the south tunnel entrance, Blackmore had his driver honk his truck's horn repeatedly.   As he was doing so, the other vehicles, one by one, pulled up either behind or alongside him. There were twenty-three in all, and all filled with supplies, machinery, and hand tools.

Jon Shultz finally heard them and crawled down off the second floor of what used to be the commissary at this facility. He was covered with dust, sand and bits of insulation.

"Good morning," he called out, walking across

the large open area that separated the outside buildings from the tracks and tunnel. "You folks must be the Air Force units. Everyone here will be so relieved you've arrived. We need your help, and probably your supplies, most desperately."

Col Blackmore walked over, and they shook hands. And within the next five minutes of their conversation, it became unquestionably clear to him, and the to the rest of the Air Force crewmen and women, that they only had time enough to quickly set up their own camp area. Then they, too, had to begin immediately working to prepare their living quarters for the upcoming year. The gate had not been secured, because there just was not time or personnel to do so.

By 1300 hours that same day, the 97 Air Force personnel were scattered throughout the complex, loading, unloading, demolishing or rebuilding. Like with the families in Amboy, much of their work was to be manual. Moreover, once the first train arrived that would only become more obvious.

For the next four days, the combined work crews were able to disassemble two buildings. From their salvaging work, they managed to stockpile enough building materials to build most of what would be needed inside the cavern. They stacked the materials in piles alongside the railroad tracks, outside the tunnel's entrance. From these classrooms, offices, toilet and shower facilities, closet and storage areas for the families' belongings would be built. Maybe now, each outdoor worker thought, one could catch some needed sleep.

And sleep they did the night of February 25th, at least until 0430 that next morning, when they were awakened by the steady blasts of a freight train, signaling its pending arrival. The engineers began to signal their arrival just after they left Beatty. Due to the length of the train, and the grade it was pulling, the five locomotive engines and one switch engine, were working at full throttle to pull and push the train a steady 5 mph. By 0700 hours, the train passed through the perimeter fence into the Yucca Mountain facility compound and stopped at the front entrance of the south tunnel.

With the two and a half hours notice that it was coming, all 197 occupants of the facility were outside to greet its arrival. It was met with a hearty cheer, not unlike how any battlefield soldiers would react to the sight of desperately needed reinforcements. Its arrival, more than anything else up to this point, signaled that a unified plan was evolving, that maybe they could realistically hope that they, and their families, might be given a reasonable chance of surviving what lay ahead.

Ernie Tam and Steven Blackmore had already gotten together with Jon Schultz and decided who would be trained as drivers or engineers for the trains. It was to be an all Army operation. The training and coordination lent itself to being under one command. And for now, Jon and Sergeant First Class Jo Ann Henry were to be the ones trained. They would be responsible to train the others, as more trains arrived. And while they were getting a crash course from the just arrived engineers and brakeman, Ernie, Lilyanne and Jenny LaCross decided how to divide and distribute the train's freight cars.

Their final decision involved disconnecting and leaving the flat cars at the south entrance for the time being. They would eventually be loaded with the recently stacked building materials and with the trucks and vehicles brought by both the Air Force and Ernie Tam's group. Once the flat cars were loaded with building materials, they would be transported to Void #3 for off- loading. Ultimately, the flat cars, when fully loaded with vehicles, the twelve tank cars with fuel, motor oil and kerosene and the five recently-arrived locomotives would all be parked behind the Amtrak train facing the southernmost end of the tunnel.

The freight cars, with their twelve months' or more supply of food and personal supplies, would be moved immediately into the cavern and parked adjacent to the three large voids. There, they would be unloaded, sorted and divided into one-month rations for every 50 families. One month's worth of supplies would be stacked in each half of a freight car. Once the cars were reloaded, they would be moved into one of the five drifts for storage and access to every group of five Amtrak sleeper cars, kitchen and lounge car. All these residential cars would be parked on the main track beside each drift. Because Ben Javitts had warned Ernie that the Vice President of Operations for Amtrak had promised that the train would be delivered no later than March 5th, the Yucca Mountain workers realized they had only six full days to accomplish all this sorting and repacking. Resolved, all the 197 personnel that could be spared were assigned to this duty.

The tank cars, already filled with fresh water, and the empty ones, to be modified for toilet facilities, would also need to be positioned in the drifts, as well, by March 5th. It was hoped the Seabees, with their welding equipment, would arrive in the next few days and would do the necessary welding modifications on the tank cars. They needed to be modified, if possible beforehand.

By nightfall, the army personnel had been trained well enough to safely operate the locomotives and switch engine. That done, Jon elected to drive the train engineers back to Las Vegas himself. To insure good will and minimize the likelihood that they would discuss what they saw today, he elected to take them to one of the larger hotels on Las Vegas Boulevard, where he rented rooms for each of them and bought them a large, midnight buffet dinner. After some drinks and gambling, Jon bid them goodbye. By the time he left, the engineers were convinced they had done their patriotic duty. None of them ever discussed the day, outside their group.

As Jon left Las Vegas, a deep sense of loss overcame him. He began to weep uncontrollably as the morning sun arrived over the Amargosa Valley. The impact of what was happening was too overpowering. He had to pull off the road and stop. Taking the time to stare into the stark, barren desert around him, he moaned aloud, "God in Heaven, what is happening? What madness has brought us to this? What is left to pray for, except please keep my family safe until they can be with me? The knowledge of all this is just too much..." Finally, after some time composing himself, he was able to drive on safely. However, he knew that soon nothing and no one would ever be the same again.

Everyone lost track of the days, following the first train's arrival. When the Seabees drove up on March 1st, dawn was spreading over the spiraling snake-like shape of Yucca Mountain. Try as you might, it was a sinister looking formation. But Ben Javitts knew being in it, probably more so than being inside any other modified structure on the planet; they could survive most outside destructive forces. The Mountain is located next to the atomic testing grounds and has experienced countless experiments being adjacent to these sites. The Repository was later designed and built to withstand eons of geological challenges. So this facility, for all its evil looking appearance and despite being mothballed for reasons unknown to him, was still a welcome site for he and is personnel after working on the Amboy Cavern.

Again, the gates were not secured when he drove the lead vehicle inside the compound. In addition, there was no one in sight and nonresponsive to their repeated calls.   Except for a mild breeze and an occasional scolding argument from a pair of cactus wrens in the scrub brush, it was eerily silent.   Outside the   south tunnel entrance were parked flat bed railcars, loaded with trucks and equipment, and before them were the empty tank cars, waiting to be modified for toilets and showers.

Realizing that everyone must be working at a feverish pace elsewhere, Ben elected to proceed by having his personnel set up camp, unload their vehicles, and then begin mounting them onto the empty flat bed railcars.   While that was being done, he immediately directed his welding teams to prepare to cut open and modify the tank cars.   There was still some lumber left on the siding, which he instructed his carpenter team to use in fashioning the superstructures on top of the tank cars.   He, too, was aware of the March 5th deadline for the arrival of the Amtrak train.   With the 50 Seabees arriving today, the Yucca Mountain workforce was essentially at full strength.   He murmured an inaudible prayer for strength and guidance for the month ahead, recalling there was so much left to do, with so very precious little time left to do it in.

With   the   Seabees   arrival,   the   combined assortment of engineers was able to work feverishly to accomplish the "Top Priority" items on the checklist. The highest was electrification of the cavern.   Along with that was the need to reposition the various train components. The locomotives at the head of the train had to be disconnected and driven completely through the five mile tunnel and out the northern exit around to the southern entrance and reconnected to the rear of the train, behind the empty flat cars.   The switch engine then had to be positioned at the head of the train, to allow it to move box and tank cars into the drifts, as they were emptied, modified, or refilled.   Once the five drifts had

426

the six box cars with twelve months of food and personal items in them, the six tank cars with drinking water and toilet facility modifications were moved in. The exception would be the first drift, which would have eight boxcars in it, for restocking the other drifts as needed. Once that was finished, the flatcars loaded with the secondhand building materials from dismantling the outside buildings were parked and unloaded into Vault #3.

Come the morning of March 5th, the main track was clear from the north entrance into the living area for the Amtrak Superliner to pull its thirty-five cars and five locomotive engines through the tunnel until it almost made contact with the flat cars, loaded with vehicles and equipment. The switch engine was moved to the south entrance for the time being. This left room at the north end of the tunnel for storage of the freight train, still to come, with its two-mile long load of rebuilding materials. And at 1000 hours, the familiar sound of a train whistle sounded off in the distance. With great fanfare, all the personnel gathered at the northern entrance, waiting for the train. One of the Army engineers walked out to the switch at the head of the teardrop circle and reversed it, which now directed the Amtrak train into the northern entrance.

To see its sleek, high sided cars move through the desolate desert was thrilling for all the personnel. Here was their home for the next six months, at the least. It fairly gleamed in the sunshine. Once it came just to the tunnel entrance, the engineers stopped it. Jon Schultz and Jo Ann got on to inspect the controls and see what was different in operating this particular engine. Luckily, there were just a few railcars that needed repositioning, and then they could bring the new train to its assigned position.

After that, Jon again requested that this train

crew allow him to take them back to Las Vegas right away. And, like before, he arranged for the crew to have rooms at the Hotel/Casino. Only this time he did not stay in town. Maybe it was fatigue, maybe it was being a little more calloused, maybe it was being a little more possessive of his status as a possible survivor or, most likely, maybe it was that he could not face not telling them what was ahead, and instead just letting them, and the rest of humanity, possibly vanish. He knew it was the latter. He could not get back to Yucca Mountain fast enough. Somebody else was going to have to return the last train crew. He could not do this again.

Once Jon left with the train crew for Las Vegas, the call went out for everyone to board the train for its ride into the tunnel. When Jo Ann finally brought it to a stop, the locomotives came to rest adjacent to Vault #1, resting a few feet away from a flat car loaded with a disassembled helicopter. And the last sleeper car was positioned about three car lengths behind Drift #5, toward the northern entrance to the cavern. The entire train extended over three quarters of a mile in length, once the shower tank cars were interspersed between the sleeping cars.

Several days were needed to complete the electrical rewiring for cooking, dishwashing and eating in the kitchen/dining cars. The two generators at the southern tunnel entrance would power the cavern and the kitchen /dining cars. A separate electrical system was to be powered by the bicycle generators after they arrived with the rebuilding supply train. In the meantime, modifications were made in the sleeper and lounge cars for using rechargeable light bulbs, which would be recharged by the residents riding these bicycles.

Finishing this electrical work was a priority over any other construction. Soon thereafter, a major effort was started to complete the carpentry work. As many personnel as could be dedicated to the project were assigned to building classrooms, erecting shelves and storage areas in the drifts for personal belongings, constructing a Communication Center and a stage in Vault #1

The erection of both a satellite dish and a transmission tower, similar to the ones installed and built above the Amboy Cavern, were undertaken by the same Seabees as did that work. The tower was a backup system, in case there was disruption of the satellite transmissions for some reason.

On March 10th, in the late afternoon, unlike the previous two train arrivals, the final freight train load of rebuilding supplies pulled to a stop at the southern tunnel entrance with no fanfare or horns blowing. The Seabees working on the communication tower on top of Yucca Mountain were the ones who spotted its approach and radioed to the Communication Center to inform them of its arrival. By now, Ernie and Ben had been able to requisition two golf carts from Nellis AFB to move more rapidly throughout the cavern at times like these. Both of them got in one and hurriedly made their way to the south entrance.

Once there, what they saw, even after all the previous trainloads, was shocking. For two miles, stretching off to the horizon was a train of mixed railcars of every description, each loaded with the materials to physically rebuild their lives in a year or so. This arrival and the final coming together of their families would signal the finalization of this non-stop ordeal. That this was a watershed event, they had no doubt.

But the train had to be backed up and moved around so that the locomotives were closest to the northern entrance and the rear of the train was adjacent to the last sleeper car by Drift #5. (see Appendix 2, Diagrams 1 and 2, "Yucca Mountain Cavern Floor

Plan") Ben radioed to the personnel working in Drift #5 and asked them to have someone get the other golf cart and drive out to the northern entrance and open those doors. He then got in one of their few remaining vehicles, parked by the southern tunnel entrance, and drove it out to the switch box. Aware of the ordeal it had been for Jon returning the previous train crews to Las Vegas, he decided he would take this final crew back, which he did almost immediately after they parked the train. . In the meantime, Ernie drove the golf cart they were in back to the Communication Center and began processing the paperwork of this train's shipment.

As was the custom when these trains arrived, Jon and Jo Ann immediately went to meet the incoming train. As Ernie drove up to the Communication Center, they quickly took keys from him and drove on to the north entrance to meet the train. . They needed to inspect and verify that they could manage the controls of the newly arrived locomotives, and that they could train others to do so, as well. Recently, they had been talking between themselves, not wanting to alarm others, about what happens once they are no longer confined to this place. What if they needed to use one of the locomotives to get help, because the roads were impassable for some reason? On the other hand, what if the tracks had been damaged as well? Considering these possibilities, they decided to ask the recently arrived train engineers if they had seen any track repairing material, stored or lying around anywhere, during their trip here.

They did ask, once the locomotives had been repositioned to the northern entrance and inspected by them. And it turned out, as a matter of fact, that the train engineers had seen some repair gondolas, at least two or three of them, filled with rails, ties, kegs of nails and fastening plates out of Beatty, parked on a siding.

Within minutes of the train being parked, Ben was hustling the recently arrived crew into his humvee. Jon and Jo Ann hitched a ride with him over to the south entrance, where they climbed aboard the switch engine and drove it over to Beatty. Before nightfall, they had been to Beatty and back, pulling three gondolas filled with the track repair supplies. They maneuvered the three gondolas around and parked them in front of this last freight train, adjacent to the locomotives. Securing the northern doors, they drove the golf cart back to the locomotives and inspected them one more time. It was their belief at that time, that nothing on this train would be disturbed for the next year.

Meanwhile, Ben did stay in Las Vegas that night, at least until about 0230 hours. He ate, gambled and drank too much. But the train crew was a cheery lot, and he thoroughly enjoyed the break. However, by the time they decided to call it a night, he knew he was, frankly, drunk. His decision to get a large mug of coffee and drive back anyway was not a good career move. Nevertheless, he thought, if this next month is heading in the direction the people around him have been told it will, a DUI would not affect his career advancement a whole lot. The main thing, he thought, as he backed up the humvee to leave the casino, was to avoid hitting something or someone. Once on the highway, he rolled down the windows, leaned back and imagined that he and his family were taking off on a long holiday. For the next two hours, he escaped reality, with the night holding him comfortably in its arms.

The next two weeks passed with a surge of construction and various modifications, all in an attempt to make the living area as ready as possible for the families. The excitement and anxiety for the cavern personnel mounted with each passing day. They knew the cavern and its interior would all be a shock for their families to see, and then, for them to realize that it was to be their new home for the next year. However, ready or not, by 2300 hours on March 23rd, the first 100 families arrived by buses and trucks at the front gate.

No one at the cavern was sure which families would be arriving first, so it was decided that all personnel would be allowed to wait outside the south entrance to meet and greet their loved ones. They also were aware that B would have just informed their family members, earlier that day, about April 1st and why they were coming here. They would all be in complete shock, from the horror of B's revelations.

Flood lamps, cots, chairs, tables and refreshments were set up outside for their arrival. In addition, because the night air was chilly to some, but outright cold to most, it was anticipated that once the cavern personnel were reunited with their families, they would begin the long hike to their living quarters. Likewise, chairs and cots had been set up along the mile-long walkway, for them to use if necessary, as they passed the parked tank, box and flatcars and locomotives.

Living area assignments had been made according to their branch of service. It was decided that maintaining closer contact with people they already knew would help, initially, to cope with their new circumstances. So, for example, the fifty Seabee families were all to be housed in the five Amtrak sleeper cars parked by Drift #1. The 100 Air Force families would be in the sleepers parked by Drifts #2 and #3; Navy and Coast Guard families by Drift #4; and Marine and Army families by Drift #5. Nothing was to be hurried during this time. Every effort had been made to finish most of the immediate living area construction, thereby allowing each family this time to be together. Fortunately, for the Amboy families, they had had more opportunities to see and make contact with one another during this period. Not so for these families. Work gangs, assigned to complete all outdoor and the remaining indoor work, would not resume their duties until March 25th.

The final group of families, including the flight crews, arrived from the Marine Base by 1030 hours on March 24th. And at 1910 hours that same night, the front gate to the Yucca Mountain Cavern was welded shut. All personnel from Nellis AFB had also arrived by truck with materials to store, catalog and use in the months and years ahead.

The northern and southern cavern doors were not sealed shut until the evening of March 31st. During that last week, the families, when they could, were encouraged to spend time outside the cavern. Everyone, by now, realized that the confinement in the tunnel was to be an unimaginable hardship, but the impact of that was lessened by his or her foreknowledge of what lay ahead for all the rest of humanity. Most people just walked or sat. Even the children did not have the will to join in much play. This final week, before April 1st, imprinted a maturity on the children rarely seen in ones their ages. When possible, most families just huddled in small groups around the Repository Grounds.

The final preparations of the Vaults were completed during this last week. Chairs and tables were brought in from the outside complex for the Auditorium and classrooms. Building the Communication Center and the Auditorium stage were finished the last day that week. Inside the Communication Center, the computer calibration and downloading of software for the satellite dish and tower communication links were finalized, completing the work in Vault #1. A small Medical Clinic was built and furnished in Vault #2. In addition, the construction of the library and shelving in Vault #3 was completed, along with the storage shelves for personal belongings in each of the five drifts. By noon on March 31st, the Yucca Mountain Cavern was as livable, or survivable, as they could make it. At 2230 hours that night a roll call was made, and all 1000 citizens were accounted for.

TWELVE: APRIL 1ST

Of the many similarities and differences between the two shelters, one of the most notable differences was that the Yucca Mountain Repository tunnel's depth and design could much better withstand devastating forces from the outside and still protect its contents. Even though, by April 1st the contents of the cavern were now human beings, rather than nuclear waste, the effect was the same. These survivors were imbedded in an underground fortress. The Amboy Cavern, on the other hand, was perched close to the top of a mountain, more exposed to the elements and atmospheric changes and subject to all tectonic activity, like a toy duck bobbing in a child's bathtub.

This made a difference on April 1st. It had been arranged, unlike for the Amboy Cavern's occupants, who on that day, were mostly in an exhaustive sleep, that by 0800 hours all inhabitants of the Yucca Mountain Cavern were to be seated in Vault #2's General Assembly area. There was nowhere near the musical talent or access to live music in their midst, but eventually a collection of hobbyists' fiddlers, banjo, guitar, mandolin and harmonica players did come forward later to provide for entertainment, square dancing, and sing-a-longs. Today, however, only recorded music was played over the Public Address System. Like Amboy, everybody gladly contributed whatever recorded music they had for everyone else to hear.

Seated on stage were Maj. Gen. Benton Scott from Nellis, Col. Steven Blackmore from McChord, Capt. Lilyanne O'Shay from San Diego, Maj. Jon Shultz from Fort Irwin, and Lt. Ben Javitts from Port Hueneme. Each were dressed in their military uniforms, but each recognized that whatever was about to happen, made this probably their last opportunity to do so. Like Amboy, it would become a simple fact of post-April 1st life that military rank and uniforms were to become unnecessary and ostentatious. Nevertheless, today, they hoped their wearing them would give everyone there a sense of comfort and stability for what lay ahead.

Also, announcements of any reports that came into the Communication Center from outside the cavern would be broadcasted throughout the day. Everyone would hear whatever there was to hear, at the same time.

Being the ranking officer, General Scott rose and came forward to speak. No amplification was necessary here either, given the acoustics throughout the underground complex.

"Morning. Ladies and gentlemen, young adults and children, my fellow citizens," he began in the most somber tone. "We, here on the stage felt, and I am sure you will agree, that being assembled here, at this time, would give us collective strength to try and bear whatever this day is to bring us. We all are aware of what B has foretold was to happen sometime today, and we have all gone to career-ending lengths to prepare for it, as we were instructed to do. Obviously, we know of no other such arrangements being made, other than those in the Amboy Cavern. We must assume, therefore, that quite possibly we will become a body, someday joined with those in Amboy, that will be entrusted to try and extend life into the distant future. We can anticipate that

436

there will be much we will never know about what happens this day and know even less who or what survives it. However, we cannot allow those unknowns to rule our lives so much that we become paralyzed.

"That this will be a time of testing, we have already seen. It is a time of testing our faiths, our dreams and hopes, our expectations and preconceptions, our very existence. The reassurances and guidance of B's directions has brought us to this point. We can only hope that B will return one day to offer us some further hope and direction. In the meantime, whatever faith, whatever God or Deity each of you pray to, do so unceasingly in these days, months, and years we may have left to us.

"We must cling to one another now. Rank will not matter, once events spiral out of control, as we've been advised they will. Our home will always be open to each of you, as I know yours will be for my family and me. We are to become a community of survivors, of faith, of dedication to the welfare of each other. And no one here will be left behind. Thank you."

Within 50 minutes each person on the stage, except Ben Javitts, had come forward and spoken words of comfort and support. When Ben came forward, he simply said, "Dear friends, I think it is time now for those of us on this stage to come down and be with our families. We can sit here for a while longer, and then please feel free to make your way back to your living quarters whenever you want. We will be broadcasting all reports that come into the Communication Office. In addition, it has been suggested that day after tomorrow we start our schedule of classes for the children and all of us adults. In the meantime, please find comfort any way you can."

At 0900 a.m., the music was replaced by the reports coming in from the Amboy Cavern. The cascade of silence from cities and reporting centers was the sad confirmation they had dreaded and tried to prepare for. Within an hour, even the Las Vegas media had been silenced. Only Amboy Cavern continued to respond to calls for verification. And at noon, there was a rumbling, with some minor shaking, but nothing compared to what the Amboy inhabitants experienced. No one was knocked to the ground, and nothing was tipped over. Like Amboy, they conjectured it was a major earthquake in the region. However, what did result from this jolting was the loss of transmission from the satellite. Something had closed down that transmission. Now the Communication Center staff had to go to the backup, line-of-sight tower, linkage between them and Amboy. Some days later, both were able to redirect and recalibrate to reestablish linkage to the same military satellite, which, for the huge amount of material to be transmitted back and forth, was a Godsend in itself.

By 12:30 p.m., the Main Auditorium was empty. The realization of what was happening was too overwhelming. Families slowly made their way back to their sleeper car rooms. The next day and a half was lost in grief and despair.

PART IV

THIRTEEN: FAMILY LIFE UNDERGROUND

Lilyanne Duke and her twin sister, Penelope or 'Penny' as she was called from birth, were born in Belton, Texas. They lived on Pearl St., within two blocks of the University of Mary Hardin-Baylor, which was an all women's college for many years. The presence of that institution and the daily reinforcement of seeing all the college students come and go by their home inspired them. They grew up believing that they could open doors of opportunity long after they left Belton.

Two influences vied for Lilyanne's choices of which door to enter. The first eventually won out, and for her family it was the more curious of the two. It was her keen interest and admiration of Fleet Admiral Chester W. Nimitz. His being born in Fredicksburg, a small town, not too many miles from her home, captivated her. What fascinated her was that he became one of naval warfare's most ingenious leaders, and yet, he was born and raised in the arid hill country of west Texas, like her.

The second influence was more pervasive. It was the countryside that surrounded her and her sister. Together, they explored, hiked and floated in this magical area throughout their youth. Belton was in a kind of transition zone. The region had gradual uplifting slopes of loose shale and gravel, which was sparsely covered by low-lying cedar trees and cottonwoods. The uplift ended at the escarpment that formed the hill country, with its canyons, plateaus, and outcrops of low mountains and many rivers. It was an area that was later to become a source of fascination and discovery for many future archeologists.

One of their favorite haunts was the property that encompassed the old Boy Scout Camp, located on the west side of the Lampasas River about four miles from town. In the late fall and winter months there were almost no scouts in the camp, and they almost had the area to themselves. It had the largest natural flowing spring in the state. Wheel ruts were carved into the bedrock by the wagon trains, escorting their herds of cattle along the Chisholm Trail. In addition, the well-preserved remains of the old gristmill race, built in 1846, coursed its way through the hillsides, ending at what used to be the grain crushing, water-powered wheelhouse. In the many limestone caves and overhangs, they found countless Indian spear points, arrowheads and potsherds. It was like the dense woods and hillsides kept secrets for all but the most dedicated and curious adventurers.

Lilyanne and Penny could not wait until those weekends to pack a lunch, ride their bicycles out to this area, and become lost in the centuries of past human habitation. Her second vocational choice was archeology, but sister eventually chose that path...

Accompanying and reinforcing her genuine interest in Admiral Nimitz, was her many raft and canoe trips down the nearby rivers. They made the 26 mile trip from Flat Rock down the Colorado River to Lake Buchanan so many times that their parents finally bought them a canoe to use on their weekend trips. Years later, she did make other raft trips down a few of the more challenging rivers of the Northwest, but none of these ever replaced her memories of those days when they essentially owned the Colorado River. Its unspoiled beauty of high cliffs, migrating birds, and gentle but, to them in those days, challenging rapids, were precious memories. The world of water won out in the end, and by her senior year in high school, she had decided to apply for a Navy ROTC scholarship to the University of Texas in Austin, which she won to her and her parent's great surprise.

Her years at the university were also filled with exploration, but now it was in the study of electrical engineering and computer science. But always, it was with the purpose in mind of how to apply her knowledge and skills to a naval career.

Throughout her final years of living in Belton and the first two at the University, she always had time to date, but anything serious and involving a commitment of some kind was unappealing. That was until she became more aware and had more contact with Raymond O'Shay. Ray was also in the NROTC at the University, and during their first two years, they shared ROTC classes and drill together. Without question, he certainly noticed her right away their freshman year. Her naturally wavy blond hair highlighted her strikingly blue green eyes and Irish-bred pale complexion, all of which was framed by her cheeks that always seemed blushed. To him, she was enchanting. Her participation in their classes was lively and often humorous. His manner was much more withdrawn, so he guessed, rightly, that she hardly noticed he was there. Being a pre medicine student, any time out of classes or labs was spent in his dorm room, or the library, studying...

However, all that changed, at the end of their sophomore year, in one of their shared classes. He, as usual, was studying for an organic chemistry exam when she plopped down beside him, asking, "Are you planning on going to the NROTC ball in two weeks?"

Stunned, to say the least, he looked around to see if she was obviously asking that question of someone else in the room. Realizing, after a quick survey of the area, she was addressing him, he answered, "I wasn't sure. It's pretty close to final exams, and I was kind of nervous about taking the time off."

"Nonsense," she replied. "I've heard your GPA is far ahead of everyone else's in our program. And I can gather by your answer that you don't even have a date yet."

"Uhh..., no I don't." He managed to reply, by now quite amazed at the direction this conversation was heading.

"Well you do now, and it's me! So what do you think of that?" she added with a warm and hearty laugh.

Shaking his head, and secretly trying to take deep breaths to keep from possibly passing out, he could only smile broadly and say, "I would really love to go to that dance with you."

What Ray did not know, again because he was continually wading up to his neck through premed classes, was that Lilyanne had noticed him. Moreover, the more she observed him, the more she realized he had something worth getting to know. He had a gentle, unassuming manner. His wit, whenever he did finally say something, either in class or in a group, was very original and clever. Moreover, he was a handsome fellow, of medium build, with an open face that invited contact. Even then, she knew he had a physician's bedside manner. He exuded compassion and humility. But mercy, she thought, was he ever shy and awkward around the girls. However, she could handle that.

And so, as the years progressed, these two

became naval officers and were eventually engaged and married after his graduation from medical school. During those four years of his medical training, she had two assignments for sea duty, once deployed on an Aegis-class frigate and once on a Nimitz-class aircraft carrier. Ray went to medical school at the University of California in San Diego, which was where Lilyanne tried to get shore duty whenever she could. Both were sharpening their professional skills during this period, and the separations only made their commitments to each other more secure.

At the time they were selected to join the Yucca Mountain naval contingent, they each had just completed a tour of sea duty, both on board an aircraft carrier. Lilyanne's deployment ended just before she was transferred to the Marine Base near Amboy. They had two children, Robin, age 9 and Anthony, age 7. Ray, by this time, was a Board Certified Diplomat in Family Medicine and General Surgery. And Lilyanne was a true naval salt, just as she dreamed she might be one day. Both their skills were invaluable before and after April 1st.

Ray was only one of three physicians in the cavern, along with three RN's, and four nursing assistants. The other two physicians were specialists in internal medicine and orthopedic surgery. Their clinic was always busy, but unlike the Amboy Cavern, it did not require critical care skills or equipment during their confinement. Aside from some minor repairs due to cuts, falls and burns and care associated with having the flu, routine childhood problems, mental health issues and a few cases of pneumonia, their practice was uneventful. That was, up until around November 30th.

It was true what Lilyanne sensed about her husband, those first impressions she had in college. His bedside manner was legend in the cavern. So much so that his colleagues chose him as the medical director, and everyone even sought his advice and counsel as he wandered the cavern in his off duty hours. The clinic hours were 10 a.m. to 4 p.m. daily, except when they had to keep someone overnight for observation and care.

Lilyanne, for her part, was kept busy managing the electrical system in the cavern. The generators required constant maintenance and refueling. She had her crew shut down the one that supplied the kitchen and lounge cars, Classrooms, and Vaults #2 and #3 after 1030 p.m. nightly. The power to the Medical Clinic came from the other generator. In addition, it was also her responsibility to maintain and keep the rosters updated as to who recharged the batteries for each sleeper car. There had to be two shifts, and each had to pedal the five power-generating bicycles for one hour. And fortunately, she was able, after all, to position these bicycles on the east side of the train, opposite the paved walkway. The first shift began at 5 a.m., and the second shift came at 5 p.m. Between these two shifts, this provided lighting inside the sleeper cars 24 hours a day, if it was needed.

Because of her extensive experience aboard aircraft carriers, it was almost automatic for her focus to shift to the challenges inside the cavern. It was as if she was still working inside one of those huge indoor, floating cities.

Her last official duty assignment was in the Communication Center, where she often had to test her computer engineering skills. Often, whenever computer problems occurred, it was due to her expertise that kept the down time to a minimum. Eventually, the information and material from the Amboy Cavern, and their responses, was routinely transferred back and forth. Without question, this Center was the lifeline of the Yucca Mountain Cavern. Through it, all their daily reports, classroom lessons, reference materials, videos, and tape recordings passed. Being able to reconnect to the satellite after the loss of transmission on April 1st, allowed them almost total access to any media materials they might need from Amboy. Both caverns considered their Centers the windows to the outside world.

In addition, and unofficially, both Lilyanne and Ray were also part-time teachers and students. Amongst all the dependent family members transferred to the cavern, there were 15 schoolteachers. To fill the teaching needs for Levels 4-7, as outlined in the Amboy Cavern's Education Framework, many of the cavern's adults had to come forward, using the curriculum materials provided by Amboy. What these volunteers lacked in teaching skills, they made up for in enthusiasm and motivation. The urgency of their mission was not lost on any student, from preschool to adult education. Lilyanne was a natural teacher. Her wit and charm, along with her sponge-like mind and girlhood-groomed sense of adventure, made her a sought after teacher. Even her own children liked attending her classes, which, to her, was the highest compliment of all.

Jo Ann Jenkins, on the other hand, knew nothing of the stability of living and growing up in the same small community. She was an Army brat, as they were called in those days. And she lived in and traveled to more countries in her first 18 years than most people did in their entire lives. Her father was a Warrant Officer, who flew helicopters. He was frequently given overseas assignments, at his own urging, to further his military career. Jo Ann had lived in Germany, Japan and Panama by the time she got her G.E.D. at age 17. And for most of that time she was home schooled by her mother. She being their only child, it was a joy for her mother to have her at home. For Jo Ann, living in so many foreign environments did help her become quite adaptive to change and challenges, but it did not foster many extroverted social skills. She gladly accepted home education and was very close to her mother.

Her two extracurricular activities that she was most passionate about were sports and things mechanical. She played squash, tennis, volleyball, baseball, and basketball whenever and wherever she could. Moreover, her athletic body allowed her the added pleasure of being good at whatever sport she competed in. However, it was probably working with and around mechanical equipment that most intrigued her. Whenever possible, she weaseled her way into the shops and hangers where her dad's helicopter crews worked. During her teenage years, the prize gift from her parents was a 1952 Chevrolet coupe, whose motor and electrical system, she completely rebuilt. Engines were her passion even at this stage in her life.

By age 18, she could volunteer for military service, which she did the day after her birthday. More than anything at that time, she wanted to be in the U.S. Army, like her dad. Maybe some would describe her as beautiful, but, without question, all would agree that she was extremely handsome. Her auburn hair had always been styled short, but the naturally tight curves highlighted her facial features. Her large hazel eyes were set wide apart, and they served as the reference point for her finely chiseled and perfectly shaped nose. Her lips, likewise, were full and complemented her large eyes. Surrounding these features was a soft appearing, but muscular face. Her face reminded you of a classical, ancient Grecian frieze of Artemis, seated with her fellow Olympians. But boys, young men or dating were uninteresting to her. She saw enough of them being in and out of her dad's shops and hangers on his various Army posts.

So it was a major surprise to her parents when,

two years after her enlistment, while at her first duty station in Korea working in an Engineering Battalion, she met and fell in love with Sergeant Vernon Henry. He was also an Army brat and worked in the Communication Company as a translation specialist. It was revealed, during the preliminary testing done when anyone first enters military service that Vern excelled in foreign languages. It was a surprise to everyone, especially to Vern, who like Jo Ann, had never had much chance to demonstrate achievement during his formal schooling. After his basic training, he spent the next year in Foreign Language School, where he achieved a Level 4 ability to speak and understand both Chinese and Korean.

An Army Chaplain married them while they were still stationed in Korea, six months after they met. Over the passage of time they had two children, who by the time their family all came to Yucca Mountain, were ages 3 and 5. The oldest was Lois, and her younger brother was Bobby. The Army so valued these two soldiers that every effort was made to have their orders coincide, allowing them always to serve together. Moreover, arrangements for daycare were provided when they were both on duty. By all measures, theirs was a good life as a military family.

A year before their transfer to Yucca Mountain, both Jo Ann and Vern were transferred to Fort Irwin, in the Mojave Desert. It was becoming one of the Army's major training posts, due to increased deployments to arid regions of the world. The Army had to expand both this post's geographical boundaries and communication capabilities, along with adding more campus buildings to accommodate this reorganization. To do so, they brought in some of the best and brightest of the Army's Corps of Engineers. And Major Jon Shultz was their commander. One of his most trusted and reliable NCO's was Sergeant First Class Jo Ann Henry. Therefore, when it came time for Maj. Shultz to select 24 personnel to join him in the deployment to Yucca Mountain, Jo Ann was one of the first he chose.

Vern helped with the expansion of the Post's Communication Center and with translating incoming messages from various countries. By now, he knew six different languages. Unlike the Amboy families, who had the miraculous transformation from B's touch or presence, the personnel at Yucca Mountain all spoke a common language. In addition, they needed Vern's skills if or when contact was made with any foreign speaking survivor.

And because of her ability to learn how to operate and to maintain equipment quickly, Maj. Shultz assigned Jo Ann to drive and teach her fellow engineers how to run the three trains' locomotives. However, for her, it did not stop there. On her own, she became involved in the upkeep and maintenance of all the train cars, freight and Amtrak alike. With a squad of ten others from her Engineering unit, they became the wardens of the trains. For some unspoken reason, except to Vern, she sensed that these trains were not to be their refuge only in this place. She seemed to know that somehow, sometime, these trains were going to have to provide them safe passage to their final destination, wherever that might eventually be.

Initially, like with everyone else, it came as a shock to her and her family that their home would be inside a tunnel for the next year, and in an Amtrak train beyond that. Their family's home was assigned to be at Drift #5, in Sleeping Car 1, Rooms 7and 8. This sleeper was the closest to the rebuilding train, at the northernmost end of the Amtrak train. And their rooms were on the upper level, directly across from one another. Having their bedrooms directly across from one another, made it easier for families to stay in touch.

The interior lighting was provided by battery charged light bulbs. It was not a brilliant light by any measure; there only being one light per room. At least the rooms were safe and illuminated. The bicycle generators provided the recharging of the batteries. A couple of these rechargeable light bulbs likewise lighted the hallways. There was no other power source available to the sleeping cars.

The configuration in most of the sleeper rooms was two seats facing each other, which during the day were left this way for studying, writing, and reading. At night, the seats folding out and the top bunk lowered down to make two single beds, each about 30 inches wide and six feet long. And this was home for most of the residents. Some sleeper rooms were larger, and the assignment of these was strictly arbitrary. No favoritism was ever shown. Like the Amboy Cavern, after April 1st, rank had no significance. The election of the civilian authority was completed by the end of May, and that marked the official end of the military chain of command. Room assignments were done with this eventuality in mind.

Storage of Jo Ann's family's possessions and extra clothing was in the rows of shelves and lockers built along one wall in Drift #5. There was not enough room in the sleeper cars for anything but the immediate clothing and bedding. With the toilets and washbasins being in the Drifts, having storage there made it easier for them to have access to their toiletries and clothes. There were no running water or toilet facilities on the train. All toilets on the train were sealed shut. Some families, especially those with small children, used the Jerry pot at night. Otherwise, all private functions took place in the modified tank cars, in either the combination toilet/basin tank car or in the shower tank car. As far as

Jo Ann knew, very few people took monthly showers. It was too easy to become chilled. However, almost everyone did use the facility for sponge-like bathing.

The kitchen car was an altogether different arrangement. It was supplied with its own electricity from 5 a.m. to 10:30 p.m. Meals were prepared in the lower kitchen area and served in the upper dining area. Each of the fifty families took turns busing and cleaning dishes. But, almost immediately, a dedicated crew of cooks began working in each of the five groups of kitchens. This meant that there was no rotating roster of kitchen duties, and it worked better for everyone that way. Each kitchen had six individuals who prepped, cleaned and prepared three meals a day.

Only the midday meal was a full course dinner. Breakfast and supper were wholesome, but very lite fare. With the limited seating, there were assigned times for families to eat as well. Each dining area had 24 booths, so the families ate in two, one-hour shifts. Jo Ann's family ate with the first group every meal.

The lounge car was where the business and serious studying took place. It was like a library, with unspoken reminders to keep all noise at a minimum. Between the lounge and the dining car, when meals were not being served, the business of the Yucca Mountain Cavern was conducted daily. The wide booth-like tables served well for the governmental and classroom work that had to be done, all in preparation for their eventual release from this place.

Jo Ann met daily at 8:30 a.m. with her train crew in the #5 Lounge car. It was at that time they outlined what needed to be done for the day. It was understood, by her crew, that everyone 18 or older had to take the Adult Education classes, but those were not given until the evening, so they had to divide their day between work, classroom assignments and possible teaching duties.

Their train duties included going back to every freight car, be it boxcar, open gondola, flatcar or container and inspect the load. Next, all loads needed to be secured tightly if they had never been secured, as was the case for the more than sixty flat cars that held the trucks, planes, boats and helicopters brought by the convoys. Further, they had to double check the ties of the preloaded freight; many of them, it turned out, had loosened during their transport to the cavern. Finally, they needed to pack the wheels with grease, check the interlocks between the cars, refuel the locomotives, recharge any ignition batteries, oil and lubricate the engines, and endlessly sort and resort the boxcars of supplies and equipment for one purpose or another. It was Jo Ann's strong belief, and later after many discussions with Jon Schultz, his as well, that the trains had to be well maintained and ready at almost a moment's notice to be able to exit the cavern.

With that in mind they, quietly and routinely, had drills with her and Jon training the other crewmembers in how to drive the locomotives and how to be able to make a rapid, staged departure. Their weekly drills gave them the confidence that they could get the northern and southern doors open and the trains moved out, each going out separate doors, in less than one hour. And Jon acknowledged years later that it was only by the persistence and ingenuity of Jo Ann that they were able to perform as well as they did in their upcoming weeks of peril. Her actions saved lives and life-preserving supplies for the Yucca Mountain families. She was, in fact, later awarded the Medal of Honor for her heroics at that time.

Captain Earnest Tam was not born in the United States or in some American military hospital overseas. He was born in Viet Nam. His father, a Major in the

Vietnamese Army, advised American units fighting in Viet Nam, and he was stationed in Pleiku. His eldest son, Earnest, was 13 years old by 1975. Ernie, as he was always affectionately called, was renamed after an American soldier who died rescuing his family years earlier. He was a very bright boy, and being around the Americans for most of his life, he had acquired a good working knowledge of English by this time.

It was in mid-March of that year when the Tam family had to flee their home and begin the long journey to find refuge in America. They traveled overland in a mass exodus of trucks and buses to Qui Nhon, on the South China Sea Coast. While there, they were finally able to barter, bribe and beg their way onto an overcrowded boat, heading to somewhere away from their beloved Viet Nam homeland. The hand of Providence, as Ernie Tam many times would recall later, reached out and let them be picked up by a U.S. Coast Guard vessel, patrolling those waters, and delivered, two weeks later, to the Navy's Subic Bay Home Port in the Philippines. As fortune would have it, in 1976 they became the first wave of Vietnamese refugees to immigrate to the United States. They, like over 200,000 of their fellow compatriots, eventually relocated permanently in Westminster, California, in Orange County.

For Ernie, it was only the beginning of a lifelong adventure and stellar record of what a recently, landed immigrant can accomplish. Because of his already existing ability to speak English, he was able to settle into high school with minimal difficulty. He was able to get quickly to the Pacific Ocean on his bicycle or by city transit, passing through Huntington Beach or Seal Beach. By doing so, his love of the ocean and his career aspirations to one-day sail on it were kept alive. Equally confirming of his hopes and dreams was his academic record, which was so impressive, that by his senior year, he was accepted into the U.S. Coast Guard Academy in New London, Connecticut. He entered the Academy in the class of '84. His choice of the Coast Guard, he later recounted, was due entirely to their rescue in the South China Sea in 1975.

Coinciding with his fortunate success in school was his being able to maintain contact with his childhood sweetheart, Victoria, or 'Vicki', Nu. She and her family, also from Pleiku, were able to escape and eventually settle in Westminster. She went on to attend Long Beach State and got her secondary education teaching credentials in chemistry and physics. Distance and the pressures of the Academy required they put off marriage until the summer of 1984, after his graduation with a B.S. in Civil Engineering. And from then, it was a steady uphill climb for Captain Tam to become one of the most respected officers in the Coast Guard. By the time they were informed of their selection to evacuate to the Yucca Mountain Repository, their children, Mary Ann was 13 and Thomas was 15. The similarity of their own children having also to become refugees did not escape the parents. However, their insight and mature level headedness were instrumental in keeping the emotional stability of their family and many others at Yucca Mountain as good as it was.

The attraction of Ernie Tam's family and Ben Javitts' was not pure coincidence. Natural leaders gravitate toward each other, and their subordinates knew the value of keeping them in those positions. Like the Amboy Cavern, general elections were held on May 30th, for cavern-wide representatives. There were to be four elected representatives from each drift, plus a mayor and a vice mayor. The citizens of Yucca Mountain chose to use the title of Mayor, rather than Chief Executive, as was done in Amboy Cavern. They felt the Chief

Executive title should be reserved for the individual who led all the caverns' citizens, once everyone was reunited. Interestingly, Benton Scott was not elected to either of the leadership offices. He did become one of the elected representatives from his drift. Ben was elected Mayor, and Ernie was Vice Mayor. And it was not long before their two families were inseparable.

Vicki Tam became the unofficial leader of the non-adult school program and Michelle Javitts became the go-to person for the adult education programs. Their contacts with the Amboy Cavern personnel about their corresponding programs were daily and pivotal for their successful outcomes. Between the Classrooms, the Library, the General Assembly Area and the study areas in the Lounge and Dining Cars, everyone had enough room to either teach, study, test, or prepare for the challenges ahead. The Communication Center remained, for the most part, off-limits to everyone but its maintenance staff, elected officials, Vicki and Michelle.

The Governing Committees that were organized in Amboy Cavern were recreated at Yucca Mountain, both for consistency and for easier communication between the two caverns. They, like the school programs, shared projected ideas and future scenarios and served generally to keep the general population informed on how governing and rebuilding would be attempted in the future. For ease of management, the heads of these committees were also the elected representatives. They all reported to Ben and Ernie. In addition, like Amboy, any decisions that affected the community required a vote by all citizens 18 or older. There were no hidden agendas. Sometimes it made for heated and very vocal debate, but everyone, in the end, felt included in the final decisions.

Just as the Final Emergence Committee was probably the most important standing committee for

Amboy, the Welfare Committee, or Safety Committee, as the Yucca Mountain citizens referred to it, was their most important one. There were too many unknowns in the Yucca Mountain complex to take anything for granted. They had no idea why the project was abandoned in the first place. Moreover, it did not take a geological genius to notice the unsettling formations that surrounded this mountain site. Maybe this region had been relatively peaceful for hundreds of millenniums, but any casual observer could tell you this area was formed out of fire and brimstone. Furthermore, their living accommodations were 1000 feet below the tunnel entrances and supposedly, 1000 feet above the then-existing water table. To them, it just did not seem like a stable environment. They had to remain alert to any changes.

To insure that as much scrutiny and documentation, as possible, was performed on a regular basis, Ben formed a rump investigative party. It had to report regularly to the Safety Committee, keeping them up to date on the conditions of the complex. These investigators were Zelma Collins, Wally Gonzaque, Jo Ann Henry, Jon Schultz, Derek Amen and Ernie, who as the Civil Engineer, was to oversee their findings.

They were charged with dividing the cavern into sections and monitoring whatever changes they observed. They, likewise, were charged with monitoring the outside atmosphere, just like was being done at the Amboy Cavern. To their relief, by August, they noticed that the level of outside radioactive contamination had significantly lessened. They credited that to the blocking effect of the high Sierra Mountain range and probably to the strong winds in this upper desert region. Unspoken, for the most part, was their assumption that the level of destruction in their immediate area was not as great as elsewhere. It was also made part of their charge to monitor the usage and depletion of drinking water and food stores. Ben knew his estimates of usage were just that. In the back of his mind he continually worried that vital supplies would be exhausted before they could be replenished.

And so life in the Yucca Mountain Cavern proceeded day to day in a predictable routine. There were many social gatherings on the weekends in the General Assembly Vault. The collection of cavern musicians played well enough for square dancing, sing-along's, and choral group concerts. They were able to rig up a large screen and devised a way to project a collection of their many DVD movies onto the screen. It was a huge success. Popcorn and rationed drinks were distributed on these occasions. A spirit of optimism began to build, and throughout the following weeks, occupants of the cavern began to think that they might endure this confinement without further threat, danger and death.

To keep their spirits intact, both a Protestant and Catholic Lay Chaplain conducted church services every Sunday. Accompanying these services, they had regular late night prayer and Bible study group meetings. However, at no time did anyone see or hear from B. That initial experience of B's appearance haunted everyone. However, any reference of B remained unspoken, out of fear others might think it never really happened. The longer the timeframe since B's appearance, the more everyone began to think that they imagined it. So, people hung on to their respective faiths, hoping that life might be granted to them, or at least to their children, and that it might be a life worth living. Morning and nighttime prayers were not mandatory, but they were now the custom in every family.

Come October 1st, the Communication Center

did get a report from Amboy Cavern on their findings that morning when they explored the area outside their cavern. It gave the Yucca Mountain populace some hope, particularly given the lower radioactivity readings they had consistently noted in their area. At a General Assembly meeting later that day, all the Yucca Mountain citizens agreed they would also wait until January 1st, to make their emergence into the outside world. At least that was the plan.

FOURTEEN: DISTURBING DISCOVERIES

As time passed, and the participants in the terrifying journey that was to take place later that December recalled, everyone seemed to agree that it began when Jo Ann Henry ran up to Ernie Tam that morning on November 3rd, and called out to him.

"Ernie," she breathlessly yelled, as she saw him start to enter the Communication Center office, "I need to let you know that something I found today might be a source of some concern."

Turning to her, he answered, "What's that Jo Ann?"

Slowing down from a hurried walk to a normal pace, she put her right hand inside his left arm and gently guided him away from the office door. What she found, she thought to herself, was probably nothing. Nevertheless, for now, her instincts told her to share her observations with Ernie only.

"I think something is happening at the end of Drift #5," she announced in hushed confidence.

"What are you saying?" He responded, with a quick twist of his head and now looking unblinkingly at her.

"It may be nothing, or possibly is may have been there all along, and I just didn't notice it, but there is moisture evident on the ground, like possible seepage is taking place."

Shaking his head and raising an eyebrow, he countered, "but isn't the water table supposedly 1000 feet below our present position?"

"Yes, that's my understanding." she answered.

"Did you check to see if the moisture was somehow coming from the ceiling or the surrounding walls?"

"Yes, I spent time checking the entire area. I'd need a tall step ladder to reach the ceiling, but upon visual inspection, the texture of the rock along the side walls and the ceiling don't appear any different for 100 feet in either direction of the seepage."

"How large an area are you talking about?"

Hesitating somewhat, she thought and replied. "It probably encompasses ten square feet. There are no rail tracks at that far end of the drift, so it was easier to estimate the area, it not being divided or broken up by the tracks."

"How far are the box cars with our supplies from that location?"

Again, she paused, answering, "Probably a couple hundred feet."

Now he turned his head away and considered what he had just heard. After a lengthy pause, he turned back to face her and replied," You'd better check this same area daily. In addition, get something to outline its present perimeter to see if the moisture is advancing, receding or is just there. Also, check the other four drifts to see if there is the same thing happening in them. If this situation progresses in Drift #5, we'll probably have to shift the stored supplies to one of the nearby drifts. We can't afford to let mildew or fungus set up in our food.

"Next, I need you to check with Lilyanne and get her to start daily monitoring and recording the ambient gas composition and temperatures in our main tunnel and inside the five drifts we're using. She needs to record daily the gas composition inside these areas, noting the oxygen, carbon dioxide, carbon monoxide and sulfur dioxide levels. In addition, she probably needs to monitor the levels of radioactivity, if she is not already doing so, inside these areas. Plus, if she has access to a hygrometer, ask her to measure the relative humidity in these areas as well.

"This may be nothing, as you say. However, for some reason this entire project, which cost us taxpayers tens of billions of dollars to build, was abandoned. Probably what you've noticed is not part of the reasons they did so, but let's at least raise a yellow caution flag for now.

"Let me know if either you are Lilyanne notice any changes. Please notify the other members of our Safety Committee about your findings, and I'll let Ben know what you've told me this morning.

"Let's have Ben, Lilyanne, and our Committee meet a week from now, at 10:30 a.m. on November 10th, in the Lounge Car at Drift #5 to report any findings. For now, only these people should be told. It's inappropriate to alarm the general population without getting further information. We must be sure something is happening to warrant causing them more trauma."

After these instructions were given, Jo Ann left and found the other members of their Committee. Collectively, they all accompanied her to the area in Drift #5 and assisted in defining and marking off the perimeter. They all then verified there were no other visible signs of moisture in the area. After this, they made a survey of the other four drifts but found nothing suspicious in any of them. Relieved, the consensus by the end of the day was that Drift #5 was probably just an anomaly, and nothing would probably come of all this monitoring.

Once Ben Javitts was informed of this observation, it was his opinion, as well, that nothing of concern was at hand. However, he agreed that they should all still meet in a week in the Lounge Car # 5, as planned. Everyone should continue to perform his or her assigned measurements and observations in the meantime.

Four of the other Safety Committee members, excluding Ernie, took one of the occupied drifts to monitor for the next week, with Jo Ann taking #5. Nothing of consequence was noted for most of the following week, which only confirmed their impression that this was a false alarm.

Until November 8th, when, on Jo Ann's daily inspection of the original area in Drift #5, unchanged since November 3rd, she noticed that it had doubled in size over the last 24 hours. Later, when she mentioned this to Lilyanne, she was told that the temperature within the cavern had been, and still was, a steady 57° F. Still puzzled, that night while discussing this with Vern, he suggested she might want to do a quick check in Drifts 6,7, and 8, the unoccupied ones, the first thing in the morning.

Soon after breakfast the next morning, she hurried over to the outer drifts and made her examination. And to her dismay, at the end of each of these drifts there was a progressively larger area of seepage. Most disturbing of all, in Drift #8 there was actually standing water.

The Safety Committee meeting that November 10th, started off in a light, almost carefree atmosphere, with an easy banter between everyone, except Jo Ann who was late arriving, having gone back to Drift #8 again to check one more time before making her report. Each person reported that Drifts 1-4 were dry and clear. Lilyanne noted there were no changes in temperature, humidity, gas composition or radioactivity levels. Then all eyes turned to Jo Ann, who arriving late was still somewhat out of breath.

"What do you have for us this morning?" Ben asked, chairing this meeting. "I trust Drift #5 is static as well."

"Unfortunately, Ben, it isn't. My observations yesterday, and reconfirmed again this morning before this meeting, is that the area of seepage has increased twice over what it was when I found it last week. Oddly, this happened over only a 24-hour period. But more important, I went ahead and checked Drifts 6, 7, and 8 as well yesterday. And all of them have progressively larger areas of seepage, except #8, which has standing water in it!"

It was at this point that the mood and intensity of this meeting changed completely. Like a small child darting out between two parked cars in front of a passing motorist, at that instant they knew things were not going to be the same again.

"Then what you have observed," Ben said after a long pause, " unfortunately, confirms that something dynamic is taking place in or around this cavern. We can only speculate what may be causing these changes, but we need to make some contingency plans. Any suggestions?"

"I'd advise we begin to think about how and where we might have to move the supplies stored in Drift #5," Ernie offered.

"Do we need to think even further ahead? Should we consider making some evacuation plans?" Jon asked.

"Well, I know you, Jo Ann and your train crews have had some mock drills, and certainly you have kept the trains in peak condition. What would you have in mind beyond that?" Ben followed up.

"Specifically, I suppose we should begin considering the order or process of evacuation... For instance, we need to agree on a process of removing the three trains from the cavern. We'd need to shift all full or partially full boxcars and tank cars, and attach them back onto the freight train. Regretfully, we also need to practice announcements over the Public Address System, just like you would anyplace else for a fire or disaster drill, and have all our people go to prearranged assembly points for evacuation or refuge." Jon suggested.

"They'd need to get on a train, and not shelter themselves in the drifts. Particularly the school kids, we need to develop a buddy system, where everyone is looking out for someone else, making sure no one is left behind." Derek added.

"What about opening the tunnel doors?" Zelma asked. "Shouldn't someone be assigned to go as quickly as possible to each exit, possibly using the two golf carts, and immediately open the doors when a signal is given to do so?"

"Does the Public Address System have speakers at the furthest ends of the main tunnel? Are the flammable tank cars and the flatbed cars, loaded with fuel bladders, closest to the exit doors?" Wally offered.

"And can the generators at the south exit be unanchored and transferred quickly onto a flatbed car for eventual use elsewhere?" Zelma inquired.

"Good questions, everyone." Ben interjected. "What would you say to them, Ernie?"

"I'd say, for now, we should still keep this information within this group, but begin our planning and pre-positioning of equipment for such an eventuality. Lilyanne can check whether the P.A. System reaches the tunnel entrances and, if not, arrange to have enough power or install large enough speakers to insure someone stationed there would easily hear the orders to open the north and south tunnel doors. Likewise, you should check to see if the generators could be disconnected relatively easily and loaded onto a flatbed car. Eventually, I would like them positioned at the front of the first train, as we prepare for this possible evacuation.

"I'd suggest we appoint Zelma and Wally to be responsible for going to the tunnel doors whenever we have a drill or an actual evacuation is ordered. Further, I would suggest that their respective golf carts always be located near their residences and that they take them wherever they go, if they are to be away from their homes for any extended time. In other words, you two will be on-call all the time, once this plan goes into effect.

"Jon and Jo Ann will check on the location of the hazardous tank and flatbed cars. It seems to me that all that material is located just inside the south entrance. It will need to be rearranged, if it isn't.

"Derek and I will work on the evacuation plan. Right now, the best option I see is that wherever someone finds themselves at the time of a drill or order for evacuation, they are to go immediately to the nearest train car, no matter whether freight or Amtrak, and get on it. We'll have to drill on having helpers for the smaller children, if school is in session at the time. In addition, Jo Ann and Jon will work with their crew on how and in what order the trains will exit. In reality, there's really only one way, and it is based on which is the nearest exit for each train's locomotives. Whatever happens, the Amtrak train will be the last train out, whichever direction it can ultimately exit. Can anyone think of something else we need to do at this time?"

Looking around the two tables, Ben could see that everyone, for now, had had about all the contingency planning they could cope with. All this news was too much of a shock for everyone. It was time to adjourn.

"Ok, then," Ben concluded, "we'll just leave it at that for now. Let's plan to meet here again in one week, same time. Continue your monitoring, and as you get your individual assignments completed, try doing some dry runs on your own. Coordination of this entire plan will have to wait until we feel it necessary to inform the general population. And I still hope that won't be necessary. Thank you, each one, for being here. Your expertise and professionalism makes it possible for me to trust you completely with my precious family's very survival. See you next week."

Sunday, November 11th, being Veterans' Day, was an occasion for an all-afternoon observance and evening celebration. Everyone dressed formally, even the children, and food was catered to the General Assembly area, along with a healthy ration of everyone's favorite beverage. The afternoon ceremony was particularly memorable, given it was in honor of all who perished on April 1st as well. And in an effort to overcome the onslaught of tragedy and loss, dinner, music and dancing highlighted the evening. The memory of this night, as bright as it was, began to fade before a gathering of this kind, or a celebration of any sort, was held again.

The Veterans' Day event was still the main topic of discussion at the dinner table where Lilyanne, Ray, and their children were eating on November 13th. They ate with the second serving in Drift #4's Kitchen/Dining Car. This was due to Ray's usually having a patient to see, or attend to, at the last minute in the Clinic. They were just finishing the meal and talking easily when there was the slightest shudder. It was almost imperceptible, except for the rippling in their water glasses, but it signaled that something was happening. The event passed almost entirely unnoticed by everyone at the table, except for Lilyanne, who had a momentary reflection about the conversations their committee had a few days earlier. It was only later that its importance was realized.

By November 15th, when the Safety Committee had their second meeting in the Lounge Car at Drift #5, there was nothing new to report, aside from one curious observation by Lilyanne's monitoring team. She reported that over the last week the temperature in the cavern, as a whole, had risen 6 degrees to 63°F. Her good news was that the radioactivity levels outside had dropped to within a high normal range. Life could be sustained safely outside, if it were necessary for someone to be out there. She preferred, however, for absolute safety, that more time passed before anyone had to be outside. After some discussion, it was agreed, given the temperature spike, that they would keep meeting weekly. It all had an ominous feel about it.

Passing unnoticed by everyone in both the Amboy and Yucca Mountain Caverns, except to Clem and Jake, was the anniversary date of November 19th. It was only a year ago this night that Clem was awakened by the presence of B in his cabin. It was certainly not a date to memorialize, Clem thought. But it was cause for the deepest reflection; so much, so very many, and now so few. And where was B? And where and how will it all end? Even as late at night as these recollections occurred, he decided to break the silence of the night, rose from his bedding, and walked over to the broadcast equipment in the Communication Center. Combing through the various recordings, he picked out several, and for the rest of that night rich and calming music filled the cavern. Doing this was the only way Clem knew how to speak to the loss and fears of everyone.

At 4:23 a.m. on November 20th, largely unnoticed by all but the lightest sleepers, a second tremor was felt in the Yucca Mountain Cavern. This one lasted 3-5 seconds, and if there had been instrumentation available to measure, it would have registered a 3.0 on the Richter scale.

The next day, when Jo Ann made her daily rounds of Drifts #5-8, she found standing water in #5. Equally disheartening, taking a thermometer with her to the other Drifts, she got a reading of 83° F. in #8.

The third Safety Committee meeting was early in the morning, on November 22nd, Thanksgiving Day, and opened with Jo Ann presenting her findings, along with Lilyanne announcing that the overall temperature of the cavern had risen another 6 degrees, over the last week, to 69° F. There followed a brief discussion of the implications of these changes and then Ben announced, "We have to make an announcement that, rather than having any Thanksgiving Day observances today, we must have a General Assembly Meeting right away, say at 11:30 a.m. We're going to have to get volunteers to start unloading the two full boxcars in Drift #5 and shift those supplies over to Drift #4's empty cars. We'll need to put the remainder of November's food supplies in the #5 Kitchen/Dining Car. This will require we use a human chain-like, assembly line to pass the goods. Because of the distance involved to Drift #4, it will probably take well over 100 people. Moreover, we need to work in shifts. Try to get three shifts, having each shift work no more than one hour at a time. We need to be started on this by 3 p.m. today."

Once again, just as was the case during most of the last year, an assembly of the cavern's occupants was taking place, for another announcement or warning. The immediacy of this meeting, interrupting their plans for Thanksgiving Day, was pointing to that same situation.

And it was with the greatest group reluctance that the citizenry of Yucca Mountain came to Vault #2. Families were huddled together, again, awaiting the next disappointment. The mood was resigned and growing more despondent, even before anyone addressed them.

Ben elected to speak for the Safety Committee. It seemed right that he should do so, given his Mayoral position. It was a bullet he couldn't dodge. Rising from the row of chairs, occupied by the Safety Committee at the back of the stage, he came forward.

"My fellow brothers and sisters, I do have a message of some gravity to give you today, but before I do, I have an even more important statement to make. Moreover, it is to be our marching orders from henceforth.

"By God, enough's, enough! What we've shared! What we've lost! What we've imagined is happening to the world outside this place! What we have ahead of us, once we are free or have to leave here! But most important of all, what we are and who we are, demands that I say to you, enough!

"From this moment on, I want each of us to resolve that we are no longer going to act or behave like victims. No matter what happens from now on, we are to shout, inwardly and outwardly, 'no more will I be a victim of terror, madness, corruption, chance or so-called bad luck.' Each of us has earned the absolute right, from this moment on, to stand-alone and together as brave, decent and loving members of a new community. We, from now on, are no longer survivors or victims! We are citizens of this place and of this world! We are no more than this, but absolutely, we are no less. Sit tall, stand tall, walk tall. Be proud of yourselves! Because, as with everything that is Holy, you deserve that. Do not let anything that I, or anyone else, say alter that feeling about yourselves. I don't suggest it. I don't recommend it. I demand it! And, again, by God, I am so proud, as are all the people assembled on this stage with me, to be a part of your company. Together, we will overcome whatever is ahead. We will have a future! We will make one happen!

"Announcing that, I must report to you some findings that have been evolving over the past three weeks. At the outset of their discovery, we took measures to monitor them, but elected not to report them to you unless or until they should become worrisome. Now they are that.

"We have water now rising to the surface of Drifts #5-8. In addition, we are experiencing a rise in overall temperature in the cavern complex, more so in the outer Drifts. The cause and consequence of these observations we don't know, but we've decided to do three things in response to it. The first was to hold this meeting. Second, immediately, starting no later than 3 p.m. today, all of us who can assist are to begin transferring the food and other supplies from the boxcars in Drift #5 to Drift #4's empty boxcars. This will have to be done by hand, in one-hour shifts. We will need at least 100 personnel for each of the three shifts. And third, we will be having some evacuation drills, starting after the movement of the supplies is completed. Details of these will be printed and posted in all the dining and lounge cars.

"As to what would happen if we should have to evacuate, I can say that Lilyanne O'Shay's group has determined that the outside atmosphere has returned essentially to normal. With each passing day, the measurements approach pre-April 1st levels. In short, we will not be in any danger, once outside, if evacuation is required. Further, on that note, if evacuation is called for, we do plan to remove all three trains from here.

They go with us. For now, and the foreseeable future, they will remain our homes, wherever we go.

"Certainly, there will be more details on all of this, as we develop the evacuation plan further. Please, give all your suggestions and input you may have to any of us. We need your collective wisdom and strength. As you leave here today, there will be slips to pick up, which will be numbered '1-3', corresponding to when you should report to Drift #5 to begin moving the stored goods. Those with the number '1' should be at Drift #5 at 3 p.m. And those with a number '2' should be there at 4 p.m., followed by anyone with a number '3' at 5 p.m. We will keep rotating until the job is finished.

"Finally, recognize that our leaving this place was the plan all along. Maybe we will have to leave under different circumstances than we anticipated, but leave it we shall. And we will have, for ourselves, a good life. That is my promise to you, and I'm sure yours' to me. God bless you one and all, and now let's go to work."

Following this, the entire audience began to clap, then one by one began standing, then chanting. It was both a chorus of solidarity and of determination.

For the next twenty-four hours, the hour-long shifts worked at unpacking, shifting and resorting into the empty boxcars. While that was being accomplished, the Safety Committee completed the plans for evacuation drills. The first one was held on Sunday, November 25th, when no one was in school; the second one was the next day, when school was in session. Certainly, it was more chaotic and time consuming. However, the drill the next day went much better, after the Buddy System was better organized. Within an hour that day, everyone was on the train and safely secured for evacuation.

Which was a needed boast to their confidence,

because on November 27th, the third earthquake occurred at 2:43 p.m.? It would have registered 5.2 on the Richter scale, and it lasted 5-8 seconds. Now objects were knocked off shelves and breakage occurred. Despite their determination and courage, peoples' nerves were shaken afterward. They were, after all, already underground. There was no quick escape to the outside when this happened. Soon enough, everyone regained their composure, knowing that the evacuation plans were in place.

The Safety Committee Meeting on November 29th had two updates that, from this point on, were posted in the dining/lounge cars for everyone to see. The temperature in the cavern had risen another 6 degrees to 75° F. By now, that was not unexpected news. Everyone knew the temperature was rising steadily. Shirtsleeves were all that was needed due to the warmth. The other finding, although not absolutely confirmed yet, was that there was possibly some traces of sulfur dioxide gas being picked up by Lilyanne's sensors in the Drift #8 area.

This was indirectly confirmed the next day, when about 10:45 a.m. the staff at the Medical Clinic noticed a gradual, but steady increase in patients coming in with complaints of increased coughing and wheezing, all signs of pending respiratory distress. By the end of that day, November 30th, all of the Clinic beds were occupied, and the medical staff was on duty around the clock, dealing with acute asthmatic and bronchial conditions. Only by sealing the doors after each time after they were opened could they insure their air quality was safe inside the Clinic. No one was in status asthmaticus, just yet. But Ray O'Shay knew it was only a matter of time.

PART V

FIFTEEN: PREMATURE EXIT

The fourth earthquake occurred at 5:32 a.m. on December 5th. Prior to then, the cavern's physical status had been relatively unchanged for the preceding five days. Everyone was hoping it would be possible to stay longer in the cavern, allowing the outside atmosphere to normalize as much as possible.   However, this latest quake was a 6.1 on the Richter scale. It prompted an immediate announcement over the P.A. System for everyone to meet at 7 a.m. in the General Assembly area.

Armed with the emergency procedures, as had been developed by the Safety Committee, Ernie rose this time to speak to the nervous, but determined, families.

"We must now prepare to leave this place," he began.   "Up to now our efforts have been to sustain, indefinitely, our presence here in the cavern, while at the same time making some preparations and taking part in drills to make an emergency exit, if conditions warranted. Now, with this latest trembler, we know there is something happening that is ominous. We will try to remain here at least one more week, during which time we have certain jobs to try to finish.

"Everyone needs to begin packing up their belongings, taking whatever you have stored in the shelves and cupboards in the Drifts and put them in the empty box cars. Label and package them to make it somewhat easier to identify when we unload later. Have only what you absolutely need with you in the Sleeper Cars. Remember, though, it's December and winter is upon us. We have been locked in this temperature-controlled environment for months, and you will not be prepared for the cold. Leave out your winter coats and blankets; pack and store everything else.

"Likewise, all the documents, books, periodicals, and manuals that are in the Library need to be repacked and placed in an empty box car. This goes, as well, for all schoolbooks, lessons, all printed material and media equipment such as audio and video tapes, CD's, flash cards, and photographs. We need all this material in one area, but please, again, try to label and store it in such as way that various materials can be retrieved easily. Make a floor plan as to where anything is stored, be it personal belongings or these printed and media materials.

"Then we need to disassemble the shelves, classrooms, library, and stage, as much as possible, and stack the salvaged material in such a way that it can be loaded into empty box or flatbed cars. We must try to save as much as we can for later use. We will leave the superstructures on the tank cars for the toilet and shower facilities. However, due to the tank cars' ladders being where the railcars connect to one another, those stairs will need to be removed and something temporary will have to be built that allows access from the tank cars' sides.

"We will be shifting the trains around within the next day or two, and this will entail driving the rebuilding supplies freight train out of here and parking it outside the cavern. After that, we will have to use the switch engine to remove all the cars from the drifts and attach them to the other freight train. The Amtrak train cannot be spliced with other rail cars. It is like one long welded body. There is no interconnection possible with the freight cars, as much as we would like to do it.

"Saying that, I think it's time for all of us to begin our final preparations. Our committee will meet again tomorrow morning; and if there is further news, we will probably announce it over the P.A. System. That will be less interruptive. Stay strong. Work safely."

The next day when the Safety Committee met, Lilyanne reported that the cavern temperature was now 81° F., an increase of 21 degrees since November 8th. The difference of this day's meeting was that all the elected representatives were present. Decisions now made required all the elected officials' input and involvement. And after some discussion, it was decided that Jon should have Jo Ann and her crew take the rebuilding freight train out the north entrance and park it well outside the perimeter of the Yucca Mountain. By doing this, it would be possible to back the Amtrak train up to where that freight train is now. Moreover, it being there would allow the switch engine to park in Drift #5. From there, the switch engine could begin the process of reconnecting the box and tank cars back onto the second freight train.

Once the meeting broke up, Jon found Jo Ann and asked her to have three of her crew meet him at the rear of the rebuilding freight train in one hour. He then consulted with Zelma, who agreed to drive her golf cart up to the north entrance and get ready to open those doors.

When the five-member train crew met an hour later, they divided and each took a side of the train, walking the length of it to check for any loose connections, straps, cables or chains. They needed to insure there would be no load shifting either in or out of the tunnel. By the time they got to the locomotives, Jo Ann took the helm of the lead locomotive. One individual stayed on the ground and hitched a ride on the last freight car as it came out of the tunnel. His job was to throw the switch at the top of the track oval, once they were outside. One crewmember got into the switch engine, which was at the head of the train, ahead of the gondolas. Jon stayed with Zelma at the entrance to help with the opening the doors and the other crewmember rode with Jo Ann.

At the agreed upon time, Zelma and Jon forced open the huge doors, and when they were fully opened, Jo Ann started the locomotive engines. Now was when her attentiveness to detail and maintenance paid off. Each locomotive started up immediately, like a well-maintained racecar engine. Slowly, she opened the throttle, causing a deafening clashing of metal throughout the tunnel, as the slack was taken up on each successive freight car for the two-mile long train. Jon later commented that the sight of that train exiting the northern tunnel, after their months of confinement, was one of the wonders of his life.

The fumes from the locomotives throttling up filled that portion of the cavern, and with the doors opening, they swept quickly into the residential area of the tunnel. Fortunately, after the multiple respiratory complications on November 30th, it was decided to turn the exhaust fans on 24 hours a day. It meant the generators were not going to be spelled, but it was a choice they had to make. In addition, to avoid further any respiratory problems, an announcement over the P.A. System instructed everyone in the cavern to cover their nose and mouth until the fumes were dissipated.

Meanwhile, the further out into the daylight Jo Ann drove the freight train, the stronger was a primordial urge for her to fully engage the throttle and speed away as fast as she could from the confines of their cloistered underworld. Looking at her crewmember, all she could say was "It's wonderful to be outside again."

He, overwhelmed at the sight and experience, could only nod.

The wonder of their exit was soon interrupted by experiencing the immediate cold. No one had foretold how cold it would be. It was December after all, and in the upper desert of the Great Basin that was to be expected. But there was nearly a foot of snow as well. It did not impede the advance of the train, but it was immediately clear to Jo Ann that this was an unexpected, and potentially, a delaying complication. She thought the engineers might have to fashion and attach some kind of snowplow on the front of the lead train. And, even though the debate was still ongoing, as to which train should be in the lead for their evacuation, at this moment it was clear to her it had to be the other freight train. For her, at this moment, it was clear that the upcoming journey was probably going to entail many unexpected hazards. To meet them, they would need the variety of heavy equipment that the other freight would be transporting.

Steadily she inched the train out of the northern entrance. Once near the switch, where the tracks head either toward Beatty or back to the southern entrance, she stopped the train and asked her crewmember to get out make sure the switch was set for the train to go towards Beatty. After he checked and reset the switch, he climbed back into the cab, and she drove on until the last car was past that switch. Then the crewmember at the rear of the train reversed the switch so she could back the train toward the southern entrance. At this point, the crewmember in the switch engine, positioned at the front of the freight train, got out and unhooked the gondolas and his lead switch engine.

The process was then reversed with the switch engine going into the northern entrance after maneuvering the gondolas well ahead on the track going to Beatty. Jo Ann's train then maneuvered through the switches again until the locomotives were now parked just outside the northern tunnel entrance. This would allow for the quickest movement of the train when the time for the final evacuation came. The switch engine was driven into Drift #5, where it was parked for now. By 5 p.m. all the switching was completed, the personnel were back inside and the northern entrance doors were again closed. Everyone piled onto Zelma's golf cart to ride back to Drift #5. The train crew was too cold and exhausted to attempt to walk that distance.

It was decided to let the train crews rest overnight, before they had to move the Amtrak train north into the area where the rebuilding freight train had been. After the Amtrak train was moved, this would allow the switch engine to maneuver the box and tank cars out of the Drifts and reattach them to the second freight train. It was hoped with all that could be done within the next day that the Amtrak train could be returned to the same general area it was, in closer to the toilet facilities.

The next day it was necessary to divide the second freight train. There was not enough room between its locomotives and the southern tunnel entrance to move it all forward to accommodate the soon-to-be added freight cars from the drifts. The Amtrak train was moved well back toward the northern entrance to give extra room for these cars. Over the course of December 7th, the drifts were emptied and their cars were reattached to the freight train. By that evening, the Amtrak train was returned to near its original position.

All the while, as this was going on, a crew of Seabees repositioned some heavy equipment to have one empty flatbed car at the rear of the train, which would be loaded with the generators when everyone was evacuated. In addition, they had to load the necessary crane and forklift on a flatbed car adjacent to the empty one for that upcoming job. Following that, they moved heavy equipment, including two bulldozers and an excavator, along with some welding rigs and flood lamps, onto flatbed cars adjacent to the locomotives. Eventually, it was hoped, the gondolas, with the track repair materials, and the switch engine would be positioned with these flatbed cars and the generators at the head of this freight train.

The Seabees last job was to fashion a snowplow, as Jo Ann discussed earlier that day with Ben, and it would be attached to the lead train, once all the cars and trains were finally assembled for the journey. It appeared the switch engine would be in the lead.

The next two days were filled with ongoing dismantling of the wooden structures the residents had built in the cavern. They then stacked, bundled and eventually loaded these materials onto and into any empty freight cars on the second freight train. This work went on for those next 48 hours non-stop. Time, everyone knew, was running out.

Then, as if the cavern did not want to ease the pressure on its occupants, on December 10th, Lilyanne's sensors picked up both a definite increase in sulfur dioxide and the beginning presence of carbon monoxide. Because the exhaust fans were already working 24 hours a day, the only other thing to do was to open both north and south tunnel doorways and see if there would be more evacuation of these gases. However, everyone on the newly informed Governing Body knew this was only a stopgap measure. If they did not act quickly, another rash of illnesses, and maybe worse, would ensue.

The decision was unanimously made by 11 a.m. that day, ready or not, the second freight train had to be driven out the southern tunnel entrance and parked outside. This would then leave room for the Amtrak train to move into the southernmost portion of the main tunnel, even extending the locomotives of that train outside. The hope was to shelter the families as long as possible in the Amtrak Sleeper cars. The cold and snow outside was too hazardous not to try at least keeping them in a portion of the tunnel.

The final measurements were taken early the next morning. In making her rounds with two other personnel, Lilyanne made note that the tunnel temperature was now 87°F. Drift #5's temperature was now 101°F. However, most astonishing and concerning of all, Drift #8's temperature was spiking at 140°F. And that was only at the drift's entrance. Despite the rising heat, a cold chill coursed through her. Something catastrophic was ahead, of that she was certain. In her conversations with geologists, Geoffrey and Patty Graham in the Amboy Cavern, it was made clear that any spiking temperature like this, along with the clustering of earthquakes, signaled the likelihood that a major underground event was eminent.

That was on December 11th, and they had hoped to stay in the cavern until the 13th, but it was only too clear now, total evacuation had to occur immediately. Climbing into one of the golf carts, she yelled out to her team members, "Come on, we have to get out of here, NOW! Leave whatever you do not have in your hands and climb on! We don't have any time to waste."

And as they drove away, a deep rumbling, or moaning, was heard far back in the main tunnel. It was clear the ground was heaving; she could see it happening along the still-lit railroad track bed.

"You must go faster!" one of her companions yelled out.

"I can't," she cried. "This is the top speed for this cart. Even if we got off and ran, we couldn't cover the distance we have to go without becoming totally exhausted. We have to try and make it on this cart."

After riding two or three minutes, they saw the rear Sleeper car of the Amtrak train. It was clear to them that panic was seizing everyone. People were starting to run out the doors of the Sleepers, blocking any passage of the golf cart. Realizing she could no longer drive, she jumped off and began to run, weaving her way through the growing mass of petrified families.

"Please don't panic! Let me through! Please, get back on board the train! It is too far for you to try to run with your children. You must let me through! I need to get someone to start the locomotives and pull the train out of the tunnel. Please! Stay back! Let me through!"

Repeatedly, she urged the families to be calm and get back onboard, as she ran from car to car. She did not have time to observe what effect she was having. Her main objective now was to get the train moving. Just then, ahead of her, she saw Jo Ann peering down from the last locomotive.

"Get us out of here, now!" Lilyanne screamed. "We cannot stay in this tunnel a minute longer. MOVE! Get this train moving!!"

By now, pieces of the ceiling were falling down around them, and it was quite evident the heat was building steadily inside the tunnel. Jumping down off the platform on the rear locomotive, Jo Ann ran as fast as she could to the lead locomotive. Within two minutes, she had it started and throttled up to pull out. Letting out a long blast of the train's horn, she tried to signal that everyone must get on board now. And because that was the signal to board the train immediately, everyone, fortunately, did so.

Surging ahead from a stand-to-start operational speed that violated the common sense and training of every engineer, Jo Ann had the entire train roaring out the tunnel within one to two minutes. It was estimated that at least 850 lives were saved by her reckless, yet life-saving act.

The second freight train had previously been pulled well ahead of the junction switch at the top of the oval, and this allowed the Amtrak train to be driven about a mile from the southern tunnel entrance. Likewise, the rebuilding train had also been moved about a mile from the northern tunnel entrance.

The atmosphere in the main Yucca Mountain tunnel, as the last train left, became saturated with sulfur and carbon dioxide gases and carbon monoxide fumes. Larger and larger chunks of the ceiling were now collapsing down onto the tracks, as the earthquake now was registering a 7.2, with its epicenter just inside Drift #8. If anyone had been able to survive standing at that drift's entrance, he or she would have noticed there was a reddish glow coming from deep inside that tunnel. The temperature at that entrance was now 197° F. The Yucca Mountain Repository's mothballed status was soon to be downgraded even further.

Despite the daily communication with Amboy about what was occurring inside Yucca Mountain, when the time came to abandon the cavern, there was no time to send a signal. Amboy, despite hourly attempts for the next three days, could not raise a signal from Yucca Mountain. That left them extremely concerned that possibly something terrible had happened before the families could get out. For the next three weeks, they had no idea whether they had all perished or if some had escaped.

When everyone was finally outside the cavern and eventually accounted for, Ben and Ernie had the representatives go to each sleeper car and instruct the families to go immediately to the main office building, adjacent to the south tunnel entrance. There was no longer any P.A. System to make announcements, which left them no choice, given the cold and snow, but to bring everyone together in one of the buildings. Eventually, the Amtrak train's internal P.A. System was repaired and operational, but that was not until just before they left Yucca Mountain permanently. From then on all announcements could be made throughout the train.

As luck would have it, the particular building where the families were to gather could be heated by large propane tanks, located adjacent to the building. It probably was part of a backup system in case of an emergency. A couple of the engineers checked it out, and managed to clear the regulators and get the pilot lights ignited. Soon there was heat throughout the building. No one was sure how long the heating would last, but it was a relief after their harrowing escape. Using extra fuel to warm only the Sleeper cars was not a luxury they could afford. They had to ration all their available fuel. These trains would need it all for the journey ahead.

The meeting started at 5 p.m. It still being the same day as their terrifying escape from the tunnel, everyone was thankful the quaking had subsided for the time being. It was the hope of the Governing Body that they could delay departure a few days to reconfigure the supply freight train and reassemble all the trains in the most survivable formation.

Once everyone was settled, whether by sitting, standing, lying, leaning, or assuming whatever position was comfortable, Ben began to speak.

"First off, I and the Governing Body are so relieved that everyone has made it out safely. I realize it was a terrifying experience, and we all know there are still grave challenges ahead of us. If possible, we are going to try to stay camped out here until the morning of December 16th. At that time, we should have the trains lined up in proper sequence, and the special equipment and the various cars positioned in the front or rear of certain trains for immediate access. Because of our panic in having to leave the cavern prematurely, many last minute jobs were left undone. Yet they have to be completed before we can hope to have a safe and reasonable chance of completing this upcoming journey into a fathomless unknown.

"The Governing Body has just determined the route we are going to take and our eventual destination. I realize not every one of you got the chance to have input on this, as events careened out of control, and we had to make some decisions without full discussion and debate. For that, we are sorry. However, we had to settle on some destination and route immediately.

"Our final decision is that we are going to Kelso, a small community with a railroad station, located about 600 miles south of here. It is located about twenty miles due west of the Amboy Cavern. Once we get somewhat settled in Kelso, we can begin to convoy over to the cavern when the time is right.

"The route we are about to take, once we leave here, begins with a 320 mile circular roadway, along what's called the 'Caliente Corridor'. This phase of our trip ends at the town of Caliente. From there it is about a 100 miles south to Moapa, traveling beside a mostly deserted stretch of dry riverbed. From Moapa, we'll travel around 90 miles, paralleling Interstate 15 through Las Vegas to Primm, on the Nevada-California border. Finally, there is the last 100 miles to Kelso.

"We cannot begin to know what we'll find along this route. It's winter. Already we see so much snow piled outside, which has to be unusual for even this time of year. And we have no idea what has occurred on April 1st. We know the atmosphere was filled with radioactivity afterwards, but we have no idea where it originated from or how. In addition, we sensed and felt, early on, that there was a major earthquake somewhere, but what effect that may have on our trip, we just don't know. We know nothing about any survivors, other than those in the Amboy Cavern. Moreover, for our immediate concern, we don't know anything about the condition of the railroad tracks that we are about to use.

"Taking all this into consideration, in the next four days, we need to accomplish the following. We must repair the buckled track on the northern spur so the rebuilding freight train can pass through the junction switch toward Beatty. We need to attach a snowplow on the front of the switch engine, which will be the lead locomotive. The plow will help clear snow off the tracks, certainly; but it will also help remove any abandoned cars or debris we encounter along the way. We have to detach the generators at the south tunnel entrance and load them onto a flatbed car. In addition, we need to reposition the flatbed cars with fuel bladders or fuel tank cars in front of each set of locomotives for refueling every 200 miles. In addition, we have to flush out the toilet tank cars with the gray water from the shower cars; we'll use 100 foot lengths of six inch corrugated black tubing to do so. Finally, we have to position these toilet tank cars at the end of the lead freight train for easier access, if the need arises to use them. Bear in mind, this trip could take weeks, and we could easily over-extend the toilet facilities in the Sleeper cars.

"In summary, we have to arrange the order of

the engines and freight cars for the first freight train, with the switch engine first, followed by the generators and flood lamps, gondolas of track repair equipment, construction and welding equipment on the flatbed cars, the fuel tank car and locomotives. After the locomotives are the remaining freight cars we have been reloading and sorting for weeks. Then the Amtrak train follows second, and the rebuilding supplies freight train is last. The total length of this train convoy will be about four and a half miles!

"And for emergencies and safety, due to the unknowns we will be facing, there will be stationed along all the trains individuals with side arms and rifles. The firearms will not be loaded with live ammunition, but each individual will carry some, in case it was needed. And there will be two boxes of dynamite in the front gondola. They could be needed depending on what size obstacles we encounter along the way.

"We will plan to leave on Sunday, December 16, after a sunrise service. It's true that this date is nowhere near Easter, but for us this day will represent a time of resurrection from the confines of our tomb here at Yucca Mountain. As I challenged each of us a few days ago about being strong, now we must also be thankful and observant. We are struggling to do our part in sustaining life. It's now time to implore the Heavenly Host to offer us guidance, peace and hope for our future. Without hesitation, each of us would like to address B as to what lies ahead, if we only could. For now, we must pray, hope and struggle on.

"As much as possible, we will try to keep this area warmed; all of us should try to limit the heat going anywhere else in this building. We must try to conserve the propane gas. Eat, rest, sleep overnight here, if you'd like. We encourage it, because the train will not be heated. The kitchen/dining cars will be operational, so you must still get your food from there.

"After this meeting, the Governing Body will be distributing the work orders for various ones of us. There will be a lot of switching of train cars the last day, so watch out for each other. We need to make sure everyone is away from the trains when this starts. I'd recommend everyone return here, except for the train crews doing the realignment and switching. There will be no more general meetings, until we meet the morning of the 16th. God's speed to us all."

The next two days saw a cold, but eager, scattering of work crews completing the jobs, previously outlined by Ben. These had to be done before the final evacuation could get underway. The temperature never got above freezing during the day, and it was well into the teens at night. Everyone was constantly amazed that the cold was so intense, and the snow so deep. Snow shovels were not items that were on anyone's supply list before the confinement, so they had to improvise, fabricating wide mouth shovels, using aluminum siding removed from the various storage buildings in the area.

By the third day after Ben's speech to everyone, it was necessary for the Governing Body to sit down and select who was doing what and where they would be stationed on the trains. Due to the length of time the trip might take, it was decided to keep families together as much as possible. There were countless assignments. Besides the train engineers and brakemen, they needed thirty personnel, ten to an eight-hour shift, to ride in the gondolas. They had to be on the lookout for track damage and be the vanguard for repairing what they found. Lookouts or observers were needed. They would take notes along the way of what they saw and heard and monitor various atmospheric conditions as the train progressed through the countryside and Las Vegas. Guards had to be posted at the front, middle and back of each of the three trains for safety and protection. Mechanics and maintenance personnel were necessary for refueling and insuring the trains were kept roadworthy. And it was no surprise to anyone that there was no lack of volunteers for these assignments. Everybody, even the children, wanted to assist and insure the trains were underway and made it to their destination.

It was finally decided that Jo Ann and Jon would be the engineers for the first freight train, and that their families would ride in the cabs of the five locomotives. Another of the crew Jo Ann and Jon had trained would act as brakeman, and this was the case for the other two trains as well. The engineers and families for the Amtrak train were Jesus Cabrera and Benton Scott, and for the rebuilding freight train, they would be Jenny La Cross and Ernie Tam. Their families would be scattered among the other locomotive cabs on each train, but they would at least be nearer to their loved ones.

The three survey and repair crews, that were to work in shifts out of the leading gondolas, were to be led by Zelma, Wally and Derek Amen. Lilyanne was in charge of the observers and monitoring crew and equipment. Steven Blackmore was to be in charge of the guards. And Ben would have, as usual, the overall responsibility of the train convoy. The Governing Body representatives, not already assigned to other duties for the journey, were to oversee the welfare of each group of Sleeper cars. They were to report any issues to Ben through their hand-held radios. Likewise, engineers, guards, gondola crews or anyone else who had responsibilities throughout the trains, were issued hand-held radios. For this train convoy, miles in length, these radios were a vital link. The last day, after the trains were rejoined in their proper configuration and alignment, this link was tested and retested until it was functional and ready.

The #1 Lounge car on the Amtrak train was to be the official convoy headquarters, for Ben and his family. Along with him, there would be Ray's makeshift medical clinic and Lilyanne's office for the collecting and categorizing information and data. All five of the kitchen/dining cars had been fully stocked with a month's worth of food supplies for all the cavern's citizens to eat..

As a way to keep the older children busy during these four days of final preparations, the Seabees fabricated 25 snow shovels; and the kids eagerly divided into three teams of fifty each, two to a shovel. They then began the process of clearing a walkway from the end of the Amtrak train, the one closest to the building everyone was taking temporary shelter in, and shoveled their way out to the second freight train and then beyond to the locomotives of the rebuilding supplies freight train. They worked clearing snow on both sides of the trains, to make it easier for anyone to work coupling, uncoupling, switching, securing and covering the loads. This effort prevented the snow from becoming compacted and, as cold as it got at night, forming ice, which would have slowed the necessary work needing to be done to a slippery crawl.

On December 15th, as soon as the sun rose over the eastern mountain range, the train crews all made their way to the two freight trains and the junction switch. The Amtrak train was to stay where it was. Come the next day, it would just pull straight ahead behind the first freight train and then the rebuilding supplies freight train would pull in behind it from the siding closest to the northern entrance. However, the two freight trains needed repeated pulling, shifting and switching. By 3:10 p.m., they had completed the process and had attached canopy covers over the gondolas and various flat cars for added protection from the weather. It was clear to everyone that the crews riding in the gondolas were going to be exposed to severe weather conditions. That was the main reason for rotating them. Extra blankets and clothes were stocked there as well, along with gas-powered floodlights to help them see while traveling, and if need be, working at night.

The first freight train was finally reassembled with the three gondolas containing hand tools, track repair supplies and flood lamps; on flatbed cars were the generators with fuel bladders, welding equipment, two bulldozers and a crane, all being pushed by the switch engine. Attached to these were five locomotives and a mile and a half of loaded freight cars, followed by two toilet and two water tank cars and finally a diesel tank car to refuel the Amtrak train. The rebuilding supplies freight train had a diesel tank car attached just behind its 5 locomotives, then 2 toilet and 2 water tank cars, and finally, the two miles of freight cars behind these.

To everyone, although no one spoke of it out of fear that the monster might awaken, the most amazing event of these last four days was what did not happen. The cavern had been quiet during these four days of preparation. Both tunnel doors had been sealed shut, so no one could imagine what was occurring inside. To their unspoken relief, they knew they would soon be pulling away from this powder keg.

Dawn on December 16th found all 1006 citizens of the soon-to-be-departed-from Yucca Mountain Cavern, six of whom were to call this shelter their birthplace, gathered in the large meeting room with the Catholic and Protestant chaplains prepared to conduct a sunrise service. It was later described as inspirational in its simplicity and reverence. Each chaplain said a prayer, offered thanks for their safe passage to this day, asked for strength and guidance for the journey to follow, and then gave the Eucharist or Communion to all in attendance. There was a final prayer when the Sacrament was completed, and the service was adjourned.

Ben, reverently and with dignity and solemnity, rose slowly, and turned to his now beloved charges and said, "Let's begin this final stage in our journey. It's time we leave this place and go make way for our new home, our new life, in our new world. You are ready. And I am so proud of each of you. Take a moment to hug those around you, and wish them God's grace and peace, and let's be on our way."

SIXTEEN: THE JOURNEY BEGINS

The propane gas was turned off at 7 a.m., as the last family was leaving the assembly hall and the doors were shut and locked. It took two more hours for all the various crews to be settled into place on their respective trains. Radio contact was established and confirmed that everyone was on board. It was time to start the engines. And once they were sufficiently warmed up, as if on cue, all three trains blew their horns at once, announcing the launching of this expedition into the unknown. The deafening sound filled the absolute silence, echoing across the valleys and mountains with a mournful cry.

When the sound of the horns had dissipated across the valley, Ben reached down inside his desk drawer and got out an audio CD and hand-written note that Clem had sent him about three weeks ago. Clem had sent it when he heard they had to leave Yucca Mountain.

The note simply said, "Hey, there Ben. We're looking forward to seeing you and your families sometime soon. Here's something for you to play as you leave your cavern confinement and when you pull into your final destination. Stay safe. Clem."

His instructions to Ben were to broadcast it throughout the trains as they pulled away, using whatever radio system they had. After that, they were then to play the other song when they finally ended their journey. Ben, smiling broadly, slipped the disk into his player and turned it on, setting the volume at its highest level.

Jo Ann pushed the throttle handle forward, and eased her freight train through the junction switch, onto the track to Beatty. Just as soon as Jesus saw her last car moving, he opened the throttle on the Amtrak train and moved it forward, away from the buildings surrounding the southern tunnel entrance. And once his train passed the junction switch, Jenny slowly advanced the rebuilding supply freight train's throttle forward, staying at least fifty yards behind the Amtrak train. When the last car on her train passed the switch, the entire train convoy, spaces between them included, now measured five miles in length. If someone could have seen it from overhead, it would have been a remarkable sight.

Jo Ann had instructions to keep her train's speed between 3-5 mph, particularly during this first leg of the trip. No one was sure, how the trains would handle; nor were the crews sure, how well they, themselves, could manage the trains. In addition, everyone knew they had some major elevations to traverse, between there and Las Vegas, and that it would be a steady climb until they passed the highest summit west of Warm Springs. They needed time to get a feel for the trains' performance and operation.

It was to become obvious that as the elevation increased so did the snow pack. The snowplow on the switch engine was going to be well used before they got to Caliente. As they got up to running speed, Jo Ann turned to Jon and said, "Can you believe it? We're finally on our way, away from that underground emerging hell! I'm afraid I'm having a dream, just wishing it were so. Pinch me, will you?"

"I know," he said. "We may never know how fortunate we were to all escape with our lives. Another geological chapter about this place is being written as we depart. It served us well during our confinement. And maybe it was still trying to keep us safe, by warning us as discretely as it could, that we had to leave. Remarkably, we were also given some time to get the trains realigned for this journey. It was a Godsend. However, I am very concerned about what all is ahead for us, but I am also convinced we are as prepared as we can be for those unknowns."

"I'm worried," she went on, "that our traveling at night may become too hazardous. This is due, in part, to you and me not riding in front of the entire train. In addition, with the switch engine headlight being so faint, even with the floodlights in the gondolas turned on, neither of these illuminates the tracks ahead of us as well as our locomotives. Because of these conditions, my feeling is that when we get into the higher elevations, with the probability of increased snow pack, that we should limit our nighttime travel."

"Good point," Jon replied. "We can discuss this with Ben and Ernie. Maybe after we pass through Goldfield, probably sometime tomorrow morning, we can raise this issue with them. For now, I'm all for just enjoying the scenery and pretending I'm taking my family on a long, overdue vacation."

"Fair enough," Jo Ann answered. "I'll encourage the crew in the switch engine to be extra diligent tonight in observing the tracks ahead, and we'll revisit this tomorrow. Today, it does feel good just to be alive."

After discussing this, both of them took the time to look at the landscape spread out before them. The heavy snowfall had carpeted the valley floors and the lower elevations of the sharply rising mountainsides in the purest, white velvet. The mountains and hillsides in this area jutted out from this white carpet in brilliant

493

orange and red plumage. Moreover, capping it off, in between the occasional cluster of clouds, was as true a blue sky as Jo Ann had ever seen. It was as if they were passing a steady stream of red, white and blue bunting. It appeared that the trains were being saluted, as if in a parade.

There was no mistaking it; this area was remote and stark. Life in this region had not been plentiful for many eons. But the bright coloration around them was as if the area recognized and gave escort to this passing of life, so fragilely sheltered in these passing trains. To Jo Ann it was a good omen.

Their lead train arrived at the outskirts of Goldfield at 5:13 a.m. the next morning. However, the switch engine noticed that there was some odd angularity to the tracks ahead and radioed Jo Ann and Jon to stop. They, in turn, alerted the train crews behind them to do the same. And, upon further investigation, the Seabees from the gondola found there was a 32-foot section of track that had to be replaced. It took until full daylight for the gondola crew to assemble the welding equipment, assorted tools, rails and ties to repair the damaged area. Then, it was another four hours before the work was completed. It was 1:30 p.m. before they could resume the trip.

During this layover, Ben and the Governing Body discussed the need to stop at least every hundred miles. This would allow everyone to get off the trains, stretch, use the tank car toilets, walk if the snowfall would allow it, and by doing so, try to decrease the families' tension and anxiety somewhat. In addition, the schedule for refueling every two hundred miles was reviewed and acknowledged as a necessary precaution as well, even though traveling at these slow speeds did not consume as much fuel. Keeping the engines running for heat and lights did. Moreover, after Jon discussed Jo

Ann's concerns about night travel, it was agreed for this portion of the journey, they would only travel during daylight hours. This decision also added to their unanticipated fuel consumption, requiring regular refueling. Everyone was in agreement with this schedule, as the trains departed Goldfield.

About fifteen miles outside Goldfield, they passed by Mud Lake's now dry lakebed, their trek inching along the barren Stonewall Flat. As slow as that was, when the trains began to climb up the progressively higher, eight degree grade towards Saulsbury Summit, their travel got even slower. It was twilight when the trains finished making the sharp, steep turn, to head east. At that moment the earthquake started.

For those individuals helping Lilyanne record observations and events along the way, one of them later noted that at 4:35 p.m. on December 17th, the earth began the violent shaking. Automatically, all the train crews brought their respective trains to a complete stop. They were on a progressive incline, but, thankfully, not near any ravine or sharp embankments. The families could exit the train safely, and that they did without any encouragement, and quickly. Not knowing at first where the epicenter might be, they looked in every direction for any clues as to what was happening. Then, one by one, individuals began to point to the south, where there was an uncommon reddish glow in the sky.

Yucca Mountain had finally begun its final convulsion into its next period of change. It was entering the disappearing stage. The first sign, which no one was around to record, was when the two sets of tunnel doors blew out, followed by an outward rush of steam, heat, rock and fire. Molten lava had been steadily oozing into Drift #8 since December 11th, and at that time, it was acting like a safety valve for the mountain. And it gave the survivors time to leave unharmed.

However, by 4:35 p.m. December 17th, time was up. It was as if two massive hands took hold of each side of Yucca Mountain's sharp ridgeline, and along the top of that ridgeline was a weakened seam, poorly stitched by some hurried, prehistoric tailor. The hands proceeded at that moment to rip and tear the ridgeline apart, along the Ghost Dance fault line. At that point, the outpouring of lava began erupting hundreds of feet upward and out into the surrounding area. Within seconds, it had covered the outbuildings next to the northern and southern tunnel entrances. The families were seeing the red glow of this lava plume.

Not that they were aware then or even for years afterwards, but at approximately that same moment, the Yucca Mountain's sister volcanic caldron at Yellowstone Park began to foretell future changes in that part of the world as well. All the geysers, steam vents, and boiling mud pots ceased their activity. It was like a giant, sucking inhalation, just before a catastrophic, uncontrollable cough. Moreover, unlike the Yucca Mountain caldron, the Yellowstone eruption was to be a pyroclastic event. The tectonic activity, begun on April 1st, which was set off by the solar outburst of energy hitting the earth, had now worked its way inland. Life on earth was becoming scarce and precious.

The families, filled with a combination of awe, horror, relief, and many questions as to what this all meant for their ongoing trip, just stood and stared in the direction they had just come from yesterday. It was quickly agreed that the trains would not be traveling that night. Instead, Ben and Ernie decided to send the switch engine ahead, with one of the gondola crews accompanying it. They could double-check the rails integrity between there and the summit. It was further agreed that the three trains would remain stationary until that survey party returned.

Few people got much sleep that night. They probably would have stayed outside all night to watch the fiery plumes and molten rocks shoot into the air, but the cold drove them back inside the train. The earthquake itself has lasted at least 45 seconds to a minute, and aftershocks were too numerous to count. Later it was assumed the size of the quake was around 8.8 on the Richter scale.

Come daylight on December 18th, the survey team returned at 6:20 a.m. There did not appear to be any direct visible damage to the tracks, but there were landslides that had to be cleared. Under that debris they might find track damage, would require laying new rail bed and track. The worst of these slides were within a half mile of the summit.

Once the gondolas and switch engine were reattached to Jo Ann's freight train, there was again the sound of three train horns blowing across the mountainsides, into the surrounding desert landscape. It was about 20 miles from the summit. Once at the first landslide, they had to stop. To clear and repair the track required the gondola team unload one of the bulldozers to help remove the dirt and boulders. The remainder of the day was spent repairing the track itself.

Wanting to get the trains off this highest point, the decision was made to have the switch engine and gondolas go ahead of the locomotives, a quarter of a mile, looking for breaks, bowing or uplifting of the rail bed. Everyone wanted to get to Warm Springs to stop and rest. This would be the first town they could actually enter. Beatty and Goldfield were about two miles from the tracks, so no one was able to check on the local population. This stop would allow them their first opportunity to see how the outside population had fared over the last nine months.

By 8 p.m., they pulled into Warm Springs.

Actually, Jo Ann's freight pulled all the way through the community, and let the Amtrak train occupy the track, extending from one end of the town to the other. More specifically, given the length of the A Train, as it was now affectionately called, it extended beyond the town's borders substantially at both ends of the train.

That night the Governing Body met to decide who should go into the town first. If there were any surprises or disturbing discoveries, they did not want the general population to be exposed to that. And to lessen exposure to anything hazardous or any chance of divulging something that might be damaging to the morale of the families, it was decided that Ben and Ernie would go into the community before anyone else. They would enter the town the next day at dawn.

Probably preventing these two envoys from making most discoveries that next day were three the feet of accumulated snow, with drifts up to six feet in and about the town. Luckily, the track cut through the town's midsection, so getting about was not as cumbersome as it might have been. What they found raised more questions than it answered; they found nothing. All the houses and shops were vacant or unoccupied, but none appeared vandalized. It was as if everyone just left or disappeared. Equally curious there were no signs of animals. The snow was in pristine condition. There were no animal tracks or footprints, aside from their own. There were no signs of a struggle. The area was certainly windswept, which they later surmised might have accounted for the mass evacuation. Maybe the elevated radioactivity levels required they evacuate completely, but where was the animal life? If anything, the place looked sterile. It was very unsettling to both officials.

After an hour's search, Ben finally spoke. "Does any of this make sense to you, Ernie? It appears that no one has occupied this town in months. And when they left, it was as if they locked their doors and closed their windows, almost as if they expected to return in a week or so. Do you think there was an organized or ordered evacuation?"

"That's certainly the most logical explanation," Ernie answered. "But it still doesn't explain why there is no life at all in this area. Something very toxic must have penetrated the region, and possibly the heavy snow pack has covered the evidence. Whatever happened, this place makes me very uncomfortable. Let's get out of here."

"Good idea. Obviously, we are not going to find any answers here, only more questions. Maybe there will be more answers if the snow wasn't so deep, but from what I'm seeing now, I'd just as soon get out of here as soon as we can. Besides, the way it feels, we could get marooned up here if a blizzard should come in," Ben replied.

Later that morning of December 19th, as Ben and Ernie boarded the trains; they noticed some snow flurries, with darkening clouds moving up the slopes from the west. It appeared certain a heavy snowstorm was in store. The safety of this convoy dictated that they had to leave immediately. Because no one had stepped off the train, due to the cold, the radio message went out to move the trains forward. With loud blasts of their horns, the last visitors to Warm Springs, for a long time to come, were leaving.

Nevertheless, if anything, they were a little too late in leaving. The rebuilding freight train was caught in the worst of it. The blizzard did materialize, but two conditions were in their favor. The snowplow at the front of the switch engine did a mighty job clearing enough of the excess snow to prevent them from stalling, and they were rapidly descending. Within the next ten miles, the storm, as ferocious as it was at the summit, had lessened to just scattered flurries.

Their descent was due south out of Warm Springs, avoiding the Reveille Range of mountains by traveling just west of them. There was still at least one to two feet of snow that had accumulated over the rails, so monitoring the track integrity was hopeless. If anything, it placed the switch engine in the hazardous position of being on the 'point', being the first to be exposed to whatever danger might be ahead.

Nevertheless, the eagerness of the switch engine and gondola crew to be leaving the area overcame any of their fears. Going downhill posed some extra demands on the locomotive engineers, trying to maintain a slow enough speed and not collide with the train in front. The grade was at least 5%, and no curves were included that might slow their descent. The roadbed pointed almost straight downward.

About 30 miles out of Warm Springs the greatest challenge to avoid a collision, thus far, occurred. Just before crossing a steel trestle bridge spanning a 750-foot deep gorge, over what used to be a dry riverbed, the switch engine crew made an emergency stop. Occasionally, the Hot River had enough runoff to drain into the National Wildhorse Management Area. However, unbeknownst to these travelers, this same river had been flowing continually, at near flood stage, for the last four months. Many months later, Geoffrey and Patty Graham, upon reflection, theorized that the alteration of the atmosphere, for whatever reason after April 1st, had apparently created a much wetter climate worldwide, along with disturbing the tectonic framework of the planet. But all of this was lost on the Yucca Mountain escapees.

And for the engineer of the switch engine, his only choice in seeing the bridge, and rightly judging that it might be unsafe, was to jam on his brakes and sound his horn. Jo Ann, unaware of why this was happening, at least had the presence of mind to do the same, as did the other trains' engineers. In retrospect, they all agreed there would have been a disaster, if the trains had not been going so slow and if the switch engine and gondola crews had not been so alert.

Everyone just sat dazed for a few minutes after this emergency stop. Thereafter, the gondola engineering crew piled out and did a bridge walkover, inspecting the tracks and the superstructure. They could only surmise what had or was happening to the supporting structure of the bridge. It was about 200 feet in length, long enough to trap and then swallow most of the locomotives in one gulp, if it collapsed under the trains' weight. Following the locomotives, most likely, would be the rest of the train. The gorge was approximately 400 feet deep, and the river was running fast and deep. It could handle a falling train. Seeing all this flowing water, heading south, gave the engineers pause, remembering the water seepage into the Yucca Mountain Cavern before they left.

Eventually, Ben, Derek, and all the Seabees and Army engineers were crawling over the structure. Sadly, their conclusion was that without some stabilization and reinforcement, the trains had no chance of passing over it safely. The prolonged force and height of the water had loosened and undermined the supporting foundation. Quickly, they all got together and eventually developed a plan to try to stabilize the bridge.

Getting out the track repair and welding equipment, some cables and large wooden beams from the back of the first train, they erected floodlights and began work on the bridge and the canyon walls on both sides of the gorge. Cables were anchored from the canyon walls to the bridge's sides for lateral stabilization. Steel rail and large wooden beams were welded and steel plated to provide extra horizontal and vertical strength. Nothing, on the other hand, could be done about reinforcing the foundation of the bridge. The water was too swift to work on the bridge's supporting structures. That had to be left to the power of prayer alone. They started their work at 2 p.m. and did not stop until noon on December 21st.

By then they thought it was safe enough to test. Jo Ann volunteered to drive the switch engine and gondolas across first. If they crossed safely, she would drive one locomotive across, then two, then the entire supply freight train. If all that was successful, then she would drive one Amtrak locomotive across, then two, then the entire Superliner train. However, before the entire Amtrak train crossed, it was decided to have all the families walk across using the double catwalks in each side of the track. The walkways each had a border fence, although it was only one strand of cable. That being the case, Ben instructed everyone to rope him or herself together for added safety and to prevent panic. Once all the families had walked over, Jo Ann would drive the empty Big A across. The logic of the people going first was that if the passenger train were lost, at least they would be with their food and some shelter supplies stored in the first freight train. It was not an option anyone wanted to consider seriously, unless there was no choice.

It took the next three hours to maneuver the trains and people across the gorge. In addition, before they left, the engineers fenced off the bridge, giving clear indication to anyone else coming along that it was unsafe. It was made clear to Jo Ann, at the time she drove the Big A across; the bridge did sag a few inches. However, she reasoned it was the heaviest train, so she felt she could drive the lighter rebuilding freight train across without incident. It was a feat of heroism recorded for later recognition.

Once the trains were refueled and reloaded with passengers and crew, the trains blew their whistles and resumed the trip at 4:30 p.m. The track took a sharp northerly turn, skirting the Worthington Peak mountain area and arcing over to descend toward Caliente. At this time, the decision was finally made, given their distance from the Yucca Mountain disaster that they could now travel at night. And by 6:10 p.m. on December 22nd, the lead train pulled into the outskirts of Caliente.

Given the experience exploring Warm Springs, and the potential for even worse revelations in Caliente, the Governing Body decided, while they were stopped that night outside the town, to allow only two people to enter the city. It was like the first astronauts on the moon. Contamination could be a problem for these two investigators during first contact with what they might find. Although the radiation readings that Lilyanne and her staff were getting were within normal limits, they were leery of the unknown.

With all in agreement, Ben and Ernie were informed they would be the ones to leave the train the next morning, the 23rd, after the Big A pulled into town and had time to assess the conditions there. Meanwhile, as these two were investigating, the trains were to refuel and be readied for the trip to Moapa, 100 miles away, and then into and through Las Vegas.

Benton Scott, who knew the area better than anyone else working on the locomotives, radioed Ben to tell him that once they arrived in Caliente, their single, essentially unused rail bed, would end. Due to the mothballed status of the Yucca Mountain Repository, he said, they had had no competing rail traffic. Nevertheless, from here on, they were to merge into one of the busiest rail corridors in America, and faced the likelihood of meeting stranded trains, left unattended on the tracks. Worse, they probably would come upon tipped over or tangled wreckage blocking their advance.

Ben, upon hearing this, realized that the only solution to this scenario would be for his Seabees and engineers to have their three work crews spread out over the large rail yard in Caliente, starting tonight, and begin cannibalizing switching junctions. They would also need to take sections of the 'S' shaped curved tracks. Their only option, if confronted by stranded trains, would be to splice into the rail bed alongside their blocked one and install a new switch and diversion track. The entire rail roadbed from this point on into and beyond Las Vegas was double tracked, and they hoped to be able to install a bypass around whatever obstacles they found.

Ben hoped his personnel would be able to remove three pairs of tracks, in other words, right and left hand curved tracks, along with their accompanying switches. That decided, the three crews loaded into the three gondolas, with their flat cars of equipment in tow, and had the switch engine move them ahead into the Caliente rail yard. They hoped to be done by the time the trains came into Caliente in the morning.

The next morning brought bright sunshine, for a change. There was little snow on the ground here, so its light cover would hide nothing. Once the Amtrak train was parked in Caliente, Ben and Ernie, once again, left the passenger train and walked into the main street area. Again, there was no one present, and everything was neat and relatively undisturbed. However, this time, they found scattered announcements posted inside various windows and doors. (see Appendix 2, fig. 12, "State of Nevada Emergency Preparedness Department Alert and Warning"). Reading these, they realized what the reason was for the haunting emptiness. Even the animals and wildlife had fled or disappeared. It was as if the mightiest wind, beyond imagining, had swept the region clean of life.

Finding that written warning everywhere convinced them there was no further purpose served by their investigations. And there were still some preparations to finish before they left for their trip into Las Vegas. Unnerved by what they had again seen, they hurriedly returned to the Superliner and met with the Governing Body in the #1 Lounge car.

Ernie addressed the group first this time. Handing out a copy of the "Warning" to the representatives to read, he began, "We basically found nothing out of the ordinary in town. That is, if you could describe there being absolutely no living being present in it, ordinary. What I mean to say is that there were no signs of struggle or destruction. It looked like someone rang a bell or sounded an alarm, and everyone, in orderly fashion, left. There appeared to be no panic and no looting. It was as if everyone wanted to take care of their personal business in the most tidy and responsible manner possible, leaving as few loose ends as they could. It was as if this was to be their last will and testament, and they wanted it to be neat and legible. They did not want those who came after, if any did, to find a mess or think they were irresponsible in some way. It was uncanny. And it really scared me. I expected chaos after reading that warning. For an instant, I thought that somehow, the hand of B was somehow involved. It was all too unbelievable, just in human terms, to explain.

"That is not to say, when we arrive in Las Vegas that we will find the same thing. Who knows what's ahead for us. I think it important to say that we must now increase our vigilance. Moreover, most importantly, we must protect our children. If for some reason, we begin to observe tragedy and carnage, I believe we must shutter our windows. No purpose will be served by their seeing total destruction, if that is what we are about to witness.

"Also, we may find the going quite slow over the next two hundred miles, with damaged tracks and stranded trains. Whenever we come upon a stranded train, I'd like Lilyanne's team to immediately exit our train and have some of the engineering personnel help her and her folks quickly examine what cargo the trains are carrying and plot exactly where they are located. Catalog this information, as completely and accurately as you can. Some of us may need to return to this area in the future to retrieve needed supplies.

"The gondola crews worked all last night to dismantle switching junctions, and our trains are now refueled. Let's plan on heading on to Moapa by 11 a.m. this morning. Be alert from here on. Maybe I am just spooked from what I've seen in Warm Springs and here in Calilente, but for the next week I would predict we have some bone-chilling revelations ahead. Watch over your families. Let's make our way onto Kelso and let nothing deter us."

SEVENTEEN: LAS VEGAS

After Ernie had finished speaking, Ben waited until their trains' whistles blew indicating they were underway, before he took his turn addressing the Governing Body.   He, too, was relieved they were moving out of Caliente.

"Ladies and gentlemen, my formality at this moment is prompted by the content of my directions. Up until now, you have known almost entirely the informal me. Conversely, for the next week or so, you will probably be dealing exclusively with the formal, more official, me.   In other words, what I have to say now needs to be taken as law.   And for that, I apologize.

"As we proceed out of this rail yard, we may or may not encounter any obstacles, as Ernie has alluded to. My best guess is that a freight train or two may delay us. But there could also be another Amtrak train as well.   If there is either of these, and we will be notified in advance if there is, I will expect you at that point to order everyone to lower the shades in every car, be it sleeper, lounge and dining, depending on the side of our train we pass the stationary train on.   I do not want the families to witness something gruesome if we can avoid it.   Hysteria will grip this company like a contagion, if we don't try to limit exposing our people to what may be seen.

"Furthermore, as we travel down the Meadow

Valley Wash from Caliente to Moapa there will be two small towns, Elgin and Carp that we pass through. We will not be stopping in either of these, unless there is an obstacle of some sort. Otherwise, this first 100 miles will be isolated from highways and congestion of any kind. But once we arrive in Moapa, we will be making our first contact with a major metropolitan area.

"We will stop in Moapa and let our families get out. However, they are to exit only on the northwestern side of the train, and they are to stay in that immediate vicinity. At that point, you are to order, and to insure it is carried out, that all windows on the southeastern side of the train, to start with, are to be shuttered until we pass completely through Las Vegas. Interstate 15 will be on that side of the train, and we have no idea what could be seen along that highway. Our trains will be traveling alongside it, from just south of Moapa, to beyond Las Vegas' southern city limits.

"We will have our lookouts and guards posted in pairs throughout all the trains. One individual, in that pair, will be scanning the area closest to the trains, and the other person will have binoculars to scan outside our immediate vicinity. They've been instructed to protect the train at all costs from intruders, if there should be any. We are not taking on passengers or stopping for any reason other than if the tracks are blocked. We have precious cargo, if you will, to protect on this train. It is our children.

"Keep your radios turned on the entire time we are underway, until we are out of Las Vegas. Ernie or I will follow up with any further orders, if need be. In short, for you and our families' protection, consider that we are now under Martial Law until we leave Las Vegas. Good luck and be alert."

Jo Ann glanced at her watch as they left the congestion of Caliente's huge rail yard. It was 11:05

a.m. The switch engine and gondola-flat cars were to remain separated and travel on their own ahead of them. Their crews had to manually throw switches and lead the three trains through the maze of tracks and debris. Their instructions were to proceed a quarter to a half mile ahead of them, continually checking the integrity of the tracks, but more importantly, warning them to stop if there was an obstruction preventing their forward movement. She was relieved there were the empty tracks beside them now. Naively, she hoped any abandoned trains they came upon would be on those tracks, heading away from Las Vegas to Salt Lake City, coming from Los Angeles/Long Beach.

Because April 1st had been on a Sunday, she also hoped the rail traffic might have been less that day along this route. Normally there are trains passing any one spot, along this corridor, every 15 minutes, 24 hours a day. A minimum of 96 trains came and went day in and day out. Plus, she thought, March and April were normally slower months for consumer spending, so maybe there were fewer shipments being off-loaded at the ports. She figured she would soon know the answer to these desperate hopes.

It was not until they were almost to Elgin, an hour later, that they passed their first train. It looked like it was probably empty grain cars heading back to Montana to be refilled.

After some discussion amongst the train engineers and Ben, it had been agreed that they could increase the train's speed to 25-30 mph along this stretch of track into Moapa, given the area's remoteness and the lack of snow covering the tracks.

And once in Elgin, they did have an abandoned freight ahead of them, but their switch engine crew was able to divert them onto a siding and skirt around it, without having to do any construction. With each train they were about to pass, Jo Ann radioed Ben to notify the representatives about lowering the shades. She did not have time to study the locomotives she passed that well, but at a glance there did not appear to be anything disturbing to see in or around them. That was to change later.

So it went until they were beyond Carp about 12 miles. At that point, there was a freight train, loaded with coal, on their side of the tracks. To go on required their engineers cut into their main line and construct and install an 'S' track and switch. This would allow them to cross over onto the empty tracks beside them. By the time Jo Ann's train rolled up to the gondolas and flat cars ahead of her, the crews were already getting out their cutting torches, starting up one of the generators, getting a switch and a pair of left hand 'S' shaped rails unloaded, shovels, picks, sledges, plates and nails.

Within four hours of frantic work, with the other two crews helping as well, they were able to jury-rig a switch mechanism and get the switch engine and gondolas to cross it without a problem. While all three of the engineering crews watched, Jo Ann slowly drove the first locomotive through the new switch. Not able to see how the weight of her engine was tolerated, she waited until the ground crew signaled everything was ok, and then she continued to pull the rest of her freight train through. At that time, the train crews split up, each heading to their respective trains, and the Amtrak and other freight train crossed over at the newly installed switch. By 5 p.m. they were on their way again, now on the opposite track.

For the next fifty miles, there were no further trains on their rail line. However, there were two heading into Las Vegas on the opposite track. It appeared Jo Ann's theory was right; there were fewer trains leaving southern California than going in, at least based on what they were seeing in the section of track.

By being able to maintain their new speed of 30 mph, they managed to pull into the outskirts of Moapa by 7:30 p.m. A collective sigh of relief was heard, throughout the trains, as they did. As a reward, once they stopped, everyone was able to get out and stretch and walk, and many did so briskly. This rail yard was even larger than the one in Caliente. And even though the depot was a jumbled mess of full and empty freight cars, it did not really matter to them. Just to be able to be outside and walk was a luxury. Their months of confinement had made them appreciate the slightest chance to be free of restrictive spaces.

The weather was clear and cold. Again, uncommonly so, they thought. So, it was not long before most families were climbing back onto the trains. Ben and Ernie conferred with each other and decided to post guards on both sides of the trains and to stay there for the night. Once again, there was no way they could travel any further in the darkness, given their proximity to Las Vegas. However, they needed to take advantage of all daylight the next few days, so the orders were issued to be up and ready to move out by 6 a.m. tomorrow, December 24th, Christmas Eve.

The upcoming holiday season had not gone unnoticed by the families; they wanted to celebrate, even under these most extraordinary circumstances. Despite the hardships, and through the ingenuity only dire conditions can demand, some families made decorations and wrapped simple gifts for the smallest children. While at the same time, others prepared for a midnight service that night in each of the five lounge cars. It was good to have a different kind of excitement and expectation for once, rather than it always seem to be fostered by another nightmare scenario.

Having completed over two-thirds of their trip to

Kelso, and with the Christmas season at hand, the families went to bed that night more reassured of their possible survival, than they had been for over a year. Even with some of them having to get up at 4:30 a.m., to be ready to shove off at 6 a.m., this did not lessen their relief. However, before everyone went to sleep that night, all the blinds were drawn in each Amtrak car, along the southeastern-facing side of the train. Instructions were given that, under no circumstances, were they to be raised until the order was given to do so. Many families secured them with whatever ties they could find to insure there was no breach of this precautionary measure.

And with dawn breaking, all the trains' locomotive staff, including the switch engine vanguard, was in position to start their engines and ready to move out. Ben then issued the order to start the engines and once they were warmed up enough, to proceed at a speed no greater than 5 mph. Even though they were still on the outskirts of Moapa, he and others knew there was no predicting what they might encounter going on from there. The switch engine crews began moving before the other trains to insure a quarter mile distance was maintained between them and the first freight train. At this distance, the gondola crews could efficiently change the necessary track switches, allowing the trains to weave through the maze of tracks onto Las Vegas.

It was just when Jo Ann's freight cleared the crowded rail yard that she, alone, saw the leading edge of what had happened on April 1st. Jon was distracted at that moment with rechecking the gauges on the control panels, and the switch engine crews were likewise consumed with focusing on the track ahead of them and changing switches. "My God! Jesus, Mary, and Joseph!!" She cried out.

"What is it?" Jon shouted, as he rose up, lifting

and turning his head to see what she was seeing. "Jesus wept!" was his only response to the same scene.

What lay beside and ahead of them were signs of a mass evacuation, which became stalled. Accompanying this was the ensuing panic and looting. Soon thereafter there followed a lethal storm of radioactive sand, dust and droplets. And finalizing these horrors were two earthquakes, one the result of a solar explosion and the other, more devastating, from Yucca Mountain itself. Rather than the ground being covered by snow, it was piled with debris, often blown into immense piles in the corners of buildings or fences. No glass-enclosed area was intact. Buildings in the town of Moapa were left standing, but they were mute skeletons. Moreover, it was devoid of all life. Nothing, except what might shift in the wind, moved.

Quickly picking up his radio, Jon called Ben and told him to instruct everyone to shutter all windows on both sides of all the Amtrak cars. When Ben asked why, his only reply was to wait a few minutes until they passed out of the rail yard, and he would see for himself. He was unable to describe it.

From that point on the snowplow on the front of the switch engine began to perform a vital job, clearing the tracks of debris that surely would have stalled the trains. Switches were changed, and the long procession of trains continued through Moapa and into some open country for about 10 miles. At that point, the tracks, for the first time, began to course alongside Interstate 15, which they then would follow almost to the Nevada border. Moreover, a few miles later, north of Exit 88 on I-15, their next shock came.

It was the switch engine crew, this time, that saw it all first. Screaming into their cab radio, on the all-channel frequency, they yelled, "The freeway is full! It's bumper to bumper with every imaginable car, truck, bus, trailer, RV, and motor home you can imagine. For as far as you can see, they're just parked! And there's no one in sight! NO ONE!!"

In addition, as was later discovered, the eight-lane freeway, on both sides of the median divider, was filled with stalled traffic heading north, from the Utah-Nevada border back through Las Vegas. In addition, there appeared to be few, if any, passengers left in the vehicles. Once the traffic jam occurred, it appeared everyone made another mass exodus, on foot, heading northeast.

Any explanation for all that they were seeing was based on evidence collected over several years and finally compiled by Fred Wailand and Ben Javitts. It probably will always remain filled with conjecture, as it was for what actually caused the extinction of the dinosaurs. Some events were uncontestable, based on direct experience and observation; others were based on various theories, relying on as much solid science as was possible at that time. In addition, B revealed some in later encounters with the families.

Global events aside, what mattered the most to the Yucca Mountain refugees was trying to determine the sequence of events in their immediate region. It appeared there were five separate, rocket propelled nuclear device detonations that affected their area the most. The most accurate of the five struck the Marine Base near Amboy in the first two hours after noon on April 1st. That explosion led to the increasingly higher radiation levels being monitored at the Amboy Cavern, and later its cloud of radioactivity drifted into the Nevada-Utah Basins.

The next four explosions did not occur until after the solar-generated disaster, when the worldwide rampage of revenge was happening. The targets for those four were Tucson, Phoenix, the Yuma Proving

Grounds and Las Vegas. However, with the glancing impact of the solar burst on the earth's rotation, the guidance systems aboard the rockets were misaligned. This cosmic force changed the targeted impact zones, and they could not be completely corrected, so the detonations occurred off target. The missile meant for Tucson struck Benson, Arizona. The one targeting Phoenix hit Florence, Arizona. In addition, the one aimed for Yuma Proving Grounds landed in the Kopa National Wildlife Refuge. The one meant for Las Vegas and Nellis AFB, most stunning of all, fell into Lake Mead just north of Temple Bar Marina, in one of the deepest areas of the lake.

The result was the instant deaths of hundreds of thousands in the major Arizona cities and countryside, along with the upheaval of radioactive sand, debris and dust into the upper atmosphere, eventually heading north toward the Utah Basin. The Lake Mead blast had two unimaginable effects. One was to spread a radioactive spray out into that same Utah Basin, to combine later with the dust and sand coming from the lower desert regions. And the other was to create an immense tidal wave that overwhelmed Boulder Dam and caused its collapse, sending a wall of water hundreds of feet high down the Colorado River. The effect of that flood was still being dealt with at the time of this writing.

Ultimately, it is theorized, the combination of all this atmospheric contamination was to centralize where all the people of southern Nevada were heading. The roadblocks and the resulting panic left people no choice but to go on foot. Tragically, by the time many were able to make it somewhere near the Nevada-Utah border, or even beyond for some, the storm clouds of radioactive mud overtook them. However, the people kept pouring into the area, unaware of what a toxic world they were entering. Weakened and ill, any who survived, even with access to the meager untainted food and potable water stores they could find, eventually perished in the months that followed.

Fred Wailand later surmised that these series of events, witnessed indirectly on April 1st, in the Amboy Cavern Communication Center, was what caused B to suffer such anguish. B knew then. The Yucca Mountain escapees were learning now.

Stunned, and almost paralyzed, the crews of the switch engine and gondolas, along with the locomotive engineers, stopped the trains and just sat dazed.

"Ladies and gentlemen," came the call over the locomotive cab radios. "This is Ben speaking, and I want each of you to focus on your job at hand. You must continue our movement through the area. We cannot stop and certainly, we cannot offer any help for what has happened here. Look straight ahead, just as you would if you were driving your cars. Do not let your attention be drawn to either side. Our families depend on your continuing forward."

Shaking her head, Jo Ann turned to Jon and asked, "Is it possible for us to continue on, with what we are seeing? Is there any hope for us? I'm feeling a sense of panic and desperation taking control of me."

"You're ok," Jon answered. "Whatever you are feeling is perfectly normal under these horrific circumstances. Take some deep breaths. Tuck your head between your knees. Say a prayer. Ask for guidance and strength. And I'll drive the train for a while. But you'll have to spell me once you get to feeling calmer."

"Thanks, Jon," she replied. "I think I'll just walk back to the next locomotive cab and check on my family. I'll be right back in about five minutes. Ok?"

"Sure. Go ahead, and please check in on my family while you are at it. Let them know I will come back in a few minutes as well."

Somehow, they did drive the trains on, mile after mile, until they had gone about 43 miles further, one mile south of exit 57 on I-15, where I-215 crossed I-15. They were almost exactly, where a rail spur cut off the main tracks, heading to Nellis AFB. And it was at this point they had their first major rail blockade. There were trucks and cars, four lanes wide, blocking the tracks. The backup was bumper to bumper, like on the freeway. Beyond this, there was a train wreck, with at least three boxcars overturned onto their track, and the other pass-through track was also blocked with a fully loaded, stalled train. It was clear to the gondola Seabees and engineers that they had at least a ten to twelve hour challenge ahead of them to clear all this and repair any damage to their track.

Communicating this situation to Ben, he had no choice but to agree to halt the trains. After he made the announcement, Benton Scott soon came rushing into the #1 Lounge car.

"Ben, I need to take three or four personnel and try to make it over to the Base. Nellis is just about two miles south of here, and I need to see if there are any survivors and check on the condition of any aircraft. If it is going to take as long as the engineers say it is to clear and repair the tracks, then I'll have time to walk over and back before we have to leave. We may be able to get some form of transportation as we are walking over. I'd like to start right away. I'll take Frances Bynum, Alfie Shoemaker, and Louise Matthews with me. I assume you'll have no objections."

"None, Benton," Ben responded, somewhat startled at his sudden entrance and request. "But please take care of yourselves. I want you all to wear hazmat suits and take a two-way radio with you. I want you to keep in touch with us at all times. Don't take chances that would require we somehow have to send someone to rescue you and delay our journey further. If you are not back by the time we are ready to leave, I'll have the trains all blow their horns for three 30-second blasts. We'll prepare to leave 30 minutes after that. Be back before then."

"Thanks, we'll get ready and be off right away."

The rescue party left by 8:35 a.m., and given the issue of diminished daylight hours, they figured they had to be back by 5 p.m., at the latest. Anticipating it would take them a total of three hours to walk there and back, they estimated there would be approximately four hours to the search the Base. Hurriedly, they began their mission by walking a half-mile along the spur rail line, down to Range Rd. From there, it was a mile and a half to the Base entrance. Not sure if the gates would be securely locked, they took a pair of wire cutters, if they had to go through the fence instead.

The walk, once they got on Range Rd. was harrowing. It was as if someone's worst nightmare was frozen in real time. Everywhere there were signs of desperation, flight and destruction. Store windows were all smashed from looting, especially for groceries, pharmaceuticals, sporting goods and bicycles. Large department stores were nothing but charred remains, as were the gas stations. It looked as if the populations' final desperate acts were ones of vandalism and cultural self-mutilation.

To insure his crew was able to maintain their composure, Benton suggested that everyone try to focus just on placing their feet, one ahead of the other. In addition, he requested that they should follow him, and he would do the scanning ahead for the safest route to walk.

Arriving at the North Gate to the Base, they found that it indeed was locked. And no one was present in the nearby guardhouse. As a result, it took them almost thirty minutes to cut a hole in the fence large enough for them to crawl through, wearing their hazmat suits. Once through, they had already decided along the way, which person would do what. Benton went directly to the Base Operations Center. Louise had to walk across the runways to the Transient East parking area and check on the McGuire and Fairchild AFB planes' condition. Alfie began a building-to-building search along the main taxiway, knocking on doors to see if any survivors responded. And Frances went to the Base warehouses to see if any food stores were left and salvageable, ones that possibly could be picked up later.

Separating once they got to the Operations Center, they agreed to meet back there at 3 p.m. The Base had two runways, each almost two miles in length and almost a quarter-mile wide. The largest airplane parking area and the Control Tower were located on the eastern side of these runways. Hangers, maintenance and supply buildings are along most of those two miles on the western side of the runways. Consequently, there was a lot of distance to cover and many buildings to check in a short amount of time. Everyone agreed to come find Alfie, if any of them completed their assignments ahead of time.

Benton found the Base Operations Center in fair condition. Because he and his staff had left the week before April 1st, he knew he would find some confusion. Apparently, all the combat planes stationed at the base that could, were scrambled, and flew off to deal with incoming enemy planes, missiles, rockets, or sea craft. And once they were launched, the Operations Center must have received the message for everyone to abandon the Base and flee to the northeast.

Over the last months, he had to fight recurring guilt over leaving the Base when he did. Certainly, being there was a harsh reminder that he had left his post prematurely. Probably, despite all his efforts of self-justification, he would always consider his actions a dereliction of duty. While it was true that by he and his staff accompanying the McCord and Fairchild AFB flight crews, they probably helped to insure the survival of the Yucca Mountain families. However, on a personal level, he likely would not ever be able to forgive himself for not staying here. To try to guarantee success in one way, he had failed completely in his duty to his overall command here at Nellis.

Because he had removed most papers and manuals that might be useful for the rebuilding of their community, he did not see anything in his office or elsewhere in the Center that appeared vital for take with him. His job here was done. Now he needed to help Alfie see if there were survivors.

Louise was already tired from their walk to the Base, so by the time she got to the cargo and refueling planes parked on the Transient East tarmac, she was nearly exhausted. Moreover, what she found was not encouraging. Of the eight McCord and Fairchild AFB planes parked there, only two seemed to have any chance of flying again. The others could only be used to provide spare parts. A couple had even been completely turned over. They had been jammed together, as if some great wave had washed them up on a beach. It was the last planes in this pile up that appeared to have fared the best. Their landing gears were no doubt inoperable, but the wings and tail sections looked intact. Her impression was that two of them could be flown again, with about a week's overhaul. She was encouraged to find that the ground tanks of jet fuel, located near these planes, appeared intact for any future use. Having finished her assignment, she, too, began to walk back across the two runways to the buildings Alfie was investigating. She could hear him banging on the metal doors as he searched.

Frances did find some food stores in the Commissary Warehouse, which had been locked, oddly enough, before everyone left. It was as if whoever did that hoped, like some miner or prospector in the mountains, that leaving his cabin stocked for any unfortunate passerby might help him or her survive. It was mostly canned goods. She took two hours to inventory what and how much food and supplies were in the building. And by 1:30 p.m., she also decided to try to find Alfie and see if he still needed help.

Alfie elected to start at the far south end of the tarmac, banging on doors with a piece of lead pipe he found by a dumpster. He hoped that by his checking these furthest buildings, if someone came along to help him, he or she could start at the closer northern end. Eventually, they would meet somewhere in the middle. It was 2:15 p.m., when he met the other three, team members as they each approached the fire station at the same time. There had been no responses to anyone's calls or banging on doors up to this point. Dejected, Alfie banged on the locked runway-side door to the Fire Station. Again, there was no response.

"Let me just go around to the back door and try there," he said with resignation.

On his way around the sides, he also banged on the basement barred windows, working his way to the back door. By the time he got there, the door was open and standing in the doorway was Master Sergeant Shepherd Fennell.

"Col Shoemaker!" he cried out. "What in heaven's name are you doing here? How did you get here?"

"Sgt. Fennell, of all people, it's you." Alfie replied. And the two of them fell into a long and warm embrace. "How did you manage to survive? Is anyone else with you?"

"Well, it sure wasn't easy. To tell you the truth, I doubt very seriously that we have survived it. We lost so many; everyone, in fact, except ourselves. Now you! Is anyone else with you?"

"Yes, there are twenty of us from the Base that survived, Gen Scott is among them."

"Yeah, I heard he left about a week before all this began. We were never sure where he and the others of you went. Then, it didn't make any difference, because each of us was fighting for our families' and our own lives. And, yes, there are seven more of us here. One woman, Gina Porter, whose husband died almost immediately, and 6 children, two of whom are her own. The children's ages range from one 7 year old, two who are 6 years old, two who are 5, and one 4 year old. We're all getting pretty weak, as you might expect."

"How did your survive in this place?" Alfie pressed.

"You probably didn't know, because the rest of us didn't either until we took shelter in here, but this building was built during the Second World War; it was used for munitions storage most of that time. It has a three level basement, all heavily reinforced. We took shelter in the bottom level, up until about a month ago, when water began to seep into it, and we had to come up to the next level. That earthquake we had about a week ago I thought was going to do us all in."

Just then, the rest of the rescue party came around the corner of the Fire Station and experienced the same shocking sight as Alfie did.

"Good Lord!" Benton exclaimed, seeing Shepherd. "Someone is alive after all. Thank God. How are you, son? Weren't you in one of Alfie's Search and Rescue units?"

"Yes I was, sir. And seeing him, just now, I can honestly say that I'm much better at this moment, General. Much...much better. It is an unbelievable relief to see you people. Come on in and meet Gina and the children."

Because of the pressures of getting back before dark to the trains, Benton, after meeting and hugging everyone, explained they all had to leave immediately. Alfie went upstairs to get two hazmat suits for the adults and some pediatric breathing equipment for the children. They would have to carry the three children who were 4 and 5 years old, as much as they could. The six and seven year olds would have to try to walk as far as they could on their own. Once they were suited up, and because the Nellis survivors had to leave everything behind, the adults reassured the children that they might be able to return one day. It was 3:20 p.m. when they began their trip back to the trains.

Through a combination of carrying, leading and coaxing, somehow the party arrived back at the Amtrak train at 5:10 p.m. Darkness had enveloped them once they got to the spur rail line, but that was like the yellow brick road to the rescuers, compared to what it was like walking in the city streets. Upon arrival at the trains, the guards challenged them briefly, but were quickly relieved it was Benton's party. The guards then immediately confirmed their safe return with Ben and Ernie. And during the day both men had decided that the trains would remain here overnight. The demolition crews were too exhausted to push on without some rest.

The reunion of these eight survivors with the other Air Force families could not have been more welcoming. And it being Christmas Eve, it was a perfect setting for the newly arrived children. If anything, their discovery and rescue, combined with the growing realization everyone might actually make it through this nightmare, made this Christmas one of the most memorable for the remainder of these Yucca Mountain families' lives. There were Christmas Eve services in each lounge car, a late dinner and then Christmas Carols sung at midnight, with all 1014 survivors gathered outside the train.

In the emptiness of that desolate and forlorn setting, their raised voices proclaimed the majesty and mystery of the true meaning of this night. Maybe the next morning they had to resume their journey into whatever obstacles awaited them, but on this night, they took a stand. They would survive. And along with their survival, they would bring the best of a past world, one that went mad and then tried to kill itself.

At 7:30 a.m. on Christmas Day, the switch engine crew started off, followed by the three trains. The debris continued to be piled higher and higher on the tracks ahead of them. Occasionally it required the switch engine to stop while gondola personnel removed the larger pieces. It was slow, but steady progress, until they had traveled ten miles further. At the Charleston Blvd. overpass, there was no moving forward. The entire overpass had collapsed onto their tracks. Finding this, a call went out to Ben, Jon, Derek, and to the other two crews of Seabees and Army engineers to come forward and assess what to do next.

After a couple of hours crawling over the snarled mess, it was decided that they had to back the trains up a mile, after they had unloaded the two bulldozers and crane, welding equipment and leaving the flatcar with the generators and flood lights at a safe distance. They then would lay dynamite charges along the track covered with the debris. After setting off the charges, they would attempt to clear enough space to allow the trains to pass. They figured it would take at least two days to do the demolition, clear the area, and then lay new track.

For the next 60 hours, that same group who initially inspected the collapsed overpass, worked steadily to repair it. By 7:45 p.m. on December 27th, the track was ready for the trains to navigate the opening. It was agreed that, as much as they wanted this place behind them, they would load up the switch engine gondolas and flatbed cars early in the morning and then head off.

Come 9 a.m. on December 28th, all the trains had cleared the newly divided rubble from the fallen overpass. For the remainder of that morning they made their way to the Las Vegas city limits, unimpeded for the most part, aside from having to install one more bypass switch to get around an abandoned train. And as they rose up the incline to clear the Las Vegas basin, a cry went up from all the trains, locomotives, and passenger cars alike. They had made it through at last. By the time they got to Primm, on the California-Nevada border, it was approaching dusk, and Ben made the decision to halt. The last leg of their journey to Kelso would be tomorrow.

EIGHTEEN: KELSO

Certainly, by December 29th, everyone was painfully anxious to be at their destination, so without any prodding from Ben, the switch engine crew and gondolas set off at dawn to clear and divert the tracks, if necessary. Eventually, it was necessary for them to install two new switches, diverting the trains first onto the left track and then back onto the right one, all to avoid long-stranded freight trains. When their trains were switched back onto right side, even though they passed six more freight trains, all these were on the left track. They were home free. The switch engine crew was able to finally relax and enjoy the magnificent scenery of the Mojave National Preserve, once they passed through the tiny desert town of Nipton.

Waiting, while the switches were being installed, always gave Lilyanne's team time to do their inventory of the abandoned freight trains. By the time they reached Kelso, they had passed or bypassed fifteen trains, five of which were of no immediate practical value to the families. Two were automobile transports, one full and the other empty. The other three were transporting grain, coal or ore. The others had mixed inventories, but scattered amongst them were box and flatbed cars loaded with food, clothing, assorted equipment and building materials. Their locations were pinpointed, as were their contents, for return trips sometime in the future. No one knew at this point when or if they would need to restock their supplies. These abandoned trains meant the families had some emergency rations. They were at least a ready reserve, if the need arose.

It should be noted that when the trains all moved forward that morning from Primm, on the California border, the families saw the large dry lakebed and surrounding barren mountainsides, and it caused them added anxiety. Seeing this foreboding sight, with no vegetation or signs of water, they began to worry, if this was like where they were going, how they could survive in such a place.

However, the landscape soon gave way to the graceful vista of what they later called the Kelso Valley, a huge expanse bordering the Providence Mountain range to the southeast and the Soda Mountains on the northwest. From the train windows, that had been shuttered until they left Las Vegas, the exhausted voyagers could look out over 15-20 miles of undeveloped and undisturbed brush and dry grassland. It had served as grazing land for ranchers up until some years ago, when it was set aside as a Preserve. For them, it was comforting to see something other than sand and rock. As their trains slowly worked their way around the Providence Mountains' foothills, they passed by Cima and the dirt road that led to the Amboy Cavern, which was now, not more than twenty miles away. When everyone was made aware of how close they were to both Amboy and Kelso, a collective sigh was heard. Their future shelters were almost within sight.

The enthusiasm was uncontrollable. Children and adults, alike, were singing and laughing. It was a time to rejoice. Like Moses leading his people out of the Egyptian desert, through the Red Sea, they sensed they had been led out of Yucca Mountain by some overseeing

Power.   Everyone, for their deliverance, repeatedly offered prayers of thanksgiving.

And at 11:50 a.m. the switch engine with its three trains in tandem, pulled into Kelso, a township founded in 1904. For years, its primary purpose was to be a watering station during the years there were steam locomotives. Kelso's landmark was, by this time, a beautifully renovated, Spanish styled, railroad station, bunkhouse and roadhouse restaurant. It served as the Headquarters for the Preserve until April 1st. Now it, and the small hamlet that surrounded it, were starkly empty and windblown. There were four sets of tracks in the town. Most recently, these extra tracks served as a holding location for freight cars and trains, waiting to be moved toward either Los Angeles or Las Vegas. Fortunately, for these new arrivals from Yucca Mountain, the tracks were empty. In addition, most importantly, the structures in town were in excellent shape. Furthermore, Lilyanne, after a quick survey of the area, declared it within safe radioactive limits.

However, before anyone could get out and start becoming acquainted with their new surroundings, Ben announced that the trains needed to be repositioned and divided for the long term. He knew this announcement would be disappointing, but there was no way the switch engine and locomotive crews could safely do what needed to be done with children and adults milling about.

So for the next two hours there were numerous disconnections and relocations. The rebuilding freight train was parked on the outermost track away from the railroad station. But it was separated, as were all the other trains, at the paved road crossing leading out of Kelso towards Amboy. This separation would allow them to truck personnel or materials over the paved road to the Amboy Cavern later. The supply freight train was positioned next, with the food, water, shower and toilet tank cars separated into five groups to be easily accessible to the five Superliner sets of sleepers, kitchen/dining and lounge cars. And the next two sets of tracks, closest to the rail station, had two sets of five sleepers on the second track and three sets on the first track, closest to the station. The third sleeper, on the first track, had to be the other side of the paved road. At least this gave the families the closest access to the station that was possible, rather than be strung out for almost a mile either way from the station.

Then at 3:00 p.m., Ben announced that everyone could disembark to come and go as they please. The state of Martial Law was now over, and for now, they were home. What followed was like a kennel of 1014 puppies being let loose all at once. The area was immediately flooded with children and adults running, jumping, skipping, exploring, and just gazing about in wonderment. Their confinement was over.

For the next two days engineering work details worked feverishly to build a wooden overhang off the trackside of the railroad station. Yet it was built substantial enough to be enclosed when the weather turned blustery. It was to serve as an overflow area for seating families whenever there were general assembly meetings. Seating would be both in the station's large interior and outside in this covered area. The ground floor of the station was modified somewhat to give clear viewing to anyone speaking by the front door, which was opposite the trackside of the building.

Everyone reached agreement that classes would begin again on January 2nd. Likewise, they agreed they would have to be held in the lounge and dining cars. The Governing Body representatives, in discussions with their families, were to decide mealtime schedules and where they would prefer to eat.

Some of the outbuildings and homes were still usable for certain functions and the upstairs of the station had sleeper rooms that were converted into offices, library and a communication center.

No one knew how long they would remain here, but, for the time being, knowing that the Amboy Cavern families were nearby, there was no nagging worry that their lives would vanish tomorrow. Like the ancient nomadic tribes through the ages, they sensed this was the closest to home they were going to have for a while. And all agreed it was lovely to be here and to be alive.

NINETEEN: EPILOGUE

There was no way to communicate with the Amboy Cavern those first few days the families were in Kelso. Their train, hand-held devices only worked for a very limited distance. And they knew it would take a few weeks to erect the necessary superstructure to talk to them. For that reason, the Governing Body decided to send a delegation over there on January 1st.

They had one of the humvees unloaded off a flatcar on the freight train and filled it with gasoline from a tank car.   Ben, Ernie and Lilyanne were designated to go over. For Ben, it would be a revelation to see how they had managed in the shelter he and his personnel had helped construct. For Ernie and Lilyanne, like for the rest of the Yucca Mountain families, they were just excited to meet their new neighbors and fellow compatriots.

Ben and the Governing Body decided that there would be a General Assembly meeting on January 1st, much later in the morning after the all-night New Year Eve's celebrations. Ben and his party left to drive over to the Amboy Cavern at 10 a.m., hoping to arrive there around noon. They decided to take the back road, out of Cima, instead of going over on the paved road. It would give them a chance to check out that road as a possible transfer route. Besides, Ben had already driven on the paved road in February, going from the Marine Base to

531

the Yucca Mountain Repository.

The Kelso General Assembly meeting started at 11 a.m. that day. Benton was the Master of Ceremonies for that meeting, and his agenda was to address school schedules, upgrading certain buildings in Kelso, some general announcements and any issues brought up by the audience. As he rose to open the meeting, a formless figure suddenly appeared beside him. Instantaneously, the audience gasped, once again, out of shock and amazement.

By noon, as anticipated, the humvee reached the top of the Providence Mountain range and began its descent toward the Amboy Cavern complex. Coincidentally, Clem had gone up with Jake for his first climb up the backside of the cavern's mountain. Just as he reached the summit, he was startled to see a vehicle slowly rise over the top of the ridgeline. Without hesitating, he turned and with Jake in tow, he ran all the way down the hillside, yelling to the families who were still filing in and out for the first time from their confinement, "Someone's coming! Someone's driving over the mountain! Look! They're coming! Someone is coming!"

Shocked and stunned at what they were hearing, the hundreds of people gathered out of the graded ledge in front of the Amboy Cavern, turned in unison, in the direction Clem was pointing, and gasped.

APPENDIX 2

Figure 1:

"HEALTH ALERT !!
YOU MAY NEED GRIEF COUNSELING
OR CRISIS INTERVENTION"

Be advised that the Clinical Psychology/Counseling and Social Worker Team has met with the Medical and Surgical members of the Amboy Cavern's Medical Facility, and it has been determined that EACH OF US are at a high risk of developing severe, life-threatening depression if we are unaware of the following symptoms and do not seek immediate professional help. Do not wait if you notice any of the following occurring. We cannot wait to intervene. The definition of severe depression, prior to April 1st, was that the symptoms had to extend over a two week period. Given our present circumstances, and what is occurring around us, we must intervene at its onset. Please note if you have any of the following:

-thoughts of suicide and/or of taking the lives of others around you.

-having feelings of unbearable loss longer than 48 hours.

-crying uncontrollably, with your loved ones unable to console you.

-not sleeping nor eating for longer than 48 hours.

-not communicating with your loved ones for longer than 48 hours.

-if already taking antidepressants, finding yourself experiencing deepening depression the last 48 hours.

-mental confusion and forgetfulness that

533

prevents you from performing your normal daily tasks.

If you have any of the above symptoms, or if any of your family members do, please do the following. Come to the Medical Facility tomorrow at 8:00 a.m. You will be interviewed by one of our Health Care Team members. Depending on your condition, any of the following five options may be taken:

1. You may be asked to begin counseling in a group setting, led by one of our staff members.

2. You may be asked to stay overnight in our Medical Facility for further observation.

3. You may be given a prescription of antidepressants.

4. You may be reassured that what you are experiencing is within the new limits of normalcy and be asked to try and help others around you to cope and to give them encouragement and hope.

5. You will be encouraged, as will everyone in the Cavern, to attend a gathering of people who share some of the same religious beliefs as you. It is hoped everyone, cavern-wide, will come to a meeting in Cave #5's Assembly Room on April 3rd, at 6 p.m. At that time we will see what space is needed for which particular observances.

Finally, your compliance with these requests is vital for your health and for that of all of us, confined as we are, for these next months. Thank you for your cooperation.

The Amboy Cavern Medical Staff

Figure 2:

"Amboy Cavern's Educational Framework"

Level 1:-Description:"Day Care/Child Development
Center"
-Ages: 0-3 years.
-Content:
1. Nurturing.
2. Early childhood development
training.
-Staff:
1. Coordinator: professional
childhood development specialist.
2. Faculty: family members,
volunteers, professional staff for
special needs if a child has
developmental obstacles.

Level 2:-Description: "Preschool"
-Ages: 3-5 years.
-Content:
1. Learning alphabet, progressing to
identifying single words.
2. Learning numbers, progressing to
working with addition, subtraction,
beginning multiplication tables.
3. Introduction elementary level
biology, botany, chemistry, and
physics.
4. Introduction to music, art, story
development.
5. Exercise class for socialization
and play.
-Staff:
1. Professional: professional

preschool teachers.

2.Faculty: teaching aides, supervised by preschool teachers.

Level 3:-Description: "Elementary Education"
    -Ages: 6-11 years.
    -Content:

        1. Develop spelling and reading skills.

        2. Develop math skills to include elementary algebra.

        3. Begin formal introduction to biology, botany, chemistry and physics.

        4. Begin formal introduction to musical instruments, painting and drawing, writing short paragraphs and stories.

        5. Exercise class for strength, endurance, agility and play.

    -Staff:

        1.Professional: professional elementary school teachers.

        2. Faculty: teaching aides, trained and supervised by elementary teachers.

Level 4:-Description: "Apprentice Program"
    -Ages: 12-17 years. (entrance into a particular program based on aptitude testing, interview, discussion with parents and past teachers; ages 12-15 years for Theory portion; ages 16-17 years for the Mentoring portion)
    -Content:

        1. Theory Program:

I

a. Continue advancing studies
in basic sciences that
correspond to the apprenticeship
program for each individual,
e.g. for engineering: physics; for
medicine: biology; for
mechanics: computers and
design; for farming: agriculture.
b. Continue music, art,
writing skill development.
c. Exercise for strength,
coordination, agility,
competition.

2. Mentoring Program:

a. Exposure and beginning
instruction, stressing theory, in
the various apprenticeship
programs using the fulltime
professionals as mentors.
b. More advancement in all
sciences, particularly in their
Apprenticeship application.
c. Continue music or art or
writing advancement, as natural
talent dictates.
d. Exercise as above.

-Staff:

1. Professional: professional middle
and high school teachers for both
Theory and Mentoring Programs.
Professionals in their respective
fields for the Mentoring
Program.
2. Faculty: teaching aides, trained
and supervised by the middle and
high school teachers, and other

537

resource personnel within the Amboy
and Marine personnel.

Level 5:-Description: "Laboratory Program"
     -Ages: 18-19 years.
     -Content: Primarily laboratory or on the
          job site experience, with fulltime
          supervision.

Level 6-Description: "Clinical Program"
     -Ages: 20 years and up.
     -Content: All training and schooling in the
          actual theater or clinic or job site with
          eventual goal of total independence.

Level 7:-Description: "Adult Education"
     -Ages: all adults.
     -Faculty: Every adult in the Amboy Cavern
          with talents/skills to share.
     -Content: (each adult is expected to enroll in
          most or all of these classes) See
          Below:

Problems	Subjects to be Taught
1. Extreme hunger:	-animal husbandry.
	-large scale organic farming.
	-orchard management/bee keeping.
	-vegetable gardening.
	-food preparation using meager resources.
2. Extreme thirst:	-well drilling/water purification techniques.
	-dairy cows/goat

management.
-milk production, processing,
pasteurization.
-growing tea/coffee/grape
plants.

3. Extreme exposure:-heating a home w/o electricity
or gas.
-cooling a home w/o
electricity or gas.
-roof, window, door,
construction, repair.
-ways to insulate and
weatherize your
home.
-sewing clothes from limited
resources.

4. Inadequate shelter:-home building above ground
level.
-home building below ground
level.
-material selection with
limited resources.

5. Serious injury: -first aid classes/CPR
training.
-hazards & mistakes to avoid
or minimize.

6. Fires/radiation: -fire prevention and
suppression.
-monitoring & management
high radiation levels.

7. Violence: -dealing with an intruder.

-dealing with a family
member.
-dealing with large scale
intrusion.

8. Poor survival skills:-managing with limited
resources/supplies.
-recycling to extend
usefulness of
resources.
-canning, drying, smoking
to preserve food.
-farming with w/o
mechanization.
-mechanical repair of
available equipment.
-medical emergency
proficiency/ALS
skills.

9. Limited transportation:-care and use of emergency
vehicles.
-building/care of
bicycle-powered
vehicles.
-horse/mule breeding, care,
tack, handling.

10. Limited power: -building/using solar power
generators.
-building & using
wind/bicycle
generators.

-Oversight: Due to the importance of Level 7, there
will   four   additions   to   the   Standing

Education Committee. They are Geoffrey
and Patricia Graham, Eric Chan and Priscilla
Roberts.
- Bibliography for Adult Education Classes:
(The material listed here is available in
Reference Section of our Cavern Library.
There are other materials as well. You must
eventually read and   study all of them.
Your survival will depend on it.)

1. Handy Farm and Home Devices and How to Make
Them compiled and designed by J.V. Bartlett. Angus
Robertson Publishers, Australia. 1985. First publisher
The Advertiser Publishing Office, Adelaide. 1945.
2. The Guide to Self-Sufficiency by John Seymour.
Popular Mechanics Books, New York. 1976.
3. Survival, Department of the Army Field Manual, FM
21-76 by Dept. of the Army. Washington, D.C. 1957.
4. The Making of Tools by Alexander G. Waygers. Van
Nostrand Reinhold Co., New York. 1973.
5. The Modern Blacksmith by Alexander G. Waygers.
Van Nostrand Reinhold Co., New York. 1974.
6. Training & Pruning Apple and Pear Trees by Robert
L. Stebbins. A Pacific Northwest Extension Publication.
1983.
7. Grafting Fruit Trees. Issued by Washington State
Cooperative Extension, Oregon State Extension and
University of Idaho. 1987.
8. Back to Basics:; How to Learn and Enjoy Traditional
American Skills. Reader's Digest.
9. Eric Sloane's America by Eric Sloane. Promontory
Press, New York. 1982.
10.First Aid by The American Red Cross. Doubleday
and Co, Inc., Garden City, New York. 2000.
11.Wood-Frame House Construction by L.O. Anderson.
Forest Service, U.S. Dept. of Agriculture. 1970.
12.Boat Building Manual by Robert M. Steward.

International Marine Publishing Co, Camden, Maine. 1984.

13.<u>Carpentry and Building Construction</u> by John L. Feirer & Gilbert R. Hutchings. Glenco Publishing Co. 1986.

14.<u>Ball Blue Book, Easy Guide to Tasty, Thrifty Canning</u>. Ball Corporation Publishers, Muncie, Indiana. 1972.

15.<u>Joy of Cooking</u> by Irma S. Rombauer and Marion Rombauer Becker. The Bobbs-Merrill Co., Inc., New York. 1979.

16.<u>The Independent Home: Living Well with Power From the Sun, Wind, and Water</u> by Michael Potts. Chelsea Publishing Co.,199

Figure 3:

"The Temporary Governing Body's April 8th
Meeting Agenda"

A. Nomination and Election Process for Permanent
Governing Body:
1. Vote for two representatives from each
25-26 family groups.
2. Candidates will campaign from April
10th to April 24th.
3. Election Day is on April 25th. Everyone
18 or older must vote.
B. Finalizing the Composition of the Permanent
Governing Body:
1. Until the Final Emergence from the
cavern, the voting members of
the Permanent Governing Body will
have 18 elected and 15 Appointed
members. The appointed are 10
junior and senior Marine officers and
4 Amboy coordinators plus Fred
Wailand. The three judges present
will not vote, nor will the three
children representatives, but both
groups will sit on committees.
C. Forming Standing Committees and Member
Selection:
1. Education Committee.
2. Governance and Judiciary Committee.
3. Financial Framework Committee.
4. Transitions Committee.
5. Welfare Committee.
6. Final Emergence Committee.
D. General Issues to be Addressed Immediately:
1. Cavern-wide noise level at certain times.

2. Establish set times for the two main
     meals to be prepared and served.
3. Establish set times for the medical clinic
     and library to be open.
4. Caution everyone on water usage and
     recycling everything possible we
     must avoid overtaxing our water
     system and avoid as much garbage
     accumulation as possible.
5. Instruct family members in not
     disposing any foreign objects into the
     toilets. If we clog the system, it could
     have devastating effects.

Signed,

   Eric Stanfield, Interim Chairman, Amboy
   Cavern Temporary Governing Body

Figure 4:

"The Global Union's Financial Framework
Flowchart"

1*   Jan. 14th Amboy & Marine families liquidate their savings, stocks, bond holdings. Total:$16,521,500.(after $73,500. For conversion).

2*   Jan. 30th each family wires these funds to a single Swiss Bank account.

3*   Mar. 15th flight leaves from Nellis AFB for Geneva to pick up all converted currency and coinage.

4*   Mar. 18th flight arrives at Marine Base and all converted U.S.$ are moved to Amboy Cavern.

April 8th Governing Body forms a committee to develop a financial structure for families.

May 29th The Global Union is constituted and its financial structure is finalized.

Central Bank formed with the funds transferred here. Total: $8,269,750.00

Reserve Bank formed half with half the funds here. Total: transferred here. Total: $8,269,750.00.

Once any gold is located, it will be converted to gold holdings, pegged @$32/oz. Any future gold located once this total is converted will be divided @$32/oz.: half to be deposited in the Central Bank and half deposited in the Reserve Bank. No private holding of gold will be permitted.

Dispersing these funds to all individuals through a Credit Union, once a surplus of goods is is possible and bartering is no longer desired.

A Community Bank is Established once 5% income tax is begun on profits from the sale of goods.

Footnotes explaining "Financial Framework Flowchart":

1*: The 75 Amboy families were requested, soon after they had their notification of acceptance for the Amboy seminar and the visit from B, to liquidate all assets and have them deposited in a nearby bank that would eventually wire these funds to a bank in Switzerland. This request was not made at the same time as the one for them to sort and pack their belongings. It was thought that would be too overwhelming to do so at one time. It was not possible to transfer these funds directly to the United States. Internal Revenue Department regulations for U.S. banks require that they be notified for any cash transactions of $10,000.00 or more. It would have taken too long to complete the full transfer, and it would have raised too many suspicions.

2*: The Swiss Bank was instructed to convert all incoming funds into U.S.$ and then to divide ¾'s of the total amount into small bills: 45 % $1.00 bills; 20%

$5.00 bills; 15% $10.00 bills; 10% $20.00 bills; 5% $50.00 bills; 5% $100.00 bills. And ¼ of the total amount into coinage: 20% 1 cent; 25% 5 cent; 25% 10 cent; 25% 25%; 5% 50 cent pieces. B's debit card number was given the Swiss bank to cover the costs of these transactions and for the necessary sorting and packaging of these bills and coinage.

3*: A single cargo plane left for Geneva, Switzerland, from Nellis AFB. Once it was loaded with the currency and coinage, it returned to the Marine Base near Amboy. From there, it was transported to the Amboy Cavern and stored in the Communications Office.

4*: Upon its returned to Nellis AFB the plane was secured, and the crew returned to the Yucca Mountain facility. It was unnecessary to transport such cargo for the Yucca Mountain families; they were bringing whatever valuables and moneys with them to the facility. It, too, would be divided equally and deposited into the Central and Reserve Banks. The total held in the Communication Center amounted to $11,776,400.00. It was transported to Kelso in the Lounge Car that Ben used as the Command Center during their journey from Yucca Mountain. Three months after their arrival in Kelso, it was combined with the Amboy funds and divided equally between the Central Bank and Reserve Bank deposits.

5*: As gold is uncovered or found it will first be applied directly to replacing the currency held in the Central Bank at a rate of $32.00/ounce of gold. The currency that is replaced will not be put into circulation, but it will be put in inactive or 'dead' storage. Once gold is located that no longer needs to be exchanged for the $8,269,750.00, then at the same rate of $32.00/ounce, it will be divided equally between the

Central and Reserve Banks. $16.00 will be stored in the Central Bank and $16.00 will be withdrawn from the inactive or 'dead' storage area and deposited in the Reserve Bank. That $16.00 is now added to the amount that can be circulated amongst the families. When that 'dead' amount is liquidated, we will have to begin printing our own paper money, using the manual printing press that we have in storage. The press will have to be kept in a secure area for safety and security. But the circulating currency will always be matched with an equal amount in gold reserves. The monetary system for the Global Union will be a full gold standard, with a hard currency basis.

The dispersing of funds from the Reserve Bank will not occur during the period immediately following the Final Emergence. For an unknown period of time the economy, such as it will be, will be in a survival mode only. There will be no need for money to exchange hands during this time. There will be no surpluses or any incidentals, as such, to purchase. Bartering will be the most common method of exchange during this survival period.

Once there are surpluses that others want to purchase, the Reserve Bank will then initiate the dispersing funds in an equal amount to everyone, either on a monthly or quarterly basis, as the situation warrants. And to start with, this amount may be as little as $15-25.00. The objective will be to start with and maintain the prices for goods as low as possible. Further, no matter how large the amount that your family transferred to the Swiss Bank, you and your family members will still only get the same amount as the others. You saved this money for your future, and that future is here. These funds will be deposited in a Credit

Union that all 941 people sheltered in the Amboy Cavern will belong to. All adults will have a vote as to how the money is distributed. The Credit Union will be a co-operative.

And when it is possible for those with a surplus of goods to make a profit on the sale of their products, then an income tax of 5% will be imposed on the profits. This money will be deposited into a Service Account in a newly established Community Bank. The funds deposited here will pay for services or goods that arise beyond our normal voluntary service, e.g. medical care and social services. The Governing Body will oversee these accounts distributions.

Finally, as the economy grows, there will be opportunities for anyone to start up businesses, establish private banks, and do whatever you think is needed or what you can make a success. Loans will be available for these ventures through the Credit Union or the private banks, if they should exist.

Figure 5:

"The Global Union's Standing Committees"

1. Educational Committee:
Clarice Delow, biology professor, Chairwoman; Rashid Batak, agriculture professor; Kita Satou, preschool teacher; Geoffrey and Patricia Graham, Amboy rebuilding group and mining engineers, Eric Chan, Marine Capt., engineering; and Priscilla Roberts, Marine Col., logistics.

2. Governance and Judiciary Committee:
Sir Colin Newton James, a judge on the Inner London Crown Court, Chairman; Michael Outler, history professor, Oxford University; Diane Crook, history professor, Cambridge University; Bertha Ann Mack, judge on 4th Federal Court of Appeals, Washington, D.C.; Amber Jens, judge on the World Court, The Hague; Cyril McGuire, associate professor of Law, Harvard Law School; and Fred Wailand, journalist.

3. Financial Framework Committee:
Eric Stanfield, Marine General, Chairman; Hershel Schweitman, mathematics professor, Tel Aviv University; Kirill Lithow, mathematics associate professor, Kiev University; Michael Outler; and Fred Wailand.

4. Transitions Committee: (encompassing birth, marriage, & death)
Ian Murphy, Marine Capt., medical unit, Chairman; Mitzi Zimmerman, clinical psychologist; Alan Parry, professor of medicine, Adelaide Medical School; Anne Parker,nurse practitioner Toronto Public Health; NancyGilcrest, Marine Major, Personnel Affairs; and three Marine family representatives: Darcy Freeman, Julie Franks, Jeb Hearn.

5. Welfare Committee:

Albert Nugama, middle school teacher, Chairman; Theresa Lieska, artist; Philip Lieska, musician; Harriet Skinner, social worker, Minor Peterson, family practice/internal medicine, St. Joseph's Medical Center, Phoenix; Nancy Gilcrest; Hasna Eunis, Marine Capt., communications unit; and three Marine family representatives: Adele Weng, Arnold Davis, Elaine Poloski.

6. Final Emergence Committee:

Patricia Graham, Chair; Jason Black, Marine Lt. Col, Mission Operations; Nancy Gilbert, Eric Chan; Rashid Batak; Hort Bauer, civil engineer, Munich; and Genji Lin, civil engineer, Shanghai.

Figure 6:

"The Global Union's Legislative, Legal and
Fiscal Principles"

I. Guiding Principles in Forming a New Government:
    A. Does it provide for meaningful survival?
    B. Does it recognize the right for basic
       freedoms?
    C. Does it promote the general welfare of
       the citizenry?
    D. Does it protect the most vulnerable?
    E. Does it insure a democratic way of
       governing?
    F. Does there now exist a financial
       framework for its success?

II. Structural Outline:
    A. Elected representatives:
       1. Chief Executive.
       2. House of Representatives.
       3. Judiciary (eventually)
    B. Composition of the three bodies:
       1. A single individual as Chief
          Executive.
       2. One elected representative for
          every 25 families or a faction
          thereof.
       3. Three Judges.
    C. Standing Committees:

III. Terms of Office:
    A. Chief Executive:
       1. One year. This will be amended
          to more or less time as living
          conditions stabilize and the
          leadership pool broadens.
          Reelection can be possible for

up to four terms in office.
2. Vote of confidence for removal
from office requires ¾
majority vote from all elected
officials and a majority vote
from the population. If a
threshold is reached, a new
election for Chief Executive
is held immediately.
B. House of Representatives:
1. One year. Reelection can be
possible for up to four terms
in office.
2. Censure and removal from office
by ¾'s majority vote from all
elected officials and a
majority vote from the
individual's constituency.
C. Standing Committees:
1. One year. Unless entire
committee is eliminated.
IV. Resources Used for Developing Principles:
A. United States Constitutional form of
government and judiciary.
B. United Kingdom Parliamentary form of
government   and
judiciary.
C. International Co-operative Alliance.
D. The Gold Standard in Theory and
History, Barry Eichengreen,
ed., Mark Flandreau, 1997.
E. Alexander Hamilton, Broadus Mitchell.
(2 vols., 1957-62).

Figure 7:

"Definition, Values and Principles of
Co-operatives"

"Statement on the Co-operative Identity"

Definition

A co-operative is an autonomous association of persons united voluntarily to meet their common economic, social, and cultural needs and aspirations through a jointly- owned and democratically-controlled enterprise

Values

Co-operatives are based on the values of self-help, self-responsibility, democracy, equality, equity and solidarity. In the tradition of their founders, co-operative members believe in the ethical values of honesty, openness, social responsibility and caring for others.

Principles

The co-operative principles are guidelines by which co-operatives put their values into practice.

1st Principle: Voluntary and Open Membership

Co-operatives are voluntary organizations, open to all persons able to use their services and willing to accept the responsibilities of membership, without gender, social, racial, political or religious discrimination.

2nd Principle: Democratic Member Control

Co-operatives are democratic organizations controlled by their members, who actively participate in setting their policies and making decisions. Men and women serving as elected representatives are accountable to the membership. In primary co-operatives members have equal voting rights (one member, one vote) and co-operatives at other levels are also organized in a democratic manner.

3rd Principle: Member Economic Participation

Members contribute equitably to, and democratically control, the capital of their co-operative. At least part of that capital is usually the common property of the co-operative. Members usually receive limited compensation, if any, on capital subscribed as a condition of membership. Members allocate surpluses for any or all of the following purposes: developing their co-operative, possibly by setting up reserves, part of which at least would be indivisible; benefiting members in proportion to their transactions with the co-operative objective; and supporting other activities approved by the membership.

4th Principle: Autonomy and Independence

Co-operatives are autonomous, self-help organizations controlled by their members. If they enter into agreements with other organizations, including governments, or raise capital from external sources, they do so on terms that ensure democratic control by their members and maintain their co-operative autonomy.

5th Principle: Education, Training and Information

Co-operatives provide education and training for their members, elected representatives, managers, and employees so they can contribute effectively to the development of their co-operatives. They inform the general public, particularly young people and opinion leaders about the nature and benefits of co-operation.

6th Principle: Co-operation among Co-operatives
Co-operatives serve their members most effectively and strengthen the co-operative movement by working together through local, national, and regional and international structures.

7th Principle: Concern for Community
Co-operatives work for the sustainable development of their communities through policies approved by their members." [1]

---

[1]   "Statement on the Co-operative Identity", by the International Co-operative Alliance. 15, route des Morillons, 1218 Grand-Saconnex, Geneva, Switzerland. Statement used with the Alliance's permission.

Figure 8:

"Ceremonial Procedure for a Burial At Sea"

"Personnel participating or attending the services must wear the Uniform of the Day. When a chaplain of appropriate faith is not available, the service may be read by the commanding officer or an officer designated by him/her. The committal service is as follows:

-Station firing squad, casket bearers and
    bugler.
-Officer's call. Pass the word "All hands
    bury the dead (the ships should be
    stopped, if practical, and colors
    displayed at half-mast).
-Assembly.
-Adjutant's call (Call to Attention).
-Bring the massed formation to Parade Rest.
-Burial Service.
    ° The Scripture (Parade Rest).
    ° The prayers (Parade Rest, heads
        bowed).
    ° The Committal (Attention, Hand
        Salute).
    ° The Benediction (Parade Rest,
        heads bowed).
    ° Fire three volleys (Attention,
        Hand Salute).
    ° Taps. Close up colors. Resume
        course and speed at
        the last note of Taps
        (Hand Salute).
    ° Encasing of the flag (Attention).
    ° Retreat (Resume normal duties).
        Officers in the funeral

procession and casket bearers may bear the mourning band on the left arm.

DECK PLAN FOR BURIAL AT SEA

Honor Platoon

□□□□□□

□□□□□□

← aft   forward→

□ Commanding officer

Bugler □   □ Chief Master at Arms

Chaplain □   □ Executive Officer

□ | | □

□   □ Body bearers

□   □

Firing Squad

□□□□□□□

PREPARATION FOR THE AT SEA DISPOSITION

There are two component parts of the ceremony of at sea disposition: religious and military. The reading of the scripture and prayers, the committal, and the benediction constitutes the religious part and may be performed by the chaplain, commanding officer, or an officer designated by him/her. All other aspects of the ceremony are performed by other military personnel.

For at sea disposition, the casketed remains are covered with the national ensign with the union placed at the head and over the left shoulder. When draped with the national ensign, the cap and sword of the deceased are not displayed.

Six or eight casket bearers (depending on the weight of the casketed remains) form according to height of both sides of the casket. Below decks, while not carrying the casket, casket bearers will uncover. At all other times they remain covered. The casket is always carried feet first.

The selected place for committal is cleared and rigged so that when the casket remains are brought on deck they may be placed securely on a stand, if necessary, with feet overboard at right angles to and extending over the side of the launching.

Attention is sounded on the bugle or passed by word of mouth as the casket bearers, preceded by the chief-master-at-arms; execute the Hand Salute as the cortege passes to the place selected for the committal. When the remains have been so placed, the Hand Salute is terminated by those in view and a sentry is posted unless the burial service is to follow immediately.

A chief petty officer is designated to take charge of the firing party of seven persons. The chief master-at-arms directs the casket bearers during the service until the flag is encased and delivered to the commanding officer.

When the honor platoon has been assembled in massed formation and has been brought to parade rest, the burial service is begun and read through to the end of the prayers. During prayers the assemblage remains covered with bowed heads. After the conclusion of the prayers the casket bearers should hold the casket and national ensign in place by hand as may be necessary before reading the committal.

When these preparations have been completed and all is in readiness, attention is sounded. The command "Firing party, Present Arms" (Honor platoon Hand Salute) is given and the reading of the committal is commenced. When the indicated word of the committal is read, the casket bearers tilt the board until the casket slides along it, under the national ensign, overboard into the sea. As it goes, the casket bearers retain the board and the national ensign on board and stand fast.

The command "Firing party, Order Arms, Parade Rest," are given and all hands bow their heads. The benediction is pronounced. Then follow the commands, "Firing party, Attention, Fire three volleys." (Honor platoon Hand Salutes and remain so until the last note of Taps). After the last volley the firing party remains at the ready position, pieces locked, until the conclusion of Taps, and salutes.

Upon completion of Taps, the firing party is brought to Order Arms. The casket bearers encase the national ensign by folding twice along the long axis of the flag. The blue field is kept to the outside. Beginning at the fly end (away from the blue field), the flag is folded with only the blue field showing. It is then presented by the chief master-at-arms to the commanding officer..."[2]

---

[2] "Burial at Sea", U.S. Dept. Navy, Naval Historical Center, Washington, D.C., Used with Permission.

Figure 9:

"The Buried Life"
By Matthew Arnold
Light flows our war of mocking words,
    and yet,
Behold, with tears mine eyes are wet!
I feel a nameless sadness o'er me roll.
Yes, yes, we know that we can jest,
We know, we know that we can smile!
But there's a something in this breast,
To which thy light words bring no rest,
And thy gay smiles no anodyne.
Give me thy hand, and hush awhile,
And turn those limpid eyes on mine,
And let me read there, love! Thy inmost
    soul.

Alas! Is even love too weak
To unlock the heart, and let it speak?
Are even lovers powerless to reveal
To one another what indeed they feel?
I knew the mass of men concealed
Their thoughts, for fear that if revealed
They would by other men be met
With blank indifference, or with blame
    reproved;
I knew they lived and moved
Tricked in disguises, alien to the rest
Of men, and alien to themselves--and
    yet
The same heart beats in every human
    breast!

But we, my love--doth a like spell
    benumb
Our hearts, our voices?--must we too be

561

dumb?

Ah! well for us, if even we,
Even for a moment, can get free
Our heart, and have our lips unchained;
For that which seals them hath been
deep-ordained!

Fate, which foresaw
How frivolous a baby man would be--
By what distractions he would be
possessed,
How he would pour himself in every
strife,
And well-nigh change his own identity--
That it might keep from his capricious
play
His genuine self, and for him to obey
Even in his own despite his being's law,
Bade through the deep recesses of our
breast
The unrewarded river of our life
Pursue with indiscernible flow its way;
And that we should not see
The buried stream, and seem to be
Eddying at large in blind uncertainty,
Though driving on with it eternally.

But often, in the world's most crowded
streets,
But often, in the din of strife,
There rises an unspeakable desire
After the knowledge of our buried life;
A thirst to spend our fire and restless
force
In tracking out our true, original course;
A longing to inquire

Into the mystery of this heart which
        beats
So wild, so deep in us--to know
Whence our lives come and where they
        go.
And many a man in his own breast then
        delves,
But deep enough, alas! none ever mines.
And we have been on many thousand
        lines,
And we have shown, on each, spirit and
        power;
But hardly have we, for one little hour,
Been on our own line, have we been
        ourselves--
Hardly had skill to utter one of all
The nameless feelings that course
        through our breast,
But they course on forever unexpressed.
And long we try in vain to speak and act
Our hidden self, and what we say and do
Is eloquent, is well--but 'tis not true!
And then we will no more be racked
With inward striving, and demand
Of all the thousand nothings of the hour
Their stupefying power;
Ah yes, and they benumb us at our call!
Yet still, from time to time, vague and
        forlorn,
From the soul's subterranean depth up
        borne
As from an infinitely distant land,
Come airs, and floating echoes, and
        convey
A melancholy into all our day.

Only--but this is rare--
When a beloved hand is laid in ours,
When, jaded with the rush and glare
Of the interminable hours,
Our eyes can in another's eyes read
     clear,
When our world-deafening ear
Is by the tones of a loved voice
     caressed--
A bolt is shot back somewhere in our
     breast,
And a lost pulse of feeling stirs again.
The eye sinks inward, and the heart lies
     plain,
And what we mean, we say, and what
     we would, we know.
A man becomes aware of his life's flow,
And hears its winding murmur; and he
     sees

The meadows where it glides, the sun,
     the breeze.

And there arrives a lull in the hot race
Wherein he doth forever chase
That flying and elusive shadow, rest.
An air of coolness plays upon his face,
And an unwonted calm pervades his
     breast,
And then he thinks he knows
The hills where his life rose,
And the sea where it goes.[3]

---

[3] <u>The Victorian Age Prose, Poetry and Drama</u> by
John Wilson Bowyer and John Lee Brooks,
Appleton-Century-Crofts, Inc. New York, pp. 484-85.

Figure 10:

"The Global Union's Memorial Service on
July 14"

Order of Service

I. Processional: (Recorded music broadcast   over
Public Address System)

II. Hymns: (Led by Amboy Cavern Choir)[1]

III. Readings from Sacred Scriptures: (Read by Lay
Leaders from each faith)
        -Islam:
                "In the Name of God, The
                Compassionate, The Merciful

                For with God
                are the keys of the unseen;
                no one knows them
                but God.
                And God knows
                what is on the land
                and in the sea;
                and not a single leaf falls
                but God knows it.
                And there is not a single grain
                in the darknesses of earth,
                nor anything green, or withered,
                but is in an open Book.

                And it is God

---

[1]   All hymns taken from the <u>Pilgrim Hymnal</u>, The
Pilgrim Press, Boston, 1963.

who takes your souls by night,
and knows what you have acquired
by day;
then resurrects you in it,
that an appointed term
may be fulfilled.
Thence your destination
is to God,
who will then acquaint you
with what you have done." (Cattle
59-60)[2]

-Buddhism:

"The Way of Practical Attainment
The Teaching of Buddha
Faith is the fire
On the long journey of human life,
faith is the best of companions;
it is the best refreshment on the
journey; and it is the greatest
possession.

Faith is the hand that receive the
Dharma (The Teachings); it is the
pure hand that receives all the
virtues. Faith is the fire that
consumes all the impurities of
worldly desires, it removes the
burden, and it is the guide that leads
one's way.

Faith removes greed, fear and pride;

---

[2] The Essential Koran, The Heart of Islam by Thomas Cleary, Harper, San Francisco. 1994 , p. 56. Used with permission.

it teaches courtesy and to respect
others; it frees one from the bondage
of circumstances; it gives one
courage to meet hardship; it gives
one power to overcome temptations;
it enables one to keep one's deeds
bright and pure; and it enriches the
mind with wisdom."[3]

- Judaism:
Genesis 6:5-14:

"And God saw that the wickedness
of man was great in the earth,
and that every imagination of the
thoughts of his heart was only
evil continually.

And it repented the Lord that he had
made man on the earth, and it
grieved him at his heart.

And the Lord said, I will destroy man
whom I have created from the face of
the earth; both man, and beast, and
the creeping thing, and the fowls of
the air; for it repenteth me that I have
made them.
But Noah found grace in the eyes of
the Lord.

---

[3] The Teaching of Buddha. Society for the
Promotion of Buddhism, Tokyo, Japan, Kosaido
Printing Co., Ltd. 1999, p. 354. Used with
permission.

These are the generations of Noah:
Noah was a just man and perfect in
his generations, and Noah walked
with God.

And Noah begat three sons, Shem,
Ham, and Japheth.

The earth also was corrupt before
God, and the earth was filled
with violence.

And God looked upon the earth, and,
behold, it was corrupt; for all
flesh had corrupted his way upon the
earth.

And God said unto Noah, The end of
all flesh is come before me; for the
earth is filled with violence through
them; and, behold, I will destroy
them with the earth.

Make thee an ark of gopher wood;
rooms shalt thou make in the ark,
and shalt pitch it within and without
with pitch.

Genesis 7:17-19, 23-24:

And the flood was forty days upon
the earth; and the waters increased,
and bare up the ark, and it was lift up
above the earth.

And the waters prevailed, and were

increased greatly upon the earth; and
the ark when upon the face of the
waters.

And every living substance was
destroyed which was upon the
face of the ground, both man, and
cattle, and the creeping things,
and the fowl of the heaven; and they
were destroyed from the earth; and
Noah only remained alive, and that
they were with him in the ark.

And the waters prevailed upon the
earth an hundred and fifty days."[4]

-Hinduism:
"Divine Manifestations
The Blessed Lord Said:

Listen further, Arjuna,
to these words that delight your
heart;
this is my utmost teaching,
which I tell you for your greatest
good.

Neither the myriad gods
nor any of the sages know
my origin; I am the source
from which gods and sages emerge.

---

[4]   The Holy Bible, Containing The Old and New
Testaments. Eyre and Spottiswoode, Ltd. London,
St James Version.

Whoever knows me as the Unborn,
the Beginningless, the great Lord
of all worlds--- he alone sees
truly and is freed from all harm."
(10.1-3)[5]

-Christianity:
Matthew 5:1-12:

"And seeing the multitudes, he went
up into a mountain; and when
he was set, his disciples came unto
him:

And he opened his mouth, and taught
them, saying,

Blessed are the poor in spirit: for
theirs is the kingdom of
heaven.

Blessed are they that mourn: for they
shall be comforted.

Blessed are the meek: for they shall
inherit the earth.

Blessed are they which do hunger
and thirst after righteousness:
for they shall be filled.

Blessed are the merciful: for they

---

[5]   Bhagavad Gita, A New Translation by Stephen
Mitchell. Three Rivers Press, New York, 2000. p.
121.

shall obtain mercy.

Blessed are the pure in heart: for they
shall see God.

Blessed are the peacemakers: for
they shall be called the children
of God.

Blessed are they which are
persecuted for righteousness' sake:
for theirs is the kingdom of heaven.

Blessed are ye, when men shall
revile you, and persecute you, and
shall say all manner of evil against
you falsely, for my sake.

Rejoice, and be exceeding glad, for
great is your reward in heaven:
for so persecuted they the prophets
which were before you."[6]

IV. Homily: (Recited by Albert Nugama)

"We have come here today to memorialize five
of our fallen, three of whom were from one family.
Each person was precious to us. Their loss has made us
aware that we must cling to each other. Life, we are
reminded, again, is a priceless gift. More and more we
are being forced to realize that we are becoming its sole
ambassadors.

---

[6] The Holy Bible, Containing the Old and New
Testaments. Eyre and Spottiswoode Ltd., London,
St. James Version.

Eventually, we will inscribe their names on a memorial plaque. And, if there are future generations beyond ours, they can search that list for those who perished, making this journey we have ahead.

What we face beyond this place is obviously unknown and unknowable. We pray, we hope and we muster on with faith, but only silence answers our deepest questions. Even given the calming effect that B's presence gave us, we still face the limitations of our humanity in times like these. What lies beyond? What is our purpose here in this place? Who is B? All these questions are in each of our hearts and souls. And they rightly should be. For this occasion is both a time to remember and to question. And to renew.

The Scriptures chosen for this morning were from each of our great faiths. Each was chosen to remind us of our common bonds. No longer can our faiths separate us. They must provide us renewal and bring us closer together. We gather here to reaffirm our relationship to our Eternal God and to reaffirm, through Scripture, God's reaffirmation of that relationship to us, both for now and for all eternity.

And, finally, we must affirm our commitment to find and nurture the commonality within each of us. Let this Memorial Service and the sacrifice of these who we mourn and memorialize be a lasting reminder of this commitment. Their deaths cannot be vain. And neither can our existence in this place and time."

V. Hymns: (Led by Amboy Cavern Choir)

VI. Recessional: (Recorded music broadcast over the Public Address System)

Figure 11:

"Yucca Mountain Check Off Work List"

Check   Date/Initial   Work Description

TOP PRIORITY

_____-Confirm 60 railroad flat cars
           for trucks and equipment.
_____-Install communication link
           with satellite disk hook up.
_____-Dismantle exterior
           buildings; put materials in #3
           vault.
_____-Perform ventilation system
           upgrade.
_____-Service the two generators;
           set extra fuel bladders in area.
_____-Perform electrical wiring,
           with separate circuit boxes
               for:
               _____ Living Area and
               five Drifts.
               _____ Kitchens.
               _____ Vaults #1,2,3.
               _____ Communication
               Center.
               _____ Perimeter of the Main
               tunnel.
_____-Insure 5 Drifts are clear and
           ready for storage of train cars.

PRIORITY

_____-Stock chairs, tables, desks

573

and build stage in Vault #1.

_____-Build classroom and
communication center; stock
both.

_____-Select personnel to be
trained as train engineers
(drivers).

WHEN POSSIBLE

_____-Find and deliver two golf
carts and chargers.

_____-Have Air Force personnel
set up camp site by South
entrance upon their arrival on
February 21st.

_____-Have Seabees set up camp
site by South Entrance upon
their arrival on March 1st.

_____-Have supply train engineers
train our personnel to operate
the switch engine and the
locomotive engines when
it arrives and before they are
taken back to Las Vegas.

Signed,
Capt. Ernie Tam

Diagram 1:
"Yucca Mountain Cavern Floor Plan".

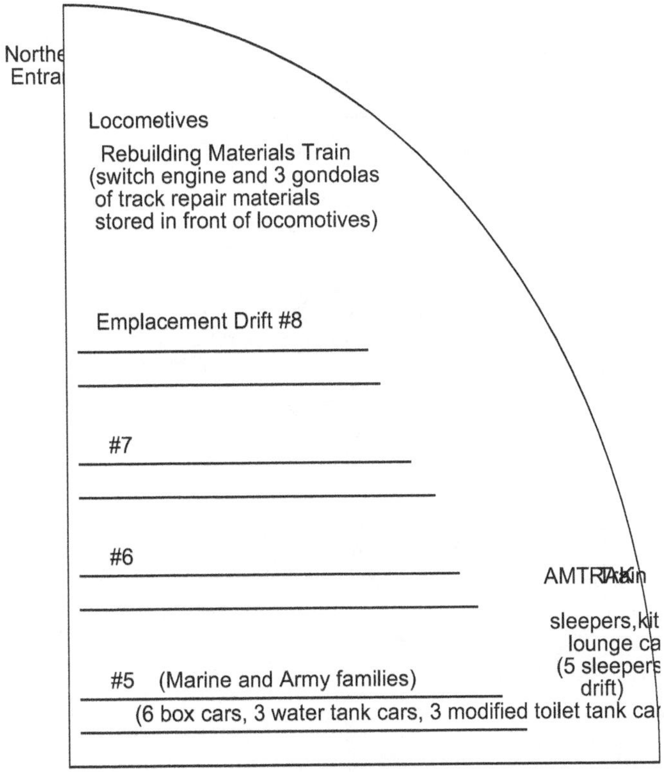

Northe
Entra

Locometives

Rebuilding Materials Train
(switch engine and 3 gondolas
of track repair materials
stored in front of locomotives)

Emplacement Drift #8

#7

#6

AMTRAK in

sleepers, kit
lounge ca
(5 sleeper
drift)

#5   (Marine and Army families)
(6 box cars, 3 water tank cars, 3 modified toilet tank car

Diagram 2:

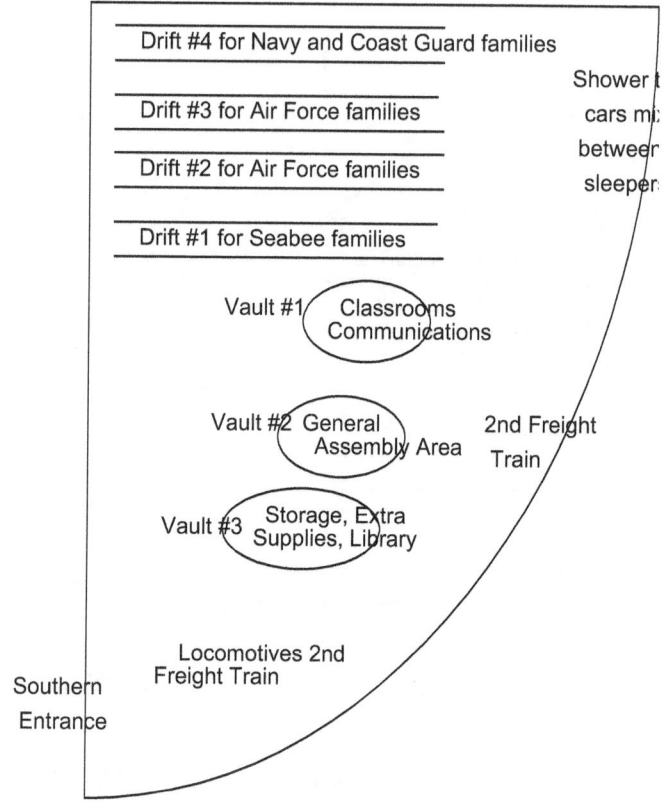

Figure 12:

"State of Nevada Emergency Preparedness

Warning"

!!!   WARNING   !!!

You and your family must leave

IMMEDIATELY!!

Drive East covering as much distance, as quickly as you can. Do not delay. This is to be your only warning.

All towns and cities, not already destroyed, are also being evacuated. The only safe areas remaining will be further East in the interior, away from Las Vegas, Salt Lake City and Denver. Go now. And may God be with you and your family.

State of Nevada Emergency Response Department
Carson City, Nevada   April 1st.

References:

1. "The Pedal-a-Watt Stationary Bike Power Generator", Convergence Technologies, Inc. 19 Tioga Lane, Pleasantville, NY 10570, 914-773-6749, email: support@econvergence.net

2.U.S. Department of Energy, Office of Civilian Radioactive Waste Management. Yucca Mountain Project. 1331 Hillshire Dr., Las Vegas, NV 89134. http://www.ocrwm.doe.gov.

3."GoldStandard",http://en.wikipedia.org/wiki/ Gold_standard.Pp 1-21.

4."All About Hantavirus; Hantavirus Pulmonary Syndrome", National Center for Infectious Diseases, Special Pathogens Branch, Division of Viral and Rickettsial Diseases, CDC, U.S. Department of Health and Human Services.

THE EMERGENCE

PART I

ONE: INTERNATIONAL SPACE STATION

Docking the Shuttle and securing it to the International Space Station had never been a simple matter for any previous mission. And for Col. Amber Peeters, the Shuttle Endeavor's Commander, even though she had done this countless times in her training at the Johnson Space Center, it was still nerve wracking for her as well. In part, this was because this, the 21st Expedition, was the last mission for the Shuttle fleet. She did not want to make any mistakes; her goal was to have a flawless mission. The Shuttles were being completely retired after this mission, something that was long overdue, she thought. And she, like all the other astronauts, was eager to start flying the Orion spacecraft. She knew her success with this mission was her ticket to going deeper into space in the Orion.

Cutbacks for NASA had required the Shuttle Program be kept in operation two years longer than originally planned. In addition, due to a worldwide recession, the international space agencies had to close down the ISS for one year. The ISS had finally been completely assembled within the year prior to its shutdown. Continued funding for its operation had become a major obstacle. Ultimately, it was decided that NASA would take complete operational control. The United Nations would assess all their member nations an annual fee to help reimburse the United States 45% of the ISS's total yearly expenses.

The launch of Col. Peeters' crew was the first mission back to the International Space Station since its deactivation. This mission was designed to restock supplies and set in motion some new experiments for long term monitoring. Most of this activity was preliminary work for the long-awaited Moon and Mars' manned missions to follow in upcoming years. They would be leaving enough supplies for 4-6 months, depending upon the size of the crews that followed them. Her mission was to last only one month. After that, the first Orion, with a crew of three, would be launched from Edwards AFB in California for a 3-month stay.

There were four crewmembers on this mission. It was not as many as usually accompanied a Shuttle mission, but one more than normally stayed for a prolonged time in the ISS. The crew consisted of Col Peeters, along with fellow American Lt. Col. Ted Huber, the Flight Engineer. Coming from Russia was Col. Oleg Norkovich, Operation Specialist; and from Poland was Major Ilse Lenowski, the Payload Commander and Mission Specialist. The crew had trained together for two weeks prior to being launched from Cape Canaveral on March 29th.

After the Shuttle docking was successfully completed and the space craft was secured, Col. Peeters called out over the intercom, "Why don't all of us heave to and get all the supplies and equipment off this ship and into the Station. If you're like me, there is so much nervous energy stored up from these last months of training and haggling; I'd like to just get that chore checked off our list. Once we have the Shuttle unloaded, we can then rest and get things sorted out. Do some house cleaning, as it were. Is that ok with everyone?"

In reply, all she heard was a chorus of agreements. "Then I'll go ahead and fire up the electrical system in the Station, tell Houston what we are about, and get some cupboard doors open. I'll work with Oleg in the Station to sort and pack the supplies away. Ilse you unload the payload bay. Ted, you suit up as well, and take what Ilse hands you and place it at the entranceway into the Station. We'll take it from there."

Because both Ilse and Oleg had not been to the Station before, she thought it best to partner each of them with either her or Ted. She had been on two previous missions, and this was Ted's second one. It was understandable that the rookies would want to spend all the spare time they could looking out at the glorious sight of earth passing beneath them.

Their average orbital altitude above the earth was 220 miles, with their perigees and apogees bracketing that distance by 40-45 miles either way. It took the station around 90 minutes to orbit the planet at that distance or they made about 15 revolutions around earth each day. It had always fascinated her that in the course of their journeys they observed 85% of the globe, where 97% of the population lived and worked.

She never tired of looking out the observation windows. They were like a magnet, continually tugging you towards them. Once you could just devote some time photographing and observing, the view was astonishing. The absolute blackness of deep space framed the brilliant blues of the oceans, the oranges, browns, reds, yellows and greens of the landmasses, and the endlessly changing whites of the cloud formations. She always began to feel like a sentinel, the longer she was able to look out. Her desire to protect this world became almost obsessive. In the vastness of the black universe surrounding them, the earth was like a sapphire buried deep in its darkened soil.

Unless they magnified their photographs, the cities had little definition, aside from the pollutants that often streamed from them, marking a hazy current of the prevailing winds. Except at night, then the lights of the cities' boundaries were dazzling. It was as if each city was a beacon, composed of a million lights, grouped together to signal their presence to any cosmic traveler. Moreover, with some magnification, she could see distinct details of any city during daylight. It was almost as if they were flying over it in a commercial airliner. And with the most powerful magnification, as was used with the military observation satellites, they could even see people on the streets and vehicles in motion. It was like she was a distant voyeur, peering into the lives of the planet's inhabitants.

The experiments that they conducted on the ISS were almost of equal fascination to her. They were able to monitor storm development and evolution, erosion, deforestation, effects and presence of atmospheric pollution, population growth and its effects, and water depth, among many others. But all of this daydreaming had to stop for now. They had begun unloading the Shuttle. She hoped it would be fully unloaded by sometime on May 31st.

They worked feverishly, with only short naps to sustain them, and by 2300 hours May 31st, the Endeavor Shuttle crew had completely off-loaded the Shuttle. It was not until after everyone had clambered back over the maze of boxes and crates crammed into the ISS that Amber returned to the Shuttle to power down its internal systems and check to make sure all hatches and doors were secured. It was midnight before each of the crew members had eaten and were ready for some uninterrupted sleep.

Amber's final duty that night was contacting Houston Control to let them know their status and to request that they not disturb her crew with anything that was not urgent for the next 24 hours. They were going to sleep. That was the last message ever sent by the Endeavor. It was also the last peaceful sleep these individuals would ever have.

Come 0800 hours New York City time or 1800 hours London time on April 1st, Amber was at her desk, entering into her logbook what had happened that day. It was basically routine housekeeping duties. The crew had slept, ate and then returned to sleep. The months of travel, training, drills and execution of the blast off had taken its toll of each of them. She was pleased at the way everyone was working as a team, solving problems with easy banter and humor, rather than getting overly excited and anxious. She anticipated this was to be a good mission. But, it was necessary to start having watches. She elected to take the first watch, from 1800 hours until 2400 hours that night, London time. After that, Ted would pull his six hour shift, etc., etc. for each of the crew for the next month. Tonight she would try to put her office area in some order, unpack a few boxes and stow away her books and papers, write a few lines in her personal diary and maybe start taking some photographs.

It was noon in New York City or 2200 hours in London. At that moment, the ISS was flying over the southern Pacific Ocean, within a few minutes of soaring by Santiago, Chile. Amber happened to be floating past one of the observation windows that had a northwesterly view. Suddenly, there was a brilliant, phosphorous-like, lingering flash in the distance. Maneuvering toward the window, concerned it might have been a collision of some kind into the Station or Shuttle; she looked out and saw, instead, that the origin of the light was off in the southeast, where Santiago was located.

Not having had any radio contact with Houston, per her instructions to them, she decided to call them, to report her sighting.

"Houston, this is the ISS calling," she announced. "Do you read me? Over."

But there was no reply.

Again, she repeated. "Houston, this is the ISS calling. I am not receiving you. Do you read me? Over."

In reply, all she heard was static. With repeated attempts, which after checking the communication console for any malfunction and finding none, her recurrent message was becoming more frantic and louder. So much so, that Ted was aroused from his sleep and came floating in to see what was wrong.

"What's happening, Amber?" he asked, almost too casually for her to not react as well, to his seeming nonchalance.

"I can't raise Houston! I've tried repeatedly, but I get only static in return! And I can't find any cause for our equipment to be malfunctioning. Besides, I was able to talk clearly to them last night. We are certainly not in a blind spot, in case one of the relay radio telescopes is off-line. We are almost exactly perpendicular to Houston, as we begin our crossing over South America."

"Let me see if I find anything that might be causing this," Ted replied. But after about ten minutes of crawling in and out of their communication gear, he could not see any loose wiring or find any electrical shorts. All the computer boards were firmly fixed into their slots. The ISS's power load was at a normal level, as was their backup unit. "Maybe it was an atmospheric disturbance of some kind. I can't find any reason either for this problem. Our equipment is in good working condition."

About this time, Ilse and Oleg floated in as well, both aware that something was not right. "Do we have a problem?" Ilse asked, with just a hint of anxiety in her voice.

"It doesn't appear we do here," Amber answered with somewhat less tension in her voice. At least, with Ted checking the equipment, she felt reassured it was not something wrong at their end. "But we are unable to communicate with Houston."

Oleg asked, "Did you notice anything unusual before you attempted your first call?"

"As a matter of fact, I did." Amber answered. "There was a brilliant flash of light in the direction of Santiago. Immediately, it got my attention, and I wanted to report it to Houston."

"Where are we located now?" Ted asked.

"We must be somewhere over central Brazil by now," Amber replied. "In fact the lights of Brasilia should be coming into view right away.

As was later recorded in the Shuttle logbook, it was just at that moment that another brilliant flash occurred in the night sky, coming from the direction of Brazil's capital city. This time three of the four astronauts witnessed it.

"Oh! My God! What was that?!!" Ilse shouted. "That was no lightening strike! There don't appear to be any clouds in the region, if the scattered surface lights we were seeing are any indication. All indications are it's a cloudless night in this region."

Then the logbook showed that a shock wave hit the ISS soon after the flash was seen. And whatever lights there may have been, coming from the large metropolitan area of Brasilia, were extinguished. Because there was to be a full moon on April 2nd, the night sky was already partially lit, enough so that they began to see the shadowy outline of a mushroom cloud rising in the distance over what used to be Brasilia.

"Oh no, that's not what I think it is? It can't be!! It just can't be!!" screamed Ilse.

"Quick, somebody," Amber yelled, "get the camera and take some photos. We must document what that is. I only pray it's not what it looks like. But, combined with the shockwave we just experienced, God forgive us, it looks like a nuclear explosion."

"Do you think that's what you saw happening in Santiago?" Oleg nervously asked. "And do you think it may even have something to do with our not being able to raise Houston?"

"How would we ever know?" Amber answered, trying now to keep her voice in as much control as she could. "But I will keep trying to raise them. We should be out over the mid-Atlantic Ocean soon, and then we'll pass by Lisbon, Portugal and on over the English Channel. That should give us views of London and Paris on the horizon. It will be about 2230 hours their time when we go by. I pray we do not see anything unusual at that time. Maybe there is some explanation for all this that we are missing. Maybe it is local terrorist madness or a renegade military coup d'état."

"While you are doing that, I'll get out all our cameras and have the three of us stationed at each of the observation windows, which should cover the views to the north, south and beneath us," Ted replied.

"And before I have to be stationed at a window, I want to turn on the all-frequency radio to see what messages we may be able to receive from any agency or country," Ilse added.

"I think, with the night we have ahead of us," Oleg sighed, "I will go into the galley and prepare some hot coffee and tea for us. I'm not as alert as I need to be."

"Good ideas, everyone," Amber replied, intermixing her comment between her repeated calls to Houston. But still there was only static in reply.

Fifteen minutes later the ISS was about fifty miles offshore from Lisbon, having passed over the Azores. To the crew's shock and horror, there was a conflagration off to their right side, where Lisbon was located. No sooner had they seen that than they were passing over western France and above the English Channel. It was while there they saw the same sight as with Lisbon and the other cities in South America. London and Paris were on fire. Within minutes the same nightmare was evident as they passed over Stockholm and Oslo. It seemed coastal cities were particular targets. Most disturbing to them, this pattern of coastal destruction appeared to confirm that Houston had probably suffered the same fate.

As they were about to pass over the polar region, Amber spoke, her voice breaking with overwhelming emotion. "Lady and gentlemen, it appears we are witnessing a global war. And we are unable to make contact or hear from anyone. All communication links appear down, for now at least. But we must stay on station. Whatever orders we did have, are now void. It appears we may be on our own.

"That being the case, for the present, I am going to request that each of you gather together pen, pencil, pad and paper, photographic equipment with any magnification adaptors you can attach and observe with, and begin making notes and taking photographs. Let me know what you need, whether it is more film, sunglasses, tablets to write on, or to be spelled for restroom duties. I will circulate to relieve and re-supply you. And call out what you see. Watch overhead and around us. There could be incoming traffic.

"Keep in mind that intercontinental ballistic

missiles, at their mid-flight phase, can be as high as 720 miles above the earth's surface. Moreover, by my rough calculations, there has to be over 1900 land and sea-based missiles scattered over the world, and with each one possibly carrying multiple warheads. In other words, that means there could be a total of over 10,000 detonations possible world-wide, if all of them were launched. We certainly cannot dodge any of these coming our way, but we can try to chronicle their passing by. Note everything you see, feel or photograph. There is nothing more we can do at this time."

"Aye, aye," was all the crew could manage to say. To attempt saying anything more was impossible. Sobbing was heard throughout the ISS cabin as each person assembled the necessary material and equipment and positioned themselves at their various locations.

From that moment on, the ISS crew fought back feelings of terror, panic, anguish, guilt and a mixture of countless others. They each held onto the hope that their families might be spared this madness. And they prayed, almost continuously, and out loud.

Passing over the polar region and the Kara Sea, off the Russian coast, Oleg was able to photograph a missile launch from the coastline. In addition, they noted were several sightings of missile vapor trails through the polar atmosphere. Passing through Russia, they were to observe scatter plumes of black smoke across their horizon. On the right side of the Shuttle the saw what used to be Moscow and Novosibirsk in flames. Further on, they saw that Beijing, Seoul, Kobe, and Kyoto were ablaze, with debris and smoke rising thousands of feet into the atmosphere. Once over Australia, they flew directly over Brisbane, covered in black smoke, as was Sydney in the distance. Finally, before passing over Antarctica, out the left side window, they saw what apparently used to be Wellington.

Their observations, as bewildering and terrifying as they were, confirmed to them that this utter madness was all-encompassing. They knew then that this war was reaching all nations, neutral or not. What may have begun as some terrorists' death wish had morphed into a massive retaliation, motivated by revenge, age-old grudges, border disputes, religious intolerance, and various political ideologies' with long-standing distrust of one another. Once over the Southern Ocean, as they scanned with high-powered optical equipment, Ted even witnessed an ocean- launched missile rise from the water. And there still was no response from Houston.

Their second pass over South America revealed further destruction of the major cities from apparent nuclear attacks. As they passed along the southern into the northern hemispheres, they noted the cities of Buenos Aires, Sao Paulo, Rio de Janeiro, Dakar, Casablanca, Madrid, Lyon, Geneva, Cologne, Rotterdam, Hamburg, Copenhagen, Helsinki and Murmansk were all under attack. Within the two hours since noon, New York City time, or 10 p.m. London time, the major cities of the world were systematically being destroyed.

However, that was not the end of it. Just as the survivors in the Amboy and Yucca Mountain Caverns had felt an earthquake, they thought, at 2 p.m. EST, the Shuttle crew likewise experienced an event of unprecedented magnitude. It was Ted who first noticed the phenomena. Calling out, he alerted the other crew members, "There is something coming towards the earth that is intensely bright and huge! It appears to be coming from the direction of the sun! I think it might….."

And at that instant, the logbook showed, the earth and their space ship was struck by a force of unparalleled strength. Because of its direction and illumination, the ISS crew later theorized it must have been a massive coronal ejection, with its fiery tongue extending through space and striking earth. If there had been any forewarning from NOAA or from scattered Observatories around the globe about its arrival, they never got it. Fortunately, their ship was blocked by 99% of the shock wave, due to their being over the north, polar region at the time of the impact. Otherwise, they would have undoubtedly been struck with such force that whatever was left of the ISS would have tumbled out of control into outer space. As it was, their location immediately changed, they were now approximately 750 miles back to the west, as the rotation of the earth had been altered by the glancing impact.

The impact zone, as they were able to pinpoint with some degree of accuracy later, was in the center of Queen Maud Land, very close to the South Pole of Antarctica. Even with the ISS being shielded by the earth, there was an atmospheric sonic boom-effect, as it were. The supersonic speed of the solar burst created a pressure wave, even in the vacuum of space that surrounded the ISS. Now rather than being over the North Pole after the impact, they were over the sea ice off the Siberian coastline. But there was no surface definition for them to really know exactly where. Between the ash, debris, smoke and fires, all of which had reduced their visibility of earth by the minute, after the solar impact, the water vapor, steam and droplets it caused made their examination of the planet's surface impossible. And it remained so for weeks.

TWO: DISCOVERY AND DECISIONS

Two months passed before the surface of the
planet was clear enough to make any definitive
observations of what had occurred on April 1st. This
delay was a source of great frustration and anxiety for
the ISS crew, as was the not knowing what might have
happened to their loved ones. All this is clearly stated in
the diaries that each one kept from that day forward.

Also clear, from their daily notations, was their
dedication to keeping records of whatever they saw, felt,
did or heard. Each one sensed that what they witnessed
may have been exclusively theirs to see. Drawing on
their individual spiritual, patriotic and/or humanitarian
motivations, each diary had a unique perspective and
voice. They were to become treasured archives in the
years to come.

Amber persisted, as did each crew member
during their assigned shifts, in trying to make radio
contact with Houston or anyone. They began to assume
the ground based microwave radio relays were damaged
or destroyed during this same period. Their S-band on
the ISS's radio spectrum remained deafeningly silent for
any human response to their calls. It was assumed the
orbiting relay satellites, some 18,000 nautical miles
above the earth, were still undamaged, but for their

purposes, they were useless. Their only hope, it seemed, was to leave their radio on continuously as they passed over any land mass, in hopes someone may be sending a message on their particular wave length.

Relieved, but with intense fear and a sense of impending doom, they charted their course to orbit across America., starting from the southern California coastline where Vandenberg AFB was located and migrating eastward with each passing orbit, until they passed over Houston, and ultimately, over Cape Canaveral. Their redirected orbits began over Polynesia in the southern Pacific Ocean, heading directly where they thought Vandenberg should be. But, passing over Vandenberg, all they saw was water.

The California shoreline, now that they could clearly observe the earth's surface, was altered. There appeared to be no cities or level land observable, fronting the ocean. The waterline now abutted the Sierra Madre and San Gabriel Mountains. From this first flyover it appeared that from the city of Santa Barbara, extending south and far into the Los Angeles Basin, all habitable land was now under water.

With each successive flyover, as they orbited eastward across the North American continent, there were staggering sights. The Sea of Cortez and the Gulf of Mexico extended far inland. Large inland cities, except for Las Vegas, had essentially disappeared. This included Salt Lake City, Boise, Colorado Springs, Denver, Calgary, Edmonton, Omaha, Kansas City, Regina, and Winnipeg. In addition, they saw the same destruction of military installations, major hubs of commerce and key industrial sites in scattered locations. Gulf Coast cities, like Houston, New Orleans and Gulfport had disappeared, whether due to nuclear detonation and/or flooding. The water line in the middle of the country extended up the rivers that fed the Gulf, extending as far as Bryan, Huntsville and Lufkin in Texas. Almost the entire states of Louisiana, Mississippi, Arkansas, Tennessee, Missouri, Illinois and Iowa had become inundated by an inland sea. And finally, on their last orbit before crossing the Atlantic Ocean, the same condition was found for Miami, Cape Canaveral, Charleston, Norfolk, Washington, D.C., Philadelphia, Baltimore, New York City and Boston. They were all gone.

They also noted signs, particularly along the eastern seaboard, of a massive tidal wave, with its accompanying mammoth piles of debris, scattered far inland. They were like giant levees, often 100 feet high, stretching horizon to horizon. All this was well beyond the present shoreline, which in itself appeared to be sometimes hundreds of miles beyond what used to be normal. It indicated that a massive tsunami had struck sometime recently. There was no way they could measure water depth due to the turbidity of the water. Nor was there any way to determine how high the ocean's water level had risen, but it was horribly clear that a massive ice melt off had occurred.

When, some weeks later, they passed over what used to be the South Pole region of Antarctica, it became evident what created the tidal waves and the high water level worldwide. There was no ice left on Antarctica. It was now a continent of exposed barren rock.

The solar impact that Ted witnessed had altered the water table and the earth's axis, shifting the North and South poles over 700 miles. They were now seeing many more active volcanoes as they passed over the Pacific Ocean's "ring of fire" and the Indonesian Archipelago. Agonizingly, if not beyond what any human could bear witnessing, throughout all these indescribable events and with all their efforts to magnify and photograph the surface of the planet, they saw no sign of human activity or movement. All life on earth, it appeared, was being threatened with extinction.

Attempting to cope with the shock of all these findings and observations, along with their continually taking photographs and making notations, they still attempted to make radio contact with anyone. It was only by the ISS crew staying occupied, that they could survive the carnage being witnessed below them. At one point, a few weeks after April 1st, they did take time to discuss and plan how to extend their food and water rations for what lay ahead. However, by June 2nd, it was clear to Amber they had to set aside considerable time to discuss their options for returning to earth.

She opened the meeting that day with a few comments, summarizing their situation. "Folks, it's clear to me we're now completely on our own. We've had no communication link established with anyone for the last two months. Furthermore, we've not seen any signs of life. I can only guess that if there are any survivors, they have gone underground, hiding somewhere away from ancient flood plains due to the vastly altered oceans' shorelines and far from the resurgent volcanic eruptions. Equally disturbing, beyond those staggering obstacles, any survivors, wherever they are, would have to have access to provisions, enough to sustain them for an extended period.

"We're witnessing the earth and its atmosphere having convulsions. And we can only assume this will be ongoing for an indefinite period of time. However, we don't have an unlimited amount of time to stay out here in space. And that's why I felt it necessary to call us all together here today.

"Our grief is, and it shall always remain, inconsolable. Likewise, that will probably be the case for our anger. All because of the utter madness that led to this fiery holocaust we witnessed below us. Then there was the apparent randomness of the universe's physical behavior that singled out earth as the destination for this solar eruption. We've witnessed both a human caused devaluing of any life and a possible, life-ending cosmic event, both of which lie far beyond the realm of human experience or adaptation. Combining these two destructive events, we're now desperately vulnerable, with little to comfort us but our anger, intermixed with our deepest fears and insecurities, and maybe for some of you, your shaken faith.

"Our psyches are like a blender of emotions, different ones sweeping up to the top of our consciousness at any given moment. And somewhere in all this, some of us try to cling to a hope or a prayer that will sustain us. Frankly, my well of faith is pretty dry right now. I say this because since April 1st, we've had no time to just be still long enough to share our thoughts and feelings. But probably that was for the best. With something so terrifying being witnessed, none of us had the emotional reserve to cope with trying to sustain each other. Our sanities were stretched thin, like a strand in a spider's web. We've all touched our breaking point, I know. And I sincerely thank you for not letting that one final filament snap.

"What comforts me, in the smallest, life-sustaining way, is the idea that somewhere there must be other survivors. And what is beginning to drive me is that we must somehow make contact with them or somehow, at the least, find a way to share the information we are gathering. The only urge I possess now, aside from a forlorn and desperate one to see my family, is to shout out to the entire universe that our humanity does matter. That we deserve to live and love and hope for a better life. That we cannot let evil or the ice coldness of the universe's whims destroy us. I, for one, want to go on. We have been documenting, possibly, humanity's last days; or, just maybe, its start of a new beginning. Unfortunately, I'm unsure we'll ever know which it will be. But I want this material we've been collecting to be available to whoever may survive.

"Moreover, at this point, I think it appropriate to announce that I no longer am a Colonel in the United States Air Force. I am now simply a citizen of a battered planet. Understandably, we've been informal with rank here in the Station. But now, I'm making this announcement my last official act. I no longer have any rank or title. Further, I'd suggest if you'd like or feel the need to, we can designate someone as the coordinator of our group. But I'd recommend we cease all military formalities. It's a waste of time. But now it's your turn to speak."

Ted, being the more animated of the four, at her invitation, quickly interjected, "I couldn't agree with you more. We must see each other as equals now and also try to compose ourselves. Whatever future we have left, and it could be short, given our options and risks of reentry and landing this Shuttle, we need the fullest trust and faith in each other. We are no longer an internationally appointed contingent of astronauts. We are now part of this planet's last inhabitants. Our duty as its citizens at this point is to get this information we've gathered to others like us."

"I agree," Ilse added, not waiting for a gesture for anyone else to speak. "Seeing the cascading destruction across our world and the loss of Warsaw and my beloved family living there, has been so emotionally and physically debilitating. But I know we must go on. After all, that does appear to be the underlying theme of all life: to go on as long as it is yours to possess. For me to try making sense of these last two months is impossible. Like you, Amber, I am so angry that this came about as it did. That humanity had so little wisdom or self-control, that it had such a homicidal sense of its own self-importance and self-righteousness, that so many had such a maniacal sense of absolute right that total destruction was a worthy goal.

"I don't think I've ever held a belief in there being a heaven. And if I could pray at this time, it would be that all those who created the environment that allowed this tragedy to happen and all those who planned and executed it would be denied any access to any form of existence after their deaths, other than one in an ever-lasting hell. It is a source of great distress to me to think that the instigators of this human-caused destruction might still be alive and burrowed away in some mountain hide out, waiting for the smoke to clear and emerge from their hellish dens to claim this world as theirs.

"Without a doubt, I think we must pursue a plan to survive our time here in space and then attempt to safely land this Shuttle. I desperately want to share what we've witnessed. The lessons it will teach those who follow us are endless. And finally, I would nominate you, Amber, as our coordinator. My reasons for doing so are because you have landed a Shuttle once already, and you've had to make preparations to do so twice."

"I concur," Oleg offered in agreement. "We need to respect our individual gifts and talents, but rank and nationality have no meaning now. My vote is for Amber to coordinate us, once we've organized a plan.

"On that point," he continued, "I would suggest we try to stay in space for at least four more months. It appears we've been able to stretch our food supplies out enough so that we could possibly stay that long and still have enough for 1-2 months, once we have landed. I'd suggest we aim for October 1st as our landing date. By then the atmosphere would be somewhat more hospitable, depending on where we can land."

"That's a good idea!" Ted interrupted. "Landing is now a pivotal issue. Where exactly? To my knowledge there were only four designated landing sites for the Shuttle: Cape Canaveral, Vandenberg AFB, Edwards AFB and White Sands Proving Grounds in New Mexico. It should be pretty clear to all of us that three of those sites are either destroyed or are under water. We only have White Sands as our remaining choice. And, honestly, I'm not sure if it has ever been used as such."

"No," Amber admitted. "At least not since the Shuttles have been doing orbital missions. There may have been a suborbital landing there once. I just don't remember. But, in any case, you're right. It is the one strip left that offers us a relatively safe landing site.

"We need to see if Holloman AFB was attacked when we pass over that area. While it's true its location is about 250 miles south of Los Alamos, which we know was destroyed; we have no information to go on from the southern part of New Mexico. I would hope any lingering radioactivity in the region would have dissipated by October 1st. We'll need that drop in radiation to occur for us to have a safe exit from the Shuttle after we have landed. Moreover, as a plus, I think the Carlsbad Caverns are located in that general vicinity, which, if we survive the landing and need shelter, it could offer us some protection for a while."

To that, everyone nodded in agreement.

The next four months were a mixture of preparations, projections, computations, securely packing their recordings and observations and extra supplies, loading the payload bay of the Shuttle, and continuing to make observations and notations of the earth's surface. During this period they did confirm that Holloman AFB was spared an attack, but there were signs of destruction elsewhere out of that immediate area.

What was alarming, to the point that it became unnerving during this same period, was the persistent radio silence. Despite there being no radio signals, their plans for leaving the ISS went ahead as they had voted. Their daily routine was purposeful and left little time to mourn or brood. It was a steely determination that drove them. And underlying it all was a seething anger.

It was into this atmosphere, on the eve of their departure from the Station that an event occurred that would possibly never have been known about, except for the in-cabin video camera. The crew had been recording their activities, non-stop, of their final days on the Shuttle, to be used later as an historic record.

There suddenly appeared a formless figure, as they were all taking a late afternoon mealtime break, their second and last meal for the day at the far end of their command module. And similar to what had happened with the Amboy and Yucca Mountain families, each astronaut glanced spontaneously at each other for confirmation of this apparition being present in their midst. Once it was confirmed that what there were seeing was real, their most silent and haunting fears rose to the surface, and each person in turn gasped, moaned, cried out and/or muttered an oath or prayer.

The figure spoke first. "Try to calm yourselves. I mean you no harm."

Thinking the figure might have been a stowaway, Amber gasped, "have you been on board since our launch from Cape Canaveral? Were you on board before we arrived to launch? My God, how long have you been here on this Station?"

"I just came here, at this very moment," the form answered.

"That can't be!" Ted challenged. "You can't

599

just appear suddenly, right before our eyes! It can't happen! This can't be happening to us!"

Oleg then reacted, reaching for something to protect him and the others, announcing "I will not let you hurt us, without a fight."

"Please," the visitor said again. "My sudden appearance is not a magic trick, nor is it a menacing act of some kind. Please let me explain."

To that response, Ilse then asked, "Are you God?"

Reacting to her question, each of the crew first looked at her in shock for asking such a question, and then twisted their heads around and stared at the shadowy form before them. By now all their eyes and mouths were wide open in stunned and transfixed disbelief. None of them could even take a breath at that moment.

"The people in the Amboy and Yucca Mountain Caverns call me B," the shadow at the end of the module replied.

"Where are these places and who are these people?" Amber asked, in a muted stutter.

"And why do they call you B?" Ted quickly added.

"It was due to the individual I first contacted, regarding what might happen on April 1st, who brought that about. Not knowing any details about me at that time or about what was possibly going to occur, along with being somewhat bewildered, he said something 'big' was apparently going to happen when I appeared to recruit him. I took the name B for 'big', in hopes of saving time by avoiding lengthy explanations.

"Amboy Cavern is in the eastern Mojave Desert of California, and Yucca Mountain Cavern is north of Las Vegas. There are two separate bands of survivors in each of these locations. Up to this time they have managed to stay alive through all you have seen in its entirety over these past months. I have appeared before them as well to help direct their course of possible survival. And I have imparted to them certain calming effects, along with some ability to interact more easily amongst themselves."

"Did you actually warn them beforehand what was to happen on April 1ˢᵗ?" Ted asked, with the volume in his voice rising.

"Yes, and certain ones were even preselected, based on their skills, experience and knowledge," B answered.

"You foretold this awful tragedy and then cherry picked the ones who survived!" Oleg exclaimed.

"Who else did you warn?" Amber asked, her own voice now displaying a hint of challenge.

"No one." B replied.

"Why?" was the automatic reaction, expressed simultaneously, by the stunned crew.

"There was not time. Plus, to do so would have endangered the ongoing plans to at least try and save a few. I had an awareness that something awful was about to happen and a possible timeline, but I hoped to divert its likelihood. Initially, a plan was instituted to avoid the human- initiated horror of that day, but it failed. And by that time, if a wider number had been informed, chaos and panic would have doomed even these two groups. Any survival thereafter would have been random and probably short term.," B explained.

"But why them?" Amber pressed.

"Because they embodied what had been accomplished by your civilization. A record, if nothing else, had to be set aside. My hope, as well, was that some individuals or families might survive, but there were, and still are, no guarantees anyone would or will."

"What about us?" Ilse countered. "We have

601

survived, at least to now. Or did you know about us and have just waited until now to appear? In other words, is our long term survival unlikely?"

"Yes, I knew about your presence here. And no, I don't know definitely what your chances are for long term survival."

"Hold on!" Amber exclaimed, now with distinct defiance in her voice. "We've been witnessing the total destruction of our homes, our countries, and our planet and somehow you've known this was going to happen. You've set aside some selected individuals, ignoring billions of others, watching us or known about us, in total anguish, recording this planetary slaughter; and you stood back, or whatever you do, and just watched!!! Who, exactly, are you? What is this really all about? If your appearance here signals what I am thinking it does, we're most likely not a part of your survival scenario. We're expendable. We, at the very least, in behalf of all doomed humanity below us, deserve some answers, if not from you, then from someone who sent you."

"It would be me who would provide the answers," B replied. "It is, after all, all my creation. You see, the 'B' could more precisely be in reference to my being 'The Beginning', the originator of it all; or what some have called, the 'Creator'. Despite all the theorizing, mathematics, cosmological conjecturing about the universe(s) origin and evolution, there still had to be that initial spark, that thought, that urge to start it all on its course. That was me. It began with me.

"Energy, space, time, and eventually matter, shaped the rest. That is up until the point that life emerged. Life was as much a wonder to me as it is to you. But nowhere, in all the masses of stars, galaxies or universes, is the variety and beauty of life as on as grand a scale as here. It was an unparalleled garden of life, not found anywhere else. And over time, with a little coaxing from me, life began to incorporate a consciousness, self-awareness and the ability to communicate. Into it I blew the whisper of the individual soul, an eternal part of me. It was my second act of creation, my second beginning, as it were. Then, I made my most daring decision of all; I gave that individual soul free will."

"That's all well and good, if it's as you say it is. There is no way I or anyone else could prove otherwise." Amber pressed, but now with rising anger in her voice. Then she challenged, "But how could you let this wanton destruction occur? If it is all so special to you, how could you let so many just pass away, dying the most horrible of deaths? Was it some kind of chess game, like something out of the Book of Job? Are we just puppets to be manipulated? Did you tire of us? How could you?" She finally wept, letting the enormity of everything sweep over her.

Visibly taken aback by Amber's outburst, B was transfixed for a few moments. "I can understand your anger and desire to want to blame something or someone," B began. "But now you must listen carefully to my words, for I too, have felt anger, immeasurable sorrow and grief since April 1st.

"Your civilization has been stalled in a spiritual adolescence for centuries. Certainly, there has been intellectual and physical progress. Your being in this space station testifies to your intellectual capabilities. And your Olympic Games attest to your progressively stronger, quicker and more agile bodies. But the countless millions, now into the billions, of lives lost due to wars, terrorist acts, tribal grudges, crime, anger and lust demonstrates, collectively, how immature spiritually you have been.

"No more. Not again. This is your fellow inhabitants' last chance, your last ark. In the first recording of an ark it was written that I directed the ark's building and caused the flood. Then afterward, I vowed never to do so again. I have let that stand, as it has been told for so long. It matters less and less now what actually happened. Be that as it may, I had no hand in the events of April 1st. Indeed, I hoped to avoid the human aspect of it. But do not misunderstand me now. I will not be the cause of the final chapter of humanity's demise, but I can sure allow it to proceed unimpeded.

"Setting this world aside for the plants, sea and land animal life, excluding humans, would not be hard to do, if humanity persists in its self-destructive patterns.

"Get it right! Put aside your anger! Find peace and satisfaction in the beauty around you. I do not insist that you worship me. How could I? You have been given free will. But my last hope for you is that you will understand worshipping a source of infinite love, beyond yourselves, will give you the strength and direction to control and conquer the baseness and coarseness of your destructive natures. It is not unlike your own hopes and prayers, through the centuries, for eternal life beyond your deaths. I have heard those prayers, and it is so. Now you must apply that same intensity of hope and prayer to overcoming the indwelling darkness inside you.

"Humility is the grandest of human virtues. It signals someone has recognized the limits of their abilities and aspirations, and that they need to find an outside source to comfort and direct them. It means someone has 'hit their psychological and spiritual wall'. Willful use of one's free will contaminates and destroys humility. And it will eventually lead to self-destruction. Faith, hope and charity are cardinal virtues in themselves, but making all that possible is having humility.

"Furthermore, it is having this humility that

allows me to speak to your souls, so often deeply hidden inside each of you. It is through your soul that I can communicate. That communication is not about war, lust, conquest or revenge. Instead, it is a conversation between you and me about creating beauty, loving, nurturing and understanding. These are the things you do best, when you are at your best.

"Be thankful, but be warned. Be relieved, but be assured. Be calmed, but be ever-alert and watchful. You are your own worst enemies. And total extinction awaits all of you unless you can grasp these truths about living your lives day-to-day.

"I have listened to and felt your anger. I have heard and felt your cries and sadness. And I, too, have been astonished and filled with the greatest sorrow by these human and cosmic disasters. One series of events on April 1st could have been avoided. The other could not. Life has few guarantees. I can offer you only two. Live your lives as I have instructed, as you should, and you will see everlasting beauty around you, even unto and beyond your deaths. Failing that and do the opposite, ignoring the things I have told you, and your world will not hear the footsteps of humanity again. There will be no more arks."

The silence that followed B's response to Amber's challenge was one only the vacuum of outer space could provide. And even this silence was still being recorded on the video camera. The figure at the end of the module remained motionless and featureless. The four crew members were frozen in different poses. One with head bowed, one looking wistfully out the window at the planet's surface as they passed over, one continually rubbing his downcast forehead back and forth, and Amber who just stared straight ahead at the shadowy form.

In a voice that was halting and octaves lower

than before, Amber finally asked, "so, then, on a much more personal level, what do you suggest or request that we do now? And, if I may be so bold, what do you plan to do now? Is there anything you could do that might give each of us some measure of peace, given what we've observed these past months and what you imply the near future may hold for us? You know that I have not been a faithful follower of a traditional faith, as uncomfortable as it makes me to say so at this moment. If anything, science has been my refuge. But, in behalf of myself, and the crew, I'd ask you to excuse our outbursts earlier and help us to deal with a reality and mission that has become too overwhelming. I honestly feel that at this moment I could lose complete control of my emotions" And saying so, she began to sob uncontrollably.

Realizing the message was spoken out of terrible disappointment and inconsolable loss, B wearily came forward toward the crew. The words just spoken gave definition to a finality and were awesome in impact, but this was not the appropriate audience for such. They had deserved better. With heads bowed, hiding their faces, B knew they were feeling deepest despair and anguish. Effortlessly, B's shroud, taking the shape of wings as it was spread out, was gently laid over the crew. In so doing, its contact infused each of the crew with reassuring peace and calm. And while doing so, B again spoke.

"Blessed are the poor in spirit: for theirs is the kingdom of heaven. Blessed are they that mourn: for they shall be comforted. Blessed are the meek: for they shall inherit the earth. Blessed are they which do hunger and thirst after righteousness: for they shall be filled. Blessed are the merciful: for they shall obtain mercy. And, dear ones assembled here at this moment with me, blessed are the pure in heart: for they shall see God. And so you have."

Saying this, B turned while still enveloping the four sitting figures, looked long and lovingly at the long-ago, now forlorn Eden passing by below and wept.

THREE: SHUTTLE REENTRY AND LANDING

The Shuttle crew, in later recounting what actually had happened during B's appearance, each separately recorded in their diaries that none could accurately recall how long they were covered with B's shroud or how much longer B stayed with them. All they could remember, following B's final words to them, was that their feelings of anger, despair and fear were gone. Their grief for the loss of life, be it family, friends, fellow countrymen or throughout the planet, remained. Amazingly, they now had the strength and indescribable will to go on. Despair was replaced with an indwelling reassurance, equally indefinable, that they were to be ok with what lay ahead for them. How and in what manner was beyond their ability to describe, but they had been given the renewed resolve and focus for what remained of their mission.

Come October 1st, the Shuttle payload bay was stacked with their food supplies, personal diaries, charts, maps, a full record of what they saw and felt from April 1st to September 30th on board the ISS, and the hundreds of photographs of earth taken during this timeframe. And the most precious cargo of all, with its additional protective wrapping against radiation of any kind, was the video tape recording of B's appearance in the command module four months ago. The crew had replayed it many times since then, including the moments B came forward to cover them and spoke the final benediction over them. The recording ended soon after that, again leaving unanswered how long B actually stayed there or how long they were in that bowed position.

The last minute details, prior to their separation from the ISS, included Amber leaving a hand written message in the command module. She placed it on the neatly rearranged operation center desk. It simply said:

"The 21st Shuttle Expedition crew departed on 1 October 2011 at 1100 hours, for our return to earth. Our destination is the White Sands Proving Grounds landing site. There are no other landing sites available to us. We pray God's grace and mercy on any and all who may find this message. This is to be the final Shuttle Expedition.
Signed:
Amber Peeters and Crew"

Oleg secured the Shuttle door leading to the ISS and then took his seat next to Ilse. Amber and Ted began the countdown sequence, and once again quickly reviewed their flight path coordinates. The Shuttle's prolonged time in space no doubt had stressed the tile shields on its underbelly, but they had to proceed in the hope that their reentry into earth's atmosphere and the landing would be successful.

Once free from the ISS, they maneuvered into the flight path they had preprogrammed into their onboard computer. It was programmed to bring them in over the mid-Pacific Ocean, almost as low as it would have been if they were landing at Edwards AFB in California. Not having Houston's cadre of engineers to rely on, they knew all too well there were no second chances with their dead stick landing at White Sands, New Mexico.

Their preliminary photographs of White Sands appeared to indicate that the landing strip there was intact, and yet they knew sand, sagebrush and debris would no doubt be likely hazards, ones they could not avoid. The plan was to have all external engines shut down, as usual, before the landing started. In addition, they would initiate shutting down as many internal systems, as well, just at touchdown, all in hopes of lessening the fire dangers. They already knew any onboard fuel was essentially exhausted. Their hope and prayers were that striking some object would not send them cart-wheeling down the runway, once they touched down.

As they swept in over Arizona, their flight path lowered well into earth's atmosphere over Albuquerque. It was then they started their southerly turn and circled over Roswell and Artesia, to approach the landing strip from the south, just north of the Army's Fort Bliss. By doing so, they did not see the area in and around Ruidoso, New Mexico, having made a wide circle around it. It had been decimated by a nuclear missile that was targeted for Holloman AFB instead. The missile was in mid-flight when the solar burst struck earth, shifting the planet's axis and scrambling the missile's coordinates. It struck near Ruidoso instead.

The landing itself was flawless. The runway was not. The crew had tried to envision and plan for the hazards and obstacles facing them in this daring and highly unlikely, successful reentry, but upon seeing the scattered debris and drifted sand covering the runway just at touchdown, it was Ted who called out, "Hold on everyone! This is going to be a rough landing!"

PART II

FOUR: JANUARY 1ST, 2012

As more and more people looked up and saw Clem, with Jake, running and twisting his way down the snowy hillside towards them, pointing to the north as he ran, they started turning their heads to see what was happening. Nothing immediately caught their attention. It was only those at the outer southern and eastern edge of the level area outside Cave #1's opening that could see something moving through the snow towards them. Eventually, a drab green vehicle could definitely be seen.

Breathless when he reached the base of the hillside, Clem leaned forward, hands on his thighs, heavily panting but still trying to maintain his gaze up the snow-covered mountainside road into their compound. Conversations and excited laughter ceased, as people began to join the growing number who turned to watch the arrival. Not knowing what happened to the Yucca Mountain families, this approaching visitor was an unknown. Fear and curiosity swirled throughout the throng.

Soon the work detail outside Cave #4 also became curious as to what everyone was stopping to watch. Their work began at 7:30 a.m. when the outside doors of Caves #1 and #4 opened for everyone to finally emerge. Even though they had the solemn duty of removing the five remains placed outside Cave #4 in July and then preparing a temporary gravesite alongside Cynthia Garr's grave, they could not help but stop and stare.

Even the children, who had finally been able to take the animals and pets outside for the first time, came to a complete stop. The animals seemed to sense the tenseness of their handlers and remained docile. Likewise, the children assigned to moving the filled dumpsters, ones which had been rolled outside Cave #4 during their confinement, were unable to continue their work.

Word soon got around, into and throughout the cavern, and by the time Ben and his party drove to the northern edge of the outdoor assembly area; all 941 survivors were standing there, transfixed at the site. (Aside: while there were the five tragic deaths in July; there were also five live births that Ian and Minor delivered during the confinement.)

Inside the humvee, the excitement that Ben, Lilyanne and Ernie were feeling became almost intolerable. Besides the rising thrill of being able to meet, and eventually unite, with the Amboy families, the snow pack over the Providence Mountains had made their trip hazardous and difficult. Unbeknownst to them, the heavy snow was another sign that a major shift in the normal amount of precipitation was occurring. There was still nearly a foot of snow on the ground even when they reached the level area in front of the Amboy Cavern. The day, however, was gloriously clear and dry, with brilliant sunshine. But it was extremely cold.

Honking the horn and waving wildly out their windows, they pulled up to the front edge of the crowd at 1 p.m. Clem, with Jake at his heels, had managed to wind his way through the crowd, many of whom were reluctant to be too near these potentially, unwelcome intruders. As the humvee stopped and Ben turned off the engine, he quickly opened his door and stepped out.

As he did, Clem, yelled out, "Ben, you folks made it!! Hey, everyone, it's the Yucca Mountain crew!! They're here!! They made it!!"

Ben, in turn, called out, "Hey, there Clem. It's such a relief to see you and all these faces."

As these two were exchanging greetings, Lilyanne and Ernie were being mobbed by the crowd. It was like the most joyous family reunion. To realize someone else had survived these last months was emotionally overwhelming to many. Everyone wanted their turn to touch and to meet the new arrivals.

At last Eric was able to make his way through the tightened mass and reach Ben. "How many are there of you? Did others survive? Are you ok?"

"We're fine. And there are 1014 of us. All but the three of us are camped out at the Kelso Railroad Station, on the other side of these mountains." Ben answered.

"Thank God," Eric cried. "What a feat! It must have been so difficult. We've been sick with worry, not being able to contact you. We had no idea what had happened to you. And it was especially concerning when our transmissions to each other ended about the time of another huge earthquake. We, honestly, feared the worst."

"It was a close call," Ben admitted. "And to this day, I'm not sure how we made it out of there; and all of us at that. We left Yucca Mountain with our three, fully loaded trains, sometime around December 16th, and got into Kelso on December 30th. I'll brief you on the details of the trip later. What we discovered along the way was beyond belief. Fortunately, we did find eight survivors along the way. But that was all." he said, shaking his head.

"You mean there was no one else alive?!!" Eric replied, aghast and astonished at what that meant.

"None that we saw or heard. And the ones we did find had the good fortune to be in a three-level basement with access to adequate supplies." Eric added.

"What caused you to have to leave so unexpectedly?" Eric asked, attempting to recover somewhat from such devastating news but still eager to get additional news about their trip.

"We had to leave sooner than we planned because Yucca Mountain, itself, became the center of a volcanic eruption, and a major one at that."

"Oh, Lord. What is that all about?" Eric stammered.

"I certainly don't know, and no one else in our group has any idea why it occurred," Ben continued. "But from all we've witnessed since then, we've concluded that both our climate and our earthly foundation are fluctuating unpredictably."

Fred Wailand had been able to maneuver himself next to the humvee and later recorded this greeting and conversation. And it was just as this conversation paused that a sudden gasping cry arose from the western edge of the crowd. Everyone, including the newcomers, turned to look in that direction. And on the hillside, about twenty feet above the level ground, there had suddenly appeared a formless figure. It was B's second appearance that day in the area. The first appearance was at 9 a.m., to deliver the same message this gathering was about to hear, to the Kelso families.

"Let me first say," B began, "how good it is to see all of you standing here today. My faith in you and in your abilities to adapt, adjust and devise ways to build, teach, heal and travel in the most adverse circumstances are a great relief to me. Your cooperation, loving and honoring each other also gives me renewed hope for your futures.

"But, once again, I must urge you on. The earthquakes and volcano you have felt and seen represent what is occurring world-wide. They are the result of an event the likes of which could not have been foretold. Your earth was struck by a fiery burst from the sun. It occurred in the midst of the raging war on April 1st. And because of the heat and force of that impact, significant and premature continental changes have been set in motion. They have resulted in massive earthquakes and volcanic eruptions.

"Sadly, you must leave this area within the next 30 days. Take everything you possibly can with you. Go east, at least as far as the nearby river. Do not build permanent shelters yet, but anchor your temporary homes the best you can, once you are relocated. Do not leave anything behind here that you plan to use later. I cannot tell you any exact date this disturbance will occur, because it is a geological event. But take heart. You are soon to be rebuilding your permanent home site. These repeated evacuations will soon be over. My hope now is that this will be your last desperate move. But move you must. This area will be transformed by what is about to happen.

"I know each of you have many questions to ask me. The time for questions and answers will come, I promise. Finish this last major move, and we will sit together in peace and calm one day. Again, I promise you that."

Upon saying this, B was gone, leaving a pall of shock and stunned disbelief throughout the families. At that moment, Eric and Ben looked at each other in puzzled amazement. It was a look of 'will this ever end for us?' coupled with 'how much more can we ask of these families?' Realizing that time was a critical factor, at this moment, to avoid the onset of panic or backlash, Ben looked at Eric and asked, "Do you mind if I say a few words to your families?"

"Be my guest," Eric replied. "For the moment I am speechless."

Climbing up on the top of their recently arrived humvee, Ben called out to the crowd, taking small, circling steps on top of the vehicle, as he did. "Ladies, gentlemen, young adults and all the children of Amboy Cavern, my colleagues and I are here to bring you greetings from all our families, recently arrived in Kelso from the Yucca Mountain Cavern. I am pleased to tell you we have a total of 1014 individuals who made it to Kelso. Before April 1st, we started out with 1000. We had six live births while in confinement and rescued eight other individuals en route to Kelso. We had no fatalities during our stay in Yucca Mountain.

"I tell you this because you need to know, at this most disappointing moment, that all of us are going to make it! We are making it! Amongst us all, we have the skills, determination, wisdom and loving devotion to overcome even this last obstacle B warned us of today. Remember the untold hardships the early settlers had traveling across the prairies and mountain ranges to establish their new homes in the western United States. We, too, are pioneers. However, this time we are heading east. We will have a better life. We will make it so.

"We had no intention of staying here in Amboy or Kelso anyway. All our rebuilding plans, once confinement was over, were to move further east. I guess you could say nothing really has changed. It's just that now we have added incentive to do so a little sooner and quicker than we would have.

"Our trains are still fully loaded, and we will provide you all the people you need to evacuate your supplies and equipment from here. There is no need to panic or despair. Those of us who just arrived here today from Kelso will meet with Eric and your leadership group immediately. They should be able to give you a detailed outline, within the next few hours, of what needs to be done to accomplish this evacuation

"And if I may, I might suggest we all get inside your shelter, out of this cold. If it's ok with Eric and your staff, why don't you plan on meeting again in your General Assembly Auditorium in three hours for our report. Is that ok Eric?"

Eric just nodded, still appearing somewhat dazed, but with a slight grin forming on his weary face.

"That's it then. Please, everyone meet back together at 4 p.m. in the Auditorium." Saying that, Ben climbed down off the humvee and escorted Lilyanne and Ernie, along with Eric, back through Cave #1's doorway into Amboy Cavern.

FIVE: THE FINAL MOVE

Glancing at Freda, Fred Wailand said, "This has to be our final move. We cannot keep up this pace of urgency and relocation. Look what those poor families from Yucca Mountain have been through already."

"I know," Freda replied. "Morale will sink to a desperate low, unless something positive and energizing is not held out this time. The losses have begun to tell on each of us. Where do you think we'll go to?"

"I don't think anyone really knows," Fred answered. "My guess is that it has to be relatively close by. But it still has to have the potential to protect and sustain us. I'd better go with Ben and Eric into this meeting and start recording what's in store for us. Tell Bernice and Megan that I'll meet you in three hours by the Auditorium's entrance."

"Take good notes," Freda advised. "We all need to know exactly what to expect."

And with a warm embrace, Fred hurried off, also entering Cave #1's portal, immediately behind Ben, Lilyanne, Ernie and Eric. Following them, the members of the Governing Body filed in one-by-one. No one looked eager. It was not a promising prelude to this most important meeting.

The next three hours were filled with heated discussions and arguments about how best to proceed.

Tempers and nerves were obviously frayed. Fred's notes of this meeting and the next month's activities were to become a vital historical record. From that record the following outline of what needed to be accomplished was developed. For detailed descriptions the reader will have to contact the Global Union's Archivist at the Library of the Union in Resolve.

The Global Union representatives, both the Yucca Mountain and the Amboy Caverns', first objective was for the Reconnaissance Teams to leave immediately to explore and select a suitable area for everyone's relocation. Alfie Shoemaker, accompanied by his five personnel from Nellis AFB, along with Pete Mendoza's three teams of five members each, was to investigate four possible sites. Alfie would take his group to the Walter's Ranch/Needles area. Pete would take one team to the Davis Dam area, along the Colorado River, which would include the towns of Laughlin and Bullhead City. The other two teams, led by Jeb Hearn and Adele Franks, were to go to the Lake Havasu City and Parker Dam areas, respectively. Each team was to be accompanied by a geologist or agriculturalist.

Due to the urgency of their missions, the teams quickly prepared, servicing their humvees, loading cans of extra fuel and food supplies for four days and leaving from the Amboy Cavern at 7 a.m. on January 3rd. Prior to their departure Ben had warned them that there would be stranded vehicles on the roadways. He tried to avoid being graphic in his descriptions, but his message was clear. Fortunately, very few vehicles either had to be avoided or even appeared to have occupants in them. The main flow of traffic out of the metropolitan areas of southern California seemed to have concentrated on Interstates 15 and 10, not I-40, the highway they were using.

After a thorough study of local maps, the teams

decided they could travel by convoy along the existing roads from the Amboy Cavern, once Alfie's team arrived from Kelso. Traveling on I-40 for 15-20 miles, Pete's team separated from the convoy on Exit 133 at Ibis, heading north on Hwy 95. Alfie's team exited just past the foothills of Dead Mountains, traveling overland to the Walter's Ranch area. It was about eight miles west of Needles, where the railroad tracks crossed under the Interstate. The other two teams planned to exit on Hwy 95 south, just east of Needles and travel straight to Lake Havasu City and Parker.

After these investigative teams separated, what each group discovered was startling. The northernmost team, led by Pete, with Patricia Boyd-Graham the accompanying geologist, found that Hwy 163 had been severely washed out two miles before they reached the Colorado River. There was no way they could travel any further by vehicle, beyond that point. As a result, over the next two days their team hiked four miles to the south, where Laughlin used to be, and then on to where Bullhead City should have been. But both had vanished. They then worked their way north into the Black Mountain canyon. The devastation they found there was beyond belief. Patricia could only assume that Hoover Dam had been breached, given the destructive, domino-like effects they were finding. The surge of steel, concrete, soil and millions of tons of water and debris rushing downstream also destroyed Davis Dam. As a result the combined watershed behind both these dams inundated these cities in a tidal surge she estimated to be 50-75 feet high. They could only guess at the damage this flood must have caused further downstream. It appeared to Patricia that the force of the water would easily course straight southward, bypassing the natural, meandering curves of the established riverbed. It was evident to everyone in this survey party that this area was so destroyed and denuded that no logical settlement could be established here.

Likewise, the two teams assigned to exploring the cities of Lake Havasu and Parker were detoured. The Interstate Highway into Needles was completely washed out one mile west of town. This required that both teams had to drive off road for almost eight miles to the south of Needles. At that point they were able to pick up Highway 95 south.

What they found, once they were able to establish on the map where Lake Havasu City was supposed to be, was that it was gone. It and Parker Dam were washed away in the flood of April 1st. But, equally shocking, they confirmed that the accumulated massive piles of debris, above the present shoreline, indicated that a huge tidal wave had struck this area. All indications were that it came from a southerly direction. Later, when the team assigned to explore Parker came to the region where the lake was supposed to be, all they found was shoreline, stretching horizon to horizon. It was salt water. It was the newly expanded Sea of Cortez.

Upon further investigation, while they traced their way back to the Amboy Cavern, the agricultural specialist assigned to their team determined that this tsunami had come inland as far as the northern Ward Valley. Its northern most debris field was just south of the railroad tracks the Yucca Mountain families were to travel on within the next week. Apparently, this was the waterline that the Amboy officials saw on October 1st, when they first tried to exit the cavern.

Alfie's team, with Geoffrey Graham serving as their geologist, was able to drive off-road, unimpeded, from Interstate 40 to the Walter's Ranch area, seven miles northeast of Needles. Located at about 600 feet elevation and west of the Colorado River, it had been spared the onrushing, raging flood waters. Geoffrey determined the ranch area was most likely spared because the main force of the water headed southeast of the existing river channel. It scoured the Fort Mohave Indian Reservation, removing all vegetation, dwellings and anything living in the area. The water continued to rampage through Needles, striking it head-on. The area was covered with huge mangled piles of rubble. They were stunned to see massive pieces of concrete, piles of building debris, even large pieces of what used to be electrical generators. Beyond that, the snowfall, certainly lighter here but still enough to cover the ground, sheltered the infinite number of smaller pieces of what was left when a civilization was reduced to tatters.

From a detailed survey, conducted by this team, it was determined that if an earthen levee, its exterior lined with the abundant ,concrete rift-raft for added protection, like often seen on seashore jetties, was built, they likely could prevent future flooding of their new settlement. The river's main channel had now moved about a mile eastward, as a result of the flood. That would give them an extra land buffer. In addition, the survey revealed there was approximately eight square miles of level land that could be used for their settlement. It would include enough land for their community, as well as for small family plots and larger acreage for crops and pasture irrigation, using the water diverted from the river. By fortifying the border this land mass at its northern and eastern edge, the land and community could be protected, not unlike what was done in the Netherlands before April 1st. It was decided. This area was to be their new home.

The second objective was initiated on January 2nd. It involved using every able-bodied Amboy Cavern and Kelso person packing, storing, and securing his or her possessions, plus doing so with any supplies or equipment in the communal areas. This objective was coordinated by Frances Bynum, and Miles Stanlowski, both of whom were in Material Operations prior to April 1st. The shipping containers, modified as homes, had to be thoroughly secured for transport. And the shipping containers, used for storage, had to be refilled with unused supplies, equipment and building materials. This task fell most heavily on those living in the Amboy Cavern; the Yucca Mountain personnel were spared most of that work due to their trains still being essentially fully loaded. But hundreds of their residents came to Amboy to help them.

Simultaneously, on January 2nd, preparations began on the third objective: transportation of all personnel and movable material to their new location. There were three locations involved in this preliminary work. They were at Amboy Cavern, Kelso and the rail line coming from Las Vegas, and each one involved assigning both transportation and engineering personnel for this last evacuation.

For the transportation of Amboy's heavy equipment, shipping containers, building materials and families, Priscilla Roberts and Margaret La Rue were the assigned coordinators. Louise Matthews and Jenny LaCross were appointed coordinators for transporting Kelso materials, 99% of which was still onboard their trains. Lilyanne O'Shay and Derek Amen were the obvious choices to supervise the return train trip towards Las Vegas. They were also to take one ten person, gondola crew for that trip, once the Kelso families were relocated. Their mission involved separating out the various rail cars that Lilyanne had previously listed and cataloged as being needed in the future. Specifically, they were to take the switch engine and gondola and bring back tank cars of fuel for the trucks, trains, and boxcars of bulk and packaged food items. The plan was to bring these cars back to Kelso for storage, unless time would allow them to transport them on to the final destination where all the families were settling.

After the reconnaissance parties returned to Amboy on January 6th, there was an immediate meeting with the combined Yucca Mountain and Amboy Governing Bodies in Amboy's Main Auditorium. The "ranch" areas, as listed on the various maps northwest of Needles, were selected unanimously as their final destination.

During that meeting it was decided that the Yucca Mountain families were to leave immediately, on their three trains, for that area. The basis of this decision was to lessen the risk of injury or death, in the event something major might occur prior to the thirty day window of opportunity that B had given them. If these survivors had learned nothing else, it was that chance was something to prepare for and avoid if possible. There was also the concern that the rail bed might be or could become impassable, which would be an almost insurmountable obstacle.

They were assigned to leave Kelso on January 10th, with the switch engine and gondolas leading the way as usual. No one knew if stranded trains would need to be bypassed or track repair would be necessary, as before. Their route would be from Kelso to Barstow, and then switch onto the tracks coming east from the towns of Cadiz and Amboy. The trip would end where the tracks were washed out west of Needles.

Lilyanne and Derek would then return to Kelso with the switch engine and one gondola car, unless they were able to secure the needed supplies from stranded trains along the way into and out of Barstow. This, as it turned out, was what they were able to do. No return trip to Kelso was necessary, to Lilyanne's great relief.

Jo Ann Henry drove the lead train as usual, but this time it was the Amtrak train.

It probably should be noted that no one, on the trains leaving Kelso, was taking time to describe what the scenery or condition of the area was like. This was primarily because it was basically unchanged from Kelso to Barstow; aside from the large sand dunes they passed about ten miles out of Kelso. All shades were pulled again when the Amtrak train maneuvered through Barstow. It was clear to Jo Ann and Derek that major looting and mob violence had occurred just proceeding the lethal radioactivity and earthquakes that have followed since then. It took three days to maneuver around stranded trains, debris and twisted track caused by earth movement, but they did arrive at their new home site, completely exhausted, on January 13th.

Assorted heavy equipment was the first to be transported from the Amboy Cavern area. It all traveled by truck along Interstate 40 to the cutoff, designated earlier by Alfie's team. Beyond that point, the flooding had destroyed most signs of any earlier habitation. Bulldozers were hauled first to begin clearing roadways from the Interstate and rail lines into the community, and also alongside the Amtrak and freight trains. Equally urgent was the need to begin preparing the levee. Given the precarious nature of their existence along the river, the engineers were anxious to erect some kind of diversionary dam in case of any unexpected flooding.

It was with this first shipment of equipment to their new home site that the fourth objective was initiated. The engineers were led by Ernie Tam, Ben Javitts, Jason Black, Doug Chan, along with Zelma Collins and Wally Gonzaque. Throughout this last emergency relocation, these individuals also coordinated the work of the twelve engineers and ten engineering instructors from the 'Amboy 75', as those selected families came to be called. After this move, all the 'Amboy 75' families' involvement, in the development of the new settlement, became paramount.

These engineers had multiple assignments. They had to prepare a foundation area on both sides of the parked Amtrak train for their modified shipping containers used for housing. These homes were to be placed side by side for protection and security for everyone, both in the train and in the container homes. Also needed was another area cleared for two storage warehouses, one for equipment and supplies, and one large building for the livestock, storage of young trees and plants and a hothouse. There also needed to be engineering plans drawn up for the irrigation channels, which would eventually provide water both for crop and pasture irrigation and for personal storage use. While doing that there needed to be ground cleared and leveled for planting crops and pastureland. Wells needed to be dug. The levees built and reinforced. And finally, land needed to be set aside and cleared for a memorial cemetery.

The fifth objective, which was indispensable to beginning the final phase of the Rebuilding Committee's goals, was to have Hasna Eudis, Jenny La Cross and Vern Henry develop and supervise construction of a communication system. The two 'Amboy 75' computer engineers were essential to their eventually constructing a center that had the capacity to broadcast over two-thirds of the globe. More than anyone, though, it was Vern's uncanny abilities that would finally give them this global outreach. Even the engineers were in awe of his capacity to improvise and adapt the equipment. Short-wave messages were being sent world-wide by February 16th.

Objective number six involved Ian Murphy, Minor Peterson, Zara Mahmood and Ray O'Shay coordinating and working with the other 29 'Amboy 75' and 30 Marine Hospital health care personnel. They were to implement the plan, worked out over the last months of confinement, for delivering health care, now that the families had emerged from their shelters. To start with they were going to have to be housed in the MASH tents, which were erected adjacent to the sleeping quarters by the Amtrak train and the shipping container homes. The Medical Clinic and Hospital would be built within the next year.

The seventh objective was to continue the schooling for the children and young adults. The adult classes, the Level VII programs, were concluded for the foreseeable future. Logistically, it was impossible to provide any facilities for more adult education at this time. Moreover, there were no adult class teachers available; they were all working to rebuild the settlement. The Level I-VI classes were to be held in the lounge and dining cars, scheduling around the two meals served each day in the dining cars. Classes started at 7 a.m. and continued until 9 p.m., in order to accommodate all the students for at least 1-2 hours of instruction each day. This arrangement had to continue until permanent classrooms were built.

The eighth objective was considered, by far, the most vital to the ultimate survival of the families. It was to develop a self-sustaining agricultural network. The eight square miles of usable land amounted to approximately 15,300 acres. Of that amount, five acres were to be allocated to each of the over 750 families. With that land, they were expected to plant vegetables and maintain a few farm animals. Much larger parcels were set aside to be used as pasture for larger herds of animals and as tilled acreage for field crops and orchards. Leaving land for the actual township, and any accompanying recreation areas, were the final designations; and they were to be situated closer to the trains and container homes.

Interestingly, over time, the consensus for who should lead and help accomplish this all-important goal of a establishing a sustainable food source was Sid and Janice Blackwell. They were ably assisted by Clarice Delow and Rashid Batok. Just the same, the 'Hoquiam Harvesters', as this couple eventually became known by, blended a common sense approach and calmness with problem solving that ushered them into the forefront of the agricultural experts and scientists. Completing this cadre were the others from the 'Amboy 75'. They consisted of the four agricultural instructors, one biologist and 13 other farmers and ranchers. It was a body that had met almost daily throughout their confinement, and they were eager and ready to begin their appointed tasks as soon as possible. It was, by all accounts, these individuals who insured the sustainability and survival of the Global Union. Within days of the ground being leveled by the engineers, they were helping build the necessary buildings and irrigation system for cultivation. Immediately 25 acres were prepared for the earliest possible cultivation.

Coming in ninth, and closely united with the eighth objective, was the transfer, boarding and care of the animals being kept in Cave #4. This objective was managed entirely by the Pet and Animal Welfare Association. The leadership of this well-known group remained Jihan and Ilhan Zandi, Hanna and Mandel Segal and Bernice and Megan Wailand, just as it was upon their immediate confinement in the Amboy Cavern. After the new shelter was finished, they supervised the transport of the animals. Distribution of the pets had to be delayed until permanent residences were established, but families could now adopt a pet and begin caring for it, while it was still boarded inside the new shelter. To the credit of the Association no animals were lost during the confinement. But, like their caregivers and everyone else in the new settlement, they were excited to be free from the cave.

The tenth and final objective was the most delicate of all. Early, on January 19th, Fred and Freda Wailand, Eric and Ann Stanfield, Clem and Jake, along with four volunteers, began their appointed task of exhuming the remains of Cynthia Garr, Roger Plant, Sylvia Marzoff, Mark and Virginia Luberaski and their son, Thomas. Following that solemn task, they placed each set of remains into hand-made caskets and loaded them onto one of two enclosed trucks and left Amboy Cavern for Amboy. Once in Amboy, they hoped to find the remains of Hazel and Ray and Rose and Harry. Upon arrival in Amboy, and after a brief search, each set of remains were located in their respective homes and gently placed into the caskets brought for them. At Clem's request, on their way to the new settlement site, he asked if they could stop by his cabin and also retrieve the remains of his wife, Elizabeth. That done, they then drove on to their new home site.

Sadly, but not totally unexpectedly, it was during the final leg of this trip towards Needles, that Jake quietly died, as he lay beside Clem in the back of one of the trucks. Clem's small diary, that was discovered some years later, had many passages in it describing the conversations that he and Jake had. It was all written-off as the ramblings of a crazy old hermit, but not for Fred, Megan and Bernice. Or for B. They all knew the truth about Clem and Jake. It was probably Jake's presence that helped keep Clem alive for this long. And it was through these two that the Amboy Cavern survivors retained an awareness of their innermost selves. The solitary, but ever-present, attentiveness of Clem and his companion Jake, provided reassurance and continuity to everyone there. Their simplicity of living and behaving gave direction to a remnant of a civilization that had become lost in complexity and self-serving pursuits. Theirs was a simple framework for a life better lived, for a future better served. Clem could only say, when he realized that Jake was gone, "Oh, my dear Jakie, how I will miss you, old friend. How so very much will I miss you..."

Arrangements for the next of kin had been made beforehand, and once the burial procession of these two trucks arrived at the newly established settlement cemetery, it was not long before final internment began. Fred's family helped Clem prepare a gravesite for Jake. In anticipation of the number of caskets they would be carrying, the other gravesites had already been prepared. Grave markers were set out, but it was not until month's later that standardized, permanent markers were placed. Clem did not think Cynthia would mind if Elizabeth and Jake's remains were resting beside her. As everyone stood back, after all the caskets had been placed into their respective graves, it was Clem who stepped forward and recited the 23rd Psalm. This was, for Clem, his final official act. Under his breath, as dusk gathered over their new home site and everyone turned to go back to their shipping container homes, parked by the Amtrak train, Clem utter quietly, "that should about do it B. Unless you have other plans for me, I'm about done here."

And, as it has been recorded in the first volume of this chronicle, it was on January 21st, that apparently Clem, too, passed away. At least that is the last date that anyone can remember seeing Clem. No one was present at his passing, nor did anyone have any idea how there came to be a marker appear at the cemetery, indicating that he did. It was Helen Plant who first noticed a new marker a few days after January 19th. Moreover, she knew that had not been there originally with those buried on that day. In her conversation with Eric and Ben, she reported that it simply said: "Clement L. Newberry, 1956-2012". The oddest thing about its sudden appearance, she also noted, was that there did not appear to be any disturbance of the ground around it.

SIX: 30 DAYS AND COUNTING

If nothing else, the Kelso and Amboy halves of the Global Union had almost limitless determination to respond, somehow, to an impending crisis. Telling themselves repeatedly that this was their last relocation or evacuation, by January 29th the last truck convoy arrived at the Resolve railhead. The name chosen for their town was the result of the general population making suggestions and then voting for it. "Resolve" won hands down.

Briefly, this record needs to outline the status in and around Resolve during the last days leading up to the settlement's last major ground-shaking challenge. The days from January 29th to February 11th passed without incident, allowing the various work crews to pursue finishing their assigned objectives unimpeded.

The container homes, with their front doors facing the sleeper cars, were set up side by side along the entire length of the Amtrak train's northern exposure. On the south side of the Amtrak train, providing a windbreak and helping to stabilize Amtrak's two-story cars, were the shipping containers, filled with food supplies, rebuilding materials and the personal property of the 'Amboy 75' families. Thick ropes and cables were stretched over the Amtrak train and secured to the containers on each side to give these higher cars added lateral stability. The rebuilding freight train was parked just behind the Amtrak train, and the other freight train was now the last of the three trains.

The toilet tank cars were intermingled amongst the sleeper cars, with an additional fifteen water tank cars converted to toilet facilities to accommodate the Amboy Cavern families. A fixed-in-place sewer system was planned for sometime in the future; but for the immediate future it existed only in everyone's dreams.

Their water supply came from two sources: the Colorado River and two freshly dug wells. The river water, for the time being, was to be used as grey water only. Radioactivity from the Lake Mead explosion had been dispersed, for the most part, over the Utah basin. Residual radiation was washed down river in the months that followed. But Lilyanne's staff kept a steady check on the level. Plus, the water flowing from the river over seven miles of freshly dug irrigation channel provided some filtering. The water was turbid but not toxic.

Interestingly, the irrigation channel's pathway was engineered to give it considerable fall from its upper reaches. This allowed the engineers to construct a hydraulic ram pump. Using an eight inch diameter drive pipe off the irrigation channel and directing the flow into a four inch diameter delivery pipe, the outflow to the community of Resolve was 48-96 gallons per minute. For the time being this was sufficient for their needs, at least until other pumps could be engineered. The uniqueness and ingenuity of this device was that the only energy required to pump the water, even into an elevated storage tank, was from the source of flowing irrigation water itself.

The two drilled wells were artesian; which meant they also did not require additional power for pumping. Geoffrey and Patricia Graham surmised the reason for the wells being free flowing was due, for the most part, from what the Yucca Mountain families experienced before and during their initial train trip to Las Vegas. Plus, there was the stunning rise in the Sea of Cortez's shoreline. From these findings, they concluded there was an ongoing and significant increase in the region's underground aquifer. The ground water level was dramatically rising. And after repeated and ongoing testing, the well water was certified as potable.

Preliminary construction of the two large warehouses and the huge barn were started on January 14th, the day after the trains arrived with the rebuilding materials. More of the same kinds of building materials from Amboy Cavern were to be coming in by truck over the next two weeks, as those warehouses were emptied and the buildings salvaged. The warehouses and the combination animal shelter/hothouse had at least a foundation and a covered roof by the end of the thirty-day grace period that B had given them. The barn did have stalls to keep the animals from wandering. The various trees, shrubs and plants were safely maintained in the transparently covered hothouse. It was the best they could do in the timeframe left to them.

Throughout Resolve, there was great anticipation to get pastures, grains and vegetables planted as soon as possible. Everyone knew their long-term survival depended on their farming skills. They could only scavenge so long. Moreover, their new settlement was still a major work-in-progress, and it was anticipated it would be so for at least another year or two. And the forecast was at least two years before the levee and rift-raft were fully in place for protection from the river's flooding. The Colorado River was now free of any artificial constraints, and springtime flooding was a serious concern. Whatever mechanized equipment and manual labor was available, during daylight hours, was used in building a secure perimeter for their farming needs. At times hundreds of individuals could be seen working on the dikes.

The final building, undergoing preliminary construction, was the Global Union's Offices. For many months, it was to be an area containing multiple shipping containers, with tarp-covered walkways between them. Inside the finished building would eventually be the Communication Center, offices of the various representatives, the court room, credit union and library. For the present, it was a hodge-podge of equipment, supplies and containers, but at least it was the beginning of a new government.

The second tented structure was the General Assembly area. Two immense circus-sized tents were joined together for these meetings. They were ready to be raised soon after the expected earthquake had occurred. And finally there were the three MASH tents. They were quickly erected and equipped for surgical, medical and public health services. And they were fully operational by January 20th.

And that is basically where everything stood come February 12th at 6:17 a.m. Overall, there was heightened since of relief and blossoming camaraderie throughout the families. Socializing, when any time allowed, was genuine and without reserve. Each person, regardless of age, was fully aware what their neighbor had or was experiencing. It was a shared history of trial, suffering and survival. But there was also the gnawing awareness of what B had warned them about. The 30 day grace period was long past. No one let their guard down, however. By now, if B foretold it, they believed it to be true. At least within this extended time, beyond the 30 warning, they had been able to better secure, stabilize and store their goods. No one knew what to expect. And time was up.

SEVEN: 6:17 a.m. FEBRUARY 12th

Earthquakes of any size, provided they are strong enough to be felt, have one thing in common. They do not announce their arrival beforehand. Nothing arrives ahead of it to prepare you. The only exception for the families in Resolve was the general warning B gave them that something powerful was going to occur in about 30 days. But even in this instance, there was no knock on anyone's front door, announcing its pending entry into their lives. Nothing unusual indicated its approach. At this time, on this day, there was suddenly a raging noise, accompanied by a violent shaking, as if some giant hand was trying to empty the last contents lodged in an oversized container, in hopes of finding a priceless gift. But there was no gift this day to stop the shaking. The noise and violent movement just got worse. Each person began to have images of the earth opening up and swallowing helpless victims. Earthquakes can be indiscriminant killers, and this one was no exception. The residents of Resolve did not experience any fatalities, but throughout the region, individuals huddled in burrows, were buried by the score.

In this instance, it was the San Andreas Fault that had come to life, with the epicenter of this earthquake estimated to be about 150 miles west of their location. Even at that distance, it was terrifying. Only by their securing everything as well as they did, including cabling over the sleeper cars, was the damage no greater than it was. However, as a search party later found out, the Amboy Cavern was totally destroyed during this event; fifty miles or so closer to the epicenter made the destructive difference.

Even closer to them, it was discovered that the railroad tracks were impassable five miles west of them, as were the Interstate Highways. The rail lines were buckled and bowed for countless miles, and overpasses had collapsed by the score. Any highway travel after this would be limited to going northwest. And it would have to be via Highway 95, northward to Searchlight, and beyond from there. The Interstates were now impassable, and train travel was impossible. Besides the limited roadways available for vehicle travel, there were the two helicopters, two fixed wing airplanes and two patrol boats. Each had to be reassembled and test driven before they could be reinstated into fulltime service. February 12th ended any other modes of travel to and from Resolve.

The terrifying shaking lasted four minutes. Since the events on April 1st, the speed of slippage along the San Andreas Fault increased from that of fingernail bed growth to the speed of a snail or slug crawling on the forest floor. At least that was what Patricia Boyd-Graham theorized months later. That increased slippage speed created unimaginable stress along the fault line, causing it to buckle for hundreds of miles along its length. The epicenter was near Banning, California. There was enough force with the quake to destabilize further the Cascadian Fault along the Oregon and Washington coasts. This, in turn, affected the North American Plate and caused reactivation of the dormant volcanoes of Mt. Adams, Rainer and Shasta. The

Northwest, extended over to Yellowstone National Park, was becoming uninhabitable.

For the citizens of Resolve, once the shaking stopped there was still no way to determine the extent of damage around them. There was so much sand and dust stirred up, that visibility was zero. It was not until noon that day that everyone felt secure enough to venture out of their quarters and be able to see clearly what had happened around them. Thankfully, the damage was minimal. Their small corner of the world was still intact.

But what was not known at that time was that the mountains of the Himalayas in Tibet, and those in Afghanistan and Pakistan were hardest hit by the changes in the tectonic plate movements. This was due to the main force of energy from the April 1st solar burst being conducted directly through the continental plates into that region. Only many decades later, during extensive, exploratory surveys of that region, was it learned that the earthquakes on February 12th, and thereafter, were so violent that the resulting landslides and cave ins buried all the hide-a-ways for the April 1st architects of terror. Their lairs collapsed, along with their schemes of total control and conquest. Nature had done what man, for all the preceding centuries appeared unable to do. Radical ideologies, century's old customs of suppression and torture were swallowed up. Nature exacted her own revenge for their misdeeds. After the February 12th global shockwaves, the pockets of survivor's worldwide were few and scattered widely over the planet.

PART III

EIGHT: SEARCH AND RESCUE

As was mentioned earlier in this chronicle, the various objectives that the Resolve families had established for themselves were ones that had no actual deadlines, other than trying to prepare, as much as possible, for the predicted earthquake. Everyone knew life would be much better if all of them were accomplished immediately.   But reality was the chancellor of their daily experiences and never-ending education.   That said, the Communication Center continued to be a work-in-progress, even as it had its initial start up on February 16th. The computer engineers and Vern were entangled in a world of electromagnetic transmissions, while the other members of their team were constructing a massive tower on the nearby mountainside, setting up satellite dishes and antennas. If anything, the frantic nature of their work epitomized the priority that search and rescue operations had for everyone.

To be able to reach out beyond their circle of survivors, to be able to communicate or at least to broadcast their presence, and then to be able to launch exploratory sorties were at the core of their emotions and thinking at this time.   Their surviving all that had gone before would be less meaningful, possibly even hollow, if they did not do everything possible to reach out, locate and rescue anyone they found. The complications of how to do all this were issues that had been discussed endlessly since April 1st. Central to whatever plan their searches embodied, being able to broadcast over the widest possible distance was central to their success and sense of accomplishment.

The initial communication link was S-band broadcasting, which they hoped to link to any orbiting satellites that might still be operational. It was the easiest to install, but probably the most unlikely to yield any results.

Next to come on line, by March 5th, were the Long Wave radio broadcasts. It had required the erection of an insulated, steel latticed aerial mast nearly 1500 feet high. To do this they used the nearby hillside for most of the elevation. Prior to this, the tallest Long Wave mast, that anyone was aware of, was in Iceland. It stood about 1300 feet high. With theirs online, they could now broadcast throughout the North and Middle American continents, following the curvature of the earth. It significantly increased their chances of making some contact with any survivors in these regions.

And finally, by March 10th, once the engineers were able to install the largest generator that was used in the Yucca Mountain Cavern, they added the last of their communication options, with the installation of Short Wave radio capability. Now they had the capability of reaching any place on earth. This was possible by the short waves being refracted by the ionosphere, the so-called "Sky wave propagation". The drawback for this form of broadcasting was that it required so much power. That was something Resolve had little to spare at this time. But installation of the generator for the still, under-construction Global Union Office Building and then dedicating the Short Wave broadcasting to night only, when it is most effective anyway, limited its impact on the community's energy needs. It required nearly 500 kilowatts of power.

With the completion of this three tier Communication Center, Hasna Eunis, Jenny La Cross, Vern and the few, determined engineers and scientists who helped, were elated. Around the clock broadcasts began, announcing the same message (see Appendix 3, fig.1, "Resolve's Message to the World"). Now it was a matter of listening for any response and keeping the equipment in running order to broadcast 20-24 hours a day. Their link with the outside world had been established.

Eric and Ben had mixed emotions with this accomplishment, not knowing how large or small the response might be. Too many people, coming too soon, and everyone's survival would be in jeopardy. Too few, and the impact of that would thrust their community into the deepest despair. Everyone was holding out hope there were some survivors, somewhere. There had to be. Now they would find out for sure. They began transmitting their message world-wide at 4:15 p.m. on March 10th.

Within a day of those first Short Wave transmissions being sent, a General Assembly meeting was called, the first since all the families had united in Resolve. Now that the two circus tents had been fully deployed and chairs and benches had been built and installed for everyone, it was possible to get all the families together in one place.

The tents, massive as they were, did not seem out of place in their surroundings. They seemed to complement the color and shape of the area. The Dead Mountain range to Resolve's immediate west, covered with odd-sized boulders, sparse scrub brush or cactus and patches of undisturbed snow and bare earth, provided a speckled tan, dusty brown backdrop. To the east, looking beyond the nearby river, the hills in the distance, that were the far border of the Indian Reservation, broke the horizon in undulating curves and provided a spectacular stage for sunrises. Closer to them, on their side of the Colorado River, both to the north and to the east, the rising levees were likewise brown, but hopefully soon to be covered with grass and topped with flowering oleanders. You could see where the fields to the north were being prepared for pastures and crops, along with the irrigation canal winding its way along the base of the western hillsides. The cultivated ground stood out against the all-white undisturbed land. And to the south, there were the ever-present endless rows of shipping containers, shielding the taller Amtrak train.

However, if you climbed up to the top of the mountains on the town's western flank, the image was vastly different. While Resolve gave some harmony to the view below, the scar in the distance left by the rampaging Colorado River in full flood, left pure chaos. For as far as one could see, either to the north or to the south, there was the dark, blackish-brown, swirling waters of the newly formed river bed. The chunks of concrete and untold amounts of scattered debris had transformed the river into a boiling, swirling beast. The river's mood and appearance could only be described as like a living fury. The old river bed was now empty of water, but left full of the scattered remnants of whatever was in the flood's path upstream. The new river was no longer a tamed, meandering source of recreation. It had regained its authority and powerful presence, one that once formed the Grand Canyon. The river's course was now straight ahead, from the Black Canyon to the Sea of Cortez. It demanded respect.

Eric and Ben worried that the contents of all these General Assembly meetings were either for announcements of doom or unexpected problems. None, recently, had been just to celebrate something or to rejoice in their being alive. They worried that these gatherings were becoming a dreaded exercise. A shift in focus was needed, rather than the content of them always being grim news or detailed plans for their survival. And in that vein they also worried that survivors guilt would become an all-consuming malady.

"How do you think we should introduce this meeting?" Ben asked, with some desperation in his voice.

"I'm not sure," Eric replied. "I do know, like you, we've got to break the cycle of awful or urgent news. I sure wish that pipe organ was assembled and ready to play. Maybe we can get the piano set up on a stage of some kind and get a few of our musicians to play."

"Good idea," Ben eagerly responded. "Let's announce it as a day of fun, like a county fair. And let's put off everything, including the business meeting, until.., say on the 13th. That will give us more time to prepare the details of what Alfie Shoemaker, Ernie, Kathryn Swisher and Steven Blackmore's group is planning to do."

"Alright. I'll talk to Albert and Dada Nugama and Philip and Theresa Lieska. Between all of them they'll be able to put together a real celebration. I'll encourage them to have entertainment, food, drink, dancing and displays of student projects from school, a petting zoo with all our pets and animals. Anything and everything they can think of that's fun. And maybe, for once, we'll just leave the search and rescue orientation and formulation meeting open for anyone interested to attend, rather than make it mandatory. We'll post notices of its content, and have Alfie's group prepare ahead of time what they purpose to do," Eric suggested.

"That's great by me," Ben answered. "And I'll talk to Ernie and Alfie about their presentation. Let's say the carnival will start at 11:00 a.m. on the 13th, and the business meeting will begin, in the main tents at 5:30 p.m., before the dinner meal and entertainment that evening."

Having decided that, the two leaders immediately began notifying the various parties who were to organize the event. It was met with great excitement by everyone, and before noon that day, everyone in Resolve knew about the fun-filled day and the optional business meeting.

Come the 13th, by the time the 5:30 meeting was scheduled to start, there were fewer than 200 hundred people attending. If nothing else did, that signaled to Ben and Eric that general assembly's had gone out of favor with most of the families, at least for the present moment. They knew it was a symptom of everyone being in a state-of-continual-crisis, and they were exhausted. Folks wanted the privilege of being able to forget for a while.

When both leaders realized the small showing was all that was going to come, they briefly called the meeting to order and asked Patricia Graham to come forward to present the agenda for the meeting. It was her duty to do so; she being the Chairwoman of the Amboy Final Emergence Committee. At exactly 5:30 p.m. she arose from her seat and came forward to face the smaller than expected crowd.

"After over a year of discussions and planning, it is now time to present the culmination of this work. Search and Rescue is at the heart of whom and what we are as a community. Despite this small attendance today, I know it doesn't represent the feeling that all of us, here in Resolve, have regarding this most selfless action. I'm going to let Ernie Tam present the outline of what will be started in the weeks to come. It will be carried out for at least the next two years, provided we have the equipment in working order and the fuel to transport us to our search and recovery areas. Thank you for coming here today. Now let's hear what Ernie has to say."

"Thanks, Pat," Ernie began, as he shuffled through a handful of wrinkled notes. "Public speaking is not one of my favorite duties. So I, for one, am very relieved to see a smaller turnout than was expected. I just hope what I have to say warrants you even being here.

"The search we are about to embark on is certainly, like everything else that has happened to all of us over these last months, unprecedented. I will break it down into two major operations.

"The first, we call the local search, which in reality is not that local. We have divided the southwestern United States into grids and soon will begin a quadrant-by-quadrant investigation by air, and when needed or possible, by sea or river. Our territorial limits for this search area are 300 miles in any direction from Resolve. This range gives us the safest out and back capability that our HH-60 Jayhawk helicopters have; and yet, it still gives them a little extra fuel for emergency responses. This allows us to search most of southern California and parts of northern Mexico, the better part of Arizona, some of Utah and a few sections of Nevada, not already covered during our recent train trip.

"We will be using our two helicopters and two fixed wing aircraft for the bulk of this searching. The two rescue boats, we had mothballed on the trains, will serve to explore the waterways and seashore areas. At present, almost as I speak, our mechanics are reassembling and tuning up these craft for these trips. The trips are self-limited by the amount of fuel we have stored or could bring here or that we will have on board when in flight. We hope to tap into underground sources of fuel, like say, at Nellis AFB, but contamination and loss due to fires, make this an unpredictable source. We have calculated that we should be able to make at least a hundred sorties by aircraft and fifty by boat, before our supplies have to be replenished.

"We will alternate using the planes first to scout the most likely areas for life. Then we will return with the helicopters for a closer inspection if there are any promising or hopeful signs of life. Likewise, the fixed wing flights will help us locate where we need to transport our collapsible and light weight boats for further inspection.

"The flight crews will be commanded by Elaine DePew and Larry Jennings. Accompanying them on all flights will be either Pete Mendoza or Jason Black and some of their personnel for ground searches, if necessary and for protection, if needed. Upon occasion, I will also pilot either one of the helicopters or the fixed wing aircraft. We hope to start these flyovers in a couple of days, sometime on March 15th. Wish us luck and safe travel.

"The second portion of these search and rescue missions is more complicated, to be sure. It entails the long range missions, both for transporting people and material. Depending on the extent of destruction that is found, the searching will become progressively more risky. We intend to transport one of the helicopters, as well, in the rescue planes. It will be used if it is impossible to land at a particular airfield, and we would have to land further away and hop-scotch our way to the intended area. It will be my particular responsibility to fly these helicopter missions. Also being transported on these long range missions will be our EMT's or medics, just as one or two would be accompanying the local helicopter missions.

"The process of beginning these flights is staged. The first stage is already underway, as of the 16th of this month, when the Communication Center began its worldwide broadcasting. The next step is organizing a party of engineers and aircraft mechanics and sending them to Nellis AFB. To get to Nellis from here, it will be necessary for this party to drive from Highway 95 north and go by way of Searchlight, Nevada, to Boulder City and work their way eventually into Nellis. All major freeway and roadways into and out of Las Vegas are impassable.

"Based on what became Benton Scott's rescue mission to Nellis, during our train trip to Kelso, his party discovered there might be two of the McCord and Fairchild planes that could be made flight worthy. It will no doubt take some time to determine and accomplish this, but that's one of the reasons we scheduled the first long range mission on June 1st, to allow time for repairs.

"Provided the planes, one for rescue and one for refueling, are returned to service, then Steven Blackwell and Kathryn Swisher will pilot those planes. Their objective will be to fly to the four rendezvous points listed in our broadcast: Redmond, Oregon; Rapid City, South Dakota; Bowling Green, Kentucky and Carlsbad, New Mexico. We are hoping these places are well enough away from large metropolitan areas and industrial or military sites to be intact for landing the planes. Also we are hoping there is fuel available in underground bunkers at Nellis to even fly these missions. Benton's survey of the base indicated there was fuel present. What we don't know is whether it is useable or not.

"Finally, when all avenues of rescuing any survivors has been exhausted, and provided there is fuel enough and the planes are able to fly and land somewhere near the sites, we hope, based on what is found during these rescue attempts, to retrieve materials from three locations for storage here in Resolve. Those materials would be from three sources: The Library of Congress, Fort Knox, and the National Archives Buildings, both in Washington D.C. and in various regional centers, such as Fort Worth, Texas; Santa Fe, New Mexico; Atlanta, Georgia and Yellowstone National Park.

"To conclude, let me honestly say, based on what we saw coming from Yucca Mountain to Kelso and then what we found once we got here, that our chances of finding pockets of life appear remote. From what B told each of us initially, you'd have to assume there were few, if any, survivors in this country or elsewhere. But, saying that, there is still no reason not to try and reach out and find others who may still be alive. We have no conceivable idea what happened, throughout the world, on April 1st, so we certainly can hope for the best. It seems logical that there are pockets of survivors scattered around, particularly, in some place like Switzerland. They've had generations to prepare for various kinds of invasions or attacks. But, of course, if there are survivors overseas, they have to make their way here to our shores. That, in itself, is almost beyond any hope of happening, but we must hold on to it for their sake. All our rescue efforts in these next two years have to be directed at discovering what really happened on April 1st last year and who may have survived it. If possible, we must bring them here to our community. Thank you."

For those who attended this meeting, once they

passed the word around to those who did not, it was clear to all that Ernie had outlined monumental undertakings. It remains, to this day, a statement of purpose all of us are proud to be associated with.

NINE: THE SEARCH BEGINS

On March 15th two events occurred that are still recognized as milestones in establishing the Global Union's passage into legitimate nationhood. The first was that Ernie Tam's team had successfully completed assembling, tuning up and servicing the fixed wing aircraft and helicopters. More importantly, he had been able to steer the intense debate, at times, to get approval for their airfield to be a mile and a half strip of Interstate 40, adjacent to the parked trains. The engineers were able to construct some temporary shelters for the four aircraft at the one end, incorporating an overpass that was still structurally sound as an additional storage and repair hanger. The crowning achievement for this crew that day was that two planes lifted off at 10:30 a.m. to begin the search for survivors, heading southeast toward Los Angeles.

Probably, at this point, it is important to note the scale of their nearly impossible task ahead. Their search area had a 300 mile radius or 600 mile diameter. Given that, the total area involved had a circumference of 18, 840 miles. Recognizing there are 360° in that circular, search area, each degree at the outer edge of that circumference would involve searching 293 miles. And they only estimated it was possible to make 100 round trip flights, with either the fixed wing planes or the helicopters. Undaunted, though, the flight crews, led by Elaine DePew and Larry Jennings took off. Only the prior experience of that Coast Guard crew, along with the expertise of Pete Mendoza's Marine recon personnel, could embolden these individuals to even attempt what lay ahead for them. It drew on the entire range sea search and rescue skills of Ernie Tam and his crew to achieve what they did. The backup helicopters were on standby in case either plane ran into trouble during their flights.

The second event of that day was the departure of the overland convoy to Nellis AFB, under the combined leadership of Benton Scott, Steven Blackwell and Kathryn Swisher. They were to maintain radio contact the entire trip and throughout their deployment at Nellis. The same was true for all the local rescue flights. It was only when this communication link was available that any of the Search and Rescue units thought it safe enough to try risking these missions.

Moreover, despite there being no sign of life, other than the individuals rescued at Nellis, an armed escort also accompanied the convoy. In addition, the medical staff of Resolve had decided, prior to the emergence on January 1st, to begin issuing Potassium Iodine tablets to everyone. This was done to combat the potential effects that residual radioactive iodine might have on anyone's thyroid gland. Safety, protection, and sustaining life of the few people who survived April 1st, and its aftermath, were the primary goals for everyone now. It was like a giant team, each individual on it maintaining vigilance and thinking of ways to foster life. Along with the three flatbed trucks, carrying empty fuel bladders, there were fifteen other vehicles, carrying supplies and equipment to hopefully resurrect and fly the two transport planes back to Resolve. In all, 43 individuals left for Nellis that day.

It was further decided, for the sake of additional backup and safety, that any time the two, local rescue planes flew off together, each one would follow the same heading, but be separated by about ten miles. It would widen the area they were searching, but it would insure quick response if there was an emergency. On this first day's search their heading was to downtown Los Angeles and on to LAX. This route was chosen because it covered the most populated areas in the region and thereby possibly increased their chances of finding someone alive.

The freeway runway served their purpose well. The take offs, their first ones, were without incident, and the planes climbed quickly into the sky, heading into a gentle westerly wind. They climbed to about 5000 feet and held that altitude throughout the flight over the high desert region. Their course took them through the unpopulated area of the Mojave Desert, skirting towns of any size. Passing over Interstate 15, just before reaching Cajon Pass, they saw again the line of stalled vehicles stretching from horizon to horizon. It was exactly as they witnessed it in the Las Vegas area. And still there were no visible signs of life.

As they started the climb to 8000 feet to safely clear the San Gabriel Mountains, just east of Mt. Baldy, both pilots noted and radioed to the Communication Center in Resolve that the forests were gone. All that was left throughout the San Gabriel and San Bernardino National Forests were untold miles of blackened bare spars and stumpage, against the white carpet of newly fallen snow. And once they cleared the crest of the mountain range and could concentrate on the view ahead, Elaine shrieked into her radio, "It's all water!! Everywhere!! All I see is water!!"

At that moment, Larry, piloting the other plane, exclaimed, "We should see Upland or Pomona out the right side of the plane and San Bernardino and Ontario out the left side. But I don't see anything except water and endless miles of floating debris. It's like a giant inland sea or bay. The waterline is right up against the San Gabriel and San Bernardino Mountain ranges. Along the shoreline, stretching as far as I can see, are huge mounds of what's left of the cities, now under water."

Descending over the basin, once they passed over the mountains, and to get a much closer look at what they were witnessing, they came down to the 1,500 foot elevation. "The water is brownish-black, with an oily bluish-purple sheen when the sun reflects off the water!" Elaine shouted. "And it's so high I don't see any structures outlined on the valley floor. Only at the outer edges of the perimeter are there any identifiable structures. The water has to be 40-50 feet deep in this area, maybe even higher. There are swells, just like you see in the open ocean. There's been a tremendous flood or tidal wave. There's been a horrible tragedy here!"

"We should be coming up on downtown Los Angeles pretty soon," Larry offered, "but, again, I don't see anything resembling superstructures of the city. In the far distance, like maybe around where Century City is supposed to be, it looks like one building is sticking out through the water. My God, the whole area has been leveled and then flooded. There is absolutely no sign of life, whatsoever. And as we fly over where Inglewood and the Los Angeles Airport is supposed to be, there is nothing but brackish water."

"Maybe we should make a wide circle out by Catalina Island and check the water level there. My map shows that the highest point on the island is Mt. Orizaba, at about 1,950 feet. Seeing the island will give us a rough estimate of the devastatingly increased water level throughout this region," Elaine suggested.

"Good idea. I'll follow behind you, and then we will split up again for the return trip," Larry answered.

Both planes dipped down to 500 feet above the water level and flew in front of the outcrop, of what used to be Catalina Island. By each of the pilots' rough estimates; it appeared that the peak was approximately 1500 feet above sea level. Quickly calculated, that meant the ocean had risen somewhere around 500 feet since April 1st. As they reported these findings back to the Communication Center in Resolve, their voices trembled with fearful wonderment. No one had any idea what had led to this catastrophe. They were certainly aware of earthquakes and a volcanic eruption, but there was nothing that would indicate a global collapse of this magnitude.

And on their return trip back to Resolve, the alteration of the landscape only deepened their fears. What should have been Newport Beach was under water. The shoreline extended into the hills of the Cleveland National Forest. But once over that ridgeline, they again were confronted by standing water through the Riverside and Morongo Valleys. And the same was seen in the Coachella Valley. The waterline there extended into Palm Springs and along the tall sand dunes bordering Desert Hot Springs. As they passed over the Joshua Tree National Park, they could see, off to the south, that the flooding was an extension of what had been the Salton Sea. Seeing that, it became clear to them why the exploratory parties found sea water covering the Parker and Lake Havasu City area. They concluded that all salt water bodies, at least in this area, had been flooded beyond their pre April 1st boundaries, and if that were the case here, it must be so throughout the world.

The final discovery for this first mission, aside from having no sightings of anything living throughout their mission, was the devastation of the Marine Base at

29 Palms. It was obvious to both pilots that a nuclear blast had targeted that Base.

Arriving back, four hours later, at Resolve's converted highway-to-runway, the two pilots and their crews were emotionally drained. They all had retained their professionalism, but at the expense of their energy reserve. Meeting them at the newly established airfield, and then seeing their exhaustion, not to mention hearing their minute-by-minute reports back in the Communication Center, Ernie, Ben and Eric decided one of them had to accompany each flight for the next few missions. And given the desperate nature of their findings, they asked Fred Wailand and Patricia Boyd-Graham to also accompany each plane to get their perspectives on what had happened. It was decided no reports would be shared with the general population until all the adjacent areas had been investigated.

To do that meant that for the next three days, for a total of eight of the proposed 100 missions, they would concentrate the searches on their western flank. The next two of those flights were routed back to the ocean area to confirm the extent of the flooding. Because of the shorter daylight hours, and because the flights took a minimum of four to five hours, not including refueling, debriefing and maintenance, only one mission a day could be conducted.

On March 16th the two planes, now also including either Eric or Ben and Patricia or Fred, headed to San Diego-Coronado. Their flight path was to cross over Indio and the Salton Sea, and both those were, indeed, covered with water. The Coachella and Thermal Valley's were covered in sea water, which was lapping up against the barren Vallecito Mountains. And by the time they crossed the charred Cleveland National Forest and looked down on what was supposed to be the metropolitan area of San Diego, they found it, too, was also under water. Only scattered hills, scrapped clear of all vegetation and life, poked up from the murky, oily and foamy sea. Like the Los Angeles basin, the surrounding mountain sides were choked with huge blackened pyres of the indescribable remains of humanity. There were no structures left, after what must have been a huge nuclear blast, to identify anything of the city of San Diego. Circling wide over the Pacific the planes came back over what would have been Tijuana, Mexico. But it, as well, was inundated with sea water, as it also appeared that Mexicali was, as seen off in the distance. Their flights back confirmed that the Sea of Cortez did extend northward to the Parker area of the Colorado River.

And the last trip to the Pacific Ocean region, for years to come, was on March 17th to the Santa Barbara area. The initial outward phase of the flight was over the eastern part of the Mojave Desert, passing over Interstate 15, with its clogged highway, which would become enshrined as an ever-lasting memorial to April 1st. But when they approached Edwards AFB and Palmdale it was clear a nuclear blast had struck this area. From the town of Mojave to the Antelope Valley the area had been fire-bombed, as had the Tehachapi forest lands to the west.

It was Eric who commented first, after a prolonged silence since their lift-off. "Elaine, after listening to the earlier radio reports from your first mission, I was thunder-struck. My wife will tell you I hardly spoke that night when I got back home. The enormity of what you described, after all we have prepared for and endured, was too much for me. And then your description of the wasteland around my commands at the 29 Palms Marine Base and at Camp Pendleton was the final blow.

"But to actually see the unfolding of this before

your eyes is something no one could really describe. To see that eternal procession of vehicles, just parked for hundreds of miles and the charred earth around Palmdale and Edwards AFB and now the burnt over-forest was beyond description. It appears there was truly a scorched-earth plan in someone's mind. What failures led to this? Was it a failure in leadership, in focus, in individual pursuits, in faith, in the brotherhood and sisterhood of humanity, in belief in the most fundamental laws of simple decency? Surely, there can be no reward for those who set this all in motion. I pray for all of us to have the strength to see this through. Now I have my doubts."

And just as he finished saying this, the planes came in sight of the ocean in the distance. As they began to pass over the mountains of the Los Padres National Forest, they saw the confirmation they had feared. The ocean's shoreline was lapping at the cliffs of this coastal mountain range. The broken pieces of a civilization had been swept up the mountain sides, eventually lodging in the reddish-orange rocky cliffs, surrounding Santa Barbara. The extraordinary height and undulated length of the debris fields, extending far to the west, were clear evidence that a massive tsunami had struck this area. There was no exposed level land. Santa Barbara was gone, under hundreds of feet of water. And as they circled around the Channel Islands, it was clear that so little land was left exposed, that no life was possible there either.

As the crews looked back at the newly shaped continent, it was Ben who finally commented. "All this now looks like what the waterline resembles along the Big Sur area up north. The ocean is lapping at cliff edges. No level land exists anymore. Even our Seabee homeport at Port Hueneme and our residence in Ventura are lost. For all of us who have seen this sight, we will forever have this horrific panorama imprinted in us. Nothing, for us, will ever be the same again. Furthermore, we've seen no signs of life; nor how could there be any, looking at all this destruction. We must now focus our searches on inland locations. None of us are equipped to deal with a steady onslaught of this kind of change and loss... let's go home, Larry."

Some time later that day, at the persistent urging from Patricia, it was agreed that the one last preplanned mission, to the Bakersfield area, should still be undertaken. While it was known that the San Joaquin Valley had indirect communication to the Pacific Ocean, by way of the Sacramento River Delta, what drove this agreement to go ahead, was the hope they would find someone in that region alive and that saltwater would not have poured into the valley.

Not wanting to waste valuable time, the planes had been serviced and refueled overnight and were ready to fly by 10:00 a.m. the next day. And by 10:30 a.m. each plane was aloft, with a heading of Bakersfield, via what was Edwards AFB. Once over the Tehachapi Mountains and in position to see the southeastern end of the San Joaquin Valley, the crews were again greeted with a massive flood. As they flew over the lower end of the valley, it appeared there had to be at least 40-50 feet of standing water, extending as far north as they could see. Only the tops of few of the taller buildings in Bakersfield were visible. Covering the remainder of the valley was every article from civilization's basement. They were floating or bobbing aimlessly, surrounded by a brown-black, oily sheen. It was as if they were looking at an overflowing grease trap. It was mournfully foul, and it was clear to everyone that the toxicity of what they were seeing was so severe it would take time, measured in eons, to neutralize this area. Their hopes were dashed. The oceans' flooding had reached inland, wherever entrance could be gained by a tributary or bay. All that was needed was a low enough elevation for this intrusion. They could only theorize what this meant for the people of the Eastern seaboard and Gulf States. It was me, one of the writers of this chronicle, while aboard one of the planes on this mission, who upon seeing this epidemic of horror below us, swore out loud, "Jesus wept."

Circling wide again to insure what they were seeing was indeed encompassing the valley as far as they could see, they eventually returned to Resolve by flying over Ridgecrest. All the while, they still hoped to see and rescue anything living. But the madness continued. The Naval Weapons Center had been struck by a powerful blast and no life was visible in that area as well.

The last four days had left the two crews solemn and exhausted. And as their coordinator, Ernie decided to give them a day's rest, after he met with them for their debriefing that evening. Without any voiced objection, he also decided that he would pilot only one plane the next day, the 19th, and head east, away from all the ocean flooding. To find someone or something alive was becoming almost like an obsession to him and to most of the other team members. Finally, it was agreed that his heading would be almost due east over Prescott, Jerome and Cottonwood, Arizona. Then he would circle around over the Flagstaff and William's area to return home. He knew the trip would be stretching the fuel capacity of the plane, but at least this trip would avoid major cities, industrial sites or military reservations and overflowing rivers or tsunami-driven oceans. Maybe someone could survive outside those target zones or natural disaster regions.

At the conclusion of the debriefing, following this last trip to the Bakersfield area, Ernie said, "We are now seeing what actually happened on April 1st. And after some discussion amongst our various scientists and engineers, they seem to agree that something of unimaginable proportions occurred, other than nuclear detonations, to cause the oceans to rise so suddenly and so high. Chances are we won't ever know why. But our focus, despite these awful revelations, has to remain continuing the search for anyone who has made it through all this. Get some needed rest tomorrow. You will all be returning to work the next day. We will continue to avoid the large metropolitan areas, such as Phoenix and Tucson, for now. Let's give our senses a rest. But we will survey all possible areas of survival, including those cities, before our local searching is finished. Now go be with your families, get some rest and thank you for your dedication."

TEN: SEARCHING EAST OF RESOLVE

Everyone in the Johnson and Bazzie families were excited about their five day trip to Chino Valley, scheduled to start on March 30th. Both husbands, Tse and Niyol, were very active in their Navajo Reservation-sponsored rodeos, held each summer. They loved to ride the broncos and the bulls. And their two boys, Shiye and Gaagii, had become quite good at calf roping and bull-dogging. The two families had very close friends they had met four years ago at their annual rodeo. For the last two years, in the spring, these friends invited them to came out to their small horse ranch, just west of the Prescott National Forest, near the small town of Chino Valley. They camped out in an open meadow, with the forest just behind them, and the husbands and boys rode horses all day for two full days. The women, Shá and Shima, and their daughters, Nizhoni and Doli, were relieved just to have them out of their way, so they could do whatever they wanted. Often, they would all pile in one of the pickups and head off to Jerome or Cottonwood. It was an ideal vacation for the families.

Arriving at 1:30 p.m. on the 30th, they quickly set up their tents and gathered some firewood for their camp stoves. They were eager to get ready for the day's only meal. Afterward, the fellows went over to the corral to inspect the horses and hang up the tack they brought with them for tomorrow's rides. It was a fine herd of Appaloosas, mixed with a few Pintos. As they stood around looking at the horses, the side bets started as to who could ride the fastest, the longest, the most difficult horse and who could rope the most accurately. Everyone was in great spirits. The owners of the property were gone for these few days, being called away to Prescott. Their oldest daughter had been seriously injured in a traffic accident. They told the two families to make themselves at home and feed and care for the horses and livestock while they were gone.

All the next day the atmosphere was filled with the spirit of competition. That evening, a grand meal of fresh-caught fish, corn bread, baked beans, potato salad and hot tea and soda was spread out under the trees, by their tents, on makeshift tables. As the sun set over the Juniper Mountains to the west, the scene was nothing short of idyllic. The cheerful gurgling creek behind their tents, where they caught the fish, was still full of water from the winter snow pack runoff. The stream was at tree line, coursing its way north to the East Verde River. The meadow in front of them was in full bloom with wild flowers and a full pasture of Timothy grass. The mixed fragrances of pine pitch, drying grass and wild flowers filled the evening air.

The land was cross-fenced with white planking, giving the setting the appearance of a western-style Kentucky horse farm. To the north of them was the ranch house, built of native logs many years ago. The one change the present owners had made to the place was to excavate and build a full basement. Beyond noticing the house's exterior, the families had no idea what was in the house, or in the basement, for that matter. They came here for the camping and horseback riding. What was inside the house was of little interest to them.

As darkness and an early spring chill spread over the valley, they finished building what soon became a fully mature campfire. Its cracking, sizzling and popping was like the finest boreal symphony to each of them; stories, dancing and singing soon followed, and lasted late into the night.

Nothing in particular had been planned for April 1st, other than once they managed to wake up, they might try riding up through the forested mountainside. They would follow the well worn animal trails, as had been their custom the two previous years they had camped here. But there certainly was no hurry to wake up and get organized.

True to their promise to each other, no one awoke before 9:00 a.m., and then there was a leisurely prepared and eaten breakfast, which they were finishing and beginning to clean up by 10:00 a.m., when the first shock wave shook them. It was like the valley and mountains surrounding them shuddered from a hard chill. Everything on the table was knocked off, as their tables collapsed. The tents flattened, and the horses began running madly about the pasture. Not living in an active earthquake region, the incident scared them. Shima and Shá began yelling to the men to gather the children together and run toward the ranch house for safety. Being out in the open scared them even more. No one knew what was going to happen next.

As they were approaching the house, Tse said he wanted to turn on their truck radio to see what was going on. And quickly everyone gathered around him, as he jumped into the front seat and turned it on. Oddly, the only station he could reach was the A.M. station, broadcasting out of Flagstaff. And the announcements were chilling.

"This is the Emergency Broadcast System that you are listening to at this time. All local broadcasting has been permanently replaced by these broadcasts. Our country is under attack. Major cities throughout our land, and apparently over the world, are being destroyed by nuclear detonations. Seek shelter immediately if you can hear this message, and God Bless America, in her time of terrible peril."

Looking at each other, they were stunned and confused what it all meant. Because all they could tune in, otherwise, was static, both Tse and Niyol could only respond with, "This must really be happening! We must find some shelter to protect the children and ourselves."

It was Shima who excitedly suggested, "What about the ranch house? It looks secure from the outside. We could at least sit on the front porch and listen to the radio announcements. Tse, you drive the pick up over by the porch, and we can listen to the radio for any other announcements. At least it's better than being out here or in the barn."

Everyone agreed and ran over to the front porch. For the next two hours they tried to comfort each other and gather their belongings from their flattened campsite. They planned to sleep on the porch until they felt it safe enough to return home. But just as they were feeling somewhat more secure and relieved, a second shock wave hit. It was from the nuclear blast of the off-course missile, intended for Phoenix. It was 1:20 p.m., and their world had gone mad.

The owners had not locked the front door, trusting that their guests would respect their belongings, as they always had in the past. It was just part of the hospitality of the West to provide access to a shelter if it was needed. Rushing inside after the second event, everyone just stood paralyzed in the living room area. It was Shá who ordered them to spread out and see what was available for them to hide in or under. And by now, they had no idea what was happening, but they knew each shockwave was stronger than the last. To them it seemed only a matter of time before something devastating hit their area. Panic was setting in.

It was Shiye who found the door to the basement and called out to everyone to let them know what he had found, when he opened it. And it was at this point the power went out. The electric generating capability at Hoover Dam ended at that moment, as Lake Mead breached the dam. All of the western United States lost electrical power, as the cascading surges necessary to compensate for this loss, overwhelmed other power generating facilities in the region.

The families scrambled to find flashlights and candles. Tse ran out to the truck and got the flashlights, lanterns and other equipment. Nivol joined him, picking up their leftover food and water. Both rushed back inside with their arms full of supplies and secured the front door behind them. Just as they did, there was a rush of air, with a mixture of sand, heat, and microscopic debris that surged through the area. With it, came the first indication of higher radioactivity levels to come.

Securing the doors and windows, everyone made their way through the basement doorway and down the full-length staircase. Shutting the door behind them, it was Niyol who noticed that the basement door was metal, and encased in a heavy metal frame. As everyone finally assembled inside the basement and began focusing their flashlights around the immense room, they could see this was no ordinary storage area. It was a shelter.

There were provisions for an extended stay there, as well as bedding, extra clothes and a special toilet/shower facility. Their friends were survivalists. As such, included in the stored equipment, there was a Geiger counter. It was Gaagii who took possession of it and began taking readings and recording them. And for the next nine months, somehow these two families survived in that space. It was a testimony to the resilience of their heritage and of their will to live.

By the following January 14th, the radioactivity levels had plummeted to consistently safe levels and the family began to wander out briefly. The ranch house had not been disturbed or looted in the intervening months, but all about them was lifeless. There were no animals or bird sounds, and it was very cold. But from that day on, they began to live upstairs, making fires in the large open fireplace to heat and cook on. They were no longer prisoners of the basement.

And it was soon thereafter that they had a family council meeting to discuss what to do next. Getting out some maps of the area, it was finally decided they would begin scouting the area and lay out markers, indicating that they were there. This was done in the off-chance of anyone ever flying over or driving by. Repeated attempts to use the emergency radio had been hopeless. Only static greeted them. But it did have short-wave capabilities, so they could only pray someday they would hear voices and a message of hope.

From January 14th, to February 17th, individual members of the two families either walked, or rode the two bicycles that belonged to the ranch's owners, up and down the highway in front of their shelter. The children painted a large wooden sign and erected it on the roadside, in front of the house, indicating they were there. It simply said, in bold lettering, "HELP! THERE ARE SURVIVORS HERE!" Over time the boys rode along Hwy 89, north to Paulden, and then eventually to where it intersected with Interstate 40. To the south, they even rode all the way to Prescott.

But it was in the clearing, adjacent to the Ernest A. Love Field airport, at the turn off for Hwy 89A, that the families decided to erect their most ambitious and visible sign. On the runway, not subject to being overgrown with weeds, they painted hundreds of rocks, large and small, with black paint, found in a nearby storeroom. In ten foot high lettering it said, "HELP US! WE ARE UP THE ROAD NORTH FROM HERE". And then, due to there being no traffic in front of their ranch house shelter, other than themselves, they laid out, in white letters, the message, "WE ARE HERE". To complete their emergency signals, they built and covered a large pile of branches, some tires, and larger timber. If anyone should come by, they would ignite a huge fire.

Throughout all this time they were moving about the area, they never found anyone alive. And there were precious few vehicles on the road. None of them would start, with either their batteries dead or their electrical system badly deteriorated from the atmospheric contamination. But none of that stopped the families from trying to rebuild an engine from their own two trucks and the spare parts they scavenged from stranded vehicles.

Then the shortwave message was heard on March 12th. They had not listened to their radio on the 10th or the 11th, when they could have heard the messages being broadcasted. It all seems hopelessly in vain, so they only turned the radio on every third day, for 10 minutes. But this day was different. They heard the message coming from Resolve. (see Appendix 3, fig. 1, "Resolve's Message to the World") And it was coming from close to Needles, California, of all places! The relief, the shock, the anticipation, all of it came pouring forth from everyone. There was laughter, crying, shouting and dancing. They were not alone. They might be reunited with others. It was overwhelming.

And then on March 19th, late that morning, the children came running into the ranch house, yelling that they thought they heard a motor, possibly even an airplane, off in the distance. What they actually heard was just that. Ernie had flown almost directly over Love Field and saw their sign on the runway. Thrilled, he called back to Resolve to report the finding. Then, banking his plane north from there he followed the highway until he thought he saw something on the highway. But he was not absolutely sure what he saw, so he flew on toward Interstate 40. Meanwhile, the families realized what was happening and ran out, just as Ernie passed overhead. Hurriedly, they pulled the tarp off the brush pile. Tse threw some fuel oil over the pile, struck a match and lit the flammable liquid. Immediately, black smoke began pouring upward, which against the clear, deep blue sky, was clearly seen for miles.

Once Ernie got to the Interstate, he knew he had missed the other sign, so he turned to go back, and there before him was the rising column of black smoke. "I've got 'um," he shouted to his crew and over the radio. There is black smoke rising where they are. Get the leaflets ready to throw out, Dawkins. I'll signal we see them, and the leaflets will give them instructions what they are to do now."(see Appendix 3, fig. 2, "Rescue Leaflets").

Packaged with 50 leaflets to a bundle, they had been preprinted in case anyone was found. If someone was found, they could be dropped, letting the survivors know that a helicopter would be coming later to pick them up. As Dawkins, Ernie's faithful aid, driver and alter-ego of some years, threw out the leaflets, he watched as the eight family members ran over to pick them up. As they pulled up to return to Resolve, all of them were waving wildly. It was a grand feeling for all in the plane that day, including this chronicler.

Because the leaflet specifically stated there

would be little room for many possessions, the families brought only their most precious items and clothing. It cautioned them that it may take a while to get the helicopters readied to return for the actual rescue, but that they were not to worry. They would return. And by 4:00 p.m. that afternoon the helicopters had landed on the highway in front of the ranch house. All the members of the Johnson and Bazzie families were dressed, packed and waiting. It was one of the most touching sights Ernie and Elaine had ever seen. Not wanting to waste precious daylight, the families were hustled on board the two aircraft, doors were secured and the helicopters, very heavily loaded, lifted off for their return to Resolve with the most precious cargo left on planet earth: Life.

ELEVEN: KITT PEAK OBSERVATORY

On March 31st, as was usual during any other sun-filled day on top of the Quinlan Mountains' 6,880 feet Kitt Peak National Observatory complex, the two solar observatories were in full operational mode. The Solis and McMath-Pierce Solar Telescopes represented the biggest, and arguably, the best solar observational platforms on the planet. They were included in an amazing assembly of 23 different telescopes, situated on this isolated peak on the Tohono O'odham Nation's reservation in the Arizona-Sonoran Desert. For an astronomer or cosmologist, this outcrop of oddly shaped buildings represented a magnificent laboratory for studying the universe's past and likely future. Here, as nowhere else in science, did the eye and the mind work so closely together to unravel the deepest mysteries of existence. Mankind's nearsightedness was brought into sharper focus in this place.

The solar telescopes had a skeleton staff on this day due to needed repairs, which were long overdue, on the roadway off Hwy 86 to the Laboratory. The Laboratory Administration agreed that the Laboratory would be closed to the public the entire week, prior to that weekend. During that time needed repairs and upgrades would also be completed in the Visitor's Center, specifically in its kitchen and the dining room.

Built in 1961, the Center was in desperate need of some rehabilitation. And now that the weekday construction work was completed, it being Saturday, three of the kitchen/dining room staff brought their families to stay and help through the weekend. They were primarily engaged in the final clean up and restocking of kitchen supplies and food. After that, the building would be ready for incoming visitors, starting April 2nd.

Each of the families lived in Sells. It was a source of pride for the families and an honor for the local tribal to have their people working in such an important place as the Laboratory. The Administration agreed to families accompanying the employees, since there were no visitors. This made for a relaxed but productive atmosphere.

Stewart Conrad, the lead scientist for the solar telescopes, had two of his staff members also working that weekend. All three scientists had brought their families there, as well. Their families all lived Tucson, and it was an equally exciting time for them to be here like this. The children were particularly enthusiastic about camping out all weekend on top of the mountain. All the families brought cots that were spread out in the dining area. Eating and sleeping was done there. It was something they would never dream of doing when visitors were about. The children of all six families knew this was a special privilege and were having one adventure after another roaming throughout the complex.

Most of the heavy work left for the weekend was being done in the basement of this building. The Laboratory at Kitt Peak was started in 1958, at the height of the Cold War. Because of the paranoia at the time, a huge reinforced basement was excavated. It was to serve as a bomb shelter for the staff of the complex. Now it was a storage area for food, water, and miscellaneous supplies. This weekend they were laying in food, water and other beverages for the upcoming spring and summer rush of visitors.

Stewart, in the meantime, was frantically tasking his staff to finish photographing and cataloging digital images for the upcoming International Symposium of Astrophysicists to be held next week in Lucerne, Switzerland. All three of them were to attend this meeting. Their designated lecture series would be to present the latest information on coronal flares and massive solar ejection events. And they hoped to take the final images over these next two days, and then complete their sorting of images and rewriting the lecture syllabus by Monday. They were to fly out of Tucson on Tuesday for the symposium.

By sunrise both telescopes were prepped and ready. There had been more activity than usual across the equatorial plane of the sun in recent days, and the staff was eager to record its evolution or cessation. The time delay, from when any particular event is visible on the solar surface, as seen by the telescope, until when the effects of that event affect earth, was about 20 minutes. From sunrise to sunset the staff took images, cross-referenced them with others taken previously, had their computers refine and enhance particular ones, and then began to see if any unusual expansion of activity might be occurring. Nothing was found to be particularly worrisome, but certainly the increased activity was noteworthy. Stewart was excited that it would make for an interesting sequencing of images for their upcoming lectures. By sunset, all three scientists were exhausted and famished. They had not eaten all day. The evening was spent with all six families eating and sharing tall tales and fables. Lights out came at midnight. They had one final day left to photograph: April 1st.

The next morning was different in that, being Sunday, the pressure was not as great to get started early at the telescope labs. Instead, the families all ate breakfast together, prepared by Stewart and his fellow workers. All six wives had the day off. All meals today were courtesy of the gentlemen. The guys, working on stocking and reorganizing the basement, were to prepare the main meal, which was to be eaten mid-afternoon.

And by 9 a.m. the scientists were at their stations in the McMath-Pierce Telescope. They were finished with taking images from the Solis scope, as of yesterday. Immediately, Stewart began downloading the images that had been preprogrammed to be taken at 8 a.m. And it was just then they saw the first astonishing image. Running into their main office, where his other two colleagues were busy working, he exclaimed, "Something highly unusual appears to be happening, and possibly it warrants notifying NOAA right away. There appears to be a series of coronal flares occurring, each more intense than the last, each reaching our further into space. They appear to be happening in 10-15 minute intervals, but that timeframe isn't fixed, and if anything, it's shortening. Roger, will you notify NOAA for us? There may soon be some disruption of satellite and radio transmissions."

"Sure thing, boss," came the chipper voice of Roger Hicker. It was, after all, a standard procedure with the lab to do so. Today's development did not seem that alarming, at least not until the next observation.

Within minutes of Roger's call, the southern hemisphere's night sky was aglow with the dancing waves of the aurora Australis, secondary to a solar flare striking earth's southern hemisphere. Within seconds thereafter, electrical transmissions were severely interrupted around the world.

At 10:00 a.m. their time or noon EST in New York City, the staff on station at the solar telescope were still studying images coming from the sun, unaware that transmissions planet-wide were not only severely disrupted, but now major cities were being destroyed. Kitt Peak was isolated for now, but not for much longer. At 11:10 a.m. Fort Huachuca time, it was also struck by a nuclear-tipped missile. That was the first sign the families at Kitt Peak had any inkling that something terrible was in progress. Being encased in their lab, the scientists could not see anything outside, but, despite the telescope being anchored and cushioned against the effects of earthquakes, they still felt the earth movements from that detonation 80-90 miles away.

Being ignorant at the time of what was happening on the planet, the three scientists' concentration was solely focused on the quickening pace of the sun's energy build up and its ever-larger explosive outbursts. Meanwhile, the wives of the six families had called their children to come into the Visitor Center from outside, when they felt the blast-caused earthquake. It was Diane, Stewart's wife, who saw the rising mushroom shaped cloud rising to their southeast when she happened to glance out the window, as the children came in. It did not seem right, she knew. It appeared too large to be just a routine military exercise. Maybe, she thought later, it was a large munitions depot that exploded. She chose not to alarm the others by telling them what she had seen.

Then at 11:40 a.m. Stu and his staff saw what, to them, was the worst sight they could imagine ever seeing on an image. The entire frame was filled with a massive tongue of orange, white and red fire heading toward earth. Nothing, even remotely theorized, had approached the size of this ejection. Immediately, looking at each other, they knew a terrible force was soon going to strike the earth.

"Roger!" Stu shouted, "Call NOAA again! Tell

them there is a massive, terminal ejection heading our way. We only have 15-20 minutes to warn others. I will collect as many digital images as I can. We must leave this building immediately. Meet me at the front door in 5 minutes."

They all ran as fast, as the notebooks and file boxes they were carrying, would let them. Breathless, they came staggering into the Visitor Center. Stewart called out, stumbling between words, "Everyone! Quick! Get into the basement! Round up all the children! We must all be down there NOW!" A quick survey revealed that the wives had already gotten the children inside, and the other three men were still at work in the basement. Just before they entered the stairwell to go downstairs, Diane motioned to Stewart to look towards the southeast.

"My God!" he stammered. "That's a cloud formation from a thermonuclear explosion! What is happening? Roger! Did you ever get in contact with NOAA that last attempt? Did they tell you anything?"

"No, Stu, I didn't," he replied, heading down the stairs. "There was only static. I guess our transmission was disrupted from the effects of that first coronal ejection."

"Or, I fear, something much worse." Stewart muttered.

Rushing down the stairs, nearly stumbling over one another, the six families entered what was to be their home for the next ten months. As the last person stepped onto the concrete basement floor, it was 12:11 p.m., Mountain Time, and the shock wave of the solar ejection striking Antarctica blew past Kitt Peak Visitor Center. At their altitude, it had a more concussive effect than if they had been at a lower elevation. The upper story of the Visitor Center was severely shaken, with all the windows blown out. The radio telescope, some

675

distance away from them, was jarred off its foundation. But that was not all, within the next ten minutes, there were two more shock waves, with accompanying thunderous roars. The two thermonuclear-tipped missiles targeted for the military's Yuma Proving Grounds and Tucson each struck 30-40 miles east of their intended targets.

Stewart and his wife seeing what they did to the southeast of them and the three scientists knowing what incalculable damage could be anticipated from the giant solar emission hitting earth, it was dreadfully logical for them to assume that the Kitt Peak area was now surrounded by lethal levels of radioactivity and destruction.

Amongst the many items left, from the establishment of this shelter in the Cold War years were a couple of Geiger counters. During reshuffling and restocking the basement shelves, the three custodial workers had found these two instruments. Naturally, still being packed in their original container boxes, they were unsure what they were for. But they did recognize the universal symbol for radioactivity on the outside of the boxes. Once they realized the subject being discussed by Stewart and Diane with everyone, following these shaking events, one of them mentioned what they had found.

Roger immediately went over to the area where the boxes were located and took one of them. Removing its faded cover, he set about preparing it for use. Soon he climbed the basement stairs to open the door into the first floor, but as he climbed higher, the readings began to climb as well. As he called the numbers out, Stewart finally said, "That's far enough Roger. You don't need to go up any further. It's as we feared. There has been some kind of nuclear warfare started. And we are now prisoners in this place, for no-telling how long. It would not surprise me if we would have to stay down here for months."

Those first few days were, as they would be for anyone in their circumstances, unbearable. They had to subdivide the full basement into small family living quarters. Eventually, they set aside an eating area and a sort of lounge area. But most importantly, they had to sort and separate the food, water and beverages, and begin the rationing each for the long struggle ahead. There was more of each upstairs in the kitchen, but for the time being there was no way to access it. Their survival depended on barely existing on meager rations. A gravity toilet system had been engineered when the shelter was first constructed, which lessened the probability of contamination. A separate toilet and wash basin was enclosed. For the next ten months these six families hovered on the edge of existence.

The lights and all electricity went off at the same time as the last two explosions. There was a brief scurry to find flashlights and candles. From that point on, any illumination was from these two sources, and they, too, were rationed. Essentially, they became cave dwellers.

Come February 2nd, the levels of radioactivity had dropped to safe levels both on the main floor of the Visitor Center and around Kitt Peak generally. And luckily, the canned food and bottled water supplies on the first floor were protected behind closed doors and packaging. They were safe to consume. All six of the families emerged from the basement, on that day, to a much different world than existed on March 31st. Like the families trying to survive upstate, outside of Chino Valley, the Kitt Peak families also had a radio. And it also had shortwave capabilities. But, like their northern compatriots, all they could hear was static. However, they were convinced whenever, or possibly if ever, there were to be messages from other survivors, it would be delivered by shortwave. Everyone took turns monitoring the shortwave band width at periodic intervals night and day.

In the meantime it was decided they needed to make their presence visually apparent, as much as they could. To begin with, they hoisted a large American flag on the flagpole outside the Visitor Center. They felt that its fluttering presence was so incongruous, compared to the general state of the area that it had to signal life was nearby. They then found a five gallon container of black, asphalt paint and two individuals climbed up onto the roof of the Visitor Center and painted "HELP US" in large letters on the white, aluminum-base, protective roof coating. The two Conrad children rode bicycles, ones that had been used by Telescope staff as their primary means of commuting within the various buildings on Kitt Peak, down to the main highway and painted the same sign at the entrance to their exit. They used white paint. And finally, as a last resort, everyone gathered together bits of dried desert brush, twigs, and branches and made a large pile in the parking lot of the Visitor Center. It was covered with weighted, plastic table clothes to keep the material dry. Cans of lighter fluid and matches were sealed and placed nearby, with instructions for anyone who heard or saw anything to run out and ignite the pile.

It was on March 12th, that they heard their first broadcast from Resolve's Communication Center. It set off shouts, cheers and hugs. They had confirmation they were not alone. They knew Needles was not that far away, and if they got too low on supplies, a few of them could strike out for there. For the time being though, they decided to wait for any over-flights. Venturing far out from their shelter was not something anyone was eager to do. After April 1st, the unknown was now recognized as both challenging and, quite possibly, very deadly.

Back at Resolve, with the plane crews more rested, Elaine and Doug again took off on the morning of March 20th, heading south east into Arizona. Their heading was toward Nogales, by way of Gila Bend. Their assumption, using this heading, was that the cities of Phoenix and Tucson were most likely destroyed and any survivors had to seek shelter well outside those areas.

At 11:50 a.m. that morning, the children of the six families were playing volleyball with a makeshift net and under-inflated ball. It was their scheduled physical education time. Their schooling had been maintained by the adults, but mostly without the benefit of books or other materials. P.E. was a welcome break for them from the grind of classes six days a week.

Today, however, their set schedule ended. And it started with the sounds of approaching aircraft. Screaming to everyone that they could hear it coming, they yelled, "Someone is coming!! Quick, light the bonfire!! Take off your shirts, wave something at them!! Hurry!!! Everyone outside! They're coming!!"

Frantically, the plastic covers were pulled off, while someone doused the pile with lighter fluid and struck a couple of matches. Soon the dry stack was ablaze, filling the air with white smoke. Combined with the smoke, the waving figures on the ground, the various large, hand-written signs, and the American flag, all this caught the attention of the aircraft. Both planes wagged their wings in response, and one threw out the leaflets as they passed over. Then, both turned, one headed back to Resolve and the other swooped down to find a safe landing area on the nearby highway.

Adults and children, alike, poured out of the Visitor Center, running around to catch one of the leaflets in mid-flight. It was true there were three scientists, of world-renown, amongst this group, but they, like everyone else, acted like the youngest child there, with pure glee and abandon.

Elaine was piloting the plane that managed to land on a clear stretch of highway. She left her co-pilot there to relay any messages to Resolve that she might send him on her hand-held radio, one of those used on the three Yucca Mountain trains. The personnel in the Communication Center needed to know the number and status of the survivors at Kitt Peak. Hurriedly, she, an EMT, and yours truly, Fred Wailand, headed up the mountainside to the survivors.

We were met a little over half way up the newly surfaced roadway by a group of happy and excited kids, along with Stewart Conrad. It was like a scene out of the newsreels at the end of the Second World War. Tattered clothing, emaciated and gaunt, it was only too clear their survival had been at a great price. I elected to stay with Stewart, rather than have him try to walk all the way back up. It was clear that would be too much for him. In time, he and I would walk down to the highway, where he would eventually board our plane for the trip back to Resolve. In the meantime, he filled me in on what they had witnessed before and after April 1st. It was a story for the ages.

Elaine and Mike Leary, the EMT, went ahead with the children and began to triage the families. There were two individuals, one Tohono male and one Kitt Peak Lab staff member's wife who needed medical attention immediately. Elaine radioed that information back to Resolve. It was decided to fly both helicopters and the other plane back, with only their pilots, leaving extra space for return passengers.

Again, by 4:20 p.m. the helicopters had landed on the Visitor Center parking lot and loaded up the two sick individuals on litters along with boxes of invaluable video images, reports and documentation. All the technical manuals had been stored in the basement and would be picked up at a later date, when the Global Union Library was finished and ready to catalog and store them. The other chopper carried one family. And the two planes carried another two families. That left nine people to rescue the next day. Roger Hicker and family volunteered to stay behind, as did the Freidrick Gott, the other scientist, and his children and Diane and their oldest son. They were plucked up the next morning by 11:30 a.m. and returned to Resolve.

It was a warm welcome by everyone in Resolve for the 32 people rescued from Arizona. Sadly, that was all of the survivors that the local rescue missions discovered in their three months of searching. They flew 97 missions. But the boats were never used. There was no sign of life anywhere near water, probably because of the massive upheavals associated with any water source in their search area. And the intense cold, undoubtedly from the combination of nuclear and volcanic debris heaved up into the atmosphere, made sustained life improbable for nearly everyone. Along with that, there was the daunting task of finding enough food and water for such an extended period of time.

In just a matter of days the newly arrived survivors were integrating themselves into the community. The Navajo and Tohono tribe members were relieved to have each other to lean on during those early days. Then gradually they began to meld into the general population, as they realized the true brotherhood and sisterhood of all present. And quite frankly, it was the native peoples, who were rescued over the next two years, who were the most humble and reverent whenever there were the return appearances of B. Something in their genetic memory, guarded and celebrated through the countless millennia, had prepared them for B's revelations. Their calm and insight was a source of inspiration and confidence for the general population in Resolve. The skills and talents they brought, that might insure Resolve's ultimate survival, were not indexed in textbooks or procedure manuals. They were of the heart and the soul.

Ernie Tam's team of rescuers had performed their jobs with dedication and resourcefulness. Their discoveries, and the information they brought back to Resolve with Steward Conrad's group, filled many gaps in their knowledge. The picture of what happened on April 1st was becoming only too clear. But now it was time to support the long range rescuers. Benton Scott's team was now in the spotlight.

TWELVE: EXTENDED RESCUES BEGIN

The trip to Nellis AFB that started on March 15th with the convoy of 43 personnel was not able to reach the Base until March 18th. There were many roadblocks once they got to Highway 93, between Boulder City and Henderson. For the majority of this team, the return was retracing the memories of their trip from Yucca Mountain on the trains. But there were a few along from the "Amboy 75" and the Marine Base near Amboy who had not, as yet, seen up close the chaos and despair of April 1st. Benton made sure none of these individuals were driving the vehicles when they turned onto Highway 93.

Often they had to weave their way through back streets, in order to get the large flatbed trucks through the congested and blocked roadways. And for everyone it was the absolute silence that greeted them, as they maneuvered their way through this overbuilt and abandoned metropolitan area that was unnerving. A deeply disturbing combination of urban, post-April 1st decay, was settling in. Drifting sand was accumulating everywhere, as if nature was attempting to erase this mistake on her canvas. No window appeared intact. Curtains fluttered out of their oddly shaped openings, left by the broken glass, whether from homes, businesses or high rise hotels, going as far up as you could see. At least that was the view of the taller buildings left standing. It all signaled, to anyone passing by, that there was no life here. Repeated earthquakes, high radiation levels and deadly shock waves had seen to that. And where drifted sand and wind-blown debris had not piled up, there were snow drifts. What all this covered was left unsaid. It was as if the elements were going to see to the burial services of this failed civilization. No help was needed.

Eventually, the convoy arrived at Nellis, coming in from the southern entrance. Benton had suggested that they set up camp at the fire station, it being the soundest building and, no doubt, the safest. From there, they would spread out to work on their various objectives. From their earlier meetings, it was determined that four objectives had to be met before they could consider launching any long range rescue missions.

First, they had to establish they could, indeed, salvage a cargo and a refueling plane from the pile up of their planes on the transit parkway. Second, they had to insure they could find usable jet fuel and be able to pump it from the underground storage bunkers to tanker trucks and fuel bladders. To do so, they needed to rehabilitate a couple of electric generators stored at the base for emergencies. And third, they had to locate a smaller bulldozer and two snowplows with blowers fit inside their cargo plane. After reviewing the missions they had ahead of them, they realized there was no way they were going to land these planes, even if they got them airworthy, on the designated airfields across the nation, unless they had the equipment to clear the tarmacs of debris and snow. And last, they had to find parachute rigging to attach to these larger pieces of equipment, along with material to make skids. If they accomplish all this, and it was a leap of faith their thinking they could, then maybe they would be able to start these long range missions.

Soon after they arrived and got settled into the firehouse, Steven Blackwell and Kathryn Swisher took their respective teams and drove around to the pile of their mangled aircraft. As reported to them, there were two planes that appeared salvageable.

Through days of tedious maneuvering and untangling, the teams finally got the two planes, each relatively intact, moved and parked in one of the larger hangers. Then the process of disassembling and reassembling both aircraft, from the wheels up began. In addition, due to the cold weather, some of the other, nearly destroyed planes were dismantled and spread out inside another, more damaged hanger. To work continuously outside was impossible, given the sudden changes in weather and the persistent cold. From inside these two hangers, the cutting torches and wrenches could begin dissecting the needed sections for reconstructing the two rescue planes.

While the majority of the personnel were involved in that work, a team of five, along with Alfie Shoemaker, Louise Matthews and Frances Bynum began the search for the fuel bunkers and the heavy equipment, as well as for the parachute paraphernalia and the skid-making materials.

Working in shifts using two restored generators, each of which enabled them to have flood lamps and a welder, they had the two planes reassembled and the engines retuned within one month of their arrival. And it was estimated that within a week they could most likely attempt a test flight of both planes. That would depend on the success of static testing the engines, sorting out some refueling issues, and being able to clear the runway for a safe take off and landing. The equipment to do the cleanup had been finally located and refurbished. It was time now to bulldoze and plow snow off the runway.

Despite Benton's reservations, both Steven Blackwell and Kathryn Swisher insisted they were going to test fly their respective planes. Their rationale was that they would be flying the cross-country missions anyway, so it was better to see right away how the planes would handle. Benton's hesitation was centered on the possibility of losing them in an aborted takeoff or landing or in mid-air power failure. But, he had to agree they were, by far, the most qualified to test fly them.

At last, on May 2nd, at 9:45 a.m. the last of the snow pack was cleared off the runway, the two planes were warmed up at the end of the tarmac and ready to proceed with take off. On board, there was a skeleton crew of just the pilot and co-pilot on each plane, leaving 41 nervous spectators standing outside the fire station waiting for their final throttle up and lift off.

Inside the cockpit Steve made the final check-off with his co-pilot and simply stated, "It's time, at last. Let's see what this ole girl can do."

The plane's jet engines roared louder and louder across the vastness of the giant Las Vegas valley. And then it moved forward, gathering speed and within 10 seconds it had lifted off the pavement. His plane was soon joined by Kathryn's. Banking to the south, after they gained some altitude, they headed toward Lake Mead and the Grand Canyon. Their flight plan was to circle around the Grand Canyon and back through Utah, around St. George and land, coming in from the north. It would take about 30-45 minutes to travel their route.

It was Steve, who while easing back on the throttle, happened to look out his window and see what used to be Lake Mead and the Hoover Dam. "Holy Mother of God," he called out on his radio, which was tuned in to both Benton at Nellis and Eric in Resolve,

686

"Lake Mead is completely drained, and the dam is gone! All that remains are water marks along the sides of the lake and jagged, twisted steel and concrete at the base of the dam. There is a scorch line on the south side shoreline. I would presume that means a blast of some kind was detonated in the area. From here, it appears the explosion occurred inside the lake itself. What have we done? What an awful mess we have left this planet in! For the love of God..."

Trying to regain his composure, he turned to his co-pilot and asked, "Do the instruments indicate that we are stable?"

"Everything checks out, sir," he replied.

"Good. Let's try to focus on the purpose of this trip, then. We have some serious flying ahead, and we need to make sure these planes can handle it."

Returning to Nellis 30 minutes later, both planes checked out ok. Now, the next step was to load the cargo plane with the bulldozer and two snow plows. It was decided that a test run was needed with them as well, but that they would do that upon their return to Resolve. Everyone was anxious to return home, and whatever glitches there were in the equipment drop, could be sorted out there.

Sleds were scrounged from storerooms and modified for each piece of equipment. Parachutes were bundled and attached to the sleds. A crew of three was to be placed in the back of the cargo plane to position the equipment and to coordinate the drops, once they were given the go ahead to parachute them.

Benton suggested the flatbed trucks with full bladders of fuel be accompanied by all the vehicles going back to Resolve, and he would return with that convoy. Nellis was set up so that the generator used to pump fuel was easily accessible to the flight and ground crews in between each separate mission. All refueling had to be done there for these planes. On May 6th, all the vehicles pulled out, leaving the air and ground crews there to fly into Resolve on May 9th. They needed the extra three days to mothball the base and get everything in order for quick refueling once their missions started. For now they had enough fuel for the first mission on June 1st, considering the refueling plane was also full as well.

All of Resolve was waiting for the arrival of the two giant planes on May 9th. The freeway had been cleared of any standing obstacles, such as mileposts, exit signs along either shoulder on the east and west bound lanes. It was determined the median strip barrier was no hazard, given the height of the landing gear and wheels. Their height gave the wings more than adequate clearance. To enable the planes to turn around and fly out of Resolve, a 100 yard wide strip of medial barrier was removed by the engineers and a U-turn access to the westbound lanes was prepared by the Seabees. All was in place and ready for the Nellis AFB planes to land.

A cry went up when everyone began to see the C-141B Starlifter, the cargo plane, come into view. But rather than align itself with the eastbound lane, it began a lower, reduced speed, run along the blocked off westbound strip. As it started this run along that course, the rear doors opened and then out started falling, parachutes attached and unfolding as the equipment fell, the bulldozer and two snowplows. They both landed in the middle of the westbound lanes and skidding to a stop within 150 feet of their first hitting the pavement. Each stopped, as if preprogrammed, within 100 feet of the screaming and cheering throng of families.

The cargo plane then swooped up and around and came in for its landing on the eastbound lane. Closely following it was the KC-135 Stratotanker, the refueling plane. Once the engines were powered down and the doors of the planes opened up, the people surged forward to greet the crews. Benton Scotts' work crews had accomplished what seemed far beyond what was likely or possible. The long range search and rescue missions were to start as scheduled. And now the search teams had time to prepare and drill for the assignment ahead.

That night there was one of the now-famous Celebrations of Life parties. The most recent rescued families had their first taste of Resolve festivities. They were unable to fully participate, due to the shock of just being rescued, but by now, even after the short time they had been in Resolve, they were impressed that this was not a frivolous, bacchanalian event. Its purpose was to salute all who were not there, to recognize their intention to preserve the best of humanity, and to declare that evil could be overcome with good, that truth could overcome deceit. It was a true celebration of a new life, through joining together the occasions of funeral and birth, the acts of separation and union, and the commitments of confession and reawakening. It was intended to welcome the future and their place in it. And it was a display, most of all, of genuine goodness.

Starting on May 20th the Communication Center began to broadcast the dates and approximate times the rescue planes would be in the air over the four different locations. And over the course of the next two years, two of the rendezvous sites yielded an amazing assembly of survivors. However, for that first trip in June, there was no sign of anyone at any of the first three sites in Oregon, South Dakota or Kentucky. Instead, there were countless changes in both the climate and the geography to document and describe. And these were occurring throughout what used to be the United States.

Their first trip on June 1st revealed the awesome impact of the volcanic eruptions along the Cascade

Mountain range. Cities on both sides of that range were affected either by large lava flows or subsonic eruptions of pyroclastic ash and rock. Many cities, like Bend, Oregon, were buried completely. The airfield outside Redmond was indistinguishable from the surrounding landscape. It was all covered in layers of ash.

On their next flight to Rapid City, they were able to see at least the western edge of the effects of Mt. Yellowstone's eruptions. This name was given to that immense formation in later years. From it, Montana, Wyoming, parts of Idaho and South Dakota were blackened, like the bottom of a skillet left too long on a cook stove. And, again, their choice of an airfield in or around Rapid City, like with Redmond, was an unfortunate mistake. There was no way to reasonably estimate the amount of ash on its Regional Airport runway. Both airfields were unusable.

And by their third mission to Kentucky on June 5th, it was evident that the continental United States was split apart. There was now an inland sea separating the eastern seaboard states from the Midwest. From the Gulf of Mexico to the Great Lakes, stretching 50-100 miles on either side of the Mississippi River, there was salt water. The eastern portion of the States was now an island. Luckily there was no damage to the Regional Airport in Bowling Green. There was just no sign of any survivors. But in New Mexico, there was a rescue, one that to this day is still discussed with wonder and amazement.

THIRTEEN: THE CARLSBAD RESCUE

It was June 7th when the long-range rescue team left Resolve for their final pick up point, of this quarter, in New Mexico. Everyone was discouraged that none of the other sites had resulted in rescues or even airfields being seen that were recognizable. Still, they were convinced there had to be more survivors than what they were finding. Their concluding assumption was that even if someone heard their repeated broadcasts, it no doubt would take considerable time to reach one of the four airfields. So, with some resignation, Steven Blackwell and his crew boarded their cargo plane and took off at 6:10 a.m., bound for Carlsbad, New Mexico.

Prior to that departure, in fact many months prior to it, on October 1st, the Shuttle made its approach to the White Sands Space Harbor landing site. Just after Ted called out a warning to everyone about the upcoming touchdown, their rear wheels touched the sand. It was at that moment that the overly-stressed, aging Shuttle landing gears declared they were no longer safe. Immediately, they buckled and collapsed, forcing the Shuttle to land on its underbelly, with its front wheel left in position, trying to keep the craft's nose up and to prevent it from burrowing into the sand. For the next quarter to half a mile, heat shields, sundry metal parts, and shredded tires were left behind them. Midway through that skidding, the front nose wheel assembly also collapsed, adding to the Shuttle's friction with the ground and bringing it to a complete stop against a large mound of drifted sand.

It all happened so fast that no one in the Shuttle had any time to react. Not that any reaction would have altered their crash landing. Remarkably, they were badly shaken up but not seriously injured. Looking around at each other, a shout of relief went up, "We made it!"

Quickly, they unfastened their seat belts and made their way to the exit door, which had been partially buried in the sand as well. With some effort, they were all able to force it open enough to, one by one, crawl out.

But at that point the effects of full gravity hit them. Of the four, it was Oleg who volunteered to try and walk back to the buildings behind them and see if he could find a transport vehicle of some kind. Amber cautioned him not to over-exert himself, but she realized they probably needed to get some distance from the Shuttle, in case certain propellants and other gases might be still left in various reservoirs. And as she looking around her, she realized they could not stay in this spot indefinitely. The white sand was almost endless to the horizon, with barren, rusty colored, life-starved mountains surrounding them. The overcast of clouds that they had observed elsewhere, covering most of the planet, seemed less so in this area. The sky was not clear, but the haze allowed some warmth of sunlight through. She knew by nightfall it would be bitterly cold, and they needed to make some kind of arrangements beforehand. It was a desolate place. "Good luck," she called out to Oleg, as he climbed over the mounded sand, plowed up by the skidding shuttle when it landed.

"I'll try to be back within two hours. Don't wait up, if I'm late." Oleg yelled back, feeling the deepest relief that they were all at least in one piece and on the ground.

What Amber did not want to admit to herself, or to the others, was that in addition to what she thought and felt about this area, she also seemed to both taste and smell the slightest hint of iodine. She knew about radioactive potassium iodide and that they had no protection against it. They had no thyroid pills, no Geiger counter to confirm or reduce her premonition, and at this moment, no shelter to shield them from it. For now, she just hoped Oleg would find some means of transport and get them away from here as quickly as possible.

For Oleg's part, he managed to stumble along, through the brilliant, white sand and over its heavier accumulation around collections of debris and scattered Shuttle parts, strewn along the runway. He thought, in passing, what a sight this must have been on a clear day, with a deep blue sky, against this sheer white background, and the reddish mountains behind. But, "not this day, nor probably on many to come," he sighed aloud. The atmosphere, from all they saw in space, has changed drastically since April 1st.

After he had walked over a mile he saw a collection of buildings in the distance. However, it was only after he had a chance to stop and rest that he was able to push on. The effects of gravity were punishing him through this physical exertion. At last, he did come abreast of the buildings, which were mostly warehouses and possibly a couple of hangers. But situated in the midst of these was the emergency response building, painted the traditional bright red. Working his way over to it, he found the doors unlocked, as they should be, and two fire engines and a full size ambulance inside.

It occurred to him that this equipment had to have been serviced relatively recently, this site being one of the emergency landing fields for their Shuttle. With that thought, he opened the rear ambulance door, climbed in and laid down on one of the two stretchers. He was done in. He had to rest before doing anything further.

After nearly an hour's nap, he finally awoke. He knew he had to muster up the strength to inspect the equipment a little further and then get one of the vehicles started and drive it back to the Shuttle crew. His survey revealed that both fire engines were fully loaded with water. Apparently, he thought, the equipment that sprayed foam must have been stored elsewhere. And all the equipment was able to be started. Their batteries were still good. He did not have time to check around for extra batteries, but he knew they would have to do so. All that done, he opened the large bay doors enough to drive the ambulance through and drove out to where the Shuttle was half buried in sand.

It was Ted who first saw the vehicle approaching them in the distance. He let out a relieved cry, "Oleg must have found something to drive. He's coming now!"

Immediately upon his arrival, Amber had everyone climb on board. Ilse and Ted, being the most exhausted, were instructed to lie on the stretchers in the back. And they immediately returned to the emergency station. There was a modest kitchen area in the building, along with three bunk beds for personnel on standby duty. Again, the facility had been prepped for their launch and was stocked with some food and water. All personnel or any sign of them, however, were nowhere to be seen. It was a puzzle they chose not to try and solve. Any more tragedy or death was beyond what their minds could handle. Like inmates in a concentration camp, who were left alive, when so many others had perished before their eyes, they had become numbed and deeply scarred. Their primary objective now was to survive long enough to deliver the compiled material they still had stored onboard the Shuttle.

After a night's rest and some land-based food, each of Amber's crew were in better spirit's the next day. Following breakfast, they all sat around a small table, probably used primarily for cribbage or solitaire, and outlined what they needed to do in the next couple of days. One thing certain, Amber knew they had to find a dosimeter of some kind or a Geiger counter to measure what radiation they were being exposed to. It had to have dissipated considerably over the last six months, but she wanted to know for sure. And, as she had hoped, Ted later that morning found a Geiger counter stored in one of the equipment rooms. In addition, he located a portable radio which had short wave capability. That was their only hope for any rescue party finding them. It would be their communication link.

During their firehouse meeting that morning, the primary topics of discussion revolved around transportation and removal of supplies and material from the Shuttle. It was decided that they would remove all the emergency gear from the fire engines and load as much of their stored goods on them as possible. And the ambulance would serve mostly as a backup for storage. They would then drive the three vehicles to the closest large town, which was Alamogordo. When they got there, they would look for another fire department and see if they could find another fire truck fully loaded with water. Their plan was to use that stored water as their back up supply. They figured it would most likely not be contaminated, although it would need to be boiled before drinking it. The third fire engine would then hold extra food supplies and any gear stored in the ambulance, freeing it up to be a shelter. They were to rig up bunk beds inside the ambulance. It would be cramped, but living onboard the ISS had conditioned each of them for living snugly.

From Alamogordo, they anticipated they would drive further southeast, away from the contamination of northern New Mexico, to Artesia. Once there, they would try to find three more fire engines. As they used up the water in the first three engines, they would switch over to the replacements and drive them to Carlsbad. They assumed there was no way to siphon or pump enough gasoline to refill any of the fire trucks. Ultimately, their plan was to exist in Carlsbad for the long term. In the back of their minds was the possibility they might need to seek shelter in the Carlsbad Caverns, if the weather turned particularly nasty over the winter months.

Returning to the Shuttle that morning, it was necessary to work as quickly as possible to remove the supplies and recordings they made during their time orbiting the earth. Amber discovered her sense of smell and taste confirmed the higher levels of radiation still present in this region. Not noticing the blast crater northeast of their present position was the reason they were somewhat puzzled at this finding. But each person worked quickly and within the next three hours everything of importance was unloaded and repacked on the fire fighting and emergency vehicles. They would secure them better once they were out of this danger zone.

Changing their plans once they got away, they decided to detour to the Alamogordo Regional Airport instead. It was Ted who suggested it might be easier to locate fire engines, fully loaded with water and topped off with fuel, there. And they were fortunate enough to find what they needed.

It was there they spent their second night, inside the newly modified, ambulance mobile home. The next morning Amber knew they needed to be on their way, despite their lingering fatigue and slow adjustment to the effects of gravity. She, with everyone's consent, assigned Ilse to drive the ambulance, and the other three would drive the fire engines. By 10:45 a.m., on the morning of October 3rd, they headed for the city of Alamogordo, and from there on to Artesia. It was over 100 miles to Artesia, but once there, they all gathered around the Geiger counter to see its present findings. The results were within normal limits. Overwhelmed with relief, they found a fire station on one of the town's main streets and pulled into its large driveway and parked for the next week.

Throughout their travels to the Artesia fire station, they were passing through the remains of a collapsed, if not already dead, society. Only they were left alive. All along the way, there was one ghastly sight after another. To even survive that journey, they had to force themselves to focus completely on their driving. Often, maneuvering their large vehicles along the highway or through the city streets became impossible, unless they pushed some vehicles aside.

The last six months since April 1st had added to the deterioration of the surroundings, with the howling winds, swirling debris, and unburied remains. It was due to these ever-present surroundings that the Shuttle crew decided they would rather push on to Carlsbad after they had rested for a week. And, without much discussion they also decided, it would be best to go directly to the Caverns. It was there they would spend whatever time necessary, before any rescue or further travel was required.

And so the hop-scotch pattern of changing vehicles continued until they arrived at the Carlsbad Caverns. And apparently it, too, had been shut down prior to April 1st. It and the Mammoth Cavern National

Park and half of the other National Parks in the country had been closed that entire fiscal year due to budget shortfalls. The national debt had finally reached the breaking point. Certain National Parks, Forests, and Monuments were shuttered, and more were planned for each, new fiscal year. There was no one at the Carlsbad Caverns when they finally arrived.

That was October 13th. And there they remained until June 6, 2012. Prior to that date they had been receiving the shortwave messages, broadcasted from Resolve. They started receiving them on March 14th, after they turned on the radio, the one day a week they did so. Realizing they had no chance of rescue until June 1st, they elected to not waste valuable battery power until then. It was on June 5th that they learned of their impending rescue at the Carlsbad City Air Terminal, 23 miles northeast of their present position. They were to be rescued on June 7th.

All day June 5th was spent reloading their recordings, log books and diaries onto one fire truck. They only took enough food and water for the next two days. They left for the airport at 11:00 a.m. on June 6th. Their survival in the Carlsbad Caverns, during those winter months, is the stuff of legends, but is not to be recounted in this chronicle. Suffice it to say, it was their will to live, and share their experiences and findings while in space, that drove them to endure and triumph over incredible adversity.

Back in Resolve, on June 7th, the flight crews were busy plotting their last flight plan for this first round of long range rescues, as fruitless as they had been up until now. At least they would not have snow drifts, lava flows and flooding conditions to deal with where they were going. They anticipated they would be able to land straight away. But they took the bulldozer, along with two engineers that would parachute in as well to unpack and drive it, in case there was scattered debris on the runway. They knew that would take time, and possibly a refueling mid-flight would be necessary if too much work had to be done. At least they tried to anticipate every scenario. Given their distance from any backup, proper preplanning was their only insurance for any success.

Their flight plan had them heading on a course southeast, about 20 miles north of Phoenix and over the White Sands National Monument, into Carlsbad City's Air Terminal. Each time they were to begin another mission, beforehand they had to return to Nellis AFB to refuel both planes. They would then return to Resolve to get last minute instructions, load the equipment and personnel and set off on their mission from there. This trip was no different.

Once in the air, the two planes flew side by side. This time the cargo plane was positioned to the left of the refueling plane, which gave them an ample opportunity to observe the destruction of the region around Tonto Basin, an area northeast of Phoenix. The missile meant for Phoenix had struck it. The resulting impact crater and forest fires left a blacked scar stretching for countless miles across the landscape. Certainly, there were no signs of life here. But the major discovery that occurred, during what was to be a very routine flight, was Steven's copilot noticing a shiny object partially buried on the old White Sands Space Shuttle landing strip. Because they flew at a much lower cruising altitude when on these missions, all in hopes of seeing any movement or signaling from the ground as they passed over, it was not hard to see that the shape of this object was that of NASA's Space Shuttle.

"Great Scott, look over here!" Kristin Stoltz, Steven's copilot cried out. "That looks just like the Shuttle, semi-buried in the sand."

Steven banked the cargo plane enough to get a glimpse and answered, "It can't be! But, by golly, I think you're right!! Let's go down to the deck and see for sure! Notify Kathryn what we are doing and why. What's this all about?! What's a Shuttle doing way out here?!!"

"Wasn't there supposed to be a Shuttle launch just before April 1st?" Kris asked.

"You know, I think you're right. And this is one of their standby emergency landing sites. Do you think that's what I'm thinking it might be?" Steve wondered out loud.

"That's a likely possibility. The Shuttles were not flying about, two or three at a time," Kris quipped.

"You have to wonder if anyone survived the landing," Steve added. "But we've got to proceed to our rendezvous location first. Probably we'll have to check this out later. Notify the Communication Center folks in Resolve about this discovery. What an amazing find! If we hadn't been on this heading, we'd never have known that it was even there. For now, let's make tracks to that airfield in Carlsbad and see if anyone is waiting for us there."

Even before they began descending to check the condition of the runway, they saw smoke rising from the direction of the airport. "Someone's there. That's for sure," Kris said excitedly. "They must have received our message about making sure we could see them. Boy!! Look at that column of smoke!"

And as they were making their first low pass, it was clear to Steve that someone had been clearing the runway for their landing. It was clear of debris its entire length. What they certainly did not know was that since the broadcasts began in March and the Shuttle crew heard them, they had been make sorties to the airfield to clean and prepare it for their rescue. It was the least they could do, they figured.

"And look!" Steve exclaimed, "There are four people waving wildly at us. Hot dog! Can you beat that! We got some survivors to rescue!! That's just great! Man alive, that's just great!! Let's get these planes down on the ground."

The landing was picture perfect for both aircraft, almost as if the planes themselves wanted to show off for the special company they were about to rescue. What could not be recognized from the air was that the four survivors were dressed in their astronaut flight suits. After the planes circled the runway and finally pulled up to the air terminal, the cargo plane turned with its tail section pointing toward the terminal. Slowly, the rear loading door was lowered and out strolled Steven Blackmore and his crew. Kathryn Swisher's crew followed them soon thereafter. Nobody wanted to miss the reunion, but nobody was prepared for the survivors they were about to meet.

Walking up to the group, Steve twisted his head slightly, thinking he kind of recognized the tattered suit's the survivors were wearing. But he quickly dismissed any logical connections, thinking instead they were probably acquired from some ruined uniform shop. Once he got closer, his impression and mood changed completely.

"My God, I recognize you," he said to Amber who was ahead of the group walking toward the newly arrived crews. "You are the commander of the last Shuttle flight that was supposed to be…. Good God, it's true; the Shuttle we saw over in White Sands was your ship…and this is your crew!!"

"That's right," Amber announced, walking up to him. Reaching out her hand to shake his, but he would have nothing of it. Quickly, he bypassed her outstretched hand and gave her a warm and welcoming-home hug.

"Welcome back, Colonel," Steve said as he pulled back from her and studied her and her crewmates. "It's an amazing sight for us to see you, and it's an honor to be able to be part of the rescue mission that finds you."

"I assure you, the feeling is mutual," replied Ted. "We were never sure if our fate was going to play out like it has for some many billions across the world."

"Let us introduce ourselves. I am Steve Blackwell. And I'll let everyone else introduce themselves."

From that point on it was a blur of introductions, questions, laughter and sad revelations. Hearing that they had a couple of vehicles loaded with supplies and recorded material and documents from the Shuttle, everyone helped form a conveyer from the fire engine and ambulance to the cargo plane's hold. No attempt was made to describe what was being loaded. There would be plenty of time for that once they got back to Resolve. The two planes took off at 4:15 p.m., expecting to arrive back home in an hour and a half. None of the Shuttle crew spoke much during that return flight. They were so relieved to be reuniting with their fellow citizens. Their emotions were too frail to be pushed with conversation at this point. The flight crew left them alone with their thoughts. There was a light drizzle, as had been the case for the last two days, when they came to a halt on the eastbound lane of the highway in Resolve. The Shuttle crew looked at each other as the plan came to a complete stop. At that point they knew they were home at last.

FOURTEEN: THE REMAINING SURVIVORS

The final rescues did not come until a year and a half later, December 5, 2013, to be exact. Despite the excellent maintenance of the two large jet aircraft, they had been unable to continue the rescue flights for the originally estimated two years. They had exhausted their usable jet fuel sources and now, somehow, had to begin searching a much wider area for any other storage sites. That being the case, after that December, all search and rescue flights were finished for the foreseeable future. And during this last year and a half of searching, they had no further sightings of survivors, other than the rescue of the Shuttle crew.

That was until that afternoon of December 5, when the first rescue began at the Boling Green-Warren Country Regional Airport. The second, and last, mission took place at the Carlsbad City Air Terminal a few days later. But before describing the actual rescues, a little background on these survivors is in order. It will help anyone who reads this account appreciate their determination and most remarkable will to live.

From the desolate, sacred hinterland of the Australian Aborigines, from the inaccessible highlands of Papua New Guinea, from the volcanic slopes of Indonesia, from the desolate reaches of Inner Mongolia and northern China, from the small, village redoubts scattered in the mountains of Kazakhstan, Pakistan,

Afghanistan, Iran and India, and from the equatorial forests and fertile interior of deepest Africa and South America came streamlets of survivors who had heard the shortwave messages that had started more than two years earlier.

What drove them was the hope and promise of being reunited into a community. And if that should occur, then it could provide them the strength and courage to face a future, whose past had become unbearable. The unknown was no longer a source of conjecture, myth or promise. It was dangerous beyond anyone's imagination. They were driven to be comforted by the company of others and maybe to be able to live and not just survive. It was the prayer of any true immigrant.

The pathway these individuals and small groups took was like the current of a stream, whose outlet was eventually to be the Atlantic Ocean. It started at the Arafura Sea, north of Australia, and moved on through the Bunda Sea, through the Java Sea, into the Bay of Bengal and the Indian Ocean. From there it passed over the Arabian Sea into the Red Sea and the flooded Suez Canal zone into the Mediterranean Sea. Finally, it moved out of the Straits of Gibraltar into the Atlantic Ocean. All along that route an amazing assortment of small and large, wind-driven sailing craft merged and then made their way eventually into the Caribbean Sea and the Gulf of Mexico. By the score, they ultimately landed inland from where San Antonio, Texas, used to be. For many, who had traveled nearly two years, the long journey ended along the shores of that state's Hill Country, 150 miles from the old Gulf coastline.

Untold hardships and losses followed them along this journey. Hunger, thirst, storms of unprecedented intensity, capsized boats, diseases and overwhelming loneliness, all took their measure. The final total of men, women and children who arrived in Carlsbad, New Mexico, in November of that year was 217. Over 5,000 refugees started this desperate odyssey almost two years before their arrival in New Mexico.

However, first it is necessary to backtrack and cover some background that will be helpful in understanding what led up to the rescue on December 5. And, for that, there must be a recounting of what occurred on and after that April 1st in eastern Switzerland.

Civil Defense in Switzerland was not something delegated to an immense government agency, which may or may not have a dysfunctional response to an emergency. It was the responsibility of each family unit. Each home had a shelter of some kind, equipped for survival and stocked with supplies. They regularly drilled on how to respond when the warning sirens sounded in every village across the country. It was not left up to the government to react to a catastrophe of some kind; it was the responsibility of the individual and the family. On that issue, there was no confusion.

By the time on April 1st that the warnings were beginning to be heard throughout the cities, towns, and villages throughout Switzerland, the detonations had already begun on her largest cities: Geneva, Zurich, Basel, even Bern and Lucerne. It was like there was an international feeling of resentment that Switzerland had been spared the warring madness of the previous two centuries and that she needed some full-fledged destruction for once. There were to be no invading armies for her to fend off that day, only the invasion of thermonuclear tipped missiles for which there was no defense.

And, as has had been the case for the rest of the planet, two hours after the detonations started, there was the massive earthquake, associated with the solar ejection impact onto Antarctica.. As mentioned before in these chronicles, this forceful impact had an almost immediate effect on the tectonic plates in northwest Africa. The Rift Valley sunk and split apart. The force of this movement transferred almost immediately into southern and middle Europe, particularly into the mountain ranges of Switzerland. Accompanying this energy transfer were avalanches, landslides, buried fortress compounds inside caves, and buildings collapsing as they were shaken off their foundations. In short, the earth began heaving under, around and over the Swiss citizenry. Even as the sirens sounded across the countryside, they were being silenced, one by one, by all the destruction. Steep-walled valleys became immense coffins. Graceful and peaceful landscapes became transformed into a geological whirlpool.

In and around Sargans, in the St. Gallen Canton, survivors were having better success at keeping alive in their one shelter. Located on the eastern border of Switzerland, nestled in a valley protected by high snow-covered mountains, for centuries Sargans had been the guardian fortress against invaders coming through Lichtenstein and Austria. It was on the northern end of where the Rhine River begins forming its magnificent canyons. Situated about 75 miles from where the Rhine empties into Lake Constance, the towns people had a modest avenue of escape along this more navigable portion of the river, if they had to in the months to come.

Sargans, in years past, was primarily a military outpost, but most recently had become more of a haven for tourists. But being in between the winter ski season and the onrush of summertime tourists, this village with a population of about 5,000 residents, was more like its old self. Nine out of ten residents there now were Swiss citizens. Each one of these individuals and families knew where the old fortifications were inside one of the cliff faces, bordering them. And if the Civil Defense sirens were ever to sound, as many as could, also knew, to evacuate immediately to this shelter and to stay there until the all-clear was sounded.

The fort in Sargans was maintained by a small garrison of ten fulltime military personnel, led by Capt. Franz Seifert. Being fulltime military personnel, they were entitled to have their families billeted with them. In their case, the military housing consisted of a small group of chalets clustered at the base of the fortification. And because April 1st was on a Sunday, everyone was at home when the sirens began to wail. Moreover, it being the highly unusual time of 7:25 p.m. when they sounded, everyone who could, either went immediately into their basements or hurried over to the old fortress. There was mild confusion at first as to why they had been warned to seek shelter. Then the reports began to come in to the fort's shortwave radio room of the holocaust underway throughout the world. Disbelief was the appropriate and usual initial reaction. But then as reports started coming in, describing the destruction of Swiss cities, the disbelief turned into gasping, crying and mournful silence.

Finally, at 9:15 p.m. the shaking began, associated with the solar-generated impact on Antarctica. With that event the whole mountain began to shake violently. And what was Sargans, disappeared under tons of snow and rock. Throughout Switzerland, what had been designed as safe havens, fortified outposts, Civil Defense assembly areas, all were buried beyond recovery or destroyed. All, except this one shelter in Sargans.

The confusion, noise and panic were impossible to control at first. Everyone, without expressing it, knew they were going to perish. And, if someone did not get the crowd under some control, that was surely going to happen. It was Capt. Seifert who first began to establish some calm in the midst of the uproar.

From the general assembly area, overcrowded with families, he rushed forward and announced, "Please, please listen to me! Your very lives depend on it! We must regain some order in here! Quiet! All of you!! QUIET!!!" he ended up shouting.

Following his command, the overflowing crowd gradually began to turn to one another and encourage some semblance of calm. Eventually, all the faces turned toward the front of the cavernously large chamber. What they saw surprised them. Standing before them was Capt. Seifert, with his hands still cupped over his mouth ready to yell again. But alongside him were his ten troops, fully armed with weapons being held across their chests. It was not a stance of parade rest.

"As of this moment, I must inform you that you are now, as is anyone else throughout Switzerland, under Martial Law. You will now have to obey me and these troops before you, without question. It appears, with whatever information we've been able to gather up to this point, that not only is Switzerland under attack, but similar destruction is happening throughout the world. And our only chance at surviving any of this, as small as that might appear to be at this moment, is for all of us to be as calm as possible, and then to think, prepare and cooperate fully. We will be organizing citizen groups to handle different issues, such as food allotments and preparation, assigning quarters for each family or lone individuals, preparing for long term residency in here, and what to do once we can safely exit this place.

"Nothing we have to do is going to be easy nor will anything be guaranteed. Before this tragedy has run its course, we will no doubt be facing untold hardships, most of which will be beyond our wildest imaginings. For now, until we can get better organized and establish some representative form of governing, I will be in charge. You must obey me and these individuals standing in front of you. If there are any canton or city leaders among us, please meet me in one hour in the fortress office. For now, you may locate yourselves and your family anywhere along the corridors or any vacant rooms you can find. The dining room will serve food at noon tomorrow. That will give us time to organize a little better. Water is available at the various water stations scattered throughout this redoubt.

"For now, you must take heart. We desperately need each other's strength, wisdom and courage. We, Swiss, are a hardy people. We cannot let ourselves sink into chaos and madness. We will prevail, somehow. And that's all I have to say for now."

The following hours, days, weeks, even months, in that fort were gradually organized for long-term survival. The facility had been expanded, some years earlier, to accommodate 1,500 soldiers, along with a six months' supply of rations. It was, as would be expected, fully self-contained. It was, after all, designed to protect the eastern entrance into Switzerland and needed to be well-staffed and well-armed.

The final tally of survivors who entered the fortress on April 1st was 1,345. Most were families, but 148 were individuals, who were caught outside their homes or who somehow became separated from their loved ones. To insure their food rations lasted much longer than six months, it was decided there would only be one meal per day. In addition to that meal there would be tea and a biscuit or some light soup for the other light nourishment during the day.

Leadership did emerge and Martial Law was ended after one month, once it was determined the populace was responding appropriately under civilian direction. And, again, like with Yucca Mountain

Cavern, Franz was elected Mayor. The duties left to the small military presence were primarily communication monitoring, police duties, and maintaining lookout outposts stationed along the cliff face overlooking the Rhine Valley before them.

The plans on what to do, once the danger of further attack ended and the life-threatening radioactivity levels reached normal levels, centered on three, linked objectives. The first was to survey what destruction had occurred in their immediate area and in a 25 mile radius around them. The second was to determine if they could sustain life in the region. And last, if they could not, it was to develop and execute a plan of evacuation to a safer locale for an eventual settlement. Different individuals were assigned to each objective and were to develop plans on how they would accomplish their assignments.

By October 1, just as was the case with Amboy Cavern in California, small groups began to leave the fort and explore the surrounding area. They found the snow depth was already far beyond what they would have had even in the middle of December. By dividing up, they each focused on one of the nearby villages of Flums, Vaduz, Bludenz and Feldkirch.

It was their hope to find other survivors and conditions conducive to living outside the fortress. But it was not to be. Switzerland was a country of pastoral views beyond every rise of a hill or bend in the road, but during their explorations, even far beyond these locales and further to the south of Sargans, nothing was found other than destruction and death. Nothing was found that might sustain life. It was grim. And because of the heavy snowfall, there was no way to begin any kind of journey away from the tragedy around them. They would have to wait until springtime.

The choice of an escape route for the Sargans

evacuees became one of default. Come spring, they would have to travel along the Rhine River. Between October 1st and the upcoming March 15th, when they tentatively planned on leaving their shelter, they would begin building the boats necessary to travel down the river. The collapse of the mountain sides around Sargans did offer them one consolation. There was an endless mixture of building materials and freshly downed timber to choose from for construction.

There was no one, single boat design that was chosen for the trip downstream. That was because there were untold obstacles ahead, which would require fording, either by carrying or towing their boats; and the larger the craft, the more the risk of it becoming lodged or impossible to maneuver. And because there was a road or rail line beside most of the river's length, especially for the 75 miles they needed to travel to Lake Constance, it was decided that all able-bodied individuals, not rowing or towing the boats, would walk. The boats would carry supplies, food, water, the weaker citizens and the children.

It was anticipated, through experience some of the residents in the fortress had had in traveling along the Rhine as far as Basel that the same unpredictable conditions would exist up until they passed beyond there. In fact, between Lake Constance and Basel there was a large series of waterfalls, which would require everyone to help to portage that stretch of the river. Once they were north of Basel, they hoped to commandeer some large, self-propelled river barges to travel the next 500 miles to the North Sea. At that point, they had no idea what would be available for them to use, if they had to move further on. Certainly, at this time, it was their fervent prayer they could reestablish a home somewhere along the way, preferably still within the boundaries of Switzerland.

711

Much of that thinking began to change when they started getting the shortwave broadcasts on March 12th from Resolve, California. The incoming messages did not alter their immediate plans to travel the Rhine to and through Lake Constance and into Konstanz. But from that point on, they would have to reconsider their options. Many of the citizens were beginning to mumble about the likelihood of having to leave Switzerland, and even the boundaries of Europe altogether, if they were ever to find a location for sustained survival. Unlike the reactions of other survivors elsewhere who heard this same message from Resolve, this tradition-bound, self-sufficient community, was more resigned than elated. Europe was gradually, but surly, becoming too cold for agricultural production and more people were beginning to realize it. For them, their homeland was uninhabitable.

Their remarkable journey began, as planned, on March 15, 2012. At that time there were 1,213 men, women and children who set off. Adding to the tragedy of April 1st was a flu epidemic that occurred in mid-January. In their confined quarters, it spread through the fort like a blanket of fog. Nowhere and no one escaped its symptoms. And over 100 died in a month's time. Because they had such a narrow window of tolerable weather to travel through northern Europe, they proceeded with their plans to leave on schedule. The plan was to be at the entrance to the North Sea by August and then to sail down the Brittany seacoast of France by October or November, by the latest. There, they would winter over. The plan was to get food from the farming communities in that area, which would sustain them through the winter months. During that time they would also try to lie in stores for the last leg of their trip. From there, they tentatively planned to head to Ireland, then onto Iceland, Greenland and

Newfoundland. Once in Newfoundland, they planned on working their way down to Maine and travel either by roadway or inner coastal waterways to Norfolk, Virginia. The final leg of this proposed journey was to travel by land to Mammoth Caverns in Kentucky by sometime in October-November, 2013. At the time they started off, this all seemed so unattainable. The consensus, after much discussion of their plans, was that they had to take this upcoming migratory escape to a safe haven one mile at a time; otherwise, they would become paralyzed with fear. So agreeing, their journey began.

The Rhine River Armada, as they eventually began to call themselves, consisted of 25 thirty foot long drift-style wooden boats, with high gunnels, and even higher bows and sterns. It was an enlargement of the smaller, rushing river drift boats seen in New Zealand and America. Each held 10 passengers and four crewmembers, along with provisions for all. In addition, there were 10 thirty foot long by twelve foot wide wooden rafts, with a crew of five, which carried their supplies. That meant 400 people were transported on the water, and 813 walked alongside and assisted the boats over and around obstacles. And while it was certainly true, the Swiss were not particularly seafaring people, they were, by nature, excellent artisans, and these boats were sturdy and safe.

The river at Sargans was still compressed by canyon walls and had many hundreds of feet to fall before reaching the North Sea. Likewise, it had to meander continuously to circumvent solid granite cliff outcrops. During this first phase of their voyage to Lake Constance, 75 miles away, they only managed to travel three miles per day. Winter snow melt had raised the river to dangerous heights and small riffles were transformed into dangerous torrents. The blackened canyon walls in this area had scars of recent landslides, but luckily the cliff faces were far enough away from the river banks to protect it from filling with debris. For this portion of the trip, the sky remained a whitish grey. They never saw the sun these next 25 days. And there was a constant chill in the air. In areas, where the snow had not melted as much, those walking had to take turns either shoveling a pathway through or around the drifts. All of this made for a slow, tedious and cheerless struggle. And gravesites were left behind, as the journey slowly progressed downstream.

A few miles before reaching the broad expanse of Lake Constance the river slowed down and widened and the snow pack around them thinned. It was a relief for everyone. The higher mountain peaks began to fade in the distance, replaced with rolling hills. The mood began to lighten as the party realized they had passed beyond the grips of the unstable mountains and the angry river. Once in Konstanz, at the western end of the Lake, they spent the next four days locating, selecting and repairing 25 more boats for the next leg of their trip. It was an odd assortment of sizes and kinds of boats, but all had to be able to move on their own. No fuel was available in this small village. Single and double hull boats were confiscated, allowing another 250 people to ride the remainder of the journey. Now only 530 were left, having to walk to Basel. Grimly, thirty-three individuals died during this first phase of their trip.

The scenery changed steadily as they made their way to Basel. Now there were more homes, although most were nearly hidden by overgrowth, along the less dramatic cliff-faced shoreline. Towns and settlements were plentiful along this second portion of their journey. But all were eerily quiet and vacant. There were fewer portages, but many more miles to cover. However, to lift their spirits somewhat, they did have several days when sunlight did break through, but the cold, though less, remained ever-present. The countryside had a little more color with some trees struggling to leaf out and marsh grasses attempting to reestablish themselves. The surrounding trees gave the slightest hint of budding greenery, against a background, otherwise dominated by whitewashed emptiness. In addition, everyone noticed the air along the river had a mildly pungent odor, as if someone was continually processing cellulose, to make paper pulp. But, tragically, it was actually the odor of decay.

Entering what used to be Basel, 45 days after leaving Konstanz, was anticipated to maybe be their first chance to see other survivors. But seeing the ruins around the city from the bomb's destruction convinced them that it was highly unlikely. Skeletons of buildings, trees and hillsides met their gaze wherever they turned. And where the blast effects ended, the scorched earth began, crossing the Rhine and into Germany, as well. Everywhere, in and along the Rhine, were sunken boats and barges. It was a tangled mess, particularly where bridges once stood. If it was not for the puzzling elevated water level, much of the river would not have been navigable. Whether it was due to snow melt or other causes, they were unaware of; the water level was at least 5-8 feet higher than normal. And it continued to rise throughout the rest of their trek down river.

Once beyond the circumference of the worst blast effects, they began to find boats and barges that were upright and intact. It was then they stopped and spent the next four days corralling five very long barges. Each had to be checked for being river-worthy and the fuel topped off, if necessary. Any goods or materials already on board had to be sorted, and then each barge was reloaded and secured with the provisions from their many smaller boats. They then erected additional shelters on the top deck and below it, much beyond what quarters already existed on each barge.

Relentlessly, the death toll from this exodus mounted steadily. Another 46 had perished from drowning, injuries, illness or suicide since leaving Konstanz. That brought their number to 1,134 survivors. And each person was finally able to board one of these five vessels for the third leg of their trip.

It must be noted at this point that there was much discussion and argument concerning two major issues. One was whether they should continue proceeding down the Rhine or try to go overland to Brittany in western France. The other was whether they should keep the larger sailing vessels they now had, in addition to the five barges, and take additional ones they might find along the way downstream.

The final decision to continue with the Rhine River hinged on the unparalleled horrors they and their children would see if they went overland. Plus, there would probably not be reliable transportation for them, given their large number. And the decision to keep and commandeer additional larger sailing vessels was made for two reasons. First, everyone needed practice crewing a sail-driven craft before they got to the open waters of the seas and oceans. Secondly, they were possibly facing a sinister situation, that being the puzzling, progressive rise of the water levels, the further they went downstream. They needed to gather the sailing boats when and where they could. It was their only insurance of passage later on. Finally, it was agreed that the barges would lead, and the sailing vessels would follow. It made for a remarkable parade, many miles long, winding down the river. This was, in a sense, their point of no return.

No one had the skills to steer these long and unwieldy barges, but Franz volunteered his barge to lead the way and everyone else to follow. They were lucky, in one respect, that the river was overflowing its bank. It meant piloting around sand bars and sunken objects were not the hazards they might have been. He steered a course mid-river for the duration of the remaining trip, while silently hoping it would last the 500 miles needed to reach Rotterdam. And the trail of barges and scattered, smaller boats trailed behind.

Starting in Mainz, Germany, they began to pass the outcrops of castles, all built in the Middle Ages. But this was also where they noted the river level was becoming significantly higher, more than an abnormally high spring runoff would cause. And it was also at this point they began to notice some scouring of the hillsides, above the high water line. It was becoming obvious, as well, that scattered debris had been deposited at that level, almost like a high tide had strewn it there. Franz radioed to the other boats to begin watching more closely for driftwood and large objects floating in the water or partially submerged. Something was not right; he just sensed it. But, all the while, they kept up their very slow movement downstream.

Occasionally, the various barges slowed down to let people off; and they would then board additional sailing boats, moored either along private docks or in sheltered yacht basins. Already, by this point, they had taken possession of two larger ketches, which would accommodate 15-20 people.

Their boats weaved in and out of curves in the river, passing village after village, old stone bulwarks atop one promontory after another, for miles. But always, they stopped at night, anchoring at the shoreline. And some days, when the wind was so strong and the visibility so poor, they stayed moored all that day. With each passing day, when the sun did shine, they noticed more vegetation spreading across the ever-present hillsides. The sight of more greenery, alone, gave them hope for something better to come.

Yet, again, it was when they came to the southern outskirts of Bonn, Germany, everyone knew something terrible, far beyond what destruction they saw before this, had happened. It was only too clear that for weeks the water level had been continuously rising above the original shoreline. Now it was at least 10 feet higher. The level was getting higher the further downstream they went; it was just the opposite of what one would expect to be happening.

Worried that something serious had or was happening, Franz ordered everyone to take turns refilling the barges' tanks at a refueling depot south of Bonn. The station was just above the elevated waterline. As it was, it required considerable time to perform this operation, due to the fuel having to be manually pumped. While this was underway, the decision was made to begin transferring some supplies from the barges onto the assorted armada of sailing craft. By now, they had accumulated 41 wind-driven vessels, a few larger ones with two and three masts. All these vessels were stripped of anything non-essential, to make room for additional passengers and cargo. There had been 227 passengers assigned to each barge when they left Basel, but with keeping a few other vessels at that point and finding the remaining 38 along the way outside Bonn, the number of passengers on the barges could now be reduced to zero.

This information was relayed to Franz and the other barge captains, as they were struggling to refuel the first barge. At that point a major conference was held to see how to proceed from there. The outcome of that meeting was that they would stay anchored at this site for up to a week. During that time, they would complete off-loading as much as they could from the barges, restock supplies from the surrounding villages, and send out a scouting party to the north of Bonn, to see what lay beyond.

They were able to find a power boat, whose engine did work and topped off its fuel tank for the scouting party. By daybreak, on the third day they were moored outside Bonn, that party took off downstream. As they entered the city limits of Bonn, via the river, what they saw was chilling. The destruction was complete. It was so horrific they elected to not divert their eyes from the river itself. As it was, they had to maneuver in and around collapsed bridges and partially exposed remains of the city. But the real, ever-lasting shock came when they had traveled about twenty miles north of Bonn. At that point the river began to spread out, forming what appeared to be a lake. And yet as they turned off the main course of the river, the further they rode west the more convinced they were this was no lake. It was the North Sea. And the hillside above the waterline showed marked effects of an immense tidal surge, like was seen by the Ernie's Search and Rescue teams in and around Los Angeles. They knew it had to have been caused by a tsunami. And the further they traveled, the more the expanse of water stretched out before them to the north and the west.

Upon their return to the moored barges and sailing ships, some seven hours later, their report was met with complete, stunned silence. Following hours of discussion, anguish and argument, it was decided that all the barges would be refueled, as previously planned, and then they would tow the various other ships out into the open waters, as far as their fuel lasted. It was hoped that by that time they would have the minimum skills to navigate their sailing ships and calm, persistent winds to sail them. Whatever charts they had, did not account for anything like this, so they would have to just dead reckon their way as they went. It was a terribly sobering meeting. They were not adventures or explorers, eagerly awaiting their next challenge or discovery. They were just a ragged band of survivors.

Within that next week they had assembled the supplies and transferred others from the barges, leaving the barges with only skeleton crews and provisions. Seven sailing vessels were tethered to each barge, as each barge maneuvered midstream in the river. The six largest sailing vessels had enough sail to maneuver unassisted down river without being towed, but they were always close enough to be attached to a barge if the need arose. On August 15, they were fully assembled and began their fourth leg of this, now improbable, journey.

Nothing prepared them for what lay 30 miles north of Bonn. There had been a steady widening of the water basin they were in, but they could still see the eastern border of the German hillsides. But once they reached this point, even that landmark disappeared and all they saw was open sea water. The North Sea had reclaimed all of The Netherlands, northern Germany and Belgium.

Hoping to keep at least some land in sight, for as long as they could, they turned the barges and flotilla northwest, forever leaving behind the guiding pathway of the Rhine River. No existing charts of the English Channel or the North Sea would help them now. Soon the water level was so deep they could no longer anchor at night. For their last, open water anchorage, all the self-designated boat captains maneuvered their five barges together in a unique moorage, securing themselves sideways to each other. By this point they were easily 50 miles from any southern shoreline.

During this meeting it was decided that they would try to continue using the barges as towing vessels, until at least they got to where they thought Brussels would be located. If their fuel was too low to push on any further, it would be at this point the sailing ships would have to assume the rest of the trip under their own power. As it turned out, they were able to tow the sailing craft as far as Dieppe, France, or at least where they estimated it lay beneath them.

By August 28th, the day they were somewhere just south of Brussels, and 90 days after leaving Basel, their numbers dwindled to 1,105 survivors. From Franz's vantage point in the barge's pilot house, he was the first to see what was still left standing in that city. Only the tallest church spires in the outskirts of the city were visible above the new water level. The rest of Brussels had been lost in one of the first blasts. To pass by these few spires, as the rolling swells of the sea were split by them, was a sight no one could accept or comprehend. It was a horrifying thought to imagine what lay just below.

The barges motored on in a northwesterly direction at a much slower pace, and as they went out further from the newly flooded shoreline, the swells got higher. By the time they reached the region around Dieppe, the barges had to be cast adrift. Their fuel tanks were nearly empty; and controlling the long craft, in the higher surf, were now impossible.

And it is probably worth mentioning at this point, that in their foraging for food and drinking water throughout their trip, they had managed to set aside enough to get them, they hoped, to landfall somewhere within a few hundred miles of their present location. By this time, they were consuming only canned food and bottled liquid. And they still were only having one small meal a day, with a very light snack in the mornings. It just kept them alive.

One final meeting of all the armadas' ships'

captains was held, as they managed to link the barges together one last time, over where Dieppe most likely lay. While there, the process of getting an agreement on the next course of action was agreed upon. They all agreed making a heading to Brest, France was hopeless. It, too, was undoubtedly underwater by now. The decision to take a dead reckon course to Land's End, on the southeastern tip of England, was finally made. Once there, they would circle it and make way to dock, somewhere along an estuary or protected bay in southern Wales. It was there they had to find quarters for the upcoming winter and try to make preparations for the trans-Atlantic crossing sometime next spring.

So while the fall storms were still in abeyance, it was decided they had to sail due west from Dieppe to Land's End. The prevailing winds were still able to assist them in making a heading that direction. That being so, they disbanded and unhooked their crafts from the barges; and the odd collection of vessels set sail, under their own wind-generated power, for Wales. Like a flock of pelicans, bobbing on the ocean's surface, their flotilla nestled together, drawing encouragement and hope from one another. By now, they were well out of sight of any land. As a rough estimate, it was determined by a couple of the more capable sailors, among the survivors, that they had approximately 400 nautical miles to sail before sighting Land's End. Moreover, it was another150 nautical miles to sail from there to Swansea, Wales. This was their destination; the area they most likely would seek shelter for the upcoming winter. At an average of two nautical miles per hour, they hoped to cover 48 miles a day and be out of the worst of the current and unpredictable winds by September 16th, and be on the north side of Land's End, sailing the last leg onto Wales. They estimated sailing that distance would not take them longer than 4-5 days, so they would be anchored in Swansea on or about September 21st.

During this passage through the English Channel, it was often a topic of conversation that since leaving the Brussels area, no one else had died. That, alone, gave them some needed hope for the future success of their voyage. And after so much hardship and struggle, the Channel, for all its unpredictable reputation, had only mild to moderate winds their entire trip. Despite the novice sailors and navigators, all the boats maintained a close, convoy-like formation, even after nightfall. The break of dawn was always anticipated with great eagerness, and some anxiety, to see if each of the ships were still in sight of one another. Only by staying constantly in touch with one another did they have the confidence to see this portion of their journey to its successful conclusion.

Rounding Land's End should have been cause for a celebration; both because they made it, and also because their navigating abilities had been sufficient to meet this challenge. But there was just not the time or the energy to do so. However, it gave them hope for what lay ahead next spring, when they had to cross the ocean.

After entering the Irish Sea, they hugged the newly formed coastline of southwestern England for shelter. The winds began to gale three days before they crossed the Bristol Channel at Ifracombe, England to head north by northwest to Swansea. With three separate storm-related delays, due to some of the smaller boats' crews having to be rescued, they finally made landfall north of Swansea on September 23rd. It was in a newly formed cove, inland from the now-flooded, Swansea airport. The airport's elevation, as indicated on their maps, was about 290 feet above the old sea level. This revelation gave them their first concrete number for the coastal flooding they had been experiencing. From all indications, they were putting ashore near the town of Ponterdawe, Wales.

Upon their arrival, and in the months to come, a series of desperate measures had to be undertaken, almost all at once. For all the sacrifices and struggles, their journey was far from over. But in terms of confronting major complications, that portion of their journey was almost over. At this point, three vital jobs had to be started: find food and water, find shelter for the upcoming winter, and find boats and material to outfit for the transoceanic crossing.

Gathering food and water was assigned to one quarter of the company. This job, in particular, was the one given to the children within the survivors. There were nearby villages they could search for these supplies and then transport to a central location. For now that location was to be Ponterdawe's town square. There, it was sorted and much of it consumed during the first weeks. Famine had nearly claimed many victims, but amazingly no further loss of life occurred during their trip from Deppe. It was like everyone was too afraid to even die. And it was in Ponterdawe's town square that shops were opened and tables and chairs set up for everyone to eat and meet.

One quarter of the company went searching for a shelter they could use during the winter. It was their insurance, in case something else terrifying happened. As it was, they also had the job of clearing a pathway from their moorage through high, tidal wave-like mounds of debris. And through this clearing, they completely offloaded the sailing vessels of whatever supplies and materials they had left. To accomplish all of these assignments, this same group divided into small crews. Some of these crews focused their searches in and around the Brecon Beacon National Park, north and further inland of their present position. Eventually they located a series of caves, so named the National Showcave Center, about 10 miles from Ponterdawe. These three limestone caves were at a higher elevation and offered them the safety they desperately longed for after these months since April 1st. And over the next weeks, one half of the survivors joined forces and began transporting goods and equipment up to the cavern and started making it habitable for the long-term.

And the other half of the survivors divided up and immediately began searching east and west of their present position for ships to use and materials to build with. They knew there was little more they could ask of their recently anchored, life-saving boats. A few of those boats were still safe enough to use for any local investigations and surveys. But, after their voyages from Bonn, everyone agreed that any attempt at crossing the Atlantic Ocean would require much larger, preferably steel-hulled, sail-rigged vessels. If possible, they had to find at least four of these ships. But going overland along the new coastline was hopeless, given the flooding and debris fields. By their estimation, the water had risen at least 350 feet from its original level. And then there was the destruction from the now widely observed aftereffects of a massive tsunami. Much of the United Kingdom's coastal areas had been flooded. They had to search the shoreline using their smaller sailboats.

Of course, these search parties were unaware of a Tall Ships regatta that was being held in conjunction with Swansea's and Cardiff celebration of their centuries-old tradition of ship building. It was a world-wide gathering of the biggest Tall Ships, including "The Eagle", the United States Coast Guard's four masts training vessel. She was one of the ships that Ernie Tam trained on when he was attending the U.S. Coast Guard Academy. And the thousands from all over the United

Kingdom came the weekend of March 30th-April 1st, 2011, to witness the parade and race down the Bristol Channel of these magnificent ships.

At 10 p.m. the night of April 1st London, Southampton and Dublin were the first targets in that region. Later, after the solar impact event on Antarctica, other cities targeted were struck, but like at Cardiff, the missiles were now off course and impacted miles away from their intended targets. But the tsunami, flooding and blast-related aftereffects leveled or ravaged the north shore area of Bristol Channel, including Cardiff and Swansea.

Oddly, however, it did not completely destroy these Tall Ships, which were anchored well offshore. The tsunami waves did tear them from their anchorage, in the middle of the Channel, and then swept them up onto the shore. Some yard arms, masts and main masts were snapped off, and the rigging was fouled beyond recognition. But it appeared the navigational instruments, for the most part, were spared, as were the hulls and their interiors.

As the first Swiss search parties discovered, five of the largest ships had been washed ashore near Neath. Among the ships stranded there was The Eagle. The ships were crowded together at the newly established waterline. This meant there would have to be an all-out effort to dredge and to use ropes and make-shift pulleys to return the ships afloat again. Once that was done, they had to build docking facilities, both to facilitate repairs and to give the crews and passengers easier access for moving supplies and equipment on board.

Finding these ships was a major boost to the morale of the survivors. From that point on, it was much easier to get the work, which had to be done, out of everyone. For the next two months, before the weather turned too impossible to work in, the concentration was on these ships. Altogether, 527 adults and older children worked night and day to get these ships upright and afloat alongside some makeshift piers. Work crews, taken from this force, went into the National Forest and cut out timber needed to rebuild the superstructure of each ship.

By December 1, the weather was turning particularly cold and windy, with snow squalls beginning to be daily occurrences. Work on the interior of the ships continued, as well as maintenance on the decks and rigging. They did not want to have a heavy ice buildup on the decks. To do so, would slow down all their rebuilding efforts and make the ships dangerously heavy and prone to capsize where they were moored. From then on, a work detail was established to break up any heavy ice buildup that might form around the hull of the ships, should a deep freeze overtake the region.

That all arranged and underway, the majority of the Swiss survivors retreated to the three Showcase Center caves. In the two months that work had been going on the sailing ships, the remainder of the expatriates worked as diligently getting their living quarters well stocked and equipped for the winter. They projected it would not be until late March or early April before any more superstructure work could be resumed on the ships.

In the meantime, many discussions were held about their upcoming final waterborne leg of this two-plus, years' journey. All residents were in attendance at these meetings. Eventually, it was decided that they would not attempt to travel to Iceland and Greenland, on the way to Newfoundland. That route added hundreds more miles to their trip, as did any attempt to go south to the Azores and then to the east coast of the United States. Instead, they would follow the traditional transatlantic shipping lanes from the tip of Ireland in an arching straight line directly to Newfoundland. Upon their sighting Newfoundland, they also decided to avoid attempting to dock their ships, given the unknowns of what the newly risen water level may be hiding. They agreed to then follow the coastline of Canada down along the Maine and New England coastline to Virginia. Ultimately, they would make landfall at or near Norfolk, Virginia. From there they hoped to take the more lightly traveled roadways in Virginia to Kentucky. On the few maps they had, it looked like they would travel on Highway 58 into Kentucky, then onto Highway 92 to Highway 90 and from there into the Mammoth Caverns area.

And after this route was laid out and accepted, it was agreed from that moment on, as soon as any ship was deemed seaworthy, a crew would be immediately assigned to it; and they would begin working on their navigation skills, develop proficiency on raising and lowering sails, and piloting the ships up and down the Channel and eventually into the Irish Sea. Each crew had to drill for months to be able to manage these large vessels in the open waters of the ocean.

And so it went until July 3, 2013. It was on that day all five of the Tall Ships set sail from their protective cove off Bristol Channel, and the 1,080 survivors, some 216 to a ship, left the safety of European soil forever. After they left the confines of the Irish Sea, they stayed within sight of the southern tip of Ireland, until they eventually made for a south-by-southwest heading to Newfoundland. There was a steady 10-15 knot east wind blowing as they turned into the open ocean. Orders went out on all the ships to unfurl all sails. The five ships were a remarkable sight, everyone agreed. Each ship took turns being on the point of the formation. The others spread out, one to each side, far enough not to take wind away from the lead vessel, and the two others were staggered behind these three, creating an inverse "V" formation.

In the final meeting of the five crews, before they left Wales, it was estimated they had about 2,500 miles of Open Ocean to travel. And at an average speed of five-ten knots/hour, they estimated it would take anywhere from 10-20 days to come within sight of Newfoundland. That is, if they did not run into a major problem that slowed them down. They hoped the sea lanes would be clear of obstacles. Certainly, at this time of year they did not expect any ice bergs to be present, particularly with their navigating at lower latitudes than originally planned. But they were wrong.

They were six days out in open waters, and the time was 0210 hours. There was no moon to help illuminate their surroundings, but they hoped that by their going so slow, they could avoid whatever might be in their way. It was the second ship on the starboard side of the lead vessel, the one furthest to the north that struck the low profile berg. It ripped a large hole just under its water line. And it began to list almost immediately, taking on the frigid North Atlantic waters. There were a few life boats on each ship, but really not enough for all its passengers. However, in this case, those asleep in the lower holds had no chance to escape. Only those already topside and those who could climb out onto the deck quickly could even begin to find safety in the life boats.

And by the time their emergency flare was seen, in the cloud-covered, breath-absorbing blackness, to alert the other ships of their distress, precious, life-sacrificing minutes, for them to alter course and come to their rescue, were lost forever. Some passengers, those who could not get into the lifeboats, were able to don life preservers. Within 10 minutes the ship rolled over and began to sink. There was no time for any of the other ships to rescue anyone on board. All they could do was pick up the ones in life rafts and the 17 who were wearing life preservers. Of those 17, six did not survive. The final tally was 102 passengers and crew who were lost that night. The total of Swiss survivors now stood at 978.

The suddenness of this event shook everyone to their very core. It was commonly felt that this venture across the ocean was, at best, like a desperate gambler's last bid. But it was how quickly it happened, giving no time for warnings, to prepare or to bid farewell. It was too impersonal, too capricious. It was like evil had morphed from a human vector to a natural one, and they could be victims of its whims anywhere, at anytime. They felt completely defenseless to deal with it. For the first time since leaving Sargans, hopelessness became epidemic.

And into this misery and grief, onto the deck of each of the four remaining ships, as the entire company of survivors on each ship stood about in silence, there suddenly appeared a shapeless form. Each separate appearance took only a few minutes, with the same message being delivered to each ship's company. And on each ship the first reaction to the presence of someone or something so foreign, so unexplained, was disbelief and shock.

The shadow began to speak at the end of their collective gasps. "I do not want you to be filled with fear and despair. You are a brave and courageous people. Maybe you are not given to as much overt expressions of faith and worship, as would be normal under the circumstances you have experienced over these past two years. But that is not a worry or bother to me. You care deeply for each other, and you mean no other any harm. From there, I can easily begin again, with the work we both have ahead of us.

"I am not a dream, nor a figment of your imagination. I will be appearing on each of your ships-at-sea tonight. You have witnessed a terrible accident, and it was just that. And I am so saddened by your sudden loss. But there is no evil intent or force lurking about and stalking you. What has occurred since April 1st has been unimaginable, even to me. Not because I cannot foresee much of what can or might happen, but that it occurred so quickly and so completely.

"You do have a shelter waiting for you at the end of this journey, and you will find comfort and peace there, I assure you. And those in that place have also seen me and heard my words. There are not many of you left on this weary planet. For that I am deeply saddened. Creation of life has no guarantee that it will last beyond an instant. But my promise to you is that I will be physically present in your midst more often, to encourage, give hope, share a love I have for you, give needed direction, and confirm that there is something more throughout the vastness of your time and place, something wondrous and grand.

"Take heart. Grieve as you should this night and always for your many losses. But you must go on. You are needed where you are headed. And you are on the right course. And so you know, there are others you will be meeting who call me 'B'. You may certainly refer to me that way as well, but to others, throughout your past history, I was referred to as God. For now, I extend to you my blessing and my peace."

Saying that, B then imparted the calming serenity that he first gave to Clem, and so many others, nearly three years before. The sobs did not stop that night, nor did the grief at their losses. But the Swiss travelers knew from those few moments on, that they were not alone in the universe and that there was reason for hope and perseverance. The conversations about B's separate appearances and the same, exact message being delivered to each separate ship convinced everyone this was not a hoax or trick of the age-old sirens of the deep. With increased confidence they sailed on that night and the many days to come.

Twenty-six days after leaving Bristol Channel, on July 29th, they first sighted St. John's, Newfoundland or the exposed outcrop of that coastal city that remained after the sea level changes of April 1st. A shout of accomplishment went out from all four ships, as they each saw the land before them. They had made the ocean crossing.

From there, they carefully made their way down the coastline of Canada, only being able to mark their progress by a few observable landmarks that stood above the new water level. From St. John's, over the next weeks, they marked their passing of the Cape Breton Highlands National Park and later of Halifax, Nova Scotia. The next landmark noted was the rocky outcrop of Acadia National Park in Maine. From there until they saw their next landmark, the remains of the Chesapeake Bay Bridge, in Virginia, the next 900 miles did not have distinguishable land marks. The flooding and destruction was so severe that the visible eastern seaboard, from their vantage point 5 miles or so off shore, was barren except for seawater.

They had prepared themselves for a landing somewhere around Norfolk, Virginia, but noting the lack of landing sites, they chose to sail about thirty miles south of the Bay Bridge and enter the flooded continental United States where they presumed False Cape State Park, Virginia used to be. Sailing slowly from there, in single file, they hoped to make landfall somewhere between Emporia and South Boston, Virginia, depending on the water level. And in fact they ran aground southwest of La Crosse, Virginia, at the junction of Highways 1 and 58 in Mecklenburg County on August 12th. The jubilation was uncontrollable. The very worst of their journey was over.

Now they had to travel overland, but they hoped the route they chose would be relatively free of obstacles and dangers. There was even the hope they might find some vehicles to transport them part of the way to the final destination of Mammoth Caverns, 500 miles away.

As the ships were purposefully being run aground, the attempt was made to bring them relatively close to one another, to limit the distance everyone would have to travel to get back and forth to land. It took a week to get the ships unloaded, and somewhat secured and protected. This was done out of reverence for their protecting and delivering them to their destination. While the unloading was being done, twenty-five individuals were selected to make their way out onto the roadways and try to find transportation for the 980 survivors.

There were two live births during the last portion of their voyage. One birth was in sight of St. John's, and his name became, automatically, Landon Sea Kaelin. His mother, Verena Kaelin, had lost her husband in the ship wreck at sea. But now Verena and her five year old daughter, Klara, had a son to help fill that loss. These two births gave the survivors reminders of what B had told them.

Fortunately for all those weary travelers, the 25 scouts did find adequate land transport. But as everyone was soon to find out, it was an odd assortment of vehicles, some requiring significant interior modifications, others only minor exterior ones. And using them required the removal, preparation and burial of April 1st victims, as was the case for the five Swansea sailing vessels they had to rebuild earlier. Eventually, a solemn and dignified burial ceremony was held in La

Crosse. Altogether, 85 graves had to be dug over those next few days, but at that, it was just a fraction of how many sailors they had buried at Pontedawe, Wales cemetery.

This same work detail also had to fashion 25 hand siphons for each individual in their group, along with finding a large storage container, and then they had to locate stranded vehicles to siphon gas from. While those jobs were being completed, areas were being cleared and prepared to drive the selected vehicles onto and parked for refitting and eventual loading of passengers and supplies.

The vehicles selected, both by necessity and by chance, were six full size buses; five 53 foot long enclosed, semi-trailer trucks; ten 24 foot long open, bobtail, mid-sized trucks; and four 53 foot long, flatbed trailer trucks. Each required some modification for their upcoming trip to the Mammoth Caverns. Most notably, the enclosed area of the semi-trailers needed to be subdivided into three tiers of continuous bunk beds. There would be 13 beds to a tier, six on each side and one at the enclosed end of the trailer. Two mattresses would be located on the aisle in the middle, for a total of 41 beds per truck. These beds were for the weakest and most exhausted Swiss survivors. The buses did not require any modification, just work on making their interiors more comfortable. They would carry the less exhausted survivors, but ones still needing to sit semi-reclined for this final portion of their journey. There would be 50 passengers per bus.

The bobtail and flat-bed trucks needed to have high side rails built and installed, along with attaching tarps around the sides and one capable of being unrolled over the top of the passengers, if need be. The bobtail trucks would carry 25 people each and the semi-trailer flatbed trucks would carry 50 each. These trucks would carry the healthiest survivors. Completing the carrying capacity of this convoy would be the 25 drivers.

Together, these vehicles would transport all 980 of the 1,213 Swiss citizens who began this evacuation so long ago, or of the 1,245 of their countrymen, women and children who were first sheltered in the Sargans fortress on April 1st. A few years after completing their journey, the names of all 365 lost since that time were inscribed on a monument erected in Resolve's Memorial Cemetery. Their suffering and sacrifice, along with those individuals who were already buried in Resolve's cemetery, were to serve as an everlasting memorial to the countless losses, worldwide, on and after April 1st. The actual day chosen for the annual recognition of their losses was not on April 1st, but on December 10th, when the last survivors from Mammoth and Carlsbad Caverns were rescued and safely relocated back in Resolve.

The final trip to Mammoth Caverns for the Swiss refugees started on August 26th, two weeks after they beached the four tall ships. They were to drive along Highways 90 to Highway 92, all the way to the Mammoth Caverns. This route spared them the stalled congestion and terrible reminders of what took place during and after April 1st. They were to travel on these lightly traveled roadways all the way. The drive, itself, only averaged 30 miles per hour; and it entailed just five hours of continuous travel each day. This was due to the multiple needs and generally exhausted condition of the passengers. Plus, there was a two day stopover due to a bus and a large truck breaking down. Arrival at Mammoth was on September 3rd, two days after the September 1st flyover by Resolve's Search and Rescue planes. As expected, they would have to wait now until December 1st for their rescue.

FIFTEEN: THE FINAL RESCUE MISSIONS

The two rescue planes took off on December 1, 2013, as usual, but this time it was for their final attempt to locate and rescue anyone. It had been one and a half years since they started these flights, and this was their last effort. Their fuel supply had been exhausted. And it had become routine and, quite frankly some of the crewmembers admitted, somewhat frustrating. The flights were long, crossing the country back and forth; and they had been fruitless since the rescue of the Shuttle crew. It was as if the entire country, aside from Resolve, had been sterilized of all human life. It seemed impossible to them that the number of survivors now living in Resolve was all that would ever survive. Certainly, they thought, there would be people coming from elsewhere, but radio silence had been complete; and there were no signs of survivors from other countries.

However, that was about to change. In anticipation of what the Swiss evacuees had heard on their shortwave radio, in now what seemed many years ago, in their fortress shelter, there should be another flyover at the Bowling Green-Warren Counties Regional Airport on December 1st. Not wanting to exhaust everyone with a potentially fruitless trip, their leadership decided to take three bus loads to the airfield. Once there, they would have the 150 people line up on the taxi

736

runway, holding large red banners, spelling out the large letters, "HELP US!" While they were doing that, the bus drivers would ignite the earlier prepared and covered pile of brush and old tires, whenever they heard the sound of approaching jet engines.

At 1 p.m. the first sound of airplane engines were heard. Immediately everyone assembled on the pavement and the diesel gas-soaked pile was lit. Black smoke billowed skyward instantaneously, creating a column that could be seen for miles.

So shocked and stunned were the flight crews, they began yelling at each other and into their radios, "Look there!! Smoke is rising in the distance! We have survivors!!! By God, we have survivors!! Send a message to Resolvle" Steve Blackmore called out, "we're going in."

For some reason, probably most likely related to Ernie Tam's long career as a Search and Rescue officer, he had accompanied this final flight. He came, along with the usual EMT's and a couple of Marines for safety, although everyone, by now, thought that was unnecessary to do so. At hearing Steve's voice exclaiming and shouting orders, Ernie spun in his seat and looked out his window, in the southeasterly direction. Staring hard, he could just make out the words formed by the red banners the Swiss survivors were waving. "You're right?" he cried excitely, "There are many people down there. It's an absolute miracle!! Thank God, someone else is alive after all."

Waving their red flags wildly back and forth, those holding them were jumping up and down overjoyed at the sight. Soon the two large planes made their landing approach and were pulled up close to them and parked. Within three minutes of landing, the rear cargo bay doors opened and the two parties rushed towards each other. Greeting the flight crews were 150 cheering, laughing, crying, jumping up and down, but very nervous survivors. What would they say? How would they be understood? Would there be room for all of them? Immediately, there was a rush of emotions and questions.

But B's presence in their midst that night in the Atlantic Ocean, where each person was touched, solved their doubts when they began to speak to the flight crews. As the flight crews poured out of the cargo door, exclaiming excitedly, "Welcome! How are you? How many of you are there? Where did you come from?" The survivors, in return, replied, in perfect English, not in their traditional French or German, the only languages they previously knew, to all their greetings and questions.

There were questions, much hugging and periods of just stunned staring at each other in amazement and awe. The outline of their story of survival staggered the flight crews. And Franz, noting the Coast Guard insignia on Ernie's uniform, which he worn as a sentimental gesture for this last rescue mission, came up to him and asked if he was, in fact, a Coast Guard officer. After it was established he was, Franz briefly told him the story about finding "The Eagle" sailing ship and how she had helped bring them to America. Ernie was so moved by this story, he wept with joy and admiration at their courage and bravery.

It was obvious to all the flight crews that these survivors had done just that, survived. Diseases of malnourishment and exposure to long term hardship had depleted their bodies' immune systems and fat reserves. They were all thin, some jaundiced with missing teeth, premature balding, sunken eyes, pale skin and signs of wounds not healing. There was a generalized weakness noted, especially when some of them tried to get up from sitting or climbing up the ramp into the cargo plane's

738

hold. Undoubtedly, they thought, vitamin deficiencies played a part in all they were seeing, with scurvy and rickets the most likely culprit, due to their having a very restricted amount of food, for an extended period of time.

But the display of joy and relief, as seen in their darkened and sunken eyes, told the rescuers these people were ready to regain their health and make a place for themselves in a new world. Steve Blackmore and Kathryn Swisher, as well as their crews, were humbled by their indescribable will to live and good humor. Even I, your chronicler of these and other events of this nature since our evacuation from Amboy, was given to shout a thankful "Halleluiah!" Across the deepening December cold and silence of that barren airfield, voices were heard to yell, "Saved at last!!" "We're saved at last!!" "Thank God, we're saved at last!!" Their voices rose in celebration.

But after 30-45 minutes, Steve and Benton informed the Swiss survivors that only 125 individuals, at the most, could be transported back to Resolve at any one time. Given the large number of evacuees, they needed to choose who left that day. Then, they informed everyone the rest would be rescued on daily flights for the next seven days. But that the remaining 25 people who came today would have to return to the Mammoth Caverns and organize the ones to come hereafter.

In addition, Steve asked me, Fred Wailand, in case you did not know who is recording this material, to search the cargo plane for some of the leaflets that were distributed in Arizona by Ernie's rescue crews, when they found those survivors. Once I found a package of 50, he had me start amending them to say, for anyone who might be at the Carlsbad City Air Terminal when we all flew back that day that their rescue would be delayed until December 9th.

And on our way back, loaded with the 125 rescued survivors, while circling the Carlsbad airport, we saw in bold lettering the words, "HELP" "RESCUE US". And out of the airport terminal building a group came running and waving their hands skyward, signaling for us to land. Instead, Steve ordered one of his crew to open the rear cargo hold door while he circled low over the air terminal and to toss the leaflets out as we went by. It was important that these desperate folks were not left wondering if or when they would be rescued. They needed to be reassured that they would not be forgotten. As the cargo plane made a third pass, it was clear they had read and understood the message and waved us good-bye for now. The lack of frantic motions indicated to everyone on board that they understood we would come back for them.

The arrival of that first flight of Swiss survivors at Resolve was at 6 p.m. The entire town of 1,999 turned out for their homecoming. The Communication Center had been alerted of their existence and kept abreast of all the crews' findings as the mission progressed. And for the next nine nights the same scene unfolded. Moreover, it was always with the same equally enthusiastic welcome for each rescued group that arrived.

Each person, who arrived, was given a thorough medical checkup, complete psychological and nutritional evaluations and a needs assessment. Unlike the survivors from Amboy, Yucca Mountain, Chino Valley, or Kitts Peak, many of the Swiss refugees were from broken families, as was the case with the Shuttle survivors. As a consequence, a large number were either alone or were orphans. Very few families arrived fully intact, as they had been when they first arrived at the Sargans' fortress on April 1st. As quickly as possible, each person, adult or child, was integrated into the community. Everyone in Resolve was thrilled to finally be part of a world-wide network of survivors, beyond those in the "Amboy 75". It had been hoped, throughout the preceding year and a half, that there would be many survivors rescued. But, in fact, there had been so few. They had become dispirited at that course of events, but now all that was changed. They were to become a safe harbor for peoples from all over the world.

And without question, the survivors at the Carlsbad Caverns were nervously waiting on December 1st at the Carlsbad Airport for someone to appear. The first of the two rescue planes, upon seeing their sign on the runway, swooped low, and opened the large, rear door to throw out leaflets. After reading them, they were reassured they would be rescued in eight more days, and waved at the planes as the turned to fly away. Since their arrival in November at the Carlsbad Caverns, their health had declined, due to the strain and hardships of their arduous journey to America.

Seeing the planes was an overwhelming experience for all of them. Many of these survivors were not accustomed to seeing such large, complicated airships or comfortable with the possibility of being thrust into the fast-paced complexity of an industrialized society. Most were still experiencing flashbacks and emotional outbursts, recalling their surviving the death-stalking voyages across so many immense bodies of water. They were filled with a mixture of relief and a growing fear of the unknown ahead of them.

Come December 9th, when the first flight arrived at Resolve's airstrip, the native families of Arizona had already sensed some of the new arrivals might need their particularly unique kind of support and insight. And sure enough, once the passengers had deplaned, it was learned that a fair number of them began their trip from the isolated desert regions of Australia, China and Outer Mongolia or the deepest jungles of New Guinea, Indonesia, Africa or South America or the remote mountains of Kazakhstan, Iran, Tibet or the Congo. Quickly, a support system was established by the Arizona families to comfort and support these new arrivals.

For much of the beginning of their seemingly endless journey, everyone had to rely on the more sophisticated skills and equipment of the technologically proficient survivors in their midst. But soon enough, for there to be anyone to survive and get to Carlsbad, their eventual destination, the skills of these native people's were the difference between the entire group perishing or completing their journey. Most importantly, now the need was for everyone in Resolve to learn from these native people. Their treasure trove of survival skills had kept them alive for centuries in their hostile, homeland environments. That knowledge was priceless now.

The rest of the next night, December 10th, when the last flight returned from Carlsbad, and into the next day, was filled with celebrations. Over time, that same date was to become the officially recognized one as the anniversary for the Global Union's formation. To mark its importance at 5 p.m. the next day, as Resolve's celebration in their newly finished Assembly Hall was about to conclude, I got out the previously recorded music Clem had instructed me to play when the new government was fully unified. The music transfixed everyone there. They stood motionless, quietly listening to the stirring music. Looking around at each other, they realized their small number of 3,196 citizens was all that was left on this most-haggard and war-ravaged world.

PART IV

SIXTEEN: SETTLING IN

In the year since the ending of the rescue
missions, the settlement of Resolve continued to take on
the permanency of an established community. Most
importantly, though, its citizens gathered here from
everywhere on the planet, were successfully planting and
harvesting their own food. Hot houses had to be
engineered and built to extend their growing season,
which had significantly shortened due to the colder
atmospheric conditions that had settled over most of the
world. The animals had to be given extra protection
against the harsher winters; they needed adequate
shelters to retreat into when necessary. And steadily,
they were extending the acreage being irrigated for their
food and for animal feed. In order to widen the skill
base of food production, all families were required to
cultivate at least one to two acres or their five acre
allotments.   The success of that program was now
clearly evident. There was enough food for day-to-day
consumption and increasingly, enough excess to start
bartering and storing for emergencies.

Likewise, during this year the Global Union
Government Building had finally been completed. It
had two floors, plus a full basement. On the first floor is
our library. Books, magazines, periodicals, papers,

videos, microfiche records, DVD's, CD's were cataloged and stored in the basement. Part of the first floor has dedicated space for research, meetings, and writing. It was in that room where this chronicle you are now reading, was composed.

Included on the rest of the first floor is the Credit Union, which was to start issuing monthly payments of $15.00 per person on December 10, 2014, in two days, when our First Anniversary was to be celebrated. Also on the first floor is the Constable's Office. We still have a ready force to protect and defend ourselves, but the general thinking now is that, because no other survivors had been located or heard from, there is little threat of any kind immediately around us. If nothing else, these trained and drilled volunteers serve as a kind of Ready-Reserve Home Guard, to be used in case of any emergency. And the last department housed on the first floor is the Communication Center. It houses our Public Address System, a small radio station that operates only certain hours each day, the Community Bulletin Board, and the nerve-center of our more sophisticated extra-terrestrial listening and image-capturing devices. That area is the pride of our scientific community.

The second floor has our Court Room, with a bench for our three judges. They hear and decide on all legal issues that are brought before them. And this is where the law professors instruct our Level 5 and 6 interns for their eventual government and legal occupations and leadership. Taking up the remainder of the space on the second floor are the offices of the Global Union's elected officials and representatives. None of these are paid positions. In fact, there are none in all of Resolve. What is important here is not what you do, so much as how you teach what you do to others, and how you work to sustain our community.

The Medical Clinic and small Hospital were actually finished well over a year ago. Building them and the school buildings were priorities for everyone. Included in the Medical Clinic is our Emergency Response equipment and offices. We have the two fire engines and three ambulances from the Marine Base near Amboy for the EMT's to use. Our hospital has 25 beds, but there has never been, as yet, a time when more than 8-10 were in use. The school buildings house every school level from preschool through the apprenticeship programs and even the ever-present, evening adult education classes. Gradually, there is less emphasis on survival skill training and more on self-expression, musical instrument instruction and dance and drama classes. And we still have talent nights, so ably coordinated by Philip and Theresa Lieska, along with Albert and Dada Nugama doing the introductions and moment-to-moment directing. They remain a great success and probably will become a permanent institution.

Our Advanced Learning Center houses our teaching and research laboratories. Knowledge for knowledge sake is still a priority. And if anything, it is pointing the way away from our past, hopefully into a brighter future. We are not motivated to make scientific breakthroughs, but we do challenge our youth to always try being on the frontiers of knowledge. Our past history is the foundation we build their learning on, both to remind them to avoid certain avenues of learning and actions and to challenge them to search for and build a better world. None of us in Resolve, even the newly settled native peoples, are afraid of science. But all of us are terrified at humanity's ability to misuse science and to distort and manipulate religious beliefs and governing bodies into doing terrible harm. We are even exploring ways we may be able to dismantle telescopes at Kitt

Peak and Palomar and transport some of them here. It would involve ferrying the Kitt Peak equipment across the Colorado River, there being no bridges left. It's a dream right now, but everyone involved believes it is might be possible to do.

Our homes or apartments, whichever you might prefer to call them, were finished about three months ago. They are two story row houses, built in large quadrangles, with entrances into and out of the interior courtyard through each of the four corners. The courtyard is a combination playground, outdoor exercise area and meeting area. This area gets a lot of use. We have built sixteen of these complexes, each able to accommodate 200 families. There are 50 families to each side.

The rationale for building the homes in this fashion was to preserve whatever heat is generated in the individual homes. There are no windows on the exterior of the buildings. And the space to build these complexes takes up much less room than individual houses would. This leaves us more available land for our agricultural needs. The assignment of living spaces was done by each family or set of individuals taking a number at random. Then those numbers were assigned to each apartment, at random. The rationale for this was that there was a strong desire by everyone to avoid establishing any cultural enclaves or choice residences being given to selected individuals. The democratic process, here in Resolve, has been taken further than was usually seen in most western cultures. We desperately wanted to build a society that was not tempted by old cultural pitfalls. Isolation, prejudice and ignorance all breed disaster. That we know only too well.

Our Transportation Center became our showpiece, if there was ever anyone to impress outside Resolve. It was built, as you might suspect, along the

Interstate Highway. It incorporated the modified highway airstrip, with hangers for the helicopters, fixed wing aircraft and large jets. There were also large warehouses built for the many trucks, earth moving equipment and humvees we had left over from the confinements. Containers and boxcars were also used for storage of tools, supplies and equipment needed to maintain all these craft and vehicles. Over time the engineers were able to transport, overland, modified tanker trucks, filled with fuel for all the stored planes and trucks. Interestingly, the train engines are also maintained and housed in their own facility. No one could say if at a future date they might not be needed again.

It is in this area that the Amtrak sleeper, lounge and dining/kitchen cars are kept and used on a regular basis for study groups, conferences or meetings. The Magazine Building was built here as well. In it is stored all the military equipment, including uniforms, arms and ammunition. The military background of so many residents in Resolve is obvious and is not held in suspicion. On the contrary, it was agreed to keep training our Home Guard on a permanent basis but maintain a low profile for our vigilance. Everyone is expected to train, and stay prepared for any emergency, be it for protection, transportation, or medical management.

The last two noteworthy structures that need to be described are the Performance Hall and the Worship Center. I will reserve the Worship Center for last, it being the last building constructed and the one most involved in the evolution of Resolve. The Performance Hall's presence and function speaks for itself. After months of struggle with Eric Stanfield's priceless pipe organ, by a host of the engineers and Philip, it was finally fully installed. Somehow he got it disassembled and shipped to the Marine Base and then on to the Amboy Caverns for storage. But there was no one accomplished enough to really do it justice. Philip tried his hand at it with minimal success. What is left now is for the music students in the Performance Arts Program to gradually increase their knowledge and ability with the piano and organ and someone to eventually become accomplished playing it. The Performance Hall easily accommodates 1,200 people at a time. And the stage is large enough to allow a full orchestra to perform or a major drama to be produced. It is the pride of the community. The basement has multiple rehearsal studios for the performers to use day or night.

Probably it should be noted, after all this discussion about the various buildings and outlying acreage that is under cultivation, that Resolve has one main road or street, with these major structures located on either side of this single road. Cultivated land surrounds the community on all sides, with the main road leading to the Transportation Center on the south end of town. Beyond the downtown, if you will, on its eastern and northern sides, there are the 15 foot high levees, with their outside walls protected by concrete slabs from the destroyed dams and buildings upstream.

Finally, I come to the Worship Center. And to discuss this I must go back almost two years ago, when the Shuttle astronauts were rescued. Following their rescue, there were two or three weeks of silence, both from them and from the leadership of Resolve about their status or experiences. But during all that time Amber and her crew were being debriefed by Eric Stanfield and Ben Javitts, whenever they were not trying to revive their malnourished and exhausted bodies and minds with proper food and rest. After countless hours of these meetings, which eventually included the scientists from Kitts Peak as well, it was decided that a general assembly of all Resolve's families had to be convened. At the center of this decision was the video recording of B's appearance inside the International Space Station. Their joint decision was that everyone should have the opportunity to see it.

It was in mid-July when that meeting was held, after the first long-range rescue missions of June 1, 2012. Eric, Ben, the Kitt's Peak scientists and the Shuttle crew all were seated on the makeshift stage, inside the double circus-size tents. The rest of Resolve's residents were sitting or standing in or around the tents. They only had three small video monitors that were mounted in the front and on each side of the stage, but speakers were scattered throughout the tents for everyone to at least hear clearly whatever was said. Later, and up to this writing, people come to our Library and check-out the video tape and watch it in wonder.

Eric rose first to address the gathering. "My fellow citizens, we, gathered here on this stage, have finally decided to call this meeting. We want each of you to have the opportunity to watch and listen to a video recording that was made aboard the International Space Station during the time our four rescued astronauts were confined there. Additionally, we have posted on several bulletin boards, scattered around the walls of these tents, still photographs of what they recorded on and after April 1st while circling earth. Between what they recorded and what the scientists rescued from Kitts Peak Observatories have shown and told us, and which are also on display here today, we think we have a pretty accurate picture of what took place when most of us were confined inside our respective caves or shelters on that day.

"Without exception, all of us on this stage today, have been both humbled and extremely distressed by our decision to show you all this material. But the decision finally came down to this: no one has the right not to show you everything. We all agreed that the process, and staggering volume of information, that was designated as 'classified', 'top secret', or 'for selected eyes only' prior to April 1st by our governmental and military authorities had become, both pathological and criminal. It was your government, your elected officials, your tax money that paid their wages. And they chose, day in and day out, to ignore your opinions, your wants and your collective common sense. This secret and silent arrogance of governing, world-wide, had become one of the root causes of the destruction on April 1st and its aftermath.

"Our hesitation in showing you this material, in fact, was based solely on its content, on its emotional impact on you, as it was on us. But, in the end, we thought then, as well as for the duration of our new society, that there shall be no more secrets, even at the expense of emotionally challenging you to your core. You have the absolute right to view and hear what we have assembled here today. You've earned that right. Never let the right of full disclosure slip away again.

"In doing this, we have decided to divide this meeting into two parts. The first part will be your viewing some composite video recordings, taken by both the Shuttle and Kitts Peak crews. After which, you may stand up and walk around the perimeter of the tents and look at the labeled, still photographs taken by these crews. We might suggest you start your walking tour here at the stage podium, and work your way around to your right. There is a sequence to the pictures that will better explain what happened during that time. After everyone has had time to look at them, we will then proceed with the second part of our meeting. Please, if you will, let us watch this first video, and then you can begin your walking tour of the still pictures on the tents' walls."

For the next three hours the families filed past the documentation of what led up to and occurred on April 1st. What you, the reader, have read throughout these three volumes, these survivors saw and read about in a matter of minutes. The impact was heartbreaking. Most did not finish the entire circuit around the tents. And because of this, the collection remains, as I have said, actively viewed in our Library to this day. It shall always remain beyond mere mortals comprehension all that led up to what happened on that day. But at the end of these three hours, everyone had taken their seats or positions back around the tents.

Again Eric rose to speak. "Now for the second part of today's gathering, I want to turn the meeting over to Amber Peeters, the commander of the Shuttle flight, some of whose pictures you've been looking at... Amber."

"Thank you, Eric. And I want to thank all of you, in behalf of myself and our crew for your unbelievable hospitality and help in getting us through our grief and poor health, after you rescued us. Your understanding and tenderness towards us has made our experience and losses bearable. You have accepted us, into your midst, as family. We can never fully repay you for your kindness. But today we will try, at least, to make a small down payment.

"What you are about to see, I realize, is not going to be the total surprise it was to us. You had, as I understand it, a prior shocking encounter with B before your confinement in the caverns. To my knowledge it has only been the families rescued from Chino Valley, Arizona and Kitts Peak Observatories that have not had that experience. Today will fix that. We have no idea if B knew we were accidentally recording this appearance. We didn't realize it ourselves until days later. But if B did, the matter was never discussed or objected to. What you are about to see and hear, in short, is what we sincerely believe is a conversation, albeit an emotionally distraught one, with our crew and God."

"It's certainly not for me or anyone else on this stage to tell you how to react or respond to this recording. That is something each person has to decide for themselves, via free will, if you will. But, seeing this again and hearing the words spoken, I personally have, for the first time, dedicated myself to attending a worship service, at least weekly, and finding solace in daily prayer. It was a choice I felt compelled to make. And now, let's view the tape. Ted, if you will, please..."

The next fifteen minutes were viewed and broadcasted throughout the tents and beyond. Once it was completed, a call went out from within the midst of the audience to please rewind and run it again. That was immediately seconded by everyone there. No one moved or spoke throughout either of the viewings. It was as if there was no question that B knew this recording was being made. And the message could not be clearer to each person who saw it. Time had run out on frivolous, free will decisions. The universal clock was now reset and ticking. It was either going to record the beginning of a new time or the end of a finished one. That was their choice now.

And so it went until the next meeting with B. No actual decision was made about any type of Worship Center until about three months later, October 15, to be exact, when another General Assembly meeting was being held, this time to discuss the final plans for various buildings and other projects with everyone. It was, as they say, strictly a business meeting. And because it was, and the discussions, decisions and plans that were finalized were important, these proceedings were being videotaped as well for historical purposes.

Ben Javitts and Doug Chan, the head building engineers for Resolve, called the meeting to order. Scattered around the tent were sketches of building plans, agricultural plots and pastures, along with specifications of the Transportation Center's expansion. They knew it could be a lengthy meeting.

But just before Ben rose to open the meeting, a now familiar form appeared on stage before everyone. Still, and particularly after everyone had seen the repeated viewings of the Shuttle video tape, there was a murmur of shock rise from everyone in the audience and on stage.

B, without introduction or apology began, by saying, "Good morning to each of you. I am so pleased to see all of you here looking as well as you do. Frankly, I am so pleased just to see you here. The migration of survivors is not done; I can assure you of that. But you are the island of refuge for anyone who does manage to survive after April 1st. Only time will tell if more people will be found or make their way to this place. I certainly hope so, and I believe so.

"My coming here today is prompted by your relatively recent viewing of an appearance I made before the Shuttle crew. Frankly, I was not aware at the time that the meeting was being recorded, but I am glad it was. I do not plan to repeat the message given on that day. You have already seen and heard enough from it. It reflects the crew's challenge toward me that each of you is entitled to express, particularly after what you have experienced and seen. I tried, in answering those challenges at that meeting, to express my views on the state of this world and the eventual outcome if nothing goes unchanged.

"Today, I want to address the issues of worship and religious faith. In other words how do you express yourselves, in a relationship with me? What is the basis of that relationship? What nurtures it? What are the obstacles to hinder it? Why even bother, as increasingly so many chose not to, before April 1ˢᵗ. To answer these questions may take some time, so please get comfortable and listen.

"To worship something or someone is the loftiest act anyone can perform. You do not worship out of fear, but from gratitude for what you have been given. You do not worship out of feeling specifically chosen, but from hope for what, everyone, has been promised. You do not worship out of selfish desire to receive more, but from peacefulness for what you already have.

"What then are these givens or gifts that can result in this gratitude, hope and peace? Briefly stated, they are life itself, the freedom to make choices, the capacity to hope and to love, the promise of everlasting life, and a voyage of wondrous discovery, both of your world and someday, one beyond its boundaries.

"And what is it about each of these gifts that either thrills or haunts you, that either causes you to accept or reject them and me. The gift of life, unfortunately in earthly terms, is and always will be, self-limited.   That's   an   insurmountable   given. Understanding that, how can someone live it to the fullest, and be grateful as well? Or asked another way, with all that you have witnessed since April 1ˢᵗ, how can someone feel grateful for even being alive at this very moment? With so much death and destruction around you, how can you feel anything but anger and guilt to be here, in this place?

"You work your way around and out of these self-destructive reactions and feelings by the givens or gifts of hope and love. You begin to realize that my love for you is boundless. Not all-powerful, but limitless in terms of what I feel for you. And, in turn, you begin to find the capacity to love each other and me, little by little. Too many confuse my capabilities with what they think or idealize they are, rather than grasping what is the truth. In the briefest terms, I am love.

"There was the beginning, the act of creating the universe, and I will take credit for that moment in time. But that, too, was an act of love, not a show of force or power. The power of love is limitless. The power of destruction and evil is self-limiting. And it was ever-fascinating to me over these past centuries that as your love for each other and for me grew; the well-spring of hope inside you became even stronger. And, as I have said before to another who used to be in your midst, it was that hope that drove me to my third act of creation, that of establishing the kingdom of heaven.

"And it's true that I have provided signposts, if you will, along the way to point to this third act of mine. I have placed in your midst, through the ages, my Son, prophets, saints, messengers, scribes, even my Spirit. But they were too subtle, too bold or too frightening. Many have believed, and of such is the Kingdom of Heaven. But too many did not, and such was the creation of the hell on April 1st.

"At this point I will digress briefly to say the cosmic event on that same day was not something I even anticipated or could control. Physical events of nature and the universe interact independent of me. Being the Creator does not entitle me to be able to control creation or have omnipotent foresight. That's part of the beauty and mystery of the universe. It's like a river in flood. It moves along a previously charted course, but easily has the capacity to flood over its banks at any time; so, too, it is with the laws of the physical universe and its behavior. Cosmic events, like that which occurred on April 1st, do and will occur. I am unable to predict or to deter them. And I have no desire to do so. To me, and to others amongst you, it's part of the beauty of creation;

and it should be left that way.

"Lastly, what part does a sense of peace play in all this? It is peacefulness that awakens in you, what I call the 'attainables'. And these are humility, humor, trust, faith, goodness and enlightenment. With these, life becomes precious and your relationship with me becomes alive and self-sustaining, through all of life's twists and turns. You become aware of and a participant in the kingdom on earth, or as the prayer intones, 'on earth as it is in heaven'.

"All this said, how then do you interact with me? Through individual and/or collective worship, through individual and/or collective prayer, through individual and/or collective faith, sometimes expressed by a religious ceremony in a house of worship or often just expressed by your individual soul reaching out to me in complete trust. No intermediaries are necessary. They might help point the way or enlighten you, but each soul has the capacity to communicate directly with me.

"So, in summary, worship or communicating with me can take many forms, through the use of sacraments, vestments, music, works of art, icons, candles, incense, statues, various symbols, and written or spoken words. All are well and good. They are the outward, visible signposts of your most precious, inward possession, your soul. Your own life-sustaining part of the universe's creation. Treasure it, guard it, nurture it and talk to me through it. I am always with you, both now, to and through all there is to come.

"Finally, let me say, I will come again to stand amongst you, as I have repeatedly said over these last three years. I never want you to feel alone or abandoned again. Listen to and understand what I say. And know my love for each of you is boundless."

The silence that filled that gathering was breathtaking. Even I, who had never been one to sense the need or desire to worship anything or anyone, other than my good fortune to have married Freda and being present for the birth and rearing of our daughters, was staggered by what I saw and heard. I know I could not have stood, if asked to do so at that time. My knees were shaking, as was the rest of me. Even for a life-long skeptic like me, I knew that after this encounter with B, I no longer was the same. You couldn't help but feel privileged to have been present and heard these words being spoken. And for the first time in my life, I began to recite a prayer, often heard, but never repeated by me, "Our father, who art…"

Eventually, Ben did rise and come forward to the edge of the stage and announce quietly, "If you don't mind, maybe the rest of today should be spent in some other way rather than meeting here. I suggest we postpone today's meeting until tomorrow at the same time."

And it was that next day that the Worship Center was planned. It was to include indoor and outdoor sanctuaries. Both areas had public and private areas for groups or individuals to find solitude and reverential quiet. As mentioned elsewhere in these chronicles, no dedicated or formal religious leadership was available in Resolve. Over time, however, there were certain individuals who became Lay Leaders, as was the case in both the Amboy and Yucca Mountain Caverns. The Worship Center was nestled closer to the hillside on the western side of town. It was eventually constructed out of native, mountain and river rock, with its outdoor area filled with flowering plants, shrubs and trees, along with fruit bearing plants and trees. It was an oasis that everyone came to many times a week for comfort, rest and guidance.

SEVENTEEN: JANUARY 1st, 2015's
CELEBRATION CEREMONY

This was the second ceremony of its kind held in Resolve. It and the Anniversary of Resolve's founding were the two major non-religious holidays observed for the next few years. Eventually, the calendar was beaming with holidays and observances of all kinds. But this day was particularly special. It was the first time everyone who had been rescued could be publicly recognized and honored.

The youth of Resolve were the ones who dictated how and when this important occasion would be observed. By a unanimous vote they decided the various celebrations should be held in common, on the same day, in the same place. It was a decision based on what gave them the greatest comfort and sense of security. Individualism was not as important to them after April 1st. Sharing and celebrating with everyone else was what they wanted. And this became a tradition that has persisted for many years to this writing. If possible, I think they would prefer to all celebrate all their birthdays once a year as well. Their strength and view of the future is one shaped by this commitment to each other. They genuinely care about one another. So it was an easy decision on the part of the Global Union's elected officials to second their wishes and proceed accordingly.

The program for this second Celebration of Life was in two parts. The first was formal; the second very informal and more to the liking of all the Resolve residents. There was to be plenty of food, drink and dancing that night in the General Assembly Hall, the last major building that needs to be mentioned. It, alone, can accommodate all of us under one roof. It's a sprawling facility, next to the Government Offices Building. It's where all our community festivities are held.

The formal program had two divisions, one that celebrated the accomplishments of the adults and one for the youth. Because the larger group to be recognized was the adults, they went first. And what followed, in a somewhat chaotic fashion, but no one seemed to mind, was the introduction and passing in review of all the survivors of the two rescue missions from the Mammoth and Carlsbad Caverns, the folks from Switzerland, the South Pacific, Asia, Africa, Southern Europe, South and Middle America. It was a parade of such proud and thankful people. Names were called out as each passed by the podium.

Next, there was the awarding of medals for bravery, the Medals of Honor. Four individuals were awarded these: Jo Ann Henry, for her instrumental and pivotal role in driving the trains from Yucca Mountain to Kelso; G. W. McCoy and Archie Davis for their heroism in risking their lives to save the people in the Amboy Caverns. And one award was given posthumously to Clement L. Newberry for his tireless work in helping the Caverns' occupants assemble, prepare and survive. In this same ceremony the next year, ten more individuals were given the Medal of Honor for the heroism shown during their journeys to the Mammoth and Carlsbad Caverns and for the crews who flew those regional and long range rescue missions.

Finally, and with the most laughter, was the

recognition of three individuals by the Global Union's Governing Body for their recent discovery. Sid Blackwell, Geoffrey and Patrician Graham were awarded the Medal of Amazingly Good Luck, as it was jokingly called, for their discovery of GOLD! It appears the three had gotten gold-hunting fever, after much of the more urgent work was completed, and after the apparent end of earthquakes and major rainstorms and flooding. They went prospecting and found a large deposit of it about fifteen miles from Resolve. Everyone who wanted to then had an opportunity to go with them and dig for the treasure. Of course, by law, all of it had to be turned over to the Government. But the thrill was in the discovery.

The second part of the celebration was dedicated to the youth; this involved passing out certificates and diplomas to all graduates from elementary, middle, high school and apprenticeship programs. This was followed by the announcement of those who had entered the just-established Advanced Studies Programs in Mathematics, Astronomy, Government and Agriculture. Next, there were the 4-H honors for those who had taken such excellent care of the animals and pets for the years leading up to this celebration. They were: Jihan and Ilhan Zandi, Hanna and Mandel Segal, Megan Wailand, and Edree Nugama. This was followed by the announcement of Resolve's first marriage engagement: Bernice Wailand and Chet Stanfield and one couple who were getting married later that day: Helen Plant and Peter Marzoff. Both Helen and Peter were from the two families whose spouses were lost to the Deer Mouse virus outbreak in the Amboy Cavern.

Following the distribution of certificates, diplomas and awards, there was an announcement of what future plans were being discussed for any outreach beyond their community. With the discovery of another large repository of usable jet fuel, two sets of long range flights were being planned to retrieve documents and gold stored at Fort Knox, Kentucky, as well as any historical archives and documents they could locate in Regional National Archive Centers, such as Fort Worth, Texas, and Santa Fe, New Mexico, provided there was any sign of these Centers being intact.

The other major venture was a flight to the Tall Ships landing site in Virginia, where 120 engineers and seamen would be dispatched to try and repair and launch The Eagle and any of the other Tall Ships. Their hope was to then sail them either through the Panama Canal, if it was intact or around the Horn to the Sea of Cortez and dock them near Parker, Arizona. During that mission, their planes would again pass over the Mammoth and Carlsbad Cavern rescue rendezvous points to check on any survivors.

The celebrations finally ended at sunrise the next day.

PART V

EIGHTEEN: EPILOGUE

By April 4th, 2015, much had happened since the Second Celebration Ceremony on January 1st. Somewhat later than was originally intended, this quarterly, all-town meeting was scheduled for this day at 10:30 a.m.

The stage in the Performing Arts Center was full of people, standing and sitting in bleachers, as were both the auditorium's balcony, first floor and isles. The Center was packed, with excited conversations and laughter filling the hall. As Eric stood to bring the audience to order and present Resolve's quarterly progress report, two figures unexpectedly came out from the side curtains and crossed over to the middle of the stage. B reached out and touched Eric, motioning him to take his seat for now. As Eric backed up to sit down, both figures moved forward to the edge of the stage and faced the audience.

The audience was immediately caught up in an unusual show of collective emotion at B's appearance, even after a rather short period of time since their last contact.   There erupted a gradual, but spreading applause, which soon included everyone.   This was followed immediately with everyone standing, even the smallest children, as they clapped. It was meant to show their deepest affection and recognition of B's role in their lives.

B nodded, which was observable, even through the hooded shroud. As the ovation began to lessen, B motioned for everyone to be seated.

"Good morning, again. It seems like only a few days ago when we last were together. Today, I have no lengthy message, instructions or directions to give you. Or, more importantly, I have no warnings either." To this, everyone again broke into clapping and occasional shouts and whistles.

"Instead," looking at the other figure who was dressed in a way no one had ever seen before, "I have someone beside me who is anxious to meet you. She accompanied me here today. And as you will see after her introductory remarks, this is a moment you have wondered and dreamed about for centuries. Your world is now about to change forever. It gives me the greatest pleasure to introduce to you...." At that moment, somehow, initiated by someone or something, strains of music began to fill the Auditorium as the other figure approached the center of the stage...

However, B's words and the music were lost on most people, because they had begun, one by one, to notice that this other figure's feet were not touching the stage floor. It was as if she was hovering in midair.

APPENDIX 3

Figure 1:

"Resolve's Message to the World"

"This message is being broadcast to you from a small group of survivors, located next to the Colorado River, along the California-Arizona border, about five miles above where Needles, California, used to be. We have 475 families, or 1,945 individuals here. Many are from nations scattered around the world. We have some search and rescue capabilities, but they are limited to the continental United States. We are unable to extend our efforts beyond this area due to scarcity of equipment and fuel. However, we will make every effort to pick up any survivors who can make it to four rendezvous points. Their locations are: Redmond, Oregon (with Lava River Cave nearby for shelter); Rapid City, South Dakota (with Jewel or Wind Caves nearby for shelter); Bowling Green, Kentucky (with Mammoth Caverns nearby for shelter); and Carlsbad, New Mexico (with Carlsbad Caverns nearby for shelter). Our first flights to these four locations will be on or about June 1st of this year.

"We will return to these same four locations three months later for the next two years, or for as long as our fuel holds out. Stay tuned for the exact date and time of our arrival. You must mark on the runways of the airfields that you are there; otherwise we will not land for your rescue. Use anything you can find to indicate you are there. The airfields for each location are: Roberts Field in Redmond, Rapid City Regional Airport, Bowling Green-Warren Co. Regional Airport, and Cavern City Air Terminal in Carlsbad.

"In addition, we plan to make repeated flights in a 300 mile radius from our location. We will be flying small fixed-wing, spotter aircraft first. If anyone is located, we will then launch rescue helicopters to pick you up. Please make your presence visible to the spotters with signs, flags, fires, whatever you can use to attract our attention. We want to find you. That is our promise.

"For any who may hear this message, who are sheltered across the ocean, in either direction, sadly you must find your own way to our shores and these four sites. We have no way to sail or fly across the seas at this time. But if you can make it to any of these pick up points, we will pick you up and give you a new home with us. Everyone is welcome. We pray for your safe journey, should anyone hear this message and act on it.

"We are the Global Union broadcast network."

Figure 2:

"Rescue Leaflets"

This leaflet is to reassure you that you have been seen. And that we will return within the day, unless bad weather or equipment problems prevent it. But we promise we will rescue you. On our return we will come in two helicopters. Clear any debris that may be tossed about by our rotary blades and hurt someone in the landing zone. Designate a landing zone that is free of wires and high overhanging objects with a large "X" laid out on the ground. Firm pavement is best, if available. Bring only your most precious small valuables with you and some clothing for each person. We may not be able to take everything you bring. Try to separate your non-clothing items in bundles of less importance in case we have to leave some behind. We have room for four people per helicopter. Thank God you are alive. You will be rescued soon. And you will be safe within a community of survivors who will embrace you warmly. Don't be scared. You'll be ok.

Signed,

The Global Union